Praise for Elmore Leonard and

FORTY LASHES LESS ONE

"Well-developed characters and dialogue with a perfect pitch . . .
this is Elmore Leonard territory."   —*Chicago Tribune*

"As welcome as a thunderstorm in a dry spell."
                                        —*Dallas Morning News*

"All the elements of his Detroit, Miami, and Atlantic City novels
are here: oblique dialogue, closely observed behavior, a certain
sunny cynicism, a melancholy courage."   —*Boston Globe*

"Leonard knows his way onto a horse and out of a gunfight as
well as he knows the special King's English spoken by his pat-
ented, not-so-lovable urban lowlifes."
                                    —*Milwaukee Journal-Sentinel*

"Classic western fare."   —*San Francisco Chronicle*

"Although known for his mysteries, Leonard has penned some
of the best western fiction ever."   —*USA Today*

"Long before his slick, dark crime comedies, Elmore Leonard
wrote some very tough and realistic westerns."
                                        —*Daily News* (New York)

Forty Lashes Less One

Also by Elmore Leonard

FICTION

Raylan
Djibouti
Comfort to the Enemy and
    Other Carl Webster Stories
Road Dogs
Up in Honey's Room
The Hot Kid
The Complete Western Stories
    of Elmore Leonard
Mr. Paradise
Fire in the Hole (previously
    titled *When the Women*
    Come Out to Dance)
Tishomingo Blues
Pagan Babies
Be Cool
The Tonto Woman and Other
    Western Stories
Cuba Libre
Out of Sight
Riding the Rap
Pronto
Rum Punch
Maximum Bob
Get Shorty
Killshot

Freaky Deaky
Touch
Bandits
Glitz
LaBrava
Stick
Cat Chaser
Split Images
Gold Coast
City Primeval
Gunsights
The Switch
The Hunted
Unknown Man #89
Swag
52 Pickup
Mr. Majestyk
Valdez Is Coming
The Moonshine War
The Big Bounce
Hombre
Last Stand at Saber River
Escape from Five Shadows
The Law at Randado
The Bounty Hunters

NONFICTION

Elmore Leonard's 10 Rules of Writing

ELMORE LEONARD

Forty Lashes Less One

WM
WILLIAM MORROW
An Imprint of HarperCollins*Publishers*

This book is a work of fiction. The characters, incidents, and dialogue are drawn from the author's imagination and are not to be construed as real. Any resemblance to actual events or persons, living or dead, is entirely coincidental.

HarperCollins books may be purchased for educational, business, or sales promotional use. For information please e-mail the Special Markets Department at SPsales@ harpercollins.com.

FIRST HARPERTORCH PAPERBACK PUBLISHED 2002.
FIRST WILLIAM MORROW PAPERBACK PUBLISHED 2013.

Library of Congress Cataloging-in-Publication Data has been applied for.

ISBN 978-0-06-228949-0

13 14 15 16 17   OV/RRD   10 9 8 7 6 5 4 3 2 1

Forty Lashes Less One

1

The train was late and didn't get into Yuma until after dark. Then the ticket agent at the depot had to telephone the prison and tell them they had better get some transportation down here. He had three people waiting on a ride up the hill: a man he had never seen before who said he was the new prison superintendent, and another man he knew was a deputy sheriff from Pima County and he had a prisoner with him, handcuffed, a big colored boy.

Whoever it was on the phone up at the prison said they had sent a man two hours ago and if the train had been on time he would have met them. The ticket agent said well, they were here now and somebody better hurry with the transportation, because the Southern Pacific didn't care for convicts hanging around the depot, even if the boy was handcuffed.

The Pima deputy said hell, it wasn't anything new; every time he delivered a man he had to sit and wait on the prison people to get off their ass. He asked the big colored boy if he minded waiting, sitting in a nice warm train depot, or would he rather be up there in one of them carved-out cells with the wind whistling in across the river? The Pima deputy said something about sweating all day and freezing at night; but the colored boy, whose name was Harold Jackson, didn't seem to be listening.

The new prison superintendent—the new, temporary superintendent—Mr. Everett Manly, heard him. He nodded, and adjusted his gold-frame glasses. He said yes, he was certainly familiar with Arizona winters, having spent seven years at the Chiricahua Apache Mission School. Mr. Manly heard himself speak and it sounded all right. It sounded natural.

On the train Mr. Manly had exchanged a few words with the deputy, but had not spoken to the colored boy. He could have asked him his name and where he was from; he could have asked him about his sentence and told him that if he behaved himself he would be treated fairly. He could have asked him if he wanted to pray. But with the Pima deputy sitting next to the colored boy—all afternoon and evening on the wicker seats, bumping and swaying, looking out at the sun haze on the desert and the distant, dark brown mountains—Mr. Manly had not been able to get the first words out, to start a conversation. He was not afraid of the colored boy, who could have been a cold-blooded killer for all he knew. It was the idea of the deputy sitting there listening that bothered him.

He thought about starting a friendly conversation with the ticket agent: ask him if he ever got up to the prison, or if he knew the superintendent, Mr. Rynning, who was in Florence at the present time seeing to the construction of the new penitentiary. He could say, "Well, it won't be long now, there won't be any more Yuma Territorial Prison," and kidding, add, "I suppose you'll be sorry to see it closed." Except maybe he wasn't supposed to talk about it in idle conversation. It had been mentioned in newspapers—"Hell-Hole on the Bluff to Open Its Doors Forever by the Spring of 1909"—pretty clever, saying *opening* its doors instead of closing them. And no doubt the station agent knew all about it. Living here he would have to. But a harmless conversation could start false rumors and speculation, and before you knew it somebody from the Bureau would write and ask how come he was going around telling everybody about official government business.

If the ticket agent brought up the subject that would be different. He could be noncommittal. "You heard the old prison's closing, huh? Well, after thirty-three years I imagine you won't be too sorry to see it happen." But the ticket agent didn't bring up the subject.

A little while later they heard the noise outside. The ticket agent looked at them through his barred window and said, "There's a motor conveyance pulling into the yard I reckon is for you people."

Mr. Manly had never ridden in an automobile before. He asked the driver what kind it was and the driver told him it was a twenty-horsepower Ford Touring Car, powerful and speedy, belonged to the superintendent, Mr. Rynning. It was comfortable, Mr. Manly said, but kind of noisy, wasn't it? He wanted to ask how much a motor rig like this cost, but there was the prison above him: the walls and the guard towers against the night sky, the towers, like little houses with pointed roofs; dark houses, nobody home. When the gravel road turned and climbed close along the south wall, Mr. Manly had to look almost straight up, and he said to the guard driving the car, "I didn't picture the walls so high." And the guard answered, "Eighteen feet up and eight feet thick. A man can't jump it and he can't bore through neither."

"My last trip up this goddamn rock pile," the Pima deputy said, sitting in the back seat with his prisoner. "I'm going to the railroad hotel and get me a bottle of whiskey and in the morning I'm taking the train home and ain't never coming back here again."

The rest of the way up the hill Mr. Manly said nothing. He would remember this night and the strange feeling of riding in a car up Prison Hill, up close to this great silent mound of adobe and granite. Yuma Territorial Prison, that he had heard stories about for years—that he could almost reach out and touch. But was it like a prison? More like a tomb of an ancient king, Mr. Manly was thinking. A pyramid. A ghostly monument. Or, if it was a prison, then one that was already deserted. Inside the walls there were more than a hundred men. Maybe a hundred and fifty counting the guards. But there was no sound or sign of life, only this motor car putt-putting up the hill, taking forever to reach the top.

What if it did take forever, Mr. Manly thought. What if they kept going and going and never reached the prison gate, but kept moving up into stoney darkness for all eternity—until the four of them realized this was God's judgment upon them. (He could hear the Pima deputy cursing and saying, "Now, wait a minute, I'm just here to deliver a prisoner!") It could happen this way, Mr. Manly thought. Who said you had to die first? Or, how did a person know when he was dead? Maybe he had died on the train. He had dozed off and opened his eyes as they were pulling into the depot—

A man sixty years old could die in his sleep. But—and here was the question—if he was dead and this was happening, why would he be condemned to darkness? What had he done wrong in his life?

Not even thinking about it very hard, he answered at once, though quietly: What have you done right? Sixty years of life, Mr. Manly thought. Thirty years as a preacher of the Holy Word, seven years as a missionary among pagan Indians. Half his life spent in God's service, and he was not sure he had converted even one soul to the Light of Truth.

They reached the top of the bluff at the west end of the prison and, coming around the corner, Mr. Manly saw the buildings that were set back from the main gate, dim shapes and cold yellow lights that framed windows and reflected on the hard-packed yard. He was aware of the buildings and thought briefly of an army post, single- and two-story structures with peaked roofs and neatly painted verandas. He heard the driver point out the guard's mess and recreation hall, the arsenal, the stable, the storehouses; he heard him say, "If you're staying in the sup'rintendent's cottage, it's over yonder by the trees."

Mr. Manly was familiar with government buildings in cleanswept areas. He had seen them at the San Carlos

5

reservation and at Fort Huachuca and at the Indian School. He was staring at the prison wall where a single light showed the main gate as an oval cavern in the pale stone, a dark tunnel entrance crisscrossed with strips of iron.

The driver looked at Mr. Manly. After a moment he said, "The sally port. It's the only way in and, I guarantee, the only way out."

Bob Fisher, the turnkey, stood waiting back of the inner gate with two of his guards. He seemed either patient or half asleep, a solemn-looking man with a heavy, drooping mustache. He didn't have them open the iron lattice door until Mr. Manly and the Pima deputy and his prisoner were within the dark enclosure of the sally port and the outer gate was bolted and locked behind them. Then he gave a sign to open up and waited for them to step into the yard light.

The Pima deputy was pulling a folded sheaf of papers out of his coat pocket, dragging along his handcuffed prisoner. "I got a boy name of Harold Jackson wants to live with you the next fifteen years." He handed the papers to the turnkey and fished in his pants pocket for the keys to the handcuffs.

Bob Fisher unfolded the papers close to his stomach and glanced at the first sheet. "We'll take care of him," he said, and folded the papers again.

Mr. Manly stood by waiting, holding his suitcase.

"I'll tell you what," the Pima deputy said. "I'll let you buy me a cup of coffee 'fore I head back."

"We'll see if we got any," Fisher said.

The Pima deputy had removed the handcuffs from the prisoner and was slipping them into his coat pocket. "I don't want to put you to any trouble," he said. "Jesus, a nice friendly person like you."

"You won't put us to any trouble," Fisher answered. His voice was low, and he seemed to put no effort or feeling into his words.

Mr. Manly kept waiting for the turnkey to notice him and greet him and have one of the guards take his suitcase; but the man stood at the edge of the yard light and didn't seem to look at any of them directly, though maybe he was looking at the prisoner, telling him with the sound of his voice that he didn't kid with anybody. What does he look like, Mr. Manly was thinking. He lowered his suitcase to the ground.

A streetcar motorman, that was it. With his gray guard uniform and gray uniform hat, the black shiny peak straight over his eyes. A tough old motorman with a sour stomach and a sour outlook from living within the confinement of a prison too many years. A man who never spoke if he didn't have to and only smiled about twice a year. The way the man's big mustache covered the sides of his mouth it would be hard to tell if he ever smiled at all.

Bob Fisher told one of the guards to take the Pima deputy over to the mess hall, then changed his mind and said no, take him outside to the guard's mess. The Pima deputy shrugged; he didn't care where he got his coffee. He took time to look at Mr. Manly and say, "Good luck, mister." As Mr. Manly said, "Good luck to you too," not looking at the turnkey now but feeling him there, the Pima deputy turned his back on them; he waited to get through the double gates and was gone.

"My name is Everett Manly," Mr. Manly said. "I expect—"

But Fisher wasn't ready for him yet. He motioned to the guards and watched as they led the prisoner off toward a low, one-room adobe. Mr. Manly waited, also watching them. He could see the shapes of buildings in the darkness of the yard, here and there a light fixed above a doorway. Past the corner of a two-story building, out across the yard, was the massive outline of a long, windowless adobe with a light above its criss-crossed iron door. Probably the main cellblock. But in the darkness he couldn't tell about the other buildings, or make any sense of the prison's layout. He had the feeling again that the place was deserted except for the turnkey and the two guards.

"I understand you've come here to take charge."

All the waiting and the man had surprised him. But all was forgiven, because the man was looking at him now, acknowledging his presence.

"I'm Everett Manly. I expect Mr. Rynning wrote you I was coming. You're—"

"Bob Fisher, turnkey."

Mr. Manly smiled. "I guess you would be the man in charge of the keys." Showing him he had a sense of humor.

"I've been in charge of the whole place since Mr. Rynning's been gone."

"Well, I'm anxious to see everything and get to work."
Mr. Manly was being sincere now, and humble. "I'm going to admit though, I haven't had much experience."

In his flat tone, Fisher said, "I understand you haven't
had any."

Mr. Manly wished they weren't standing here alone.
"No *prison* experience, that's true. But I've dealt with
people all my life, Mr. Fisher, and nobody's told me yet
convicts aren't people." He smiled again, still humble
and willing to learn.

"Nobody will have to tell you," Fisher said. "You'll
find out yourself."

He turned and walked off toward the one-room
adobe. Mr. Manly had no choice but to pick up his suitcase and follow—Lord, with the awful feeling again and
wishing he hadn't put so many books in with his clothes;
the suitcase weighed a ton and he probably looked like
an idiot walking with quick little steps and the thing
banging against his leg. And then he was grateful and
felt good again, because Bob Fisher was holding the
door open for him and let him go inside first, into the
lighted room where the colored boy was jackknifed over
a table without any clothes on and the two guards were
standing on either side of him.

One of the guards pulled him up and turned him
around by the arm as Fisher closed the door. "He's
clean," the guard said. "Nothing hid away down him or
up him."

"He needs a hosing is all," the other guard said.

Fisher came across the plank floor, his eyes on the
prisoner. "He ain't worked up a sweat yet."

9

"Jesus," the first guard said, "don't get close to him. He stinks to high heaven."

Mr. Manly put down his suitcase. "That's a long dusty train ride, my friend." Then, smiling a little, he added, "I wouldn't mind a bath myself."

The two guards looked over at him, then at Fisher, who was still facing the prisoner. "That's your new boss," Fisher said, "come to take Mr. Rynning's place while he's gone. See he gets all the bath water he wants. This boy here washes tomorrow with the others, after he's put in a day's work."

Mr. Manly said, "I didn't intend that to sound like I'm interfering with your customs or regulations—"

Fisher looked over at him now, waiting.

"I only meant it was sooty and dirty aboard the train."

Fisher waited until he was sure Mr. Manly had nothing more to say. Then he turned his attention to the prisoner again. One of the guards was handing the man a folded uniform and a broad-brimmed sweat-stained hat. Fisher watched him as he put the clothes on the table, shook open the pants and stepped into them: faded, striped gray and white convict pants that were short and barely reached to the man's high-top shoes. While he was buttoning up, Fisher opened the sheaf of papers the Pima deputy had given him, his gaze holding on the first sheet. "It says here you're Harold Jackson."

"Yes-suh, captain."

The Negro came to attention as Fisher looked up, a hint of surprise in his solemn expression. He seemed to study the prisoner more closely now and took his time before saying, "You ain't ever been here before, but you been somewhere. Where was it you served time, boy?"

"Fort Leavenworth, captain."

"You were in the army?"

"Yes-suh, captain."

"I never knew a nigger that was in the army. How long were you in it?"

"Over in Cuba eight months, captain. At Leavenworth four years hard labor."

"Well, they learned you some manners," Fisher said, "but they didn't learn you how to stay out of prison, did they? These papers say you killed a man. Is that right?"

"Yes-suh, captain."

"What'd you kill him with?"

"I hit him with a piece of pipe, captain."

"You robbing him?"

"No-suh, captain, we jes' fighting."

Mr. Manly cleared his throat. The pause held, and he said quickly, "Coming here he never gave the deputy any trouble, not once."

Fisher took his time as he looked around. He said, "I generally talk to a new man and find out who he is or who he believes he is, and we get a few things straightened out at the start." He paused. "If it's all right with you."

"Please go ahead," Mr. Manly said. "I just wanted to say he never acted smart on the trip, or was abusive. I doubt he said more than a couple words."

"That's fine." Fisher nodded patiently before looking at Harold Jackson again. "You're our last nigger," he said to him. "You're the only one we got now, and we want you to be a good boy and work hard and do whatever you're told. Show you we mean it, we're going to help you out at first, give you something to keep you out of trouble."

There was a wooden box underneath the table. Mr. Manly didn't notice it until one of the guards stooped down and, with the rattling sound of chains, brought out a pair of leg-irons and a ball-peen hammer.

Mr. Manly couldn't hold back. "But he hasn't done anything yet!"

"No, sir," Bob Fisher said, "and he ain't about to with chains on his legs." He came over to Mr. Manly and, surprising him, picked up his suitcase and moved him through the door, closing it firmly behind them.

Outside, Fisher paused. "I'll get somebody to tote your bag over to Mr. Rynning's cottage. I expect you'll be most comfortable there."

"I appreciate it."

"Take your bath if you want one, have something to eat and a night's sleep—there's no sense in showing you around now—all right?"

"What are you going to do to the colored boy?"

"We're going to put him in a cell, if that's all right."

"But the leg-irons."

"He'll wear them a week. See what they feel like."

"I guess I'm just not used to your ways," Mr. Manly said. "I mean prison ways." He could feel the silence again among the darkened stone buildings and high walls. The turnkey walked off toward the empty, lighted area by the main gate. Mr. Manly had to step quickly to catch up with him. "I mean I believe a man should have a chance to prove himself first," he said, "before he's judged."

"They're judged before they get here."

"But putting leg-irons on them—"

"Not all of them. Just the ones I think need them, so they'll know what irons feel like."

Mr. Manly knew what he wanted to say, but he didn't have the right words. "I mean, don't they hurt terrible?"

"I sure hope so," Fisher answered.

As they came to the lighted area, a guard leaning against the iron grill of the gate straightened and adjusted his hat. Fisher let the guard know he had seen him, then stopped and put down the suitcase.

"This Harold Jackson," Fisher said. "Maybe you didn't hear him. He killed a man. He didn't miss Sunday school. He beat a man to death with an iron pipe."

"I know—I heard him."

"That's the kind of people we get here. Lot of them. They come in, we don't know what's on their minds. We don't know if they're going to behave or cause trouble or try and run or try and kill somebody else."

"I understand that part all right."

"Some of them we got to show right away who's running this place."

Mr. Manly was frowning. "But this boy Harold Jackson, he seemed all right. He was polite, said yes-sir to you. Why'd you put leg-irons on him?"

Now it was Fisher's turn to look puzzled. "You saw him same as I did."

"I don't know what you mean."

"I mean he's a nigger, ain't he?"

13

Looking up at the turnkey, Mr. Manly's gold-frame spectacles glistened in the overhead light. "You're saying that's the only reason you put leg-irons on him?"

"If I could tell all the bad ones," Bob Fisher said, "as easy as I can tell a nigger, I believe I'd be sup'rintendent."

Jesus Christ, the man was even dumber than he looked. He could have told him a few more things: sixteen years at Yuma, nine years as turnkey, and he hadn't seen a nigger yet who didn't need to wear irons or spend some time in the snake den. It was the way they were, either lazy or crazy; you had to beat 'em to make 'em work, or chain 'em to keep 'em in line. He would like to see just one good nigger. Or one good, hard-working Indian for that matter. Or a Mexican you could trust. Or a preacher who knew enough to keep his nose in church and out of other people's business.

Bob Fisher had been told two weeks earlier, in a letter from Mr. Rynning, that an acting superintendent would soon be coming to Yuma.

Mr. Rynning's letter had said: "Not an experienced penal administrator, by the way, but, of all things, a preacher, an ordained minister of the Holy Word Church who has been wrestling with devils in Indian schools for several years and evidently feels qualified to match his strength against convicts. This is not my doing. Mr. Manly's name came to me through the Bureau as someone who, if not eminently qualified, is at least conveniently located and willing to take the job on a temporary basis. (The poor fellow must be desperate.

Or, perhaps misplaced and the Bureau doesn't know what else to do with him but send him to prison, out of harm's way.) He has had some administrative experience and, having worked on an Apache reservation, must know something about inventory control and logistics. The bureau insists on an active administrator at Yuma while, in the same breath, they strongly suggest I remain in Florence during the new prison's final stage of preparation. Hence, you will be meeting your new superintendent in the very near future. Knowing you will oblige him with your utmost cooperation I remain . . ."

Mr. Rynning remained in Florence while Bob Fisher remained in Yuma with a Holy Word Pentacostal preacher looking over his shoulder.

The clock on the wall of the superintendent's office said ten after nine. Fisher, behind the big mahogany desk, folded Mr. Rynning's letter and put it in his breast pocket. After seeing Mr. Manly through the gate, he had come up here to pick up his personal file. No sense in leaving anything here if the preacher was going to occupy the office. The little four-eyed son of a bitch, maybe a few days here would scare hell out of him and run him back to Sunday school. Turning in the swivel chair, Fisher could see the reflection of the room in the darkened window glass and could see himself sitting at the desk; with a thumb and first finger he smoothed his mustache and continued to fool with it as he looked at the clock again.

Still ten after nine. He was off duty; had been since six. Had waited two hours for the preacher.

It was too early to go home: his old lady would still be

up and he'd have to look at her and listen to her talk for an hour or more. Too early to go home, and too late to watch the two women convicts take their bath in the cook shack. They always finished and were gone by eight-thirty, quarter to nine. He had been looking forward to watching them tonight, especially Norma Davis. Jesus, she had big ones, and a nice round white fanny. The Mexican girl was smaller, like all the Mexican girls he had ever seen; she was all right, though; especially with the soapy water on her brown skin. It was a shame; he hadn't watched them in about four nights. If the train had been on time he could have met the preacher and still got over to the cook shack before eight-thirty. It was like the little son of a bitch's train to be late. There was something about him, something that told Fisher the man couldn't do anything right, and would mess up anything he took part in.

Tomorrow he'd show him around and answer all his dumb questions.

Tonight—he could stare at the clock for an hour and go home.

He could stare out at the empty yard and hope for something to happen. He could pull a surprise inspection of the guard posts, maybe catch somebody sleeping.

He could stop at a saloon on the way home. Or go down to Frank Shelby's cell, No. 14, and buy a pint of tequila off him.

What Bob Fisher did, he pulled out the papers on the new prisoner, Harold Jackson, and started reading about him.

* * *

One of the guards asked Harold Jackson if he'd ever worn leg-irons before. Sitting tired, hunch-shouldered on the floor, he said yeah. They looked down at him and he looked up at them, coming full awake but not showing it, and said yes-suh, he believed it was two times. That's all, if the captain didn't count the prison farm. He'd wore irons there because they liked everybody working outside the jail to wear irons. It wasn't on account he had done anything.

The guard said all right, that was enough. They give him a blanket and took him shuffling across the dark yard to the main cell block, then through the iron-cage gate where bare overhead lights showed the stone passageway and the cell doors on both sides. The guards didn't say anything to him. They stopped at Cell No. 8, unlocked the door, pushed him inside, and clanged the ironwork shut behind him.

As their steps faded in the passageway, Harold Jackson could make out two tiers of bunks and feel the closeness of the walls and was aware of a man breathing in his sleep. He wasn't sure how many were in this cell. He let his eyes get used to the darkness before he took a step, then another, the leg chains clinking in the silence. The back wall wasn't three steps away. The bunks, three decks high on both sides of him, were close enough to touch. Which would make this a six-man room, he figured, about eight feet by nine feet. Blanket-covered shapes lay close to him in the middle bunks. He couldn't make out the top ones and didn't want to feel around;

but he could see the bottom racks were empty. Harold Jackson squatted on the floor and ducked into the right-side bunk.

The three-tiered bunks and the smell of the place reminded him of the troopship, though it had been awful hot down in the hold. Ten days sweating down in that dark hold while the ship was tied up at Tampa and they wouldn't let any of the Negro troops go ashore, not even to walk the dock and stretch their legs. He never did learn the name of that ship, and he didn't care. When they landed at Siboney, Harold Jackson walked off through the jungle and up into the hills. For two weeks he stayed with a Cuban family and ate sugar cane and got a kick out of how they couldn't speak any English, though they were Negro, same as he was. When he had rested and felt good he returned to the base and they threw him in the stockade. They said he was a deserter. He said he came back, didn't he? They said he was still a deserter.

He had never been in a cell that was this cold. Not even at Leavenworth. Up there in the Kansas winter the cold times were in the exercise yard, stamping your feet and moving to keep warm; the cell was all right, maybe a little cold sometimes. That was a funny thing, most of the jails he remembered as being hot: the prison farm wagon that was like a circus cage and the city jails and the army stockade in Cuba. He'd be sitting on a bench sweating or laying in the rack sweating, slapping mosquitoes, scratching, or watching the cockroaches fooling around and running nowhere. Cockroaches never looked like they knew where they were going. No, the heat was all right. The heat, the bugs were like part of being in jail. The cold was something he would have to get used to. Pretend it was hot. Pretend he was in Cuba. If he had to pick a jail to be in, out of all the places—if somebody said, "You got to go to jail for ten years, but we let you pick the place"—he'd pick the stockade at Siboney. Not because it was a good jail, but because it was in Cuba, and Cuba was a nice-looking place, with the ocean and the trees and plenty of shade. That's a long way away, Harold Jackson said to himself. You ain't going to see it again.

There wasn't any wind. The cold just lay over him and didn't go away. His body was all right; it was his feet and his hands. Harold Jackson rolled to his side to reach down below the leg-irons that dug hard into his ankles and work his shoes off, then put his hands, palms together like he was praying, between the warmth of his legs. There was no use worrying about where he was. He would think of Cuba and go to sleep.

In the morning, in the moments before opening his eyes, he wasn't sure where he was. He was confused because a minute ago he'd have sworn he'd been holding a piece of sugar cane, the purple peeled back in knife strips and he was sucking, chewing the pulp to draw out the sweet juice. But he wasn't holding any cane now, and he wasn't in Cuba.

The bunk jiggled, strained, and moved back in place as somebody got down from above him. There were sounds of movement in the small cell, at least two men.

"You don't believe it, take a look."

"Jesus Christ," another voice said, a younger voice. "What's he doing in here?"

Both of them white voices. Harold Jackson could feel them standing between the bunks. He opened his eyes a little bit at a time until he was looking at prison-striped legs. It wasn't much lighter in the cell than before, when he'd gone to sleep, but he could see the stripes all right and he knew that outside it was morning.

A pair of legs swung down from the opposite bunk and hung there, wool socks and yellow toenails poking out of holes. "What're you looking at?" this one said, his voice low and heavy with sleep.

"We got a coon in here with us," the younger voice said.

The legs came down and the space was filled with faded, dirty convict stripes. Harold Jackson turned his head a little and raised his eyes. His gaze met theirs as they hunched over to look at him, studying him as if he was something they had never seen before. There was a heavy-boned, beard-stubbled face; a blond baby-boy face; and a skinny, slick-haired face with a big cavalry mustache that drooped over the corners of the man's mouth.

"Somebody made a mistake," the big man said. "In the dark."

"Joe Dean seen him right away."

"I smelled him," the one with the cavalry mustache said.

"Jesus," the younger one said now, "wait till Shelby finds out."

Harold Jackson came out of the bunk, rising slowly, uncoiling and bringing up his shoulders to stand eye to eye with the biggest of the three. He stared at the man's dead-looking deep-set eyes and at the hairs sticking out of a nose that was scarred and one time had been broken. "You gentlemen excuse me," Harold Jackson said, moving past the young boy and the one who was called Joe Dean. He stood with his back to them and aimed at the slop bucket against the wall.

They didn't say anything at first; just stared at him. But as Harold Jackson started to go the younger one murmured, "Jesus Christ—" as if awed, or saying a prayer. He stared at Harold as long as he could, then broke for the door and began yelling through the ironwork, "Guard! Guard! Goddamn it, there's a nigger in here pissing in our toilet!"

2

Raymond San Carlos heard the sound of Junior's voice before he made out the words: somebody yelling—for a guard. Somebody gone crazy, or afraid of something. Something happening in one of the cells close by. He heard quick footsteps now, going past, and turned his head enough to look from his bunk to the door.

It was morning. The electric lights were off in the cell block and it was dark now, the way a barn with its doors open is dark. He could hear other voices now and footsteps and, getting louder, the metal-ringing sound of the guards banging crowbars on the cell doors—good morning, get up and go to the toilet and put your shoes on and fold your blankets—the iron clanging coming closer, until it was almost to them and the convict above Raymond San Carlos yelled, "All right, we hear you! God Almighty—" The other convict in the cell, across from him in an upper bunk, said, "I'd like to wake them sons of bitches up some time." The man above Raymond said, "Break their goddamn eardrums." The other man said, "No, I'd empty slop pails on 'em." And the crow-

23

bar clanged against the door and was past them, banging, clanging down the passageway.

Another guard came along in a few minutes and unlocked each cell. Raymond was ready by the time he got to them, standing by the door to be first out. One of the convicts in the cell poked Raymond in the back and, when he turned around, pointed to the bucket.

"It ain't my turn," Raymond said.

"If I want you to empty it," the convict said, his partner close behind him, looking over his shoulder, "then it's your turn."

Raymond shrugged and they stood aside to let him edge past them. He could argue with them and they could pound his head against the stone wall and say he fell out of his bunk. He could pick up the slop bucket and say, "Hey," and when they turned around he could throw it at them. Thinking about it afterward would be good, but the getting beat up and pounded against the wall wouldn't be good. Or they might stick his face in a bucket. God, he'd get sick, and every time he thought of it after he'd get sick.

He had learned to hold onto himself and think ahead, looking at the good results and the bad results, and decide quickly if doing something was worth it. One time he hadn't held onto himself—the time he worked for the Sedona cattle people up on Oak Creek—and it was the reason he was here.

He had held on at first, for about a year while the other riders—some of them—kidded him about having a fancy name like Raymond San Carlos when he was Apache Indian down to the soles of his feet. Chiricahua

Apache, they said. Maybe a little taller than most, but look at them black beady eyes and the flat nose. Pure Indin.

The Sedona hands got tired of it after a while; all except two boys who wouldn't leave him alone: a boy named Buzz Moore and another one they called Eljay. They kept at him every day. One of them would say, "What's that in his hair?" and pretend to pick something out, holding it between two fingers and studying it closely. "Why, it's some fuzz off a turkey feather, must have got stuck there from his headdress." Sometimes when it was hot and dry one of these two would look up at the sky and say, "Hey, chief, commence dancing and see if you can get us some rain down here." They asked him if he ever thought about white women, which he would never in his life ever get to have. They'd drink whiskey in front of him and not give him any, saying it was against the law to give an Indian firewater. Things like that.

At first it hadn't been too hard to hold on and go along with the kidding. Riding for Sedona was a good job, and worth it. Raymond would usually grin and say nothing. A couple of times he tried to tell them he was American and only his name was Mexican. He had made up what he thought was a pretty good story.

"See, my father's name was Armando de San Carlos y Zamora. He was born in Mexico, I don't know where, but I know he come up here to find work and that's when he met my mother who's an American, Maria Ramirez, and they got married. So when I'm born here, I'm American too."

He remembered Buzz Moore saying, "Maria Ramirez? What kind of American name is that?"

The other one, Eljay, who never let him alone, said, "So are Apache Indins American if you want to call everybody who's born in this country American. But anybody knows Indins ain't citizens. And if you ain't a citizen, you ain't American." He said to Raymond, "You ever vote?"

"I ain't never been where there was anything to vote about," Raymond answered.

"You go to school?"

"A couple of years."

"Then you don't know anything about what is a U. S. citizen. Can you read and write?"

Raymond shook his head.

"There you are," Eljay said.

Buzz Moore said then, "His daddy could have been Indin. They got Indins in Mexico like anywhere else. Why old Geronimo himself lived down there and could have sired a whole tribe of little Indins."

And Eljay said, "You want to know the simple truth? He's Chiricahua Apache, born and reared on the San Carlos Indin reservation, and that's how he got his fancy name. Made it up so people wouldn't think he was Indin."

"Well," Buzz Moore said, "he could be some part Mexican."

"If that's so," Eljay said, "what we got here is a red greaser."

They got a kick out of that and called him the red greaser through the winter and into April—until the day up in the high meadows they were gathering spring calves and their mammas and chasing them down to the valley graze. They were using revolvers and shotguns part of the time to scare the stock out of the brush stands and box canyons and keep them moving. Raymond remembered the feel of the 12-gauge Remington, holding it pointed up with the stock tight against his thigh. He would fire it this way when he was chasing stock—aiming straight up—and would feel the Remington kick against his leg. He kept off by himself most of the day, enjoying the good feeling of being alone in high country. He remembered the day vividly: the clean line of the peaks towering against the sky, the shadowed canyons and the slopes spotted yellow with arrowroot blossoms. He liked the silence; he liked being here alone and not having to think about anything or talk to anybody.

It wasn't until the end of the day he realized how sore his leg was from the shotgun butt punching it. Raymond swung down off the sorrel he'd been riding and limped noticeably as he walked toward the cook fire. Eljay was standing there. Eljay took one look and said, "Hey, greaser, is that some kind of one-legged Indin dance you're doing?" Raymond stopped. He raised the Remington and shot Eljay square in the chest with both loads.

On this morning in February, 1909, as he picked up the slop bucket and followed his two cellmates out into the passageway. Raymond had served almost four years of a life sentence for second-degree murder.

The guard, R. E. Baylis, didn't lay his crowbar against No. 14, the last door at the east end of the cellblock. He opened the door and stepped inside and waited for Frank Shelby to look up from his bunk.

"You need to be on the supply detail today?" R. E. Baylis asked.

"What's today?"

"Tuesday."

"Tomorrow," Shelby said. "What's it like out?"

"Bright and fair, going to be warm."

"Put me on an outside detail."

"We got a party building a wall over by the cemetery."

"Hauling the bricks?"

"Bricks already there."

"That'll be all right," Shelby said. He sat up, swinging his legs over the side of the bunk. He was alone in the cell, in the upper of a double bunk. The triple bunk opposite him was stacked with cardboard boxes and a wooden crate and a few canvas sacks. A shelf and mirror hung from the back wall. There was also a chair by the wall with a hole cut out of the seat and a bucket underneath. A roll of toilet paper rested on one of the arms. The convicts called the chair Shelby's throne. "Get somebody to empty the bucket, will you?" Looking at the guard again, Shelby said, "You need anything?"

R. E. Baylis touched his breast pocket. "Well, I guess I could use some chew."

"Box right by your head," Shelby said. "I got Mail Pouch and Red Man. Or I got some Copenhagen if you want."

R. E. Baylis fished a hand in the box. "I might as well take a couple—case I don't see you again today."

"You know where to find me." Shelby dropped to the floor, pulled on half-boots, hopping a couple of times to keep his balance, then ran a hand through his dark hair as he straightened up, standing now in his boots and long underwear. "I believe I was supposed to get a clean outfit today."

"Washing machine broke down yesterday."

"Tomorrow then for sure, uh?" Shelby had an easy, unhurried way of talking. It was known that he never raised his voice or got excited. They said the way you told if he was mad or irritated, he would fool with his mustache; he would keep smoothing it down with two fingers until he decided what had to be done and either did it himself or had somebody else do it. Frank Shelby was serving forty-five years for armed robbery and second-degree murder and had brought three of his men with him to Yuma, each of them found guilty on the same counts and serving thirty years apiece.

Junior was one of them. He banged through the cell door as Shelby was getting into his prison stripes, buttoning his coat. "You got your mean go-to-hell look on this morning," Shelby said. "Was that you yelling just now?"

"They stuck a nigger in our cell last night while we was asleep." Junior turned to nail the guard with his look, putting the blame on him.

"It wasn't me," R. E. Baylis said. "I just come on duty."

"You don't throw his black ass out, we will," Junior said. By Jesus, this was Worley Lewis, Jr. talking, nineteen-year-old convict going on forty-nine before he would ever see the outside of a penitentiary, but he was one of Frank Shelby's own and that said he could stand up to a guard and mouth him if he had a good enough reason. "I'm telling you, Soonzy'll kill the son of a bitch."

"I'll find out why—" the guard began.

"It was a mistake," Shelby said. "Put him in the wrong cell is all."

"He's in there now, great big buck. Joe Dean seen him first, woke me up, and I swear I couldn't believe my eyes."

Shelby went over to the mirror and picked up a comb from the shelf. "It's nothing to get upset about," he said, making a part and slanting the dark hair carefully across his forehead. "Tonight they'll put him someplace else."

"Well, if we can," the guard said.

Shelby was watching him in the mirror: the gray-looking man in the gray guard uniform, R. E. Baylis, who might have been a town constable or a deputy sheriff twenty years ago. "What's the trouble?" Shelby asked.

"I mean he might have been ordered put there, I don't know."

"Ordered by who?"

"Bob Fisher. I say I don't know for sure."

Shelby turned from the mirror. "Bob don't want any trouble."

"Course not."

"Then why would he want to put Sambo in with my boys?"

"I say, I don't know."

Shelby came toward him now, noticing the activity out in the passageway, the convicts standing around and talking, moving slowly as the guards began to form them into two rows. Shelby put a hand on the guard's shoulder. "Mr. Baylis," he said, "don't worry about it. You don't want to ask Bob Fisher; we'll get Sambo out of there ourselves."

"We don't want nobody hurt or anything."

The guard kept looking at him, but Shelby was finished. As far as he was concerned, it was done. He said to Junior, "Give Soonzy the tobacco. You take the soap and stuff."

"It's my turn to keep the tally."

"Don't give me that look, boy."

Junior dropped his tone. "I lugged a box yesterday."

"All right, you handle the tally, Joe Dean carries the soap and stuff." Shelby paused, as if he was going to say something else, then looked at the guard. "Why don't you have the colored boy empty my throne bucket?"

"It don't matter to me," the guard said.

So he pulled Harold Jackson out of line and told him to get down to No. 14—as Joe Dean, Soonzy, and Junior moved along the double row of convicts in the dim passageway and sold them tobacco and cigarette paper, four kinds of plug and scrap, and little tins of snuff, matches, sugar cubes, stick candy, soap bars, sewing needles and thread, playing cards, red bandana handkerchiefs,

31

shoelaces, and combs. They didn't take money; it would waste too much time and they only had ten minutes to go down the double line of eighty-seven men. Junior put the purchase amount in the tally book and the customer had one week to pay. If he didn't pay in a week, he couldn't buy any more stuff until he did. If he didn't pay in two weeks Junior and Soonzy would get him in a cell alone and hit him a few times or stomp the man's ribs and kidneys. If a customer wanted tequila or mescal, or corn whiskey when they had it, he'd come around to No. 14 after supper, before the doors were shut for the night, and pay a dollar a half-pint, put up in medicine bottles from the sick ward that occupied the second floor of the cell block. Shelby only sold alcohol in the morning to three or four of the convicts who needed it first thing or would never get through the day. What most of them wanted was just a day's worth of tobacco and some paper to roll it in.

When the figure appeared outside the iron lattice Shelby said, "Come on in," and watched the big colored boy's reaction as he entered: his gaze shifting twice to take in the double bunk and the boxes and the throne, knowing right away this was a one-man cell.

"I'm Mr. Shelby."

"I'm Mr. Jackson," Harold said.

Frank Shelby touched his mustache. He smoothed it to the sides once, then let his hand drop to the edge of his bunk. His eyes remained on the impassive dark face that did not move now and was looking directly at him.

"Where you from, Mr. Jackson?"

"From Leavenworth."

That was it. Big time con in a desert prison hole. "This place doesn't look like much after the federal pen, uh?"

"I been to some was worse, some better."

"What'd you get sent here for?"

"I killed a man was bothering me."

"You get life?"

"Fifteen years."

"Then you didn't kill a man. You must've killed another colored boy." Shelby waited.

Harold Jackson said nothing. He could wait too.

"I'm right, ain't I?" Shelby said.

"The man said for me to come in here."

"He told you, but it was me said for you to come in."

Harold Jackson waited again. "You saying you the man here?"

"Ask any of them out there," Shelby said. "The guards, anybody."

"You bring me in to tell me about yourself?"

"No, I brought you in to empty my slop bucket."

"Who did it before I come?"

"Anybody I told."

"If you got people willing, you better call one of them." Harold turned and had a hand on the door when Shelby stopped him.

"Hey, Sambo—"

Harold came around enough to look at him. "How'd you know that was my name?"

"Boy, you are sure starting off wrong," Shelby said. "I believe you need to be by yourself a while and think it over."

Harold didn't have anything to say to that. He turned

to the door again and left the man standing there playing with his mustache.

As he fell in at the end of the prisoner line, guard named R. E. Baylis gave him a funny look and came over.

"Where's Shelby's bucket at?"

"I guess it's still in there, captain."

"How come he didn't have you take it?"

Harold Jackson stood at attention, looking past the man's face to the stone wall of the passageway. "You'll have to ask him about that, captain."

"Here they come," Bob Fisher said. "Look over there."

Mr. Manly moved quickly from the side of the desk to the window to watch the double file of convicts coming this way. He was anxious to see everything this morning, especially the convicts.

"Is that all of them?"

"In the main cell block. About ninety."

"I thought there'd be more." Mr. Manly studied the double file closely but wasn't able to single out Harold Jackson. All the convicts looked alike. No, that was wrong; they didn't all look alike.

"Since we're shutting down we haven't been getting as many."

"They're all different, aren't they?"

"How's that?" Bob Fisher said.

Mr. Manly didn't answer, or didn't hear him. He stood at the window of the superintendent's office—the largest of a row of offices over the mess hall—and watched the convicts as they came across the yard, passed beyond the end of a low adobe, and came into view again almost directly below the window. The line reached the door of the mess hall and came to a stop.

Their uniforms looked the same, all of them wearing prison stripes, all faded gray and white. It was the hats that were different, light-colored felt hats and a few straw hats, almost identical hats, but all worn at a different angle: straight, low over the eyes, to the side, cocked like a dandy would wear his hat, the brim funneled, the brim up in front, the brim down all around. The hats were as different as the men must be different. He should make a note of that. See if anything had been written on the subject: determining a man's character by the way he wore his hat. But there wasn't a note pad or any paper on the desk and he didn't want to ask Fisher for it right at the moment.

He was looking down at all the hats. He couldn't see any of their faces clearly, and wouldn't unless a man looked up. Nobody was looking up.

They were all looking back toward the yard. Most of them turning now so they wouldn't have to strain their necks. All those men suddenly interested in something and turning to look.

"The women convicts," Bob Fisher said.

Mr. Manly saw them then. My God—two women.

Fisher pressed closer to him at the window. Mr. Manly could smell tobacco on the man's breath. "They just come out of the latrine, that adobe there," Fisher said. "Now watch them boys eyeing them."

The two women walked down the line of convicts, keeping about ten feet away, seeming at ease and not in any hurry, but not looking at the men either.

"Taking their time and giving the boys sweet hell, aren't they? Don't hear a sound, they're so busy licking their lips."

Mr. Manly glanced quickly at the convicts. The way they were looking, it was more likely their mouths were hanging open. It gave him a funny feeling, the men dead serious and no one making a sound.

"My," Fisher said, "how they'd like to reach out and grab a handful of what them girls have got."

"Women—" Mr. Manly said almost as a question. Nobody had told him there were women at Yuma.

A light-brown-haired one and a dark-haired one that looked to be Mexican. Lord God, two good-looking women walking past those men like they were strolling in the park. Mr. Manly couldn't believe they were convicts. They were *women*. The little dark-haired one wore a striped dress—smaller stripes than the men's outfits— that could be a dress she'd bought anywhere. The brown-haired one, taller and a little older, though she couldn't be thirty yet, wore a striped blouse with the top buttons undone, a white canvas belt and a gray skirt that clung to the movement of her hips as she walked and flared out as it reached to her ankles.

"Tacha Reyes," Fisher said

"Pardon me?"

"The little chilipicker. She's been here six months of a ten-year sentence. I doubt she'll serve it all though. She behaves herself pretty good."

"What did she do? I mean to be here."

"Killed a man with a knife, she claimed was trying to make her do dirty things."

"Did the other one—kill somebody?"

"Norma Davis? Hell, no. Norma likes to do dirty things. She was a whore till she took up armed robbery and got caught holding up the Citizens' Bank of Prescott, Arizona. Man with her, her partner, was shot dead."

"A woman," Mr. Manly said. "I can't believe a woman would do that."

"With a Colt forty-four," Fisher said. "She shot a policeman during the hold-up but didn't kill him. Listen, you want to keep a pretty picture of women in your head don't get close to Norma. She's serving ten years for armed robbery and attempted murder."

The women were inside the mess hall now. Mr. Manly wanted to ask more questions about them, but he was afraid of sounding too interested and Fisher might get the wrong idea. "I notice some of the men are carrying buckets," he said.

"The latrine detail." Fisher pointed to the low adobe. "They'll go in there and empty them. That's the toilet and wash house, everything sewered clear out to the river. There—now the men are going into mess. They got fifteen minutes to eat, then ten minutes to go to the toilet before the work details form out in the exercise yard."

"Do you give them exercises to do?"

"We give them enough work they don't need any exercise," Fisher answered.

Mr. Manly raised his eyes to look out at the empty yard and was surprised to see a lone convict coming across from the cellblock.

"Why isn't that one with the others?"

Bob Fisher didn't answer right way. Finally he said, "That's Frank Shelby."

"Is he a trusty?"

"Not exactly. He's got some special jobs he does around here."

Mr. Manly let it go. There were too many other things he wanted to know about. Like all the adobe buildings scattered around, a whole row of them over to the left, at the far end of the mess hall. He wondered where the women lived, but didn't ask that.

Well, there was the cook shack over there and the tailor shop, where they made the uniforms. Bob Fisher pointed out the small one-story adobes. Some equipment sheds, a storehouse, the reception hut they were in last night. The mattress factory and the wagon works had been shut down six months ago. Over the main cellblock was the hospital, but the doctor had gone to Florence to set up a sick ward at the new prison. Anybody broke a leg now or crushed his hand working the rocks, they sent for a town doctor.

And the chaplain, Mr. Manly asked casually. Was he still here?

No, there wasn't any chaplain. The last one retired and they decided to wait till after the move to get another. There wasn't many of the convicts prayed anyway.

How would you know that? Mr. Manly wanted to

ask him. But he said, "What are those doors way down there?"

At the far end of the yard he could make out several iron-grill doors, black oval shapes, doorways carved into the solid rock. The doors didn't lead outside, he could tell that, because the top of the east wall and two of the guard towers were still a good piece beyond.

"Starting over back of the main cellblock, you can't see it from here," Bob Fisher said, "a gate leads into the TB cellblock and exercise yard."

"You've got consumptives here?"

"Like any place else. I believe four right now." Fisher hurried on before Mr. Manly could interrupt again. "The doors you can see—one's the crazy hole. Anybody gets mean loco they go in there till they calm down. The next one they call the snake den's a punishment cell."

"Why is it called—"

"I don't know, I guess a snake come in through the air shaft one time. The last door there on the right goes into the women's cellblock. You seen them. We just got the two right now."

There, he could ask about them again and it would sound natural. "The one you said, Norma something, has she been here long?"

"Norma Davis. I believe about a year and a half."

"Do the men ever—I mean I guess you have to sort of watch over the women."

"Mister, we have to watch over everybody."

"But being women—don't they have to have their own, you know, facilities and bath?"

Fisher looked right at Mr. Manly now. "They take a bath in the cook shack three, four times a week."

"In the cook shack." Mr. Manly nodded, surprised. "After the cooks are gone, of course."

"At night," Fisher said. He studied Mr. Manly's profile—the soft pinkish face and gold-frame glasses pressed close to the windowpane—little Bible teacher looking out over his prison and still thinking about Norma Davis, asking harmless sounding questions about the women.

Fisher said quietly, "You want to see them?"

Mr. Manly straightened, looking at Fisher now with a startled expression. "What do you mean?"

"I wondered if you wanted to go downstairs and have another look at Norma and Tacha."

"I want to see everything," Mr. Manly said. "Everything you have here to show me."

3

When Frank Shelby entered the mess hall he stepped in line ahead of Junior. In front of him, Soonzy and Joe Dean looked around.

"You take care of it?" Junior asked him.

"He needs some time in the snake den," Shelby said.

Soonzy was looking back down the line. "Where's he at?"

"Last one coming in."

"I'll handle him," Junior said.

Shelby shook his head. "I want somebody else to start it. You and Soonzy break it up and get in some licks."

"No problem," Junior said. "The spook's already got leg-irons on."

They picked up tin plates and cups and passed in front of the serving tables for their beans, salt-dried beef, bread, and coffee. Soonzy and Joe Dean waited, letting Shelby go ahead of them. He paused a moment, holding his food, looking out over the long twelve-man tables and benches that were not yet half filled. Joe Dean moved up next to him. "I see plenty of people that owe us money."

41

"No, I see the one I want. The Indin," Shelby said, and started for his table.

Raymond San Carlos was pushing his spoon into the beans that were pretty good but would be a lot better with some ketchup. He looked up as Frank Shelby and Junior put their plates down across from him. He hurried and took the spoonful of beans, then took another one more slowly. He knew they had picked him for something. He was sure of it when Soonzy sat down on one side of him and Joe Dean stepped in on the other. Joe Dean acted surprised at seeing him. "Well, Raymond San Carlos," he said, "how are you today?"

"I'm pretty good, I guess."

Junior said, "What're you pretty good at, Raymond?"

"I don't know—some things, I guess."

"You fight pretty good?"

It's coming, Raymond said to himself, and told himself to be very calm and not look away from this little boy son-of-a-bitch friend of Frank Shelby's. He said, "I fight sometimes. Why, you want to fight me?"

"Jesus," Junior said. "Listen to him."

Raymond smiled. "I thought that's what you meant." He picked up his coffee and took a sip.

"Don't drink it," Shelby said.

Raymond looked directly at him for the first time. "My coffee?"

"You see that colored boy? He's picking up his plate." As Raymond looked over Shelby said, "After he sits down I want you to go over and dump your coffee right on his woolly head."

He was at the serving table now, big shoulders and narrow hips. Some of the others from the latrine had come in behind him. He was not the biggest man in the line, but he was the tallest and seemed to have the longest arms.

"You want me to fight him?"

"I said I want you to pour your coffee on his head," Shelby answered. "That's all I said to do. You understand that, or you want me to tell you in sign language?"

Harold Jackson took a place at the end of a table. There were two men at the other end. Shifting his gaze past them as he took a bite of bread, he could see Frank Shelby and the mouthy kid and, opposite them, the big one you would have to hit with a pipe or a pick handle to knock down, and the skinny one, Joe Dean, with the beard that looked like ass fur off a sick dog. The dark-skinned man with them, who was getting up now, he hadn't seen before.

There were five guards in the room. No windows. One door. A stairway—at the end of the room behind the serving tables—where the turnkey and the little man from the train were coming down the stairs now: little man who said he was going to be in charge, looking all around—my, what a fine big mess hall—looking and following the turnkey, who never changed his face, looking at the grub now, nodding, smiling—yes, that would sure stick to their ribs—taking a cup of coffee the turnkey offered him and tasting it. Two of the guards walked over and now the little man was shaking hands with them.

That was when Harold felt somebody behind him brush him, and the hot coffee hitting his head was like a shock, coming into his eyes and feeling as if it was all over him.

Behind him, Raymond said, "What'd you hit my arm for?"

Harold wiped a hand down over his face, twisting around and looking up to see the dark-skinned man who had been with Shelby, an Indian-looking man standing, waiting for him. He knew Shelby was watching, Shelby and anybody else who had seen it happen.

"What's the matter with you?" Harold said.

Raymond didn't move. "I want to know why you hit my arm."

"I'll hit your mouth, boy, you want. But I ain't going to do it here."

Raymond let him have the tin plate, backhanding the edge of it across his eyes, and Harold was off the bench, grabbing Raymond's wrist as Raymond hit him in the face with the coffee cup. Harold didn't get to swing. A fist cracked against his cheekbone from the blind side. He was hit again on the other side of the face, kicked in the small of the back, and grabbed by both arms and around his neck and arched backward until he was look-ing at the ceiling. There were faces looking at him, the dark-skinned boy looking at him calmly, people pressing in close, then a guard's hat and another, and the turnkey's face with the mustache and the expression that didn't change.

"Like he went crazy," Junior said. "Just reared up and hit this boy."

"I was going past," Raymond said.

Junior was nodding. "That's right. Frank seen it first,

we look over and this spook has got Raymond by the neck. Frank says help him, and me and Soonzy grabbed the spook quick as we could."

The turnkey reached out, but Harold didn't feel his hand. He was looking past him.

"Let him up," Fisher said.

Somebody kicked him again as they jerked him to his feet and let go of his arms. Harold felt his nose throbbing and felt something wet in his eyes. When he wiped at his eyes he saw the red blood on his fingers and could feel it running down his face now. The turnkey's face was raised; he was looking off somewhere.

Fisher said, "You saw it, Frank?"

Shelby was still sitting at his table. He nodded slowly. "Same as Junior told you. That colored boy started it. Raymond hit him to get free, but he wouldn't let go till Junior and Soonzy got over there and pinned him."

"That's all?"

"That's all," Shelby said.

"Anybody else see it start?" Fisher looked around. The convicts met his gaze as it passed over them. They waited as Fisher took his time, letting the silence in the room lengthen. When he looked at Harold Jackson again there was a moment when he seemed about to say something to him. The moment passed. He turned away and walked back to the food tables where Mr. Manly was waiting, his hands folded in front of him, his eyes wide open behind the gold-frame glasses.

"You want to see the snake den," Bob Fisher said. "Come on, we got somebody else wants to see it too."

* * *

After breakfast, as the work details were forming in the yard, the turnkey and the new superintendent and two guards marched Harold Jackson past the groups all the way to the snake den at the back of the yard.

Raymond San Carlos looked at the colored boy as he went by. He had never seen him before this morning. Nobody would see him now for about a week. It didn't matter. Dumb nigger had done something to Shelby and would have to learn, that's all.

While Raymond was still watching them—going one at a time into the cell now—one of the guards, R. E. Baylis, pulled him out of the stone quarry gang and took him over to another detail. Raymond couldn't figure it out until he saw Shelby in the group and knew Shelby had arranged it. A reward for pouring coffee on a man. He was out of that man-breaking quarry and on Shelby's detail because he'd done what he was told. Why not?

As a guard with a Winchester marched them out the main gate Raymond was thinking: Why not do it the easy way? Maybe things were going to be better and this was the beginning of it: get in with Shelby, work for him; have all the cigarettes he wanted, some tequila at night to put him to sleep, no hard-labor details. He could be out of here maybe in twenty years if he never did nothing to wear leg-irons or get put in the snake den. Twenty years, he would be almost fifty years old. He couldn't change that. Or he could do whatever he felt like doing and not smile at people like Frank Shelby and Junior and the two convicts in his cell. He could get his head pounded against the stone wall and spend the rest of his life here. It was a lot to think about, but it made the most sense to get in with Shelby. He would be as dumb as the nigger if he didn't.

Outside the walls, the eight-man detail was marched past the water cistern—their gaze going up the mound of earth past the stonework to the guard tower that looked like a bandstand sitting up there, a nice shady pavilion where a rapid-fire weapon was trained on the main gate—then down the grade to a path that took them along the bluff overlooking the river. They followed it until they reached the cemetery.

Beyond the rows of headstones an adobe wall, low, and uneven, under construction, stood two to three feet high on the riverside of the cemetery.

Junior said, "What do they want a wall for? Them boys don't have to be kept in."

"They want a wall," Shelby said, "because it's a good place for a wall and there ain't nothing else for us to do."

Raymond agreed four year's worth to that. The work was to keep them busy. Everybody knew they would be moving out of here soon, but every day they pounded rocks into gravel for the roads and made adobe bricks and built and repaired walls and levees and cleared brush along the riverbank. It was a wide river with a current—down the slope and across the flat stretch of mud beach to the water—maybe a hundred yards across. There was nothing on the other side—no houses, only a low bank and what looked to be heavy brush. The land over there could be a swamp or a desert; nobody had ever said what it was like, only that it was California.

All morning they laid the big adobe bricks in place, gradually raising the level string higher as they worked on a section of wall at a time. It was dirty, muddy work, and hot out in the open. Raymond couldn't figure out why Shelby was on this detail, unless he felt he needed sunshine and exercise. He laid about half as many bricks as anybody else, and didn't talk to anybody except his three friends. It surprised Raymond when Shelby began working on the other side of the wall from him and told him he had done all right in the mess hall this morning. Raymond nodded; he didn't know what to say. A few minutes went by before Shelby spoke again.

"You want to join us?"

Raymond looked at him. "You mean work for you?"

"I mean go with us," Shelby said. He tapped a brick in place with the handle of his trowel and sliced off the mortar oozing out from under the brick. "Don't look around. Say yes or no."

"I don't know where you're going."

"I know you don't. You say yes or no before I tell you."

"All right," Raymond said. "Yes."

"Can you swim?"

"You mean the river?"

"It's the only thing I see around here to swim," Shelby said. "I'm not going to explain it all now."

"I don't know—"

"Yes, you do, Raymond. You're going to run for the river when I tell you. You're going to swim straight across and find a boat hidden in the brush, put there for us, and you're going to row back fast as you can and meet us swimming over."

"If we're all swimming what do you want the boat for?"

"In case anybody can't make it all the way."

"I'm not sure I can, even."

"You're going to find out," Shelby said.

"How wide is it here?"

"Three hundred fifty feet. That's not so far."

The river had looked cool and inviting before; not to swim across, but to sit in and splash around and get clean after sweating all morning in the adobe mud.

"There's a current—"

"Don't think about it. Just swim."

"But the guard—what about him?"

"We'll take care of the guard."

"I don't understand how we going to do it." He was frowning in the sunlight trying to figure it out.

"Raymond, I say run, you run. All right?"

"You don't give me any time to think about it."

"That's right," Shelby said. "When I leave here you come over the wall and start working on this side." He got up and moved down the wall about ten or twelve feet to where Soonzy and Junior were working.

Raymond stepped over the three-foot section of wall with his mortar bucket and continued working, facing the guard now who was about thirty feet away, sitting on a rise of ground with the Winchester across his lap and smoking a cigarette. Beyond him, a hundred yards or so up the slope, the prison wall and the guard tower at the northwest corner stood against the sky. The guard up there could be looking this way or he could be looking inside, into the yard of the TB cellblock. Make a run for the river with two guns within range. Maybe three, counting the main tower. There was some brush, though, a little cover before he got to the mud flat. But once they saw him, the whistle would blow and they'd be out here like they came up out of the ground, some of them shooting and some of them getting the boat, wherever the boat was kept. He didn't have to stay with Shelby, he could go up to the high country this spring and live by himself. Maybe through the summer. Then go some place nobody knew him and get work. Maybe Mexico.

Joe Dean came along with a wheelbarrow and scooped mortar into Raymond's bucket. "If we're not worried," Joe Dean said, leaning on the wall, "what're you nervous about?"

Raymond didn't look up at him. He didn't like to look at the man's mouth and tobacco-stained teeth showing in his beard. He didn't like having anything to do with the man. He didn't like having anything to do with Junior or Soonzy either. Or with Frank Shelby when he thought about it honestly and didn't get it mixed up with cigarettes and tequila. But he would work with them and swim the river with them to get out of this place. He said to Joe Dean, "I'm ready any time you are."

Joe Dean squinted up at the sun, then let his gaze come down to the guard. "It won't be long," he said, and moved off with his wheelbarrow.

The way they worked it, Shelby kept his eye on the guard. He waited until the man started looking for the chow wagon that would be coming around the corner from the main gate any time now. He waited until the guard was finally half-turned, looking up the slope, then gave a nod to Junior.

Junior jabbed his trowel into the foot of the man working next to him.

The man let out a scream and the guard was on his feet at once, coming down from the rise.

Shelby waited until the guard was hunched over the man, trying to get a look at the foot. The other convicts were crowding in for a look too and the man was holding his ankle, rocking back and forth and moaning. The guard told him goddamn-it, sit still and let him see it.

Shelby looked over at Raymond San Carlos, who was standing now, the wall in front of him as high as his hips. Shelby nodded and turned to the group around the injured man. As he pushed Joe Dean aside he glanced around again to see the wall empty where Raymond had been standing. "What time is it?" he said.

Joe Dean took out his pocket watch. "Eleven-fifty about."

"Exactly."

"Eleven-fifty-two."

Shelby took the watch from Joe Dean as he leaned in to see the clean tear in the toe of the man's shoe and the blood starting to come out. He waited a moment before moving over next to the wall. The guard was asking what happened and Junior was trying to explain how he'd tripped over the goddamn mortar bucket and, throwing his hand out as he fell, his trowel had hit the man's shoe. His foot, the guard said—you stabbed him.

Well, he hadn't meant to, Junior told the guard. Jesus, if he'd meant to, he wouldn't have stabbed him in the foot, would he?

From the wall Shelby watched Raymond moving quickly through the brush clumps and not looking back—very good—not hesitating until he was at the edge of the mud flats, a tiny figure way down there, something striped, hunched over in the bushes and looking around now. Go on, Shelby said, looking at the watch. What're you waiting for? It was eleven fifty-three.

The guard was telling the man to take his shoes off, he wasn't going to do it for him; and goddamn-it, get back and give him some air.

When Shelby looked down the slope again Raymond was in the water knee-deep, sliding into it; in a moment only his head was showing. Like he knew what he was doing, Shelby thought.

Between moans the injured man said Oh God, he believed his toes were cut off. Junior said maybe one or two; no trowel was going to take off all a man's toes, 'less you come down hard with the edge; maybe that would do it.

Twenty yards out. Raymond wasn't too good a swimmer, about average. Well, that was all right. If he was average then the watch would show an average time. He sure seemed to be moving slow though. Swimming was slow work.

When the chow wagon comes, the guard said, we'll take him up in it. Two of you men go with him.

It's coming now, somebody said.

There it was, poking along close to the wall, a driver and a helper on the seat, one of the trusties. The guard stood up and yelled for them to get down here. Shelby took time to watch the injured man as he ground his teeth together and eased his shoe off. He wasn't wearing any socks. His toes were a mess of blood, but at least they all seemed to be there. He was lucky.

Raymond was more than halfway across now. The guard was motioning to the wagon, trying to hurry it. So Shelby watched Raymond: just a speck out there, you'd have to know where to look to find him. Wouldn't that be something if he made it? God Almighty, dumb Indin probably could if he knew what to do once he got across. Or if he had some help waiting. But he'd look for the boat that wasn't there and run off through the brush and see all that empty land stretching nowhere.

Eleven fifty-six. He'd be splashing around out there another minute easy before he reached the bank.

Shelby walked past the group around the injured man and called out to the guard who had gone partway up the slope, "Hey, mister!" When the guard looked around Shelby said, "I think there's somebody out there in the water."

The guard hesitated, but not more than a moment before he got over to the wall. He must have had a trained eye, because he spotted Raymond right away and fired the Winchester in the air. Three times in rapid succession.

Joe Dean looked up as Shelby handed him his pocket watch. "He make it?" Joe Dean asked.

53

"Just about."

"How many minutes?"

"Figure five anyway, as a good average."

Junior said to Shelby, "What do you think?"

"Well, it's a slow way out of here," Shelby answered. "But least we know how long it takes now and we can think on it."

Mr. Manly jumped in his chair and swiveled around to the window when the whistle went off, a high, shrieking sound that ripped through the stillness of the office and seemed to be coming from directly overhead. The first thing he thought of, immediately, was, *somebody's trying to escape*! His first day here . . .

Only there wasn't a soul outside. No convicts, no guards running across the yard with guns.

Of course—they were all off on work details.

When he pressed close to the window Mr. Manly saw the woman, Norma Davis, standing in the door of the tailor shop. Way down at the end of the mess hall. He knew it was Norma, and not the other one. Standing with her hands on her hips, as if she was listening— Lord, as the awful piercing whistle kept blowing. After a few moments she turned and went inside again. Not too concerned about it.

Maybe it wasn't an escape. Maybe it was something else. Mr. Manly went down the hall and opened the doors, looking into empty offices, some that hadn't been used in months. He turned back and, as he reached the end of the hall and the door leading to the outside stairway, the whistle stopped. He waited, then cautiously opened the door and went outside. He could see the front gate from here: both barred doors closed and the inside and outside guards at their posts. He could call to the inside guard, ask him what was going on.

And what if the man looked up at him on the stairs and said it was the noon dinner whistle? It was just about twelve.

Or what if it was an exercise he was supposed to know about? Or a fire drill. Or anything for that matter that a prison superintendent should be aware of. The guard would tell him, "That's the whistle to stop work for dinner, sir," and not say anything else, but his look would be enough.

Mr. Manly didn't know where else he might go, or where he might find the turnkey. So he went back to his office and continued reading the history file on Harold Jackson.

Born Fort Valley, Georgia, September 11, 1879.

Mr. Manly had already read that part. Field hand. No formal education. Arrested in Georgia and Florida several times for disorderly conduct, resisting arrest, striking an officer of the law. Served eighteen months on a Florida prison farm for assault. Inducted into the army April 22, 1898. Assigned to the 24th Infantry Regiment in Tampa, Florida, June 5. Shipped to Cuba.

He was going to read that part over again about Harold Jackson deserting and being court-martialed.

But Bob Fisher, the turnkey, walked in. He didn't knock, he walked in. He looked at Mr. Manly and nodded, then gazed about the room. "If there's something you don't like about this office, we got some others down the hall.

"Caught one of them trying to swim the river, just about the other side when we spotted him." Fisher stopped as Mr. Manly held up his hand and rose from the desk.

"Not right now," Mr. Manly said. "I'm going to go have my dinner. You can give me a written report this afternoon."

Walking past Fisher wasn't as hard as he thought it would be. Out in the hall Mr. Manly paused and looked back in the office. "I assume you've put the man in the snake den."

Fisher nodded.

"Bring me his file along with your report, Bob." Mr. Manly turned and was gone.

4

Harold Jackson recognized the man in the few moments the door was open and the guards were shoving him inside. As the man turned to brace himself Harold saw his face against the outside sunlight, the dark-skinned face, the one in the mess hall. The door slammed closed and they were in darkness. Harold's eyes were used to it after half a day in here. He could see the man feeling his way along the wall until he was on the other side of the ten-by-ten-foot stone cell. It had been almost pitch dark all morning. Now, at midday, a faint light came through the air hole that was about as big around as a stovepipe and tunneled down through the domed ceiling. He could see the man's legs good, then part of his body as he sat down on the bare dirt floor. Harold drew up his legs and stretched them out again so the leg-iron chains would clink and rattle—in case the man didn't know he was here.

Raymond knew. Coming in, he had seen the figure sitting against the wall and had seen his eyes open and close as the sunlight hit his face, black against blackness, a striped animal in his burrow hole. Raymond knew. He had hit the man a good lick across the eyes with his tin plate, and if the man wanted to do something about it, now it was up to him. Raymond would wait, ready for him—while he pictured again Frank Shelby standing by the wall and tried to read Shelby's face.

The guards had brought him back in the skiff, making him row with his arms dead-tired, and dragged him wet and muddy all the way up the hill to the cemetery. Frank Shelby was still there. All of them were, and a man sitting on the ground, his foot bloody. Raymond had wanted to tell Shelby there wasn't any boat over there, and he wanted Shelby to tell him, somehow, what had gone wrong. He remembered Shelby staring at him, but not saying anything with his eyes or his expression. Just staring. Maybe he wasn't picturing Shelby's face clearly now, or maybe he had missed a certain look or gesture from him. He would have time to think about it. Thirty days in here. No mattress, no blanket, no slop bucket, use the corner, or piss on the nigger if he tried something. If the nigger hadn't done something to Shelby he wouldn't be here and you wouldn't be here, Raymond thought. Bread and water for thirty days, but they would take the nigger out before that and he would be alone. There were men they took from here to the crazy hole after being alone in the darkness too long. It can happen if you think about being here and nothing else, Raymond said to himself. So don't think about it. Go over and hit the nigger hard in the face and get it over with. God, if he wasn't so tired.

Kick him in the face to start, Harold was thinking, as he picked at the dried blood crusted on the bridge of his nose. Two and a half steps and aim it for his cheekbone, either side. That would be the way, if he didn't have on the irons and eighteen inches of chain links. He try kicking the man, he'd land flat on his back and the man would be on top of him. He try sneaking up, the man would hear the chain. 'Less the man was asleep and he worked over and got the chain around the man's neck and crossed his legs and stretched and kicked hard. Then they come in and say what happen? And he say I don't know, captain, the man must have choked on his bread. They say yeah, bread can kill a man all right; you stay in here with the bread the rest of your life. So the best thing would be to stand up and let the man stand up and hit him straightaway and beat him enough but not too much. Beat him just right.

He said, "Hey, boy, you ready?"

"Any time," Raymond answered.

"Get up then."

Raymond moved stiffly, bringing up his knees to rise.

"What's the matter with you?"

"I'll tell you something," Raymond said. "If you're any good, maybe you won't get beat too bad. But after I sleep and rest my arms and legs I'll break your jaw."

"What's the matters with your arms and legs?"

"From swimming the river."

Harold Jackson stared at him, interested. He hadn't thought of why the man had been put in here. Now he remembered the whistle. "You saying you tried to bust out?"

"I got across."

"How many of you?"

Raymond hesitated. "I went alone."

"And they over there waiting."

"Nobody was waiting. They come in a boat."

"Broad daylight—man, you must be one dumb Indin fella."

Raymond's legs cramped as he started to rise, and he had to ease down again, slowly.

"We got time," Harold Jackson said. "Don't be in a hurry to get yourself injured."

"Tomorrow," Raymond said, "when the sun's over the hole and I can see your black nigger face in here."

Harold saw the chain around the man's neck and his legs straining to pull it tight. "Indin, you're going to need plenty medicine before I'm through with you."

"The only thing I'm worried about is catching you," Raymond said. "I hear a nigger would rather run than fight."

"Any running I do, red brother, is going to be right at your head."

"I got to see that."

"Keep your eyes open, Indin. You won't see nothing once I get to you."

There was a silence before Raymond said, "I'll tell you something. It don't matter, but I want you to know it anyway. I'm no Indian. I'm Mexican born in the United States, in the territory of Arizona."

"Yeah," Harold Jackson said. "Well, I'm Filipina born in Fort Valley, Georgia."

"Field nigger is what you are."

"Digger Indin talking, eats rats and weed roots."

"I got to listen to a goddamn field hand."

"I've worked some fields," Harold said. "I've plowed and picked cotton, I've skinned mules and dug privies and I've busted rock. But I ain't never followed behind another convict and emptied his bucket for him. White or black. *Nobody.*"

Raymond's tone was lower. "You saw me carrying a bucket this morning?"

"Man, I don't have to see you, I know you carry one every morning. Frank Shelby says dive into it, you dive."

"Who says I work for Frank Shelby?"

"He say scratch my ass, you scratch it. He say go pour your coffee on that nigger's head, you jump up and do it. Man, if I'm a field nigger you ain't no better than a house nigger." Harold Jackson laughed out loud. "Red nigger, that's all you are, boy. A different color but the same thing."

The pain in Raymond's thighs couldn't hold him this time. He lunged for the dark figure across the cell to drive into him and slam his black skull against the wall. But he went in high. Harold got under him and dumped him and rolled to his feet. They met in the middle of the cell, in the dim shaft of light from the air hole, and beat each other with fists until they grappled and kneed and strained against each other and finally went down.

When the guard came in with their bread and water, they were fighting on the hard-packed floor. He yelled to another guard who came fast with a wheelbarrow, pushing it through the door and the short passageway into the cell. They shoveled sand at Harold and Raymond, throwing it stinging hard into their faces until they broke apart and lay gasping on the floor. A little while later another guard came in with irons and chained them to ring bolts on opposite sides of the cell. The door slammed closed and again they were in darkness.

Bob Fisher came through the main gate at eight-fifteen that evening, not letting on he was in a hurry as he crossed the lighted area toward the convicts' mess hall.

He'd wanted to get back by eight—about the time they'd be bringing the two women out of their cellblock and over to the cook shack. But his wife had started in again about staying here and not wanting to move to Florence. She said after sixteen years in this house it was their *home*. She said a rolling stone gathered no moss, and that it wasn't good to be moving all the time. He reminded her they had moved twice in twenty-seven years, counting the move from Missouri. She said then it was about time they settled; a family should stay put, once it planted roots. What family? he asked her. Me and you? His wife said she didn't know anybody in Florence and wasn't sure she wanted to. She didn't even know if there was a Baptist church in Florence. What if there wasn't? What was she supposed to do then? Bob Fisher said that maybe she would keep her fat ass home for a change and do some cooking and baking, instead of sitting with them other fatties all day making patchwork quilts and bad-mouthing everybody in town who wasn't a paid-up member of the church. He didn't honestly care where she spent her time, or whether she baked pies and cakes or not. It was something to throw at her when she started in nagging about staying in Yuma. She said how could anybody cook for a person who came home at all hours with whiskey stinking up his breath? Yes, he had stopped and had a drink at the railroad hotel, because he'd had to talk to the express agent about moving equipment to Florence. Florence, his wife said. She wished she had never heard the name—the same name as her cousin who was still living in Sedalia, but now she didn't even like to think of her cousin any more and they had grown up together as little girls. Bob Fisher couldn't picture his wife as a little girl. No, that tub of fat couldn't have ever been a little girl. He didn't tell her that. He told her he had to get back to the prison, and left without finishing his coffee.

Fisher walked past the outside stairway and turned the corner of the mess hall. There were lights across the way in the main cellblock. He moved out into the yard enough to look up at the second floor of the mess hall and saw a light on in the superintendent's office. The little Sunday school teacher was still there, or had come back after supper. Before going home Fisher had brought in his written report of the escape and the file on Raymond San Carlos. The Sunday school teacher had been putting his books away, taking them out of a suitcase and lining them up evenly on the shelf. He'd said just lay the report on the desk and turned back to his books. What would he be doing now? Probably reading his Bible.

Past the latrine adobe Fisher walked over to the mess hall and tried the door. Locked for the night. Now he moved down the length of the building, keeping close to the shadowed wall though moving at a leisurely pace— just out for a stroll, checking around, if anybody was curious. At the end of the building he stopped and looked both ways before crossing over into the narrow darkness between the cook-shack adobe and the tailor shop.

Now all he had to do was find the right brick to get a free show. About chin-high it was, on the right side of the cook-shack chimney that stuck out from the wall about a foot and would partly hide him as he pressed in close. Fisher worked a finger in on both sides of the brick that had been chipped loose some months before, and pulled it out as slowly as he could. He didn't look inside right away; no, he always put the brick on the ground first and set himself, his feet wide apart and his shoulders hunched a little so the opening would be exactly at eye level. They would be just past the black iron range, this side of the work table where they always placed the washtub, with the bare electric light on right above them.

Fisher looked in. Goddamn Almighty, just in time.

Just as Norma Davis was taking off her striped shirt, already unbuttoned, slipping it off her shoulders to let loose those round white ninnies that were like nothing he had ever seen before. Beauties, and she knew it, too, the way she stuck them out, standing with her hands on her hips and her belly a round little mound curving down into her skirt. What was she waiting for? Come on, Fisher said, take the skirt off and get in the tub. He didn't like it when they only washed from the waist up. With all the rock dust in the air and bugs from the mattresses and sweating under those heavy skirts, a lick-and-a-promise, armpits-and-neck wash wasn't any good. They had to wash theirselves all over to be clean and healthy.

Maybe he could write it into the regulations: Women convicts must take a full bath every other day. Or maybe every day.

The Mexican girl, Tacha Reyes, appeared from the left, coming from the end of the stove with a big pan of steaming water, and poured it into the washtub. Tacha was still dressed. Fisher could tell by her hair she hadn't bathed yet. She had to wait on Norma first, looking at Norma now as she felt the water. Tacha had a nice face; she was just a little skinny. Maybe give her more to eat—

Norma was taking off her skirt. Yes, *sir,* and that was all she had. No underwear on. Bare-ass naked with black stockings that come up over her knees. Norma turned, leaning against the work table to pull the stockings off, and Bob Fisher was looking at the whole show. He watched her lay her stockings on the table. He watched her pull her hair back with both hands and look down at her ninnies as she twisted the hair around so it would stay. He watched her step over to the tub, scratching under one of her arms, and say, "If it's too hot I'll put you in it."

"It should be all right," Tacha said.

Another voice, not in the room but out behind him, a voice he knew, said, "Guard, what's the matter? Are you sick?"

Twisting around, Bob Fisher hit the peak of his hat on the chimney edge and was straightening it, his back to the wall, as Mr. Manly came into the space between the buildings.

"It's me," Fisher said.

"Oh, I didn't know who it was."

"Making the rounds. I generally check all the buildings before I go to bed."

Mr. Manly nodded. "I thought somebody was sick, the way you were leaning against the wall."

"No, I feel fine. Hardly ever been sick."

"It was the way you were standing, like you were throwing up."

"No, I was just taking a look in here. Dark places you got to check good." He couldn't see Mr. Manly's eyes, but he knew the little son of a bitch was looking right at him, staring at him, or past him, where part of the brick opening might be showing and he could see light coming through. "You ready to go," Fisher said, "I'll walk you over to the gate."

He came out from the wall to close in on Mr. Manly and block his view; but he was too late.

"What's that hole?" Mr. Manly said.

"A hole?"

"Behind you, I can see something—"

Bob Fisher turned to look at the opening, then at Mr. Manly again. "Keep your voice down."

"Why? What is it?"

"I wasn't going to say anything. I mean it's something I generally check on myself. But," Fisher said, "if you want to take a look, help yourself."

Mr. Manly frowned. He felt funny now standing here in the darkness. He said in a hushed tone, "Who's in there?"

"Go ahead, take a look."

Through the slit of the opening something moved, somebody in the room. Mr. Manly stepped close to the wall and peered in.

The light glinted momentarily on his glasses as his head came around, his eyes wide open.

"She doesn't have any clothes on!"

"Shhhh." Fisher pressed a finger to his heavy mustache. "Look and see what they're doing."

"She's bare-naked, washing herself."

"We want to be sure that's all," Fisher said.

"What?"

"Go on, see what she's doing."

Mr. Manly leaned against the wall, showing he was calm and not in any hurry. He peered in again, as though looking around a corner. Gradually his head turned until his full face was pressed against the opening.

What Norma was doing, she was sliding a bar of yellow soap over her belly and down her thighs, moving her legs apart, and coming back up with the soap almost to her breasts before she slid it down again in a slow circular motion. Mr. Manly couldn't take his eyes off her. He watched the Mexican girl bring a kettle and pour water over Norma's shoulders, and watched the suds run down between her breasts, Lord Jesus, through the valley and over the fertile plain and to the dark forest. He could feel his heart beating and feel Bob Fisher close behind him. He had to quit looking now; Lord, it was long enough. It was too long. He wanted to clear his throat. She was turning around and he got a glimpse of her behind as he pulled his face from the opening and stepped away.

67

"Washing herself," Mr. Manly said. "That's all I could see she was doing."

Bob Fisher nodded. "I hoped that was all." He stooped to pick up the brick and paused with it at the opening. "You want to look at Tacha?"

"I think I've seen enough to know what they're doing," Mr. Manly answered. He walked out to the open yard and waited there for Fisher to replace the brick and follow him out.

"What I want to know is what you're doing spying on them."

"Spying? I was checking, like I told you, to see they're not doing anything wrong."

"What do you mean, wrong?"

"Anything that ain't natural, then. You know what I mean. Two women together without any clothes on—I want to know there ain't any funny business going on."

"She was washing herself."

"Yes, sir," Fisher said, "that's all I saw too. The thing is, you never know when they might start."

Mr. Manly could still see her, the bar of yellow soap moving over her body. "I've never heard of anything like that. They're both *women*."

"I'll agree with you there," Fisher said, "but in a prison you never know. We got men with no women, and women with no men, and I'll tell you we got to keep our eyes open if we don't want any funny business."

"I've heard tell of men," Mr. Manly said—the sudsy water running down between her breasts—"but *women*. What do you suppose they do?"

"I hope I never find out," Fisher said. He meant it, too.

He got Mr. Manly out of there before the women came out and saw them standing in the yard; he walked Mr. Manly over to the main gate and asked him if he had read the report on the escape attempt.

Mr. Manly said yes, and that he thought it showed the guards to be very alert. He wondered, though, wasn't this Raymond San Carlos the same one the Negro has assaulted in the mess hall? The very same, Fisher said. Then wasn't it dangerous to put them both in the same cell? Dangerous to who? Fisher asked. To *them*, they were liable to start fighting again and try and kill each other. They already tried, Fisher said. They were chained to the floor now out of each other's reach. Mr. Manly asked how long they would leave them like that, and Fisher said until they made up their minds to be good and kind to each other. Mr. Manly said that could be never if there was a grudge between them. Fisher said it didn't matter to him, it was up to the two boys.

Fisher waited in the lighted area as Mr. Manly passed through the double gates of the sally port and walked off toward the superintendent's cottage. He was pretty sure Mr. Manly had believed his story, that he was checking on the women to see they didn't do queer things. He'd also bet a dollar the little Sunday school teacher wouldn't make him chink the hole up either.

That was dumb, taking all his books over to the office. Mr. Manly sat in the living room of the superintendent's cottage, in his robe and slippers, and didn't have a thing to read. His Bible was on the night table in the bedroom. Yes, and he'd made a note to look up what St. Paul said about being in prison, something about all he'd gone through and how one had to have perseverance. He saw Norma Davis rubbing the bar of soap over her body, sliding it up and down. No—what he wished he'd brought were the file records of the two boys in the snake den. He would have to talk to them when they got out. Say to them, look, boys, fighting never solved anything. Now forget your differences and shake hands.

They were different all right, a Negro and an Indian. But they were alike too.

Both here for murder. Both born the same year. Both had served time. Both had sketchy backgrounds and no living relatives anybody knew of. The deserter and the deserted.

A man raised on a share-crop farm in Georgia; joined the army and, four months later, was listed as a deserter. Court-martialed, sentenced to hard labor.

A man raised on the San Carlos Indian reservation; deserted by his Apache renegade father before he was born. Father believed killed in Mexico; mother's whereabouts unknown.

Both of them in the snake den now, a little room carved out of stone, with no light and hardly any air. Waiting to get at each other.

Maybe the sooner he talked to them the better. Bring them both out in ten days—no matter what Bob Fisher thought about it. Ten days was long enough. They needed spiritual guidance as much as they needed corporal punishment. He'd tell Fisher in the morning.

As soon as Mr. Manly got into bed he started thinking of Norma Davis again, seeing her clearly with the bare light right over her and her body gleaming with soap and water. He saw her in the room then, her body still slippery-looking in the moonlight that was coming through the window. Before she could reach the bed, Mr. Manly switched on the night-table lamp, grabbed hold of his Bible and leafed as fast as he could to St. Paul's letters to the Corinthians.

For nine days neither of them spoke. They sat facing each other, their leg-irons chained to ring bolts that were cemented in the floor. Harold would stand and stretch and lean against the wall and Raymond would watch him. Later on Raymond would get up for a while and Harold would watch. They never stood up at the same time or looked at each other directly. There was silence except for the sound of the chains when they moved. Each pretended to be alone in the darkness of the cell, though each was intently aware of the other's presence. Every day about noon a guard brought them hardtack and water. The guard was not allowed to speak to them, and neither of them spoke to him. It was funny their not talking, he told the other guards. It was spooky. He had never known a man in the snake den not to talk a storm when he was brought his bread and water. But these two sat there as if they had been hypnotized.

The morning of the tenth day Raymond said, "They going to let you out today." The sound of his voice was strange, like someone else's voice. He wanted to clear his throat, but wouldn't let himself do it with the other man watching him. He said, "Don't go anywhere, because when I get out of here I'm going to come looking for you."

"I be waiting," was all Harold Jackson said.

At midday the sun appeared in the air shaft and gradually faded. Nobody brought their bread and water. They had been hungry for the first few days but were not hungry now. They waited and it was early evening when the guard came in with a hammer and pounded the ring bolts open, both of them, Raymond watching him curiously but not saying anything. Another guard came in with shovels and a bucket of sand and told them to clean up their mess.

Bob Fisher was waiting outside. He watched them come out blinking and squinting in the daylight, both of them filthy stinking dirty, the Negro with a growth of beard and the Indian's bony face hollowed and sick-looking. He watched their gaze creep over the yard toward the main cellblock where the convicts were standing around and sitting by the wall, most of them looking this way.

"You can be good children," Fisher said, "or you can go back in there, I don't care which. I catch you fighting, twenty days. I catch you looking mean, twenty days." He looked directly at Raymond. "I catch you swimming again, thirty days and leg-irons a year. You understand me?"

For supper they had fried mush and syrup, all they wanted. After, they were marched over to the main cellblock. Raymond looked for Frank Shelby in the groups standing around outside, but didn't see him. He saw Junior and nodded. Junior gave him a deadpan look. The guard, R. E. Baylis, told them to get their blankets and any gear they wanted to bring along.

"You putting us in another cell?" Raymond asked him. "How about make it different cells? Ten days, I'll smell him the rest of my life."

"Come on," Baylis said. He marched them down the passageway and through the rear gate of the cellblock.

"Wait a minute," Raymond said. "Where we going?"

The guard looked around at him. "Didn't nobody tell you? You two boys are going to live in the TB yard."

5

———◆———

A work detail was making adobe bricks over by the south wall, inside the yard. They mixed mud and water and straw, stirred it into a heavy wet paste and poured it into wooden forms. There were bricks drying all along the base of the wall and scrap lumber from the forms and stacks of finished bricks, ready to be used here or sold in town.

Harold Jackson and Raymond San Carlos had to come across the yard with their wheelbarrows to pick up bricks and haul them back to the TB cellblock that was like a prison within a prison: a walled-off area with its own exercise yard. There were eight cells here, in a row facing the yard, half of them empty. The four tubercular convicts stayed in their cells most of the time or sat in the shade and watched Harold and Raymond work, giving them advice and telling them when a line of bricks wasn't straight. They were working on the face wall of the empty cells, tearing out the weathered, crumbling adobe and putting in new bricks; repairing cells that would probably never again be occupied. This was their main job. They worked at it side by side without saying

75

a word to each other. They also had to bring the tubercular convicts their meals, and sometimes get cough medicine from the sick ward. A guard gave them white cotton doctor masks they could put on over their nose and mouth for whenever they went into the TB cells; but the masks were hot and hard to breathe through, so they didn't wear them after the first day. They used the masks, and a few rags they found, to pad the leg-irons where the metal dug into their ankles.

The third day out of the snake den Raymond began talking to the convicts on the brick detail. He recognized Joe Dean in the group, but didn't speak to him directly. He said, man alive, it was good to breathe fresh air again and feel the sun. He took off his hat and looked up at the sky. All the convicts except Joe Dean went on working. Raymond said, even being over with the lungers was better than the snake den. He said somebody must have made a mistake, he was supposed to be in thirty days for trying to escape, but they let him out after ten. Raymond smiled; he said he wasn't going to mention it to them, though.

Joe Dean was watching him, leaning on his shovel. "You take care of him yet?"

"Take care of who?" Raymond asked him.

"The nigger boy. I hear he stomped you."

"Nobody stomped me. Where'd you hear that?"

"Had to chain him up."

"They chained us both."

"Looks like you're partners now," Joe Dean said.

"I'm not partners with him. They make us work together, that's all."

"You going to fight him?"

"Sure, when I get a chance."

"He don't look too anxious," another convict said. "That nigger's a big old boy."

"I got to wait for the right time," Raymond said. "That's all."

He came back later for another wheelbarrow load of bricks and stood watching them as they worked the mud and mixed in straw. Finally he asked if anybody had seen Frank around.

"Frank who you talking about?" Joe Dean asked.

"Frank Shelby."

"Listen to him," Joe Dean said. "He wants to know has anybody seen Frank."

"I got to talk to him," Raymond said. "See if he can get me out of there."

"Scared of TB, huh?"

"I mean being with the black boy. I got enough of him."

"I thought you wanted to fight him."

"I don't know," Joe Dean said. "It sounds to me like you're scared to start it."

"I don't want no more of the snake den. That's the only thing stopping me."

"You want to see Frank Shelby," one of the other convicts said, "there he is." The man nodded and Raymond looked around.

Shelby must have just come out of the mess hall. He stood by the end-gate of a freight wagon that Junior and Soonzy and a couple of other convicts were unloading. There was no guard with them, unless he was inside. Raymond looked up at the guard on the south wall.

"I'll tell you something," Joe Dean said. "You can forget about Frank helping you."

Raymond was watching the guard. "You know, uh? You know him so good he's got you working in this adobe slop."

"Sometimes we take bricks to town," Joe Dean said. "You think on it if you don't understand what I mean."

"I got other things to think on."

As the guard on the south wall turned and started for the tower at the far end of the yard, Raymond picked up his wheelbarrow and headed for the mess hall.

Shelby didn't look up right away. He was studying a bill of lading attached to a clipboard, checking things off. He said to Junior, "The case right by your foot, that should be one of ours."

"Says twenty-four jars of Louisiana cane syrup."

"It's corn whiskey." Shelby still didn't look up, but he said then, "What do you want?"

"They let me out of the snake den," Raymond said. "I was suppose to be in thirty days, they let me out."

Shelby looked at him now. "Yeah?"

"I wondered if you fixed it."

"Not me."

"I thought sure." He waited as Shelby looked in the wagon and at the clipboard again. "Say, what happened at the river? I thought you were going to come right behind me."

"It didn't work out that way."

"Man, I thought I had made it. But I couldn't find no boat over there."

"I guess you didn't look in the right place," Shelby said.

"I looked where you told me. Man, it was work. I don't like swimming so much." He watched Shelby studying the clipboard. "I was wondering—you know I'm over in a TB cell now."

Shelby didn't say anything.

"I was wondering if you could fix it, get me out of there."

"Why?"

"I got to be with that nigger all the time."

"He's got to be with you," Shelby said, "so you're even."

Raymond grinned. "I never thought of it that way." He waited again. "What do you think?"

"About what?"

"About getting me back with everybody."

Shelby started fooling with his mustache, smoothing it with his fingers. "Why do you think anybody wants you back?"

Raymond didn't grin this time. "I did what you told me," he said seriously. "Listen, I'll work for you any time you want."

"I'm not hiring today."

"Well, what about getting me out of the TB yard?"

Shelby looked at him. He said, "Boy, why would I do that? I'm the one had you put there. Now you say one more word Soonzy is going to come down off the wagon and break both your arms."

Shelby watched Raymond pick up his wheelbarrow and walk away. "Goddamn Indin is no better than a nigger," he said to Junior. "You treat them nice one time and you got them hanging around the rest of your life."

When Raymond got back to the brick detail Joe Dean said, "Well, what did he say?"

"He's going to see what he can do," Raymond answered. He didn't feel like talking any more, and was busy loading bricks when Harold Jackson came across the yard with his wheelbarrow. Harold wore his hat pointed low over his eyes. He didn't have a shirt on and, holding the wheelbarrow handles, his shoulders and arm muscles were bunched and hard-looking. One of the convicts saw him first and said to Raymond, "Here comes your buddy." The other convicts working the adobe mud looked up and stood leaning on their shovels and hoes as Harold Jackson approached.

Raymond didn't look at him. He stacked another brick in the wheelbarrow and got set to pick up the handles. He heard one of the convicts say, "This here Indian says you won't fight him. Says you're scared. Is that right?"

"I fight him any time he wants."

Raymond had to look up then. Harold was staring at him.

"Well, I don't know," the convict said. "You and him talk about fighting, but nobody's raised a hand yet."

"It must be they're both scared," Joe Dean said. "Or it's because they're buddies. All alone in that snake den they got to liking each other. Guard comes in thinks they're rassling on the floor—man, they're not fighting, they're buggering each other."

The other convicts grinned and laughed, and one of them said, "Jesus Christ, what they are, they're sweethearts."

Raymond saw Harold Jackson take one step and hit the man in the face as hard as he could. Raymond wanted to say no, don't do it. It was a strange thing and happened quickly as the man spun toward him and Raymond put up his hands. One moment he was going to catch the man, keep him from falling against him. The next moment he balled up a fist and drove it into the man's face, right out in the open yard, the dumbest thing he had ever done, but doing it now and not stopping or thinking, going for Joe Dean now and busting him hard in the mouth as he tried to bring up his shovel. God, it felt good, a wild hot feeling, letting go and stepping into them and swinging hard at all the faces he had been wanting to smash and pound against a wall.

Harold Jackson held back a moment, staring at the crazy Indian, until somebody was coming at him with a shovel and he had to grab the handle and twist and chop it across the man's head. If he could get room and swing the shovel—but there were too many of them too close, seven men in the brick detail and a couple more, Junior and Soonzy, who came running over from the supply detail and grabbed hunks of lumber and started clubbing at the two wild men.

By the time the guard on the south wall fired his Winchester in the air and a guard came running over from the mess hall, Harold lay stunned in the adobe muck; Raymond was sprawled next to him and neither of them moved.

"Lord," Junior said, "we had to take sticks this time to get them apart."

Soonzy shook his head. "I busted mine on that nigger, he went right on fighting."

"They're a scrappy pair," Junior said, "but they sure are dumb, ain't they?"

Bob Fisher told the guard to hose them off and throw them in the snake den. He told Soonzy and Junior and the men on the brick detail to get back to work. Chained? the guard wanted to know. Chained, Fisher said, and walked off toward the stairs at the end of the mess hall, noticing the convicts who had come out of the adobe huts and equipment sheds, brought out by the guard's rifle fire, all of them looking toward the two men lying in the mud. He noticed Frank Shelby and some convicts by the freight wagon. He noticed the cooks in their white aprons, and the two women, Norma and Tacha, over by the tailor shop.

Fisher went up the stairs and down the hall to the superintendent's office. As he walked in, Mr. Manly turned from the window.

"The same two," Fisher said.

"It looked like they were all fighting." Mr. Manly glanced at the window again.

"You want a written report?"

"I'd like to know what happened."

"Those two start fighting. The other boys try to pull

them apart and the two start swinging at everybody. Got to hit 'em with shovels to put 'em down."

"I didn't see them fighting each other."

"Then you must have missed that part." Past Mr. Manly's thoughtful expression—through the window and down in the yard—he saw a convict walking toward the tailor shop with a bundle under his arm. Frank Shelby. This far away he knew it was Shelby. Norma Davis stood in the door waiting for him.

"Soon as I heard the shots," Mr. Manly said, "I looked out. They were separated, like two groups fighting. They didn't look close enough to have been fighting each other."

Bob Fisher waited. "You want a written report?"

"What're you going to do to them?"

"I told them before, they start fighting they go back in the snake den. Twenty days. They know it, so it won't be any surprise."

"Twenty days in there seems like a long time."

"I hope to tell you it is," Fisher said.

"I was going to talk to them when they got out the other day. I meant to—I don't know, I put it off and then I guess some other things came up."

Fisher could see Shelby at the tailor shop now, close to the woman, talking to her. She turned and they both went inside.

"I'm not saying I could have prevented their fighting, but you never know, do you? Maybe if I *had* spoken to them, got them to shake hands—you understand what I mean, Bob?"

Fisher pulled his gaze away from the tailor shop to the little man by the window. "Well, I don't know about that."

"It could have made a difference."

"I never seen talking work much on anybody."

"But twenty days in there," Mr. Manly said, "and it could be my fault, because I didn't talk to them." He paused. "Don't you think, Bob, in this case, you ought to give them no more than ten days? You said yourself ten days was a long time. Then soon as they come out I'll talk to them."

"That Indian was supposed to be in thirty days," Fisher said, "and you changed it to ten. Now I've already told them twenty and you want to cut it down again. I tell a convict one thing and you say something else and we begin to have problems."

"I'm only asking," Mr. Manly said, "because if I could have done something, if I'm the one to blame, then it wouldn't be fair to those two boys."

"Mister, they're convicts. They do what we tell them. Anything."

Mr. Manly agreed, nodding. "That's true, we give the orders and they have to obey. But we still have to be fair, no matter who we're dealing with."

Bob Fisher wondered what the hell he was doing here arguing with this little four-eyed squirt. He said, "They don't know anything about this. They don't know you meant to talk to them."

"But I know it," Mr. Manly said, "and the more I think about it the more I know I got to talk to them." He paused. "Soon."

Fisher saw it coming, happening right before his eyes, the little squirt's mind working behind his gold-frame glasses.

"Yes, maybe you ought to bring them in tomorrow."

"Just a minute ago you said ten days—"

"Do you have any children, Bob?"

The question stopped Fisher. He shook his head slowly, watching Mr. Manly.

"Well, I'm sure you know anyway you got to have patience with children. Sure, you got to punish them sometimes, but first you got to teach them right from wrong and be certain they understand it."

"I guess my wife's got something wrong with her. She never had any kids."

"That's God's will, Bob. What I'm getting at, these two boys here, Harold and Raymond, they're just like children." Mr. Manly held up his hand. "I know what you're going to say, these boys wasn't caught stealing candy, they took a life. And I say that's true. But still they're like little children. They're grown in body but not in mind. They got the appetites and temptations of grown men. They fight and carry on and, Lord knows, they have committed murder, for which they are now paying the price. But we don't want no more murders around here, do we, Bob? No, sir. Nor do we want to punish anybody for something that isn't their fault. We got two murderers wanting to kill each other. Two mean-looking boys we chain up in a dungeon. But Bob, tell me something. Has anybody ever spoke kindly to them? I mean has anybody ever helped them overcome the hold the devil's got on them? Has anybody ever showed them the path of righteousness, or explained to them Almighty God's justice and the meaning of ever-lasting salvation?"

Jesus Christ, Bob Fisher said—not to Mr. Manly, to himself. He had to get out of here; he didn't need any sermons today. He nodded thoughtfully and said to Mr. Manly, "I'll bring them in here whenever you want."

When Junior and Soonzy came back from clubbing the Indian and the colored boy, Frank Shelby told them to get finished with the unloading. He told them to leave a bottle of whiskey in the wagon for the freight driver and take the rest of it to his cell. Soonzy said Jesus, that nigger had a hard head, and showed everybody around how the hunk of wood was splintered. Junior said my, but they were dumb to start a fight out in the yard. This old boy over there called them sweethearts and that had started them swinging. If they wanted to fight, they should have it out in a cell some night. A convict standing there said, boy, he'd like to see that. It would be a good fight.

Shelby was looking at Norma Davis outside the tailor shop. He knew she was waiting for him, but what the convict said caught in his mind and he looked at the man.

"Which one would you bet on?"

"I think I'd have to pick the nigger," the convict said. "The way he's built."

Shelby looked around at Soonzy. "Who'd you pick?"

"I don't think neither of them look like much."

"I said who'd you pick."

"I don't know. I guess the nigger."

"How about in the mess hall," Shelby said. "The Indin showed he's got nerve. Pretty quick, too, the way he laid that plate across the boy's eyes."

"He's quick," Junior said.

"Quick and stronger than he looks," Shelby said. "You saw him swimming against the river current."

"Well, he's big for an Indin," Junior said. "Big and quick and, as Frank says, he's got some nerve. Another thing, you don't see no marks on him from their fighting in the snake den. He might be more'n the nigger can handle."

"I'd say you could bet either way on that fight," Shelby said. He told Junior to hand him the bundle for the tailor shop—a bolt of prison cloth wrapped in brown paper—and walked off with it.

Most of them, Shelby was thinking, would bet on the nigger. Get enough cons to bet on the Indin and it could be a pretty good pot. If he organized the betting, handled the whole thing, he could take about ten percent for the house. Offer some long-shot side bets and cover those himself. First, though, he'd have to present the idea to Bob Fisher. A prize fight. Fisher would ask what for and he'd say two reasons. Entertain the cons and settle the problem of the two boys fighting. Decide a winner and the matter would be ended. Once he worked out the side bets and the odds.

"Bringing me a present?" Norma asked him.

Shelby reached the shade of the building and looked up at her in the doorway. "I got a present for you, but it ain't in this bundle."

"I bet I know what it is."

"I bet you ought to. Who's inside?"

"Just Tacha and the old man."

"Well, you better invite me in," Shelby said, "before I start stripping you right here."

"Little anxious today?"

"I believe it's been over a week."

"Almost two weeks," Norma said. "Is there somebody else?"

"Two times I was on my way here," Shelby said, "Fisher stopped me and sent me on a work detail."

"I thought you got along with him."

"It's the first time he's pulled anything like that."

"You think he knows about us?"

"I imagine he does."

"He watches me and Tacha take a bath."

"He comes in?"

"No, there's a loose brick in the wall he pulls out. One time, after I was through, I peeked out the door and saw him sneaking off."

Shelby grinned. "Dirty old bastard."

"Maybe he doesn't feel so old."

"I bet he'd like to have some at that." Shelby nodded slowly. "I just bet he would."

Norma was watching him. "Now what are you thinking?"

"But he wouldn't want anybody to know about it. That's why he don't come in when you're taking a bath. Tacha's there."

Norma smiled. "I can see your evil mind working. If Tacha wasn't there—"

"Yes, sir, then he'd come in."

"Ask if I wanted him to soap my back."

"Front and back. I can see him," Shelby said. "One thing leads to another. After the first time, he don't soap you. No, sir, he gets right to it."

"Then one night you come in"—Norma giggled—"and catch the head guard molesting a woman convict."

Shelby shook his head, grinning.

"He's trying to pull his pants on in a hurry and you say, Good evening, Mr. Fisher. How are tricks?"

"God *damn*," Shelby said. "that's good."

"He's trying to button his pants and stick his shirt in and thinking as hard as he can for something to say." Norma kept giggling and trying not to. "He says, uh—"

"What does he say?"

"He says, 'I just come in for some coffee. Can I get you a cup, Mr. Shelby?' And you say, 'No, thank you. I was just on my way to see the superintendent.' He says, 'About what, Mr. Shelby?' And you say, 'About how some of the guards have been messing with the women convicts.'"

"It's an idea," Shelby said, "but I don't know of anything he can do for me except open the gate and he ain't going to do that, no matter what I get on him. No, I was wondering—if you and him got to be good friends—what he might tell you if you were to ask him."

Norma raised her arm and used the sleeve to wipe the wetness from her eyes. "What might he tell me?"

"Like what day we're supposed to move out of here. If we're going by train. If we're all going at once, or in groups." Shelby spoke quietly and watched her begin to nod her head as she thought about it. "Once we know when we're moving we can begin to make plans. I can talk to my brother Virgil, when he comes to visit, get him working on the outside. But we got to know *when*."

Norma was picturing herself in the cook shack with Fisher. "It would have to be the way I asked him. So he wouldn't suspect anything."

"Honey, you'd know better than I could tell you."

"I suppose once I got him comfortable with me."

"You won't have any trouble at all."

"It'll probably be a few times before he relaxes."

"Get him to think you like him. A man will believe anything when he's got his pants off."

"We might be having a cup of coffee after and I'll make a little face and look around the kitchen and say, 'Gee, honey, I wish there was some place else we could go.'"

"Ask him about the new prison."

"That's what I'm leading to," Norma said. "I'll tell him I hope we'll have a better place than this. Then I'll say, like I just thought of it, 'By the way, honey, when are we going to this new prison?'"

"Ask him if he's ever done it on a train?"

"I'll think of a way. I bet he's a horny old bastard."

"So much the better. He's probably never got it off a good-looking woman before in his life."

"Thank you."

"You're welcome."

"The only thing is what to do about Tacha."

"I'll have to think on that," Shelby said.

"Maybe he'd like both of us."

"Honey, he don't even have dreams like that any-more."

Tacha Reyes looked up from her sewing machine as they came into the shop and Shelby dropped the bundle on the work table. The old man, who had been a tailor here for twenty-six years since murdering his wife, continued working. He sat hunched over with his legs crossed, sewing a button to a striped convict coat.

Norma didn't say anything to them. She followed Shelby into the back room where the supplies and bolts of material were kept. The first few times they went back there together she said they were going to inventory the material or look over the thread supply or count buttons. Now she didn't bother. They went into the room and closed the door.

Tacha sat quietly, not moving. She told herself she shouldn't listen, but she always did. Sometimes she heard Norma, the faint sound of her laughing in there; she never heard Frank Shelby. He was always quiet.

Like the man who owned the café in St. David. He would come up behind her when she was working in the kitchen and almost before she heard him he would be touching her, putting his hands on her hips and bringing them up under her arms, pretending to be counting her ribs and asking how come she was so skinny, how come, huh, didn't she like the cooking here? And when she twisted away from him—what was the matter, didn't she like working here?

"How can he come in," Tacha said, "do whatever he wants?"

The tailor glanced over at the stock-room door. He didn't look at Tacha. "Norma isn't complaining."

"She's as bad as he is."

"I wouldn't know about that."

"She does whatever he wants. But he's a convict, like any of them."

"I'll agree he's a convict," the tailor said.

"You're afraid to even talk about him."

"I'll agree to that too," the tailor said.

"Some people can do whatever they want. Other people have to let them." Tacha was silent again. What good was talking about it?

The owner of the café in St. David thought he could do whatever he wanted because he paid her seven dollars a week and said she didn't have to stay if she didn't want to. He would kiss her and she would have to close her eyes hard and hold her breath and feel his hand coming up over her breast. Her sister had said so what, he touches you a little. Where else are you going to make seven dollars a week? But I don't want him to, Tacha had said. I don't love him. And her sister had told her she was crazy. You don't have to love a man even to marry him. This man was providing for her and she should look at it that way. He gave her something, she should give him something.

She gave him the blade of a butcher knife late one afternoon when no one was in the café and the cook had gone to the outhouse. She jabbed the knife into him because he was hurting her, forcing her back over the kitchen table, smothering her with his weight and not giving her a chance to speak, to tell him she wanted to quit. Her fingers touched the knife on the table and, in that little moment of panic, as his hand went under her skirt and up between her legs, she pushed the knife into his stomach. She would remember his funny, surprised expression and remember him pushing away from her again with his weight, and looking down at the knife handle, touching it gently with both hands then, standing still, as if afraid to move, and looking down at the knife. She remembered saying, "I didn't mean to—" and thinking, Take it out, you can do whatever you want to me, I didn't mean to do this.

"Some people lead," the tailor said, "some follow."

Tacha looked over at him, hunched over his sewing. "Why can Frank Shelby do whatever he wants?"

"Not everything, he can't."

"Why can he go in there with her?"

"Ask him when he's through."

"Do you know something?" Tacha said. "You never answer a question."

"I've been here—" the tailor began, and stopped as the outside door opened.

Bob Fisher stepped inside. He closed the door quietly behind him, his gaze going to the stock room, then to Tacha and past her to the tailor.

"Where's Norma at?"

Tacha waited. When she knew the tailor wasn't going to answer she said, "Don't you know where she is?"

Fisher's dull expression returned to Tacha. "I ask a question, I don't need a question back."

"She's in there," Tacha said.

"I thought I saw a convict come in here."

"He's in there with her."

"Doing what?"

"Doing *it*," Tacha said. "What do you think?"

Bob Fisher took time to give her a look before he walked over to the stock room. Then he didn't hesitate: he pushed the door and let it bang wide open and stood looking at them on the flat bolts of striped prison material they had spread on the floor, at the two of them lying close and pulling apart, at their upturned faces that were momentarily startled.

"You through?" Fisher said.

Shelby started to grin and shake his head. "I guess you caught us, boss."

Tacha could see Norma's skirt pulled up and her bare thighs. She saw Shelby, behind Fisher, getting to his feet. He was buttoning the top of his pants now. Norma was sitting up, slowly buttoning her blouse, then touching her hair, brushing it away from her face.

Tacha and the tailor began working again as Fisher looked around at them. He motioned Norma to get up. "You go on to your cell till I'm ready for you."

Shelby waited, while Norma gave Fisher a look and a shrug and walked out. He said then, "Were me and her doing something wrong? Against regulations?"

"You come with me," Fisher said.

Once outside, they moved off across the yard, toward the far end of the mess hall. Fisher held his set expression as his gaze moved about the yard. Shelby couldn't figure him out.

"Where we going?"

"I want to tell the new superintendent what you were doing."

"I didn't know of any law against it."

Fisher kept walking.

"What's going on?" Shelby said. Christ, the man was actually taking him in. Before they got to the latrine adobe Shelby said, "Well, I wanted to talk to him anyway." He paused. "About this guard that watches the girls take their bath. Pulls loose a brick and peeks in at them."

Fisher took six strides before saying, "She know who this guard is?"

"You bet," Shelby said.

"Then tell the sup'rintendent."

Son of a bitch. He was bluffing. Shelby glanced at him, but couldn't tell a thing from the man's expression.

Just past the latrine Shelby said, "I imagine this guard has got a real eyeful, oh man, but looking ain't near anything like doing, I'll tell you, 'cause I've done both. That Norma has got a natural-born instinct for pleasing a man. You know what she does?"

Fisher didn't answer.

Shelby waited, but not too long. "She knows secret things I bet there ain't ten women in the world can do. I been to Memphis, I been to Tulsa, to Nogales, I know what I'm talking about. You feel her mouth brushing your face and whispering dirty things in your ear—you know something? Once a man's had some of that woman—I mean somebody outside—he'd allow himself to be locked up in this place the rest of his life if he thought he could get some every other night. Get her right after she comes out of the bath."

Shelby paused to let Fisher think about it. As they were nearing the outside stairs he said, "Man, I tell you, anybody seen her bare-ass naked knows that's got to be a woman built for pleasure."

"Upstairs," Fisher said.

Shelby went up two steps and paused, looking around over his shoulder. "The thing is, though. She don't give it out to nobody but me. Less I say it's all right." Shelby looked right at his eyes. "You understand me, boss?"

Mr. Manly heard them coming down the hall. He swiveled around from the window and moved the two file folders to one side of the desk, covering the Bible. He picked up a pencil. On his note pad were written the names *Harold Jackson* and *Raymond San Carlos*, both underlined, and the notations: *Ten days will be Feb. 23, 1909. Talk to both at same time. Ref. to St. Paul to the Corinthians 11:19–33 and 12:1–9.*

When the knock came he said, "Come in" at once, but didn't look up until he knew they were in the room, close to the desk, and he had written on the note paper: *See Ephesians* 4:1–6.

Bob Fisher came right out with it. "He wants to tell you something."

In that moment Shelby had no idea what he would say; because Fisher wasn't bluffing and wasn't afraid of him; because Fisher stood up and was a tough son of a bitch and wasn't going to lie and lose face in front of any con. Maybe Fisher would deny the accusation, say prove it. Shelby didn't know what Fisher would do. He needed time to think. The next moment Mr. Manly was smiling up at him.

"I'm sorry I don't know everybody's name yet."

"This is Frank Shelby," Fisher said. "He wants to tell you something."

Shelby watched the little man rise and offer his hand and say, "I'm Everett Manly, your new superintendent." He watched Mr. Manly sit down again and look off somewhere.

"Frank Shelby . . . Shelby . . . forty-five years for armed robbery. Is that right?"

Shelby nodded.

"Forty-five years," Mr. Manly said. "That's a long time. Are you working to get some time off for good behavior?"

"I sure am," Shelby said. He didn't know if the man was serious or not, but he said it.

"How long have you been here at Yuma?"

"Little over a year."

"Have you got a good record here? Keep out of fights and trouble?"

"Yes, *sir*."

"Ever been in the snake den?"

"No, sir."

"Got two boys in there now for fighting, you know."

Shelby smiled a little and shook his head. "It's funny you should mention them," he said. "Those two boys are what I wanted to talk to you about."

Bob Fisher turned to look at him but didn't say a word.

"I was wondering," Shelby went on, "what you'd think of us staging a prize fight between those two boys?"

"A prize fight?" Mr. Manly frowned. "Don't you think they've done enough fighting? Lord, it seems all they like to do is fight."

"They keep fighting," Shelby said, "because they never get it settled. But, I figure, once they have it out there'll be peace between them. You see what I mean?"

Mr. Manly began to nod, slowly. "Maybe."

"We could get them some boxing gloves in town. I don't mean the prison pay for them. We could take us up a collection among the convicts."

"I sure never thought of fighting as a way to achieve peace. Bob, have you?"

Fisher said quietly, "No, I haven't."

Shelby shrugged. "Well, peace always seems to follow a war."

"You got a point there, Frank."

"I know the convicts would enjoy it. I mean it would keep their minds occupied a while. They don't get much entertainment here."

"That's another good point," Mr. Manly said.

Shelby waited as Mr. Manly nodded, looking as if he was falling asleep. "Well, that's all I had to say. I sure hope you give it some thought, if just for the sake of those two boys. So they can get it settled."

"I promise you I will," Mr. Manly said. "Bob, what do you think about it? Off-hand."

"I been in prison work a long time," Fisher said. "I never heard of anything like this."

"I'll tell you what, boys. Let me think on it." Mr. Manly got up out of the chair, extending a hand to Shelby. "It's nice meeting you, Frank. You keep up the good work and you'll be out of here before you know it."

"Sir," Shelby said, "I surely hope so."

Bob Fisher didn't say a word until they were down the stairs and Shelby was heading off along the side of the building, in the shade.

"Where you going?"

Shelby turned, a few steps away. "See about some chow."

"You can lose your privileges," Fisher said. "All of them inside one minute."

Go easy, Shelby thought, and said, "It's up to you."

"I can give it all to somebody else. The stuff you sell, the booze, the soft jobs. I pick somebody, the tough boys will side with him and once it's done he's the man inside and you're another con on the rock pile."

"I'm not arguing with you," Shelby said. "I used my head and put together what I got. You allow it because I keep the cons in line and it makes your job easier. You didn't give me a thing when I started."

"Maybe not, but I can sure take it all away from you."

"I know that."

"I will, less you stay clear of Norma Davis."

Shelby started to smile—he couldn't help it—even with Fisher's grim, serious face staring at him.

"Watch yourself," Fisher said. "You say the wrong thing, it's done. I'm telling you to keep away from the women. You don't, you lose everything you got."

That was all Bob Fisher had to say. He turned and went back up the stairs. Shelby watched him, feeling better than he'd felt in days. He sure would keep away from the women. He'd give Norma all the room she needed. The state Bob Fisher was in, Norma would have his pants off him before the week was out.

6

---❖---

"Boys, I tell you the Lord loves us all as His children; but you cross Him and He can be mean as a roaring lion. Not mean because he hates you boys, no-sir; mean because he hates sin and evil so much. You don't believe me, read your Psalms, fifty, twenty-two, where it says, 'Now consider this, ye that forget God, lest I tear you in pieces'—you hear that?—'tear you in *pieces* and there be none to deliver. . . . ' None to deliver means there ain't nothing left of you."

Mr. Manly couldn't tell a thing from their expressions. Sometimes they were looking at him, sometimes they weren't. Their heads didn't move much. Their eyes did. Raymond's eyes would go to the window and stay there a while. Harold would stare at the wall or the bookcase, and look as if he was asleep with his eyes open.

Mr. Manly flipped back a few pages in his Bible. When he looked up again his glasses gleamed in the overhead light. He had brought the two boys out of the snake den after only three days this time. Bob Fisher hadn't said a word. He'd marched them over, got them fed and cleaned up, and here they were. Here, but some-where else in their minds. Standing across the desk fif-teen, twenty minutes now, and Mr. Manly wondered if either of them had listened to a word he'd said.

"Again in the Psalms, boys, chapter eleven, sixth verse, it says, 'Upon the wicked shall rain snares, fire and brimstone and a horrible tempest'—that's like a storm—'and this shall be the portion of their cup.'

"Raymond, look at me. 'He that keepeth the com-mandments keepeth his own soul'—Proverbs, chapter nineteen, verse sixteen—'but he that despiseth His way shall die.'

"Harold Jackson of Fort Valley, Georgia, 'There shall be no reward for the evil man.' That's Proverbs again, twenty-four, twenty. 'The candle of the wicked shall be put out.' Harold, you understand that?"

"Yes-suh, captain."

"What does it mean?"

"It mean they put out your candle."

"It means God will put *you* out. You're the candle, Harold. If you're evil you get no reward and the Lord God will snuff out your life. You want that to happen?"

"No-suh, captain."

"Raymond, you want to have your life snuffed out?"

"No, sir, I don't want no part of that."

"It will happen as sure as it is written in the Book. Harold, you believe in the Book?"

"What book is that, captain?"

"The Holy Bible."

"Yes-suh, I believe it."

"Raymond, you believe it?"

"What is that again?"

"Do you believe in the Holy Bible as being the inspired word of Almighty God as told by Him directly into the ears of the boys that wrote it?"

"I guess so," Raymond said.

"Raymond, you don't guess about your salvation. You believe in Holy Scripture and its truths, or you don't."

"I believe it," Raymond said.

"Have you ever been to church?"

"I think so. When I was little."

"Harold, you ever attend services?"

"You mean was I in the arm service, captain?"

"I mean have you ever been to church."

"Yes, I been there, captain."

"When was the last time?"

"Let's see," Harold said. "I think I went in Cuba one time."

"You *think* you went to church?"

"They talk in this language I don't know what they saying, captain."

"That was ten years ago," Mr. Manly said, "and you don't know if it was a church service or not."

"I think it was."

"Raymond, what about you?"

"Yes, sir, when I was little, all the time."

"What do you remember?"

"About Jesus and all. You know, how they nail him to this cross."

"Do you know the Ten Commandments?"

"I think I know some of them," Raymond said. "Thou shall not steal. Thou shall not commit adultery."

"Thou shalt not kill," Mr. Manly prompted.

"Thou shall not kill. That's one of them."

"The one that sent you here. Both of you. And now you're disobeying that commandment again by fighting. Did you know that? When you fight you break the Lord's commandment against killing?"

"What if you only hit him?" Raymond asked. "Beat him up good, but he don't die."

"It's the same thing. Look, when you hit somebody you hurt him a little bit or you hurt him a lot. When you kill somebody you hurt him for good. So hitting is the same as killing without going all the way. You understand that, Harold?"

"What was that, captain?"

Mr. Manly swiveled around slowly to look out the window, toward the convicts standing by the main cellblock. Close to a hundred men here, and only a handful of them, at the most, understood the Divine Word. Mr. Manly was sixty years old and knew he would never have time to teach them all. He only had a few months here before the place was closed. Then what? He had to do what he could, that's all. He had to begin somewhere, even if his work was never finished.

He came around again to face them and said, "Boys, the Lord has put it on the line to us. He says you got to keep His commandments. He says you don't keep them, you die. That doesn't mean you die and they put in a grave—no-sir. It means you die and go straight down to

104

hell to suffer the fires of the damned. Raymond, you ever burn yourself?"

"Yes, sir, my hand one time."

"Boys, imagine getting burned all over for the rest of your life by the hottest fire you ever saw, hotter'n a blast furnace."

"You'd die," Raymond said.

"Only it doesn't kill you," Mr. Manly said quickly. "See, it's a special kind of fire that hurts terrible but never burns you up."

They looked at him, or seemed to be looking at him; he wasn't sure.

He tried again. "Like just your head is sticking out of the fire. You understand? So it don't suffocate you. But, boy, these flames are licking at your body and it's so hot you're a-screaming your lungs out, 'Water, water, somebody give me just a drop of water—please!' But it's too late, because far as you're concerned the Lord is fresh out of mercy."

Raymond was looking at the window again and Harold was studying the wall.

"Hell—" Mr. Manly began. He was silent for a while before he said, "It's a terrible place to be and I'm glad you boys are determined not to go there."

Harold said, "Where's that, captain?"

After they were gone Mr. Manly could still see them standing there. He got up and walked around them, picturing them from the back now, seeing the Negro's heavy, sloping shoulders, the Indian standing with a slight cock to his hip, hands loose at his sides. He'd like to stick a pin in them to see if they jumped. He'd like to holler in their ears. What's the matter with you? Don't you understand plain English? Are you too ignorant, or are you too full of evil? Answer me!

If they didn't understand the Holy Word, how was he ever going to preach it to them? He raised his eyes to the high ceiling and said, "Lord, if You're going to send me sinners, send me some with schooling, will you, please?"

He hadn't meant to say it out loud. In the silence that followed he hurried around the desk to sit down again.

Maybe that was the answer, though, and saying it out loud was the sign. Save somebody else, somebody who'd understand him, instead of two boys who couldn't even read and write. Sixty years old, he didn't have time to start saving illiterates. Somebody like Frank Shelby. Save him.

No, Frank was already trying. It was pretty clear he'd seen the error of his past life and was trying to correct it.

Norma Davis.

Get Norma in here and ask her if she was ready to accept the Lord Jesus Christ as her saviour. If she hadn't already.

No, something told Mr. Manly she hadn't yet. She was in for robbery, had shot a man, and had been arrested for prostitution in Wichita, Kansas. It wasn't likely she'd had time to be saved. She looked smart though.

Sit her down there, Mr. Manly thought.

He wasn't sure how he'd begin, but he'd get around

to picking some whores out of the Bible to tell her about—like that woman at the well. Jesus knew she was a whore, but He was still friendly and talked to her. See, He wasn't uppity about whores, they were just sinners to him like any other sinners. Take the time they're stoning the whore and He stops them, saying, Wait, only whoever of ye is without sin may cast a stone. And they had to quit doing it. See, Norma, we are all of us sinners in one way or another.

He kept looking at the way her top buttons were undone and the blouse was pulled open so he could see part of the valley between her breasts.

Where the soap had run down and over her belly.

She was sitting there trying to tempt him. Sure, she'd try to tempt him, try to show him up as a hypocrite.

She would undo a couple more buttons and he'd watch her calmly. He would say quietly, shaking his head slowly, "Norma, Norma."

She'd pull that blouse wide open and her eyes and her breasts would be staring right smack at him.

Sit back in the swivel chair then; show her he was at ease. Keep the expression very calm. And kindly.

She'd get up and lean over the desk then so they'd hang down. Great big round things with big reddish-brown tips. Then she'd jiggle them a little and he'd say in his quiet voice, "Norma, what are you doing that for? Don't you feel silly?"

Maybe he wouldn't ask her if she felt silly, but he'd say something.

She'd see she wasn't getting him, so then she'd take off her belt and slowly undo her skirt, watching him all the time, and let it fall. She'd back off a little bit and put her hands on her hips so he could see her good.

"Norma, child, cover your nakedness."

No, sir, that wasn't going to stop her. She was coming around the desk now. She'd stepped out of the skirt and was taking off the blouse, all the way off, coming toward him now without a stitch on.

He had better stand up, or it would be hard to talk to her.

Mr. Manly rose from the chair. He reached out to place his hands on Norma's bare shoulders and, smiling gently, said, "Child, 'If ye live after the flesh ye shall die'—Romans, eight, thirteen—'but if ye mortify the deeds of the body, ye shall live.'"

From the doorway Bob Fisher said, "Excuse me."

Mr. Manly came around, seeing the open door that had been left open when the two went out; he dropped his hands awkwardly to the edge of the desk.

Bob Fisher kept staring at him.

"I was just seeing if I could remember a particular verse from Romans," Mr. Manly said.

"How'd you do with Harold and Raymond?"

"It's too early to tell. I want to see them again in the morning."

"They got work to do."

"In the morning," Mr. Manly said.

Bob Fisher thought it over, then nodded and left the office. Walking down the hall, he was thinking that the little preacher may have been trying to remember a verse, but he sure looked like a man about to get laid.

* * *

Lord, give me these two, Mr. Manly said to the window and to the yard below. Give me a sign that they understand and are willing to receive the Lord Jesus Christ into their hearts.

He didn't mean a tongue of fire had to appear over the two boys' heads, or they had to get knocked to the ground the way St. Paul did. All they had to do was show some interest, a willingness to accept their salvation.

Lord, I need these two to prove my worthiness and devotion as a preacher of your Holy Writ. I need them to show for thirty years service in your ministry. Lord, I need them for my record, and I expect You know it.

Sit them down this time. Maybe that would help. Mr. Manly turned from the window and told them to take chairs. "Over there," he said. "Bring them up close to the desk."

They hesitated, looking around. It seemed to take them forever to carry the chairs over, their leg chains clinking on the wooden floor. He waited until they were settled, both of them looking past him, seeing what there was to see at this lower angle than yesterday.

"I'm going to tell you something. I know you both had humble beginnings. You were poor, you've been hungry, you've experienced all kinds of hardships and you've spent time in jail. Well, I never been to jail before I got sent here by the Bureau"—Mr. Manly paused as he grinned; neither of them noticing it—"I'll tell you though, I'll bet you I didn't begin any better off than you boys did. I was born in Clayburn County, Tennessee—either of you been there?"

Raymond shook his head. Harold said nothing.

"Well, it's in the mountains. I didn't visit Knoxville till I was fifteen years old, and it wasn't forty miles from home. I could've stayed there and farmed, or I could have run off and got into trouble. But you know what I did? I joined the Holy Word Pentacostal Youth Crusade and pledged myself to the service of the Lord Jesus. I preached over twenty years in Tennessee and Kentucky before coming out here to devote the rest of my life to mission work—the rest of it, five years, ten years. You know when your time is up and the Lord's going to call you?"

Harold Jackson's eyes were closed.

"Harold"—the eyes came open—"you don't know when you're going to die, do you?"

"No-suh, captain."

"Are you ready to die?"

"No-suh, captain. I don't think I ever be ready."

"St. Paul was ready."

"Yes-suh."

"Not at first he wasn't. Not until the Lord knocked him smack off his horse with a bolt of lightning and said, 'Saul, Saul, why do you persecuteth me?' Paul was a Jew-boy at that time and he was persecuting the Christians. Did you know that, Raymond?"

"No, I never knew that."

"Yes, sir, before he became Paul he was a Jew-boy name of Saul, used to put Christians to death, kill them in terrible ways. But once he become a Christian himself he made up for all the bad things he'd done by his own suffering. Raymond, you ever been stoned?"

"Like with rocks?"

"Hit with big rocks."

"I don't think so."

"Harold, you ever been shipwrecked?"

"I don't recall, captain."

Mr. Manly opened his Bible. "You boys think you've experienced hardships, listen, I'm going to read you something. From two Corinthians. 'Brethren, gladly you put up with fools, because you are wise . . . ' Let me skip down. 'But whereas any man is bold . . . Are they ministers of Christ?' Here it is ' . . . in many more labors, in lashes above measure, often exposed to death. From the Jews'—listen to this—'five times I received forty lashes less one. Thrice I was scourged, once I was stoned, thrice I suffered shipwreck, a night and a day I was adrift on the sea; on journeyings often, in perils from floods, in perils from robbers, in perils from my own nation . . . in labor and hardships, in many sleepless nights, in hunger and thirst, in fastings often, in cold and nakedness.' "

Mr. Manly looked up. "Here's the thing, boys. St. Paul asked God three times to let him up from all these hardships. And you know what God said to him?" Mr. Manly's gaze dropped to the book. "He said, 'My grace is sufficient for thee, for strength is made perfect in weakness.' "

Now Mr. Manly sat back, just barely smiling, looking expectantly from Raymond to Harold, waiting for one of them to speak. Either one, he didn't care.

He didn't even care what they said, as long as one of them spoke.

Raymond was looking down at his hands, fooling with one of his fingernails. Harold was looking down too, his head bent low, and his eyes could have been open or closed.

"Strength—did you hear that, boys?—is made perfect in weakness."

He waited.

He could ask them what it meant.

He began thinking about the words. If you're weak the Lord helps you. Or strength stands out more in a weak person. Like it's more perfect, more complete, when a weak person gets strong.

No, that wasn't what it meant.

It meant no matter how weak you were you could get strong if you wanted.

Maybe. Or else it was the part just before which was the important part. God saying My grace is sufficient for thee. That's right, no matter what the temptaion was.

Norma Davis could come in here and show herself and do all kinds of terrible things—God's grace would be sufficient. That was good to know.

It wasn't helping those two boys any, though. He had to watch that, thinking of himself more than them. They were the ones had to be saved. They had wandered from the truth and it was up to him to bring them back. For . . . 'whoever brings back a sinner from the error of his ways will save his own soul from death'—James, five-something—'and it will cover a multitude of sins.' "

That was the whole thing. If he could save these two boys he'd have nothing to worry about the rest of his life. He could maybe even slip once in a while—give in to temptation—without fear of his soul getting sent to hell. He wouldn't give in on purpose. You couldn't do that. But if somebody dragged you in and you went in scrapping, that was different.

"Boys," Mr. Manly said, "whoever brings back a sinner saves his own soul from death and it will cover a multitude of sins. Now do you want your souls to be saved, or don't you?"

Mr. Manly spent two days reading and studying before he called Raymond and Harold into the office again.

While they were standing by the desk he asked them how they were getting along. Neither of them wanted to answer that. He asked if there had been any trouble between them since the last time they were here. They both said no, sir. He asked if there had been any mean words between them. They said no, sir. Then it looked like they were getting somewhere, Mr. Manly said, and told them to bring the chairs over and sit down.

" 'We know,' " he said to Raymond, " 'that we have passed from death unto life because we love the brethren. He that loveth not his brethren abideth in death.' " Mr. Manly looked at Harold Jackson. " 'Whoever hateth his brother is a murderer, and ye know that no murderer hath eternal life abiding in him.' James, chapter three, the fourteenth and fifteenth verses."

They were looking at him. That was good. They weren't squinting or frowning, as if they were trying to figure out the words, or nodding agreement; but by golly they were looking at him and not out the window.

"Brethren means brother," he said. "You know that.

It doesn't mean just your real brother, if you happen to have any brothers. It means everybody's your brethren. You two are brethren and I'm your brethren, everybody here at Yuma and everybody in the whole world, we are all brethren of Jesus Christ and sons of Almighty God. Even women. What I'm talking about, even women are your brethren, but we don't have to get into that. I'm saying we are all related by blood and I'll tell you why. You listening?"

Raymond's gaze came away from the window, his eyes opening wide with interest.

Harold said, "Yes-suh, captain."

"We are all related," Mr. Manly said, watching them, "because we all come from the first two people in the world, old Adam and Eve, who started the human race. They had children and their children had children and the children's children had some more, and it kept going that way until the whole world become populated."

Harold Jackson said, "Who did the children marry?"

"They married each other."

"I mean children in the same family."

Mr. Manly nodded. "Each other. They married among theirselves."

"You mean a boy did it with his sister?"

"Oh," Mr. Manly said. "Yes, but it was different then. God said it was all right because it was the only way to get the earth populated. See, in just a few generations you got so many people they're marrying cousins now, and second cousins, and a couple hundred years it's not even like they're kin any more."

Mr. Manly decided not to tell them about Adam living to be nine hundred and thirty and Seth and Enoch and Kenan and Methuselah, all of them getting up past nine hundred years old before they died. He had to leave out details or it might confuse them. It was enough to tell them how the population multiplied and the people gradually spread all over the world.

"If we all come from the same people," Raymond said, "where do niggers come from?"

So Mr. Manly had to tell them about Noah and his three sons, Shem, Ham, and Japheth, and how Ham made some dirty remark on seeing his daddy sleeping naked after drinking too much wine. For that Noah banished Ham and made his son a "slave of slaves." Ham and his family had most likely gone on down to Africa and that was where niggers came from, descendents of Ham.

Harold Jackson said, "Where does it say Indins come from?"

Mr. Manly shook his head. "It don't say and it don't matter. People moved all over the world, and those living in a certain place got to look alike on account of the climate. So now you got your white race, your yellow race, and your black race."

"What's an Indin?" Harold said. "What race?"

"They're not sure," Mr. Manly answered. "Probably somewhere in between. Like yellow with a little nigger thrown in. You can call it the Indian race if you want. The colored race is the only one mentioned in the Bible, on account of the story of Noah and Ham."

Harold said, "How do they know everybody was white before that?"

Mr. Manly frowned. What kind of a question was that? "They just know it. I guess because Adam and Eve was white." He said then, "There's nothing wrong with being a nigger. God made you a nigger for a reason. I mean some people have to be niggers and some have to be Indians. Some have to be white. But we are all still brethren."

Harold's eyes remained on Mr. Manly. "It say in the Bible this man went to Africa?"

"It wasn't called Africa then, but they're pretty sure that's where he went. His people multiplied and before you know it they're living all over Africa and that's how you got your different tribes. Your Zulus. Your Pygmies. You got your—oh, all different ones with those African names."

"Zulus," Harold Jackson said. "I heard something about Zulus one time."

Mr. Manly leaned forward on the edge of the desk. "What did you hear about them?"

"I don't know. I remember somebody talking about Zulus. Somebody saying the word."

"Harold, you know something? For all you know you might be a Zulu yourself."

Harold gave him a funny look. "I was born in Fort Valley, Georgia."

"Where was your mama and daddy born?"

"Fort Valley."

"Where was your granddaddy born?"

"I don't know."

"Or your great-granddaddy. You know, he might have been born in Africa and brought over here as a slave. Maybe not him, but somebody before him, a kin of yours, was brought over. All your kin before him lived in Africa, and if they lived in a certain part of Africa then, by golly, they were Zulus."

Mr. Manly had a book about Africa in his collection. He remembered a drawing of a Zulu warrior, a tall Negro standing with a spear and a slender black and white cowhide shield.

He said, "Harold, your people are fine hunters and warriors. Oh, they're heathen, they paint theirselves up red and yellow and wear beads made out of lion's claws; but, Harold, they got to kill the lion first, with spears, and you don't go out and kill a lion unless you got plenty of nerve."

"With a spear, huh?" Harold said.

"Long spear they use, and this shield made out of cowhide. Some of them grow little beards and cut holes in the lobes of their ears and stick in these big hunks of dried sugar cane, if I remember correctly."

"They have sugar cane?"

"That's what it said in the book."

"They had a lot of sugar cane in Cuba. I never see anybody put it in their ear."

"Like earrings," Mr. Manly said. "I imagine they use all kinds of things. Gold, silver, if they got it."

"What do they wear?"

"Oh, just a little skimpy outfit. Some kind of cloth or animal skin around their middle. Nothing up here. Wait a second," Mr. Manly said. He went over to his book-case. He found the book right away, but had to skim through it twice before he found the picture and laid the book open in front of Harold. "There. That's your Zulu warrior."

Harold hunched over the book. As he studied the picture Mr. Manly said, "Something else I remember. It says in there these Zulus can run. I mean *run*. The boys training to be warriors, they'd run twenty miles, take a little rest and run some more. Run thirty-forty miles a day isn't anything for a Zulu. Then go out and kill a lion. Or a elephant."

Mr. Manly noticed Raymond San Carlos glancing over at the book and he said quickly, "Same with your Indians; especially your desert tribes, like the Apaches. They can run all day long, I understand, and not take a drink of water till sundown. They know where to find water, too, way out in the middle of the desert. Man told me once, when Apaches are going where they know there isn't any water they take a horse's intestine and fill it full of water and wrap it around their bodies. He said he'd match an Apache Indian against a camel for traveling across the desert without any water."

"There's plenty of water," Raymond said, "if you know where to look."

"That's what I understand."

"Some of the older men at San Carlos, they'd take us boys and make us go up in the mountains and stay there two, three days without food or water."

"You did that?"

"Plenty of times."

"You'd find water?"

"Sure, and something to eat. Not much, but enough to hold us."

"Say, I just read in the paper," Mr. Manly said. "You know who died the other day? Geronimo."

"Is that right?"

"Fort Sill, Oklahoma. Died of pneumonia."

"That's too bad," Raymond said. "I mean I think he would rather have got killed fighting."

"You ever seen him? No, you would have been too young."

"Sure, I seen him. Listen, I'll tell you something I never told anybody. My father was in his band. Geronimo's."

"Is that a fact?"

"He was killed in Mexico when the soldiers went down there."

"My goodness," Mr. Manly said, "we're talking about warriors, you're the son of an Apache warrior."

"I never told anybody that."

"Why not? I'd think you'd be proud to tell it."

"It doesn't do me any good."

"But if it's true—"

"You think I'm lying?"

"I mean since it's a fact, why not tell it?"

"It don't make any difference to me. I could be Apache, I could be Mexican, I'm in Yuma the rest of my life."

"But you're living that life," Mr. Manly said. "If a person's an Indian then he should look at himself as an Indian. Like I told Harold, God made him a nigger for a reason. All right, God made you an Indian. There's nothing wrong with being an Indian. Why, do you know that about half our states have Indian names? Mississippi.

The state I come from, Tennessee. Arizona. The Colorado River out yonder. Yuma."

"I don't know," Harold said, "that spear looks like it could break easy."

Mr. Manly looked over at him and at the book. "They know how to make 'em."

"They fight other people?"

"Sure they did. Beat 'em, too. What I understand, your Zulus owned most of the southern part of Africa, took it from other tribes and ruled over them."

"Never got beat, uh?"

"Not that I ever heard of. No, sir, they're the greatest warriors in Africa."

"Nobody ever beat the Apache," Raymond said, "till the U. S. Army come with all their goddamn guns."

"Raymond, don't ever take the Lord's name in vain like that."

"Apaches beat the Pimas, the Papagos, Maricopas—took anything we wanted from them."

"Well, I don't hold with raiding and killing," Mr. Manly said, "but I'll tell you there is something noble about your uneducated savage that you don't see in a lot of white men. I mean just the way your warrior stands, up straight with his shoulders back and never says too much, doesn't talk just to hear himself, like a lot of white people I know. I'll tell you something else, boys. Savage warriors have never been known to lie or go back on their word, and that's a fact. Man up at the reservation told me that Indians don't even have a word in their language for lie. Same thing with your Zulus. I reckon if a boy can run all day long and kill lions with a spear, he don't ever *have* to lie."

"I never heard of Apaches with spears," Raymond said.

"Oh, yes, they had them. And bows and arrows."

Harold was waiting. "I expect the Zulus got guns now, don't they?"

"I don't know about that," Mr. Manly answered. "Maybe they don't need guns. Figure spears are good enough." A smile touched his mouth as he looked across the desk at Raymond and Harold. "The thing that tickles me," he said, "I'm liable to have a couple of real honest-to-goodness Apache and Zulu warriors sitting right here in my office and I didn't even know it."

That evening, when Bob Fisher got back after supper, the guard at the sally port told him Mr. Manly wanted to see him right away. Fisher asked him what for, and the guard said how was he supposed to know. Fisher told the man to watch his mouth, and headed across the compound to see what the little squirt wanted.

Fisher paused by the stairs and looked over toward the cook shack. The women would be starting their bath about now.

Mr. Manly was writing something, but put it aside as Fisher came in. He said, "Pull up a chair," and seemed anxious to talk.

"There's a couple of things I got to do yet tonight."

"I wanted to talk to you about our Apache and our Zulu."

"How's that?"

"Raymond and Harold. I've been thinking about Frank Shelby's idea—he seems like a pretty sensible young man, doesn't he?"

Jesus Christ, Bob Fisher thought. He said, "I guess he's smart enough."

Mr. Manly smiled. "Though not smart enough to stay out of jail. Well, I've been thinking about this boxing-match idea. I want you to know I've given it a lot of thought."

Fisher waited.

"I want Frank Shelby to understand it too—you might mention it to him if you see him before I do."

"I'll tell him," Fisher said. He started to go.

"Hey, I haven't told you what I decided."

Fisher turned to the desk again.

"I've been thinking—a boxing match wouldn't be too good. We want them to stop fighting and we tell them to go ahead and fight. That doesn't sound right, does it?"

"I'll tell him that."

"You're sure in a hurry this evening, Bob."

"It's time I made the rounds is all."

"Well, I could walk around with you if you want and we could talk."

"That's all right," Fisher said, "go ahead."

"Well, as I said, we won't have the boxing match. You know what we're going to have instead?"

"What?"

"We're going to have a race. I mean Harold and Raymond are going to have a race."

"A race," Fisher said.

"A foot race. The faster man wins and gets some kind of a prize, but I haven't figured that part of it out yet."

"They're going to run a race," Fisher said.

"Out in the exercise yard. Down to the far end and back, maybe a couple of times."

"When do you want this race held?"

"Tomorrow I guess, during free time."

"You figure it'll stop them fighting, uh?"

"We don't have anything to lose," Mr. Manly said. "A good race might just do the trick."

Get out of here, Bob Fisher thought. He said, "Well, I'll tell them."

"I've already done that."

"I'll tell Frank Shelby then." Fisher edged toward the door and got his hand on the knob.

"You know what it is?" Mr. Manly was leaning back in his chair with a peaceful, thoughtful expression. "It's sort of a race of races," he said. "You know what I mean? The Negro against the Indian, black man against red man. I don't mean to prove that one's better than the other. I mean as a way to stir up their pride and get them interested in doing something with theirselves. You know what I mean?"

Bob Fisher stared at him.

"See, the way I figure them—" Mr. Manly motioned to the chair again. "Sit down, Bob, I'll tell you how I see these two boys, and why I believe we can help them."

By the time Fisher got down to the yard, the women had taken their bath. They were back in their cellblock and he had to find R. E. Baylis for the keys.

"I already locked everybody in," the guard said.

123

"I know you did. That's why I need the keys."

"Is there something wrong somewhere?"

Bob Fisher had never wanted to look at that woman as bad as he did this evening. God, he felt like he *had* to look at her, but everybody was getting in his way, wasting time. His wife at supper nagging at him again about moving to Florence. The little squirt preacher who believed he could save a couple of bad convicts. Now a slow-witted guard asking him questions.

"Just give me the keys," Fisher said.

He didn't go over there directly. He walked past the TB cellblock first and looked in at the empty yard, at the lantern light showing in most of the cells and the dark ovals of the cells that were not occupied. The nigger and the Indian were in separate cells. They were doing a fair job on the wall; but, Jesus, they'd get it done a lot sooner if the little squirt would let them work instead of wasting time preaching to them. Now foot races. God Almighty.

Once you were through the gate of the women's cellblock, the area was more like a room than a yard—a little closed-in courtyard and two cells carved into the granite wall.

There was lantern light in both cells. Fisher looked in at Tacha first and asked her what she was doing. Tacha was sitting on a stool in the smoky dimness of the cell. She said, "I'm reading," and looked down at the book again. Bob Fisher told himself to take it easy now and not to be impatient. He looked in Tacha's cell almost a minute longer before moving on to Norma's.

She was stretched out in her bunk, staring right at

him when he looked through the iron strips of the door. A blanket covered her, but one bare arm and shoulder were out of the blanket and, Jesus, it didn't look like she had any clothes on. His gaze moved around the cell to show he wasn't too interested in her.

"Everything all right?"

"That's a funny thing to ask," Norma said. "Like this is a hotel."

"I haven't looked in here in a while."

"I know you haven't."

"You need another blanket or anything?"

"What's anything?"

"I mean like kerosene for the lantern."

"I think there's enough. The light's awful low though."

"Turn it up."

"I can't. I think the wick's stuck. Or else it's burned down."

"You want me to take a look at it?"

"Would you? I'd appreciate it."

Bob Fisher brought the ring of keys out of his coat pocket with the key to Norma's cell in his hand. As he opened the door and came in, Norma raised up on one elbow, holding the blanket in front of her. He didn't look at her; he went right to the lamp and peered in through the smoky glass. As he turned the wick up slowly, the light grew brighter, then dimmed again as he turned it down.

"It seems all right now." Fisher glanced at her, twisted bare back. He tried the lantern a few more times, twist-

ing the wick up and down and knowing her bare back—
and that meant her bare front too—wasn't four feet
away from him. "It must've been stuck," he said.

"I guess it was. Will you turn it down now? Just so
there's a nice glow."

"How's that?"

"That's perfect."

"I think you got enough wick in there."

"I think so. Do you want to get in bed with me?"

"Jesus Christ," Bob Fisher said.

"Well, do you?"

"You're a nervy thing, aren't you?"

Norma twisted around a little more and let the blanket fall. "I can't help it."

"You can't help what?"

"If I want you to do it to me."

"Jesus," Bob Fisher said. He looked at the cell door
and then at Norma again, cleared his throat and said in
a lower tone, "I never heard a girl asking for it before."

"Well," Norma said, throwing the blanket aside as
she got up from the bunk and moved toward him,
"you're hearing it now, daddy."

"Listen, Tacha's right next door."

"She can't see us."

"She can hear."

"Then we'll whisper." Norma began unbuttoning his
coat.

"We can't do nothing here."

"Why not?"

"One of the guards might come by."

"Now you're teasing me. Nobody's allowed in here at night, and you know it."

"Boy, you got big ones."

"There, now slip your coat off."

"I can't stay here more'n a few minutes."

"Then quit talking," Norma said.

7

Frank Shelby said, "A race, what do you mean, a race?"

"I mean a foot race," Fisher told him. "The nigger and the Indin are going to run a race from one end of the yard to the other and back again, and you and every convict in this place are going to be out here to watch it."

"A race," Shelby said again. "Nobody cares about any foot race."

"You don't have to care," Fisher said. "I'm not asking you to care. I'm telling you to close your store and get everybody's ass out of the cellblock. They can stand here or over along the south wall. Ten minutes, I want everybody out."

"This is supposed to be our free time."

"I'll tell you when you get free time."

"What if we want to make some bets?"

"I don't care, long as you keep it quiet. I don't want any arguments, or have to hit anybody over the head."

"Ten minutes, it doesn't give us much time to figure out how to bet."

"You don't know who's going to win," Fisher said. "What's the difference?"

About half the convicts were already in the yard. Fisher waited for the rest of them to file out: the card players and the convicts who could afford Frank Shelby's whiskey and the ones who were always in their bunks between working and eating. They came out of the cellblock and stood around waiting for something to happen. The guards up on the wall came out of the towers and looked around too, as if they didn't know what was going on. Bob Fisher hadn't told any of them about the race. It wouldn't take more than a couple of minutes. He told the convicts to keep the middle area of the yard clear. They started asking him what was going on, but he walked away from them toward the mess hall. It was good that he did. When Mr. Manly appeared on the stairway at the end of the building Fisher was able to get to him before he reached the yard.

"You better stay up on the stairs."

Mr. Manly looked surprised. "I was going over there with the convicts."

"It's happened a sup'rintendent's been grabbed and a knife put at his throat till the gate was opened."

"You go among the convicts; all the guards do."

"But if any of us are grabbed the gate stays closed. They know that. They don't know about you."

"I just wanted to mingle a little," Mr. Manly said. He looked out toward the yard. "Are they ready?"

"Soon as they get their leg-irons off."

A few minutes later, Raymond and Harold were brought down the length of the yard. The convicts watched them, and a few called out to them. Mr. Manly didn't hear what they said, but he noticed neither Raymond nor Harold looked over that way. When they reached the stairs he said. "Well, boys, are you ready?"

"You want us to run," Raymond said. "You wasn't kidding, uh?"

"Course I wasn't."

"I don't know. We just got the irons off. My legs feel funny."

"You want to warm up first?"

Harold Jackson said, "I'm ready any time he is."

Raymond shrugged. "Let's run the race."

Mr. Manly made sure they understood—down to the end of the yard, touch the wall between the snake den and the women's cellblock, and come back past the stairs, a distance Mr. Manly figured to be about a hundred and twenty yards or so. He and Mr. Fisher would be at the top of the stairs in the judge's stand. Mr. Fisher would fire off a revolver as the starting signal. "So," Mr. Manly said, "if you boys are ready—"

There was some noise from the convicts as Raymond and Harold took off as the shot was fired and passed the main cellblock in a dead heat. Raymond hit the far wall and came off in one motion. Harold stumbled and dug hard on the way back but was five or six yards behind Raymond going across the finish.

They stood with their hands on their hips breathing in and out while Mr. Manly leaned over the rail of the stair landing, smiling down at them. He said, "Hey, boys, you sure gave it the old try. Rest a few minutes and we'll run it again."

Raymond looked over at Harold. They got down again and went off with the sound of the revolver, Raymond letting Harold set the pace this time, staying with him and not kicking out ahead until they were almost to the finish line. This time he took it by two strides, with the convicts yelling at them to *run*.

Raymond could feel his chest burning now. He walked around breathing with his mouth open, looking up at the sky that was fading to gray with the sun below the west wall, walking around in little circles and seeing Mr. Manly up there now. As Raymond turned away he heard Harold say, "Let's do it again," and he had to go along.

Harold dug all the way this time; he felt his thighs knotting and pushed it some more, down and back and, with the convicts yelling, came in a good seven strides ahead of the Indian. Right away Harold said, "Let's do it again."

In the fourth race he was again six or seven strides faster than Raymond.

In the fifth race, neither of them looked as if he was going to make it back to the finish. They ran pumping their arms and gasping for air, and Harold might have been ahead by a half-stride past the stairs; but Raymond stumbled and fell forward trying to catch himself, and it was hard to tell who won. There wasn't a sound from the convicts this time. Some of them weren't even looking this way. They were milling around, smoking cigarettes, talking among themselves.

Mr. Manly wasn't watching the convicts. He was leaning over the railing looking down at his two boys: at Raymond lying stretched out on his back and at Harold sitting, leaning back on his hands with his face raised to the sky.

"Hey, boys," Mr. Manly called, "you know what I want you to do now? First I want you to get up. Come on, boys, get up on your feet. Raymond, you hear me?"

"He looks like he's out," Fisher said.

"No, he's all right. See?"

Mr. Manly leaned closer over the rail. "Now I want you two to walk up to each other. Go on, do as I say. It won't hurt you. Now I want you both to reach out and shake hands. . . .

"Don't look up here. Look at each other and shake hands."

Mr. Manly started to grin and, by golly, he really felt good. "Bob, look at that."

"I see it," Fisher said.

Mr. Manly called out now, "Boys, by the time you get done running together you're going to be good friends. You wait and see."

The next day, while they were working on the face wall in the TB cellblock, Raymond was squatting down mixing mortar in a bucket and groaned as he got to his feet. "Goddamn legs," he said.

"I know what you mean," Harold said. He was laying a brick, tapping it into place with the handle of his trowel, and hesitated as he heard his own voice and realized he had spoken to Raymond. He didn't look over at him; he picked up another brick and laid it in place. It was quiet in the yard. The tubercular convicts were in their cells, out of the heat and the sun. Harold could hear a switch-engine working, way down the hill in the Southern Pacific yard; he could hear the freight cars banging together as they were coupled.

After a minute or so Raymond said, "I can't hardly walk today."

"From running," Harold said.

"They don't put the leg-irons back on, uh?"

"I wondered if they forgot to."

"I think so. They wouldn't leave them off unless they forgot."

There was silence again until Harold said, "They can leave them off, it's all right with me."

"Sure," Raymond said, "I don't care they leave them off."

"Place in Florida, this prison farm, you got to wear them all the time."

"Yeah? I hope I never get sent there."

"You ever been to Cuba?"

"No, I never have."

"That's a fine place. I believe I like to go back there sometime."

"Live there?"

"Maybe. I don't know."

"Look like we need some more bricks," Raymond said.

The convicts mixing the adobe mud straightened up with their shovels in front of them as Raymond and Harold came across the yard pushing their wheelbarrows. Joe Dean stepped around to the other side of the mud so he could keep an eye on the south-wall tower guard. He waited until the two boys were close, heading for the brick pile.

"Well, now," Joe Dean said, "I believe it's the two sweethearts."

"If they come back for some more," another convict said, "I'm going to cut somebody this time."

Joe Dean watched them begin loading the wheelbarrows. "See, what they do," he said. "they start a ruckus so they'll get sent to the snake den. Sure, they get in there, just the two of them. Man, they hug and kiss, do all kinds of things to each other."

"That is Mr. Joe Dean talking," Harold said. "I believe he wants to get hit in the mouth with a 'dobe brick."

"I want to see you try that," Joe Dean said.

"Sometime when the guard ain't looking," Harold said. "Maybe when you ain't looking either."

They finished loading their wheelbarrows and left.

In the mess hall at supper they sat across one end of a table. No one else sat with them. Raymond looked around at the convicts hunched over eating. No one seemed aware of them. They were all talking or concentrating on their food. He said to Harold, "Goddamn beans, they always got to burn them."

"I've had worse beans," Harold said. "Worse everything. What I like is some chicken, that's what I miss. Chicken's good."

"I like a beefsteak. With peppers and catsup."

"Beefsteak's good too. You like fried fish?"

"I never had it."

"You never had fish?"

"I don't think so."

"Man, where you been you never had fish?"

"I don't know, I never had it."

"We got a big river right outside."

"I never seen anybody fishing."

"How long it take you to swim across?"

"Maybe five minutes."

"That's a long time to swim."

"Too long. They get a boat out quick."

"Anybody try to dig out of here?"

"I never heard of it," Raymond said. "The ones that go they always run from a work detail, outside."

"Anybody make it?"

"Not since I been here."

"Man start running he got to know where he's going. He got to have a place to go to." Harold looked up from his plate. "How long you here for?"

"Life."

"That's a long time, ain't it?"

They were back at work on the cell wall the next day when a guard came and got them. It was about mid-afternoon. Neither of them asked where they were going; they figured they were going to hear another sermon from the man. They marched in front of the guard down the length of the yard and past the brick detail. When they got near the mess hall they veered a little toward the stairway and the guard said, "Keep going, straight ahead."

Raymond and Harold couldn't believe it. The guard marched them through the gates of the sally port and right up to Mr. Rynning's twenty-horsepower Ford Touring Car.

"Let me try to explain it to you again," Mr. Manly said to Bob Fisher. "I believe these boys have got to develop some pride in theirselves. I don't mean they're supposed to get uppity with us. I mean they got to look at theirselves as man in the sight of men, and children in the eyes of God."

"Well, I don't know anything about that part," Bob Fisher said. "To me they are a couple of bad cons, and if you want my advice based on years of dealing with these people, we put their leg-irons back on."

"They can't run in leg-irons."

"I know they can't. They need to work and they need to get knocked down a few times. A convict stands up to you, you better knock him down quick."

"Have they stood up to you, Bob?"

"One of them served time in Leavenworth, the other one tried to swim the river and they're both trying to kill one another. I call that standing up to me."

"You say they're hard cases, Bob, and I say they're like little children, because they're just now beginning to learn about living with their fellowman, which to them means living with white men and getting along with white men."

"Long as they're here," Fisher said, "they damn well better. We only got one set of rules."

Mr. Manly shook his head. "I don't mean to change the rules for them." It was harder to explain than he thought it would be. He couldn't look right at Fisher; the man's solemn expression, across the desk, distracted him. He would glance at Fisher and then look down at the sheet of paper that was partly covered with oval shapes that were like shields, and long thin lines that curved awkwardly into spearheads. "I don't mean to treat them as privileged characters either. But we're not going to turn them into white men, are we?"

"We sure aren't."

"We're not going to tell them they're just as good as white men, are we?"

"I don't see how we could do that," Fisher said.

"So we tell them what an Indian is good at and what a nigger is good at."

"Niggers lie and Indians steal."

"Bob, we tell them what they're good at as members of their race. We already got it started. We tell them Indians and niggers are the best runners in the world."

"I guess if they're scared enough."

"We train them hard and, by golly, they begin to believe it."

"Yeah?"

"Once they begin to believe in something, they begin to believe in themselves."

"Yeah?"

"That's all there is to it."

"Well, maybe you ought to get some white boys to run against them."

"Bob, I'm not interested in them running *races*. This has got to do with distance and endurance. Being able to do something no one else in this prison can do. That race out in the yard was all wrong, more I think about it."

"Frank Shelby said he figured the men wouldn't mind seeing different kinds of races instead of just back and forth. He said run them all over and have them jump things—like climb up the wall on ropes, see who can get to the top first. He said he thought the men would get a kick out of that."

"Bob, this is a show. It doesn't prove nothing. I'm talking about these boys running *miles*."

"Miles, uh?"

"Like their granddaddies used to do."

"How's that?"

"Like Harold Jackson's people back in Africa. Bob, they kill lions with *spears*."

"Harold killed a man with a lead pipe."

"There," Mr. Manly said. "That's the difference. That's what he's become because he's forgot what it's like to be a Zulu nigger warrior."

Jesus Christ, Bob Fisher said to himself. The little squirt shouldn't be sitting behind the desk, he should be over in the goddamn crazy hole. He said, "You want them to run miles, uh?"

"Start them out a few miles a day. Work up to ten miles, twenty miles. We'll see how they do."

"Well, it will be something to see, all right, them running back and forth across the yard. I imagine the convicts will make a few remarks to them. The two boys get riled up and lose their temper, they're back in the snake den and I don't see you've made any progress at all."

"I've already thought of that," Mr. Manly said. "They're not going to run in the yard. They're going to run outside."

* * *

The convicts putting up the adobe wall out at the cemetery were the first ones to see them. A man raised up to
stretch the kinks out of his back and said, "Look-it up
there!"

They heard the Ford Touring Car as they looked
around and saw it up on the slope, moving along the
north wall with the two boys running behind it. Nobody
could figure it out. Somebody asked what were they
chasing the car for. Another convict said they weren't
chasing the car, they were being taken somewhere. See,
there was a guard in the back seat with a rifle. They
could see him good against the pale wall of the prison.
Nobody had ever seen convicts taken somewhere like
that. Any time the car went out it went down to Yuma,
but no convicts were ever in the car or behind it or anywhere near it. One of the convicts asked the work-detail
guard where he supposed they were going. The guard
said it beat him. That motor car belonged to Mr. Rynning and was only used for official business.

It was the stone-quarry gang that saw them next.
They looked squinting up through the white dust and
saw the Ford Touring Car and the two boys running to
keep up with it, about twenty feet behind the car and
just barely visible in all the dust the car was raising. The
stone-quarry gang watched until the car was past the
open rim and the only thing left to see was the dust hanging in the sunlight. Somebody said they certainly had it
ass-backwards; the car was supposed to be chasing the
cons. They tried to figure it out, but nobody had an answer that made much sense.

Two guards and two convicts, including Joe Dean, coming back in the wagon from delivering a load of adobe bricks in town, saw them next—saw them pass right by on the road—and Joe Dean and the other convict and the two guards turned around and watched them until the car crossed the railroad tracks and passed behind some depot sheds. Joe Dean said he could understand why the guards didn't want the spook and the Indian riding with them, but he still had never seen anything like it in all the time he'd been here. The guards said they had never seen anything like it either. There was funny things going on. Those two had raced each other, maybe they were racing the car now. Joe Dean said Goddamn, this was the craziest prison he had ever been in.

That first day, the best they could run in one stretch was a little over a mile. They did that once: down prison hill and along the railroad tracks and out back of town, out into the country. Most of the time, in the three hours they were out, they would run as far as they could, seldom more than a quarter of a mile—then have to quit and walk for a while, breathing hard with their mouths open and their lungs on fire. They would drop thirty to forty feet back of the car and the guard with the Winchester would yell at them to come on, get the lead out of their feet.

Harold said to Raymond, "I had any lead in my feet I'd take and hit that man in the mouth with it."

"We tell him we got to rest," Raymond said.

They did that twice, sat down at the side of the road

in the meadow grass and watched the guard coming with the rifle and the car backing up through its own dust. The first time the guard pointed the rifle and yelled for them to get on their feet. Harold told him they couldn't move and asked him if he was going to shoot them for being tired.

"Captain, we *want* to run, but our legs won't mind what we tell them."

So the guard gave them five minutes and they sat back in the grass to let their muscles relax and stared at the distant mountains while the guards sat in the car smoking their cigarettes.

Harold said to Raymond, "What are we doing this for?"

Raymond gave him a funny look. "Because we're tired, what do you think?"

"I mean running. What are we running for?"

"They say to run, we run."

"It's that little preacher."

"Sure it is. What do you think, these guards thought of it?"

"That little man's crazy, ain't he?"

"I don't know," Raymond said. "Most of the time I don't understand him. He's got something in his head about running."

"Running's all right if you in a hurry and you know where you going."

"That road don't go anywhere."

"What's up ahead?"

"The desert," Raymond said. "Maybe after a while you come to a town."

"You know how to drive that thing?"

"A car? I never even been in one."

Harold was chewing on a weed stem, looking at the car. "It would be nice to have a ride home, wouldn't it?"

"It might be worth the running," Raymond said.

The guard got them up and they ran some more. They ran and walked and ran again for almost another mile, and this time when they went down they stretched out full length: Harold on his stomach, head down and his arms propping him up; Raymond on his back with his chest rising and falling.

After ten minutes the guard said all right, they were starting back now. Neither of them moved as the car turned around and rolled past them. The guard asked if they heard him. He said goddamn-it, they better get up quick. Harold said captain, their legs hurt so bad it didn't look like they could make it. The guard levered a cartridge into the chamber of the Winchester and said their legs would hurt one hell of a lot more with a .44 slug shot through them. They got up and fell in behind the car. Once they tried to run and had to stop within a dozen yards. It wasn't any use, Harold said. The legs wouldn't do what they was told. They could walk though. All right, the guard said, then walk. But god-*damn*, they were so slow, poking along, he had to keep yelling at them to come on. After a while, still not in sight of the railroad tracks, the guard driving said to the other guard, if they didn't hurry they were going to miss supper call. The guard with the Winchester said well, what was he supposed to do about it? The guard driving said it looked like there was only one thing they *could* do.

Raymond liked it when the car stopped and the guard with the rifle, looking like he wanted to kill them, said all right, goddamn-it, get in.

Harold liked it when they drove past the cemetery work detail filing back to prison. The convicts had moved off the road and were looking back, waiting for the car. As they went by Harold raised one hand and waved. He said to Raymond, "Look at them poor boys. I believe they convicts."

8

———◆◆◆———

"You know why they won't try to escape?" Mr. Manly said.

Bob Fisher stood at the desk and didn't say anything, because the answer was going to come from the little preacher anyway.

"Because they see the good in this. They realize this is their chance to become something."

"Running across a pasture field."

"You know what I mean."

"Take a man outside enough times," Fisher said, "he'll run for the hills."

"Not these two boys."

"Any two. They been outside every day for a week and they're smelling fresh air."

"Two weeks, and they can run three miles without stopping," Mr. Manly said. "Another couple of weeks I want to see them running five miles, maybe six."

"They'll run as long as it's easier than working."

Mr. Manly smiled a little. "I see you don't know them very well."

"I have known them all my life," Bob Fisher said.

"When running becomes harder than working, they'll figure a way to get out of it. They'll break each other's legs if they have to."

"All right, then I'll talk to them again. You can be present, Bob, and I'll prove to you you're wrong."

"I understand you write a weekly report to Mr. Rynning," Fisher said. "Have you told him what you're doing?"

"As a matter of fact, I have."

"You told him you got them running outside?"

"I told him I'm trying something out on two boys considered incorrigible, a program that combines spiritual teaching and physical exercise. He's made no mention to me what he thinks. But if you want to write to him, Bob, go right ahead."

"If it's all the same to you," Fisher said, "I want it on the record I didn't have nothing to do with this in any way at all."

Three miles wasn't so bad and it was easier to breathe at the end of the stretch. It didn't feel as if their lungs were burning any more. They would walk for a few minutes and run another mile and then walk again. Maybe they could do it again, run another mile before resting. But why do it if they didn't have to, if the guards didn't expect it? They would run a little way and when Raymond or Harold would call out they had to rest the car and would stop and wait for them.

"I think we could do it," Raymond said.

"Sure we could."

"Maybe run four, five miles at the start."

"We could do that too," Harold said, "but why would we want to?"

"I mean to see if we could do it."

"Man, we could run five miles right now if we wanted."

"I don't know."

"If we had something to run for. All I see it doing is getting us tired."

"It's better than laying adobes, or working on the rock pile."

"I believe you're right there," Harold said.

"Well," Raymond said, "we can try four miles, five miles at any time we want. What's the hurry?"

"What's the hurry," Harold said. "I wish that son of a bitch would give us a cigarette. Look at him sucking on it and blowing the smoke out. Man."

They were getting along all right with the guards, because the guards were finding out this was pretty good duty, driving around the countryside in a Ford Touring Car. Ride around for a few hours. Smoke any time they wanted. Put the canvas top up if it got too hot in the sun. The guards weren't dumb, though. They stayed away from trees and the riverbank, keeping to open range country once they had followed the railroad tracks out beyond town.

The idea of a train going by interested Harold. He pictured them running along the road where it was close to the tracks and the train coming up behind them out of the depot, not moving too fast. As the guards watched the train, Harold saw himself and Raymond break through the weeds to the gravel roadbed, run with the

147

train and swing up on one of those iron-rung ladders they had on boxcars. Then the good part. The guards are watching the train and all of a sudden the guards see them on the boxcar—*waving to them*.

"Waving good-bye," Harold said to Raymond when they were resting one time and he told him about it.

Raymond was grinning. "They see the train going away, they don't know what to do."

"Oh, they take a couple of shots," Harold said. "But they so excited, man, they can't even hit the train."

"We're waving bye-bye."

"Yeah, while they shooting at us."

"It would be something, all right." Raymond had to wipe his eyes.

After a minute Harold said, "Where does the train go to?"

"I don't know. I guess different places."

"That's the trouble," Harold said. "You got to know where you going. You can't stay on the train. Sooner or later you got to get off and start running again."

"You think we could run five miles, uh?"

"If we wanted to," Harold said.

It was about a week later that Mr. Manly woke up in the middle of the night and said out loud in the bedroom, "All right, if you're going to keep worrying about it, why don't you see for yourself what they're doing?"

That's what he did the next day: hopped in the front seat of the Ford Touring Car and went along to watch the two boys do their road work.

It didn't bother the guard driving too much. He had less to say was all. But the guard with the Winchester yelled at Raymond and Harold more than he ever did before to come on, pick 'em up, keep closer to the car. Mr. Manly said the dust was probably bothering them. The guard said it was bothering him too, because he had to see them before he could watch them. He said you get a con outside you watch him every second.

Raymond and Harold ran three miles and saw Mr. Manly looking at his watch. Later on, when they were resting, he came over and squatted down in the grass with them.

"Three miles in twenty-five minutes," he said. "That's pretty good. You reckon you could cover five miles in an hour?"

"I don't think so," Raymond said. "It's not us, we want to do it. It's our legs."

"Well, wanting something is half of getting it," Mr. Manly said. "I mean if you want something bad enough."

"Sure, we want to do it."

"Why?"

"Why? Well, I guess because we got to do it."

"You just said you wanted to."

"Yeah, we like to run."

"And I'm asking you why." Mr. Manly waited a moment. "Somebody told me all you fellas want to do is get out of work."

"Who tole you that?"

"It doesn't matter who it was. You know what I told him? I told him he didn't know you boys very well. I told him you were working harder now, running, than you ever worked in your life."

"That's right," Raymond said.

"Because you see a chance of doing something nobody else in the prison can do. Run twenty miles in a day."

Raymond said, "You want us to run twenty miles?"

"*You* want to run twenty miles. You're an Apache Indian, aren't you? And Harold's a Zulu. Well, by golly, an Apache Indian and a Zulu can run twenty miles, thirty miles a day, and there ain't a white man in this territory can say that."

"You want us to run twenty miles?" Raymond said again.

"I want you to start thinking of who you are, that's what I want. I want you to start thinking like warriors for a change instead of like convicts."

Raymond was watching him, nodding as he listened. He said, "Do these waryers think different than other people?"

"They think of who they are." An angry little edge came into Mr. Manly's tone. "They got pride in their tribe and their job, and everything they do is to make them better warriors—the way they live, the way they dress, the way they train to harden theirselves, the way they go without food or water to show their bodies their willpower is in charge here and, by golly, their bodies better do what they're told. Raymond, you say you're Apache Indian?"

"Yes, sir, that's right."

"Harold, you believe you're a Zulu?"

"Yes-suh, captain, a Zulu."

"Then prove it to me, both of you. Let me see how good you are."

As Mr. Manly got to his feet he glanced over at the guards, feeling a little funny now in the silence and wondering if they had been listening. Well, so what if they had? He was superintendent, wasn't he? And he answered right back, You're darn right.

"You boys get ready for some real training," he said now. "I'm taking you at your word."

Raymond waited until he walked away and had reached the car. "Who do you think tole him we're doing this to get out of work?"

"I don't know," Harold said. "Who do you think?"

"I think that son of a bitch Frank Shelby."

"Yeah," Harold said, "he'd do it, wouldn't he?"

On Visiting Day the mess-hall tables were placed in a single line, dividing the room down the middle. The visitors remained on one side and the convicts on the other. Friends and relatives could sit down facing each other if they found a place at the tables; but they couldn't touch, not even hands, and a visitor was not allowed to pass anything to a convict.

Frank Shelby always got a place at the tables and his visitor was always his brother, a slightly older and heavier brother, but used to taking orders from Frank.

Virgil Shelby said, "By May for sure."

"I don't want a month," Frank said. "I want a day."

"I'm telling you what I know. They're done building the place, they're doing something inside the walls now and they won't let anybody in."

"You can talk to a workman."

"I talked to plenty of workmen. They don't know anything."

"What about the railroad?"

"Same thing. Old boys in the saloon talk about moving the convicts, but they don't know when."

"Somebody knows."

"Maybe they don't. Frank, what are you worried about? Whatever the day is we're going to be ready. I've been over and across that rail line eight times—nine times now—and I know just where I'm going to take you off that train."

"You're talking too loud."

Virgil took time to look down the table both ways, at the convicts hunched over the tables shoulder to shoulder and their visitors crowded in on this side, everyone trying to talk naturally without being overheard. When Virgil looked at his brother again, he said, "What I want to know is how many?"

"Me. Junior, Soonzy, Joe Dean. Norma." Frank Shelby paused. "No, we don't need to take Norma."

"It's up to you."

"No, we don't need her."

"That's four. I want to know you're together, all in the same place, because once we hit that train there's going to be striped suits running all over the countryside."

"That might be all right."

"It could be. Give them some people to chase after. But it could mess things up too."

"Well, right now all I hear is you wondering what's going to happen. You come with more than that, or I live the next forty years in Florence, Arizona."

"I'm going to stay in Yuma a while, see what I can find out about the train. You need any money?" Virgil asked.

"If I have to buy some guards. I don't know, get me three, four hundred."

"I'll send it in with the stores. Anything else?"

"A good idea, buddy."

"Don't worry, Frank, we're going to get you out. I'll swear to it."

"Yeah, well, I'll see you."

"Next month," Virgil said. He turned to swing a leg over the bench, then looked at his brother again. "Something funny I seen coming here—these two convicts running behind a Ford automobile. What do you suppose they was doing, Frank?"

Shelby had to tear his pants nearly off to see Norma again. He ripped them down the in-seam from crotch to ankle and told the warehouse guard he'd caught them on some bailing wire and, man, it had almost fixed him good. The guard said to get another pair out of stores. Shelby said all right, and he'd leave his ripped pants at the tailor's on the way back. The guard knew what Shelby was up to; he accepted the sack of Bull Durham Shelby offered and played the game with him. It wasn't hurting anybody.

So he got his new pants and headed for the tailor shop. As soon as he was inside, Norma Davis came off the work table, where she was sitting smoking a cigarette, and went into the stock room. Shelby threw the ripped pants at the tailor, told Tacha to watch out the window for Bob Fisher, and followed Norma into the back room, closing the door behind him.

"He's not as sure of himself as he used to be," Tacha said. "He's worried."

The tailor was studying the ripped seam closely.

Tacha was looking out the window, at the colorless tone of the yard in sunlight: adobe and granite and black shadow lines in the glare. The brick detail was at work across the yard, but she couldn't hear them. She listened for sounds, out in the yard and in the room behind her, but there were none.

"They're quiet in there, uh?"

The tailor said nothing.

"You expect them to make sounds like animals, those two. That old turnkey makes sounds. God, like he's dying. Like somebody stuck a knife—" Tacha stopped.

"I don't know what you're talking about," the tailor said.

"I'm talking about Mr. Fisher, the turnkey, the sounds he makes when he's in her cell."

"And I don't want to know." The tailor kept his head low over his sewing machine.

"He sneaks in at night—"

"I said I don't want to hear about it."

"He hasn't been coming very long. Just the past few

weeks. Not every night either. He makes some excuse to go in there, like to fix the lantern or search the place for I don't know what. One time she say, 'Oh, I think there is a tarantula in here,' and the turnkey hurries in there to kill it. I want to say to him, knowing he's taking off his pants then, 'Hey, mister, that's a funny thing to kill a tarantula with.'"

"I'm not listening to you," the tailor said. "Not a word."

In the closeness of the stock room Shelby stepped back to rest his arm on one of the shelves. Watching Norma, he loosened his hat, setting it lightly on his forehead. "Goodness," he said, "I didn't even take off my hat, did I?"

Norma let her skirt fall. She smoothed it over her hips and began buttoning her blouse. "I feel like a mare, standing like that."

"Honey, you don't look like a mare. I believe you are about the trickiest thing I ever met."

"I know a few more ways."

"I bet you do, for a fact."

"That old man, he breathes through his nose right in your ear. Real loud, like he's having heart failure."

Shelby grinned. "That would be something. He has a stroke while he's in there with you."

"I'll tell you, he isn't any fun at all."

"You ain't loving him for the pleasure, sweetheart. You're supposed to be finding out things."

"He doesn't know yet when we're going."

"You asked him?"

"I said to him, 'I will sure be glad to get out of this place.' He said it wouldn't be much longer and I said, 'Oh, when are we leaving here?' He said he didn't know for sure, probably in a couple of months."

"We got to know the day," Shelby said.

"Well, if he don't know it he can't hardly tell me, can he?"

"Maybe he can find it out."

"From who?"

"I don't know. The superintendent, somebody."

"That little fella, he walks around, he looks like he's lost, can't find his mama."

"Well, mama, maybe you should talk to him."

"Get him to come to my cell."

"Jesus, you'd eat him up."

Norma giggled. "You say terrible things."

"I mean by the time you're through there wouldn't be nothing left of him."

"If *you're* through, you better get out of here."

"I talked to Virgil. He doesn't know anything either."

"Don't worry," Norma said. "One of us'll find out. I just want to be sure you take me along when the time comes."

Shelby gave her a nice little sad smile and shook his head slowly. "Sweetheart," he said, "how could I go anywhere without you?"

Good timing, Norma Davis believed, was one of the most important things in life. You had to think of the other person. You had to know his moods and reactions and know the right moment to spring little surprises.

You didn't want the person getting too excited and ruining everything before it was time.

That's why she brought Bob Fisher along for almost two months before she told him her secret.

It was strange; like instinct. One night, as she heard the key turning in the iron door of the cellblock, she knew it was Bob and, for some reason, she also knew she was going to tell him tonight. Though not right away.

First he had to go through his act. He had to look in at Tacha and ask her what was she doing, reading? Then he had to come over and see Norma in the bunk and look around the cell for a minute and ask if everything was all right. Norma was ready. She told him she had a terrible sore ankle and would he look at it and see if it was sprained or anything. She got him in there and then had to slow down and be patient while he actually, honest to God, looked at her ankle and said in a loud voice it looked all right to him. He whispered after that, getting out of his coat and into the bunk with her, but raising up every once in a while to look at the cell door.

Norma said, "What's the matter?"

"Tacha, she can hear everything."

"If she bothers you, why don't you put her some place else?"

"This is the women's block. There isn't any place else."

Norma got her hand inside his shirt and started fooling with the hair on his chest. "How does Tacha look to you?"

"Cut it out, it tickles," Fisher said. "What do you mean, how does she look?"

"I don't know, I don' think she looks so good. I hear her coughing at night."

"Listen, I only got a few minutes."

Norma handled the next part of it, making him believe he was driving her wild, and as he lay on the edge of the bunk breathing out of his nose, she told him her secret.

She said, "Guess what? I know somebody who's planning to escape."

That got him up and leaning over her again.

"Who?"

"I heard once," Norma said, "if you help the authorities here they'll help you."

"Who is it?"

"I heard of convicts who helped stop men trying to escape and got pardoned. Is that right?"

"It's happened."

"They were freed?"

"That's right."

"You think it might happen again?"

"It could. Who's going out?"

"Not out of here. From the train. You think if I found out all about it and told you I'd get a pardon?"

"I think you might," Fisher said. "I can't promise, but you'd have a good chance."

"It's Frank Shelby."

"That's what I thought."

"His brother Virgil's going to help him."

"Where do they jump the train?"

"Frank doesn't know yet, but soon as I find out I'll tell you."

"You promise?"

"Cross my heart."

"You're a sweet girl, Norma. You know that?"

She smiled at him in the dim glow of the lantern and said, "I try to be."

Another week passed before Bob Fisher thought of something else Norma had said.

He was in the tailor shop that day, just checking, not for any special reason. Tacha looked up at him and said, "Norma's not here."

"I can see that."

"She's at the toilet—if you're looking for her."

"I'm not looking for her," Fisher said.

He wasn't sure if Tacha was smiling then or not—like telling him she knew all about him. Little Mexican bitch, she had better not try to get smart with him.

It was then he thought of what Norma had said. About Tacha not looking so good. Coughing at night.

Hell, yes, Bob Fisher said to himself and wondered why he hadn't thought of it before. There was only one place around here to put anybody who was coughing sick. Over in the TB cellblock.

9

The guard, R. E. Baylis, was instructed to move the Mexican girl to the TB area after work, right before supper. It sounded easy enough.

But when he told Tacha she held back and didn't want to go. What for? Look at her. Did she look like she had TB? She wasn't even sick. R. E. Baylis told her to get her things, she was going over there and that's all there was to it. She asked him if Mr. Fisher had given the order, and when he said sure, Tacha said she thought so; she should have known he would do something like this. Goddamn-it, R. E. Baylis thought, he didn't have to explain anything to her. He did though. He said it must be they were sending her over there to help out—bring the lungers their food, get them their medicine. He said there were two boys in there supposed to be looking after the lungers, but nobody had seen much of them the past couple of months or so, what with all the running they were doing. They would go out early in the morning, just about the time it was getting light, and generally not get back until the afternoon. He said some of the guards were talking about them, how they had changed;

161

but he hadn't seen them in a while. Tacha only half listened to him. She wasn't interested in the two convicts, she was thinking about the TB cellblock and wondering what it would be like to live there. She remembered the two he was talking about; she knew them by sight. Though when she walked into the TB yard and saw them again, she did not recognize them immediately as the same two men.

R. E. Baylis got a close look at them and went to find Bob Fisher.

"She give you any trouble?" Fisher asked.

He sat at a table in the empty mess hall with a cup of coffee in front of him. The cooks were bringing in the serving pans and setting up for supper.

"No trouble once I got her there," R. E. Baylis said. "What I want to know is what the Indin and the nigger are doing?"

"I don't know anything about them and don't want to know. They're Mr. Manly's private convicts." Fisher held his cup close to his face and would lean in to sip at it.

"Haven't you seen them lately?"

"I see them go by once in a while, going out the gate."

"But you haven't been over there? You haven't seen them close?"

"Whatever he's got them doing isn't any of my business. I told him I don't want no part of it."

"You don't care what they're doing?"

"I got an inventory of equipment and stores have to be tallied before we ship out of here and that ain't very long away."

"You don't care if they made spears," R. E. Baylis said, "and they're throwing them at a board stuck in the ground?"

Bob Fisher started coughing and spilled some of his coffee down the front of his uniform.

Mr. Manly said, "Yes, I know they got spears. Made of bamboo fishing poles and brick-laying trowels stuck into one end for the point. If a man can use a trowel to work with all day, why can't he use one for exercise?"

"Because a spear is a weapon," Fisher said. "You can kill a man with it."

"Bob, you got some kind of stain there on your uniform."

"What I mean is you don't let convicts make *spears*."

"Why not, if they're for a good purpose?"

No, Bob Fisher said to himself—with R. E. Baylis standing next to him, listening to it all—this time, goddamn-it, don't let him mix you up. He said, "Mr. Manly, for some reason I seem to have trouble understanding you."

"What is it you don't understand, Bob?"

"Every time I come up here, it's like you and me are talking about two different things. I come in, I know what the rules are here and I know what I want to say. Then you begin talking and it's like we get onto something else."

"We look at a question from different points of view," Mr. Manly said. "That's all it is."

"All right, R. E. Baylis here says they got spears. I

haven't been over to see for myself. We was down-stairs—I don't know, something told me I should see you about it first."

"I'm glad you did."

"How long have they had 'em?"

"About two weeks. Bob, they run fourteen miles yesterday. Only stopped three times to rest."

"I don't see what that's got to do with the spears."

"Well, you said you wanted it to show in the record you're not having anything to do with this business. Isn't that right?"

"I want it to show I'm against their being taken out-side."

"I haven't told you anything what's going on, have I?"

"I haven't asked neither."

"That's right. This is the first time you've mentioned those boys in over two months. You don't know what I'm teaching them, but you come in here and tell me they can't have spears."

"It's in the rules."

"It says in the rules they can't have spears for any pur-pose whatsoever?"

"It say a man found with a weapon is to be put under maximum security for no less than ten days."

"You mean put in the snake den."

"I sure do."

"You believe those two boys have been found with weapons?"

"When you make a spear out of a trowel, it becomes a weapon."

"But what if I was the one told them to make the spears?"

"I was afraid you might say that."

"As a matter of fact, I got them the fishing poles myself. Bought them in town."

"Bought them in town," Bob Fisher said. His head seemed to nod a little as he stared at Mr. Manly. "This here is what I meant before about not understanding some things. I would sure like to know why you want them to have spears?"

"Bob," Mr. Manly said, "that's the only way to learn, isn't it? Ask questions." He looked up past Fisher then, at the wall clock. "Say, it's about supper time already."

"Mr. Manly, I'll wait on supper if you'll explain them spears to me."

"I'll do better than that," Mr. Manly said, "I'll show you. First though we got to get us a pitcher of ice water."

"I'll even pass on that," Fisher said. "I'm not thirsty *or* hungry."

Mr. Manly gave him a patient, understanding grin. "The ice water isn't for us, Bob."

"No sir," Fisher said. He was nodding again, very slowly, solemnly. "I should've known better, shouldn't I?"

Tacha remembered them from months before wearing leg-irons and pushing the wheelbarrows. She remembered the Negro working without a shirt on and remembered thinking the other one tall for an Indian. She had never spoken to them or watched them for a definite reason. She had probably not been closer than fifty feet to either of them. But she was aware now of the striking change in their appearance and at first it gave her a strange, tense feeling. She was afraid of them.

The guard had looked as if he was afraid of them too, and maybe that was part of the strange feeling. He didn't tell her which cell was to be hers. He stared at the Indian and the Negro, who were across the sixty-foot yard by the wall, and then hurried away, leaving her here.

As soon as he was gone the tubercular convicts began talking to her. One of them asked if she had come to live with them. When she nodded he said she could bunk with him if she wanted. They laughed and another one said no, come on in his cell, he would show her a fine old time. She didn't like the way they stared at her. They sat in front of their cells on stools and a wooden bunk frame and looked as if they had been there a long time and seldom shaved or washed themselves.

She wasn't sure if the Indian and the Negro were watching her. The Indian was holding something that looked like a fishing pole. The Negro was standing by an upright board that was as tall as he was and seemed to be nailed to a post. Another of the poles was sticking out of the board. Neither of them was wearing a shirt; that was the first thing she noticed about them from across the yard.

They came over when she turned to look at the cells and one of the tubercular convicts told her again to come on, put her blanket and stuff in with his. Now, when she looked around, not knowing what to do, she saw them approaching.

She saw the Indian's hair, how long it was, covering his ears, and the striped red and black cloth he wore as a headband. She saw the Negro's mustache that curved around his mouth into a short beard and the cuts on his face, like knife scars, that slanted down from both of his cheekbones. This was when she was afraid of them, as they walked up to her.

"The cell on the end," Raymond said. "Why don't you take that one?"

She made herself hold his gaze. "Who else is in there, you?"

"Nobody else."

Harold said, "You got the TB?"

"I don't have it yet."

"You do something to Frank Shelby?"

"Maybe I did," she said, "I don't know."

"If you don't have the TB," Harold said, "you did something to somebody."

She began to feel less afraid already, talking to them, and yet she knew there was something different about their faces and the way they looked at her. "I think the turnkey, Mr. Fisher, did it," Tacha said, "so I wouldn't see him going in with Norma."

"I guess there are all kinds of things going on," Harold said. "They put you in here, it's not so bad. It was cold at night when we first come, colder than the big cellblock, but now it's all right." He glanced toward the tubercular convicts. "Don't worry about the scarecrows. They won't hurt you."

"They lock everybody in at night," Raymond said. "During the day one of them tries something, you can run."

That was a strange thing too: being afraid of them at first because of the way they looked, then hearing them say not to worry and feeling at ease with them, believing them.

Raymond said, "We fixed up that cell for you. It's like a new one."

She was inside unrolling her bedding when the guard returned with the superintendent and the turnkey, Mr. Fisher. She heard one of them say, "Harold, come out here," and she looked up to see them through the open doorway: the little man in the dark suit and two in guard uniforms, one of them, R. E. Baylis, holding a dented tin pitcher. The Indian was still in the yard, not far from them, but she didn't see the Negro. The superintendent was looking toward her cell now, squinting into the dim interior.

Mr. Manly wanted to keep an eye on Bob Fisher and watch his reactions, but seeing the woman distracted him.

"Who's that in there, Norma Davis?"

"The other one," Fisher said, "the Mexican."

"I didn't see any report on her being sick."

"She's working here. Your two boys run off, there's nobody to fetch things for the lungers."

Mr. Manly didn't like to look at the tubercular convicts; they gave him a creepy feeling, the way they sat there all day like lizzards and never seemed to move. He gave them a glance and called again, "Harold, come on out here."

The Negro was buttoning a prison shirt as he appeared in the doorway. "You want me, captain?"

"Come over here, will you?"

Mr. Manly was watching Fisher now. The man's flat open-eyed expression tickled him: old Bob Fisher staring at Harold, then looking over at Raymond, then back at Harold again, trying to figure out the change that had come over them. The change was something more than just their appearance. It was something Mr. Manly felt, and he was pretty sure now Bob Fisher was feeling it too.

"What's the matter, Bob, ain't you ever seen an Apache or a Zulu before?"

"I seen Apaches."

"Then what're you staring at?"

Fisher looked over at Harold again. "What're them cuts on his face?"

"Tell him, Harold."

"They tribal marks, captain."

Fisher said, "What the hell tribe's a field nigger belong to?"

Harold touched his face, feeling the welts of scar tissue that were not yet completely healed. He said, "My tribe, captain."

"He cut his own face like that?"

Fisher kept staring at the Negro as Mr. Manly said, "He saw it in a Africa book I got—picture of a native with these marks like tattoos on his face. I didn't tell him to do it, you understand. He just figured it would be all right, I guess. Isn't that so, Harold?"

"Yes-suh, captain."

"Same with Raymond. He figured if he's a full-blooded Apache Indian then he should let his hair grow and wear one of them bands."

"We come over here to look at spears," Fisher said.

Mr. Manly frowned, shaking his head. "Don't you see the connection yet? A spear is part of a warrior's get-up, like a tool is to a working man. Listen, I told you, didn't I, these boys can run fifteen miles in a day now and only stop a couple of times to rest."

"I thought it was fourteen miles," Fisher said.

"Fourteen, fifteen—here's the thing. They can run that far *and* go from morning to supper time without a drink of water, any time they want."

"A man will do that in the snake den if I make him." Bob Fisher wasn't backing off this time.

Mr. Manly wasn't letting go. "Inside," he said, "is different than running out in the hot sun. Listen, they each pour theirselves a cup of water in the morning and you know what they do? They see who can go all day without taking a drink or more than a couple of sips." He held his hand out to R. E. Baylis and said, "Let me have the pitcher." Then he looked at Raymond and Harold again. "Which of you won today?"

"I did," Raymond said.

"Let's see your cups."

Raymond went into his cell and was back in a moment with a tin cup in each hand. "He drank his. See, I got some left."

"Then you get the pitcher of ice water," Mr. Manly said. "And, Harold, you get to watch him drink it."

Raymond raised the pitcher and drank out of the side of it, not taking very much before lowering it again and holding it in front of him.

"See that?" Mr. Manly said. "He knows better than to gulp it down. One day Raymond wins, the next day Harold gets the ice water. I mean they can both do it any time they want."

"I would sure like to see them spears," Fisher said.

Mr. Manly asked Harold where they were and he said, "Over yonder by the wall, captain."

Tacha watched them cross the yard. The Negro waited for the Indian to put the pitcher on the ground and she noticed they gave each other a look as they fell in behind the little man in the dark suit and the two guards. They were over by the wall a few minutes talking while Mr. Fisher hefted one of the bamboo spears and felt the point of it with his finger. Then the superintendent took the spear from him and gave it to the Indian. The Negro picked up the other spear from against the wall and they came back this way, toward the cells, at least a dozen paces before turning around. Beyond them, the group moved away from the upright board. The Indian and the Negro faced the target for a moment, then stepped back several more feet, noticing Tacha now in the doorway of her cell.

She said, "You're going to hit that, way down there?"

"Not today," Raymond answered.

Everyone in the yard was watching them now. They raised the spears shoulder high, took aim with their outstretched left arms pointing, and threw them hard in a low arc, almost at the same moment. Both spears fell short and skidded along the ground past the board to stop at the base of the wall.

Raymond and Harold waited. In the group across the yard Mr. Manly seemed to be doing the talking, gesturing with his hands. He was facing Bob Fisher and did not look over this way. After a few minutes they left the yard, and now Mr. Manly, as he went through the gate last, looked over and waved.

"Well," Raymond said—he stooped to pick up the tin pitcher—"who wants some ice water?"

Within a few days Tacha realized that, since moving to the TB cellblock, she felt better—whether it made sense or not. Maybe part of the feeling was being outside most of the day and not bent over a sewing machine listening to Norma or trying to talk to the old man. Already that seemed like a long time ago. She was happier now. She even enjoyed being with the tubercular convicts and didn't mind the way they talked to her sometimes, saying she was a pretty good nurse though they would sure rather have her be something else. They needed to talk like men so she smiled and didn't take anything they said as an offense.

In the afternoon the Apache and the Zulu would come in through the gate, walking slowly, carrying their shirts. One of the tubercular convicts would yell over, asking how far they had run and one or the other would tell them twelve, fifteen, sixteen miles. They would drink the water in their cups. One of the convicts would fill the cups again from the bucket they kept in the shade. After drinking the second cup they would decide who the winner would be that day and pour just a little more water into his cup, leaving the other one empty. The TB convicts got a kick out of this and always laughed. Every day it was the same. They drank the water and then went into the cell to lie on their bunks. In less than an hour the TB convicts would be yelling for them to come out and start throwing their spears. They would get out their money or rolled cigarettes when the Apache and the Zulu appeared and, after letting them warm up a few minutes, at least two of the convicts would bet on every throw. Later on, after the work crews were in for the day, there would be convicts over from the main yard watching through the gate. None of them ever came into the TB yard. They were betting too and would yell at the Apache and the Zulu—calling them by those names—to hit the board, cut the son of a bitch dead center. Frank Shelby appeared at the gate only once. After that the convicts had to pay to watch and make bets. Soonzy, Junior, and Joe Dean were at the grillwork every day during free time.

Harold Jackson, the Zulu, walked over to the gate one time. He said, "How come we do all the work, you make all the money?"

Junior told him to get back over there and start throwing his goddamn spear or whatever it was.

Harold let the convicts get a good look at his face scars before he walked away. After the next throw, when he and Raymond were pulling their spears out of the board, Harold said, "Somebody always telling you what to do, huh?"

"Every place you go," Raymond said.

They were good with the spears. Though when the convicts from the outside yard were at the gate watching they never threw from farther than thirty-five feet away, or tried to place the spears in a particular part of the board. If they wanted to, they could hit the board high or low at the same time.

It was Tacha who noticed their work shoes coming apart from the running and made moccasins for them, sewing them by hand—calf-high Apache moccasins she fashioned out of old leather water bags and feed sacks.

And it was Tacha who told Raymond he should put war paint on his face. He wasn't scarey enough looking.

"Where do you get war paint?" Raymond asked her. "At the store?"

"I think from berries."

"Well, I don't see no berries around here."

The next day she got iodine and a can of white enamel from the sick ward and, after supper, sat Raymond on a stool and painted a white streak across the bridge of his nose from cheekbone to cheekbone, and orange-red iodine stripes along the jawline to his chin.

Harold Jackson liked it, so Tacha painted a white stripe across his forehead and another one down between his eyes to the tip of his nose.

"Hey, we waryers now," Raymond said.

They looked at themselves in Tacha's hand mirror and both of them grinned. They were pretty mean-looking boys. Harold said, "Lady, what else do these waryers put on?"

Tacha said she guessed anything they wanted. She opened a little sack and gave Raymond two strands of turquoise beads, a string for around his neck and another string, doubled, for around his right arm, up high.

She asked Harold if he wanted a ring for his nose. He said no, thank you, lady, but remembered Mr. Manly talking about the Zulus putting chunks of sugar cane in their ear lobes and he let Tacha pierce one of his ears and attach a single gold earring. It looked good with the tribal scars and the mustache that curved into a short beard. "All I need me is a lion to spear," Harold said. He was Harold Jackson the Zulu, and he could feel it without looking in the mirror.

He didn't talk to Raymond about the feeling because he knew Raymond, in a way of his own, Raymond the Apache, had the same feeling. In front of the convicts who watched them throw spears or in front of the two guards who took them out to run, Harold could look at Raymond, their eyes would meet for a moment and each knew what the other was thinking. They didn't talk very much, even to each other. They walked slowly and seemed to expend no extra effort in their movements. They knew they could do something no other men in the prison could do—they could run all day and go without water—and it was part of the good feeling.

They began to put fresh paint on their faces almost every day, in the afternoon before they threw the spears.

10

The evening Junior and Joe Dean came for them they were sitting out in front of the cells with Tacha. It was after supper, just beginning to get dark. For a little while Tacha had been pretending to tell them their fortunes, using an old deck of cards and turning them up one at a time in the fading light. She told Harold she saw him sleeping under a banana tree with a big smile on his face. Sure, Cuba, Harold said. With the next card she saw him killing a lion with his spear and Harold was saying they didn't have no lions in Cuba, when Junior came up to them. Joe Dean stood over a little way with his hands in his pockets, watching.

"Frank wants to see you," Junior said. "Both of you." He took time to look at Tacha while he waited for them to get up. When neither of them moved he said, "You hear me? Frank wants you."

"What's he want?" Harold said.

"He's going to want me to kick your ass you don't get moving."

Raymond looked at Harold, and Harold looked at

Raymond. Finally they got up and followed them across the yard, though they moved so goddamn slow Worley Lewis, Jr. had to keep waiting for them with his hands on his hips, telling them to come on, *move*. They looked back once and saw Joe Dean still over by the cells. He seemed to be waiting for them to leave.

Soonzy was in the passageway of the main cellblock, standing in the light that was coming from No. 14. He motioned them inside.

They went into the cell, then stopped short. Frank Shelby was sitting on his throne reading a newspaper, hunched over before his own shadow on the back wall. He didn't look up; he made them wait several minutes before he finally rose, pulled up his pants and buckled his belt. Junior and Soonzy crowded the doorway behind them.

"Come closer to the light," Shelby said. He waited for them to move into the space between the bunks, to where the electric overhead light, with its tin shield, was almost directly above them.

"I want to ask you two something. I want to know how come you got your faces painted up like that."

They kept looking at him, but neither of them spoke.

"You going to tell me?"

"I don't know," Raymond said. "I guess it's hard to explain."

"Did anybody tell you to put it on?"

"No, we done it ourselves."

"Has this Mr. Manly seen it?"

"Yeah, but he didn't say nothing."

"You just figured it would be a good idea, uh?"

"I don't know," Raymond said. "We just done it, I guess."

"You want to look like a couple of circus clowns, is that it?"

"No, we didn't think of that."

"Maybe you want to look like a wild Indin," Shelby said, "and him, he wants to look like some kind of boogey-man native. Maybe that's it."

Raymond shrugged. "Maybe something like that. It's hard to explain."

"What does Mr. Jackson say about it?"

"If you know why we put it on," Harold said, "what are you asking us for?"

"Because it bothers me," Shelby answered. "I can't believe anybody would want to look like a nigger native. Even a nigger. Same as I can't believe anybody would want to look like a Wild West Show Indin 'less he was paid to do it. Somebody paying you, Raymond?"

"Nobody's paying us."

"See, Raymond, what bothers me—how can we learn people like you to act like white men if you're going to play you're savages? You see what I mean? You want to move back in this cellblock, but who do you think would want to live with you?"

"We're not white men," Raymond said.

"Jesus Christ, I know that. I'm saying if you want to live with white men then you got to try to act like white men. You start playing you're an Apache and a god-damn Zulu or something, that's the same as saying you don't want to be a white man, and that's what bothers me something awful, when I see that going on."

There was a little space of silence before Harold said, "What do you want us to do?"

"We'll do it," Shelby said. "We're going to remind you how you're supposed to act."

Soonzy took Harold from behind with a fist in his hair and a forearm around his neck. He dragged Harold backward and as Raymond turned, Junior stepped in and hit Raymond with a belt wrapped around his fist. He had to hit Raymond again before he could get a good hold on him and pull him out of the cell. Joe Dean and a half-dozen convicts were waiting in the passageway. They got Raymond and Harold down on their backs on the cement. They sat on their legs and a convict stood on each of their outstretched hands and arms while another man got down and pulled their hair tight to keep them from moving their heads. Then Joe Dean took a brush and the can of enamel Tacha had got from the sick ward and painted both of their faces pure white.

When R. E. Baylis came through to lock up, Shelby told him to look at the goddamn mess out there, white paint all over the cement and dirty words painted on the wall. He said that nigger and his red nigger friend sneaked over and started messing up the place, but they caught the two and painted them as a lesson. Shelby said to R. E. Baylis goddamn-it, why didn't he throw them in the snake den so they would quit bothering people. R. E. Baylis said he would tell Bob Fisher.

The next morning after breakfast, Shelby came out of

the mess hall frowning in the sunlight and looking over the work details forming in the yard. He was walking toward the supply group when somebody called his name from behind. Bob Fisher was standing by the mess hall door: grim-looking tough old son of a bitch in his gray sack guard uniform. Shelby sure didn't want to, but he walked back to where the turnkey was standing.

"They don't know how to write even their names," Fisher said.

"Well"—Shelby took a moment to think—"maybe they got the paint for somebody else do to it."

"Joe Dean got the paint."

"Joe did that?"

"Him and Soonzy and Junior are going to clean it up before they go to work."

"Well, if they did it—"

"You're going to help them."

"Me? I'm on the supply detail. You know that."

"Or you can go with the quarry gang," Fisher said. "It don't make any difference to me."

"Quarry gang?" Shelby grinned to show Fisher he thought he was kidding. "I don't believe I ever done that kind of work."

"You'll do it if I say so."

"Listen, just because we painted those two boys up. We were teaching them a lesson, that's all. Christ, they go around here thinking they're something the way they fixed theirselves up—somebody had to teach them."

"I do the teaching here," Fisher said. "I'm teaching that to you right now."

Dumb, stone-face guard son of a bitch. Shelby said,

"Well," half-turning to look off thoughtfully toward the work groups waiting in the yard. "I hope those people don't get sore about this. You know how it is, how they listen to me and trust me. If they figure I'm getting treated unfair, they're liable to sit right down and not move from the yard, every one of them."

"If you believe that," Fisher said, "you better tell them I'll shoot the first man that sits down, and if they all sit down at once I'll shoot you."

Shelby waited. He didn't look at Bob Fisher; he kept his gaze on the convicts. After a moment he said, "You're kneeling on me for a reason, aren't you? You're waiting to see me make a terrible mistake."

"I believe you've already made it," Fisher said. He turned and went into the mess hall.

Scraping paint off cement was better than working in the quarry. It was hot in the passageway, but there was no sun beating down on them and they weren't breathing chalk dust. Shelby sat in his cell and let Junior, Soonzy, and Joe Dean do the work, until Bob Fisher came by. Fisher didn't say anything; he looked in at him and Shelby came out and picked up a trowel and started scraping. When Fisher was gone, Shelby sat back on his heels and said, "I'm going to bust me a guard, I'll tell you, if that man's anywhere near us when we leave."

The scraping stopped as he spoke, as Junior and Soonzy and Joe Dean waited to hear whatever he had to say.

"There is something bothering him," Shelby said. "He wants to nail me down. He could do it any time he feels like it, couldn't he? He could put me in the quarry or the snake den—that man could chain me to the wall. But he's waiting on something."

Joe Dean said, "Waiting on what?"

"I don't know. Unless he's telling me he knows what's going on. He could be saying, 'I got my eye on you, buddy. I'm waiting for you to make the wrong move.'"

"What could he know?" Joe Dean said. "We don't know anything ourselves."

"He could know we're thinking about it."

"He could be guessing."

"I mean," Shelby said, "he could *know*. Norma could have told him. She's the only other person who could."

Junior was frowning. "What would Norma want to tell him for?"

"Jesus Christ," Shelby said, "because she's Norma. She don't need a reason, she does what she feels like doing. Listen, she needs money she gets herself a forty-four and pours liquor into some crazy boy and they try and rob a goddamn *bank*. She's seeing Bob Fisher, and she's the only one could have told him anything."

"I say he's guessing," Joe Dean said. "The time's coming to move all these convicts, he's nervous at the thought of it, and starts guessing we're up to something."

"That could be right," Shelby said. "But the only way I can find out for sure is to talk to Norma." He was silent a moment. "I don't know. With old Bob watching every move I got to stay clear of the tailor shop."

"Why don't we bring her over here?" Junior said. "Right after supper everybody's in the yard. Shoot, we can get her in here, anywhere you want, no trouble."

"Hey, boy," Shelby grinned, "now you're talking."

Jesus, yes, what was he worrying about that old man turnkey for? He had to watch that and never worry out loud or raise his voice or lose his temper. He had to watch when little pissy-ant started to bother him. The Indin and the nigger had bothered him. It wasn't even important; but goddamn-it, it had bothered him and he had done something about it. See—but because of it Bob Fisher had come down on him and this was not anytime to get Bob Fisher nervous and watchful. Never trust a nervous person unless you've got a gun on him. That was a rule. And when you've got the gun on him shoot him or hit him with it, quick, but don't let him start crying and begging for his life and spilling the goddamn payroll all over the floor—the way it had happened in the paymaster's office at the Cornelia Mine near Ajo. They would have been out of there before the security guards arrived if he hadn't spilled the money. The paymaster would be alive if he hadn't spilled the money, and they wouldn't be in Yuma. There was such a thing as bad luck. Anything could happen during a holdup. But there had been five payroll and bank robberies before the Cornelia Mine job where no one had spilled the money or reached for a gun or walked in unexpectedly. They had been successful because they had kept calm and in control, and that was the way they had to do it again, to get out of here.

It had surely bothered him though—the way the Indin and the nigger had painted their faces.

*   *   *

Junior pushed through the mess-hall door behind Norma as she went out, and told her to go visit Tacha. That's how easy it was. When Norma got to the TB yard Joe Dean, standing by the gate, nodded toward the first cell. She saw Tacha sitting over a ways with the Indian and the Negro, and noticed there was something strange about them: they looked sick, with a gray pallor to their skin, even the Negro. Norma looked at Joe Dean and again he nodded toward the first cell.

Soonzy stepped out and walked past her as she approached the doorway. Shelby was waiting inside, standing with an arm on the upper bunk. He didn't grin or reach for her, he said, "How're you getting along with your boyfriend?"

"He still hasn't told me anything, if that's what you mean."

"I'm more interested in what you might have told him."

Norma smiled and seemed to relax. "You know, as I walked in here I thought you were a little tense about something."

"You haven't answered my question."

"What is it I might have told him?"

"Come on, Norma."

"I mean what's there to tell him? You don't have any plan you've told me about."

"I don't know," Shelby said, "it looks to me like you got your own plan."

"I ask him. Every time he comes in I bring it up. 'Honey, when are we going to get out of this awful place?' But he won't tell me anything."

"You were pretty sure one time you could squeeze it out of him."

"I don't believe he knows any more than we do."

"I'll tell you what," Shelby said. "I'll give you three more days to find out. You don't know anything by then, I don't see any reason to take you with us."

Norma took her time. She kept her eyes on Shelby, holding him and waiting a little, then stepped in close so that she was almost touching him with her body. She waited again before saying, quietly, "What're you being so mean for?"

Shelby said, "Man." He said, "Come on, Norma, if I want to put you on the bunk I'll put you on the bunk. Don't give me no sweetheart talk, all right? I want you to tell me if you're working something with that old man. Now hold on—I want you to keep looking right at me and tell me to my face yes or no—yes, 'I have told him,' or no, 'I have not told him.' "

Norma put on a frown now that brought her eyebrows together and gave her a nice hurt look.

"Frank, what do you want me to tell you?" She spaced the words to show how honest and truthful she was being, knowing that her upturned, frowning face was pretty nice and that her breasts were about an inch away from the upcurve of his belly.

She looked good all right, and if he put her down on the bunk she'd be something. But Frank Shelby was looking at a train and keeping calm, keeping his voice down, and he said, "Norma, if you don't find out anything in three days you don't leave this place."

It was Sunday, Visiting Day, that Mr. Manly decided he would make an announcement. He called Bob Fisher into his office to tell him, then thought better of it—Fisher would only object and argue—so he began talking about Raymond and Harold instead of his announcement.

"I'll tell you," Mr. Manly said, "I'm not so much interested in who did it as I am in *why* they did it. They got paint in their eyes, in their nose. They had to wash theirselves in gasoline and then they didn't get it all off."

"Well, there's no way of finding out now," Fisher said. "You ask them, there isn't anybody knows a thing."

"The men who did it know."

"Well, sure, the ones that did it."

"I'd like to know what a man thinks like would paint another person."

"They were painting theirselves before."

"I believe you see the difference, Bob."

"These are convicts," Fisher said. "They get mean they don't need a reason. It's the way they are."

"I'm thinking I better talk to them."

"But we don't know who done it."

"I mean talk to all of them. I want to talk to them about something else any way."

"About what?"

"Maybe I can make the person who did it come forward and admit it."

"Mister, if you believe that you don't know anything a-tall about convicts. You talked to Raymond and Harold, didn't you?"

"Yes, I did."

"And they won't even tell you who done it, will they?"

"I can't understand that."

"Because they're convicts. They know if they ever told you they'd get their heads beat against a cell wall. This is between them and the other convicts. If the convicts don't want them to paint up like savages then I believe we should stay out of it and let them settle it theirselves."

"But they've got rights—the two boys. What about them?"

"I don't know. I'm not talking about justice," Fisher said. "I'm talking about running a prison. If the convicts want these two to act a certain way or not act a certain way, we should keep out of it. It keeps them quiet and it don't cost us a cent. When you push against the whole convict body it had better be important and you had better be ready to shoot and kill people if they push back."

"I told them they could put on their paint if they wanted."

"Well, that's up to you," Fisher said. "Or it's up to them. I notice they been keeping their faces clean."

When Mr. Manly didn't speak right away, Fisher said, "If it's all right with you I want to get downstairs and keep an eye on things. It's Visiting Day."

Mr. Manly looked up. "That's right, it is. You know, I didn't tell you I been wanting to make an announcement. I believe I'll do it right now—sure, while some of them have their relatives here visiting." Mr. Manly's expression was bright and cheerful, as if he thought this was sure a swell idea.

* * *

"I don't know what you're doing," Shelby said, "but so far it isn't worth a rat's ass, is it?" He sat facing his brother, Virgil, who was leaning in against the table and looking directly at Frank to show he was sincere and doing everything he could to find out when the goddamn train was leaving. There were convicts and their visitors all the way down the line of tables that divided the mess hall: hunched over talking, filling the room with a low hum of voices.

"It ain't like looking up a schedule," Virgil said. "I believe this would be a special train, two or three cars probably. All right, I ask a lot of questions over at the railroad yard they begin wondering who I am, and somebody says hey, that's Virgil Shelby. His brother's up on the hill."

"That's Virgil Shelby," Frank said. "Jesus, do you believe people know who you are? You could be a mine engineer. You could be interested in hauling in equipment and you ask how they handle special trains. 'You ever put on a special run? You do? Like what kind?' Jesus, I mean you got to use your head and think for a change."

"Frank, I'm ready. I don't need to know more than a day ahead when you leave. I got me some good boys and, I'm telling you, we're going to *do* it."

"You're going to do what?"

"Get you off that train."

"How?"

"Stop it if we have to."

"How, Virgil?"

"Dynamite the track."

"Then what?"

"Then climb aboard."

"With the guards shooting at you?"

"You got to be doing something too," Virgil said. "Inside the train."

"I'm doing something right now. I'm seeing you don't know what you're talking about. And unless we know when the train leaves and where it stops, we're not going to be able to work out a plan. Do you see that, Virgil?"

"The train goes to Florence. We know that."

"Do we know if it stops anywhere? If it stops, Virgil, wouldn't that be the place to get on?"

"If it stops."

"That's right. That's what you got to find out. Because how are you going to know where to wait and when to wait if you don't know when the train's leaving here? Virgil, are you listening to me?"

His brother was looking past him at something. Shelby glanced over his shoulder. He turned then and kept looking as Mr. Manly, with Bob Fisher on the stairs at the far end of the mess hall, said, "May I have your attention a moment, please?"

Mr. Manly waited until the hum of voices trailed off and he saw the faces down the line of tables looking toward him: upturned, solemn faces, like people in church waiting for the sermon. Mr. Manly grinned. He always liked to open with a light touch.

He said, "I'm not going to make a speech, if any of you are worried about that. I just want to make a brief announcement while your relatives and loved ones are here. It will save the boys writing to tell you and I know some of them don't write as often as they should. By the way, I'm Everett Manly, the acting superintendent here in Mr. Rynning's absence." He paused to clear his throat.

"Now then—I am very pleased to announce that this will be the last Visiting Day at Yuma Territorial Prison. A week from tomorrow the first group of men will leave on the Southern Pacific for the new penitentiary at Florence, a fine new place I think you all are going to be very pleased with. Now you won't be able to tell your relatives or loved ones what day exactly you'll be leaving, but I promise you in three weeks everybody will be out of here and this place will open its doors forever and become a page in history. That's about all I can tell you right now for the present. However, if any of you have questions I will be glad to try and answer them."

Frank Shelby kept looking at the little man on the stairway. He said to himself, It's a trick. But the longer he stared at him—the little fellow standing up there waiting for questions—he knew Mr. Manly was telling the truth.

Virgil said, "Well, I guess that answers the question, doesn't it?"

Shelby didn't look at his brother. He was afraid he might lose his temper and hit Virgil in the mouth.

11

⬥

For three sacks of Mail Pouch, R. E. Baylis told Shelby the convicts would be sent out in groups of about forty at a time, going over every other day, it looked like, on the regular morning run.

R. E. Baylis even got Shelby a Southern Pacific schedule. Leave Yuma at 6:15 A.M. Pass through Sentinel at 8:56; no stop unless they needed coal or water. They'd stop at Gila at 9:51, where they'd be fed on the train; no one allowed off. They'd arrive in Phoenix at 2:40 P.M., switch the cars over to a Phoenix & Eastern train and arrive at Florence about 5:30 P.M. Bob Fisher planned to make the first run and the last one, the first one to see what the trip was like and the last one so he could lock up and officially hand over the keys.

Shelby asked R. E. Baylis if he would put him and his friends down for the first run, because they were sure anxious to get out of here. R. E. Baylis said he didn't know if it could be done, but maybe he could try to arrange it. Shelby gave him fifty dollars to try as hard as he could.

The guard told Bob Fisher about Shelby's request,

since Fisher would see the list anyway. Why the first train? Fisher wanted to know. What was the difference? R. E. Baylis asked. All the trains were going to the penitentiary. Fisher put himself in Shelby's place and thought about it a while. Maybe Shelby was anxious to leave, that could be a fact. But it wasn't the reason he wanted to be on the first train. It was so he would know exactly which train he'd be on, so he could tell somebody outside.

Fisher said all right, tell him he could go on the first train. But then, when the time came, they'd pull Shelby out of line and hold him for the last train. "I want him riding with me," Fisher said, "but not before I look over the route."

It bothered R. E. Baylis because Shelby had always treated him square and given him tobacco and things. He stopped by Shelby's cell that evening and said Lord, he could sure use that fifty dollars, but he would give it back. Bob Fisher was making them go on the last train. Shelby looked pretty disappointed. By God, he was big about it though. He let R. E. Baylis keep the fifty dollars anyway.

The next morning when he saw Junior and Soonzy and Joe Dean, Shelby grinned and said, "Boys, always trust a son of a bitch to be a son of a bitch. We're taking the last train."

All he had to do now was to get a letter of instructions to Virgil at the railroad hotel in Yuma. For a couple more sacks of Mail Pouch R. E. Baylis would probably deliver it personally.

*   *   *

Virgil Shelby and his three men arrived at Stout's Hotel in Gila on a Wednesday afternoon. Mr. Stout and a couple of Southern Pacific division men in the lobby got a kick out of these dudes who said they were heading south into the Saucedas to do some prospecting. All they had were bedrolls and rifles and a pack mule loaded with suitcases. The dudes were as serious about it though as they were ignorant. They bought four remount horses at the livery and two 50-pound cases of No. 1 dynamite at Tom Child's trading store, and on Thursday morning they rode out of Gila. They rode south two miles before turning west and doubling back to follow the train tracks.

They arrived in sight of the Southern Pacific water stop at Sentinel that evening and from a grove of trees studied the wooden buildings and frame structure that stood silently against a dark line of palo verdes. A water tank, a coaling shed, a section house and a little one-room station with a light showing in the window, that's all there was here.

As soon as Virgil saw the place he knew Frank was right again. Sometimes it made him mad when he sounded dumb in front of his brother. He had finished the sixth grade and Frank had gone on to the seventh or eighth. Maybe when Frank was looking at him, waiting, he would say the wrong thing or sound dumb; but Jesus, he had gone into places with a gun and put the gun in a man's face and got what he wanted. Frank didn't have to worry about him going in with a gun. He had not found out the important facts of the matter talking to the railroad people. He had not thought up the plan in all the time he'd had to do it. But he could sure do what Frank said in his letter. He had three good boys who would go with him for two hundred and fifty dollars each and bring the guns and know how to use them. These boys drank too much and got in fights, but they were the captains for this kind of work. Try and pick them. Try and get three fellows who had the nerve to stop a prison train and take off the people you wanted and do it right, without a lot of shooting and getting nervous and running off into the desert and hiding in a cave. He wished he had more like them, but these three said they could do the job and would put their guns on anybody for two hundred and fifty dollars.

He had a man named Howard Crowder who had worked for railroad lines in both the United States and Mexico, before he turned to holding up trains and spent ten years in Yuma.

He had an old hand named Dancey who had ridden with him and Frank before, and had been with them at the Cornelia Mine payroll robbery and had got away.

He had a third one named Billy Santos who had smuggled across the border whatever could be carried and was worth anything and knew all the trails and water holes south of here.

Five o'clock the next morning it still looked good and still looked easy as they walked into the little station at Sentinel with their suitcases and asked the S.P. man when the next eastbound train was coming through.

The S.P. man said 8:56 this morning, but that train

was not due to stop on account of it was carrying convicts some place.

Virgil asked him if there was anybody over in the section house. The S.P. man said no, he was alone. A crew had gone out on the 8:45 to Gila the night before and another crew was coming from Yuma sometime today.

Virgil looked over at Billy Santos. Billy went outside. Howard Crowder and Dancey remained sitting on the bench. The suitcases and bedrolls and rifles and two cases of dynamite were on the floor by them. No, the S.P. man behind the counter said, they couldn't take the 8:56, though they could get on the 8:48 this evening if they wanted to hang around all day. But what will you do with your horses? he said then. You rode in here, didn't you?

Virgil was at the counter now. He nodded to the telegrapher's key on the desk behind the S.P. man and said, "I hope you can work that thing, mister."

The S.P. man said, "Sure, I can work it. Else I wouldn't be here."

"That's good," Virgil said. "It's better if they hear a touch they are used to hearing."

The S.P. man gave Virgil a funny look, then let his gaze shift over to the two men on the bench with all the gear in front of them. They looked back at him; they didn't move or say anything. The S.P. man was wondering if he should send a message to the division office at Gila; tell them there were three dudes hanging around here with rifles and dynamite and ask if they had been seen in Gila the day before. He could probably get away with it. How would these people know what he was saying? Just then the Mexican-looking one came back in, his eyes on the one standing by the counter, and shook his head.

Virgil said, "You all might as well get dressed."

The S.P. man watched them open the suitcases and take out gray and white convict suits. He watched them pull the pants and coats on over the clothes they were wearing and shove revolvers down into the pants and button the coats. One of them brought a double-barrel shotgun out of a suitcase in two pieces and sat down to fit the stock to the barrels. Watching them, the S.P. man said to Virgil Shelby, "Hey, what's going on? What is this?"

"This is how you stop a train," Virgil told him. "These are prisoners that escaped off the train that come through the day before yesterday."

"Nobody escaped," the S.P. man said.

Virgil nodded up and down. "Yes, they did, mister, and I'm the deputy sheriff of Maricopa County who's going to put them back on the train for Florence."

"If you're a deputy of this county," the S.P. man said, "then you're a new one."

"All right," Virgil said, "I'm a new one."

"If you're one at all."

Virgil pulled a .44 revolver from inside his coat and pointed it in the S.P. man's face. He said, "All you got to do is telegraph the Yuma depot at exactly six A.M. with a message for the prison superintendent, Mr. Everett Manly. You're going to say three escaped convicts are being held here at Sentinel and you request the train to stop and take them aboard. You also request an immediate answer and, mister," Virgil said, "I don't want you to send it one word different than I tell it to you. You understand?"

The S.P. man nodded. "I understand, but it ain't going to work. If three were missing at the head-count when they got to Florence, they would have already told Yuma about it."

"That's a fact," Virgil said. "That's why we had somebody wire the prison from Phoenix Wednesday night and report three missing." Virgil looked around then and said, "Howard?"

The one named Howard Crowder had a silver dollar in his hand. He began tapping the coin rapidly on the wooden bench next to him in sharp longs and shorts that were loud in the closed room. Virgil watched the expression on the S.P. man's face, the mouth come open a little.

"You understand that too?" Virgil asked him.

The S.P. man nodded.

"What did he say?"

"He said, 'Send correct message or you are a dead man.' "

"I'm happy you understand it," Virgil said.

The S.P. man watched the one named Dancey pry open a wooden case that was marked *High Explosives—Dangerous* and take out a paraffin-coated packet of dynamite sticks. He watched Dancey get out a coil of copper wire and detonator caps and work the wire gently into the open end of the cap and then crimp the end closed with his teeth. The Mexican-looking one was taking a box plunger out of a canvas bag. The S.P. man said to himself, My God, somebody is going to get killed and I am going to see it.

At six A.M. he sent the message to the depot at Yuma, where they would then be loading the convicts onto the train.

The Southern Pacific equipment that left Yuma that Friday morning was made up of a 4-4-0 locomotive, a baggage car, two day coaches for regular passengers (though only eleven people were aboard), another baggage car, and an old wooden coach from the Cannanea-Rio Yaqui-El Pacifico line. The last twenty-seven convicts to leave the prison were locked inside this coach along with Bob Fisher and three armed guards. Behind, bringing up the rear, was a caboose that carried Mr. Manly and three more guards.

Bob Fisher had personally made up the list of prisoners for this last run to Florence: only twenty-seven, including Frank Shelby and his bunch. Most of the others were short-term prisoners and trusties who wouldn't be expected to make trouble. A small, semi-harmless group which, Bob Fisher believed, would make it easy for him to keep an eye on Shelby. Also aboard were the TB convicts, the two women and Harold Jackson and Raymond San Carlos.

Harold and Raymond were near the rear of the coach. The only ones behind them were Bob Fisher and the guards. Ahead of them were the TB convicts, then two rows of empty seats, then the rest of the prisoners scattered along both sides of the aisle in the back-to-back straw seats. The two women were in the front of the coach. The doors at both ends were padlocked. The windows were glass, but they were not made to open.

Before the train was five minutes out of Yuma every convict in the coach knew they were going to stop in Sentinel to pick up three men who had escaped on Wednesday and had been recaptured the next day. There was a lot of talk about who the three were.

Bob Fisher didn't say a word. He sat patiently waiting for the train to reach Sentinel, thinking about the message they had received Wednesday evening: *Three convicts missing on arrival Phoenix. Local and county authorities alerted.* Signed, *Sheriff, Maricopa County.* What bothered Fisher, there had been no information sent from Florence, nothing from Mr. Rynning, no further word from anybody until the wire was received at the depot this morning. Mr. Manly had wired back they would stop for the prisoners and Bob Fisher had not said a word to anybody since. Something wasn't right and he had to think it through.

About 7:30 A.M., halfway to Sentinel, Fisher said to the guard sitting next to him, "Put your gun on Frank Shelby and don't move it till we get to Florence."

Harold Jackson, next to the window, looked out at the flat desert country that stretched to distant dark mounds, mountains that would take a day to reach on foot, maybe half a day if a man was to run. But a mountain was nothing to run to. There was nothing out there but sky and rocks and desert growth that looked as if it would never die, but offered a man no hope of life. It was the same land he had looked at a few months before, going in the other direction, sitting in the same upright straw seat handcuffed to a sheriff's man. The Indian sitting next to him now nudged his arm and Harold looked up.

The Davis woman was coming down the aisle from the front of the coach. She passed them and a moment later Harold heard the door to the toilet open and close. Looking out the window again, Harold said, "What's out there, that way?"

"Mexico," Raymond answered. "Across the desert and the mountain, and if you can find water, Mexico."

"You know where the water is?"

"First twenty-five, thirty miles there isn't any."

"What about after that?"

"I know some places."

"You could find them?"

"I'm not going through the window if that's what you're thinking about."

"The train's going to stop in Sentinel."

"They open the door to put people on," Raymond said. "They ain't letting anybody off."

"We don't know what they going to do," Harold said, "till we get there." He heard the woman come out of the toilet compartment and waited for her to walk past.

She didn't appear. Harold turned to look out the window across the aisle. Over his shoulder he could see the Davis woman standing by Bob Fisher's seat. She was saying something but keeping her voice down and he couldn't make out the words. He heard Fisher though.

Fisher said, "Is that right?" The woman said something else and Fisher said, "If you don't know where what's the good of telling me? How are you helping? Anybody could say what you're saying and if it turns out right try to get credit. But you haven't told me nothing yet."

"All right," Norma Davis said. "It's going to be at Sentinel."

"You could be guessing, for all I know."

"Take my word," the woman said.

Bob Fisher didn't say anything for a while. The train swayed and clicked along the tracks and there was no sound behind Harold Jackson. He glanced over his shoulder. Fisher was getting up, handing his revolver to the guard sitting across the aisle. Then he was past Harold, walking up the aisle and holding the woman by the arm to move her along ahead of him.

Frank Shelby looked up as they stopped at his seat. He was sitting with Junior; Soonzy and Joe Dean were facing them.

"This lady says you're going to try to escape," Fisher said to Shelby. "What do you think about that?"

Shelby's shoulders and head swayed slightly with the motion of the train. He looked up at Fisher and Norma, looking from one to the other before he said, "If I haven't told her any such thing, how would she know?"

"She says you're getting off at Sentinel."

"Well, if she tells me how I'm going to do it and it sounds good, I might try it." Shelby grinned a little. "Do you believe her?"

"I believe she might be telling a story," Fisher said,

"but I also believe it might be true. That's why I've got a gun pointed at your head till we get to Florence. Do you understand me?"

"I sure do." Shelby nodded, looking straight up at Bob Fisher. He said then, "Do you mind if I have a talk with Norma? I'd like to know why she's making up stories."

"She's all yours," Fisher said.

Harold nudged Raymond. They watched Fisher coming back down the aisle. Beyond him they saw Junior get up to give the Davis woman his seat. Tacha was turned around watching. She moved over close to the window as Junior approached her and sat down.

Behind Harold and Raymond one of the guards said, "You letting the woman sit with the men?"

"They're all the same as far as I can see," Fisher answered. "All convicts."

Virgil Shelby, holding a shotgun across his arm, was out on the platform when the train came into sight. He heard it and saw its smoke first, then spotted the locomotive way down the tracks. This was the worst part, right now, seeing the train getting bigger and bigger and seeing the steam blowing out with the screeching sound of the brakes. The locomotive was rolling slowly as it came past the coaling shed and the water tower, easing into the station, rolling past the platform now hissing steam, the engine and the baggage cars and the two coaches with the half-dozen faces in the windows looking out at him. He could feel those people staring at him, wondering who he was. Virgil didn't look back at them. He kept his eyes on the last coach and caboose and saw them jerk to a stop before reaching the platform—out on open ground just this side of the water tower.

"Come on out," Virgil said to the station house.

Howard Crowder and Dancey and Billy Santos came out into the sunlight through the open door. Their hands were behind their backs, as though they might have been tied. Virgil moved them out of the doorway, down to the end of the platform and stood them against the wall of the building: three convicts waiting to be put aboard a prison train, tired-looking, beaten, their hat brims pulled down against the bright morning glare.

Virgil watched Bob Fisher, followed by another guard with a rifle come down the step-rungs at the far end of the prison coach. Two more guards with rifles were coming along the side of the caboose and somebody else was in the caboose window: a man wearing glasses who was sticking his head out and saying something to the two guards who had come out of the prison coach.

Bob Fisher didn't look around at Mr. Manly in the caboose window. He kept his gaze on the three convicts and the man with the shotgun. He called out, "What're the names of those men you got?"

"I'm just delivering these people," Virgil called back. "I wasn't introduced to them."

Bob Fisher and the guard with him and the two guards from the caboose came on past the prison coach but stopped before they reached the platform.

"You the only one guarding them?" Fisher asked.

"Yes, sir, I'm the one found them, I'm the one brought them in."

"I've seen you some place," Fisher said.

"Sure, delivering a prisoner. About a year ago."

"Where's the station man at?"

"He's inside."

"Call him out."

"I reckon he heard you." Virgil looked over his shoulder as the S.P. man appeared in the doorway. "There he is. Hey, listen, you want these three boys or don't you? I been watching them all night, I'm tired."

"I want to know who they are," Fisher said. "If you're not going to tell me, I want them to call out their names."

There was silence. Virgil knew the time had come and he had to put the shotgun on Fisher and fill up the silence and get this thing done right now, or else drop the gun and forget the whole thing. No more than eight seconds passed in the silence, though it seemed like eight minutes to Virgil. Bob Fisher's hand went inside his coat and Virgil didn't have to think about it any more. He heard glass shatter as somebody kicked through a window in the prison coach. Bob Fisher drew a revolver, half turning toward the prison coach at the same time, but not turning quickly enough as Virgil put the shotgun on him and gave him a load point-blank in the side of the chest. And as the guards saw Fisher go down and were raising their rifles the three men in convict clothes brought their revolvers from behind their backs and fired as fast as they could swing their guns from one gray suit to another. All three guards were dropped where they stood, though one of them, on his knees, shot Billy Santos through the head before Virgil could get his shotgun on the man and finish him with the second load.

A rifle came out the caboose window and a barrel smashed the glass of a window in the prison coach, but it was too late. Virgil was pressed close to the side of the baggage car, out of the line of fire, and the two men in prison clothes had the S.P. man and were using him for a shield as they backed into the station house.

Virgil could look directly across the platform to the open doorway. He took time to reload the shotgun. He looked up and down the length of the train, then over at the doorway again.

"Hey, Dancey," Virgil called over, "send that train man out with the dynamite."

He had to wait a little bit before the S.P. man appeared in the doorway, straining to hold the fifty-pound case in his arms, having trouble with the dead weight, or else terrified of what he was holding.

"Walk down to the end of the platform with it," Virgil told him, "so they can see what you got. When you come back, walk up by that first passenger coach. Where everybody's looking out the window."

Jesus, the man could hardly take a step he was so scared of dropping the case. When he was down at the end of the platform, the copper wire trailing behind him and leading into the station. Virgil stepped away from the baggage car and called out, "Hey, you guards! You hear me? Throw out your guns and come out with your hands in the air, or we're going to put dynamite under a passenger coach and blow everybody clear to hell. You hear me?"

They heard him.

Mr. Manly and the three guards who were left came out to stand by the caboose. The prisoners began to yell and break the windows on both sides of the coach, but they quieted down when Frank Shelby and his three boys walked off the train and wouldn't let anybody else follow.

They are going to shoot us, Mr. Manly said to himself. He saw Frank Shelby looking toward them. Then Frank was looking at the dead guards and at Bob Fisher in particular. "I wish you hadn't of killed him," he heard Shelby say.

"I had to," the man with the shotgun said.

And then Shelby said, "I wanted to do it."

Junior said that if he hadn't kicked out the window they might still be in there. That was all they said for a while that Mr. Manly heard. Shelby and his three convict friends went into the station house. They came out a few minutes later wearing work clothes and might have been ranch hands for all anybody would know to look at them.

Mr. Manly didn't see who it was that placed the case of dynamite at the front end of the train, under the cow-catcher, but saw one of them playing out the wire back along the platform and around the off side of the station house. Standing on the platform, Frank Shelby and the one with the shotgun seemed to be in a serious conversa-

FORTY LASHES LESS ONE

tion. Then Frank said something to Junior, who boarded the train again and brought out Norma Davis. Mr. Manly could see she was frightened, as if afraid they were going to shoot her or do something to her. Junior and Joe Dean took her into the station house. Frank Shelby came over then. Mr. Manly expected him to draw a gun.

"Four of us are leaving," Shelby said. "You can have the rest."

"What about the woman?"

"I mean five of us. Norma's going along."

"You're not going to harm her, are you?" Shelby kept staring at him, and Mr. Manly couldn't think straight. All he could say was, "I hope you know that what you're doing is wrong, an offense against Almighty God as well as your fellowman."

"Jesus Christ," Shelby said, and walked away.

Lord, help me, Mr. Manly said, and called out, "Frank, listen to me."

But Shelby didn't look back. The platform was deserted now except for the Mexican-looking man who lay dead with his arm hanging over the edge. They were mounting horses on the other side of the station. Mr. Manly could hear the horses. Then, from where he stood, he could see several of the horses past the corner of the building. He saw Junior stand in his stirrups to reach the telegraph wire at the edge of the roof and cut it with a knife. Another man was on the ground, stooped over a wooden box. Shelby nodded to him and kicked his horse, heading out into the open desert, away from

209

the station. As the rest of them followed, raising a thin dust cloud, the man on the ground pushed down on the box.

The dynamite charge raised the front end of the loco-motive off the track, derailed the first baggage car and sent the coaches slamming back against each other, twisting the couplings and tearing loose the end car, rolling it a hundred feet down the track. Mr. Manly dropped flat with the awful, ear-splitting sound of the explosion. He wasn't sure if he threw himself down or was knocked down by the concussion. When he opened his eyes there was dirt in his mouth, his head throbbed as if he had been hit with a hammer, and for a minute or so he could see nothing but smoke or dust or steam from the engine, a cloud that enveloped the station and lay heavily over the platform.

He heard men's voices. He was aware of one of the guards lying close to him and looked to see if the man was hurt. The guard was pushing himself up, shaking his head. Mr. Manly got quickly to his feet and looked around. The caboose was no longer behind him; it was down the track and the prison coach was only a few feet away where the convicts were coming out, coughing and waving at the smoke with their hands. Mr. Manly called out, "Is anybody hurt?"

No one answered him directly. The convicts were standing around; they seemed dazed. No one was at-tempting to run away. He saw one of the guards with a rifle now on the platform, holding the gun on the prison-ers, who were paying no attention to him. At the other end of the platform there were a few people from the passenger coach. They stood looking at the locomotive that was shooting white steam and stood leaning awkwardly toward the platform, as if it might fall over any minute.

He wanted to be doing something. He had to be doing something. Five prisoners gone, four guards dead, a train blown up, telegraph line cut, no idea when help would come or where to go from here. He could hear Mr. Rynning saying, "You let them do all that? Man, this is your responsibility and you'll answer for it."

"Captain, you want us to follow them?"

Mr. Manly turned, not recognizing the voice at first. Harold Jackson, the Zulu, was standing next to him.

"What? I'm sorry, I didn't hear you."

"I said, you want us to follow them? Me and Raymond."

Mr. Manly perked up. "There are horses here?"

"No-suh, man say the nearest horses are at Gila. That's most of a day's ride."

"Then how would you expect to follow them?"

"We run, captain."

"There are eight of them—on horses."

"We don't mean to fight them, captain. We mean maybe we can follow them and see which way they go. Then when you get some help, you know, maybe we can tell this help where they went."

"They'll be thirty miles away before dark."

"So will we, captain."

"Follow them on foot—"

"Yes-suh, only we would have to go right now. Captain, they going to run those horses at first to get some distance and we would have to run the first five, six miles, no stopping, to keep their dust in sight. Raymond say it's all flat and open, no water. Just some little bushes. We don't have to follow them all day. We see where they going and get back here at dark."

Mr. Manly was frowning, looking around because, Lord, there was too much to think about at one time. He said, "I can't send convicts to chase after convicts. My God."

"They do it in Florida, captain. Trusties handle the dogs. I seen it."

"I have to get the telegraph wire fixed, that's the main thing."

"I hear the train man say they busted his key, he don't know if he can fix it," Harold Jackson said. "You going to sit here till tonight before anybody come—while Frank Shelby and them are making distance. But if me and the Apache follow them we can leave signs."

Mr. Manly noticed Raymond San Carlos now behind Harold. Raymond was nodding. "Sure," he said, "we can leave pieces of our clothes for them to follow if you give us something else to wear. Maybe you should give us some guns too, in case we get close to them, or for firing signals."

"I can't do that," Mr. Manly said. "No, I can't give you guns."

"How about our spears then?" Raymond said. "We get hungry we could use the spears maybe to stick something."

"The spears might be all right." Mr. Manly nodded.

"Spears and two canteens of water," Raymond said. "And the other clothes. Some people see us they won't think we're convicts running away."

"Pair of pants and a shirt," Mr. Manly said.

"And a couple of blankets. In case we don't get back before dark and we got to sleep outside. We can get our bedrolls and the spears," Raymond said. "They're with all the baggage in that car we loaded."

"You'd try to be back before dark?"

"Yes, sir, we don't like to sleep outside if we don't have to."

"Well," Mr. Manly said. He paused. He was trying to think of an alternative. He didn't believe that sending these two out would do any good. He pictured them coming back at dusk and sinking to the ground exhausted. But at least it would be doing something—now. Mr. Rynning or somebody would ask him, What did you do? And he'd say, I sent trackers out after them. I got these two boys that are runners. He said, "Well, find your stuff and get started. I'll tell the guards."

They left the water stop at Sentinel running almost due south. They ran several hundred yards before looking back to see the smoke still hanging in a dull cloud over the buildings and the palo verde trees. They ran for another half-mile or so, loping easily and not speaking, carrying their spears and their new guard-gray pants and shirts wrapped in their blanket rolls. They ran until they reached a gradual rise and ran down the other side to find themselves in a shallow wash, out of sight of the water stop.

They looked at each other now. Harold grinned and Raymond grinned. They sat down on the bank of the wash and began laughing, until soon both of them had tears in their eyes.

12

——— ❖ ———

Harold said, "What way do we go?"

Raymond got up on the bank of the dry wash and stood looking out at the desert that was a flat burned-out waste as far as they could see. There were patches of dusty scrub growth, but no cactus or trees from here to the dark rise of the mountains to the south.

"That way," Raymond said. "To the Crater Mountains and down to the Little Ajos. Two days we come to Ajo, the town, steal some horses, go on south to Bates Well. The next day we come to Quitobaquito, a little water-hole village, and cross the border. After that, I don't know."

"Three days, uh?"

"Without horses."

"Frank Shelby, he going the same way?"

"He could go to Clarkstown instead of Ajo. They near each other. One the white man's town, the other the Mexican town."

"But he's going the same way we are."

"There isn't no other way south from here."

"I'd like to get him in front of me one minute," Harold said.

"Man," Raymond said, "you would have to move fast to get him first."

"Maybe we run into him sometime."

"Only if we run," Raymond said.

Harold was silent a moment. "If we did, we'd get out of here quicker, wouldn't we? If we run."

"Sure, maybe save a day. If we're any good."

"You think we couldn't run to those mountains?"

"Sure we could, we wanted to."

"Is there water?"

"There used to be."

"Then that's probably where he's heading to camp tonight, uh? What do you think?"

"He's got to go that way. He might as well."

"We was to get there tonight," Harold said, "we might run into him."

"We might run into all of them."

"Not if we saw them first. Waited for him to get alone."

Raymond grinned. "Play with him a little."

"Man, that would be good, wouldn't it?" Harold said. "Scare him some."

"Scare hell out of him."

"Paint his face," Harold said. He began to smile thinking about it.

"Take his clothes. Paint him all over."

"Now you talking. You got any?"

"I brought some iodine and a little bottle of white.

Listen," Raymond said, "we're going that way. Why don't we take a little run and see how Frank's doing?"

Harold stood up. When they had tied their blanket rolls across one shoulder and picked up their spears, the Apache and the Zulu began their run across the southern Arizona desert.

They ran ten miles in the furnace heat of sand and rock and dry, white-crusted playas and didn't break their stride until the sun was directly overhead. They walked a mile and ran another mile before they stopped to rest and allowed themselves a drink of water from the canteens, a short drink and then a mouthful they held in their mouths while they screwed closed the canteens and hung them over their shoulders again. They rested fifteen minutes and before the tiredness could creep in to stiffen their legs they stood up without a word and started off again toward the mountains.

For a mile or so they would be aware of their running. Then, in time, they would become lost in the monotonous stride of their pace, running, but each somewhere else in his mind, seeing cool mountain pastures or palm trees or thinking of nothing at all, running and hearing themselves sucking the heated air in and letting it out, but not feeling the agony of running. They had learned to do this in the past months, to detach themselves and be inside or outside the running man but not part of him for long minutes at a time. When they broke stride they would always walk and sometimes run again before resting. At times they felt they were getting no closer to the mountains, though finally the slopes began to take shape, changing from a dark mass to dun-colored slopes and shadowed contours. At mid-afternoon they saw the first trace of dust rising in the distance. Both of them saw it and they kept their eyes on the wispy, moving cloud that would rise and vanish against the sky. The dust was something good to watch and seeing it was better than stretching out in the grass and going to sleep. It meant Frank Shelby was only a few miles ahead of them.

They came to the arroyo in the shadowed foothills of the Crater Mountains a little after five o'clock. There was good brush cover here and a natural road that would take them up into high country. They would camp above Shelby if they could and watch him, Ray-mond said, but first he had to go out and find the son of a bitch. You rest, he told Harold, and the Zulu gave him a deadpan look and stared at him until he was gone. Harold sat back against the cool, shaded wall of the gul-ley. He wouldn't let himself go to sleep though. He kept his eyes open and waited for the Apache, listening and not moving, letting the tight weariness ease out of his body. By the time Raymond returned the arroyo was dark. The only light they could see were sun reflections on the high peaks above them.

"They're in some trees," Raymond said, "about a half-mile from here. Taking it easy, they even got a fire."

"All of them there?"

"I count eight, eight horses."

"Can we get close?"

"Right above them. Frank's put two men up in the rocks—they can see all around the camp."

"What do you think?" Harold said.

"I think we should take the two in the rocks. See what Frank does in the morning when nobody's there."

The grin spread over Harold's face. That sounded pretty good.

They slept for a few hours and when they woke up it was night. Harold touched Raymond. The Indian sat up without making a sound. He opened a canvas bag and took out the small bottles of iodine and white paint and they began to get ready.

There was no sun yet on this side of the mountain, still cold dark in the early morning when Virgil Shelby came down out of the rocks and crossed the open slope to the trees. He could make out his brother and the woman by the fire. He could hear the horses and knew Frank's men were saddling them and gathering up their gear.

Frank and the woman looked up as Virgil approached, and Frank said, "They coming?"

"I don't know. I didn't see them."

"What do you mean you didn't see them?"

"They weren't up there."

Frank Shelby got up off the ground. He dumped his coffee as he walked to the edge of the trees to look up at the tumbled rocks and the escarpment that rose steeply against the sky.

"They're asleep somewhere," he said. "You must've looked the wrong places."

"I looked all over up there."

"They're asleep," Shelby said. "Go on up there and look again."

When Virgil came back the second time Frank said, Jesus Christ, what good are you? And sent Junior and Joe Dean up into the rocks. When they came down he went up himself to have a look and was still up there as the sunlight began to spread over the slope and they could feel the heat of day coming down on them.

"There's no sign of anything," Virgil said. "There's no sign they were even here."

"I put them here," Frank Shelby said. "One right where you're standing, Dancey over about a hundred feet. I put them here myself."

"Well, they're not here now," Virgil said.

"Jesus Christ, I know that." Frank looked over at Junior and Soonzy. "You counted the horses?"

"We'd a-heard them taking horses."

"I asked if you counted them!"

"Christ, we got them saddled. I don't have to count them."

"Then they walked away," Frank Shelby said, his tone quieter now.

Virgil shook his head. "I hadn't paid them yet."

"They walked away," Shelby said again. "I don't know why, but they did."

"Can you see Dancey walking off into the mountains?" Virgil said. "I'm telling you I hadn't *paid* them."

"There's nothing up there could have carried them off. No animal, no man. There is no sign they did anything but walk away," Shelby said, "and that's the way we're going to leave it."

He said no more until they were down in the trees again, ready to ride out. Nobody said anything.

Then Frank told Joe Dean he was to ride ahead of them like a point man. Virgil, he said, was to stay closer in the hills and ride swing, though he would also be ahead of them looking for natural trails.

"Looking for trails," Virgil said. "If you believe those two men walked off, then what is it that's tightening up your hind end?"

"You're older than me," Frank said, "but no bigger, and I will sure close your mouth if you want it done."

"Jesus, can't you take some kidding?"

"Not from you," his brother said.

They were in a high meadow that had taken more than an hour to reach, at least a thousand feet above Shelby's camp. Dancey and Howard Crowder sat on the ground close to each other. The Apache and the Zulu stood off from them leaning on their spears, their blankets laid over their shoulders as they waited for the sun to spread across the field. They would be leaving in a few minutes. They planned to get out ahead of Shelby and be waiting for him. These two, Dancey and Crowder, they would leave here. They had taken their revolvers and gun belts, the only things they wanted from them.

"They're going to kill us," Dancey whispered.

Howard Crowder told him for God sake to keep quiet, they'd hear him.

They had been in the meadow most of the night, brought here after each had been sitting in the rocks, drowsing, and had felt the spear point at the back of his neck. They hadn't got a good look at the two yet. They believed both were Indians—even though there were no

Indians around here, and no Indians had carried spears in fifty years. Then they would have to be loco Indians escaped from an asylum or kicked out of their village. That's what they were. That's why Dancey believed they were going to kill him and Howard.

Finally, in the morning light, when the Zulu walked over to them and Dancey got a close look at his face— God Almighty, with the paint and the scars and the short pointed beard and the earring—he closed his eyes and expected to feel the spear in his chest any second.

Harold said, "You two wait here till after we're gone."

Dancey opened his eyes and Howard Crowder said, "What?"

"We're going to leave, then you can find your way out of here."

Howard Crowder said, "But we don't know where we are."

"You up on a mountain."

"How do we get down?"

"You look around for a while you find a trail. By that time your friends will be gone without you, so you might as well go home." Howard started to turn away.

"Wait a minute," Howard Crowder said. "We don't have horses, we don't have any food or water. How are we supposed to get across the desert?"

"It's up to you," Harold said. "Walk if you want or stay here and die, it's up to you."

"We didn't do nothing to you," Dancey said.

Harold looked at him. "That's why we haven't killed you."

"Then what do you want us for?"

"We don't want you," Harold said. "We want Frank Shelby."

Virgil rejoined the group at noon to report he hadn't seen a thing, not any natural trail either that would save them time. They were into the foothills of the Little Ajos and he sure wished Billy Santos had not got shot in the head in the train station, because Billy would have had them to Clarkstown by now. They would be sitting at a table with cold beer and fried meat instead of squatting on the ground eating hash out of a can. He asked if he should stay with the group now. Norma Davis looked pretty good even if she was kind of sweaty and dirty; she was built and had nice long hair. He wouldn't mind riding with her a while and maybe arranging something for that night.

Frank, it looked like, was still not talking. Virgil asked him again if he should stay with the group and this time Frank said no and told him to finish his grub and ride out. He said, "Find the road to Clarkstown or don't bother coming back, because there would be no use of having you around."

So Virgil and Joe Dean rode out about fifteen minutes ahead of the others. When they split up Virgil worked his way deeper into the foothills to look for some kind of a road. He crossed brush slopes and arroyos, holding to a south-southeast course, but he didn't see anything that resembled even a foot path. It was a few hours after leaving the group, about three o'clock in the afternoon, that Virgil came across the Indian and it was the damnedest thing he'd ever seen in his life.

There he was out in the middle of nowhere sitting at the shady edge of a mesquite thicket wrapped in an army blanket. A real Apache Indian, red headband and all and even with some paint on his face and a staff or something that was sticking out of the bushes. It looked like a fishing pole. That was the first thing Virgil thought of: an Apache Indian out in the desert fishing in a mesquite patch—the damnedest thing he'd ever seen.

Virgil said, "Hey, Indin, you sabe English any?"

Raymond San Carlos remained squatted on the ground. He nodded once.

"I'm looking for the road to Clarkstown."

Raymond shook his head now. "I don't know."

"You speak pretty good. Tell me something, what're you doing out here?"

"I'm not doing nothing."

"You live around here?"

Raymond pointed off to the side. "Not far."

"How come you got that paint on your face?"

"I just put it there."

"How come if you live around here you don't know where Clarkstown is?"

"I don't know."

"Jesus, you must be a dumb Indin. Have you seen anybody else come through here today?"

"Nobody."

"You haven't seen me, have you?"

"What?"

"You haven't seen nobody and you haven't seen me either."

224

Raymond said nothing.

"I don't know," Virgil said now. "Some sheriff's people ask you you're liable to tell them, aren't you? You got family around here?"

"Nobody else."

"Just you all alone. Nobody would miss you then, would they? Listen, buddy, I don't mean anything personal, but I'm afraid you seeing me isn't a good idea. I'm going to have to shoot you."

Raymond stood up now, slowly.

"You can run if you want," Virgil said, "or you can stand there and take it, I don't care; but don't start hollering and carrying on. All right?"

Virgil was wearing a shoulder rig under his coat. He looked down as he unbuttoned the one button, drew a .44 Colt and looked up to see something coming at him and gasped as if the wind was knocked out of him as he grabbed hold of the fishing pole sticking out of his chest and saw the Indian standing there watching him and saw the sky and the sun, and that was all.

Raymond dragged Virgil's body into the mesquite. He left his spear in there too. He had two revolvers, a Winchester rifle and a horse. He didn't need a spear any more.

Joe Dean's horse smelled water. He was sure of it, so he let the animal have its head and Joe Dean went along for the ride—down into a wide canyon that was green and yellow with spring growth. When he saw the cottonwoods and then the round soft shape of the willows against the canyon slope, Joe Dean patted the horse's neck and guided him with the reins again.

It was a still pool, but not stagnant, undercutting a shelf of rock and mirroring the cliffs and canyon walls. Joe Dean dismounted. He led his horse down a bank of shale to the pool, then went belly-down at the edge and drank with his face in the water. He drank all he wanted before emptying the little bit left in his canteen and filling it to the top. Then he stretched out and drank again. He wished he had time to strip off his clothes and dive in. But he had better get the others first or Frank would see he'd bathed and start kicking and screaming again. Once he got them here they would probably all want to take a bath. That would be something, Norma in there with them, grabbing some of her under the water when Frank wasn't looking. Then she'd get out and lie up there on the bank to dry off in the sun. Nice soft white body—

Joe Dean was pushing himself up, looking at the pool and aware now of the reflections in the still water: the slope of the canyon wall high above, the shelf of rock behind him, sandy brown, and something else, something dark that resembled a man's shape, and he felt that cold prickly feeling up between his shoulder blades to his neck.

It was probably a crevice, shadowed inside. It couldn't be a man. Joe Dean got to his feet, then turned around and looked up.

Harold Jackson—bare to the waist, and a blanket over one shoulder, with his beard and tribal scars and streak of white paint—stood looking down at him from the rock shelf.

"How you doing?" Harold said. "You get enough water?"

Joe Dean stared at him. He didn't answer right away. God, no. He was thinking and trying to decide quickly if it was a good thing or a bad thing to be looking up at Harold Jackson at a water hole in the Little Ajo Mountains.

He said finally, "How'd you get here?"

"Same way you did."

"You got away after we left?"

"Looks like it, don't it?"

"Well, that must've been something. Just you?"

"No, Raymond come with me."

"I don't see him. Where is he?"

"He's around some place."

"If there wasn't any horses left, how'd you get here?"

"How you think?"

"I'm asking you, Sambo."

"We run, Joe."

"You're saying you run here all the way from Sentinel?"

"Well, we stop last night," Harold said, and kept watching him. "Up in the Crater Mountains."

"Is that right? We camped up there too."

"I know you did," Harold said.

Joe Dean was silent for a long moment before he said, "You killed Howard and Dancey, didn't you?"

"No, we never killed them. We let them go."

"What do you want?"

"Not you, Joe. Unless you want to take part."

Joe Dean's revolver was in his belt. He didn't see a gun or a knife or anything on Harold, just the blanket over his shoulder and covering his arm. It looked like it would be pretty easy. So he drew his revolver.

As he did, though, Harold pulled the blanket across his body with his left hand. His right hand came up holding Howard Crowder's .44 and he shot Joe Dean with it three times in the chest. And now Harold had two revolvers, a rifle, and a horse. He left Joe Dean lying next to the pool for Shelby to find.

They had passed Clarkstown, Shelby decided. Missed it. Which meant they were still in the Little Ajo Mountains, past the chance of having a sit-down hot meal today, but that much closer to the border. That part was all right. What bothered him, they had not seen Virgil or Joe Dean since noon.

It was almost four o'clock now. Junior and Soonzy were riding ahead about thirty yards. Norma was keeping up with Shelby, staying close, afraid of him but more afraid of falling behind and finding herself alone. If Shelby didn't know where they were, Norma knew that she, by herself, would never find her way out. She had no idea why Shelby had brought her, other than at Virgil's request to have a woman along. No one had approached her in the camp last night. She knew, though, once they were across the border and the men relaxed and quit looking behind them, one of them, probably Virgil, would come to her with that fixed expression on his face and she would take him on and be nice to him as long as she had no other choice.

"We were through here one time," Shelby said. "We went up through Copper Canyon to Clarkstown the morning we went after the Cornelia Mine payroll. I don't see any familiar sights, though. It all looks the same."

She knew he wasn't speaking to her directly. He was thinking out loud, or stoking his confidence with the sound of his own voice.

"From here what we want to hit is Growler Pass," Shelby said. "Top the pass and we're at Bates Well. Then we got two ways to go. Southeast to Dripping Springs and on down to Sonoyta. Or a shorter trail to the border through Quitobaquito. I haven't decided yet which way we'll go. When Virgil comes in I'll ask him if Billy Santos said anything about which trail's best this time of the year."

"What happened to the two men last night?" Norma asked him.

Shelby didn't answer. She wasn't sure if she should ask him again. Before she could decide, Junior was riding back toward them and Shelby had reined in to wait for him.

Junior was grinning. "I believe Joe Dean's found us some water. His tracks lead into that canyon yonder and it's chock-full of green brush and willow trees."

"There's a tank somewhere in these hills," Shelby said.

"Well, I believe we've found it," Junior said.

They found the natural tank at the end of the canyon. They found Joe Dean lying with his head and outstretched arms in the still water. And they found planted in the sand next to him, sticking straight up, a spear made of a bamboo fishing pole and a mortar trowel.

13

They camped on high ground south of Bates Well and in the morning came down through giant saguaro country, down through a hollow in the hills to within sight of Quitobaquito.

There it was, a row of weathered adobes and stock pens beyond a water hole that resembled a shallow, stagnant lake—a worn-out village on the bank of a dying pool that was rimmed with rushes and weeds and a few stunted trees.

Shelby didn't like it.

He had pictured a green oasis and found a dusty, desert water hole. He had imagined a village where they could trade for food and fresh horses, a gateway to Mexico with the border lying not far beyond the village, across the Rio Sonoyta.

He didn't like the look of the place. He didn't like not seeing any people over there. He didn't like the open fifty yards between here and the water hole.

He waited in a cover of rocks and brush with Norma and Junior and Soonzy behind him, and Mexico waiting less than a mile away. They could go around Quitobaquito. But if they did, where was the next water? The Sonoyta could be dried up, for all he knew. They could head for Santo Domingo, a fair-sized town that shouldn't be too far away. But what if they missed it? There was water right in front of them and, goddamn-it, they were going to have some, all they wanted. But he hesitated, studying the village, waiting for some sign of life other than a dog barking, and remembering Joe Dean with the three bullets in his chest.

Junior said, "Jesus, are we gong to sit here in the sun all day?"

"I'll let you know," Shelby said.

"You want me to get the water?"

"I did, I would have told you."

"Well, then tell me, goddamn-it. You think I'm scared to?"

Soonzy settled it. He said, "I think maybe everybody's off some place to a wedding or something. That's probably what it is. These people, somebody dies or gets married, they come from all over."

"Maybe," Shelby said.

"I don't see no other way but for me to go in there and find out. What do you say, Frank?"

After a moment Shelby nodded. "All right, go take a look."

"If it's the nigger and the Indin," Soonzy said, "if they're in there, I'll bring 'em out."

Raymond held the wooden shutter open an inch, enough so he could watch Soonzy coming in from the east end of the village, mounted, a rifle across his lap. Riding right in, Raymond thought. Dumb, or sure of himself, or maybe both. He could stick a .44 out the window and shoot him as he went by. Except that it would be a risk. He couldn't afford to miss and have Soonzy shooting in here. Raymond let the shutter close.

He pressed a finger to his lips and turned to the fourteen people, the men and women and children who were huddled in the dim room, sitting on the floor and looking up at him now, watching silently, even the two smallest children. The people were Mexican and Papago. They wore white cotton and cast-off clothes. They had lived here all their lives and they were used to armed men riding through Quitobaquito. Raymond had told them these were bad men coming who might steal from them and harm them. They believed him and they waited in silence. Now they could hear the horse's hoofs on the hard-packed street. Raymond stood by the door with a revolver in his hand. The sound of the horse passed. Raymond waited, then opened the door a crack and looked out. Soonzy was nowhere in sight.

If anybody was going to shoot at anybody going for water, Soonzy decided, it would have to be from one of the adobes facing the water hole. There was a tree in the backyard of the first one that would block a clear shot across the hole. So that left him only two places to search—two low-roofed, crumbling adobes that stood bare in the sunlight, showing their worn bricks and looking like part of the land.

Soonzy stayed close to the walls on the front side of the street. When he came to the first adobe facing the water hole, he reached down to push the door open, ducked his head, and walked his horse inside.

He came out into the backyard on foot, holding a revolver now, and seeing just one end of the water hole because the tree was in the way. From the next adobe, though, a person would have a clear shot. There weren't any side windows, which was good. It let Soonzy walk right up to the place. He edged around the corner, following his revolver to the back door and got right up against the boards so he could listen. He gave himself time; there was no hurry. Then he was glad he did when the sound came from inside, a little creaking sound, like a door or a window being opened.

Harold eased open the front door a little more. He still couldn't see anything. The man had been down at the end of the street, coming this way on his horse big as anything, and now he was gone. He looked down half a block and across the street, at the adobe, where Raymond was waiting with the people, keeping them quiet and out of the way. He saw Raymond coming out; Harold wanted to wave to him to get inside. What was he doing?

The back door banged open and Soonzy was standing in the room covering him with a Colt revolver.

"Got you," Soonzy said. "Throw the gun outside and turn this way. Where's that red nigger at?"

"You mean Raymond?" Harold said. "He left. I don't know where he went."

"Which one of you shot Joe Dean, you or him?"

"I did. I haven't seen Raymond since before that."

FORTY LASHES LESS ONE

"What'd you do with Virgil?"

"I don't think I know any Virgil."

"Frank's brother. He took us off the train."

"I haven't seen him."

"You want me to pull the trigger?"

"I guess you'll pull it whether I tell or not." Harold felt the door behind him touch the heel of his right foot. He had not moved the foot, but now he felt the door push gently against it.

"I'll tell Frank Shelby," Harold said then. "How'll that be? You take me to Frank I'll tell him where his brother is and them other two boys. But if you shoot me he won't ever know where his brother's at, will he? He's liable to get mad at somebody."

Soonzy had to think about that. He wasn't going to be talked into anything he didn't want to do. He said, "Whether I shoot you now or later you're still going to be dead."

"It's up to you," Harold said.

"All right, turn around and open the door."

"Yes-suh, captain," Harold said.

He opened the door and stepped aside and Raymond, in the doorway, fired twice and hit Soonzy dead center both times.

Shelby and Junior and Norma Davis heard the shots. They sounded far off, but the reports were thin and clear and unmistakable. Soonzy had gone into the village. Two shots were fired and Soonzy had not come out. They crouched fifty yards from water with empty canteens and the border less than a mile away.

Norma said they should go back to Bates Well. They could be there by evening, get water, and take the other trail south.

And run into a posse coming down from Gila, Shelby said. They didn't have time enough even to wait here till dark. They had to go with water or go without it, but they had to go, now.

So Junior said Jesus, give me the goddamn canteens or we will be here all day. He said maybe those two could paint theirselves up and bushwack a man, but he would bet ten dollars gold they couldn't shoot worth a damn for any distance. He'd get the water and be back in a minute. Shelby told Junior he would return fire and cover him if they started shooting, and Junior said that was mighty big of him.

"There," Raymond said. "You see him?"

Harold looked out past the door frame to the water hole. "Whereabouts?"

Raymond was at the window of the adobe. "He worked his way over to the right, coming in on the other side of the tree. You'll see him in a minute."

"Which one?"

"It looked like Junior."

"He can't sit still, can he?"

"I guess he's thirsty," Raymond said. "There he is. He thinks that tree's hiding him."

Harold could see him now, over to the right a little, approaching the bank of the water hole, running across the open in a hunch-shouldered crouch, keeping his head down behind nothing.

"How far do you think?" Raymond said.

Harold raised his Winchester and put the front sight on Junior. "Hundred yards, a little more."

"Can you hit him?"

Harold watched Junior slide down the sandy bank and begin filling the canteens, four of them, kneeling in the water and filling them one at a time. "Yeah, I can hit him," Harold said, and he was thinking, *He's taking too long. He should fill them all at once, push them under and hold them down.*

"What do you think?" Raymond said.

"I don't know."

"He ever do anything to you?"

"He done enough."

"I don't know either," Raymond said.

"He'd kill you. He wouldn't have to think about it."

"I guess he would."

"He'd enjoy it."

"I don't know," Raymond said. "It's different, seeing him when he don't see us."

"Well," Harold said, "if he gets the water we might not see him again. We might not see Frank Shelby again either. You want Frank?"

"I guess so."

"I do too," Harold said.

They let Junior come up the bank with the canteens, up to the rim before they shot him. Both fired at once and Junior slid back down to the edge of the still pool.

Norma looked at it this way: they would either give up, or they would be killed. Giving up would be taking a chance. But it would be less chancey if she gave up on her own, without Shelby. After all, Shelby had forced her to come along and that was a fact, whether the Indian and the Negro realized it or not. She had never been really unkind to them in prison; she had had nothing to do with them. So there was no reason for them to harm her now—once she explained she was more on their side than on Frank's. If they were feeling mean and had rape on their mind, well, she could handle that easily enough.

There was one canteen left, Joe Dean's. Norma picked it up and waited for Shelby's reaction.

"They'll shoot you too," he said.

"I don't think so."

"Why, because you're a woman?"

"That might help."

"God Almighty, you don't know them, do you?"

"I know they've got nothing against me. They're mad at you, Frank, not me."

"They've killed six people we know of. You just watched them gun Junior—and you're going to walk out there in the open?"

"Do you believe I might have a chance?"

Shelby paused. "A skinny one."

"Skinny or not, it's the only one we have, isn't it?"

"You'd put your life up to help me?"

"I'm just as thirsty as you are."

"Norma, I don't know—two days ago you were trying to turn me in."

"That's a long story, and if we get out of here we can talk about it sometime, Frank."

"You really believe you can do it."

"I want to so bad."

Boy, she was something. She was a tough, good-looking woman, and by God, maybe she could pull it. Frank said, "It might work. You know it?"

"I'm going way around to the side," Norma said, "where those bushes are. Honey, if they start shooting—"

"You're going to make it, Norma, I know you are. I got a feeling about this and I *know* it's going to work." He gave her a hug and rubbed his hand gently up and down her back, which was damp with perspiration. He said, "You hurry back now."

Norma said, "I will, sweetheart."

Watching her cross the open ground, Shelby got his rifle up between a notch in the rocks and put it on the middle adobe across the water hole. Norma was approaching from the left, the same way Junior had gone in, but circling wider than Junior had, going way around and now approaching the pool where tall rushes grew along the bank. Duck down in there, Shelby said. But Norma kept going, circling the water hole, following the bank as it curved around toward the far side. Jesus, she had nerve; she was heading for the bushes almost to the other side. But then she was past the bushes. She was running. She was into the yard where the big tree stood before Shelby said, "Goddamn you!" out loud, and swung his Winchester on the moving figure in the striped skirt. He fired and levered and fired two more before they opened up from the house and he had to go down behind the rocks. By the time he looked again she was inside.

* * *

Frank Shelby gave up an hour later. He waved a flour sack at them for a while, then brought the three horses down out of the brush and led them around the water hole toward the row of adobes. He had figured out most of what he was going to say. The tone was the important thing. Take them by surprise. Bluff them. Push them off balance. They'd expect him to run and hide, but instead he was walking up to them. He could talk to them. Christ, a dumb nigger and an Indin who'd been taking orders and saying yes-sir all their lives. They had run scared from the train and had been scared into killing. That's what happened. They were scared to death of being caught and taken back to prison. So he would have to be gentle with them at first and calm them down, the way you'd calm a green horse that was nervous and skittish. There, there, boys, what's all this commotion about? Show them he wasn't afraid, and gradually take charge. Take care of Norma also. God, he was dying to get his hands on Norma.

Harold and Raymond came out of the adobe first, with rifles, though not pointing them at him. Norma came out behind them and moved over to the side, grinning at him, goddamn her. It made Shelby mad, though it didn't hold his attention. Harold and Raymond did that with their painted faces staring at him; no expression, just staring, waiting for him.

As he reached the yard Shelby grinned and said, "Boys, I believe it's about time we cut out this foolishness. What do you say?"

Harold and Raymond waited.

Shelby said, "I mean what are we doing shooting at each other for? We're on the same side. We spent months together in that hell hole on the bluff and, by Jesus, we jumped the train together, didn't we?"

Harold and Raymond waited.

Shelby said, "If there was some misunderstanding you had with my men we can talk about it later because, boys, right now I believe we should get over that border before we do any more standing around talking."

And Harold and Raymond waited.

Shelby did too, a moment. He said then, "Have I done anything to you? Outside of a little pissy-ass difference we had, haven't I always treated you boys fair? What do you want from me? You want me to pay you something? I'll tell you what, I'll pay you both to hire on and ride with me. What do you say?"

Harold Jackson said, "You're going to ride with us, man. Free."

"To where?"

"Back to Sentinel."

Norma started laughing as Shelby said, "Jesus, are you crazy? What are you talking about, back to Sentinel? You mean back to *prison*?"

"That's right," Harold said. "Me and Raymond decide that's the thing you'd like the worst."

She stopped laughing altogether as Raymond said, "You're going too, lady."

"Why?" Norma looked dazed, taken completely by surprise. "I'm not with him. What have I ever done to you?"

241

"Nobody has ever done anything to us," Raymond said to Harold. "Did you know that?"

The section gang that arrived from Gila told Mr. Manly no, they had not heard any news yet. There were posses out from the Sand Tank Mountains to the Little Ajos, but nobody had reported seeing anything. At least it had not been reported to the railroad.

They asked Mr. Manly how long he had been here at Sentinel and he told them five days, since the escape. He didn't tell them Mr. Rynning had wired and instructed him to stay. "You have five days," Mr. Rynning said. "If the convict pair you released do not return, report same to the sheriff, Maricopa. Report in person to me."

Mr. Manly took that to mean he was to wait here five full days and leave the morning of the sixth. The first two days there had been a mob here. Railroad people with equipment, a half-dozen guards that had been sent over from Florence, and the Maricopa sheriff, who had been here getting statements and the descriptions of the escaped convicts. He had told the Maricopa sheriff about sending out the two trackers and the man had said, trackers? Where did you get trackers? He told him and the man had stared at him with a funny look. It was the sheriff who must have told Mr. Rynning about Harold and Raymond.

The railroad had sent an engine with a crane to lift the locomotive and the baggage car onto the track. Then the train had to be pulled all the way to the yard at Gila, where a new locomotive was hooked up and the prisoners were taken on to Florence. There had certainly been a lot of excitement those two days. Since then the place had been deserted except for the telegrapher and the section gang. They were usually busy and it gave Mr. Manly time to think of what he would tell Mr. Rynning.

It wasn't an easy thing to explain: trusting two convicts enough to let them go off alone. Two murderers, Mr. Rynning would say. Yes, that was true; but he had still trusted them. And until this morning he had expected to see them again. That was the sad part. He sincerely believed he had made progress with Harold and Raymond. He believed he had taught them something worthwhile about life, about living with their fellowman. But evidently he had been wrong. Or, to look at it honestly, he had failed. Another failure after forty years of failures.

He was in the station house late in the afternoon of the fifth day, talking to the telegrapher, passing time. Neither had spoken for a while when the telegrapher said, "You hear something?" He went to the window and said, "Riders coming in." After a pause he said, "Lord in heaven!" And Mr. Manly knew.

He was off the bench and outside, standing there waiting for them, grinning, beaming, as they rode up: his Apache and his Zulu—thank you, God, just look at them!—bringing in Frank Shelby and the woman with ropes around their necks, bringing them in tied fast and making Mr. Manly, at this moment, the happiest man on earth.

Mr. Manly said, "I don't believe it. Boys, I am looking at it and I don't believe it. Do you know there are posses all over the country looking for these people?"

"We passed some of them," Raymond said.

"They still after the others?"

"I guess they are," Raymond said.

"Boys, I'll tell you, I've been waiting here for days, worried sick about you. I even began to wonder—I hate to say it but it's true—I even began to wonder if you were coming back. Now listen, I want to hear all about it, but first I want to say this. For what you've done here, for your loyalty and courage, risking your lives to bring these people back—which you didn't even have to do—I am going to personally see that you're treated like white men at Florence and are given decent work to do."

The Apache and the Zulu sat easily in their saddles watching Mr. Manly, their painted faces staring at him without expression.

"I'll tell you something else," Mr. Manly said. "You keep your record clean at Florence, I'll go before the prison board myself and make a formal request that your sentences be commuted, which means cut way down." Mr. Manly was beaming. He said, "Fellas, what do you think of that?"

They continued to watch him until Harold Jackson the Zulu, leaning on his saddle horn, said to Mr. Manly, "Fuck you, captain."

They let go of the ropes that led to Frank Shelby and the woman. They turned their horses in tight circles and rode out, leaving a mist of fine dust hanging in the air.

ELMORE LEONARD
THE UNDISPUTED MASTER OF THE CRIME NOVEL

RAYLAN
A Raylan Givens Novel
Available in Paperback and eBook

DJIBOUTI
Available in Paperback and eBook

ROAD DOGS
Available in Paperback and eBook

COMFORT TO THE ENEMY AND OTHER CARL WEBSTER STORIES
Available in Paperback and eBook

MR. PARADISE
Available in Paperback and eBook

THE HUNTED
Available in Paperback and eBook

FIRE IN THE HOLE
Available in Paperback and eBook
Stories, Including One Featuring Raylan Givens

GOLD COAST
Available in Paperback and eBook

MR. MAJESTYK
Available in Paperback and eBook

CUBA LIBRE
Available in Paperback and eBook

MAXIMUM BOB
Available in Paperback and eBook

RIDING THE RAP
A Raylan Givens Novel
Available in Paperback and eBook

PRONTO
A Raylan Givens Novel
Available in Paperback and eBook

RUM PUNCH
Available in Paperback and eBook

GET SHORTY
Available in Paperback and eBook

TISHOMINGO BLUES
Available in Paperback and eBook

KILLSHOT
Available in Paperback and eBook

FREAKY DEAKY
Available in Paperback and eBook

BANDITS   Available in Paperback and eBook

GLITZ   Available in Paperback and eBook

STICK   Available in Paperback and eBook

CAT CHASER   Available in Paperback and eBook

SPLIT IMAGES   Available in Paperback and eBook

CITY PRIMEVAL   Available in Paperback and eBook

THE MOONSHINE WAR   Available in Paperback and eBook

HOMBRE   Available in Paperback and eBook

THE SWITCH   Available in Paperback and eBook

OUT OF SIGHT   Available in Paperback and eBook

SWAG   Available in Paperback and eBook

LaBRAVA   Available in Paperback and eBook

VALDEZ IS COMING   Available in Paperback and eBook

NOW AVAILABLE

52 PICKUP   Available in Paperback and eBook

BE COOL   Available in Paperback and eBook

GUNSIGHTS   Available in Paperback and eBook

THE HOT KID   Available in Paperback and eBook

LAST STAND AT
SABER RIVER   Available in Paperback and eBook

PAGAN BABIES   Available in Paperback and eBook

TOUCH   Available in Paperback and eBook

UNKNOWN MAN #89   Available in Paperback and eBook

UP IN HONEY'S
ROOM   Available in Paperback and eBook

Available wherever books are sold.

Fodor's

W9-DHH-971

SEATTLE

4th Edition

**Where to Stay and Eat
for All Budgets**

**Must-See Sights
and Local Secrets**

Ratings You Can Trust

Fodor's Travel Publications   New York, Toronto, London, Sydney, Auckland
www.fodors.com

FODOR'S SEATTLE
Editor: Paul Eisenberg

Editorial Production: Tom Holton
Editorial Contributor: Carissa Bluestone
Maps & Illustrations: David Lindroth cartographer; Bob Blake and Rebecca Baer, *map editors*
Design: Fabrizio LaRocca, *creative director*; Guido Caroti, Siobhan O'Hare, *art directors*; Melanie Marin, *senior picture editor*; Moon Sun Kim, *cover designer*
Cover Photo (Seattle Art Museum): David Ball/Index Stock Imagery/Jupiter Images
Production/Manufacturing: Steve Slawsky

Fourth Edition

ISBN 978-1-4000-1854-3

ISSN 1531-3417

SPECIAL SALES

This book is available at special discounts for bulk purchases for sales promotions or premiums. Special editions, including personalized covers, excerpts of existing books, and corporate imprints, can be created in large quantities for special needs. For more information, write to Special Markets/Premium Sales, 1745 Broadway, MD 6-2, New York, New York 10019, or e-mail specialmarkets@randomhouse.com.

AN IMPORTANT TIP & AN INVITATION

Although all prices, opening times, and other details in this book are based on information supplied to us at press time, changes occur all the time in the travel world, and Fodor's cannot accept responsibility for facts that become outdated or for inadvertent errors or omissions. So **always confirm information when it matters,** especially if you're making a detour to visit a specific place. Your experiences—positive and negative—matter to us. If we have missed or misstated something, **please write to us.** We follow up on all suggestions. Contact the Seattle editor at editors@fodors.com or c/o Fodor's at 1745 Broadway, New York, NY 10019.

PRINTED IN THE UNITED STATES OF AMERICA
10 9 8 7 6 5 4 3 2 1

Be a Fodor's Correspondent

Your opinion matters. It matters to us. It matters to your fellow Fodor's travelers, too. And we'd like to hear it. In fact, we need to hear it.

When you share your experiences and opinions, you become an active member of the Fodor's community. That means we'll not only use your feedback to make our books better, but we'll publish your names and comments whenever possible. Throughout our guides, look for "Word of Mouth," excerpts of your unvarnished feedback.

Here's how you can help improve Fodor's for all of us.

Tell us when we're right. We rely on local writers to give you an insider's perspective. But our writers and staff editors—who are the best in the business—depend on you. Your positive feedback is a vote to renew our recommendations for the next edition.

Tell us when we're wrong. We're proud that we update most of our guides every year. But we're not perfect. Things change. Hotels cut services. Museums change hours. Charming cafés lose charm. If our writer didn't quite capture the essence of a place, tell us how you'd do it differently. If any of our descriptions are inaccurate or inadequate, we'll incorporate your changes in the next edition and will correct factual errors at fodors.com immediately.

Tell us what to include. You probably have had fantastic travel experiences that aren't yet in Fodor's. Why not share them with a community of like-minded travelers? Maybe you chanced upon a beach or bistro or B&B that you don't want to keep to yourself. Tell us why we should include it. And share your discoveries and experiences with everyone directly at fodors.com. Your input may lead us to add a new listing or highlight a place we cover with a "Highly Recommended" star or with our highest rating, "Fodor's Choice."

Give us your opinion instantly at our feedback center at www.fodors.com/feedback. You may also e-mail editors@fodors.com with the subject line "Seattle Editor." Or send your nominations, comments, and complaints by mail to Seattle Editor, Fodor's, 1745 Broadway, New York, NY 10019.

You and travelers like you are the heart of the Fodor's community. Make our community richer by sharing your experiences. Be a Fodor's correspondent.

Happy traveling!

Tim Jarrell, Publisher

CONTENTS

ABOUT
THIS BOOK

Sometimes you find terrific travel experiences and sometimes they just find you. But usually the burden is on you to select the right combination of experiences. That's where our ratings come in.

As travelers we've all discovered a place so wonderful that its worthiness is obvious. And sometimes that place is so unique that superlatives don't do it justice: you just have to be there to know. These sights, properties, and experiences get our highest rating, **Fodor's Choice,** indicated by orange stars throughout this book.

Black stars highlight sights and properties we deem **Highly Recommended,** places that our writers, editors, and readers praise again and again for consistency and excellence.

By default, there's another category: any place we include in this book is by definition worth your time, unless we say otherwise. And we will.

Disagree with any of our choices? Care to nominate a place or suggest that we rate one more highly? Visit our feedback center at www.fodors. com/feedback.

Hotel and restaurant price categories from ¢ to $$$$ are defined in the opening pages of the Where to Eat and Where to Stay chapters. For attractions, we always give standard adult admission fees; reductions are usually available for children, students, and senior citizens. Want to pay with plastic? **AE, D, DC, MC, V** following restaurant and hotel listings indicate whether American Express, Discover, Diner's Club, MasterCard, and Visa are accepted.

Unless we state otherwise, restaurants are open for lunch and dinner daily. We mention dress only when there's a specific requirement and reservations only when they're essential or not accepted—it's always best to book ahead.

Hotels have private bath, phone, TV, and air-conditioning and operate on the European Plan (aka EP, meaning without meals), unless we specify that they use the Continental Plan (CP, with a Continental breakfast), Breakfast Plan (BP, with a full breakfast), or Modified American Plan (MAP, with breakfast and dinner) or are all-inclusive (including all meals and most activities). We always list facili-

ties but not whether you'll be charged an extra fee to use them, so when pricing accommodations, find out what's included.

Many Listings

★	Fodor's Choice
★	Highly recommended
⊠	Physical address
✛	Directions
⌖	Mailing address
☎	Telephone
🖷	Fax
⊕	On the Web
✎	E-mail
🎫	Admission fee
☉	Open/closed times
Ⓜ	Metro stations
▭	Credit cards

Hotels & Restaurants

🏨	Hotel
⇥	Number of rooms
⬦	Facilities
🍽	Meal plans
✕	Restaurant
⬟	Reservations
↘	Smoking
🍷	BYOB
✕🏨	Hotel with restaurant that warrants a visit

Outdoors

🏌	Golf
⛺	Camping

Other

☺	Family-friendly
⇨	See also
⊠	Branch address
☞	Take note

6

WHAT'S WHERE

Seattle is a sprawling city defined by many beautiful bodies of water. On the west is the Puget Sound. On the east is massive Lake Washington. The city sits in the middle, bisected by highway I–5 and further divvied up by more lakes and canals. As a reminder that real wilderness is not too far away, the city also has amazing views of two major mountain ranges, the Olympics and the Cascades, and on clear days, Mt. Rainier looms over the southern side so impressively, even lifelong Seattleites never cease to be amazed by it.

The Lake Washington Ship Canal, which is fairly far north of the city center, separates Seattle's northern residential neighborhoods from the central and business areas.

As Seattle continues to develop at a fast rate, the lines between its neighborhoods and suburbs continue to blur; boundaries are often set more by local opinion than anything else. New neighborhood names have started to pop up as developers have begun filling in the long-neglected spaces between the core neighborhoods, and as artists and hipsters move farther out of the pricey central neighborhoods and start populating what were once industrial areas. However, the city's main neighborhoods generally break down as follows.

DOWNTOWN

Downtown, the most general descriptor possible for a fairly large swath of the city core, is easy to pick out—it's the only part of the city with skyscrapers. It's clearly bounded on the west by Elliott Bay and the waterfront and on the east by I–5, and stretches north to south from Virginia Street to Yesler Way. Seattle's business district and governmental buildings are here, and the neighborhood is also a center for shopping and dining, as well as the location of most of the city's hotels and popular tourist spots, including Pike Place Market. Downtown's famous piers include the must-see Seattle Aquarium and are the departure points for ferries to the nearby islands of the Puget Sound. Almost all visitors to Seattle spend at least some time exploring this neighborhood, if only because it's where all of the major hotels are. But because there is still a dearth of residential buildings in the area, despite all its attractions, Downtown has yet to feel like a cohesive part of the true Seattle experience. That said, if you want to feel like you're actually in a big city—instead of a strung-together collection of small towns—you'll really enjoy Downtown and its pockets of grit and glamour.

BELLTOWN	Just north of Downtown is Belltown, so close actually, they often seem like one big neighborhood. The neighborhood stretches north to Denny Way, though most of the action happens between 1st and 4th avenues and between Bell and Virginia streets. Belltown used to be a low-rent, high-crime area, but today, the only evidence of its past is the presence of homeless people and addicts and the signs and storefronts of a few nonprofit organizations trying to help them out. Beyond that, Belltown is nothing less then heaven for yuppies and scenesters. Luxury condos have replaced many of the low-income apartments, old storefronts and union halls have been converted into see-and-be-seen restaurants and art galleries, and upscale boutiques have made Belltown a more-interesting shopping area than Downtown. Belltown is alive late into the night, especially on weekends, though it's extremely quiet on weekdays and weekend mornings. Even if you're a bit turned off by the neighborhood's trendy—and at times, slightly snooty—air, don't write it off completely. Unlike Downtown, people actually do live here, and the cultural and nightlife offerings are more eclectic than they may first appear.
SEATTLE CENTER & LOWER QUEEN ANNE	Queen Anne Hill rises from Denny Way to the Lake Washington Ship Canal to the north. At the bottom is the Space Needle, the Key Arena (home to the Sonics), and the Seattle Center, the site of the Experience Music Project museum and many cultural activities, including the increasingly popular Bumbershoot festival. The neighborhood above it, Queen Anne, is divided into two parts. Lower Queen Anne stretches from the Seattle Center up to roughly Galer Street, with its main commercial district centered around Queen Anne Avenue. Despite being prime real estate it's still rather mixed, and the businesses along the lower stretch of Queen Anne Avenue include both trendy restaurants and a few independent stores. The few mid-range and budget accommodations here are a better bet than the lower-priced motels stuck in odd and unattractive areas of Downtown.
UPPER QUEEN ANNE & MAGNOLIA	Upper Queen Anne starts roughly at Galer Street and stretches all the way up the hill—centering around Queen Anne Avenue—to Nickerson Street by the ship canal. To the west (after 15th Avenue West) is Magnolia; to the east, Aurora Avenue and Lake Union. Upper Queen Anne has elegant upscale houses and fashionable restaurants and shops. There's a lot of

WHAT'S WHERE

	money in this neighborhood, and unfortunately, sometimes a lot of attitude to go with it. That said, Seattle is a very young city, and travelers who tire of twentysomethings (and thirty-somethings who act like them) may be happy to find that this is one place where the grown-ups seem to congregate. Many of the tree-lined streets in both Upper Queen Anne and Magnolia have great panoramas of Puget Sound and the Olympic or Cascade mountains. Magnolia, though it has lovely homes to gawk at, is mostly notable for the stunning Discovery Park, which has both forested trails and strollable beachfronts.
PIONEER SQUARE	Pioneer Square is a compact area directly south of Downtown. It is Seattle's oldest neighborhood, which means it has pretty redbrick and sandstone buildings not found elsewhere in the city. Because of this, the neighborhood receives an undue amount of hype from most guidebooks and tourism brochures. Truth is, while the galleries and antiques shops in the area are truly great and there are certainly worse places to spend an hour or two, the neighborhood itself is not nearly as captivating as it's often made to sound. Overall, it's got a shabbiness to it that clashes with the carefully maintained historic buildings, many of which are occupied by tourist-trap shops. Like most of Seattle's neighborhoods, Pioneer Square has enough variety and a few real gems that almost any traveler will find something to hold their interest, but don't plan your trip around it.
INTERNATIONAL DISTRICT	Once called Chinatown, the International District has expanded its roots to include Japanese, Vietnamese, Cambodian, Malaysian, and Filipino traditions. Known locally as the I.D., the neighborhood is southeast of Downtown. Small produce markets thrive here, making it a great place to shop for exotic ingredients and to enjoy authentic Asian foods. The I.D. is not a tightly packed neighborhood and isn't the best place for a leisurely stroll; most people come here specifically to visit the two-story Uwajimaya supermarket.
CENTRAL DISTRICT	The Downtown hub of Seattle's African-American community is also referred to as the Central District. It lies east of Downtown, adjacent to Capitol Hill and First Hill. In the 1940s, this part of town nurtured a dynamic jazz scene; its high school (Garfield High) was Jimi Hendrix's alma mater. In more-recent years, the area has suffered from neglect and economic blight, though it's now starting to be redeveloped (though not necessarily with the best interests of its current

	residents in mind). The neighborhood has a few beautiful and beloved churches, street art, and some great home-style restaurants, but does not have many tourist sights and therefore doesn't usually inspire many visitors to linger.
FIRST HILL	This compact neighborhood is sandwiched between Downtown and Capitol Hill, bordered by E. Union Street to the north and I–5 to the west. Sometimes referred to as "Pill Hill" for its abundance of hospitals and medical offices, it runs roughly south past Madison to James Street and east nearly to Broadway. During the day you'll see mostly working professionals—doctors, nurses, and patients hurrying to appointments, and the thirtysomethings who live here in posh condos and studio apartments—strolling briskly to and from their Downtown jobs. After dark and on weekends it's dead.
CAPITOL HILL	Northeast of Downtown and east of I–5 is Capitol Hill, a neighborhood with two faces. On one side, it's an incredibly young and hip neighborhood, full of artists, musicians, hipsters, and students hailing from three nearby schools, including Seattle University. Broadway, which runs north–south, caters to students with cheap restaurants and clothing shops. Pike and Pine streets, which parallel each other, make up the Pike–Pine corridor, which has many cool boutiques, cafés, and nightspots, popular with both undergrads and postgrads. On the other side, it's an elegant and pretty neighborhood, with tree-lined streets, 19th-century mansions, and Frederick Law Olmsted's Volunteer Park, where you'll find the Asian Art Museum. Though development of luxury condos threatens to homogenize the neighborhood, for now Capitol Hill is one of the city's most diverse neighborhoods. It was *the* gay and lesbian community for a while and still remains its heart and soul.
FREMONT & PHINNEY RIDGE	Above the Lake Washington Ship Canal are the northern neighborhoods, which are primarily residential but are also considered (whether officially or unofficially) part of Seattle proper. Fremont is the first neighborhood across the canal from Downtown. Though Fremont used to be the neighborhood for artists and freaks, it has become much more upscale in the past few years. It's now an interesting mix of pricey boutiques and dusty vintage stores, coffee shops and restaurants. Its commercial center is compact and conducive to strolling. A trail and benches along the waterfront allow you to watch boats and kayakers go by—a terrific way to pass part of a lazy afternoon. Heading up Fremont Avenue, you'll

WHAT'S WHERE

	come across another small commercial strip before cresting the big hill and entering the mostly residential Phinney Ridge, notable for Woodland Park and its zoo.
BALLARD	West and north of Fremont is Ballard, which skirts the mouth of Shilshole Bay and whose main attraction is the fun-to-tour Chittenden Locks, which connect Lake Washington to the Puget Sound. Ballard is the winter home for the Alaskan fishing fleet, which includes vessels that range from tiny salmon trollers to large factory trawlers. Once low-key and humble, the neighborhood's complexion has been changed by the hipsters and artists who have fled Capitol Hill and Fremont. As more bars, restaurants, and boutiques open along picturesque Ballard Avenue and busy NW Market Street, the area also has become increasingly popular with young couples and young families, looking for affordable apartments and single-family houses that are close to a thriving commercial strip.
WALLINGFORD & GREEN LAKE	Paralleling Fremont directly to the east is Wallingford, a large residential neighborhood that keeps a low profile. You'll find rows and rows of cute single-family houses on tree-lined streets that are great to wander around—and easier to navigate than Fremont's hills. On Wallingford's commercial strip, you'll find everything from the lowbrow (an erotic bakeshop) to the highbrow (a wonderful poetry bookstore). Wallingford also goes all the way south to the ship canal, and although most people think of the great Gas Works Park as a Fremont attraction, it's actually in this neighborhood. Directly north of Wallingford is Green Lake, a favorite place of many Seattleites. This is no tranquil park—the paved path that circles the lake is always packed with joggers (many of them pushing baby carriages), bikers, rollerbladers, and dog walkers.
UNIVERSITY DISTRICT	Northeast of Lake Union and east of I–5, this area encircles the University of Washington, the vast campus of which stretches from Portage Bay to Union Bay. The U-District, as it's almost always referred to, does have a certain energy thanks to the student population, but overall, this neighborhood doesn't usually warrant a special trip, especially if you've only got a few days in the city. Getting here from nearly anywhere in the city can be nettlesome; during the day, traffic and parking in the U-District can be nightmarish. However, the U-Dub campus is beautiful, there are two excellent museums close to the campus, University Avenue (known as The Ave) is known

for its cheap ethnic eateries, and there are a few good movie theaters and coffee shops in the vicinity.

WEST SEATTLE	South of the city and on a peninsula just across Elliott Bay lies West Seattle. Today the neighborhood is a mix of rich and poor; as prices have skyrocketed in Seattle proper, many people have fled to West Seattle in search of affordable housing, which is now probably hard to find. On a drive through it, you'll pass miles of beautiful beaches. Its center, called The Junction, has some great shops and restaurants along California Avenue. Gorgeous Alki Beach sweeps around the area's perimeter, offering views of the Puget Sound and the Seattle skyline. Lincoln Park, a sprawling, forested tract of land near the Fauntleroy ferry terminal, is a fine place to hike, bike, blade, and relax on the beach.
THE EASTSIDE	On the eastern shore of Lake Washington are the suburbs of Issaquah, Bellevue, Kirkland, and Redmond. Three-quarters of a century ago, Bellevue was a pleasant little town in the country, with rows of shops along Main Street serving the farmers who grew strawberries. Today it's synonymous with money, and it's a mini-city with its own skyline. It has an art museum of note and a commercial core that includes a lot of high-end shops and restaurants.
	Kirkland's business district, along the Lake Street waterfront, is lined with shops, restaurants, pubs, and parks, though it does feel somewhat artificial. At the height of summer, it's often warm enough to swim in the sheltered waters of Lake Washington.
	A string of pretty parks makes Redmond an inviting place to experience the outdoors, and the 13-mi Sammamish River Trail is an attraction for locals and tourists alike. The rapidly expanding city is today one of the country's most powerful business capitals thanks to the presence of such companies as Microsoft, Nintendo, and Eddie Bauer. Although there are several good malls and a lot of generic strip-mall stores, this isn't a place to shop—locals come here either to work or to play.
	Issaquah, a developing area southeast of Bellevue, is also a great place to hike, boat, or horseback ride. The surrounding Cougar, Tiger, and Squak mountain foothills—dubbed the Issaquah Alps—are older than the Cascade range and pocketed with caves, parks, and trails.

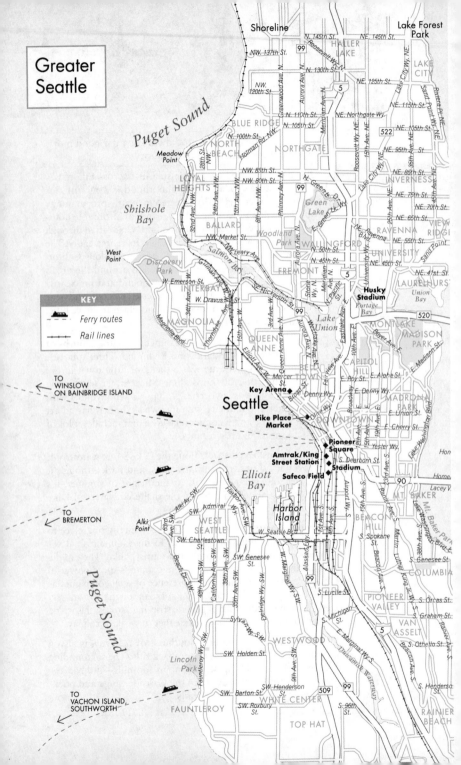

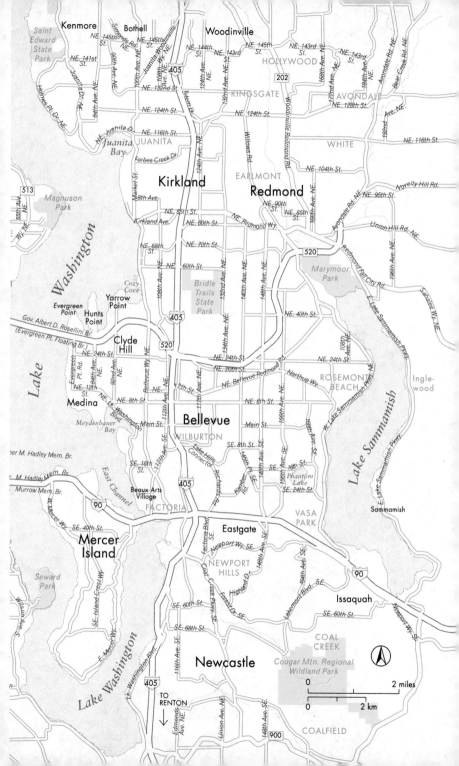

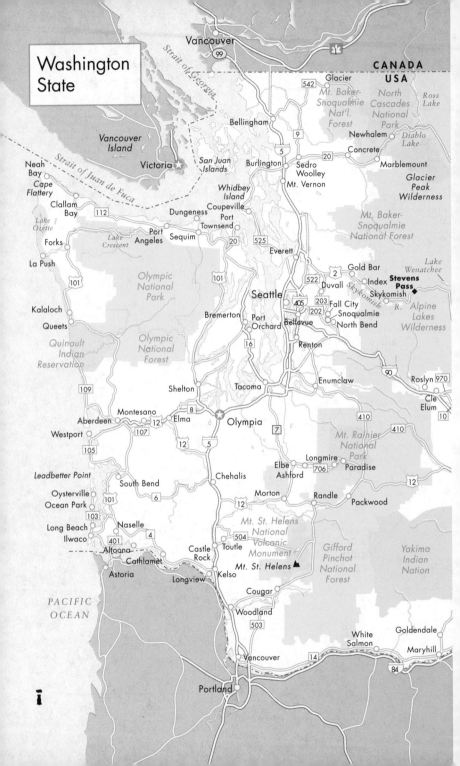

BRITISH COLUMBIA

CANADA
USA

Okanogan National Forest

Okanogan National Forest

Colville National Forest

Colville National Forest

IDAHO

Tonasket

Republic

Colville

Washington Pass
◆ 20

Winthrop

Twisp

Chewuch R.

21

25 195

Chewelah

Stehekin

Carlton

Okanogan

Colville Indian Reservation

Methow

Brewster

Columbia River

155

Franklin D. Roosevelt Lake

Newport

Lake Chelan

Grand Coulee Coulee Dam

Spokane Indian Reservation

231

Wenatchee National Forest

Chelan

Banks Lake

174

Wilbur

291

97

155

2

Davenport

Spokane

Coeur d'Alene

Leavenworth

Cashmere

◆ Sun Lakes State Park

17

28

Sprague

Wenatchee

97

Columbia River

Ephrata

Moses Lake

Ritzville

90

195

Ellensburg

Potholes Res.

◆ Ginkgo Petrified Forest State Park

26

Othello

Washtucna

Colfax

26

Pullman

395

Yakima

Snake R.

Pomeroy

Wapato

Zillah

Dayton

Toppenish

82

Richland Pasco

Umatilla National Forest

97

Prosser

Kennewick

Walla Walla

221

12

14

Columbia River

84

Pendleton

OREGON

0   40 miles
0   60 km

QUINTESSENTIAL SEATTLE

The Great Outdoors

Yeah, it rains a lot...in winter. But summers are gorgeous (as are most falls and springs), and with a major mountain range on each side and Mt. Rainier always looking over its shoulder, it's no wonder that Seattle is obsessed with the outdoors. The best adventures—heading north to hike in the Cascade range, south to hike in Mt. Rainier or Mt. St. Helens national parks, southwest to camp, hike, and spot wildlife in Olympic National Park, or across the Sound to explore one of many nearby islands on foot or by canoe or kayak—involve leaving the city, but even within Seattle proper, there's plenty to do. Kayaking is one of the easiest sports to try, thanks to the abundance of water; many people paddle around Portage Bay in the northeast corner of the city. There's really no excuse not to try something: highways easily take you to base points and numerous trails.

Coffee

It may be a cliché, but coffee is a huge part of Seattle's cultural identity. Starbucks has enough local fans to be a presence here, but to understand the coffee culture—and to get a great cup of coffee—visit the independent shops and local mini-chains, several of which manage to roast their own beans on-site without burning them. A Seattleite's relationship with coffee ranges from grabbing the daily quick fix in the morning to spending half the day at a local shop where every barista knows their name (and coffee order), reading, chatting with friends, or tapping away on a laptop. Many coffee shops pull double duty as art galleries, and some of them even pull double duty as *good* art galleries. Occasionally, shops feature hard-to-get coffees at special "cupping" events, which take on the structure and feel of wine tastings.

If you want to enjoy the Emerald City like a local, start by familiarizing yourself with some of its passions.

Pacific Northwest Cuisine

With such an active population, and easy access to the best the sea and the land have to offer, it's no wonder that eating well is so important to Seattleites. Pacific Northwest dishes emphasize fresh, locally produced ingredients; even some of the fanciest restaurants get their ingredients from the city's farmer's markets, Pike Place Market, and in some cases from their chef's own organic farms. These fresh, seasonal ingredients can be combined in straightforward ways—inventive takes on American comfort food is a recent trend—or fused with European and Asian influences. Many of Seattle's chefs have gained their fame through their ambitious takes on Pacific Northwest cuisine, but you don't have to spend big bucks for a taste: many bistros, bakeries, and cafés use local and organic ingredients as a matter of principle.

Music

First things first, grunge is over. It's mystifying that this term is still used to describe all manner of the city's carefully disheveled indie rockers. Grunge peaked in the early '90s and was on the decline by 1996 (some would argue even earlier than that), and today you're more likely to catch alt-country bands, post-emo songwriters, or The Shins sound-alikes than anything resembling grunge. Today the city's love of music is demonstrated more outside of its clubs than in them. You can see it in the independent record shops where staff members handwrite meandering, sometimes poetic recommendations, in the continued success of local label Sub Pop Records, in the nearly mainstream support for alternative radio station KEXP, in the health of midsize venues that can draw national acts, and the tendency of baristas to treat their shifts like DJ sessions.

WHEN TO GO

The Pacific Northwest climate is most enjoyable from May through October. July through September is mostly rain-free, with pleasantly warm days reaching into the mid-70s and 80s. Although the weather can be dodgy, spring and fall are also excellent times to visit, as accommodation, transport, and tour costs are usually much lower (and the crowds much thinner). Most people associate all things Washington with the evergreen, but Seattle has a lot of deciduous trees and therefore, great fall colors; in spring, trees are full of blossoms, especially in the northern residential neighborhoods. If you want snow, head for the nearby mountains, as temperatures rarely dip below the low 40s here, even in winter. When it does snow in Seattle (usually in December or January), everything grinds to a halt.

Climate

Seattle's climate is surprisingly benign for a city that's farther north then Québec City. The coastal regions are uniformly mild, and inland regions are protected against the ocean's blustery winter winds by the Olympic mountain range. The Cascades stand guard on Seattle's opposite side, keeping the bitter temperatures of eastern Washington from reaching the coast.

Seattle has an average of only 36 inches of rainfall a year—less than New York, Chicago, or Miami. The wetness, however, is concentrated in winter, when cloudy skies and drizzly weather persist. More than 75% of Seattle's annual precipitation occurs from October through March. That said, thanks to global climate change, Seattle's weather has gotten less predictable; 2006's summer started slow but was characterized by a heat wave that kept temperatures in the high

90s for days, and a similar but shorter heat wave struck in July 2007. Winter, which is usually just a gray, mild, drizzly affair, included in 2006 Noah-and-the-ark deluges that knocked out power in some areas for days, as well as hail, snow, and bright, sunny days with temperatures in the low 30s. Either bring layers or be prepared to buy them.

Forecasts **Weather Channel Connection** (☎ 900/932–8437 95¢ per min from a Touch-Tone phone ⊕ www.weather.com).

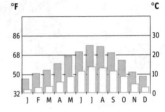

IF YOU LIKE

Arts & Culture

The Great Outdoors gets so much attention it's easy to overlook Seattle's Great Indoors—its myriad galleries, museums, and cinemas. The city teems with visual artists and sculptors; several excellent film festivals attest to the number of resident cinephiles. Nearly every local coffee shop (and many restaurants, bars, and stores) serves as an impromptu art gallery; some even hold official openings with food, drinks, and music when exhibits change.

A great way to get an overview of Seattle's art scene—and do some socializing in the process—is to participate in one of the city's many **art walks,** which include stops at galleries, coffeehouses that have rotating art exhibits, restaurants, shops, and public works of art in all their quirky glory. The biggest walk is the First Thursday Art Walk (first Thursday of every month from 6 PM to 8 PM ⊕*www.pioneersquare.org/first_thursday. html*), which starts at Main Street and Occidental and takes you through Pioneer Square, the city's gallery district, as well as to some Downtown spots. There are also smaller, though no-less-interesting, walks in Capitol Hill (first Thursdays from 7 PM to 9 PM, ⊕*www.myspace.com/ 2tue*), Fremont (first Fridays from 6 PM to 8 PM, ☎ 206/632–1500), and Ballard (second Saturdays from 6 PM to 9 PM, ☎ 206/784–9705, ⊕*www.ballardchamber. com*).

The grand dame of the art scene, the **Seattle Art Museum** has reopened after a massive expansion and remodel. SAM's outdoor branch, the newly opened **Olympic Sculpture Park,** is where striking sculptures compete with views of the Puget Sound.

A nonprofit that aids Seattle's budding filmmakers, the **Northwest Film Forum** has the scoop on independent film in the Northwest and worldwide. At NWFF's hip screening room, film geeks can catch hard-to-find documentaries and feature films or just revisit classic films from masters like Jean Renoir and Akira Kurosawa.

Water

No, not the kind of water that falls from the winter sky in depressing amounts. Seattle is bounded and sliced by impressive stretches of blue. Even longtime residents can be found gawking at the mountain-backed Puget Sound and its bays.

A must-see on any itinerary, the **Seattle Aquarium** shows you what's going on underneath the surface, with special exhibits concerning the marine and river ecosystems of the Pacific Northwest. The Underwater Dome and Window on Washington Waters exhibits allow you to be surrounded by colorful fish and small sharks without having to dive into frigid waters.

Get an up-close look at all sorts of craft from research boats to posh yachts as they navigate the Lake Washington Ship Canal and the **Ballard Locks.** After your tour, head to Ray's Boathouse to dine on seafood while gazing at the blue waters of Shilshole Bay.

If you're not content with views alone, **rent a kayak** from Agua Verde Paddle Club and tool around the ship canal; head into Lake Union to see Seattle's famous houseboats.

On hot days, the swimming rafts in **Lake Washington** turn into impromptu party

IF YOU LIKE

barges. There are several beaches along the western shore of this massive lake, many of which have lifeguards and other amenities. The eastern shore of **Green Lake** also has a beach and swimming raft and offers a more-subdued dip—a good way to cool off after you join Seattleites in a long jog around the lake's path.

Lazy Days

When you live in such a pretty area, you quickly learn how to just kick back and enjoy it. Despite all the activities and sports they participate in, Seattleites understand that relaxation is at a premium these days and slowing the pace and spending a few quiet hours away from distractions is good for the soul.

Grab a few books, **find a coffee shop**, and spend a few hours reading, writing postcards, or watching the human parade. The porch of Fremont Coffee Company is particularly conducive to loitering as are Caffe Fiore in Queen Anne and the Panama Hotel Tea and Coffee House in the International District. But anyplace where the music's not too loud will do.

Instead of jostling with joggers around Green Lake or power-walking in Discovery Park, head to **Gasworks Park** and stake out a piece of green. From the park's rolling hills you can idly watch the boats in Lake Union or even fly a kite—the Gasworks Park Kite Shop is right around the corner at Stone Way and N. 34th Street.

Take the ferry to **Vashon Island**. Rent a bike, and you can tool around past parkland, farmland, and orchards—there's not much else to do out there. Pop into galleries and crafts shops if you feel so inclined. Or just find a piece of beach and park yourself there for a few hours.

Wining & Dining

It's no secret that Seattle has excellent restaurants, as well as an obsession with wine (both Northwest and international varieties) that is second only to its obsession with coffee. A wine list is never an afterthought at the city's best restaurants, and it's never difficult to find a place that does food and drink equally well.

Purple Cafe and Wine Bar is the first stop for the indecisive. You can get anything from baked Brie with apricot preserves to meat loaf. You can also order flights of three or four different wines, paired with cheeses, if you have trouble choosing from the wine list, which is so long it has a table of contents.

Out of all of the city's current favorite restaurants, **Cremant** and **Union** get a special nod for excellent wine lists and food that never disappoints. Cremant serves simple but savory traditional French country cooking, and, of course, cremant, a sparkling French wine. Union does seafood and Pacific Northwest flavors to perfection and includes many Northwest wines along with impressive choices from Italy, France, and Germany.

The Herbfarm, in the city's eastern suburbs, takes special-occasion dining to a whole new level. You'll get no fewer than nine courses and five or six paired wines, along with commentary from the chef and owners.

To indulge during daylight hours, **create the perfect picnic** with food from Salumi in Pioneer Square and a few choice bottles from the Pike & Western Wine Shop near the Pike Place Market.

ON THE CALENDAR

		The Seattle Convention and Visitor's Bureau Web site, www.visitseattle.org/cultural, has a searchable calendar of events and links to festival information sites listed by month. Here are some of our favorites.
WINTER	December	**Winterfest** takes place every weekend of the month at the Seattle Center. This family-oriented festival includes free concerts, a tree lighting ceremony, a holiday carousel, and crafts workshops.
SPRING	April	**Seattle Cherry Blossom Festival** celebrates Japanese arts and family traditions with costumes, music, crafts, ceremonies, and the famous Taiko drummers. **Taste of Washington** (☎206/667–9463 ⊕www.tastewashington.org) is the state's biggest wine-tasting festival. Washington winemakers and sommeliers from the city lead tastings; over two days, you can sample nearly 200 wines.
	Late May	The **University District Street Fair** (☎206/547–4417 ⊕streetfair.udistrictchamber.org) begins with a parade that merges into an avenue lined with crafts booths, food stalls, the well-known produce market, and stages for local bands and performance artists. **Northwest Folklife Festival** (☎206/684–7300 ⊕www.nwfolklife.org) features both Pacific Northwest musicians and national and world performers. The excellent **Seattle International Film Festival** *(SIFF)* (☎206/324–9997 ⊕www.seattlefilm.com), which runs until mid-June, presents more than 200 features in three weeks at various locations around town. Highlights include the New Directors Showcase, the Children's Film Fest, and the Secret Festival.
SUMMER	June	The **Pike Place Market Festival** (⊕www.pikeplacemarketstreetfestival.com) celebrates the famed Downtown market, and includes tastings, chef demos, and free children's activities including a dog parade. The **Pioneer Square Fire Festival** (⊕www.pioneersquare.org/fire.html) highlights the city's firefighting history, beginning with the Great Fire of 1889, with contests and lots of music and food. **Pagdiriwang** celebrates the joy of Philippine traditions at the Seattle Center. **Seattle Pride Festival** (⊕www.seattlepride.org), which has events at the Seattle Center includes the Northwest's biggest gay, lesbian, and transgender pride parade. The classic **Fremont Summer Solstice Parade** (⊕www.fremontartscouncil.org) celebrates the unique, unusual, and truly bizarre perfor-

ON THE
CALENDAR

	mance and visual artists who live and work in the neighborhood. The parade starts with naked bicyclists, some wearing body paint, others wearing nothing but a smile.
Early July	**Independence Day** in Seattle means two spectacular celebrations. Gasworks Park is the site of a day of entertainment, culminating in orchestral music (usually provided by the Seattle Symphony) and a fireworks display over Lake Union. A full slate of activities unwinds on the other side of Queen Anne Hill at the Fourth of Jul-Ivar Celebration—named for Ivar's seafood restaurant, a Seattle institution—before the skies light up over Elliott Bay.
Late July	The **Ballard Seafood Fest** (⊕*www.seafoodfest.org*) rates as one of the best neighborhood feasts, with its salmon bake and lutefisk-eating contest. **Bite of Seattle** (☎*425/283–5050* ⊕*www.biteofseattle.com*) serves up sumptuous specialties from the city's finest restaurants and includes demonstrations from Seattle's celebrity chefs.
July-August	**Seafair** (☎*206/728–0123* ⊕*www.seafair.com*), Seattle's biggest festival of the year (really a collection of smaller regional events), kicks off with a torchlight parade through Downtown and culminates in hydroplane races on Lake Washington. Pista Sa Nayon, a Filipino festival, and Bon Odori, a Japanese festival, are part of Seafair.
FALL September	**Bumbershoot** (⊕*www.bumbershoot.org*), a Seattle arts festival held Labor Day weekend, presents more than 400 performers in music, dance, theater, comedy, and the visual and literary arts. The best way to peruse all the events and buy tickets is to go online; however, local papers like *The Stranger* usually list events. **Festa Italia** (⊕*www.festaseattle.com*) is a weeklong celebration of Seattle's Italian community at the Seattle Center and Seward Park. The **Fremont Oktoberfest** (⊕*www.fremontoktoberfest.com*), which actually takes place over one weekend at the end of September, serves up great suds, food, and music along the waterfront.
October	**Earshot Jazz Festival** (⊕*www.earshot.org*) showcases hundreds of performers, both local and national, over several weeks. It may be your only chance to hear a lot of good jazz in Seattle.

GREAT ITINERARIES

SEATTLE HIGHLIGHTS

Though Seattle's not always the easiest city to navigate, it's small enough that you can see a great deal of it in a week. If you've only got a long weekend here you can easily mix and match any of the days in this itinerary. Before you explore, you'll need three things: comfortable walking shoes, layered clothing, and a flexible mind-set: It's easy and advisable to meander off-track.

Day 1: The Market & Downtown's Major Sights

Spend the first day seeing some of the major sights around Downtown. Get up early and stroll to Pike Place Market. Grab a latte or have a hearty breakfast at a market café, and spend the morning wandering through the fish, fruit, flower, and crafts stalls. When you've had your fill of the market, head farther Downtown to the Seattle Art Museum or take the steps down to the docks and visit the Seattle Aquarium. Stop at a simple restaurant like El Puerco Lloron to grab a bite to eat. If you're not too tired, head up to Belltown for a little late-afternoon shopping. Have dinner and drinks in either Belltown or Downtown—both have terrific restaurants that will give you your first taste of that famous Pacific Northwest cuisine. Head back to your hotel and collapse, knowing you won't have to rise with the sun the next day.

Day 2: Seattle Center or Pioneer Square

Take the two-minute monorail ride from Downtown's Westlake Center to the Seattle Center. Head up the Space Needle for 360-degree city views. Afterward take in one of Seattle Center's many ground-level attractions: the Pacific Science Center, the Children's Museum, the Experience Music Project, or the Science Fiction Experience museum. There aren't many good lunch options in Queen Anne, though if you're willing to head up Queen Anne Avenue North to Galer Street, the Five Spot Café is open all day. Otherwise, just grab what you can find and then walk southwest down Broad Street to the Olympic Sculpture Park. From there, drive or take the bus down to the International District. Visit the Uwajimaya superstore, stroll the streets, and have dinner in one of the neighborhood's many restaurants.

If you can do without the Space Needle, skip Seattle Center and start your day by riding the trolley past the docks to Pioneer Square. Tour a few galleries, peek into some shops, and then head to the International District for more exploring—don't miss the Wing Luke Asian Museum. Head up to Kobe Terrace Park before dinner for a break and views of Elliott Bay. If you still want to see the Space Needle, you can go after dinner; the observation deck is open until 11 PM or midnight most nights.

Day 3: Side Trips from the City

Now that you've seen a little bit of the city, it's time to leave and get a little closer to nature. Start the day on the early side and get outside. Hikers almost have too many options, but know that Mt. Rainier National Park never disappoints. Plan a whole day for any hiking excursion—between hiking time and driving time, you'll probably need it. And bring sunblock. When you return to the city, tired and probably ravenous, grab a hearty, casual meal and maybe an art flick—Capitol Hill's a great neighborhood in which to find both, as are Wallingford and the

GREAT
ITINERARIES

U-District. Fremont sometimes has seasonal outdoor movies.

If you'd rather take to the water, get on a ferry and check out either Bainbridge or Vashon islands. Bainbridge is very built up and is starting to have traffic problems, but it's pretty and has large swaths of protected land with trails. Vashon is decidedly more agricultural and low-key. The most popular way to explore either island is by bicycle, though note that Bainbridge has some killer hills. Both islands have beach strolls. Bainbridge also has many shops and good restaurants, so it's easy to grab a bite here before heading back into the city. You'll need less time to explore the islands than you'll need to do a hiking excursion, so you can probably see one or two sights Downtown before going to the pier. If you haven't made it to the aquarium yet, its proximity to the ferry makes it a great option.

Day 4: Stepping Off the Tourist Trail

Since you covered Downtown on Days 1 and 2, today you can sleep in a bit and explore the vastly differing residential neighborhoods. Go east to Capitol Hill for great shopping, strolling, and people-watching. Or head north of the Lake Washington Ship Canal to Fremont and Ballard. Wherever you end up, you can start your day by having a leisurely breakfast or coffee fix at an independent coffee shop. To stretch your legs, make the rounds at Volunteer Park in Capitol Hill or follow the Burke-Gilman Trail from Fremont Center to Gasworks Park. Visitors of all ages find both the Woodland Park Zoo (slightly north of Fremont) and the Ballard Locks captivating, so consider a visit to one or the other. In either Capitol Hill or in the northern neighborhoods, you'll have no problem rounding out the

TIPS

■ The market and waterfront attractions are open daily all year.

■ The ride to the top of the Needle is not worth the money if the day is hazy, overcast, or rainy.

■ Remember that Pioneer Square's galleries may not be open on Monday. They do, however, have late hours on the first Thursday of every month.

■ When leaving the city for an all-day hiking trip, try to time things so that you're not hitting I-5 during evening rush hour. Unless you get a very early start—or don't leave until 9:30 AM or 10 AM—you probably won't be able to avoid sitting in some morning rush-hour traffic.

day by ducking into shops and grabbing a great meal. If you're looking for a late night, you'll find plenty of nightlife options in both areas, too.

Day 5: Last Rays of Sun & Loose Ends

Spend at least half of your last day in Seattle outside, exploring Discovery Park or heading up to the University District to rent kayaks from Agua Verde Paddle Club for a trip around Portage Bay or into Lake Washington. Linger in your favorite neighborhood (you'll have one by now). Note that you can combine a park visit with kayaking if you head to the Washington Park Arboretum and Japanese Garden first. From there, it's a quick trip to the U-District.

Exploring Seattle

WORD OF MOUTH

"Walk along the waterfront (interesting parks and shops), then hike the stairs to the Pike Street Market, then, if there's time, walk on down to the Aquarium or the other way to the Ferry Terminal and 'walk on' to Whidbey Island, or drive up to Snoqualmie Falls and have a wonderful breakfast. Go to the Museum of Flight if you're interested and have a look at our way of life, then decide if you want to live here. Most days are overcast but cool, we have terrible traffic but low crime, it's damp in winter and dark in evening, summers are absolutely glorious . . . just depends on what you like . . . lots of people love it, some can't wait to get away to sunnier climates. Hope you enjoy your visit."

—clarasong

Updated
by Carissa
Bluestone

SEATTLE IS DEFINED BY WATER. There's no use denying the city's damp weather, or the fact that its skies are cloudy for much of the year. Seattleites don't tan, goes the joke, they rust. But Seattle is also defined by the rivers, lakes, and canals that bisect its steep green hills, creating distinctive microlandscapes along the water's edge. Fishing boats, floating homes, swank yacht clubs, and waterfront restaurants exist side by side.

A city is defined by its people as well as its weather or geography, and the people of Seattle—a half million or so within the city proper, another 3.5 million in the surrounding Puget Sound region—are a diversified bunch. Seattle has long had a vibrant Asian and Asian-American population, and well-established communities of Scandinavians, African-Americans, Jews, Native Americans, and Latinos live here, too. It's impossible to generalize about such a varied group, but the prototypical Seattleite was once pithily summed up by a *New Yorker* cartoon in which one arch-browed East Coast matron says to another, "They're backpacky, but nice."

Seattle's climate fosters an easygoing lifestyle. Overcast days and long winter nights have made the city a haven for moviegoers and book readers. Hollywood often tests new films here, and residents' per-capita book purchases are among North America's highest. Seattle has all the trappings of a metropolitan hub—two daily newspapers; a state-of-the-art convention center; professional sports teams; a diverse music club scene; and top-notch ballet, opera, symphony, and theater companies. A major seaport, the city is a vital link in Pacific Rim trade.

During the last few decades, the population has boomed, thanks to such corporate giants as Microsoft, Nintendo, Alaska Airlines, Boeing, and Weyerhauser, as well as a plenitude of start-up sporting companies, travel-based businesses, and dot-com operations. This growth will only continue as the city is now actively courting the biotech industry. Seattle's expansion has led to the usual big-city problems: increases in crime, homelessness, and traffic congestion. Many residents have fled east and north to the ever-growing suburbs of Bellevue, Kirkland, Redmond, Issaquah, Shoreline, and Bothell, and south to Renton, Kent, and Federal Way—all of which have swollen from quiet communities into sizable cities. Despite all the growing pains, though, Seattleites have a great love for their community and its natural surroundings; hence their firm commitment to maintaining the area's reputation as one of the country's most livable places.

Seattle, like Rome, is built on seven hills. As a visitor, you're likely to spend much of your time on only two of them (Capitol Hill and Queen Anne Hill), but the seven rises are indeed the most definitive element of the city's natural and spiritual landscape. Years of largely thoughtful building practices have kept tall buildings from obscuring the lines of sight, maintaining vistas in most directions and around most every turn. This may change as population increases and tourism booms are answered with more high-rises both Downtown and in formerly residential neighborhoods, but for now the skyline remains small and relatively spread out. The hills are lofty, privileged perches from which residents are constantly reminded of the beauty of the forests, mountains, and waters lying just beyond the city.

To know Seattle is to know its distinctive neighborhoods. Because of the hills, comfortable walking shoes are a must. But before you go charging off, ready to pack each day full of activities, remember that to know Seattle is also to know when to relax. The city has much to see, but make sure you pencil in time to kick back with a cup of coffee or organic herbal tea and enjoy the beauty around you, whether you're gazing at the peaks of the Olympics or Cascades or at an artistically landscaped garden in front of a classic Northwest bungalow.

DOWNTOWN & BELLTOWN

The Elliott Bay waterfront is the heart and soul of Downtown. Stretching along its waters is historic Pike Place Market, the city's biggest (and most crowded) tourist attraction and the source of the fresh, local ingredients used by so many of the city's restaurants. The Seattle Aquarium and the Maritime Discovery Center are on the docks here, close to the ferries that take commuters and tourists to the islands of the Puget Sound.

Though its boundaries are bit blurry, Downtown mostly refers to an area that's bounded on the west by Elliott Bay and the waterfront and on the east by I-5, and stretches north to south from Virginia Street to Yesler Way.

Downtown is one of the hardest areas of the city to sum up—in sharp contrast to the residential neighborhoods, it doesn't really have a personality of its own. Although developers are starting to build luxury condos here, trying to lure people from the leafy outlying neighborhoods with the carrot of "convenience," the neighborhood is still mostly a business hub. Except for the heavily touristed areas around the market and the piers, and the always frenetic 5th Avenue shopping district, a lot of Downtown can seem deserted, even at times when it should be busy (say, a weekend afternoon). Although most Seattleites abandon the area when the clock strikes 5, many return to eat in the city's finest restaurants or see concerts or shows at several arts venues. Visitors will get to know Downtown well—all of the major hotels are clustered here, as are most of the traditional sights. The city trades more on its beauty, outdoorsy spirit, and distinct neighborhood experiences than its museums and monuments, but Downtown is notable for providing the most "urban" atmosphere the city has to offer, as well as many of the check-em-off-the-list sights.

Just north and slightly west of Downtown is Belltown. The neighborhood's boundaries are, roughly, from Elliott Bay east to 6th Avenue, and north from Virginia Street to Denny Way, though most of the action happens between 1st and 4th avenues and between Bell and Virginia streets. Not too long ago, Belltown was home to some of the most unwanted real estate in the city; the only scenesters around were starving artists. Today, Belltown is yuppie heaven, with many luxury condos, trendy restaurants, an ever-increasing number of boutiques, and bars where people actually dress up. You can still find remnants of its edgy past—the outreach and recovery programs that aid the homeless and drug addicted, a gallery exhibiting urban street art, a punk-rock vinyl shop—but Belltown is almost unrecognizable to long-term residents. Regardless, the Belltown of today, changed though it is, is far more interesting than some other Downtown areas, which can swing from being very touristy to very sterile and business-centric. Though the number of homeless people in the neighborhood can be intimidating to some, Belltown is generally safe during the day and can be really pleasant to stroll around.

■TIP→ **Both Downtown and Belltown are very easy to get around on foot— walking from one neighborhood to the other is easy, too—but if you head down to the waterfront, be prepared for some killer hills on the way back east toward your hotel.**

WHAT TO SEE

★ ❽ **BLVD/Roq La Rue.** If you get tired of looking at totem poles, glass sculptures, and austere black-and-white photos, swing by these sister galleries for a different take on contemporary Northwest art. Cheeky surrealist pop art hangs in Roq La Rue, which is not solely Northwest focused; urban street art from the region populates BLVD. Kirsten Anderson, the owner of both galleries, is well known for injecting some much-needed life into the city's gallery scene by exhibiting work that often gets ignored by traditional venues in spaces that are as professional as all the rest. ⊠ *BLVD, 2316 2nd Ave., Belltown* ⊕ *www.blvdart.com* ⊠ *Roq La Rue, 2312 2nd Ave., Belltown* ☎ *206/374–8977* ⊕ *www. roqlarue.com* ⊠ *Free* ⊗ *Wed., Thurs., and Sat. 1–6; Fri. 1–7.*

❼ **Friesen.** This small, sophisticated gallery on the ground floor of the Washington Mutual building is one of the most respected fine-art spaces in the city. You won't necessarily find the cutting edge here, but you will find paintings, sculpture, and glass pieces from talented international artists. ⊠ *1210 2nd Ave., Downtown* ☎ *206/628–9501* ⊕ *www.friesengallery.com* ⊠ *Free* ⊗ *Tues.–Fri. 10–6, Sat. 11–5.*

☺ ❺ **Odyssey Maritime Discovery Center.** Cultural and educational exhibits on Puget Sound and ocean trade are the focus of this waterfront attraction. Learn all about the Northwest's fishing traditions with hands-on exhibits that include kayaking over computer-generated waters, loading a container ship, and listening in on boats radioing one another on Elliott Bay just outside. You can also shop the on-site fish market, dine on the catch of the day at the seafood restaurant, or spy on boaters docking at the marina or cruise ships putting into port. ⊠ *2205 Alaskan Way, Pier 66, Belltown* ☎ *206/374–4000* ⊕ *www.ody.org* ⊠ *$7* ⊗ *Wed. and Thurs. 10–3, Fri. 10–4, weekends 11–5.*

❿ **Olympic Sculpture Park.** After much fuss and a lot of waiting, the Olympic Fodor'sChoice Sculpture Park opened in January 2007. The 9-acre open-air expanse
★ nestled between Belltown and Elliott Bay is a scenic outdoor branch of the Seattle Art Museum. Follow a zigzag path through a variety of nat-

ural settings dotted with waterfalls and fishponds. Around the grasses, blossoms, and water features are scattered an amazing variety of over-size, handmade pieces from some of the Northwest's notable visual artists. Though some of the pieces are very interesting, they're all completely upstaged by the views from the upper tier of the park. On clear days, you'll get near-perfect views of the water with the jagged, snow-capped Olympic Mountains in the background. The PACCAR Pavilion has a gift shop, café, and more information about the park. ✉ *Western Ave. between Broad and Bay Sts., Belltown* ☎ *206/645-3100* ✉ *Free* ☉ *Park daily sunrise–sunset. PACCAR Pavilion May–Sept., Tues.–Sun. 10–5, Fri. until 9; Oct.–Apr. Tues.–Sun. 10–4.*

Fodor's Choice ★

❶ Pike Place Market. Like many historical sites whose importance is taken for granted, this institution started small. It dates from 1907, when the city issued permits allowing farmers to sell produce from wagons parked at Pike Place. Later the city built permanent stalls. At one time the market was a madhouse of vendors hawking their produce and haggling with customers over prices. Some fishmongers still carry on this kind of frenzied banter, but chances are you won't get them to waver on their prices. Urban renewal almost killed the market, but a group of residents, led by the late architect Victor Steinbrueck, rallied and voted it a historical asset in 1973. Many buildings have been restored, and the complex is connected to the waterfront by stairs and elevators. Booths sell seafood—which can be packed in dry ice for your flight home—produce, cheese, wine, spices, tea, coffee, and crafts. There are also several restaurants. The flower market is a must-see.

Free maps, available at several locations throughout the market, distinguish among the various types of shops and stalls. Farmers, who come to the market from as far away as the Yakima Valley, east of the Cascade Mountains, have first dibs on the tables, known as "farmers' tables," where they display and sell their own vegetables, fruits, or flowers. Vendors in the so-called high stalls often have fruits and vegetables or crafts that they've purchased locally to sell here. The superb quality of the high-stall produce helps to set Seattle's dining standards.

The shopkeepers who rent stores in the market sell such things as packaged food items, art, curios, pets, and more. Most of the shops are nothing special, catering to the massive number of tourists that make their way through here in high season, but there are a few gems here and there. Because the market is along a bluff, the main arcade stretches down the cliff face for several stories; many shops are below street level. Other shops and restaurants are in buildings east of Pike Place and west of Western Avenue. The information booth is at 1st and Pike.

Tours of the market are given daily and cost $8. Note that you must make reservations for tours at least a day in advance.

Everyone visits the market, which means it is often infuriatingly crowded, especially when cruise ships are in port. During high season, you might never find a quiet corner, but getting to the market early

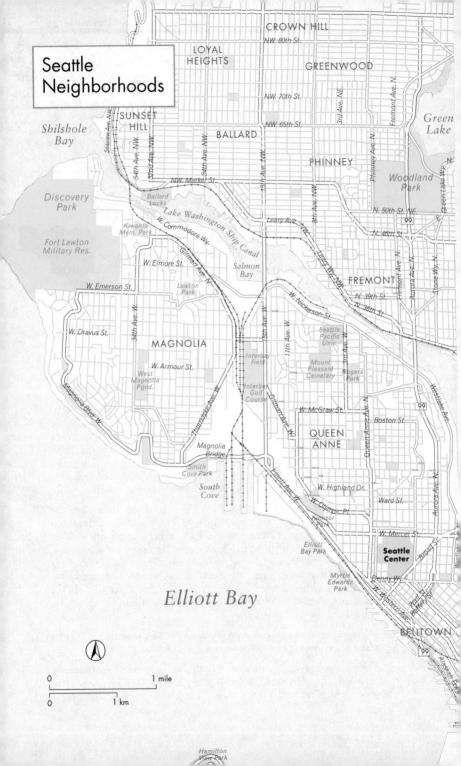

Seattle
Neighborhoods

CROWN HILL
NW. 80th St.

LOYAL
HEIGHTS

GREENWOOD

SUNSET
HILL

NW. 70th St.

Shilshole
Bay

NW. 65th St.

BALLARD

PHINNEY

Green
Lake

Woodland
Park

NW. Market St.

Discovery
Park

Ballard
Locks

Lake Washington Ship Canal

Leary Ave. NW.

N. 50th St. NE.

99

N. 46th St.

Kiwanis
Mem. Park

W. Commodore Wy.

Fort Lawton
Military Res.

W. Elmore St.

Gilman Ave. N.

Salmon
Bay

FREMONT

W. Emerson St.

Lawton
Park

N. 39th St.

W. Nickerson St.

N. 36th St.

W. Dravus St.

Seattle
Pacific
Univ.

MAGNOLIA

W. Armour St.

West
Magnolia
Pgnd.

Interbay
Field

Mount
Pleasant
Cemetery

Rogers
Park

Interbay
Golf
Course

W. McGraw St.

Magnolia
Bridge

Boston St.

QUEEN
ANNE

99

Smith
Cove Park

South
Cove

W. Highland Dr.

Ward St.

Elliott
Bay Park

Kinnear
Park

W. Olympic Pl.

W. Mercer St.

Seattle
Center

Myrtle
Edwards
Park

Denny Wy.

Elliott Bay

BELLTOWN

99

0   1 mile

0   1 km

Hamilton
View Park

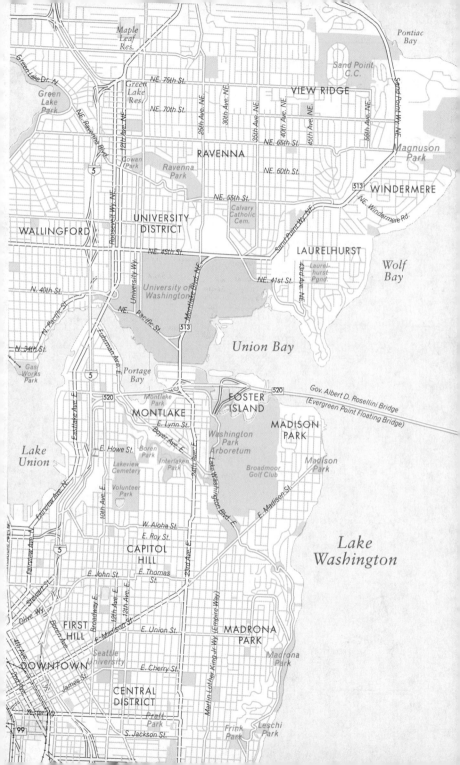

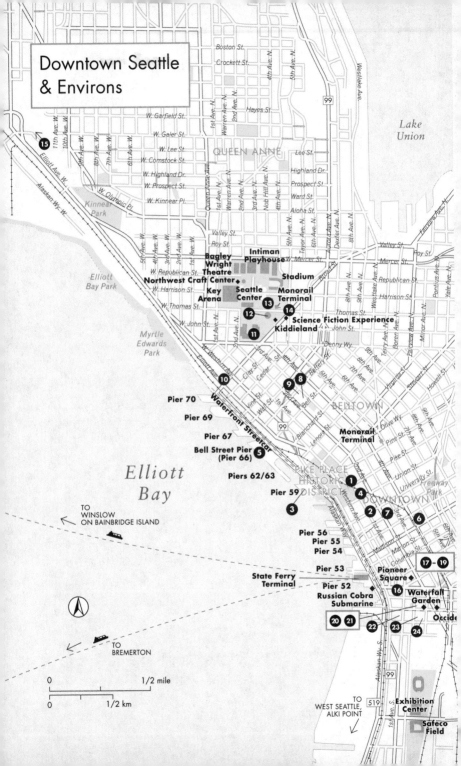

Downtown Seattle & Environs

Boston St.
Crockett St.

W. Garfield St.
W. Galer St.
QUEEN ANNE
W. Lee St.
W. Comstock St.
Highland Dr.
W. Highland Dr.
Prospect St.
W. Prospect St.
Ward St.
W. Kinnear Pl.
Aloha St.

15

Kinnear Park

Elliott Bay Park

Valley St.
Roy St.
Intiman Playhouse
Bagley Wright Theatre
W. Republican St.
Mercer St.
Northwest Craft Center
Stadium
W. Harrison St.
Monorail Terminal
Key Arena
Seattle Center
W. Thomas St.
13
12
Science Fiction Experience
Kiddieland
11
Denny Wy.

Myrtle Edwards Park

Thomas St.
John St.

10

Pier 70
Waterfront Streetcar
Pier 69
Pier 67
BELLTOWN
Bell Street Pier (Pier 66)
9 **8**
5
Monorail Terminal
Piers 62/63
Pine St.
PIKE PLACE HISTORIC DISTRICT
Pike St.
Pier 59
1
3
Union St.
4
University St.
Freeway Park
DOWNTOWN
Pier 56
2 **7**
6
Pier 55
Pier 54
Madison St.
Columbia St.
Marion St.
Pier 53
17 – **19**
State Ferry Terminal
Pioneer Square
Pier 52
16
Waterfall Garden
Russian Cobra Submarine
Occide
20 **21**
22 **23**
24

Elliott Bay

TO WINSLOW ON BAINBRIDGE ISLAND

TO BREMERTON

0   1/2 mile
0   1/2 km

Lake Union

TO WEST SEATTLE, ALKI POINT

519
Exhibition Center

Safeco Field

(around 8 AM) is probably your best bet.

There are numerous garages in the area, including one affiliated with the market itself (the Public Market Parking Garage at 1531 Western Avenue), at which you can get validated parking from many merchants; some restaurants offer free parking at this garage after 5 PM. You'll also find several pay lots farther south on Western Avenue. ⊠*Pike Pl. at Pike St., west of 1st Ave., Downtown* ☎*206/682–7453* ⊕*www.pikeplacemarket.org* ⊗*Stall hrs vary: 1st-level shops Mon.–Sat. 10–6, Sun. 11–5; underground shops daily 11–5.*

> ## THE MARKET AT NIGHT
>
> If you want to see the historic area, but can't deal with the crowds, visit in the evening when most of the shops and stalls are shutting down—and several bars and restaurants are just getting going. You won't get to see the fish throwers or the tables crowded with bouquets of fresh flowers and produce, but the nighttime view of the market can be a very romantic one, especially just after a rainstorm when the damp cobblestones reflect its lights.

OFF THE BEATEN PATH

Russian Cobra Submarine. Just south of the ferry terminals, you can tour the torpedo rooms, sonar and radar areas, and crew quarters of a Russian-built Foxtrot Class attack submarine. From 1974 through 1994, this 284-foot sub patrolled the Arctic, Indian, and Pacific oceans on secret Cold War missions. Around 80 crew members spent up to three months at sea in this vessel, which had only three showers and two toilets. ⊠*Pier 48, 101 Alaskan Way, Downtown* ☎*206/223–1767* ⊕*www.russiancobra.com* ☑*$10* ⊗*Sept.–May, daily 9–5:30; June–Aug., daily 9–8.*

Fodor'sChoice ★

☺ ❸ Seattle Aquarium. The aquarium should call itself Otters R Us—you could spend hours just watching the delightful antics of the sea otters and their river cousins. The partially open-air Marine Mammal section also includes harbor seals and fur seals, and, unlike at some aquariums, you get unimpeded, close-up views of the animals from two levels—you can see them sleeping on the rocks or gliding around the water's surface and then go down a floor to watch them as they dive to the bottoms of their pools. If that weren't enough entertainment for one day, the Underwater Dome surrounds you with colorful schools of fish. The tide pool room, usually the most anticlimactic part of an aquarium, is spectacular—tanks and touch pools are bursting with neon-color anemones and starfish. ■TIP→ **Spend a few minutes in front of the octopus tank even if you don't detect any movement. Your patience will be rewarded if you get to see this amazing creature shimmy up the side of the tank.** If you're visiting in fall or winter, dress warmly—the Marine Mammal area is on the waterfront and catches all of those chilly Puget Sound breezes. ⊠*Pier 59 off Alaskan Way, Downtown* ☎*206/386–4300* ⊕*www.seattleaquarium.org* ☑*$12.50* ⊗*Daily 9:30–5.*

★ ❷ Seattle Art Museum. Long the pride of the city's art scene, SAM is now better than ever after a massive expansion that connects the iconic old building on University Street (where sculptor Jonathan Borofsky's several-stories-high *Hammering Man* still pounds away) to a sleek, light-filled high-rise space around the corner on 1st Avenue and Union Street. As you enter, you'll have the option of wandering around two floors of free public space. The first floor includes the museum's shop; a café that focuses on local, fresh ingredients; and drop-in workshops where the whole family can get creative. The second floor features free exhibitions, including awe-inspiring large-scale installations. The third and fourth floors are dedicated to the museum's extensive permanent collection—surveying Asian, Native American, African, Oceanic, and pre-Columbian art—and special exhibitions; admission is charged for these floors. Among the highlights are the anonymous 14th-century Buddhist masterwork *Monk at the Moment of Enlightenment* and Jackson Pollock's *Sea Change*. The expansion also brought some exciting new pieces to the permanent collection from such artists as Georgia O'Keefe, John Singer Sargent, Mary Cassatt, and Jasper Johns. Murals, interactive video installations, and unimpeded views of the city thread the galleries together, meaning there's more to gawk at than the collections. ⊠ *1300 1st Ave., Downtown* ☎ *206/654–3100* ⊕ *www.seattleartmuseum.org* ⊠ *$13, free 1st Thurs. of month* ☉ *Tues.–Wed. and weekends 10–5, Thurs. and Fri. 10–9, 1st Thurs. until midnight.*

❻ Seattle Central Library. The structure that resembles a spaceship covered in delicate spiderweb threads is the hub of Seattle's 25-branch library system. Designed by Dutch architect Rem Koolhaas, the 11-story building houses 1.4 million books—the nonfiction titles on a four-level "book spiral" with continuous access—plus 400 computers, an auditorium, a "mixing chamber" floor of information desks, an area with materials in languages other than English, and a café. Floors zigzagging upward are visible from outside the metal facade. Intersecting beams, pipes, and trusses ensure that the costly building ($159 million plus) can withstand the region's earthquakes. Tours focusing on the building's architecture are offered several times a week on a first-come, first-served basis; call for a current schedule. The reading room on the 10th floor has views of the city and the water. ⊠ *1000 4th Ave., Downtown* ☎ *206/386–4636* ⊕ *www.spl.org* ☉ *Mon.–Thurs. 10–8, Fri. and Sat. 10–6, Sun. noon–6.*

❾ Suyama Space. The brainchild of art advocate and noted local architect George Suyama, this gallery exhibits mostly large-scale, site-specific installations that are often mathematical in nature (and at times a little obtuse). A recent exhibit entitled "All things long to persist in their being" consisted of timbers arranged to replicate the nautilus shell, one of nature's most studied designs. Unlike many of Seattle's galleries, this is not a commercial venue—it's kept afloat solely through grants and donations—which is just another reason to take a stroll through the lofty space. ⊠ *2324 2nd Ave., Belltown* ☎ *206/256–0809* ⊕ *www.suyamapetersondeguchi.com* ⊠ *Free* ☉ *Weekdays 9–5.*

❹ William Traver Gallery. A classic gallery space with white walls and creaky, uneven wood floors, William Traver is like a little slice of Soho in Seattle—without the attitude. Light pours in from large picture windows. The focus is on high-price (tens of thousands of dollars) glass art from local and international artists. Pieces are exquisite—never too whimsical or gaudy—and the staff is extremely courteous to those of us who can only enjoy this place as a museum and not a shop. After you're done tiptoeing around the gallery, head back downstairs and around the corner to Vetri, which sells glass art and objects from emerging artists at steep but much-more-reasonable prices. ⊠ *110 Union St., Downtown* ☎*206/587–6501* ⊕*www.travergallery.com* ✉*Free* ⊗*Tues.–Fri. 10–6, Sat. 10–5, Sun. noon–5.*

> **THE BEST OF BOTH WORLDS**
>
> At the Olympic Sculpture Park, photographers can kill two birds with one stone. Head up the path to Alexander Calder's arresting *Eagle* sculpture—take the quintessential water-and-mountains shot and then turn around to get a great shot of the Space Needle with *Eagle* in the foreground.

SEATTLE CENTER & QUEEN ANNE

You're certainly in no danger of driving right past the Seattle Center. Not only is the area home to Seattle's version of the Eiffel tower, the Space Needle, but it is anchored by Frank Gehry's wild Experience Music Project building. Almost all visitors make their way here at least once, whether to visit the museums, catch a concert or show at one of the many performing arts venues, or cheer on the Sonics at the Key Arena.

The 74-acre complex was built for the 1962 World's Fair. A rolling green campus organized around the massive International Fountain. Among the arts groups based here are the Seattle Repertory Theatre, Intiman Theatre, the Seattle Opera, and the Pacific Northwest Ballet. The center hosts several professional sports teams: the Seattle Supersonics (NBA basketball), Sounders (soccer), Seadogs (indoor soccer), and Thunderbirds (amateur hockey). It's also the site of three of the area's largest summer festivals: the Northwest Folklife Festival, Bite of Seattle, and Bumbershoot.

Traffic and parking can be nightmarish during games and large-scale special events, so try to take public transportation (like the monorail) or a cab.

Just west of the Seattle Center is the intersection of Queen Anne Avenue N and Denny Way. This marks the start of the Queen Anne neighborhood, which stretches all the way up formidable Queen Anne Hill to the ship canal. The neighborhood is split into Upper and Lower Queen Anne and the two neighborhoods are quite different. Lower Queen Anne is a mixed-income neighborhood that has a small, interesting mix of independent record and book stores; laid-back, postgame pubs; and a few upmarket restaurants and bars. Past Aloha Street, the neighborhood starts to look more upscale and suburbanish, and at Galer Street a separate commercial district starts marking the heart of wealthy Upper

1

Queen Anne. With the exception of the Seattle Center, Queen Anne doesn't have many sights, but the residential streets west of Queen Anne Avenue in Upper Queen Anne are fun to tool around in if you want to get a look at some of Seattle's most expensive real estate. The wealth extends to the Magnolia neighborhood, the northwest corner of the hill west of 15th Avenue NW. There's only one sight to see in Magnolia, but it's a terrific one—gorgeous Discovery Park.

Buses trudge up Queen Anne Avenue, making the commercial districts easy to reach from Downtown or the Seattle Center; the rest of the neighborhood will require a car to tour. Buses also drop you close to the West Government Way entrance to Discovery Park; from Lower Queen Anne, the trip shouldn't take more than 20 minutes, and the park is well worth the detour from any area of town.

WHAT TO SEE

☺ **⑬ The Children's Museum.** Enter this colorful, spacious museum off the Seattle Center food court through a Northwest wilderness setting, with winding trails, hollow logs, and a waterfall. From here, you can explore a global village where rooms with kid-friendly props show everyday life in Ghana, the Philippines, and Japan. Another neighborhood contains an American post office, a fire station, and a grocery store. Cog City is a giant game of pipes, pulleys, and balls; and kids can test their talent in a mock recording studio. There's a small play area for toddlers, and lots of crafts to help kids learn more about the exhibits. ⊠*Seattle Center House, 305 Harrison St., Queen Anne* ☎*206/441–1768* ⊕*www.thechildrensmuseum.org* ⊡*$7.50* ☉*Weekdays 10–5, weekends 10–6.*

OFF THE BEATEN PATH

Center for Wooden Boats. Though slightly off the main drag at the south end of Lake Union, the center is a great place to launch your expedition if you're interested in exploring the water (or just the waterfront). Check out the 1897 schooner *Wawona* and the other historic vessels on display, watch the staff at work on a restoration, rent a boat at the Oarhouse for a sail around the lake, or have a picnic. ⊠*1010 Valley St., Queen Anne* ☎*206/382–2628* ⊕*www.cwb.org* ⊡*Free* ☉*Museum Jun.–Aug., daily 10–8; Sep.–Oct. and Mar.–May, daily 10–6; Nov.–Feb., daily 10–5. Boat rentals start at noon most days; call to confirm hrs.*

⑮ Discovery Park.
Fodor'sChoice
★
Discovery Park is Seattle's largest park, and it has an amazing variety of terrain: cool forest trails that can feel as secluded as mountain hikes lead to meadows, saltwater beaches, sand dunes, a lighthouse, and views that include Puget Sound, the Cascades, and the Olympics. There are 2.8 mi of trails through this urban wilderness, but the North Beach Trail, which takes you along the shore to the lighthouse, is a must-see. Head to the South Bluff Trail to get a view of Mt. Rainier and the skyline. The park has several entrances—if you want to stop at the visitor center to pick up a trail map before exploring, use the main entrance at Government Way. The North Parking Lot is much closer to the North Beach Trail and to Ballard and Fremont, if you're coming from that direction. To get to here from Downtown take

15th Avenue NW and get off at the Emerson Street exit onto W. Emerson. Make a right onto 23rd Avenue W, then a left onto Commodore Way, which will lead you to the park's north entrance. **TIP→ Note that the park is easily reached from Ballard and Fremont. It's sometimes easier to combine a park day with an exploration of those neighborhoods than with a busy Downtown itinerary.** ✉ *3801 W. Government Way, Magnolia* ✣ *From Downtown Seattle to the main entrance: Take Elliott Ave. north until it becomes 15th Ave. NW. Take the Dravus St. exit and turn left on Dravus at the stoplight. Turn right on 20th Ave. W, which becomes Gilman Ave. W. Gilman eventually becomes W. Government Way; follow the road into the park* ☎ *206/386–4236* 🌐 *www.cityofseattle.net/parks* 🎫 *Free* ⏲ *Park daily 6 AM–11 PM, visitor center Tues.–Sun. 8:30–5.*

MONORAIL MINUTES

Seattle Center is in an awkward part of the city, but the monorail that runs from Westlake Center (5th Avenue and Pine Street) makes getting here easy from Downtown. The monorail runs daily from 9 AM to 11 PM, with departures every ten minutes. The ride takes about two minutes.

14 **Experience Music Project.** Seattle's most controversial architectural statement is the 140,000-square-foot interactive museum celebrating American popular music. Architect Frank Gehry drew inspiration from electric guitars to achieve the building's curvy design, though it looks more like open-heart surgery than a musical instrument. Regardless, it stands out among the city's cookie-cutter high-rises and therefore it's a fitting backdrop for the world's largest collection of Jimi Hendrix memorabilia, which is flanked by a gallery of guitars once owned by Bob Dylan, Hank Williams, Kurt Cobain, and the bands Pearl Jam, Soundgarden, and the Kingsmen. Experiment with instruments and recording equipment in the interactive Sound Lab, or attend performances or workshops in the Sky Church concert hall, JBL Theater, or Liquid Lounge bar. ✉ *5th Ave. between Broad and Thomas Sts., Queen Anne* ☎ *206/367–5483* 🌐 *www.emplive.org* 🎫 *$19.95* ⏲ *May 25–Sept. 3, Mon. and Wed.–Sun. 10–5; rest of yr, daily 10–8.*

11 **Pacific Science Center.** With about 200 indoor and outdoor hands-on exhibits and a state-of-the-art planetarium, this is a great place for both kids and grown-ups. The startling dinosaur exhibit is complete with moving robotic creatures, while Tech Zones has robots and virtual-reality games. Machines analyze human physiology in Body Works. The tropical butterfly house is stocked with farm-raised chrysalides weekly; other creatures live in the woodland and tide pool areas. Next door, IMAX movies and laser rock shows run daily. ✉ *200 2nd Ave. N, Queen Anne* ☎ *206/443–2844* 🌐 *www.pacsci.org* 🎫 *Center $10, IMAX $8, light shows $5–$8* ⏲ *Weekdays 10–5, weekends 10–6.*

Science Fiction Experience. Another Paul Allen brainchild in Seattle Center, this museum has an advisory board—Arthur C. Clarke, Ray Bradbury, Octavia Butler, Orson Scott Card, Syne Mitchell, Kim Stanley Robinson, and Greg Bear, among many others—that reads like the equivalent of a science fiction fan's fantasy baseball team. But this museum is not just for mouth-breathers: the best science fiction writers have always tackled major themes, and the Brave New Worlds exhibit explores the different visions science fiction has produced regarding our future. There's more-lighthearted fun, too: Spacedock surveys the genre's coolest spaceships and trekkies can head to the Armory to see a Klingon dagger up close. ⊠ *5th Ave. between Broad and Thomas Sts., Queen Anne* ☎ *206/724-3284* ⊕ *www. sfhomeworld.org* ⬚ *$12.95* ⊙ *May 25–Sept. 3, Mon. and Wed.–Sun. 10–5; rest of yr, daily 10–8.*

🐣 ★ ⑫ **Space Needle.** The distinctive exterior of the 520-foot-high Space Needle is visible throughout much

> **CHIEF SEATTLE**
>
> At the southeast corner of Seattle Center stands a statue of Chief Seattle, of the Duwamish tribe. Seattle was among the first Native Americans to have contact with the white explorers who came to the region. He was viewed as a great leader and peacemaker by his fellow tribesmen and as a friendly contact by the white settlers. The sculpture was created by local artist James Wehn in 1912 and dedicated by the chief's great-great granddaughter, Myrtle Loughery, on Founder's Day, November 13, 1912.

of the city—but the view from the inside out is even better. A 42-second elevator ride up to the circular observation deck yields 360-degree vistas of Elliott Bay, Queen Anne Hill, the University of Washington campus, and the Cascade Range. The Needle was built just in time for the World's Fair in 1962, but has since been refurbished with educational signs, interactive trivia game stations for kids, and the glass-enclosed SpaceBase store and Pavilion spiraling around the base of the tower. Don't waste your money dining at the top-floor SkyCity revolving restaurant; though eating there gets you free admission to the observation deck, the food is overpriced and often mediocre. ■ TIP→ **And don't bother doing the trip at all on rainy days.** Note that if you can't decide whether you want the daytime or nighttime view, for $17 you can buy a ticket that allows you to visit twice in one day. ⊠ *5th Ave. and Broad St., Queen Anne* ☎ *206/905–2100* ⊕ *www.spaceneedle.com* ⬚ *$14* ⊙ *Sun.–Thurs. 9* AM–*11* PM, *Fri. and Sat. 9* AM–*midnight.*

PIONEER SQUARE

The Pioneer Square district, directly south of Downtown, is Seattle's oldest neighborhood, and it pushes its historical cache hard in every brochure and guidebook. It certainly attracts visitors because of its elegantly renovated (or in many cases replica) turn-of-the-20th-century redbrick buildings. The district's most unique structure, the 42-story Smith Tower on Second Avenue and Yesler Way, was the tallest building west of the Mississippi when it was completed in 1914; today, its observation deck is a great place to get views of the city if you don't want to deal with the Space Needle.

Though its history is pretty clear, the role Pioneer Square plays in the city today is harder to define. It's undeniably the center of the arts scene—there are more galleries in this small neighborhood then we have room to list, and they make up the majority of the neighborhood's sights. ■TIP➡ First Thursday art walks are perhaps the best time to see Pioneer Square, when animated crowds walk from gallery to gallery, viewing the new exhibitions. That said, the neighborhood is no longer a center for artists per se, as rents have risen in a way that doesn't reflect the value of the neighborhood; only established gallery owners have the cash to rent lofty spaces in heavily trafficked areas. The neighborhood had begun to go upscale before the dot.com bust and developers are again eyeballing the area, ready to make it another Belltown, but so far the rising rents have only succeeded in creating a bunch of empty storefronts and the feeling that the neighborhood is at its most incohesive, being pushed and pulled in too many directions at once.

> **A MUST-STOP PHOTO OP**
>
> Kerry Park on W. Highland Drive between 2nd and 3rd Avenues West has outstanding views of the city and the water. It's an all-time favorite spot for snapshots—be prepared to share the view with bus and van tours. If you're heading north on Queen Anne Avenue N, turn left onto W. Highland Drive.

By day, you'll see a mix of Downtown workers and tourists strolling the area, though the local parks are mainly inhabited by homeless people. Pioneer Square has a well-known nightlife scene, but unfortunately these days, it's a much-derided one thanks to the meat-market vibe of many of the clubs and the high chance that the night will end with overadrenalized men fighting on the street.

Nowadays, when Seattleites speak of Pioneer Square they usually speak of the love they have for certain unique neighborhood institutions—Elliott Bay Books, Bud's Jazz Records, Zeitgeist coffeehouse, a certain gallery, a friend's loft apartment—than the love they have for the neighborhood as a whole. Pioneer Square is always worth a visit, but reactions vary. Anyone seriously interested in doing the gallery circuit will be thrilled. Anyone looking for a vibrant, picture-perfect historic district that invites hours of contented strolling will be seriously underwhelmed. Most people combine Pioneer Square with a trip to the International District, which together would make a full day of touring.

WHAT TO SEE

㉔ Klondike Gold Rush National Historical Park. A redbrick building with wooden floors and soaring ceilings contains a small museum illustrating Seattle's role in the 1897–98 gold rush in northwestern Canada's Klondike region. Displays show antique mining equipment, and the walls are lined with photos of gold diggers, explorers, and the hopeful families who followed them. Film presentations, gold-panning demonstrations, and rotating exhibits are scheduled throughout the year. Other sectors of this park are in southeast Alaska. ✉117 S. Main St., Pioneer Square ☎206/553–7220 ⊕www.nps.gov/klse/index.htm ☞Free ☉Daily 9–5.

Occidental Park. This picturesque cobblestone "park" and the ivy-covered wall on its western boundary show up in a lot of brochures. It's the geographical heart of the historic neighborhood—too bad its current layout is not that historic at all. Though it once was the site of the Savoy Hotel, the park actually spent a lot of time as a parking lot before the restoration of the neighborhood started in the late 1960s and early '70s. It can be lovely on sunny days, and there's a small outdoor café in seasonable weather. Note, however, that this square is known as a place where homeless people congregate; depending on how intense the panhandling activity is, it may be more of a stroll-through then a sit-down-and-linger. The square is best avoided at night because of drug activity.

OFF THE BEATEN PATH

Safeco Field. This 47,000-seat, grass turf, open-air baseball stadium with a retractable roof is the home of the Seattle Mariners. If you want to see the stadium in all its glory, take the one-hour tour, which brings you onto the field, into the dugouts, back to the press and locker rooms, and up to the posh box seats. Wear comfortable shoes. Tours depart from the Team Store on First Avenue, and you purchase your tickets here, too. Afterward, head across the street to the Pyramid Alehouse for a brew. ⊠ *1st Ave. S, Sodo* ☎ *206/622–4487* ⊕ *www.mariners. mlb.com* ⊡ *$7* ⊙ *Apr.–Oct. nongame-day tours at 10:30, 12:30, and 2:30, game-day tours at 10:30 and 12:30; Nov.–Mar. tours Tues.–Sun. at 12:30 and 2:30.*

Underground Tour. Despite being touristy and a bit corny at times, this tour of the vestiges of Seattle's subterranean passageways and businesses (they were once above ground) is still a lot of fun. It's very informative, too—if you're interested in the general history of the city or anecdotes about the city's early politicians and residents, you'll appreciate it that much more. Note that even though it sounds like an adventure, young kids will probably be bored, as there's not much to see at the specific sites, which are more used as launching points for the stories. Comfortable shoes and an appreciation of bad puns are musts. Several tours are offered daily and schedules change month to month: call or visit the Web site for a full list of tour times. ⊠ *608 1st Ave., Pioneer Square* ☎ *206/682–4646* ⊕ *www.undergroundtour.com* ⊡ *$11* ⊙ *Tours daily; call for schedules.*

Waterfall Garden. Probably the best outdoor place to take a break is this small garden surrounding a 22-foot artificial waterfall that cascades over large granite stones. There are a few café tables; before heading over, grab some lunch to go from Grand Central Baking Company in the Grand Central Arcade on 1st Avenue S and Washington Street. ⊠ *Corner of S. Main St. and 2nd Ave. S, Pioneer Square.*

GALLERIES **Davidson Galleries.** Showing three
⑳ types of work, Davidson actually
consists of two buildings. Davidson
Contemporary is the newer space
on S. Washington Street; it focuses
on contemporary paintings and
sculptures. The Occidental Avenue
branch houses an impressive stock
of antique prints, as well as contemporary drawings and prints.
Though the antique print department is more of a specialized interest, the contemporary print exhibits
are always interesting and worth a
look. ⊠ *Davidson Contemporary:
310 S. Washington St., Pioneer
Square* ☎ *206/624–7684* ⊘ *Tues.–Sat. 11–5:30* ⊠ *Print Center: 313
Occidental Ave. S, Pioneer Square* ☎ *206/624–1324* ⊘ *Tues.–Sat. 10–
5:30* ⊕ *www.davidsongalleries.com* ⊠ *Free.*

> **SKID ROW**
>
> Today's Yesler Way was the
> original "Skid Row," where in the
> 1880s timber was sent to the
> sawmill on a skid of small logs
> laid crossways and greased so
> that the cut trees would slide
> down to the mill. The area later
> grew into Seattle's first center of
> commerce. Many of the buildings
> you see today are replicas of the
> wood-frame structures destroyed
> by fire in 1889.

★ ⑱ **Foster/White Gallery.** One of the Seattle art scene's heaviest hitters, Fos-
ter/White has digs as impressive as the works it shows: a century-old
building with high ceilings and 7,000 square feet of exhibition space.
Internationally acclaimed glass artist Dale Chihuly, and paintings,
sculpture, and drawings by Northwest masters Kenneth Callahan,
Mark Tobey, and George Tsutakawa are on permanent display. There's
another equally impressive branch in Rainier Square at 5th Avenue
and Union Street. ⊠ *220 3rd Ave. S, Pioneer Square* ☎ *206/622–2833*
⊕ *www.fosterwhite.com* ⊠ *Free* ⊘ *Tues.–Sat. 10–6.*

⑯ **Gallery 110.** Gallery 110 works with a collective of 60 artists, showing
pieces in its small space that are edgy, energetic, and sometimes just
plain weird. Occasionally, special exhibits will involve work from outside the collective and its affiliates—a recent show spotlighted the best
work from a collective in Portland. ⊠ *110 S. Washington St., Pioneer
Square* ☎ *206/624–9336* ⊕ *www.gallery110.com* ⊠ *Free* ⊘ *Wed.–Sat.
noon–5.*

⑲ **G. Gibson Gallery.** Vintage and contemporary photography is always on
exhibit here, including retrospectives from major artists like Walker
Evans, but G. Gibson also shows contemporary paintings, sculpture,
and mixed-media pieces. This is another institution of the Seattle art
scene, and the gallery's taste is always impeccable. ⊠ *300 S. Washington St., Pioneer Square* ☎ *206/587–4033* ⊕ *www.ggibsongallery.com*
⊠ *Free* ⊘ *Tues.–Fri. 11–5:30, Sat. 11–5.*

⑰ **Greg Kucera Gallery.** One of the most important destinations on the
Fodor'sChoice First Thursday gallery walk, this gorgeous space is a top venue for
★ national and regional artists. Be sure to check out the outdoor sculpture deck on the second level. If you can only stomach one gallery
visit, this is the place to go. You'll see big names that you might recognize along with newer artists and the thematic group shows are

consistently well thought out and well presented. ⊠*212 3rd Ave. S, Pioneer Square* ☎*206/624–0770* ⊕*www.gregkucera.com* ✉*Free* ⊙*Tues.–Sat. 10:30–5:30.*

㉑ Grover/Thurston Gallery. Twenty Northwest artists are represented in this historic space. Shows, which can be either solo or group exhibitions, are often fun, as many of the artists create wry pieces, many of which seem more like fine art imitating folk art. ⊠*309 Occidental Ave. S, Pioneer Square* ☎*206/223–0816* ⊕*www.groverthurston.com* ✉*Free* ⊙*Tues.–Sat. 11–5.*

★ ㉓ Stonington Gallery. You'll see plenty of cheesy tribal art knockoffs in tourist-trap shops, but this elegant gallery will give you a real look at the best contemporary work of Northwest Coast and Alaska tribal members (and artists from these regions working in the native style). Three floors exhibit wood carvings, paintings, sculpture, and mixed-media pieces. ⊠*119 S. Jackson St., Pioneer Square* ☎*206/405–4040* ⊕*www.stoningtongallery.com* ✉*Free* ⊙*Weekdays 10–6, Sat. 10–5:30, Sun. noon–5.*

㉒ wall space. Seattle doesn't have many spaces devoted solely to photography, which makes wall space notable among Pioneer Square's umpteen galleries. Equal attention is giving to Ansel Adams–style black-and-white prints and to the new possibilities and genres that are emerging thanks to digital technologies. ⊠*600 3rd Ave., Suite 332, Pioneer Square* ☎*206/330–9137* ⊕*www.wallspaceseattle.com* ✉*Free* ⊙*Tues.–Sat. 10:30–5:30.*

INTERNATIONAL DISTRICT

Bright welcome banners and 12-foot fiberglass dragons spinning in the wind capture the Asian spirit of the expanding International District (formerly called Chinatown). The I.D., as it's locally known, began as a haven for Chinese workers who came to the United States to work on the transcontinental railroad. The community has remained largely intact despite anti-Chinese riots and the forced eviction of Chinese residents during the 1880s and the internment of Japanese-Americans during World War II. About one-third of the residents are Chinese, one-third are Filipino, and another third come from elsewhere in Asia or the Pacific islands. The I.D. stretches from 4th Avenue to 12th Avenue and between Yesler Way and S. Dearborn Street. Although today the main business anchor is the Uwajimaya Japanese superstore, there are also many small Asian restaurants, herbalists, acupuncturists, antiques shops, and private clubs for gambling and socializing. Note that the area is more diffuse than similar communities in larger cities like San Francisco and New York. You won't find the densely packed streets chockablock with tiny storefronts and markets that spill out onto the sidewalk—scenes that have become synonymous with the word "Chinatown." Many of Seattle's Asian communities have moved farther south and north, past the city's borders.

The I.D. is a very popular lunchtime spot with Downtown office workers and a popular dinner spot with many Seattleites. ■TIP→ **You should definitely make a meal here part of your visit.** Look for the diamond-shape dragon signs in store windows—these establishments will give you a free-parking token. Check out ⊕*www.cidbia.org* for information on events and festivals in the neighborhood.

WHAT TO SEE

㉕ **Kobe Terrace.** Seattle's sister city of Kobe, Japan, donated a 200-year-old stone lantern to adorn this small hillside park. Despite being so close to I–5, the terrace is a peaceful place to stroll through and enjoy views of the city, the water, and, if you're lucky, Mt. Rainier; a few benches line the gravel paths. The herb gardens you see are part of the Danny Woo Community Gardens, tended to by the neighborhood's residents. ⊠*Main St. between 6th Ave. S and 7th Ave. S, International Distritct* ⊡*Free* ☉*Daily dawn–dusk.*

★ ㉗ **Uwajimaya.** Everyone makes a stop at this fantastic Japanese supermarket. A 30-foot-long red Chinese dragon stretches above colorful mounds of fresh produce and aisles of exotic packaged goods from countries throughout Asia. A busy food court serves sushi, Japanese bento-box meals, Chinese stir-fry combos, Korean barbecue, Hawaiian plates, Vietnamese spring rolls, and an assortment of teas and tapioca drinks. This is a great place to pick up all sorts of snacks; dessert lovers won't know which way to turn first. The housewares section is well stocked with dishes, cookware, appliances, textiles, and gifts. There's also a card section, a Hello Kitty corner, and Yuriko's cosmetics, where you can find Shiseido products that are usually available only in Japan. Last but not least, there's a small branch of the famous Kinokuniya bookstore chain. The large parking lot is free for one hour with a minimum $5 purchase (which will be no problem) or two hours with a minimum $10 purchase—don't forget to have your ticket validated by the cashiers. ⊠*600 5th Ave. S, International District* ☏*206/624–6248* ⊕*www.uwajimaya.com* ☉*Mon.–Sat. 9 AM–10 PM, Sun. 9–9.*

㉖ **Wing Luke Asian Museum.** Named for the Northwest's first Asian-American elected official, this small, well-organized museum surveys the history and cultures of people from Asia and the Pacific islands who settled in the Pacific Northwest. Alongside the costumes, fabrics, crafts, and photographs that kids will love, the museum also provides sophisticated looks at how immigrants and their descendants have transformed and been transformed by American culture. The most poignant and sobering part of the museum is an excellent multimedia exhibit dealing with the internment of Japanese-American citizens in camps during World War II. ■TIP→ **The museum is a great place to start your tour of the I.D., as it will provide a context to the neighborhood and the communities living here that you won't get by simply wandering around.** ⊠*407 7th Ave. S, International District* ☏*206/623–5124* ⊕*www.wingluke.org* ⊡*$4, free 1st Thurs. of month* ☉*Tues.–Fri. 11–4:30, weekends noon–4.*

Fodor'sChoice ★

FIRST HILL & THE CENTRAL DISTRICT

Smack between Downtown and Capitol Hill, First Hill is an odd mix of sterile-looking medical facility buildings (earning it the nickname "Pill Hill"), old brick buildings that look like they belong on a college campus, newer residential towers, and a few tree-lined streets. There are a few businesses along Boren Avenue, but they're mostly unremarkable. The main draw of the neighborhood is the Frye Art Museum, which is well worth a detour.

The Central District, or the "C.D.," lies south of Capitol Hill and east of the I.D. Its boundaries are roughly 12th Avenue on the west, Martin Luther King Jr. Boulevard on the east, E. Madision to the north, and S. Jackson Street to the south. Though it can still be considered the center of Seattle's African-American community (other major neighborhoods are outside the city's borders), the area started to change in the late 1990s. As all downtown areas of Seattle rapidly develop, it is facing an even more-awkward transitional period. Community groups are working hard to ensure that the "revitalization" of the area doesn't come at the expense of stripping the city's oldest residential neighborhood of its history or breaking up and pricing out the community that's hung in there during years of economic blight.

WHAT TO SEE

FIRST HILL

Frye Art Museum. The Frye was a forgotten museum for a while, haunted only by Seattleites who would come to visit their favorite paintings from the permanent collection—mostly 19th- and 20th-century representational pieces depicting pastoral scenes. But a new curator shook the Frye out of its stupor and now in addition to its beloved permanent collection, this elegant building plays host to eclectic and often avant-garde rotating exhibits. Recent shows have included morbid pencil drawings from Robyn O'Neil; a large collection of pieces from illustrator Henry Darger's mad-genius, 15,000-page, unpublished manuscript; and a retrospective of works from the Leipzeig Art Academy. No matter what's going on in the stark, brightly lighted back galleries, it always seems to blend well with the permanent collection, which occupies two hushed and elegant galleries with velvet couches and dark-blue and purple walls—the latter usually serving as either an amuse-bouche or after-dinner mint to the featured exhibits. The museum is small enough that you can move through it in an hour, but you could easily spend more time here, too. The café has a small courtyard and real entrées in addition to sandwiches and sweets. ⊠ *704 Terry Ave., First Hill* ☎ *206/622–9250* ⊕ *www.fryeart.org* ✉ *Free* ☉ *Tues.–Sat. 10–5 (Thurs. until 8), Sun. noon–5.*

Fodor'sChoice ★

THE CENTRAL DISTRICT

Crespinel Martin Luther King Jr. Mural. Heading west on Cherry Street in the Central Area, you'll see a 17-foot-tall mural of Dr. Martin Luther King Jr. Pacific Northwest artist James Crespinel painted the mural in the summer of 1995 on the eastern face of the building that houses Catfish Corner, a soul-food take-out place. ⊠ *Corner of Martin Luther King Jr. Way and Cherry St., Central District.*

㉝ Douglass Truth Neighborhood Library. Originally named the Yesler Library after Seattle businessman Henry Yesler, this simple brick, schoolhouse-style building is a hub of activity. Architects W. Marbury Somervell and Harlan Thomas designed the library, which opened in 1914 and today contains more than 9,000 books—many focusing on local and international experiences of African-Americans. At the request of local residents, who preferred that the name reflect the neighborhood's diversity, the library was renamed after Frederick Douglass and Sojourner Truth in 1975. ✉ *2300 E. Yesler Way, Central Area* ☎ *206/684–4704* ⊕ *www.spl.org* ⊘ *Mon.–Thurs. 10–9, Fri. 11:30–6, Sat. 10–6, Sun. 1–5.*

㉙ First African Methodist Episcopal Church. Founded in 1886, the state's oldest African-American church and the community's nexus has operated out of this historic building since 1912. The gospel choir is one of the city's best, and discussions with and among intellectuals, authors, artists, and the community are regularly scheduled. Rapidly growing church attendance—with 600 more members just since 2000—has led to an extra service out of a satellite site in Kent. ✉ *1522 14th Ave., Central Area* ☎ *206/324–3664* ⊕ *www.fameseattle.org* ⊘ *Sun. 7:30 and 11, Kent service 9:30.*

㉚ Mount Zion Baptist Church. Gospel-music fans are drawn to the church of the state's largest African-American congregation. The church's first gatherings began in 1890; back then its prayer meetings were held in people's houses and in a store. The church was incorporated in 1903, and after a number of moves, settled in its current simple but sturdy brick building. Eighteen stained-glass windows, each with an original design that honors a key African-American figure, glow within the sanctuary. Beneath the bell tower, James Washington's sculpture *The Oracle of Truth,* a gray boulder carved with the image of a lamb, is dedicated to children struggling to find truth. ✉ *1634 19th Ave., Central Area* ☎ *206/322–6500* ⊕ *www.mountzion.net* ⊘ *Services Sun. 7:30 and 10:45.*

CAPITOL HILL

With its mix of theaters and churches, coffeehouses and nightclubs, stately homes and student apartments, Capitol Hill still deserves its reputation as Seattle's most eclectic neighborhood. Though new money is starting to change the neighborhood—several luxury condo developments will strip part of the Pike–Pine corridor of its most beloved institutions and much of its personality—Capitol Hill has very loyal residents, and it will still take some time to turn the artsy, hip neighborhood into a string of cell phone stores and FedEx/Kinko's branches.

Though it has a deserved reputation for its nightlife, Capitol Hill is also the best neighborhood in the city to spend a few daylight hours strolling around. Old brick buildings; modern, interesting apartment buildings; colorfully painted two-story homes; and what can rightfully be called mansions all occupy the same area. There are plenty of cute shops to browse in (though most of them sell variations of the same retro-vintage hipster accoutrements) and quite a few fantastic coffee shops to kick back in. ■TIP➔ **Nothing gets going here too early, so unless you want to check out the parks in the morning, save your visit for the afternoon. After some strolling and shopping, stick around for dinner and barhopping.**

You can walk to the Hill from Downtown, taking Pine Street across I–5 to Melrose Avenue, but keep in mind that touring the neighborhood will require a lot of walking, so you might want to plan to take the bus or cab in one or both directions. Note that trying to find street parking here can be maddening, and many streets are zoned (i.e., only residents with the proper permits can park there). There are, however, quite a few pay lots, and though the ones closest to Seattle University tend to fill up on weekdays, you should be able to find something.

WHAT TO SEE

36 Ballard Fetherston Gallery. As you make your way down the Pike–Pine corridor, this airy, contemporary space is a great diversion, especially if you want to feel like you've done more with the day than shop or people-watch. The bright abstract works (mainly paintings) will pop out enough to beckon you in, even amid all the activity on this stretch of the road. High-quality shows present thought-provoking yet often playful and humorous works from nationally known names as well as local talent—often done in striking, saturated colors. ✉ *818 E. Pike St., Capitol Hill* ☎ *206/322–9440* ⊕ *www.ballardfetherstongallery. com* ✆ *Free* ⊘ *Tues.–Sat. 11–5.*

35 Broadway Shopping District. Seattle's youth culture, old money, gay scene, and everything in between all converge on this lively, if somewhat scuzzy stretch of Broadway E between E. Denny Way and E. Roy Street. It's a cluttered stretch of cheap restaurants (with a one or two more-upscale-looking cafés thrown into the mix), even cheaper clothing stores, a few interesting books and records shops, and a few bars. Most of the good shopping, eating, and drinking is along the Pike–Pine corridor or on side streets, and it's a real stretch to claim as some guidebooks do that Broadway is the epicenter of Seattle's counterculture (whatever that means), but a lot of people still find the area compelling because of its human parade. It's also one of the few areas in Seattle that can claim to have a consistently lively street life, and despite some aggressive panhandlers and the occasional twitchy meth-head, the avenue is generally safe at all hours. If you really want to see Seattle in all its quirky glory, head to Dick's Drive-In around 1 AM on a weekend night (or around 11:30 AM the next morning). Between Pine and Roy streets artist Jack Mackie inlaid seven sets of bronze dancing footprints demonstrating the steps for the tango, the waltz, the fox-trot, and others. Look closely at the steps near Roy Street to see coffee beans in the concrete, a nod to the region's love affair with java. Near Pine Street is a bronze effigy of one of the city's most worshiped rock-and-roll icons, Jimi Hendrix. You might see someone leave an offering—a flower, a cigarette, or even a joint—in his outstretched fingers.

39 Lakeview Cemetery. One of the region's most beautiful cemeteries looks east toward Lake Washington from its elevated hillside directly north of Volunteer Park. Bruce Lee's grave and that of his son Brandon are the most visited sites. Several of Seattle's founding families are also interred here (their bodies were moved from a pioneer cemetery when Denny Hill was leveled to make room for the motels, car dealerships, and parking lots of the Denny Regrade south of Lake Union). Ask for a map at the cemetery office. ⊠ *1554 15th Ave. E, Capitol Hill* ☎ *206/322–1582* ▧ *Free* ⊘ *Mon.–Sat. 9–4:30.*

37 Martin-Zambito Fine Art. If you're interested in Northwest regional art, this gallery is a must. But don't expect a "greatest hits" collection here—David Martin and Dominic Zambito are well known in Seattle's art scene for expanding the study of regional Northwest art namely by uncovering little-known, unknown, or long-forgotten artists, many of them women. Their research has extended the history of the genre to the late 1800s (before they started digging, most collections started in the 1940s). Their exhibits consist of mostly paintings and photographs and tend to focus on WPA and Depression-era works. ⊠ *721 E. Pike St., Capitol Hill* ☎ *206/726–9509* ⊕ *www.martin-zambito.com* ▧ *Free* ⊘ *Tues.–Sat. 11–6.*

31 Photographic Center Northwest. A small, starkly attractive gallery space occupies the front of this photo education center. Student work is often on display, but this gallery is not just a repository for end-of-workshop projects. Curated shows often feature well-respected photographers, whose work ranges from journalistic to fantastical. The gallery is convenient to the Pike–Pine corridor—it's a few blocks south of Pike—but if you're not a photography buff, you may want to save the detour for an evening when you plan to eat at Lark or drink at Licorous, both of which are a few steps away. ⊠ *900 12th Ave., Capitol Hill* ⊕ *www.pcnw.org* ▧ *Free* ⊘ *Mon. and Sun. noon–9:30, Tues.–Fri. 9–9:30, Sat. 9–5.*

34 Pike–Pine Corridor. Nowadays, more people consider this, not Broadway, the heart of the Hill. The so-called corridor begins at the corners of Pike and Pine streets (which run parallel) and Melrose Avenue. You'll find a bunch of interesting businesses as soon as you enter the area, including the Baguette Box and Bauhaus coffee shop; Faire, another great coffee shop, is just a few blocks north on E. Olive Way. So, if you need some sustenance, grab a coffee and a sandwich and head east on either Pike or Pine. Pine is a slightly more-pleasant walk, but Pike has more stores—and unless you're here in the evening, it's the stores that will be the main draw. The architecture along both streets is a mix of older buildings with small storefronts, a few taller buildings that have loft office spaces, and garages and warehouses (some converted, some not). The best plan of attack is to follow either street to 11th Avenue, which skirts Cal Anderson Park—a small, pleasant park with a unusual conic fountain and reflecting pool, and a great place to take a break after walking and shopping. The park can be either very quiet or filled with all kinds of activities from softball games to impromptu concerts from a neighborhood marching band. If you want a coffee or a snack, cross the park to its northeastern corner, across the street from which is Vivace Roasteria.

38 **Volunteer Park.** High above the mansions of North Capitol Hill sits 45-acre Volunteer Park, a grassy expanse perfect for picnicking, sunbathing, reading, and strolling. You can tell this is one of the city's older parks by the size of the trees and the rhododendrons, many of which were planted more than a hundred years ago. The Olmsted Brothers, the premier landscape architects of the day, helped with the final design in 1904, and the park has changed surprisingly little since then. The manicured look of the park is a sharp contrast to the wilds of Discovery Park or the Washington Park Arboretum, but the design suits the needs of the densely populated neighborhood well—after all, Capitol Hill residents need someplace to set up Ultimate Frisbee games. A small wading pool by the water tower is extremely popular with families on hot summer days.

Beside the lake in the center of the park is the **Seattle Asian Art Museum** (☎ *206/654–3100* ⊕ *www.seattleartmuseum.org* ✉ *$5, free 1st Thurs. and Sat. of month* ☉ *Tues.–Sun. 10–5, Thurs. until 9; call for tour schedule*). This 1933 art moderne edifice fits surprisingly well with the stark plaza stretching from the front door to the edge of a bluff, and with the lush plants of Volunteer Park. The museum's collections include thousands of paintings, sculptures, pottery, and textiles from China, Japan, India, Korea, and several Southeast Asian countries. It's a small place, and doesn't take long to move through, but it usually has one or two surprises to keep you around a bit longer, such as the enigmatic short films shown in its theater. Children's crafts tables provide activities related to current exhibits, and free gallery tours are available by appointment. Across from the museum is the **Volunteer Park Conservatory** (☎ *206/684–4743*). This Victorian-style greenhouse has a magnificent (if cramped) collection of tropical plants. The Anna Clise Orchid Collection, begun in 1919, is at its most spectacular in late fall and early winter, when most of the flowers are in full bloom. The conservatory also has some splendid palm trees, a well-stocked koi pond, and, almost incongruously, a collection of cacti and other succulents. Climbing the 108 steps of the old water tower yields some decent views of the city over the park's tree line as well as some old photos and maps of the park. A focal point of the park, at the western edge of the 445-foot-high hill and in front of the Asian Art Museum, is Isamu Noguchi's sculpture *Black Sun,* carved from a 30-ton block of black granite. Many seem to enjoy taking photos of the Space Needle framed in the 9-foot, 9-inch hole of the "sun." ✉ *Park entrance: 14th Ave. E at Prospect St., Capitol Hill* ⊕ *www.ci.seattle.wa.us/seattle/parks/parkspaces/volpark.htm* ✉ *Free* ☉ *Park daily sunrise–sunset; conservatory May–mid-Sept., daily 10–7, otherwise 10–4.*

♻ ★ **40** **Washington Park Arboretum.** As far as the area's green spaces go, Volunteer Park gets all the attention, but this 230-acre arboretum is far more beautiful. On calm weekdays, the place feels really secluded; though there are trails, you feel like you're freer to roam here than at Discovery Park. The seasons are always on full display: in warm winters, flowering cherries and plums bloom in its protected valleys as early as late February, while the flowering shrubs in Rhododendron Glen and Azalea Way are in full bloom March through June. In autumn, trees and shrubs glow in hues of crimson, pumpkin, and lemon; in winter, plantings chosen specially for their stark and colorful branches dominate the landscape. From March through October, visit the peaceful **Japanese Garden** (☎206/684–4725 ✉$3$3), a compressed world of mountains, forests, rivers, lakes, and tablelands, open daily from 10 AM until sunset. The pond, lined with blooming water irises in spring, has turtles and brightly colored koi. An authentic Japanese teahouse is reserved for tea ceremonies and instruction on the art of serving tea. The Graham Visitors Center at the park's north end has descriptions of the arboretum's flora and fauna, which include 130 endangered plants, as well as brochures, a garden gift shop, and walking-tour maps. ✉2300 Arboretum Dr. E, Capitol Hill ☎206/543–8800 arboretum, 206/684–4725 Japanese garden ⊕http://depts. washington.edu/wpa ✉Free ⊙Park daily 7 AM–sunset, visitor center daily 10–4.

> **THE SWEETEST STRETCH**
>
> Roy Street between Broadway E and Harvard Avenue is a quiet and quaint little street that looks more Europe than Seattle. In addition to some nice shops, you'll find a great coffee shop, Joe Bar, which is a good place to get a crepe in the morning on your way to Volunteer Park. The Massage Sanctuary around the corner on Broadway is excellent. Just strolling down Roy and then heading north on Harvard or Boylston to Prospect and hooking back around down Broadway E past the Bacon Mansion is also pleasurable.

FREMONT & BALLARD

If you ever wondered where the center of the universe is, look no further—the self-styled "Republic of Fremont" was declared just this by its residents in the 1960s. For many years, Fremont enjoyed its reputation as Seattle's most eccentric neighborhood, home to hippies, starving artists, bikers, and rat-race dropouts. But Fremont has lost a lot of its artist cache as the stores along its main strip turn more upscale, luxury condos and town houses appear above the neighborhood's warren of small houses, and rising rents send many longtime residents reluctantly packing (many to nearby Ballard). On weekends, the downtown strip sometimes looks like one big frat party, as a bunch of new bars draw in a very young crowd from Downtown Seattle, the University District, and the city's suburbs.

During the week, however, this pretty neighborhood is peaceful, friendly, and still very much embodies that accepting, laid-back attitude that made it famous. There are a few quintessential sights—mostly works of public art—as well as a few nice boutiques and vintage stores, but the main reason to come to Fremont is to stroll around Fremont Center and along the waterfront, spend a few hours in a coffeehouse, and "just be." The concentration of great restaurants also makes the neighborhood a good midweek dinner and drinks spot.

Ballard, directly to the west of Fremont, is everyone's sweetheart. Seattle residents of all stripes can't help but hold some affection for this neighborhood, even as it enters a new, less-humble phase of existence. Ballard used to be almost exclusively Scandinavian and working-class; it was the logical home for the Swedish and Norwegian immigrants who worked in the area's fishing, shipbuilding, and lumber industries. Reminders of its origins still exist—most literally in the Nordic Heritage Museum—but the neighborhood is undergoing inevitable changes as the number of artists, hipsters, and young professionals (many of whom have been priced out of Fremont and Capitol Hill) increases. Trendy restaurants, upscale furniture stores, and boutiques have popped up all along NW Market Street and Ballard Avenue, the neighborhood's main commercial strips. But no matter how tidy it gets, Ballard doesn't feel as gentrified as Fremont—or as taken with its own coolness as Capitol Hill. Ballard doesn't have many sights; you'll spend more time strolling, shopping, and hanging out than crossing attractions off your list. It's got a great little nightlife and restaurant scene on Ballard Avenue, so you may want to time your visit for later in the day. Ballard Avenue is also the most attractive street in the neighborhood—head here if you want to stroll and window-shop.

Note that the neighborhood is more spread out than it appears on a map. For example, even walking west from the heart of Market Street to the locks and back can be tiring (and not particularly scenic). If you're bringing a car, you'll want to take advantage of the pay parking lot at the locks and then drive back to the commercial area, where you should be able to find street parking. Continuing on to the marina and Golden Gardens Park may not be worth the effort if you don't have a car.

WHAT TO SEE

FREMONT
41
Fremont Center. The neighborhood's small center is comprised of two short strips: Fremont Avenue heading north from the Fremont Bridge to N. 39th Street, and a few blocks of N. 36th Street as it veers west off Fremont Avenue toward Ballard. Both streets have an eclectic bunch of shops, cafés, bars, and small businesses. The area also contains most of Fremont's sights.

Beneath the Aurora Bridge at N. 36th Street lurks the 18-foot-tall *Fremont Troll,* clutching a Volkswagen Beetle in his massive left hand. The giant watches over the neighborhood, and even allows people to crawl up onto his shoulders for the obligatory photo. The troll appeared in 1991, commissioned by the Fremont Arts Council. Like all of Fremont's sculptures, he can't escape a little playful decoration—around Halloween, he's given a bicycle-wheel rim as a nose ring and a giant spider crawls on his shoulder.

When Russian counterrevolutionaries knocked over a 7-ton **statue of Lenin** in 1989, they couldn't have known it would end up in Fremont. A man named Lewis Carpenter toted the statue from Slovakia to Seattle in 1989, and when he died in 1994, it made its way to the neighborhood's Sunday flea market. Soon ousted from this den of capitalism,

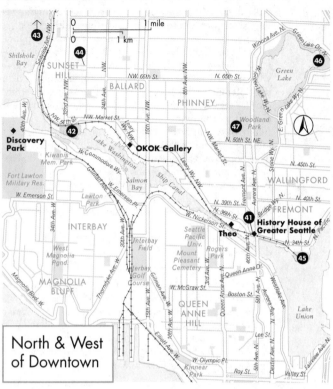

North & West
of Downtown

the bronze Bolshevik now stands proudly in front of a burrito joint on N. 36th Street, between Fremont and Evanston avenues. During Gay Pride Weekend, the commissar is sometimes decked out in pink (skirt, hat, lipstick, and pasties) from head to toe.

Fremont's signature statue, *Waiting for the Interurban,* is a cast aluminum sculpture of five figures, one holding a small child. The Interurban was a light-rail system that operated in the '40s. Residents enjoy dressing and ornamenting the figures for just about any joyful occasion, from retirements to birthdays to declarations of love. Look closely at the dog circling the legs of one figure and you'll see it wears the face of a bearded, ornery-looking man. As the story goes, the onetime honorary mayor of Fremont, Armen Stepanian, was upset with Richard Beyer for choosing himself as the artist to create the statue when no one else applied to the Fremont Arts Council for the job. Beyer had the final word in the brouhaha by putting Stepanian's face on the canine. The sculpture's home is on N. 34th Street, just over the Fremont Bridge at Fremont Avenue.

On the corner of N. 35th Street and Evanston Avenue, look up to spot the 53-foot, Russian-built **Fremont Rocket,** which marks the official center of the center of the universe.

1

There's a lovely stretch of the **Burke-Gilman Trail** along the canal on the west side of the Fremont Bridge. Watch kayakers and small craft float down the river; several benches along the path make it easy to linger for hours.

History House of Greater Seattle. This small museum celebrates the history of Seattle's neighborhoods, mostly through displays of old photographs. ■TIP→ **It's a great way to get a tiny glimpse of the Seattle of yesteryear, especially if you don't have time to go to the Museum of History & Industry in Montlake.** The museum's entrance is bound to grab your eye as you walk by: the iron-wrought gates look like tree branches sprouting colorful houses, butterflies, and the Space Needle; behind them is a fun sculpture garden. ⊠790 N. 34th St., Fremont ☎206/675–8875 ⊕www.historyhouse.org ⊠1$ ⊗Wed.–Sun., noon–5.

★ ⊙ **Theo.** If it weren't for a tiny sign on the sidewalk pointing the way, you'd never know that Fremont has its own chocolate factory. Theo is relatively new to the Northwest's growing artisan chocolate scene, but it has already taken the city by storm, thanks to the high quality of its chocolate and the inventive creations of its head chocolatier. Theo uses only organic, Fair Trade cocoa beans, usually in high percentages—yielding darker, less-sweet, and more-complex flavors then some of their competitors. You'll see Theo chocolate bars for sale in tons of local businesses, from the typical (coffee shops) to the inexplicable (garden stores?!). Stop by the factory to buy exquisite truffles—made daily in small batches—with unusual flavors like basil and lemongrass. The superfriendly staff is extremely generous with samples. You can go behind the scenes as well: tours are offered daily at 1 PM and 3 PM; reservations aren't always necessary, but it's a good idea to call and make sure there's a spot, particularly on weekends. ⊠3400 Phinney Ave. N, Fremont ☎206/632–5100 ⊕www.theochocolate.com ⊠Tour $5 ⊗Store daily 11–5.

BALLARD   **Ballard Locks.** Though staring at a canal may not seem terribly exciting,
⊙ ★ ㊷   the locks—an important passage in the 8-mi Lake Washington Ship Canal that connects Puget Sound's saltwater Shilshole Bay to freshwater Lake Washington and Lake Union—are definitely worth a visit if you're in the area. The canal is quite pretty, especially on a sunny summer day, and you don't have to be an engineering buff to enjoy watching this fascinating system in action. In addition to boat traffic, the locks see an estimated half million salmon and trout make the journey from saltwater to fresh each year with the help of a nearby fish ladder. Finally, a trip to the locks isn't complete without a stroll around the 7-acre Carl English Jr. Botanic Garden. Guided tours of the locks are available; however, the brochure from the visitor center and the plaques by the locks will give you plenty of information if you don't have time for a tour. ⊠3015 NW 54th St., Ballard ⊹From Fremont, head north on Leary Way NW, west on NW Market St., and south on 54th St. ☎206/783–7059 ⊠Free ⊗Locks daily 7 AM–9 PM; visitor center May–Sept., daily 10–6; Oct.–Apr., Thurs.–Mon. 11–4; call for tour information.

43 Golden Gardens Park. There are 3 mi of forest trails in this 87-acre park, but most people come here to sunbathe, brave the cold waters of Puget Sound for a swim, or just sit on the beach. The stretch of sand closest to the parking lot has a snack bar, picnic tables, and restrooms—and the greatest concentration of people. As you walk farther north, the crowds thin out considerably and you'll have no problem finding a peaceful spot or empty bench. And with the Shilshole Bay Marina so close by, you can bet there will be a lot of white sails in the water to make the view of the sound and the Olympic Mountains in the distance that much more enjoyable. Though there is a large parking lot, finding parking here can be challenging, especially on sunny weekends. Be prepared to circle. ⊠ *8498 Seaview Pl. NW, Ballard* ☎ *206/684–4075* ⊠ *Free* ☉ *Daily 6 AM–11:30 PM.*

44 Nordic Heritage Museum. The only educational institute in the country to focus solely on Nordic cultures, this museum in a massive 1900s schoolhouse traces Scandinavian art, artifacts, and heritage all the way from Viking times. Behind the redbrick walls, nine permanent galleries on three floors give an in-depth look at how immigrants from Denmark, Finland, Iceland, Norway, and Sweden came to America and settled in the Pacific Northwest. Among the finds are textiles, china, books, tools, and photographs. Delve into Nordic history in the library; learn a few phrases at the on-site Scandinavian Language Institute; or join in a class or children's program on Nordic arts and crafts. The temporary galleries display paintings, sculpture, and photography by contemporary artists. ⊠ *3014 NW 67th St., Ballard* ☎ *206/789–5707* ⊕ *www.nordicmuseum.org* ⊠ *$6* ☉ *Tues.–Sat. 10–4, Sun. noon–4.*

OKOK Gallery. Part gallery, part store, part rocket-ship ride into pop surrealism, OKOK is a welcome sign that Ballard may finally be able to make a gallery scene work. In a converted garage, OKOK has a white-walled, spotlighted exhibition space showing emerging artists, and a retail space that sells art books and odd, clever toys and collectibles—Sex Pistols action figures, anyone? It's kind of like Archie McPhee's for art majors and hipsters, though Seattleites of all stripes tend to find something to love about this place. ⊠ *5107 Ballard Ave. NW, Ballard* ☎ *206/789–6242* ⊕ *www.weareokok.com* ⊠ *Free* ☉ *Tues.–Sat. noon–6, Sun. 11–5.*

WALLINGFORD & GREEN LAKE

Directly east of Fremont is Wallingford, a low-key residential neighborhood with lovely Craftsman houses. Its main commercial drag is NE 45th Street from Stone Way to I–5, with most of its notable shops and restaurants clustered within a six-block strip. Wallingford's even more laid-back and low profile than Fremont or Ballard, and outside of a few parks, it has no sights per se. But 45th has an eclectic group of shops, from a gourmet beer store to an erotic bakery to a Hawaiiana merchant, along with a great coffee shop.

Free Ballard

Around town you might see bumper stickers or T-shirts with the slogan "Free Ballard." The unofficial motto of the northern neighborhood came about in 2002 as its growth—and the lack of responsible city planning to respond to it—caused a slew of zoning and quality-of-life headaches. The Ballard Chamber of Commerce used "Free Ballard" as a rallying cry to give frustrated residents a voice and get the attention of city hall in a fun way.

You see, Ballard used to be its own city; it wasn't a part of Seattle until 1907 when Ballard residents voted to be "annexed" by the city. The citizens of Ballard were responding to a water crisis—which would be solved by becoming part of Seattle—as well as to myriad promises of new and bet-

ter public services made by Seattle's mayor. Over the years no one's been particularly impressed by how well the City of Seattle has lived up to those long-ago promises; in some ways, Ballard still functions like an autonomous municipality (certain services like street cleaning are still not provided by the city).

Today Ballard residents old and new adopt the slogan for many reasons. Although a few people would like to see Ballard revert to being its own city, many simply see it as a way to express neighborhood pride—a way to remind them and the rest of Seattle that Ballard's unique heritage and way of life must be preserved as it become's one of the hottest neighborhoods in which to live.

There's not as much to do in the Green Lake neighborhood, besides making endless circles around the lake. But if you're roaming around the northern neighborhoods, the lake is worth a detour to get some light exercise while seeing a terrific cross section of Seattle's residents.

WHAT TO SEE

 ★ **45** **Gasworks Park.** Though technically in Wallingford, this lovely park can be easily reached from Fremont Center by strolling along the waterfront Burke-Gilman Trail—remember to stay in the clearly designated pedestrian lane, as you'll be sharing the trail with many other walkers, joggers, and speed-demon bicyclists. The park gets its name from the hulking remains of an old gas plant, which, far from being an eyesore, actually lends some character to the otherwise open, hilly, 20-acre park. Get a good view of Downtown Seattle from the zodiac sculpture at the top of the hill, or feed the ducks on the lake. The sand-bottom playground has monkey bars, wooden platforms, and a spinning metal merry-go-round. Crowds throng to picnic and enjoy outdoor summer concerts, movies, and the Fourth of July fireworks display over Lake Union. ⊠ *North end of Lake Union, N. Northlake Way and Meridian Ave. N, Wallingford* ⊙ *Daily 4* AM–11:30 PM.

46 **Green Lake.** This beautiful 342-acre park is a favorite of Seattleites, who jog, blade, bike, and walk their dogs along the 2.8-mi paved path that surrounds the lake. Beaches on both the east and west sides (around 72nd Street) have lifeguards and swimming rafts. Boats, canoes, kayaks, and paddleboats can be rented at Greenlake Boat Rental on the eastern side of the lake. There are also basketball and tennis courts and baseball and soccer fields. A first-rate play area includes a giant sandbox, swings, slides, and all the climbing equipment a child could ever dream of—plus lots of grassy areas and benches where adults can take a break. The park is generally packed, especially on weekends. And you'd better love dogs: the canine-to-human ratio here is just about even. Surrounding the park are lovely middle- and upper-class homes, plus a compact commercial district where you can grab some snacks after your walk. ⊠*E. Green Lake Dr. N and W. Green Lake Dr. N, Green Lake* ☎*206/684–4075 general info, 206/527–0171 Greenlake Boat Rental* ⊕*www.seattle.gov/parks.*

☾ ★ ㊼ **Woodland Park Zoo.** Many of the 300 species of animals in this 92-acre botanical garden roam freely in habitat areas. A jaguar exhibit is the center of the Tropical Rain Forest area, where rare cats, frogs, and birds evoke South American jungles. The Butterflies & Blooms exhibit ($1) shows off the amazing beauty and variety of the winged creatures and describes their relationship with local flora. With authentic thatch-roof buildings, the African Village has a replica schoolroom overlooking animals roaming the savanna; the Asian Elephant Forest Trail takes you through a Thai village; and the Northern Trail winds past rocky habitats where brown bears, wolves, mountain goats, and otters scramble and play. The terrain is mostly flat, making it easy for wheelchairs and strollers (which can be rented) to negotiate. The zoo has parking for $4; it's a small price to pay to avoid the headache of searching for a space on the street. ⊠*5500 Phinney Ave. N, Phinney Ridge* ☎*206/684–4800* ⊕*www.zoo.org* ▤*Oct.–Apr. $10.50, May–Sept. $15* ☉*Oct.–Apr., daily 9:30–4; May–Sept., daily 9:30–6.*

UNIVERSITY DISTRICT

The U-District, as everyone calls it, is exactly what it sounds like: an extended campus for the students of the University of Washington (UW or "U-Dub" to locals). U-Dub, founded in 1861 in Downtown Seattle, is respected for its research and graduate programs in medicine, nursing, oceanography, Asian studies, drama, physiology, and social work, among many fields.

This area isn't of tremendous interest to most visitors—there aren't many sights to see; driving around the area is a headache, and parking is even worse; and whatever you do, you'll do it in the company of legions of students. That said, there are two museums close to the campus, one if which is the excellent Henry Art Gallery. You can combine a museum stop with a stroll to the campus's lovely main plaza (called Red Square after its brick paving) for a view of both college life and Mt. Rainier. When you get hungry, just head up University Way (simply known as The Ave) for a great selection of cheap ethnic food; the major action along The Ave, which includes coffeehouses, restaurants, bars, shops, and cinemas, is between 42nd and 50th streets. If you want to tour the campus beyond the obligatory stop at Red Square, the university has a visitor center at 4014 University Way NE (at the corner of NE Campus Parkway).

Can You Say "Geoduck"?

So you packed Gore-Tex, khakis, and sensible shoes, and you've mastered the art of ordering complicated espresso drinks with urbane insouciance. Now if only you could pronounce Puyallup without raising local eyebrows. Here's a guide to a few of the Northwest's tongue-twisters.

Alki (AL-ki). Rhymes with high; the point where settlers first landed in this area.

Geoduck (GOOEY-duck). Gigantic clam grown in Puget (PEW-jet) Sound, sometimes weighing in at more than 20 pounds. Often surrounded by gaping tourists at Pike Place Market.

Kalaloch (KLAY-lock). Popular scenic stretch on the wild Pacific side of the Olympic Peninsula.

Poulsbo (PAULS-bo). Charming Scandinavian town on Bainbridge Island treasured for its Norwegian bakeries.

Puyallup (pew-AL-up). Home of the Western Washington Fair, a monthlong shindig held each September. Key phrase: "Do the Puyallup."

Sequim (skwim). Rhymes with swim. Between the Olympic Mountains and the Strait of Juan de Fuca (FEW-kah). Famous for Dungeness (dun-jen-NESS) crabs.

Tacoma (Tah-CO-mah). Growing city 30 mi south of Seattle.

Yakima Valley (YAK-him-uh). South-central Washington's picturesque wine country.

For the record, Washington's neighbor to the south is Oregon (OR-eh-gun), Spokane (spo-KAN) is eastern Washington's largest city, Lake Chelan (sha-LAN) is a spectacular body of water southwest of the Methow (MET-how) Valley, and that snowcapped volcano to the south is Mt. Rainier (ray-NEAR).

⚠ **Parking is really hard to come by, especially on weekends, but don't let your frustration tempt you to park in the Safeway lot or in any other privately owned lot while you explore the area. It may seem like there's no one watching, but you will get ticketed.**

WHAT TO SEE

🕑 ㊽ **Burke Museum of Natural History and Culture.** Totem poles mark the entrance to this museum, where exhibits survey the land and cultures of the Pacific Northwest. Highlights include artifacts from Washington's 35 Native American tribes, dinosaur skeletons, and dioramas depicting the traditions of Pacific Rim cultures. An adjacent ethnobotanical garden is planted with species that were important to the region's Native American communities. For $1 more on the admission price, you get same-day admission to the Henry Art Gallery. ✉ *University of Washington campus, 17th Ave. NE and NE 45th St., University District* ☎ *206/543–5590* ⊕ *www.washington.edu/burkemuseum* ✑ *$8, free 1st Thurs. of month* 🕔 *Daily 10–5, 1st Thurs. of each month 10–8.*

★ ㊾ **Henry Art Gallery.** The Henry is perhaps the best reason to take a side trip to the U-District. The large gallery consistently presents sophisticated and thought-provoking work. A notable recent example: large-scale installations by environmental artist Maya Lin. Exhibits pull from many different genres and include mixed media, photography, 19th-

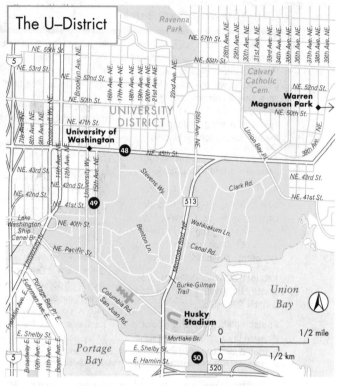

The U–District

and 20th-century paintings, and textiles from the permanent collection. Its permanent installation, *Light Reign,* is a "Skyspace" from artist James Turrell—an elliptical chamber that allows visitors to view the sky (more than a few people have used this as a meditation spot); at night the chamber is illuminated by thousands of LED lights. ⊠ *University of Washington campus, 15th Ave. NE and NE 41st St., University District* ☎ *206/543–2280* ⊕ *www.henryart.org* ⊠ *$10* ⊙ *Tues.–Sun. 11–5, Thurs. until 8.*

⟳ ⑤⓪ **Museum of History & Industry.** Few places are better equipped to help you get a handle on the history of the Pacific Northwest. Since 1952 this museum has collected objects (some dating to 1780) that chronicle the region's economic, social, and cultural history. Factory and mining equipment, gramophones, clothing, newspapers, and everyday items from yesteryear are all on display, many along the re-created Seattle street from the 1880s. The interactive exhibits encourage kids to have fun and learn. On weekends look for educational presentations, family workshops, and historical walks. Students, teachers, and history buffs are always roaming the vast museum library. ⊠ *2700 24th Ave. E, across Montlake Bridge from University, on south side of Union Bay, Montlake* ☎ *206/324–1126* ⊕ *www.seattlehistory.org* ⊠ *$7, free 1st Thurs. of month* ⊙ *Daily 10–5, 1st Thurs. of month 10–8.*

CLOSE UP

Art to Go

Bus shelters around the city are adorned with paintings to ease the boredom of waiting, but no work is more colorful than the Metro Transportation Tunnel, the mile-long bus tunnel that runs underground between the Convention Center (at Terry Avenue and Pine Street) and the International District. Among the artwork near the route's six stations are three 35-foot-long city-sanctioned murals—designed and installed by local artists Fay Jones, Gene Gentry McMahon, and Roger Shimomura—that provide abstract cartoonish interpretations of Downtown landmarks and street scenes in glorious palettes.

It's also hard to miss the sculptures at the stops along the way. A favorite is the awe-inspiring *Temple of Music,* created by Erin Shie Palmer, which tantalizes concertgoers bound for Benaroya Hall from the University Street Station. Best of all, you don't have to pay to see these works, since the tunnel falls within the city's "ride free zone." There are entrances to the tunnel at Ninth Avenue and Pine Street, at the Westlake Center Mall, at Third Avenue between Union and Seneca streets, at Third Avenue between Jefferson Street and Yesler Way, and at Fifth Avenue South and South Jackson Street.

OFF THE BEATEN PATH

Northwest Puppet Museum. In a renovated church in the Maple Leaf neighborhood, the only puppet center in the Northwest highlights the renowned marionettes of the Carter family, professional puppeteers trained by masters from Italy, Romania, and China. For their talents they have received a Fulbright Award and a UNIMA/USA Citation of Excellence, the highest award in American puppet theater. Performances are open to the public on weekends. Recent shows include *The Nutcracker, The Travels of Babar,* and *The Adventures of Sinbad.* Also on-site are a museum, theater, research library, picnic area, playground, and shop where puppet-making workshops and marionette classes are held. ⊠ *9123 15th Ave. NE, University District* ⊹ *Take I–5 north, Exit 171 to Lake City Way, turn left on 15th Ave. NE and continue to 92nd St.* ☎ *206/523–2579* ⊕ *www.nwpuppet.org* ✉ *Varies by performance* ⊙ *Call for performance and workshop schedules.*

Warren Magnuson Park. Jutting into Lake Washington northeast of the University District is this beachside area, also called Sand Point–Magnuson Park. Innovative art is threaded through the grounds, including *Soundgarden,* a series of aluminum tubes mounted to catch the wind and create flutelike music. (Yes, Seattle's famous band named itself after this sculpture.) Morning walkers and joggers often rest on the whale-shape benches to watch the sun rise over Lake Washington—a spectacle that's especially lovely when accompanied by this gentle sound track. The sculpture is in the northern part of the park, through the turnstile and across *Moby Dick* Bridge (embedded with quotes from Melville's novel). To get here from the U-District, you can follow 45th Street east past the University Village shopping center until it turns into Sand Point Way and then follow Sand Point until you reach the park. If you're coming from Downtown, take I–5 to the 65th Street exit and head east on 65th until you reach the park. Note that traffic around University Village is usually pretty slow, especially on weekends. ⊠*Park entrance: Sand Point Way NE at 65th St., Sand Point* ⊕*www.seattle. gov/parks/magnuson.*

WEST SEATTLE

Cross the bridge to West Seattle and it's another world altogether. Jutting out into Elliott Bay and Puget Sound, separated from the city by the Duwamish waterway, this suburb covers most of the city's western peninsula—and, indeed, it has an identity of its own. The first white settlers parked their boat at Alki Point in 1851, planning to build a major city here until they discovered a deeper logging port at today's Pioneer Square. Alki Point Lighthouse sits on the peninsula's northwest tip, a place for classic sunset views. In summer, throngs hang out at Alki Beach—Seattle's taste of California—while others head for the trails and playgrounds of Lincoln Park to the west. The main shopping and dining areas line Alki Avenue, next to the beach, and California and Fauntleroy avenues on the way to the ferry docks.

WHAT TO SEE

Alki Point. Part beach and part park, threaded by biking and running paths, this is the place where David Denny, John Low, and Lee Terry arrived in September 1851, ready to found a city. They stayed here for six months before moving to what is now Pioneer Square; a marker shows where they landed. Also in the park is one of 195 Lady Liberty replicas found around the country. This one, near the 2700 block of Alki Avenue SW, was erected by Boy Scouts in 1952 as part of their national "Strengthening the Arm of Liberty" campaign. The so-called Miss Liberty (or Little Liberty) is a popular meeting point for beachfront picnics and dates. Marvel at the lustrous 50 acres of rugged oldgrowth forest at **Schmitz Park** (⊠*5551 SW Admiral Way, West Seattle*), steps from Alki Beach. Along the neighborhood's southwest edge, near the Fauntleroy ferry terminal, **Lincoln Park** (⊠*5551 SW Admiral Way, West Seattle*) sets acres of old forests, rocky beaches, and such recreational facilities as a playground, a pool, and tennis courts, against views of Puget Sound.

OFF THE BEATEN PATH

Museum of Flight. Boeing, the world's largest builder of aircraft, was founded in Seattle in 1916. So it's not surprising that this facility at Boeing Field, south of the International District, is one of the city's best museums. It's especially fun for kids, who can climb in many of the aircraft and pretend to fly, make flight-related crafts, or attend special programs. The Red Barn, Boeing's original airplane factory, houses an exhibit on the history of flight. The Great Gallery, a dramatic structure designed by Ibsen Nelson, contains more than 20 vintage airplanes. The Personal Courage Wing showcases World War I and World War II fighter planes. ⊠*9404 E. Marginal Way S, Tukwila* ⊹*Take I–5 south to Exit 158, turn right on Marginal Way S* ☎*206/764–5720* ⊕*www. museumofflight.org* ⊡*$14* ⊙*Daily 10–5, 1st Thurs. of every month until 9* PM.

West Seattle Junction. Walk through West Seattle's business district, amid the small restaurants, shops, and businesses, and you'll come across works of art depicting scenes from local history. A few play tricks with perspective, reminiscent of the paintings Wile E. Coyote used in his attempts to trick the Roadrunner. *The Junction* is a perfect example: If not for the row of neatly trimmed laurel bushes just beneath the wall upon which it's painted, you might be tempted to walk right into the picture's 1918 street scene, painted from the perspective of a streetcar. Another mural is taken from a postcard of 1920s Alki. The most colorful, however, is the *The Hi-Yu Parade,* with its rendition of a *Wizard of Oz*–theme float reminding locals of a 1973 summer celebration. ⊠*Along California Ave. SW and Fauntleroy Way SW (between 44th and 47th Aves.), West Seattle* ⊕*www.westseattle.com/site/murals.*

THE EASTSIDE

On the far side of Lake Washington is East King County, the center of which is Bellevue, a fast-growing city with its own downtown, hotels and restaurants, and a music and performance center. North of Bellevue, Woodinville is best known for the Chateau Ste. Michelle and Columbia wineries and the Redhook Brewery, any of which make fun day trips. Buses run to Bellevue, but it's easier to get here—and to the wineries—by car. Note that during rush hour, traffic across the 520 bridge is a nightmare.

WHAT TO SEE

Bellevue Arts Museum. A real feather in Bellevue's cap, this museum presents sophisticated exhibits on craft and design, with a focus on regional artists. Past exhibitions have included glass art from the Pilchuck Glass School Gallery, mixed media from Thomas Mann made from objects and debris found in New Orleans post-Katrina, and a collection of contemporary tapestries. There is no permanent collection. The dramatic puzzle piece–looking building, which really stands out in Bellevue's somewhat uninspired core, is worth the trip alone. In late July, the museum hosts the Bellevue Arts and Crafts Fair, which involves more than 300 local artists and craftspeople. ⊠*510 Bellevue Way NE, Bellevue* ☎*425/519–0770* ⊕*www.bellevuearts.org* ☜*$7* ☉*Tues.–Thurs. and Sat. 10–5:30, Fri. 10–9, Sun. noon–5:30.*

Bellevue Botanical Gardens. This beautiful, 36-acre public area in the middle of Wilburton Hill Park is encircled by spectacular perennial borders, brilliant rhododendron displays, and patches of alpine and rock gardens. Docents lead tours of the gardens nearly every day at 2 PM. ■TIP➜The Yao Japanese garden is beautiful in fall, when the leaves change. One of the most interesting features of the park is the Waterwise Garden, which was planted with greenery that needs little water in summer to demonstrate that not all great gardens require wasteful daily drenchings with a hose or sprinkler system. When you're tired of manicured gardens, take the Lost Meadow Trail, which winds through a heavily forested area, to see nature's disorganized beauty. The gardens are a short drive from Bellevue's core. ⊠*12001 Main St., Bellevue*

☎ *425/452–2750* ⊕*www.bellevuebotanical.org* ✎*Free* ⊙*Gardens daily dawn–dusk, visitor center daily 9–4.*

↻ **Burke-Gilman/Sammamish River Trail.** The 27-mi-long, paved Burke-Gilman Trail runs from Seattle's Gasworks Park, on Lake Union, east along an old railroad right-of-way along the ship canal and then north along Lake Washington's western shore. At Blyth Park in Bothell, the trail becomes the Sammamish River Trail and continues for 10 mi to Marymoor Park, in Redmond. Energetic Seattleites take the trail to Marymoor for the annual Heritage Festival and Fourth of July Fireworks. Except for a stretch of the Sammamish River Trail between Woodinville and Marymoor Park where horses are permitted on a parallel trail, the path is limited to walkers, runners, and bicyclists. ✛ *Take I–90 east to north I–405, then Exit 23 east (Hwy. 522) to Woodinville* ⊠.

Chateau Ste. Michelle Winery. One of the state's oldest wineries is 15 mi northeast of Seattle on 87 wooded acres. Once part of the estate of lumber baron Fred Stimson, it includes the original trout ponds, a carriage house, a caretaker's cottage, formal gardens, and the 1912 family manor house (which is on the National Register of Historic Places). Complimentary wine tastings and cellar tours run throughout the day. ■TIP➡ **Reservations are required for private tours, one week in advance.** You're also invited to picnic and explore the grounds on your own; the wineshop sells delicatessen items. In summer Chateau Ste. Michelle hosts nationally known performers and arts events in its amphitheater. ⊠ *14111 NE 145th St., Woodinville* ✛ *From Downtown Seattle take I–90 east to north I–405; take Exit 23 east (Hwy. 522) to Woodinville exit* ☎ *425/415–3300* ⊕ *www.ste-michelle.com* ✎ *Free* ⊙ *Daily 10–5.*

Columbia Winery. A group of UW professors founded this winery in 1962, making it the state's oldest. Using only European vinifera-style grapes grown in eastern Washington, the founders' aim was to take advantage of the fact that the vineyards share the same latitude as the best wine-producing areas of France. Complimentary wine tastings are held daily; cellar tours are on weekends. The gift shop is open year-round and sells wines and wine-related merchandise. Columbia hosts special food-and-wine events throughout the year. Columbia's vintages aren't as good as Chateau Ste. Michelle's, though some of its higher-end bottles aren't bad. ⊠ *14030 NE 145th St., Woodinville* ✛ *From Downtown Seattle take I–90 east to north I–405; take Exit 23 east (Hwy. 522) to Woodinville exit, go right. Go right again on 175th St., and left on Hwy. 202* ☎ *425/488–2776 or 800/488–2347* ⊕ *www. columbiawinery.com* ✎ *Free* ⊙ *Winery daily 10–6. Tours weekdays at 3:30; Sat. at 11, noon, 3, 4, and 5; Sun. at 11, 2, 3, 4, and 5.*

OFF THE BEATEN PATH

Jimi Hendrix Grave Site. Since his death in 1970, the famed guitarist has rested in Greenwood Cemetery. The site includes a memorial with a domed roof and granite columns. ⊠ *3rd and Monroe Sts., Renton* ✛ *Take I–5 south to I–405 north and the WA–169 south (SE Maple Valley Hwy.) exit, keeping left at fork in the ramp. Merge onto SE*

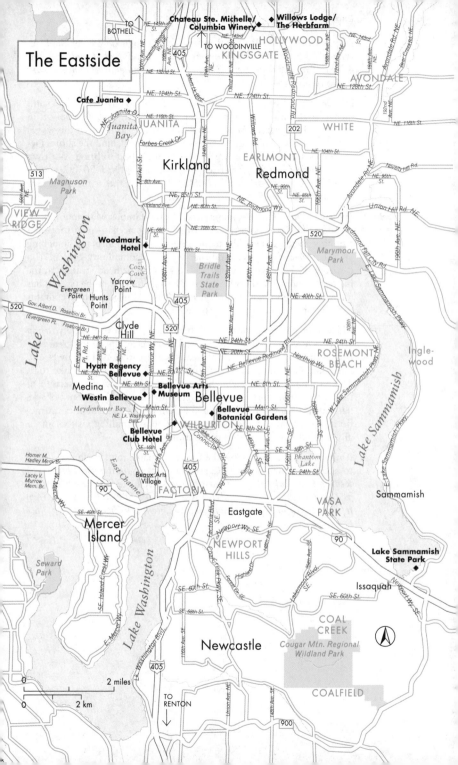

The Eastside

TO BOTHELL

NE 145th St.

Chateau Ste. Michelle/ Columbia Winery ◆   **Willows Lodge/ The Herbfarm** ◆

NE 143rd

TO WOODINVILLE

HOLLYWOOD

KINGSGATE

NE 132nd St.

NE 124th St.

NE 124th St.

AVONDALE

NE 128th St.

NE 116th St.

NE 116th St.

Cafe Juanita ◆

Juanita Bay

JUANITA

WHITE

202

Forbes Creek Dr.

Kirkland

EARLMONT

Redmond

NE 104th St.

513

Magnuson Park

Union Hill Rd. NE

VIEW RIDGE

8th Ave.

NE 85th St.

NE 85th St.

Kirkland Ave.

NE 80th St.

NE 80th St.

NE 70th St.

520

NE 68th St.

NE 68th St.

Woodmark Hotel ◆

NE 60th St.

Marymoor Park

Washington

Cozy Cove

Bridle Trails State Park

Yarrow Point

NE 40th St.

Evergreen Point

Hunts Point

Ingle-wood

520

Gov. Albert D. Rosellini Br.

(Evergreen Pt. Floating Br.)

NE 24th St.

NE 24th St.

Clyde Hill

520

NE 20th St.

ROSEMONT BEACH

Lake

405

NE Bellevue-Redmond Rd.

Hyatt Regency Bellevue ◆

NE 12th

NE 8th St.

NE 8th St.

Medina

Westin Bellevue ◆

Bellevue Arts Museum ◆

Bellevue

Meydenbauer Bay

Main St.

Main St.

Bellevue Botanical Gardens ◆

WILBURTON

SE 8th St.

Bellevue Club Hotel ◆

SE 16th St.

Phantom Lake

Lake Sammamish

Homer M. Hadley Mem. Br.

SE 24th St.

Lacey V. Murrow Mem. Br.

Beaux Arts Village

FACTORIA

90

SE 40th St.

Eastgate

VASA PARK

Sammamish

Mercer Island

NEWPORT HILLS

Newport Wy. SE

90

Seward Park

Lake Sammamish State Park ◆

SE 60th St.

Issaquah

SE 60th St.

Lake Washington

SE 68th St.

COAL CREEK

Newcastle

Cougar Mtn. Regional Wildland Park

405

TO RENTON

COALFIELD

900

0   2 miles

0   2 km

Maple Valley Hwy./WA–169 north. Take a right on Sunset Blvd. N, then a right at NE 3rd St. Continue 1 mi, as NE 3rd St. becomes NE 4th St. Turn right at the 3rd light ⊕*www.jimihendrixmemorial.com* ☉ *Daily sunrise–sunset.*

Lake Sammamish State Park. Eastsiders flock to this day-use park in summer to soak up the sunshine on the sandy beach, then to cool off in the frigid lake waters. Speedboats and kayaks zip through the waves out past the swimming float; hikers follow trails behind the shore. Picnic tables are crowded on weekends—and it's best to bring your own basket rather than test the greasy concessions. ✉*Off I–90W, Issaquah* ☎*425/455–7010 or 800/233–0321* ⊕*www.parks.wa.gov* ☞*Free* ☉ *Daily dawn–dusk.*

★ ☺ **Marymoor Park.** This 640-acre park has the famous Marymoor Velodrome—the Pacific Northwest's sole cycling arena—a 45-foot-high climbing rock, game fields, tennis courts, a model airplane launching area, off-leash dog space, and the Pea Patch community garden. You can row on Lake Sammamish, fish off a pier, or head straight to the picnic grounds or to the Willowmoor Farm, an estate in the park. It has a Dutch-style windmill and the historic Clise Mansion, which contains the Marymoor Museum of Eastside History.

Marymoor has some of the best bird-watching in this largely urban area. It's possible to spot some 24 resident species, including great blue herons, belted kingfishers, buffleheads, short-eared and barn owls, and red-tailed hawks. Occasionally, bald eagles soar past the lakefront. The Sammamish River, which flows through the western section of the park, is an important salmon spawning stream. King County Parks naturalists periodically give guided wildlife tours. With all these attractions, it's no wonder the park has more than 1 million visitors annually—about ¼ of the state's population.

Ambitious hikers can follow the Burke-Gilman/Sammamish River Trail to access the park on foot. ✉*6046 W. Lake Sammamish Pkwy. NE, Redmond* ⊹*Take Rte. 520 east to the West Lake Sammamish Pkwy. exit. Turn right (southbound) on W. Lake Sammamish Pkwy. NE. Turn left at the traffic light* ⊕*www.metrokc.gov/parks/marymoor* ☉ *Daily 8 AM–dusk.*

Where to Eat

WORD OF MOUTH

"Some of my favorite restaurants in Seattle include Le Pichet, which is French bistro fare, the Flying Fish, for excellent seafood, and the Dahlia Lounge, which is a Tom Douglas restaurant. If you go to the Dahlia Lounge, you have to try the coconut pie. It is heavenly!"

—BetsyinKY

Updated
by Carissa
Bluestone

WHAT WAS ONCE A MEAT-AND-POTATOES town is now a culinary capital in its own right. It started with Chinese, Japanese, and French chefs who were inspired by the quality of local produce and seafood and able to cater to an upwardly mobile clientele spawned by the region's software industry. Young American chefs soon moved in and, applying lessons learned from their foreign-born mentors, raised the quality of local cookery even higher. Seattle's culinary revolution seems never-ending.

Seattle has a little bit of everything—well, almost everything—but the city is particularly strong on the following cuisines: its own regional take on American cooking, French, Japanese, and Thai. Latin American offerings are improving but there are still very few great *tacquerias*. The influx of transplanted East Coasters has given the two-fisted sandwich scene a boost, but has yet to produce great pizzerias. Seattle does have quite a few outstanding bakeries, whose breads and desserts you'll see touted on the menus of many restaurants. Though Seattleites consume a lot of seafood and meat, vegetarians and vegans will be happy here, too—the city has several noteworthy vegetarian spots whose offerings go beyond grilled tofu or pasta.

Seattle's chefs are nothing if not inventive. Some have gone off the culinary deep end as the fusion-cooking fad has reached its peak—dining at celebrity chef–owned restaurants can feel like being a judge on "Iron Chef": a roller-coaster ride of amazing new flavors and incredible misfires. Two dominant themes have emerged in the past few years: On one hand, perhaps in response to all the experimentation, it seems like the most popular places these days are doing versions of American comfort food (mac and cheese seems to show up in the strangest places) and very traditional European cooking. On the other hand, many spots are going the opposite route with an all-over-the-map menu of mostly small plates. It's hard to say where the scene will go next as celebrity chefs continue to try to outdo each other, but one thing's for sure: they'll all continue using the high-quality ingredients that makes Pacific Northwest cooking famous, meaning that even their missteps are far more palatable than the successes of restaurants in other food towns.

Although dining well in Seattle isn't cheap, you'll still pay far less for a fancy meal here than in Los Angeles, San Francisco, or New York. What's more, ■TIP➜ most of Seattle's finest restaurants have bar menus from which you can create a respectable meal out of small plates for half the price of a sit-down dinner.

WHAT IT COSTS				
¢	$	$$	$$$	$$$$
AT DINNER under $8	$8–$16	$16–$24	$24–$32	over $32

Prices are per person for a main course, excluding tax and tip.

KNOW-HOW

MEALTIMES

Many of Seattle's better restaurants serve only dinner and are closed Sunday; quite a few are closed Monday. Many that serve lunch during the week do not do so on weekends, though they may offer brunch, which is an increasingly popular activity in Seattle. Unless otherwise noted, the restaurants listed are open daily for lunch and dinner. Seattle restaurants generally serve food until 10 or 11 PM on weekdays and often much later on Friday and Saturday. Outside the city, restaurants stop serving around 9 PM. Though there are a few spots that offer good breakfast menus throughout the week, for locals, breakfast is generally an eat-at-home or a quick grab-a-cup-of-coffee affair. Consequently, most coffeehouses carry terrific pastries and breads from the city's best bakeries.

RESERVATIONS

Seattleites dine out often, so reservations are always a good idea. Reviews note only where they are essential or not accepted. Reservations can often be made a day in advance, but you might have to make them a week or two ahead at the most popular restaurants. If you've just arrived in town and heard about a popular restaurant, it doesn't hurt to call—you'll likely be able to get a reservation for midweek when even hot restaurants don't always reach capacity.

SMOKING

Smoking in restaurants and bars is prohibited in Washington State.

TIPPING

Though tip jars at coffeehouses are usually stuffed with dollar bills, Seattleites are not usually extravagant tippers. Most Seattleites tip 12%–15%. You should leave at least 20% if the service was outstanding, or the server or kitchen fulfilled special requests. A 16%–18% gratuity will automatically be added to bills for larger parties—be sure to check your receipt before adding a tip, or ask your server to be certain.

WHAT TO WEAR

Seattle dining is very informal. It's almost a little too informal—though the city's lack of pretension is one of its charms, the crowd at even the fancier Downtown spots can be downright frumpy. Almost no restaurants require jackets and ties; however, business casual is usually a safe way to go if you're off to a spendy or trendy restaurant. We mention dress only when men are required to wear a jacket or a jacket and tie.

WINE, BEER & SPIRITS

The liquor laws in the state of Washington are stringent. Spirits are sold only in state-run liquor stores, and liquor stores are closed Sunday. The laws are less strict regarding wine and beer, which can be readily found in grocery and convenience stores; in fact, the variety of wines and specialty beers sold in most grocery stores is quite astounding, though it's easy to get stuck with a bad bottle if you don't know what you're looking for.

2

COFFEEHOUSES

Most coffeehouses open by 6 AM on weekdays and no later than 8 AM on weekends; closing hours vary greatly. All coffeehouses are open seven days a week. Almost all accept debit and credit cards, though you may be charged a small fee to use a card if your total is less than $5. Remember to throw some change or a buck or two into the tip jar—baristas, like waiters, depend on tips to help them make a living. Tipping well is also a nice gesture if you plan to spend hours in a place, using the Wi-Fi while nursing one drink.

Most independent coffee shops offer free, unlimited Wi-Fi to customers. The exception to the rule is the local mini-chain Caffe Lladro, which offers only 65 minutes of Wi-Fi with purchase (you're given a log-in code at the register). Of all the big chains, Tully's is the one that offers free Wi-Fi in all locations.

■ TIP→ **Most coffeehouses have a "bus your own table" policy, especially small, independent ones with overworked baristas and long lines.** You're expected to clean up after yourself when you leave. Throw out your trash and place flatware, glasses, and dishes in the black plastic tubs next to the garbage cans. This is something Seattleites do automatically.

DOWNTOWN & BELLTOWN

Cherry Street Coffee House. The coolest branch of this Downtown mini-chain blends the best of old and new Belltown. The interior, with its swaths of cherry red and bright greens, is funky while being sophisticated enough to appeal to the neighborhood's newer, more-monied residents. The coffee, which is the same blend used at Capitol Hill's B&O Espresso, is always good, and there's a small menu of tasty sandwiches. Mornings and weekends can be busy, but weekday afternoons are usually calm and you'll probably be able to snag one of the window seats looking out onto First Avenue. Note that the place closes at 5 PM. ⊠2121 1st Ave., Belltown ☎206/441–7676 ⊠103 Cherry St., Pioneer Square ☎206/621–9372 ⊠808 3rd Ave., Downtown ☎206/442–9372 ⊕www.cherrystreetcoffeehouse.com.

Macrina Bakery. Though not a coffee shop in the strictest sense—it's a bakery with a small café that's very popular for breakfast and brunch—Macrina deserves a mention because a) it serves great coffee, and b) it has the best baked goods in Belltown. Though it's usually too frenzied to invite the hours of idleness that other coffee shops may inspire, Macrina is a great place to take a break on your way to or from the Olympic Sculpture Park—get an iced latte and a piece of ridiculously rich cake. ⊠2408 1st Ave., Belltown ☎206/448–4032 ⊕www.macrinabakery.com.

PIONEER SQUARE & THE INTERNATIONAL DISTRICT

Panama Hotel Tea and Coffee Shop. On the ground floor of the historic Panama Hotel is a serene teahouse with tons of personality and a subtle Asian flair that reflects its former life as a Japanese bathhouse. The space is lovely, with exposed-brick walls, shiny, hardwood floors, and black-and-white photos of old Seattle (many of them relating to the history of the city's Japanese immigrants). Kick back with an individual pot of tea—there are dozens of varieties—or an espresso. This is a good place to bring a book, as it's usually calm and quiet. No credit cards. ✉ *605½ S. Main St., International District* ☎ *206/223-9242* ⊕ *www. panamahotel.net.*

★ **Zeitgeist Coffee.** Not only is Zeitgeist one of the few decent coffee shops in the southern part of the city core, it is also a local favorite. Even Seattleites who don't particularly like Pioneer Square will happily hunt for parking to spend a few hours here, maybe stopping by Elliott Bay Book Company first, which is around the corner on First Avenue. Housed in one of Pioneer Square's great brick buildings, with high ceilings and a few artfully exposed ducts and pipes, Zeitgeist has a simple, classy look that's the perfect backdrop for the frequent art shows held here. You'll feel smarter just sitting in here. ✉ *171 S. Jackson St., Pioneer Square* ☎ *206/583-0497* ⊕ *http://zeitgeistcoffee.com.*

QUEEN ANNE & SEATTLE CENTER

★ **Caffe Fiore.** Blissfully removed from the hubbub of Queen Anne Avenue, the Queen Anne branch of this mini-chain (the other branch is tucked away in the northern reaches of Ballard) is in the bottom floor of a house that's been painted and decorated to match the brand's deep-cocoa-and-burnt-orange logo—it's a very cozy spot to spend a few hours. The coffee is some of the best in the city—in fact, you'll see Caffe Fiore roasts sold in other shops. ✉ *224 W. Galer St., Queen Anne* ☎ *206/282-1441* ⊕ *www.caffefiore.com.*

El Diablo. El Diablo is a Latin coffeehouse that serves Cuban-style coffee and delicious, authentic Mexican hot chocolate. If you don't want coffee, you can also get a *batido,* a Cuban shake made with real fruit. The interior is splashed with bright yellows, reds, blues, and purples, and most surfaces are covered with murals. It's a bit loud, both in appearance and in noise level—it seems like customers should be sitting around piles of chips and guacamole and giant margaritas, not mugs of coffee—but it's fun and certainly unique among Seattle's java stops. El Diablo is open late (until midnight on Friday and Saturday and until 11 all other days) and has live music several nights a week. At night, they serve sangria and beer, too. ✉ *1811 Queen Anne Ave. N, Queen Anne* ☎ *206/285-0693* ⊕ *www.eldiablocoffee.com.*

CAPITOL HILL

B&O Espresso. A cute, cozy neighborhood favorite that looks like a funky, shabby-chic version of a Victorian tearoom, B&O was one of Seattle's earliest purveyors of the latte, and the drinks are still great. The on-site bakery turns out great desserts. The place is always packed for weekend brunch. It's less of a hipster scene than some of the Hill's coffeehouses. ✉ *204 Belmont Ave. E, Capitol Hill* ☎ *206/322-5028.*

Bauhaus. A great place to people-watch if you enjoy watching people— from punk rockers to professors—take themselves too seriously. Attitudey patrons aside, the coffee's good, the baristas are always pleasant, and the bi-level space is big enough that you won't have to fight for room to lay down your laptop. The bookshelf-lined walls (full of art and architecture books) make the interior of this café a little more interesting than most. ✉ *301 E. Pine St., Capitol Hill* ☎ *206/625-1600.*

Faire Gallery Cafe. Another coffee shop that does double, make that triple, duty, Faire offers coffee and sandwiches, art exhibitions, and live music in its small bi-level space. If that isn't enough to keep you occupied, there are also a few board games lying around. The café, which is quite a bit calmer than some of its competitors in the busy Pike–Pine corridor, is a great place to chill out before or after slogging around the Hill. There's live jazz every Sunday starting at 8 PM. ⊠ *1351 E. Olive Way, Capitol Hill* ☎*652–9444* ⊕*www.fairegallerycafe.com.*

Joe Bar. Tiny Joe Bar is one of the most charming coffee shops in the city, partly thanks to its location on a serene side street and partly thanks to its intimate yet cheery space. Light pours in through the storefront, which is made up almost entirely of leaded glass panels. A few café tables are perched in front of lime-green walls; a small mezzanine and a few outdoor tables provide some additional seating. Joe Bar serves savory crepes in the morning and beer and wine in the evening, making it more than a place to get your caffeine fix. The coffee isn't the best in the city, but it's pretty good. ⊠ *810 E. Roy St., Capitol Hill* ☎*206/324–0407* ⊕*www.joebar.org.*

★ **Victrola Coffee & Art.** Victrola is probably the most loved of Capitol Hill's many coffeehouses, and it's easy to see why. The space is lovely, the coffee and pastries are fantastic, the baristas are skillful, and everyone, from soccer moms to indie rockers, is made to feel like this neighborhood spot exists just for them. Unfortunately, it can be hard to score a table here, especially if you have a big group. If 15th Avenue is too far off the beaten path for you, there's a new branch on Pike between Melrose and Bellevue. ⊠ *411 15th Ave. E, Capitol Hill* ☎*206/325–6520* ⊕*www.victrolacoffee.net.*

Fodor'sChoice
★ **Vivace Roasteria.** Vivace is considered by many to be the home of Seattle's finest espresso. In fact, they're so dedicated to serving espresso, they don't even offer drip coffee. A long, curving bar and checkerboard floor add some character to a space that might otherwise look like a diner. The place has got a great energy—lively and bustling, where Hill residents tap on laptops and students from the nearby colleges hold study groups—but it's not necessarily a good spot for a quiet read. There's another branch right across the way from REI on Yale Avenue. ⊠ *901 E. Denny Way, Capitol Hill* ☎*206/860–5869* ⊕*www. espressovivace.com.*

FREMONT

★ **Fremont Coffee Company.** This is a second home (and office) to many writers, freelancers, students, and assorted Fremont residents. It helps that the coffeehouse is actually a small house with a wonderful wraparound porch, and that the baristas are some of the friendliest in the city. The coffee's great, too. Inside seating is less comfortable, so save this one for a sunny day. ⊠ *459 N. 36th St., Fremont* ☎*206/632–3633* ⊕*www.fremontcoffee.net.*

Lighthouse Roasters. The lone retail outfit for a popular roasting house whose blends are used in many restaurants and cafés is a popular neighborhood spot off the tourist track (it requires cresting that nasty hill that you can see from more-accessible perches on N 36th Street). Every day of the week, you'll find folks gathered on the wooden benches outside the cheery yellow storefront or on the set of concrete steps adjacent to the building. No Wi-Fi. ✉*400 N. 43rd St., Fremont* ☎*206/634–3140* ⊕*www.lighthouseroasters.com.*

BALLARD

Mr. Spots Chai House. Mr. Spots does indeed serve a mean chai, in addition to the usual coffee drinks and café nibbles. This place is very unassuming, almost self-consciously so—the furniture is a mix of fabric-draped secondhand-store chairs and sofas and wicker chairs and wood tables that could have had a first life in a hotel lobby. Poetry readings, live music, and open-mike sessions occur nightly—as for daytime entertainment, maybe one of the baristas will sing along with the stereo. As befitting a chai house, there's a healthy dose of hippie here—from the cheesy Tibetan crafts and aromatherapy oils on sale to some of the customers, who seem to be straight from central casting—but the crowd is usually pretty mixed. ✉*5463 Leary Way, Ballard* ☎*206/297–2424* ⊕*www.chaihouse.com.*

WALLINGFORD & GREEN LAKE

Teahouse Kuan Yin. If you're looking for Asian chic or Victorian elegance, go elsewhere—as far as atmosphere and decor are concerned, Kuan Yin could double as a curry house, with its warm yellow walls and its takeout-joint tables decorated with bright Indian-print tablecloths. But serenity reigns here—turn off that cell phone—and you'll find regulars quietly chatting, reading, and studying. The tea selection is outstanding and the knowledgeable staff will help you choose one. Rich scones, berry pies, and green-tea ice cream leaven the mix. ✉*1911 N. 45th St., Wallingford* ☎*206/632–2055.*

★ **Zoka.** This bustling coffeehouse halfway between Green Lake and Wallingford sees everyone from UW law students to old-school hippies playing chess or Chinese checkers. It's often busy and sometimes the line for drinks can get long, but you'll usually find a spot—the place is spacious and loaded with tables and couches. Despite the fact that everyone here seems to be intently wrapped up in something—whether it be a laptop screen, textbook, or conversation about how they plan to save the world once their postgraduate work is done—Zoka can be a great place to kick back in for a few hours and the burst of energy is especially welcome on slow, rainy days. ✉*2200 N. 56th St., Wallingford* ☎*206/545–4277* ⊕*www.zokacoffee.com.*

UNIVERSITY DISTRICT

Trabant Chai Lounge. A trip here would be worth it for the chai alone (which comes in so many varieties, you'll be staring at the menu board for at least 10 minutes), but Trabant is special because it offers the best of the college coffeehouse experience. Sure, you'll see school clubs and activist groups in intense discussions, but this place hardly feels like an extension of the UW cafeteria. It's a colorful, happily laid-back place to work, chat, or just check your e-mail at one of the shared computers. If you're concerned about being 30 years older than everyone else in the room, don't worry—they'll just assume you're a professor. ✉*1309 NE 45th St., University District* ☎*206/675–0668* ⊕*www.trabantchailounge.com.*

World Cup. Some of Ravenna, the calmer residential neighborhood to the north of the U-District, must have trickled down here, because amid a strip of college bars and a comedy club is a classy little coffeehouse and wineshop. Yup, you read that correctly. One half of World Cup is a pretty little café with ornately carved, heavy wooden chairs and tables; the other half is literally a wall of wine bottles. You can get a coffee, tea, or chai along with a tasty sandwich or panini. In the evening you can relax with a glass of wine or port and play a game of chess or one of the board games stacked against one wall. Wednesday nights host either wine tastings or trivia contests and there is often live music on Saturday nights. ■TIP➔ This is a great place to stop before heading over to the Grand Illusion cinema for an art flick. ⊠ *5200 Roosevelt Way NE, University District* ☎*206/729–4929* ⊕*www.worldcupespressoandwine.com.*

RESTAURANTS

DOWNTOWN

AMERICAN

$$–$$$$ ✕ **13 Coins.** 13 Coins is a wonderful oddity. One of the few restaurants open 24 hours a day, the place nearly defies description. To say it seems stuck in time, circa 1967, would be true, but it's really stuck in another universe altogether. Maybe it's those ridiculously out-of-proportion, high-back booths, but the place reminds us of Alice's mad tea party presided over by waiters who stumbled into a wormhole somewhere in Brooklyn, New York. Service is downright entertaining—half the fun of coming here, especially late at night, is listening to the waiters and cooks banter as dishes are whisked around. The food is upscale diner fare, consistently good but a bit overpriced. Though the menu does include some standbys like a good cheesesteak and huge frittatas—don't expect hamburgers, fries, and mozzarella sticks here. Menu benchmarks include liver and onions, jumbo shrimp on ice, and platters of steak and pasta big enough to stuff a logger. Seafood dishes aren't quite up to Seattle's high standards, but the steamed clams and the baked king salmon fillet are decent. ⊠ *1125 Boren Ave. N, Downtown* ☎*206/682–2513* ⊕*www.13coins.com* ⚑*Reservations not accepted* ▤*AE, D, MC, V.*

$$–$$$ ✕ **Place Pigalle.** Large windows look out on Elliott Bay in this cozy spot tucked behind a meat vendor in Pike Place Market's main arcade. In nice weather, open windows let in the fresh salt breeze. Flowers brighten each table, and the staff is warm and welcoming. Despite its name, this restaurant only has a few French flourishes on an otherwise American/Pacific Northwest menu. Go for the rich oyster stew, the Dungeness crab (in season), or the fish of the day. Local microbrews are usually on tap, and the wine list is thoughtfully compact. ⊠ *81 Pike Pl. Market, Downtown* ☎*206/624–1756* ▤*AE, MC, V* ☾*Closed Sun.*

$–$$ ✕ **Matt's in the Market.** Your first dinner at Matt's is like a first date you
Fodor'sChoice hope will never end. The crown jewel of the Market-area restaurants,
★ Matt's redefined intimate dining and personal service when it opened

2

its 23-seat spot on the second floor of the Corner Market Building. A recent expansion nearly doubled the amount of seats, but the basics remain: a lunch counter perfect for grabbing a delicious po'boy or cup of gumbo, an inviting space with simple adornments like clear glass vases filled with flowers from the market, a seasonal menu that synthesizes the best picks from the restaurant's neighbors, and an excellent wine list. At dinner, starters might include such delectable items as Manila clams steamed in beer, herbs, and chilies; entrées always include at least one catch of the day and one good vegetarian option. And yes, there is a Matt—he's a hell of a nice guy and is often in the restaurant chatting with regulars. ⊠ *94 Pike St., Suite 32, Downtown* ☎*206/467–7909* ⊕*www.mattsinthemarket.com* ⌑ *Reservations essential* ▤*MC, V* ⊗*Closed Sun.*

¢–$ ✕**FareStart.** The homeless men and women who operate this café, a project of the FareStart job-training program, prepare an American-style lunch of sandwiches, burgers, and fries during the week. Reservations are essential for the $25 Thursday dinner, prepared by a guest chef from a restaurant such as Ray's Boathouse or the Metropolitan Grill. The cuisine changes with the chef. Whenever you go, you're assured a great meal for a great cause and a real taste of Seattle's community spirit. ⊠ *700 Virginia St., Downtown* ☎*206/443–1233* ⊕*www.fare-start.org* ▤*D, MC, V* ⊗*No lunch weekends. No dinner Fri.–Wed.*

¢–$ ✕**Three Girls Bakery.** Pike Place Market is such a tourist trap that the selection of quick and cheap lunch options is pretty dismal. Rest assured that Three Girls Bakery knows how to make a sandwich and they don't skimp on the fillings. Soups are also very good and of course the baked goods are outstanding. This isn't a place to enjoy a sit-down meal, and service can be a bit brusque, so plan on taking your meatloaf sandwich and macaroons elsewhere. ⊠ *1514 Pike Pl., Downtown* ☎*206/622–1045* ▤*No credit cards.*

ECLECTIC

$$–$$$ ✕**Andaluca.** This secluded spot downstairs at the Mayflower Park Hotel offers a synthesis of fresh local ingredients and Mediterranean flavors. Small plates can act as starters or be combined for a satisfying meal. A Dungeness crab tower with avocado, hearts of palm, and gazpacho salsa is cool and light, while the beef tenderloin with pears and blue cheese is a glorious trip to the opposite end of the sensory spectrum. Cozy booth seating makes this a great spot for a romantic dinner. ⊠ *407 Olive Way, Downtown* ☎*206/382–6999* ⊕*www.anda-luca.com* ▤*AE, D, DC, MC, V.*

$–$$ ✕**Marazul.** Does the world really need another "fusion tapas" place? Probably not, but Marazul has added something positive to Seattle's dining scene. The tapas are literally all over the map—Cuban, Caribbean, and pan-Asian influences are responsible for items like miso seviche and Jamaican jerk salmon sushi, most of which are very successful experiments. A vague island theme (and gallons of premium and hard-to-find rums) holds everything together, but don't expect steel-drum music and giant drinks with umbrellas—Marazul is hip and sexy, with its mix of exotic woods, its gorgeous copper-accented rum bar, and its separate tatami room. Even the gimmicky touches like mah-jongg

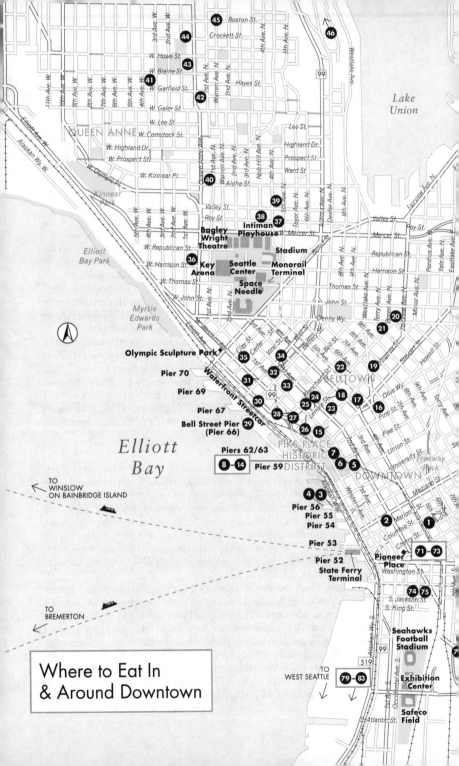

Downtown	
Andaluca	**17**
Campagne	**13**
Copacabana	**9**
Dahlia Lounge	**18**
Elliott's Oyster House	**4**
Emmett Watson's Oyster Bar	**8**
FareStart	**19**
Il Fornaio	**16**
Marazul	**21**
Matt's in the Market	**6**
Maximilien	**14**
McCormick's Fish House	**1**
Metropolitan Grill	**2**
Le Pichet	**15**
Pink Door	**10**
Place Pigalle	**12**
El Puerco Lloron	**11**
Steamers	**3**
13 Coins	**20**
Three Girls Bakery	**7**
Union	**5**

Belltown	
Anthony's Pier 66	**29**
Brasa	**23**
Cascadia	**33**
Cherry Street Coffee	**26**
Etta's Seafood	**28**
Flying Fish	**27**
El Gaucho	**31**
Macrina Bakery	**32**
Mike's East Coast Sandwiches	**35**
Palace Kitchen	**22**
Restaurant Zoë	**25**
Saito's Japanese Café and Bar	**24**
Shiro's	**34**
Six Seven	**30**

Queen Anne	
Bahn Thai	**37**
Bamboo Garden	**38**
Caffe Fiore	**41**
Canlis	**46**
Chinoise Café	**45**
Crow	**39**
Dick's Drive-In	**36**
El Diablo	**43**
Five Spot	**42**
Paragon	**44**
Veil	**40**

I.D. & Pioneer Square	
Cafe Paloma	**71**
Chinoise Café	**78**
Green Leaf	**65**
Hing Loon	**76**
Linyen	**66**
Malay Satay Hut	**63**
Maneki	**68**
Mitchelli's	**73**
Panama Hotel	**70**
Salumi	**75**
Sichuanese Cuisine	**64**
Takohachi	**69**
Il Terrazzo Carmine	**72**
Top Gun	**67**
Uwajimaya Village Food Court	**77**
Zeitgeist	**74**

Central District	
Assimba Ethiopian Cuisine	**61**
Ezell's Fried Chicken	**62**

Capitol Hill	
B&O Expresso	**54**
Ballet	**59**
Bauhaus	**57**
Café Septieme	**51**
Coastal Kitchen	**50**
Crave	**60**
Dick's Drive-In	**52**
Dinette	**55**
Faire Gallery/Cafe	**56**
Honeyhole Sandwiches	**58**
Jamjuree	**48**
Joe Bar	**47**
Victrola Coffee & Art	**49**
Vivace Roasteria	**53**

West Seattle	
Alki Bakery	**79**
Endolyne Joe's	**80**
Ephesus Restaurant	**81**
Luna Park Café	**82**
Salty's on Alki	**83**

and dominos games at the bar and world music on the sound system are fun and tastefully executed. Patio seating is available in summer. Breakfast and lunch are served daily, a novel concept for a trendy spot. ⊠*2200 Westlake Ave., South Lake Union* ☎*206/654–8170* ⊕*www. marazulrestaurant.com* ▤*MC, V.*

FRENCH

$$–$$$$ ✕**Maximilien.** Despite its great views of the sound and the Olympic Mountains, romantic Maximilien remains a well-kept secret. That's because it's tucked away in Pike Place Market behind Market Spice and a butcher shop, and it's not easy to find unless you know the way. Persevere; you'll be delighted. Under previous owner François Kissel, Maximilien was one of Julia Child's favorite Seattle restaurants. Nothing much has changed under the current owner (and former employee) Axel Macé: the bistro-style food is still very good, and the mood is still very French. ⊠*1333 5th Ave., Downtown* ☎*206/682-7270* ▤*AE, D, DC, MC, V.*

$$–$$$ ✕**Campagne.** The white walls, picture windows, snowy linens, fresh flowers, and candles at this urbane restaurant overlooking Pike Place Market and Elliott Bay evoke Provence. So does the robust French country fare, with starters such as seafood sausage, and calamari fillets with ground almonds. Main plates include panfried scallops with a green-peppercorn-and-tarragon sauce, cinnamon-roasted quail served with carrot and orange essence, and Oregon rabbit with an apricot-cider-and-green-peppercorn sauce. ∎TIP→ **Campagne is open only for dinner, but the adjacent Café Campagne serves breakfast, lunch, and dinner daily.** ⊠*Inn at the Market, 86 Pine St., Downtown* ☎*206/728-2800* ⊕*www.campagnerestaurant.com* ⌲*Reservations essential* ▤*AE, DC, MC, V* ☽*No lunch.*

$–$$
Fodor'sChoice
★
✕**Le Pichet.** Slate tabletops, tile floor, and rolled-zinc bar transport you out of Downtown Seattle and into Paris, 1934. Blackboards spell out the specials. Wines are served from the earthenware *pichets* that inspired the brasserie's name. The menu is heartbreakingly French: at lunch there are rustic pâtés and *jambon et fromage* (ham-and-cheese) sandwiches on crusty baguettes; dinner sees homemade sausages, daily fish specials, and steak tartare. The roast chicken (for two) takes an hour to prepare and is worth every second you'll wait. It's enough to make you think the French invented soul food. Dinner reservations are essential. ⊠*1933 1st Ave., Downtown* ☎*206/256-1499* ⊕*www. lepichetseattle.com* ▤*MC, V.*

ITALIAN

$–$$ ✕**Pink Door.** With its Post Alley entrance and meager signage, many enjoy the Pink Door's speakeasy-ness almost as much as the savory Italian food. In warm months patrons partake on the deck shaded by a grape arbor while enjoying the stunning view of Elliott Bay. The roasted garlic and tapenade are eminently shareable appetizers; spaghetti *alla puttanesca* (with anchovies, capers, and tomatoes), and cioppino are standout entrées, though nothing stands too far out—people come here mostly for the atmosphere. The whimsical bar is often crowded, the staff is saucy and irreverent, and cabaret acts regularly perform on a

CLOSE UP

On the Menu

Seattle is a food city, with easy access to an incredible bounty of foods from land and sea, both wild and farm-raised. Many Seattleites tend kitchen gardens, hunt and fish, trap crabs, dig clams, harvest berries in season, and cross the mountains to pick fruit in the Wenatchee and Yakima valleys. Gathering fresh foods at the source has honed local palates: Seattleites know—by taste, smell, and touch—when foods are fresh and at their peak.

Wild salmon has played an important role in local cookery, but its importance has diminished due to a decades-long decline in stocks. Still plentiful are halibut, rockfish, Dungeness crab, spot prawns, and geoduck clams as well as blackberries, huckleberries, mushrooms, and wild greens.

Seattle's chefs purchase ingredients whenever possible from regional farms, orchards, and dairies. Asparagus, tomatoes, and hot peppers arrive from the Yakima Valley; mild onions from Walla Walla; apricots and pears from Wenatchee; apples from Lake Chelan. Lamb and beef come from dryland pastures, while clams and

oysters are harvested from tidal flats in Samish Bay, the Hood Canal, and Willapa Bay. Even salmon is now farmed, and thus available year-round. Pike Place Market, a local institution since 1907, is another source of high-quality ingredients.

Because Seattle is a multiethnic city, local cooks and chefs have evolved several cooking styles. Preparations can be very plain, such as razor clams dipped in milk, egg, and cracker crumbs and panfried, or complex, like meat and seafood dishes enhanced by fruit sauces in the Sephardic tradition. Local chefs' obsessions with the freshest seasonal ingredients may make it difficult to get the same dish twice—especially at top-notch restaurants, where menus change seasonally, if not daily.

Comfort food has its niche here, too, with yummy clam chowder, buttermilk-batter fried chicken with mashed potatoes, pasta and smoked salmon, and pan-roasted breast of duck with aromatic spices. No Northwest meal is complete, of course, without a bottle of wine from a regional winery or ale from a local microbrewery.

small corner stage. There's no place quite like it. ⊠*1919 Post Alley, Downtown* ☎*206/443–3241* ⊕*www.thepinkdoor.net* ⌲*Reservations essential* ⊟*AE, MC, V* ⊘*No lunch Sun.*

¢–$$ ✕**Il Fornaio.** This Italian restaurant dominates the Pacific Place Mall that houses it. When shopping, there seems to be an opportunity to give them your custom at every turn. There's a casual café on the street level, then an even more-casual espresso counter on the mall's first level, and finally the elegant full-service dining room. Though the fresh breads and wood-fired pizzas are widely acclaimed, the entire menu has much to offer. Noteworthy are the seasonal antipasti, vegetarian minestrone, handmade ravioli stuffed with Swiss chard, and the rosemary-scented rotisserie chicken. ⊠*600 Pine St., Downtown* ☎*206/264–0994* ⊕*www.ilfornaio.com* ⊟*AE, DC, MC, V.*

LATIN

$ ✕**Copacabana.** Much of the strategy that preserved Pike Place Market in the 1960s was hatched at this small Bolivian café. The food served here includes such tasty fare as spicy shrimp soup, *saltenas* (savory meat-and-vegetable pies), paella, and *pescado á la Español* (halibut in a saffron-tomato-onion sauce). Tasty food, cold beer, and great views are good reasons to linger. ⊠*1520 1st Ave., Downtown* ☎*206/622–6359* ⌂*Reservations not accepted* ⊟*AE, D, MC, V* ☉*No dinner weekdays or Sun.*

MEXICAN

¢–$ ✕**El Puerco Lloron.** This funky, cafeteria-style diner has some open-air terrace seating on the Pike Place Market Hill Climb, offering views of Elliott Bay on sunny days. It's also got some of Seattle's best and most authentic Mexican cooking—simple, tasty, and inexpensive. More-ambitious highlights include perfect *chiles rellenos* (mild green peppers that are breaded, stuffed with cheese, and fried) and a particularly flavorful guacamole. ⊠*501 Western Ave., Downtown* ☎*206/624–0541* ⊟*AE, MC, V.*

PACIFIC NORTHWEST

$$$–$$$$ ✕**Dahlia Lounge.** Romantic Dahlia started the valentine-red walls trend and it's still working its magic on Seattle couples. It's cozy and then some, but the food plays its part, too. Crab cakes, served as an entrée or an appetizer, lead an ever-changing regionally oriented menu. Other standouts are seared ahi tuna, near-perfect gnocchi, and such desserts as coconut-cream pie and fresh fruit cobblers. Seattle's most energetic restaurateur, chef-owner Tom Douglas also owns Etta's Seafood in Pike Place Market, and the excellent Palace Kitchen on Fifth Avenue. But Dahlia is the one that makes your heart go pitter-patter. ⊠*2001 4th Ave., Downtown* ☎*206/682–4142* ⊕*www.tomdouglas.com/dahlia* ⌂*Reservations essential* ⊟*AE, D, DC, MC, V* ☉*No lunch weekends.*

★ $$$ ✕**Union.** Don't expect to be overwhelmed by wacky design elements or mystified by culinary acrobatics. Do expect to be filled with an inexplicable feeling of well-being when you look back on your meal weeks or even months later. Dining at Union is a special experience, but everything about the place is so understated, the experience may take a while to process. Though from the street the restaurant looks very sleek and a little standoffish (yes, there are an awful lot of red and gray accents), the space becomes very cozy once you settle in; everyone seems like they're either regulars or want to be regulars, and you'll be free to relax here and savor every bite. Fresh ingredients come from Pike Place Market and the menu changes daily to accommodate what's available. Seafood is the strong point—no one cooks a scallop better than Union—but selections always include some type of pork dish, as well as fowl. Entrées are outstanding and reasonably priced, but you might opt to concoct a meal out of starters, which are more fun and inventive. The Dungeness crab salad with avocado and basil oil is always on the menu and it's a must. The wine list is excellent and servers are great at giving advice on which bottle to select. ⊠*1400 1st Ave., Downtown* ☎*206/838–8000* ⊕*www.unionseattle.com* ⊟*AE, MC, V* ☉*No lunch.*

SEAFOOD

$–$$$$ ✕**Elliott's Oyster House.** No place in Seattle serves better Dungeness crab or oysters than Elliott's, which has gotten the presentation of fresh seafood down to a fine art. You can't go wrong with the local rock-fish or salmon. The dining room is bright, and there's a great view of Elliott Bay and of the harbor tour boats next door. On sunny days the place is packed with diners from all over the country who have come to learn what Seattle is all about. That said, the crowd is usually split fifty-fifty between tourists and locals, as Seattleites still fully embrace this place, especially the raw-bar happy hour. ⊠*Pier 56 off Alaskan Way, Downtown* ☎*206/623–4340* ⊕*http://elliottsoysterhouse.com* ⊟*AE, DC, MC, V.*

$–$$ ✕**McCormick's Fish House.** Happy hours at this restaurant are popular with the after-work crowd; prices are great (there's a $2 bar menu), and the selection is good—burgers, spring rolls, taquitas, oysters, and more. The dining room specializes in typical steak and seafood fare. The raw bar here has the largest selection of oysters in town. There's open-air dining in front. The food and good times are so consistent here that even chain-hating Seattleites don't mind patronizing the place. ⊠*722 4th Ave., Downtown* ☎*206/682–3900* ⊕*www.mccormicksandschmicks.com* ⊟*AE, D, DC, MC, V* ⊙*No lunch weekends.*

★ ¢–$ ✕**Emmett Watson's Oyster Bar.** This unpretentious spot can be hard to find—it's in the back of Pike Place Market's Soames-Dunn Building, facing a small flower-bedecked courtyard. But for those who know their oysters, finding this place is worth the effort. Not only are the oysters very fresh and the beer icy cold, but both are inexpensive and available in any number of varieties. If you don't like oysters, try the salmon soup or the fish-and-chips—flaky pieces of fish with very little grease. ⊠*1916 Pike Pl., Downtown* ☎*206/448–7721* ⚖*Reservations not accepted* ⊟*No credit cards* ⊙*No dinner Sun.*

¢–$ ✕**Steamers.** This friendly restaurant serves fish-and-chips, freshly steamed clams, and other local seafood favorites in a casual setting a small step above fast-food takeout. The flame-broiled burgers are tasty, too. On sunny days you can sit outside on the dock and have your steamers and beer alfresco. ∎TIP➔ **Its location near the aquarium means it's pretty touristy, but the food's much better than at the equally touristy Ivar's.** ⊠*Pier 56 off Alaskan Way, Downtown* ☎*206/623–2066* ⚖*Reservations not accepted* ⊟*D, MC, V.*

STEAK

$$$–$$$$ ✕**Metropolitan Grill.** This favorite lunch spot of the white-collar crowd is not for timid eaters: custom-aged mesquite-broiled steaks—arguably the best in Seattle—are huge and come with baked potatoes or pasta. Even the veal chop is extra thick. Lamb, chicken, and seafood entrées are also on the menu. The Met's take on a steak house is either "classic" or a caricature, depending on how you take to the cigar-and-cognac vibe: waiters wear tuxes, fixtures are made of brass and the bar is made of black marble, and the crowd is comprised of Seattle's relatively small population of movers and shakers. ⊠*818 2nd Ave., Downtown* ☎*206/624–3287* ⊕*www.themetropolitangrill.com* ⊟*AE, D, DC, MC, V* ⊙*No lunch weekends.*

BELLTOWN

AMERICAN

★ **$$-$$$** ✕ **Restaurant Zoë.** Reservations are sought after at this chic eatery on a high-trafficked corner. Its tall windows, lively bar scene, and charming waitstaff add to the popularity, which comes mainly from its inspired kitchen. The talents of chef-owner Scott Staples can be seen in his house-smoked hanger steak served with mashed potatoes, parsnips, and veal jus and his pan-seared sea scallops served over asparagus herb risotto with smoked bacon and blood-orange vinaigrette. Zoë is a great representative of the kind of fine dining experience that Seattle excels at, wherein a sleek, urban space, upscale cooking, and a hip crowd that enjoys people-watching come together to create not a pretentious, overblown, and overpriced spectacle, but a place that is unfailingly laid-back, comfortable, and satisfying. Reservations are recommended. ⊠ *2137 2nd Ave., Belltown* ☎ *206/256–2060* ⊕ *www.restaurantzoe. com* ⊟ *AE, D, MC, V* ⊗ *No lunch.*

¢ ✕ **Mike's East Coast Sandwiches.** Okay, so the name's a little obnoxious, but we can forgive Mike (who hails from Philadelphia) since he's offering office workers and hungry wanderers hearty grilled sandwiches that are the polar opposite of the polite panini. There is a sandwich called the East Coast, which is exactly the kind of cholesterol-bomb Italian sub that might make East Coasters homesick. However, unlike most East Coast delis, this one also has decent selections for vegetarians, and the bread used for all sandwiches is top-notch. There are a few simple tables inside, but good luck snagging one during the lunch rush. Mike's opens at 8 AM for breakfast. ⊠ *113 Cedar St., Belltown* ☎ *206/818–1744* ⊟ *No credit cards* ⊗ *Closed Sun. No dinner.*

ECLECTIC

$-$$$ ✕ **Palace Kitchen.** The star of this chic yet convivial Tom Douglas eatery (he's also responsible for Dahlia Lounge, Etta's, Lola, and Serious Pie) may be the 45-foot bar, but the real show takes place in the giant open kitchen at the back. Sausages, sweet-pea ravioli, salmon carpaccio, and a nightly selection of exotic cheeses vie for your attention on the ever-changing menu of small plates. There are also always a few entrées, 10 fantastic desserts, and a rotisserie special from the apple-wood grill. ⊠ *2030 5th Ave., Belltown* ☎ *206/448–2001* ⊟ *AE, D, DC, MC, V* ⊗ *No lunch.*

JAPANESE

$-$$$ ✕ **Saito's Japanese Café and Bar.** Fusion won't fly at this Belltown restaurant, sushi bar, and lounge. Traditional appetizers include *kaarage* (marinated, breaded, and deep-fried chicken), *gyoza* (steamed pork dumplings), and *kakifry* (panfried oysters). Aside from the gorgeous sushi and sashimi, there are many other items to consider, including the *unajyu* (broiled freshwater eel with a tangy sweet sauce) and *salmon misozuke* (brushed with red miso, baked slowly, and served with caramelized turnips). The full bar stocks more than 30 different sakes. Saito's is a tad fancier than the average sushi joint—the skylight's a nice touch—but it's tame compared to Belltown's trendy spots. There are a variety of seating options, but sushi buffs should plant themselves at the bar, where they can merely point to whatever looks good and perhaps even ask the chefs to improvise on a roll or two. ⊠*2122 2nd Ave., Belltown* ☎*206/728–1333* ⊕*www.saitos-cafe.com* ▤*AE, D, DC, MC, V* ⊘*Closed Sun. and Mon. No lunch Sat.*

$–$$$ ✗**Shiro's.** Shiro Kashiba is the most famous sushi chef in Seattle; he's been in town for going on 40 years and he still takes the time to helm the sushi bar at his popular restaurant. If you get a seat in front of Shiro, don't be shy—this is one place where ordering *omakase* (chef's choice) is almost a must. Willfully unconcerned with atmosphere, this simple spot is a real curiosity amid Belltown's chic establishments, though it does seem to be charging Belltown prices for simpler pleasures like teriyaki and tempura dinners. Be forewarned that the place has a reputation for spotty table service. ⊠*2401 2nd Ave., Belltown* ☎*206/443–9844* ⊕*www.shiros.com* ▤*AE, MC, V* ⊘*No lunch.*

MEDITERRANEAN

$$–$$$ ✗**Brasa.** When famous Seattle chefs set out to open their own restaurants, the results are often even more spectacular than they were in the places they left behind. That's certainly true for Brasa, which is still a Seattle favorite many years after Tamara Murphy, formerly of Campagne, opened its Belltown doors. The paella and roast suckling pig seem to be getting all the praise these days. More traditional are the beef tenderloin and wild king salmon. ■TIP➔ **If you don't want to shell out the big bucks for dinner, join in on one of the city's most popular happy hours. The lounge serves tapas, small plates, pizzas, and sandwiches.** The dimly lighted space is sexy and Brasa is a good place to sample the chichi Belltown scene in an established restaurant that has some substance to go with its style. ⊠*2107 3rd Ave., Belltown* ☎*206/728–4220* ⊕*http://brasa.com* ⌁*Reservations essential* ▤*AE, DC, MC, V* ⊘*No lunch.*

PACIFIC NORTHWEST

$$$–$$$$ ✗**Cascadia.** Water flows over the "rain window," a 9-foot-long panel of glass, etched with a design of the Cascade mountain range, that separates the kitchen and the cherrywood-paneled dining room at this elegant restaurant. Chef Kerry Sear uses fresh regional produce, seafood, meat, and game to create memorable meals, which might include smoked Oregon Muscovy duck with pears and creamed collard greens, marinated sea bass with roasted potatoes and caviar dressing, or crab steak with chanterelles. Seven-course tasting menus ($55–$90) showcase the Northwest's culinary best. That said, most locals swing by Cascadia to snarf down delicious miniburgers at the bar or on the patio; happy hour is extremely popular. Sear occasionally offers tours of Pike Place Market followed by lunch at Cascadia, as well as one-day cooking classes. ⊠*2328 1st Ave., Belltown* ☎*206/448–8884* ⊕*www.cascadiarestaurant.com* ⌁*Reservations essential* ▤*AE, DC, MC, V* ⊘*Closed Sun. No lunch.*

SEAFOOD

$$$–$$$$ ✗**Six Seven.** Like the hotel that houses it, Six Seven would be noteworthy for its views alone—Elliott Bay and the Puget Sound are laid out before you, especially if you opt to dine at the café tables lining the

deck (note that it can get windy out there). But it's not just sparkling blue water that brings people in for pricey Asian-influenced seafood and chops. The dining room is done in the same country-cabin chic as the hotel, complete with natural-stone fireplaces and fake trees the likes of which you've never seen (the restaurant's central columns are wrapped in bark and have branches sticking out of them). The quality of the food is pretty consistent, and if you want views and seafood in a settling that's a little more elegant and serene than Anthony's Pier 66 or Ray's Boathouse in Ballard, this is a good place to splurge. Lunch is a good deal and you won't lose that view to the setting sun. If you're not a big spender, the restaurant also has a comfortable bar area with its own "snack" menu (roasted prawns, calamari, crab cakes, Waygu hamburgers, and the like) and well-poured specialty drinks that really pack a wallop. Though you won't necessarily be right up against the glass, you'll be able to see the water from the bar. ⊠*In Edgewater Hotel, 2411 Alaskan Way, Pier 67, Belltown* ☏*206/728–7000* ⊕*www. edgewaterhotel.com* ⊟*AE, DC, MC, V.*

$-$$$$ ✕**Anthony's Pier 66.** This touristy spot still makes the grade because the views are outstanding (make sure to ask for a window table) and the simply prepared fresh fish and shellfish are consistently good, if not outstanding or terribly creative. Anthony's Bell Street Diner and Anthony's Fish Bar are in the same complex, so unless you have your heart set on more-formal dining in Pier 66, shop around and see which scene appeals to you most. Pier 66 offers the most extensive and expensive menu. The Bell Street Diner is more casual and offers snack-type foods like seafood tempura, shrimp gumbo, and burgers and tacos. The Fish Bar offers counter service and decent fish-and-chips for those looking for a quick lunch. All three spaces have deck seating in summer. Dining and dress are casual, though you might want to upgrade to business casual or casual chic for dining at Pier 66. ⊠*2201 Alaskan Way (Bell St./Pier 66), Belltown* ☏*206/448–6688* ⊕*www.anthonys. com* ⊟*AE, D, MC, V.*

★ $$-$$$ ✕**Flying Fish.** Chef-owner Christine Keff got the idea for Flying Fish on a trip to Thailand; she was impressed by the simplicity and quality of the seafood dishes grilled up in beachside restaurants. Even after a decade, the Flying Fish has stayed true to its inspiration: the fish is some of the freshest you'll find in Seattle, every ingredient is organic, and the dishes, while inventive, never get too busy. The menu changes daily, but you'll often find seafood and shellfish prepared with Thai curries and seasonings, and you'll always have the option of the delicious no-nonsense fried chicken. This joint is always jumping; dinner reservations are strongly recommended. ⊠*2234 1st Ave., Belltown* ☏*206/728–8595* ⊕*http://flyingfish.com* ⊟*AE, DC, MC, V* ⊘*No lunch weekends.*

$-$$$ ✕**Etta's Seafood.** Tom Douglas's restaurant near Pike Place Market has a stylish whimsical design and views of Victor Steinbrueck Park. Etta's is the happy medium between the pricey, sleek Downtown restaurants and the cheap yet lovable holes-in-the-wall like Emmett Watson's. The Dungeness crab cakes have always been one of Douglas's signatures and they are a must, as are the various Washington oysters on the half shell. Brunch, served weekends, is the best meal here—it always includes zesty seafood omelets, but the chef also does justice to French toast, eggs and bacon, and Mexican-influenced breakfast dishes. ✉ *2020 Western Ave., Belltown* ☎ *206/443–6000* ⊕ *www.tomdouglas.com/ettas* ▤ *AE, D, DC, MC, V.*

STEAK HOUSE

$$$–$$$$ ✗ **El Gaucho.** Dress to impress here—you don't want to be outclassed by the waistcoated waitstaff that coolly navigates the packed floor of this retro steak house. El Gaucho serves some of the city's most basic, most satisfying fare in a swanky, expansive room. For the complete show, order the items prepared table-side. From the flaming lamb shish kebab to the cool Caesar salad (possibly the city's best), the virtuoso presentation seems to make everything taste better. Ritzy yet comfortable, El Gaucho makes you relax no matter how stressful your day. Of course, you may get heart palpitations once again when you get the bill—by virtue of its entrée sticker shock alone it's likely the most expensive restaurant in Seattle (the smallest steak on the menu is $39). ✉ *2505 1st Ave., Belltown* ☎ *206/728–1337* ⊕ *www.elgaucho.com* ♦ *Reservations essential* ▤ *AE, MC, V* ◷ *No lunch.*

QUEEN ANNE

AMERICAN

★ $$$–$$$$ ✗ **Canlis.** Canlis has been setting the standard for fancy living since the 1950s. And although there are no longer kimono-clad waitresses, the food and the views overlooking Lake Union are still remarkable. Besides the famous steaks, there are equally famous Quilcene Bay oysters and fresh fish in season. Every year since 1997 Canlis has been the recipient of *Wine Spectator* magazine's Grand Award for its wine list and service. Note that if you want a table on a Friday or Saturday, you should make your reservation at least three weeks in advance. ✉ *2576 Aurora Ave. N, Queen Anne* ☎ *206/283–3313* ⊕ *www. canlis.com* ♦ *Reservations essential* Jacket required ▤ *AE, DC, MC, V* ◷ *Closed Sun. No lunch.*

★ $$–$$$ ✗ **Veil.** Everything in Veil is white, from the leather banquettes to the curtains. It's not the most inspired design choice—didn't this trend come and go in New York about five years ago?—but different textures and little pink lights keep the place from looking too washed out. It's also very different for Seattle, which has managed to bring out the inner curmudgeon in every Seattleite, many of whom seem willing to ignore how outstanding the food is to decry Veil's attempts to be chic and trendy. But Chef Shannon Galusha is an alumni of French Laundry and her restrained menu has allowed Veil to survive both its own hype and the barbs thrown by locals. The braised short rib, for example, comes lightly sauced and punctuated by two perfectly round, crispy, buttery croquettes; the presentation is lovely, but nothing distracts you from the meat, which is so tender you could eat it with a spoon. Desserts are slightly more whimsical than entrées (for example, a banana-and-Nutella crepe with red banana ice cream) and are an absolute must. Don't be disappointed by the small portions—every bite will be good (and extremely rich). Dine midweek if you want quiet and the full attention of your server. Reservations are essential on Friday and Saturday. There is a separate lounge that offers a small-plates menu. ⊠ *555 Aloha St., Queen Anne* ☎ *206/216–0600* ⊕ *www.veilrestaurant.com* ⊟ *AE, MC, V* ⊗ *Closed Sun. and Mon. No lunch* .

$–$$ ✕ **Crow.** It's easy to dismiss Crow as an amalgam of too many recent trends: it's got the converted warehouse space complete with artfully exposed ductwork, the modern comfort food menu, and a list of shareable small plates. But this bistro has proved it has staying power and is fast becoming a neighborhood institution. The food is the main component of locals' loyalty; share some appetizers and then move on to the pan-roasted chicken wrapped in prosciutto or the wonderful house lasagna with Italian sausage. Service is good, even on busy nights. ⊠ *823 5th Ave. N, Queen Anne* ☎ *206/283–8800* ⊕ *www.crowseattle. com* ⊟ *MC, V* ⊗ *No lunch.*

$–$$ ✕ **Five Spot.** Up the hill from Seattle Center, the unpretentious Five Spot has a regional American menu that makes a new stop every four months or so—Key West, Little Italy, New Orleans, Santa Fe, and the fictitious "Springfield" are just a few. At the restaurant's cousins, the Coastal Kitchen in Capitol Hill, and Endolyne Joe's in West Seattle, the same rotating menu strategy applies, with more-international flavor but equally satisfying results. This is a popular spot for Sunday brunch. ⊠ *1502 Queen Anne Ave. N, Queen Anne* ☎ *206/285–7768* ⊕ *www. chowfoods.com/five* ⊟ *MC, V.*

$–$$ ✕ **Paragon.** A comfortable neighborhood bistro, Paragon has a classy bar out front and a dining room in back that serves rustic Northwest cuisine. Look for skirt steak, lemon chicken, and pork chops as well as fresh fish. ⊠ *2125 Queen Anne Ave. N, Queen Anne* ☎ *206/283–4548* ⊕ *www.paragonseattle.com* ⊟ *AE, MC, V.*

CHINESE

$ ✕ **Bamboo Garden.** You can't tell that from the menu, but the Bamboo Garden serves some of the city's best vegetarian (and kosher) food. The Chinese dishes are listed by their traditional names even though all of the "meat"—including fish, chicken, pork, and beef—is made from gluten or other vegetarian substitutes. The dining room is simple, with the usual Asian accoutrements. ⊠ *364 Roy St., Queen Anne* ☎ *206/282–6616* ⊟ *AE, D, MC, V.*

PAN-ASIAN

$ ✕ **Chinoise Café.** This small, very popular neighborhood café with tightly packed-in tables serves a number of simple Asian dishes, from sushi and *bento* boxes to seafood stir-fried with black-bean sauce, and Vietnamese spring rolls. ⊠ *12 Boston St., Queen Anne* ☎ *206/284–6671* ⊠ *610 5th Ave. S, International District* ☎ *206/254–0413* ⊟ *AE, D, DC, MC, V.*

THAI

¢–$ ✕ **Bahn Thai.** Because of the variety and high quality of its dishes, Bahn Thai, a pioneer in local Thai food, is still one of the city's best and most popular places, so it's a good idea to make a reservation. Start your meal with a skewer of tangy chicken or pork satay, or with the *tod mun goong* (spicy fish cake), and continue with hot-and-sour soup, and one of the many prawn or fish dishes. The deep-fried fish with garlic sauce is particularly good—and you can order it extra spicy. Evenings here are relaxed and romantic. ⊠ *409 Roy St., Queen Anne* ☎ *206/283–0444* ⊕ *www.bahnthaimenu.com* ⊟ *AE, DC, MC, V* ⊙ *No lunch weekends.*

INTERNATIONAL DISTRICT & PIONEER SQUARE

CAFÉ

¢–$ ✕ **Cafe Paloma.** You might swoon over the interior of this tiny café close to several art galleries, with its decorative bronze trays and big baskets full of glossy eggplants and tomatoes. Along with coffee service, there's light lunch and dinner fare (served Thursday–Saturday in summer only) with a Mediterranean/Turkish accent: handmade dolmas, hummus, and baba ghanoush (an eggplant puree made with yogurt—not tahini—in this case). The daily lunch specials can veer toward down-home American, though: a juicy pork tenderloin is frequently the centerpiece of the midday meal. ⊠ *93 Yesler Way, Pioneer Square* ☎ *206/405–1920* ⊟ *MC, V.*

CHINESE

$–$$$ ✕ **Top Gun.** This modest storefront restaurant brims with regulars devoted to the dim sum served daily from 10 until 3. House specialties include succulent *siu mai* (steamed pork dumplings), fried cubes of tofu with prawns, pork-filled *hum bao*, salt-and-pepper squid, and crisp *gai-lan* (Chinese broccoli) drizzled with a soy sauce–based dressing. Save room for the dessert cart: the buttery, bite-size egg tarts melt in your mouth, and the mango pudding turns many first-timers into repeat customers. ⊠ *668 S. King St., International District* ☎ *206/623–6606* ⊟ *MC, V.*

$ ✕ **Hing Loon.** Food magic happens in this eatery with bright fluorescent lighting, shiny linoleum floors, and large, round, laminate tables. Although many Chinese chefs may head to Linyen after hours, this is where they purportedly come for noodles. The walls are covered with menu specials handwritten (in Cantonese and English) on paper place mats. Employ the friendly waitstaff to help make your selections. Dishes of particular note are the stuffed eggplant, crispy fried chicken, *Funn* noodles, and any of the seafood offerings. ⊠ *628 S. Weller St., International District* ☎ *206/682–2828* ⊟ *DC, MC, V.*

$ ✕ **Linyen.** If it weren't in the International District, you'd consider this elegant restaurant an upscale American café. But don't let the interior decoration fool you: the first-rate food is authentically Asian. This is the place where Chinese chefs come to eat late at night after they've closed their own kitchens. Favorite dishes include the honey walnut prawns and the Peking duck. ⊠ *424 7th Ave. S, International District* ☎ *206/622–8181* ⊟ *AE, MC, V.*

¢ ✕ **Sichuanese Cuisine.** For cheap and greasy but oh-so-good Szechuan cooking head to this hole-in-the-wall in the Asian Plaza strip mall east of I–5. Dry-cooked string beans (available with a variety of meats), spicy Szechuanese ravioli, and the *Ma Po Tofu* (a spicy combination of tofu and minced pork) are favorites; the hot pot is popular and good, but whether it's the best in town is still heavily disputed. ✉ *1048 S. Jackson St., International District* ☎ *206/720–1690* ⊕ *http://sichuan. cwok.com* ▤ *AE, MC, V.*

ITALIAN

$$–$$$$ ✕ **Il Terrazzo Carmine.** Ceiling-to-floor draperies lend the dining room understated dignity, and intoxicating aromas waft from the kitchen. The chef blends Tuscan-style and regional southern Italian cooking to create soul-satisfying dishes such as veal osso buco, homemade ravioli, pasta with seafood, and roast duck with wild cherry sauce. Reservations are recommended. ✉ *411 1st Ave. S, Pioneer Square* ☎ *206/467–7797* ⊕ *http://ilterrazzocarmine.com* ▤ *AE, D, DC, MC, V* ⊘ *Closed Sun. No lunch Sat.*

$ ✕ **Mitchelli's.** Although the food is good, Trattoria Mitchelli is important for another reason: it's open until 4 AM most nights, and opens at 7 AM. Its Pioneer Square location may account for this, as many pub crawlers find "the Trat" a hospitable establishment for winding up an evening (and for getting some much-needed late-night/early-morning sustenance). The food is traditional—thin crust, apple-wood-fired pizzas; sizable pasta dishes; Caesar salads with anchovies (if you want them). ✉ *84 Yesler Way, Pioneer Square* ☎ *206/623–3883* ⊕ *http://mitchellis. com* ⌦ *Reservations not accepted* ▤ *AE, MC, V.*

¢–$ ✕ **Salumi.** The kind chef-owner Armandino Batali (father of famed New
Fodor'sChoice   York chef Mario Batali) doles out samples of his fabulous house-cured
★   meats while you wait for a table (which you must be willing to share) at this postage-stamp of a place. Order a meatball, oxtail, sausage, or lamb sandwich. The house wine served at lunch is strong, inexpensive, and good. Most people do opt for takeout, though, the line for which goes out the door. Note that Salumi is only open from 11 to 4. ✉ *309 3rd Ave. S, Pioneer Square* ☎ *206/621–8772* ▤ *AE, D, DC, MC, V* ⊘ *Closed Sat.–Mon.*

JAPANESE

¢–$ ✕ **Maneki.** Maneki has been in its current location since the 1940s and although it's no longer a hidden gem that caters to in-the-know locals and chefs from other Japanese restaurants in the area, the food isn't any less authentic. The sushi is very good, but just as popular are the small plates meant to lay a foundation for lots of sake consumption. Rice-paper lamps and screens add a little bit of old Japan to the otherwise uninspiring space. Larger parties can reserve a tatami room. This place is a mob scene on weekends—don't even think about coming here without a reservation. ✉ *304 6th Ave. S, International District* ☎ *622–2631* ⊕ *www.manekirestaurant.com* ▤ *V* ⊘ *Closed Mon. No lunch .*

¢–$ ✕ **Takohachi.** Comfort food at a comfortable price is the name of the game at this popular little restaurant. The emphasis is on fried foods such as *tonkatsu* (breaded pork cutlet) and *kaarage* (breaded boneless chicken), but the *nabe* (cabbage soup) is also quite delicious. There are only two types of sushi on the menu—California roll and a *battera* (mackerel and sweet rice stuffed in a fried tofu pouch)—and neither is available at lunch. ✉ *610 S. Jackson St., International District* ☎ *206/682–1828* ▤ *MC, V* ⊘ *Closed Sun. No lunch Sat.*

MALAYSIAN

¢–$ ✕**Malay Satay Hut.** Grilled flat breads, called *roti canai* (unstuffed) and *roti relur* (stuffed with egg, green onion, and red pepper), are a specialty here. The roti are served with a curry dipping sauce studded with chunks of chicken and potato. Other menu favorites include Buddhist Yam Pot (scallops and prawns served in a ring of cooked shredded yam), Belachan string beans (string beans and prawns tossed in a spicy sauce), mango chicken, any of the curries, and the banana pancakes. ✉ *212 12th Ave. S, International District* ☎ *206/324–4091* ⊕ *www. malaysatayhut.com* ▤ *MC, V.*

PAN-ASIAN

★ ¢–$ ✕**Uwajimaya Village Food Court.** Not only an outstanding grocery and gift shop, Uwajimaya also has a hoppin' food court offering a quick tour of Asian cuisines at lunch-counter prices. For Japanese or Chinese, the deli offers sushi, teriyaki, and barbecued duck. For Vietnamese food, try the fresh spring rolls, served with hot chili sauce, at Saigon Bistro. Shilla has Korean grilled beef and kim chee stew, and there are Filipino *lumpia* (spring rolls) to be found at Inay's Kitchen. The Honeymoon Tea Shop sells pearl tea, a cold drink served with a fat straw for sucking up the tapioca balls at the bottom of the cup. ✉ *600 5th Ave. S, International District* ☎ *206/624–6248* ▤ *MC, V.*

VIETNAMESE

★ ¢–$ ✕**Green Leaf.** Locals pack this friendly, cute café for an expansive menu of fresh, well-prepared Vietnamese staples. The quality of the food—the *pho*, spring rolls, *bahn xeo* (the Vietnamese version of an omelet), and lemongrass chicken are just a few standouts—and reasonable prices would be enough to make it an instant I.D. favorite, but Green Leaf also proves you don't have to sacrifice ambience to get cheap, authentic Asian food in Seattle: The walls are painted a soft yellow; you'll find bamboo embellishments on lighting fixtures, tables, and chairs; and instead of glaring fluorescents, you'll get dim mood lighting in the evening. The staff greets everyone as though they're regulars. And there are plenty of regulars, enough to fill the tiny 10-table eatery, so reservations for dinner are recommended. ✉ *418 8th Ave. S, International District* ☎ *206/340–1388* ▤ *MC, V.*

CENTRAL DISTRICT

AMERICAN

¢–$ ✕**Ezell's Fried Chicken.** Hands down, this is *the* place in Seattle for fried chicken. From the counter you can watch cooks bread the chicken pieces before tossing them into deep fryers. Both original and spicy flavors are terrific, but be warned that the spicy is exactly that. The rolls are big, fluffy, and baked in generously greased muffin tins. Here you'll also find Faygo sodas. Ezell's is across from Garfield High School (alma mater of Quincy Jones and Jimi Hendrix), so you'll want to steer clear during the lunch hour to avoid the stampede of students. ✉ *501 23rd Ave., Central District* ☎ *206/324–4141* ▤ *No credit cards.*

Where to Refuel Around Town

Here are some places to consider when you are short on time or cash. A few are chains; most are locally owned. Some have seating, some don't, but all are popular, quick, affordable, and central.

Dick's Drive-In. Seattle's classic burger chain has several locations. Only the Queen Anne branch has seating.

El Puerco Lloron. Authentic Mexican food served cafeteria-style on the Pike Place Market Hill Climb.

Gourmet Groceries. Many higher-end grocery stores and natural markets offer a wide variety of freshly prepared items from salads to paninis to personal pizzas. Madison Market in Capitol Hill, Whole Foods in South Lake Union and University District, and PCC in Fremont have the best selection. Whole Foods and PCC have seating; all are open late (Whole Foods until 10 PM, PCC until midnight, Madison Market until 11 PM).

Il Fornaio. Both the café and the espresso bar on the first floor of Pacific Place mall have coffee, salads, sandwiches, and seating.

Mike's East Coast Sandwiches. Grilled sandwiches overflowing with hearty fillings and a great mac and cheese are served up at this Belltown deli.

Steamers. Great fish-and-chips and both indoor and outdoor seating on Pier 56 are very close to some of the waterfront's main attractions.

Uwajimaya Village Food Court. Several stands sell Asian fast foods in the heart of Seattle's International District. Uwajimaya's deli carries Japanese and Chinese dishes, Inay's Kitchen specializes in Filipino cuisine. Aloha Plates serves—you guessed it—Hawaiian. The long shared tables are often crowded.

ETHIOPIAN

¢–$ ✕ **Assimba Ethiopian Cuisine.** Eat with your hands here using *dabo*, bread made with semolina, spiced with cumin, and basted with butter and oil. Chef Messelu Feide Messeret has attracted quite a following by offering both traditional fare and twists on tradition: the Assimba combo is a house favorite—Messeret takes a typically vegetarian dish and covers it with an Ethiopian beef sauce. ✉ *2722 E. Cherry St., Central District* ☎ *206/322–1019* ▭ *AE, D, DC, MC, V* ⊘ *Closed Sun.*

CAPITOL HILL & ENVIRONS

Capitol Hill is a major dining destination, and the adjacent neighborhoods of Madison Park and Madrona also have their own mini–dining scenes. The greatest concentration of restaurants is in and around the Pike–Pine corridor, but there are a few spots along 15th Avenue between Harrison and Mercer, 19th Avenue between Mercer and Aloha, 34th Avenue between Spring and Pike in Madrona, and along E Madison Street just south of the Washington Park Arboretum.

Note that the best lunch options are closer to the action in the core of Capitol Hill and even there your choices are more limited than you may think—many restaurants only open for dinner and weekend brunches.

Reservations are a good idea Thursday through Sunday nights, unless you don't mind dining after 9 PM.

AMERICAN

★ $$–$$$ ✕**Crush.** Crush could describe the feeling many people have for this pretty restaurant, but it could also describe the state of the tiny foyer on a Saturday night. It's in a converted two-story house (there are dining rooms on both levels), but that's rarely apparent—the beige-and-brown palette and the anachronistic '60s space-age white chairs look like they belong in a Downtown space. The food is very tasty, but it is also very heavy, and therefore not always appropriate for hot summer days. The braised short ribs are Crush's signature dish, and they're so good that as far as we're concerned, the menu could begin and end right there. However, seafood dishes are also quite competent, if not as outstanding as at Union. Some of the desserts are overly ambitious, but others are as out of this world as those strange chairs. The place doesn't seem to have one particular demographic—you'll see cranky gourmands, couples, Belltown girls in beaded halter tops, Madison Park families, Capitol Hill hipsters, and so on. Despite the clamor for a table on the weekend, servers remain serene and you'll never be rushed out the door. ✉*2319 E. Madison St., Madison Park* ☎*206/302–7874* ⊕*www. chefjasonwilson.com* ⚖*Reservations essential* ▭*AE, MC, V* ◷*Closed Sun. and Mon. No lunch.*

★ $ ✕**Crave.** Upscale comfort food is almost as popular in this city as Asian fusion, and Crave gets the gold star for its wonderful takes on American standards, its cool industrial-chic space, and its espresso bar that opens at 7 AM. Grilled cheese is made with sharp cheddar, apple slices, and sourdough bread. Mac and cheese has fontina cheese and shiitake mushrooms; the smoked paprika chicken comes with a spring pea–and–hominy succotash. On weekends, brunch replaces lunch service; try a pomegranate mimosa with your French toast or omelet. The dining room is tiny and fills up fast; service suffers a bit when it gets busy. One note of warning: though dining here is usually a pleasant experience, don't expect any of your fellow customers to be in a good mood—the crowd is mixed, but is often heavy with angst-ridden hipsters discussing their relationship problems. ✉*1621 12th Ave., Capitol Hill* ☎*206/388–0526* ⊕*www.cravefood.com* ▭*MC, V.*

¢–$ ✕**Cafe Septième.** Everyone in Capitol Hill has been to Septième at least once. It's one of the more-reliable (and attractive) restaurants along a congested stretch of Broadway, and it has accommodating hours (9 AM to midnight daily) in a neighborhood where there's a dearth of good mid-range lunch spots. It looks like a French bistro, with its red-walled dining room, banquettes, and tables draped in white cloths, but it mostly serves such American standards as burgers, biscuits and gravy, and sandwiches; at dinner you'll also get pasta and seafood options. It's hard to save room for dessert here, but try anyway—the cakes and tarts in the glass case are as good as they look. ✉*214 Broadway E, Capitol Hill* ☎*206/860–8858* ▭*AE, MC, V.*

¢   ✕**Dick's Drive-In.** This local chain of orange hamburger stands has changed little since the 1950s. The fries are hand-cut, the shakes are hand-dipped (i.e., made with hard ice cream), and the burgers are just great. The top-of-the-line burger, Dick's Deluxe ($2.08), has two beef patties, American cheese, lettuce, and onions, and is slathered in their special tartar sauce, but most folks swear by the frill-free plain cheeseburger ($1.20). Open until 2 AM daily, these drive-ins are as popular with families and students as they are with folks girding themselves against hangovers after a night out on the town. The original Dick's is the Wallingford branch, but the Capitol Hill one is more of a local landmark, thanks to its visibility and to the freak show it becomes after the bars let out on weekends. ✉*1115 Broadway E, Capitol Hill* ☎*206/323–1300* ▭*No credit cards* ✉*111 NE 45th St., Wallingford* ☎*206/632–5125* ✉*500 Queen Anne Ave. N, Queen Anne* ☎*206/285–5155* ▭*No credit cards.*

¢   ✕**Honeyhole Sandwiches.** It's like someone took a ubiquitous sandwich chain store and gave it a soul—and a few piercings. Order your sandwich at the counter and grab a seat. While you're waiting, you can stare at the dizzying mix of local art, plants, fabrics, and fishnets that hang on the red walls and from the ceiling. The hot sandwiches are the way to go here—the cold ones can be a little dry and bread-heavy. Sandwiches come in two sizes; the 4-inch "mini" will be enough for most appetites. After 5 PM, this place makes a seamless transition into . . . a bar that serves sandwiches. ✉*703 E. Pike St., Capitol Hill* ☎*206/709–1399* ▭*MC, V.*

ECLECTIC

$–$$ ✕**Dinette.** For Dinette only, we will abandon our skepticism regarding gimmicks: their main claim to fame is fancy toast and we love them dearly for it. Granted, the clams with chorizo, the gnocchi, and the daily seafood specials are all very good, but it's memories of toast that linger. A focus on seasonal ingredients means that the toppings on said toast change regularly but they're always mouthwatering: broccoli rabe with red peppers and fontina; anchovies with arugula and Serrano ham; or Gorgonzola and walnuts. The space couldn't be cozier. Dimly lighted but not dark and brooding, Dinette is all soft blues and creams and gold-foil details. ✉*1514 E. Olive Way, Capitol Hill* ☎*206/328–2282* ⊕*www.dinetteseattle.com* ⌨*Reservations not accepted* ▭*MC, V* ⊘*Closed Sun. and Mon. No lunch.*

FRENCH

★ $$–$$$$ ✕**Rover's.** The restaurant of Thierry Rautureau, one of the Northwest's most imaginative chefs, is an essential destination. Sea scallops, venison, squab, lobster, and rabbit are frequent offerings (vegetarian items are also available) on the prix-fixe menu. Traditional accoutrements such as foie gras and truffles pay homage to Rautureau's French roots, but bold combinations of local ingredients are evidence of his wanderlust. The service at Rover's is excellent—friendly but unobtrusive—the setting romantic, and the presentation stunning. ✉*2808 E. Madison St., Madison Valley* ☎*206/325–7442* ⌨*Reservations essential* ▭*AE, MC, V* ⊘*Closed Mon. No lunch Sat.–Thurs.*

2

$$–$$$ ✕**Madison Park Cafe.** Karen Binder's small, vaguely French neighborhood café is a local institution. Although this spot is also widely known for its weekend brunches, recent years have brought a greater emphasis on the dinner service. Popular dishes on the ever-changing evening menu have included cassoulet, oysters in a Pernod cream sauce, pepper steak, and traditional rack of lamb. For warm-weather dining, there's a secluded cobblestone courtyard shaded by trees and scented by more than 12 species of lilies. In summer, foods cooked on an outdoor brick grill add to the delicious aromas wafting from the kitchen. ✉*1807 42nd Ave. E, Madison Park* ☎*206/324–2626* ▭*AE, V* ⊗*Closed Mon. No dinner Sun.*

$$ ✕**Crémant.** Chef-owner Scott Emerick's homage to traditional French country cooking is, interestingly enough, a modern, almost spare conglomerate of grays and whites—much of the gray coming from unadorned concrete walls. The menu, on the other hand, is made up almost entirely of the classics. It'll be mighty difficult to resist ordering the steak frites as you watch piles of golden fries being whisked to other tables, but nothing tops the savory bouillabaisse. The roasted marrow bones appetizer, a rarity in Seattle, may be hard to stomach visually, but it makes such a wonderfully tender and salty spread that it'll be hard to go back to simply buttering your bread. Rich desserts and an excellent cheese selection ensure that you'll linger even longer. Dining at Crémant can be either be romantic or casual and jovial, depending on the night and the company you're with. The crowd is fairly mixed, with graying foodies in dress shirts sitting next to denim-clad guys who look like they just finished their barista shifts. ✉*1423 34th Ave., Madrona* ☎*206/322–4600* ⊕*www.cremantseattle.com* ⌁*Reservations essential* ▭*AE, MC, V* ⊗*No lunch.*

Fodor's Choice
★

PAN-ASIAN

¢–$ ✕**Ballet.** It's so easy to walk right past this place—if you don't take the time to read the awning carefully, you'd assume it was fronting a dusty copy shop or a particularly depressing dance studio. But this simple, family-run spot is much beloved of residents and folks who work in the neighborhood for providing Capitol Hill with cheap and consistently delicious Pan-Asian staples. Ballet is particularly strong on Vietnamese standards—try the pho—but the menu ranges from Thai to Chinese to Japanese. There are many vegetarian and vegan options, too, made with all manner of fake meats. If the decor doesn't do it for you, get your order to go and head to Cal Anderson Park a few blocks north. ✉*914 E. Pike St., Capitol Hill* ☎*206/328–7983* ▭*AE, MC, V* ⊗*Closed Sun.*

SEAFOOD

$–$$ ✕**Coastal Kitchen.** Local restaurant gurus Jeremy Hardy and Peter Levy hit on a surefire formula with their hearty seafood meals prepared according to a rotating menu that highlights the cuisines of such far-flung coastal places as Oaxaca, Vietnam, and Barcelona, to name just a few. The focus changes quarterly, and experiments don't always work, but you can't knock their adventurous spirit. Besides, you always have the option to forgo the specials and order perfectly prepared fish fillets—lightly seasoned and either grilled or pan-seared—and there are never complaints about the roast chicken with creamy mashed potatoes or the marinated pork chop. Nice enough for a date but laid-back enough to bring the kids, Coastal Kitchen has many loyal regulars and it anchors the 15th Avenue strip. ⊠*429 15th Ave. E, Capitol Hill* ☎*206/322–1145* ⊕*www.chowfoods.com/coastal* ▤*MC, V.*

SOUTHERN

$–$$ ✕**Kingfish Cafe.** Good Southern cooking is such a novelty in Seattle that the three sisters who own and operate Kingfish are local celebrities. Here you can get a good po'boy with green tomatoes, fried chicken, pulled pork, scrumptious crab cakes, and, of course, sweet potato pie. The place is spare but elegant, with photographs culled from family albums. Be prepared to wait for a table at dinner. ⊠*602 19th Ave. E, Capitol Hill* ☎*206/320–8757* ⚄*Reservations not accepted* ▤*MC, V* ☉*Closed Tues. No dinner Sun. No lunch Mon.*

SPANISH

$$–$$$ ✕**Harvest Vine.** Going to this tiny tapas-and-wine bar can be an adventure or trial, depending on your state of mind. First of all, it's in Madison Park, not at all close to anything, really. Secondly, limited seating means that unless you come early or score a reservation (they only hold a few tables each night for reservations), you might be waiting a while when you get here. But if you think you can shrug off those annoyances, do seek out this restaurant. The Basque tapas are outstanding; no matter what congenial owner Jose Jimenez de Jimenez puts together—chorizo with grilled bread, pan-seared tuna belly with vanilla bean–infused oil—he never goes wrong. There is an impressive wine and sherry list that focuses on Basque region wines. ⊠*2701 E. Madison St., Madison Park* ☎*206/320–9771* ▤*MC, V* ☉*No lunch.*

THAI

If you don't feel like hoofing it to 15th Avenue for Thai food, Rom Mai Thai and Siam on Broadway (conveniently located across the street from each other on Broadway near Roy Street) are both solid choices.

¢–$ ✕**Jamjuree.** Jamjuree has become the Hill's go-to spot for tasty Thai food in a place that is casual without being a hole in the wall. It's a basic but well-coordinated restaurant with wooden booths and tables; a counter with retro-looking bar stools and a few parasols and statues adds a tiny bit of flair to an otherwise restrained space. You'll find all the standard curries and noodle dishes here, but before you automatically order pad thai, consider the daily specials, which are more inventive and usually good. ⊠*509 15th Ave. E Capitol Hill* ☎*206/323–4255* ⊕*www.jamjuree.com* ▤*AE, MC, V.*

VEGETARIAN

$–$$ ✕**Cafe Flora.** This sweet restaurant off the beaten path in the leafy Madison Park neighborhood offers vegetarian and vegan food for grown-ups who want more than grilled tofu but don't want to splurge at Carmelita in Greenwood. The menu changes frequently, though the chefs tend to keep things simple, offering dishes like black-bean burgers with spicy aioli, polenta with leeks and spinach, and the very popular

"Oaxaca tacos" (corn tortillas filled with potatoes and four types of cheese) at both lunch and dinner. Make sure you sit in the "Atrium," which has a stone fountain, skylight, slate floors, and garden-style café tables and chairs—the other dining room is nice, too, but it's more generic and reminiscent of the kind of upscale coffeeshop you'd find on the ground floor of a mid-range chain hotel. Brunch is very popular— great waffles made with fresh seasonal fruits—-but the hectic scene kind of mars the serenity of the place, which is an important part of the equation. ✉*2901 E. Madison St., Madison Park* ☎*206/325–9100* ⊕*www.cafeflora.com* ▭*MC, V.*

VIETNAMESE

$–$$ ✕**Monsoon.** If you want pho or congee, don't come here. Sure, you can often get both items at Monsoon, but they're so overpriced, you're better off going the fusion route. Favorites like caramelized gulf shrimp served with jasmine rice, the catfish clay pot with chili-lime sauce, and venison with curry and glass noodles blend Vietnamese and Pacific Northwest elements. Exotic homemade ice creams include jackfruit or lychee and muscat, but the restaurant's most famous dessert is the coconut crème caramel. The wine cellar has more than 230 varieties, including many French selections. When you're tired of the holes-in-the-wall in the I.D., but still crave Southeast Asian cooking, treat yourself to Monsoon. Reservations are recommended. ✉*615 19th Ave. E, Capitol Hill* ☎*206/325–2111* ▭*MC, V* ⊗*No lunch.*

WEST SEATTLE

AMERICAN

$–$$ ✕**Endolyne Joe's.** The creators of the Coastal Kitchen have found their latest home at what was once the last stop on the trolley car line from Alki to Fauntleroy. Here you'll find pan-roasted mussels, breaded flounder, and chicken dredged in crunchy corn flakes and fried. The brick and old-growth timbers of the structure, which was built in the '20s, have been used to their full advantage to give the room an authentic saloon flavor. As always with this group of restaurants, the sundaes are dreamy, with special honors going to the coconut ice cream hot fudge sundae served with homemade coconut brittle. ✉*9261 45th St. SW, West Seattle* ☎*206/937–5637* ⊕*www.chowfoods.com/endolyne* ▭*MC, V.*

$ ✕**Luna Park Cafe.** This place is about as retro as it gets, complete with tabletop jukeboxes. Actually, it's not really retro, since the café has never changed. It's still more or less what it was in the '60s—an upscale sit-down hamburger and sandwich joint that has updated by adding vegetarian "burgers" and espresso to its menu. But the milk shakes are as rich as ever, the breakfasts are as huge as always, and the burgers are still satisfying. The Luna Park is one of the best places in the city to take children. ✉*2918 SW Avalon Way, West Seattle* ☎*206/935–7250* ▭*AE, D, MC, V.*

CAFÉ

¢ ✕ **Alki Bakery.** Delicious fruit pies and pillowy cakes fill the café's attractive display case. But before you indulge, order a colorful salad or fettuccine with roasted vegetables, and take in the wide, calming view of the Olympic Mountains and Bainbridge Island. This bakery does a brisk business and also owns a retail outlet in Georgetown, south Seattle. ✉ *2738 Alki Ave. SW, West Seattle* ☎ *206/935–1352* 🖃 *AE, D, MC, V.*

GREEK

$–$$ ✕ **Ephesus Restaurant.** Neighborhood joints like this one are well worth the trip west. With a garden that provides a good amount of the restaurant's produce—Ephesus is in an old house—you can expect the emphasis to be on fresh, seasonal fare. If it's summer, order a salad; in winter try one of the *topraks* (oven-baked stews made with chunks of meat, potatoes, onions, and other veggies). They're rich and comforting on a cold and rainy day. ✉ *5245 California Ave. SW, West Seattle* ☎ *206/937–3302* ⚑ *Reservations essential* 🖃 *MC, V* ⊗ *No lunch.*

SEAFOOD

$$–$$$ ✕ **Salty's on Alki.** Famed for its Sunday and holiday brunches and its view of Seattle's skyline across the harbor, Salty's offers more in the way of quantity than quality—and a bit too much of its namesake ingredient. But it's a couple of steps up from the mainstream seafood chains. And, oh, that view. ✉ *1936 Harbor Ave. W (just past port complex), West Seattle* ☎ *206/937–1600* 🖃 *AE, MC, V.*

LAKE UNION

AMERICAN

¢–$ ✕ **14 Carrot Cafe.** This popular breakfast and lunch place has changed owners several times in the last two decades, yet somehow the restaurant stays the same. Only the cinnamon rolls are not as good as they used to be. But specials such as biscuits in gravy and the pancakes du jour still sell like hotcakes. The egg dishes are consistently good, and the Tahitian French toast, made with tahini, is as popular as ever. Don't get upset about the crowd packing the place on weekends: most live within walking distance, and this is their neighborhood café. ✉ *2305 Eastlake Ave. E, Eastlake* ☎ *206/324–1442* 🖃 *MC, V* ⊗ *No dinner.*

ITALIAN

$–$$$ ✕ **Serafina.** To many loyal patrons, Serafina is *the* perfect neighborhood café. And then there's the romance: burnt-sienna walls topped by a forest-green ceiling convey the feeling of a lush (and perhaps decadent) garden villa—a sense heightened by the small sheltered courtyard out back. Menu highlights include grilled eggplant layered and baked with prosciutto, goat cheese, and tomatoes, and the fresh mussels steamed with smoked tomatoes, *harissa* (spicy hot sauce made with chilies, garlic, cumin, coriander, and olive oil), leeks, and sweet vermouth. Live jazz every Friday through Sunday (and occasionally on Wednesday and Thursday, too) should be considered a plus, but be forewarned that it can be kind of difficult to hold a conversation while the band is playing. ✉ *2043 Eastlake Ave. E, Eastlake* ☎ *206/323–0807* ⊕ *www.serafinaseattle.com* ☰ *AE, DC, MC, V* ⊘ *No lunch Sat.*

MAGNOLIA

AMERICAN

¢–$ ✕ **Maggie Bluff's.** Supercasual and kid friendly, this spot right on the marina is popular with boaters coming in from a day at sea. On nice days there is outdoor seating, for the rainy days you can watch the weather and the bobbing sailboats from indoors. The menu is filled with burgers, Caesar salads, buffalo wings, and the like. The full bar maintains a selection of local brews on tap. ✉ *2601 W. Marina Pl., Magnolia* ☎ *206/283–8322* ☰ *AE, D, MC, V.*

¢ ✕ **Red Mill.** Burgers here are superbly crafted by a crack assembly-line staff. You can order one dressed simply, with lettuce and smoky "Mill Sauce" mayo, or more elaborately, with menu combinations of luscious roasted Anaheim peppers, blue cheese, red onion jam, or Tillamook cheddar. Vegetarians note: order the meatless patties as substitutions on the regular burger menu, rather than from the veggie menu—the regular burger buns and dressings are much better. ✉ *1613 W. Dravus, Magnolia* ☎ *206/284–6363* ✉ *316 N. 67th St., Greenwood* ☎ *206/783–6362* ☰ *No credit cards.*

SEAFOOD

$$–$$$$ ✕ **Palisade.** The short ride to the Magnolia neighborhood yields a stunning view back across the bay to the lights of Downtown. And there's no better place to take in the vista than this restaurant at the Elliott Bay Marina. Palisade scores points for its playfully exotic ambience—complete with an indoor saltwater pond. As for the food, the simpler preparations, especially the signature plank-broiled salmon, are most satisfying. Maggie Bluff's, an informal café downstairs, is a great spot for lunch on a breezy summer afternoon. ✉ *2601 W. Marina Pl., Magnolia* ✛ *From Downtown, take Elliott Ave. northwest across Magnolia Bridge to Elliott Bay Marina exit* ☎ *206/285–1000* ⊕ *www.palisaderestaurant.com* ☰ *AE, D, DC, MC, V.*

FREMONT

AMERICAN

$$ ✕ **35th Street Bistro.** The 35th Street Bistro replaced the vaunted Still Life Cafe, which was the epitome of all things Fremont back when the hood was more hippie than yuppie. Although the white tablecloths, good wine list, and the generic bistro-ness of the place suggest that Downtown has moved in uptown, the ghosts of the Still Life must still linger—this place is as casual as some of Fremont's less-flashy eateries, service goes beyond warm into personable, and organic foods populate the menu. The menu is seasonal, but roasted chicken, lamb porterhouse, and fresh seafood are usually on it. ✉ *709 N. 35th St., Fremont* ☎ *206/547–9850* ⊕ *www.35bistro.com* ☰ *V* ⊘ *No lunch Mon.*

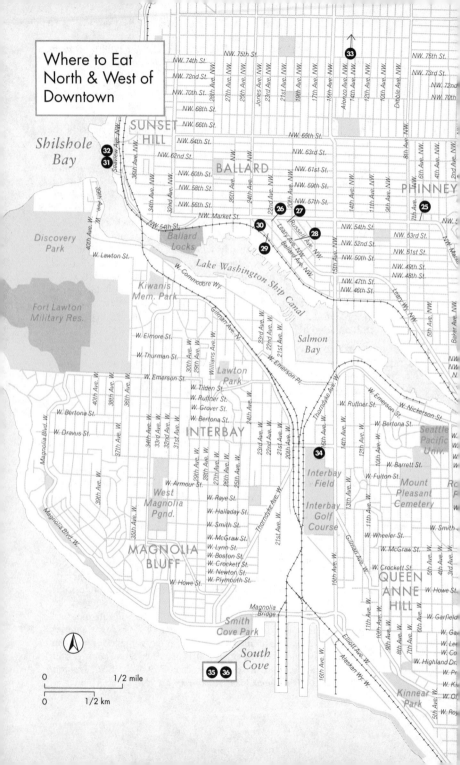

Where to Eat
North & West of
Downtown

Shilshole Bay

SUNSET HILL

BALLARD

PHINNEY

Discovery Park

Fort Lawton Military Res.

Kiwanis Mem. Park

Ballard Locks

Lake Washington Ship Canal

Salmon Bay

Lawton Park

INTERBAY

West Magnolia Pgnd.

MAGNOLIA BLUFF

Seattle Pacific Univ.

Mount Pleasant Cemetery

Interbay Field

Interbay Golf Course

QUEEN ANNE HILL

Magnolia Bridge

Smith Cove Park

South Cove

Kinnear Park

0   1/2 mile

0   1/2 km

2

CUBAN

$ ✕**Paseo.** The centerpiece of Lorenzo Lorenzo's slim Cuban-influenced
Fodor'sChoice menu is the mouthwatering Midnight Cuban sandwich. The marinated
★ pork sandwich, topped with sautéed onions and served on a chewy
baguette, is doused with an amazing sauce (the ingredients of which
are known only by Lorenzo) that keeps folks coming back for more.
The entrées are also delicious, from scallops with cilantro to prawns in
a spicy red sauce. This place is so small, it's more like a glorified lunch
truck than a sit-down eatery. There are a few tables, but don't count on
getting a seat—Paseo gets so busy the line usually snakes way out the
door, and most people opt for takeout. ⊠ *4225 Fremont Ave. N, Fremont* ☎ *206/545-7440* ▤ *No credit cards* ☾ *Closed Sun and Mon.*

ITALIAN

$–$$ ✕**Asteroid Café.** Many customers come here just to sit at the bar for the
Thursday-night jazz jams, but that's not a reflection on the food, which
is some of the best Italian in the city—so good, in fact, that Brad's has
some serious competition right in its own neighborhood. The space is
a little strange—it's tucked into the closest thing Fremont has to a strip
mall, wedged between a pub and a 24-Hour Fitness—but the owners
have managed to create a spot that is both classy and cozy. This is a
great place to order duck, especially if it's one of the daily specials;
the rigatoni *alla salsiccia* (with Italian sausage in a tomato, basil, and
cream sauce) has been a crowd pleaser since the Asteroid operated out
of its first tiny storefront in Wallingford. ⊠ *3601 Fremont Ave., Fremont* ☎ *206/547-9000* ⊕ *www.asteroidcafe.com* ▤ *AE, DC, MC, V*
☾ *Closed Sun. No lunch Sat.*

★ $–$$ ✕**Brad's Swingside Cafe.** You've probably dreamed of finding a place
like this—cozy, eclectic, and dear to the heart of the owner. Lots of
people share this dream, so you can expect to wait a while on weekends. Chef-owner Brad Inserra, who likes to come out and chat—so
long as you don't dis the Pittsburgh Pirates—bills Swingside as Seattle's
"best little Italian restaurant," but don't come expecting spaghetti and
meatballs. You will find imaginative dishes like lamb-and-venison stew
with coconut milk, orange, and mango. Be sure to ask the server what
wine Inserra recommends. He's always right. ⊠ *4212 Fremont Ave.
N, Fremont* ☎ *206/633-4057* ⊛ *Reservations not accepted* ▤ *MC, V*
☾ *Closed Sun. and Mon. No lunch.*

MEXICAN

$–$$ ✕**El Camino.** Loose, loud, and funky, this Fremont storefront restaurant
gives its own irreverent Northwest interpretation of Mexican cuisine.
Rock-shrimp quesadillas, chipotle-pepper and garlic sea bass, and duck
with a spicy green sauce are typical of the kitchen's gentle spin. Even a
green salad becomes transformed with toasted pumpkin seeds on crispy
romaine with a cool garlic, lime juice, and cilantro dressing. Weekend
brunches are also excellent—everything from standard scrambled eggs
and bacon to Mexican favorites like *chilaquiles* are done well. ⊠ *607
N. 35th St., Fremont* ☎ *206/632-7303* ▤ *AE, DC, MC, V* ☾ *Closed
Mon. No lunch weekdays.*

2

SUSHI

¢ ✕**Blue C Sushi.** Black banquettes, young sushi chefs, and a giant projection screen showing quirky Japanese TV shows and music videos make Blue C suitable for discerning hipsters, but it has become a true neighborhood haunt, attracting families, friends, and first dates. Despite its trendy interior, this place is lots of fun—just try suppressing a grin as colorful plates of nigiri, sashimi, sushi rolls, and tempura dishes chug past you on a conveyor belt. Simply grab whatever looks good. The color of the plate indicates the price of the dish; your server tallies your bill when you're done. This place gets packed on weekends, but there's an upstairs bar to wait in or you can opt for takeout. The daily happy hour (4–6) is one of the best deals in town—you can get $1 sushi in the bar, with the purchase of one beverage. ✉*3411 Fremont Ave. N, Fremont* ☎*206/633–3411* ✉*University Village, 4601 26th Ave. NE, University District* ☎*206/525–4601* ⊕*www.bluecsushi.com* ⌁*Reservations not accepted* ▭*MC, V.*

SEAFOOD

$$–$$$ ✕**Ponti.** Working in a placid canal-side location, in a villalike setting a stone's throw from the Fremont and Aurora bridges, chef Alvin Binuya builds culinary bridges between Northwest ingredients and Mediterranean and Asian techniques. Alaskan king crab legs with a chardonnay butter and herb mayonnaise demonstrate the kitchen's classic restraint; the grilled mahimahi with satsuma potato gratin and shallot jus walks on the wilder side. ✉*3014 3rd Ave. N, Fremont* ☎*206/284–3000* ⊕*www.pontiseafoodgrill.com* ▭*AE, DC, MC, V* ⊗*No lunch.*

THAI

★ ¢–$ ✕**Kwanjai Thai.** The flashier Jai Thai restaurant on Fremont Avenue might catch a lot of visitors as they get off the bus, but locals know to keep walking down 36th Street to a little house that produces some of the best Thai food in Seattle. Kwanjai serves simple, authentic (just check out grandma chopping vegetables in the open kitchen) dishes; curries are very good, as are the seafood specials. Be careful when you tell them how spicy you want your food—even two stars can be hot enough to make your nose run. This is a no-frills kind of place, but the tangerine walls and warm lighting make it cozy at night. ✉*469 N. 36th St., Fremont* ☎*206/632–3656* ⌁*Reservations not accepted* ▭*AE, MC, V* ⊗*No lunch weekends.*

BALLARD

Downtown Ballard isn't very big, but it sure has a lot of eateries—everything from chains to five-star dining. The best restaurants are on Ballard Avenue, but NW Market Street has the majority of cheap lunch spots.

Great Harvest Bread Company on Market and 22nd Street is the place to stop for delicious baked goods. ▪TIP➔ **And before you settle on a chain for a cheap sandwich, head to the Other Coast Café on Ballard Avenue between 20th and 22nd streets.** You'll get great deli sandwiches made with better-quality ingredients—the Ragin' Cajun sandwich is the clear favorite among regulars.

AMERICAN

★ $–$$$ ✕**Wild Mountain Café.** For both an off-the-beaten-path experience and a healthy dose of the West Coast approach to life, take a detour to this adorable purple house. You won't get more of a "like dining in a friend's living room" feeling anywhere else—no rooms were gutted in the house's remodel, so you actually are dining in the living room . . . and the den . . . and the guest room. As for the food, Wild Mountain may never be one of the city's top restaurants, but it serves consistently good and simple American fare made with fresh, organic ingredients, including comfort-food favorites like mac and cheese and a version of chicken Parmesan with panko as breading. Breakfast includes a variety of scrambles, tahini-stuffed French toast, and, of course, granola. ■TIP➔ This may be the most sustainable restaurant in Seattle—almost all materials used to create the restaurant (including the kitchen wares) are salvaged, secondhand, or reclaimed and kitchen scraps go into a compost bin that in turn feeds the restaurant's garden. ☒*1408 NW 85th St., Ballard* ☎*206/297-9453* ⊕*www.wildmtncafe.com* ☰*MC, V.*

¢–$ ✕**Hi-Life.** The Hi-Life is the most versatile restaurant in Ballard. In a converted firehouse, the echoey space has the familiar feeling of a TGI Friday's, which makes it a safe bet for families, but it also has personality enough to appeal to everyone from yuppies sending messages on their Blackberrys to tattooed hipsters nursing hangovers with heaping portions of rich French toast. From morning until night, the Hi-Life has something to satisfy—you can get small plates, full entrées, wood-fired pizzas, breakfast until 3 PM, and so on. The standards are done very well—salads and burgers never disappoint—but the kitchen can also handle more-creative dishes like chorizo-and-shrimp empanadas and breaded oxtail with marscarpone polenta. Note that Hi-Life does close for two hours between lunch and dinner from 3 PM to 5 PM. ☒*5425 Russell Ave. NW, Ballard* ☎*206/784-7272* ⊕*www.chowfoods.com/hilife* ☰*MC, V.*

FRENCH

★ $$$$ ✕**Le Gourmand.** On an unattractive corner somewhere halfway between Ballard and Fremont is one of the city's definitive French restaurants. The intimate, rustic-chic spot doesn't quite know if it's an unassuming bistro or a romantic, special-occasion dining room, but it sure knows how to charge for the experience. This will be one of the most expensive meals you'll have in the city, but if chef-owner Bruce Naftaly and staff are on their game, it will also be one of the best. Naftaly uses classic French techniques and locally grown ingredients to create stunning dishes such as his roast duckling with black currant sauce (using homemade cassis); or king salmon poached in champagne and gooseberry sauce. Pastry chef Sara Naftaly's dessert menu might include a flourless chocolate cake with raspberries and almond crème anglaise. Though the tasting menus seem like a good deal, patrons seem to prefer ordering à la carte. ■TIP➔ If you don't want to pay sky-high prices for the full experience, go next door to Sambar and order from an abbreviated bar menu. ⊠*425 NW Market St., Ballard* ☎*206/784–3463* ⌇*Reservations essential* ⊟*AE, MC, V.*

ITALIAN

$-$$ ✕**Volterra.** For those who favor Italian cooking over French, Volterra has eclipsed Le Gourmand as Ballard's special-occasion restaurant. It's another victim of the deep-red-walls syndrome that Seattle can't seem to rid itself of, but with its black-and-white accents, skylight, and large framed photos of Italy, it's very attractive nonetheless. The restaurant gets the most attention for dishes like wild boar tenderloin and fresh seafood baked in parchment, but it's not too taken with itself to offer something as simple as linguine in clam sauce. The long wine list features many Tuscan wines, as well as selections from other Italian regions. ⊠*5411 Ballard Ave. NW, Ballard* ☎*206/789–5100* ⊕*www.volterrarestaurant.com* ⊟*AE, DC, MC, V* ⊟*No lunch.*

MEXICAN

★ ¢–$ ✕**La Carta de Oaxaca.** True to its name, this restaurant serves traditional Mexican cooking, with Oaxacan accents. The mole negro is a must, served over chicken or pork; another standout is the *albondigas* (a spicy vegetable soup with meatballs). The menu is small plates, which works out to your advantage because you won't have to choose just one savory dish. The small space is sleek: the open kitchen is enclosed by a stainless-steel bar, the walls are covered in gorgeous black-and-white photos wedged together like puzzle pieces, and the light wood tables and black chairs and banquettes look more Scandinavian than Mexican. The place gets very crowded on weekends, and stays busy until late, though if you have a small party you usually don't have to wait too long for a table. ☎*206/782–8722* ⊕*www.lacartadeoaxaca.com* ⊟*AE, DC, MC, V* ⊙*No lunch Sun. and Mon.*

¢–$ ✕**Senor Moose.** Before you resign yourself to waiting in line for brunch at the Dish Café (the most obvious choice for brunch in the area), head a little farther down Leary Way into Ballard to Senor Moose. Looking like a cross between a truck-stop diner and a Tex-Mex restaurant, this tiny café has outstanding breakfast options, including traditional favorites from every region of Mexico. Wait for a space in the tiny dining room or belly up to the counter and read the paper (someone will have one to share) or just watch the frenetic activity as everything from soup to salsa is made from scratch. Lunch and dinner are just as good as *desayunos,* with delectable pork *carnitas* and chorizo from the state of Michoacan being favorites. ⊠*5242 Leary Ave. NW, Ballard* ☎*206/784–5568* ⊟*AE, MC, V* ⊙*No dinner Sun. and Mon.*

SEAFOOD

$$–$$$$ ✕**Anthony's Homeport.** This is a comfortable waterfront restaurant where ample outside dining in protected nooks allows you a sea breeze and great views without getting blasted by gales. The seafood preparations are as good as those of the more-upscale Ray's, next door. But this restaurant's true claim to fame rests on its annual Oyster Olympics, a madcap oyster-shucking, oyster-judging, oyster-slurping event held in late March. ⊠*6135 Seaview Ave. NW (at Shilshole Marina), Ballard* ☎*206/783–0780* ⊟*AE, MC, V.*

★ $$–$$$$ ✕ **Ray's Boathouse.** The view of Shilshole Bay might be the big draw here, but the seafood is also impeccably fresh and well prepared. Perennial favorites include broiled salmon, Kasu sake–marinated cod, Dungeness crab, and regional oysters on the half shell. Ray's has a split personality: there's a fancy dining room downstairs (reservations essential) and a casual café and bar upstairs (reservations not accepted). In warm weather you can sit on the deck outside the café and watch the parade of fishing boats, tugs, and pleasure craft floating past, almost right below your table. Be forewarned that during happy hour (or early-bird special time) in high season the café feels extremely touristy—jam-packed with sour-faced retirees and frazzled parents dragging kids around by the elbows—and service suffers greatly because of the crowds. ✉6049 Seaview Ave. NW, Ballard ☎206/789–3770 ⊕www.rays.com ☐AE, DC, MC, V.

GREENWOOD & PHINNEY

If none of the restaurants below strike your fancy, you can find many more options along Phinney and Greenwood avenues (Phinney turns into Greenwood), especially in the 70s and 80s. Reliable lunch options include Gordito's Healthy Mexican Food (85th Street right off Greenwood Avenue), Zeek's Pizza (Phinney Avenue at 60th Street), and Red Mill Burgers (Phinney Avenue at 67th Street).

AMERICAN

¢–$ ✕ **Pete's Egg Nest.** You'll notice right away that almost everybody knows everybody else here. This is truly a neighborhood restaurant where locals meet over breakfast and lunch to shoot the breeze or nurse hangovers. No one ever seems in a hurry, which means waits for weekend brunch can be long. The food here is not just inexpensive, it's truly tasty and well prepared, making Pete's one of the best and most-reliable breakfast spots in the city. Obviously, huge omelets are the first order of business here, but the pancakes are excellent, too. The interior is nothing to speak of—it looks like someone wedged a diner into a realtor's storefront. ✉7717 Greenwood Ave. N, Greenwood ☎206/784–5348 ☐MC, V ◷No dinner.

PACIFIC NORTHWEST

$$–$$$ ✕ **Stumbling Goat.** Stubbornly cranking out delicious regional fare for years, the Stumbling Goat sure knows its way around a farmers' market—you'll find the freshest organic ingredients here (from local producers, of course) and no missteps in the presentation, which is kept simple to let those fresh flavors shine. The menu changes quite frequently, but you'll find hearty dishes like risottos made with seasonal vegetables, mini–Waygu beef burgers, and in-season fish served with greens and potatoes. Though it's a bit spendy for this neck of the woods, the Stumbling Goat definitely belongs in Greenwood. The place has enough quirks—from its name (surely an ode to the excellent wine and cheese offerings) to the red walls and velvet accents in its dining room to its peach-hue happy-hour den campily named the Enchantress Lounge—to be thought of as a neighborhood bistro first

and a gourmet experience second. ✉*6722 Greenwood Ave., Greenwood* ☎*206/784–3535* ⊕*www.stumblinggoatbistro.com* ▤*MC, V* ✸*Closed Mon. No lunch.*

VEGETARIAN

★ $$ ✕**Carmelita.** Perhaps the best of Seattle's upscale vegetarian spots, Carmelita could convert a carnivore with the smells emanating from the kitchen alone. Everything on the menu is fresh and well prepared: from the beet ravioli to gourmet pizza topped with red-onion marmalade and fontina to the root-vegetable potpie. You will not notice the absence of fish, fowl, or meat stocks in the preparations. This is a popular place, so reservations are recommended. The dining room is lovely, paying homage to the natural world with lots of wood, oil paintings of poppies, and leaf shapes on the ceiling, but if the weather's nice, request a spot on the garden-shrouded patio. ✉*7314 Greenwood Ave., Greenwood* ☎*206/706–7703* ⊕*www.carmelita.net* ▤*MC, V* ✸*Closed Mon. No lunch.*

WALLINGFORD & GREEN LAKE

Wallingford has plenty of options for a casual meal. Along 45th Street, you'll also find quite a few cheap and decent (if not spectacular) sushi spots, one or two curry houses, and a few dinerlike establishments serving reliable comfort food. Green Lake has fewer spots of note, though the midway point between the two neighborhoods, around N 56th Street between Meridien and Kensington streets has several choices from an Elysian Brewing Company pub to a Japanese bakery.

PACIFIC NORTHWEST

$$–$$$ ✕**Eva.** This is a great off-the-beaten-path place to try mildly ambitious Pacific Northwest fusion cooking and local wines. The white tablecloths and sometimes-stuffy patrons are what you'd expect at a higher-end place, but the friendly staff, eager chef, and reasonable prices confirm that this little bistro would rather be a neighborhood institution than a haughty five-star any day. Seafood is well represented, as are naturally raised meats and organic ingredients. ✉*2227 N. 56th St., Wallingford* ☎*206/633–3538* ▤*AE, MC, V* ✸*No lunch.*

$$–$$$ ✕**Nell's.** Chef-owner Philip Mihalski's ever-changing menu focuses on coaxing maximum performance from the freshest of seasonal regional ingredients. Employing broadly European techniques, Mihalski creates such dishes as seared sea scallops with a curry cream sauce and shavings of black truffle over a puree of cauliflower, and poached halibut in Kaffir lime broth with roasted spring onions. Suggested appetizers include a fantastic onion tart with hazelnut butter and Jerusalem artichoke chips, and seared foie gras in duck broth over a puree of turnips. The outstanding service makes up for the somewhat forgettable interior, the best feature of which is peekaboo views of Green Lake. ✉*6804 E. Greenlake Way N, Green Lake* ☎*206/524–4044* ▤*AE, MC, V* ✸*No lunch.*

★ $–$$$ ✕**Tilth.** The city was so excited about Tilth, it made *Seattle Metropolitan Magazine*'s annual "Best Restaurants" issue mere weeks after opening.

A certified organic restaurant (a real rarity; it's incredibly difficult for a restaurant to get certification), Tilth serves up wonderful, inventive dishes that can be had as small plates or full entrées—the mini–duck burgers and pork belly deserve special mentions. It's not the sort of place you'd expect to find on Wallingford's busy commercial strip: a Crafts-man house, painted a leafy green, has been lovingly spruced up. The tiny dining room—backed by an open kitchen—occupies the ground floor and has an accidental elegance. Though overall dining here is a wonder-ful experience, Tilth has two notable drawbacks: the service can be a bit snotty—a big no-no in laid-back Wallingford—and the acoustics are terrible (be prepared to shout across your tiny table if you dine during peak hours). Tilth serves brunch on the weekends. ✉ *1411 N. 45th St., Wallingford* ☎ *206/633–0801* ⊕ *www.tilthrestaurant.com* ⚑ *Reserva-tions essential* ⊟ *MC, V* ⊗ *Closed Mon. No lunch.*

PIZZA

☺ $ ✕**Tutta Bella.** It's very hard to find good pizza in Seattle—even those spots deemed the best in the city serve sad approximations of the clas-sic slice. So, better to abandon the search for the cheap slice and go the gourmet route. Tutta Bella serves authentic Neopolitan-style pizzas that are made with organic local and imported ingredients and baked in a wood-fired oven. Crusts are thin but wonderfully chewy and sauces are light and tangy. They go easy on the cheese, so be sure to order extra cheese if that's what you're craving. The salads are excellent, too. Takeout is available, but many people opt to sit down in the spacious dining room, which has more of a café vibe than that of a typical pizza house. Tutta Bella is very family friendly, but it's also nice enough to serve as a first-date spot, and as the evening progresses you'll see plenty of couples and groups of friends sipping wine and beer as they enjoy their pies. The place gets packed on weekends, and although there is a small lot adjacent to the building, finding parking can be a problem when it fills up. ✉ *4411 Stone Way N, Wallingford* ☎ *206/633–3800* ⊕ *www.tuttabellapizza.com* ⊟ *AE, DC, MC, V.*

SEAFOOD

$–$$$ ✕**Ivar's Salmon House.** This long dining room facing Lake Union has original Northwest Indian artwork collected by the former owner. You can dine inside (ask for a window table), but you really want to snag a table on the deck for views of Lake Union and Downtown. It's all about the Sunday brunch buffet here, though you pretty much can't go wrong with any salmon dish for lunch or dinner and the views get even more spectacular at sunset. The other Ivar's locations in town are uninspiring, but this one lives up to the hype. ✉ *401 NE Northlake Way, Wallingford* ☎ *206/632–0767* ⊕ *www.ivars.net* ⊟ *AE, DC, MC, V.*

THAI

$–$$ ✕**May Thai.** May (named after the owner), is in a reconstructed tradi-
Fodor's Choice   tional teak home, which sticks out like a sore thumb (or a wonderful
★   beacon) on an otherwise uninspiring strip in Wallingford. The bar on the lower floor is downright sexy—dim, painted in reds and purples, with comfortable booths and candlelit corners. But to really focus on

the food, head up the curving staircase to the elegant dining room. Though many people are quick to dismiss upscale or expensive Thai food as "inauthentic," that charge is completely unfounded here (when they say spicy, they mean spicy) and it's a pleasure to get a menu that is much more concise than at cheaper places, and food that is much more artfully prepared. The pad thai, usually a glutinous, flavorless mess at most places, is complex and comes with some of its ingredients laid out in a banana leaf; you mix them in as you see fit. The *grapao kaidow* (meat sautéed in a garlic basil sauce accompanied by a fried egg over rice) is excellent; and the tart, spicy *tom ka* soups, whether made with shrimp or chicken, are the best in the city. Don't miss the specialty cocktails made with fresh juices. ✉*1612 N. 45th St., Wallingford* ☎*206/675–0037* ⊕*www.mayrestaurant.com* ▤*AE, DC, MC, V* ⊘*No lunch.*

UNIVERSITY DISTRICT

Not surprisingly, the University District is good for cheap ethnic eats and not so good for fine dining—or dining in places where the tables aren't sticky, for that matter. It's worth strolling up and down The Ave (University Way NE) to see if anything beckons to you before settling on a spot.

If you don't mind doing the lunch buffet thing, head to Araya Vegetarian Place on 45th Street between 11th and 12th avenues. It is beloved of UW students for providing a buffet of a great array of vegetarian Thai dishes for about $7.

AMERICAN

$ ✕**Portage Bay Cafe.** This lovely breakfast and lunch spot is a great alternative if you want to avoid busy University Avenue. Everything's organic here, from the produce piled on the breakfast bar to the breads used to make amazing French toast. At lunch, you'll find sandwiches, salads, and burgers, as well as a few fancier dishes like crab cakes, catfish and ahi fillets, and pork chops. ✉*4130 Roosevelt Ave. NE, University District* ☎*206/547–8230* ⊕*www.portagebaycafe.com* ▤*AE, DC, MC, V* ⊘*No dinner.*

BRAZILIAN

$–$$ ✕**Tempero Do Brasil.** Folks come from far afield to this festive place for a taste of Brazil. The popular cod, prawn, and halibut dishes simmered in coconut-based sauces are complex and satisfying; entrées arrive with moist, chewy, long-grain rice and delectable black beans. For a larger meal, try the charbroiled Argentine steak, *bife grelhado*. Finish with cold passion-fruit mousse or tangy guava paste served with farmer's cheese, and strong dark coffee. The outstanding food, attention to detail, and earnest staff make dining here a pleasure. The airy patio is perfect for icy Brazilian cocktails in summer. Note that this is at the very top of The Ave; it's a long walk from the campus. It's also very pricey for simple Brazilian food, so make sure that's really what you're craving before trekking out here. ✉*5628 University Way NE, Uni-*

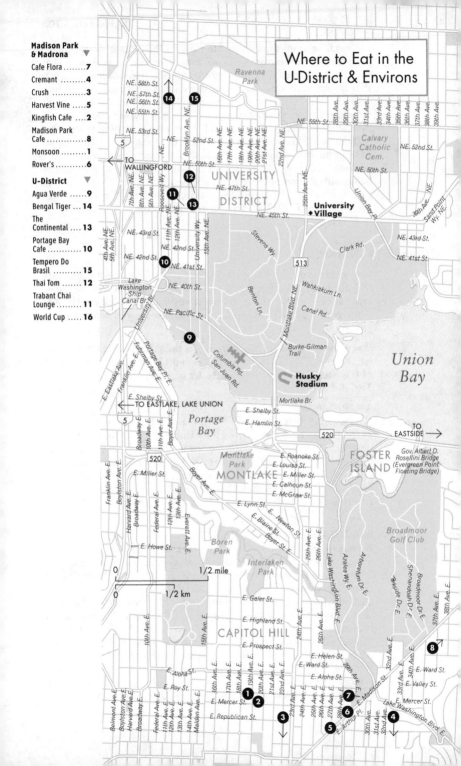

Where to Eat in the U-District & Environs

versity District ☎206/523–6229 ⊕*www.temperodobrasil.net* ☰*AE,
DC, MC, V* ☉*Closed Mon. No lunch.*

GREEK

¢–$ ✕**The Continental.** This Greek diner and pastry shop is popular with UW
students and professors. Breakfast, which might include a tomato-and-
feta omelet, is served all day. Heartier lunch and dinner options include
gyros, chicken and beef souvlaki, and reliable seafood dishes. Most of
the baking is done on-premises; save room for some baklava. ✉*4549
University Way NE, University District* ☎206/632–4700 ☰*AE, D,
MC, V.*

INDIAN

$ ✕**Bengal Tiger.** Though the immensely popular Taste of India (down the
street at the corner of 55th) has a much better ambience—no thought
has been put into deco at this no-frills restaurant—Bengal Tiger has
become the new neighborhood favorite thanks to its authentic (which
often means very spicy) dishes. Most of the menu will yield familiar
words—naan, tandoor, vindaloo, tikka masala—but there are a few
East Indian items not normally found in curry houses dominated by
northern Indian specialties. The lunch buffet is $8. ✉*6510 Roosevelt
Way, University District* ☎206/985–0041 ☰*MC, V.*

MEXICAN

¢–$ ✕**Agua Verde.** You can rent kayaks at Agua Verde, which is on a street
bordering Portage Bay and surrounded by boat repair shops. The food
here has been described as Baja California Mexican, which may refer
as much to the bright, beachy colors as it does to the cuisine. Tacos
aren't dripping with grease, cheese, or sour cream, and choices include
fish and chili-chicken. With a nod to the U-District diet, there are lots
of vegetarian items. Regulars swear by the black-bean cakes and *man-
godillas,* quesadillas with mango and poblano chilies. ✉*1303 NE
Boat St., University District* ☎206/545–8570 ⊕*www.aguaverde.com*
☰*MC, V* ☉*Closed Sun.*

THAI

★ ¢–$ ✕**Thai Tom.** This might be the cheapest Thai restaurant in town, but
rock-bottom prices aren't the only reason this place is always packed—
the food is delicious, authentic, and spicy (two stars is usually pretty
hot). The garlic chicken is one of the chef's favorite dishes, so it's not
surprising that it rates high among the customers. Pad thai is rich and
flavorful instead of oily. Tables can be hard to come by during the dinner rush, but there's usually space at the counter that lines the open
kitchen. ✉*4543 University Ave., University District* ☎206/548–9548
☰*No credit cards* ☉*Closed Sun. No lunch Sat.*

WORTH A SPECIAL TRIP

ITALIAN

$$–$$$
FodorśChoice
★
✕**Cafe Juanita.** There are so many ways for an expensive, "destination" restaurant to go overboard, making itself nothing more than a special-occasion spectacle, but Cafe Juanita manages to get everything just right. The space is refined without being too designy or too posh, and the food, much of which has a northern Italian influence, is also perfectly balanced: you won't find needlessly flashy fusion cooking or heavy sauces that obliterate subtle flavors. If you've ever had a bad experience with lamb, you must order it here; one bite of the tender saddle of Oregon lamb will expunge all memories of tough wedding entrées or greasy falafel-stand horrors. The daily fish specials are also worth the plunge, especially when the menu's featuring whole fish. Even the "seasonal fruit" offering—so often the most boring item on a dessert menu—is finally done some justice here: instead of being smothered in too-sweet creams or syrups, local strawberries are marinated in balsamic vinegar, sprinkled with black pepper, and topped with a mild gelato. To top it all off, the restaurant has an excellent wine list. Cafe Juanita prides itself on using fresh, local, and organic ingredients; this is hardly a unique feature among Seattle restaurants, but if you need to convince someone (or yourself) that local and organic foods taste (and look) better, this should be your first stop. ⚠ **Avoid trying to drive here during rush hour—dealing with traffic on the 520 bridge is not an auspicious start to such a great meal.** ✉9702 NE 120th Pl., Kirkland ☎425/823–1505 ⊕www.cafejuanita.com ⊟MC, V ⊗Closed Mon. No lunch.

PACIFIC NORTHWEST

★ **$$$$**
✕**The Herbfarm.** You may want to fast before dining at the Herbfarm. You'll get no fewer than nine courses here—it's the closest thing the Northwest has to Spain's famous El Bulli restaurant. "Dinner" takes at least four hours and includes five fine Northwest wines, so you may also want to arrange for transportation to and from the restaurant. Before you tuck in, you'll be treated to a tour of the garden, so you'll be able to see exactly where most of your meal's ingredients are coming from. The dining room itself is in a century-old farmhouse and is reminiscent of a country estate—whether said estate is in France, England, or the Pacific Northwest is your call, but it's probably the only place in the Seattle area where you can imagine being part of a dinner party at the summer home of a magnate or baron. The set menus change weekly; if you have dietary restrictions, it's essential to call ahead to make sure that you won't be confronted with a menu full of things you can't eat. With all products coming from the farm, or other local growers and suppliers, you can always expect fresh seafood and shellfish, artisanal cheeses, and luscious seasonal fruits. ✉14590 NE 145th St., Woodinville ☎425/485–5300 ⊕www.theherbfarm.com ⚑Reservations essential ⊟AE, MC, V ⊗No lunch.

Popular with Parents

Just as Seattle is serious about its food, we're serious about ensuring that no parent leaves town without knowing why. Here are some picks you and your kids will enjoy.

Anthony's Pier 66, Downtown. Children are welcome at the fish bar (where they mix a mean Shirley Temple) and in the more-formal dining room. Kids love to watch the tugboats and ferries in the busy harbor.

Blue C Sushi, Fremont. Kids love watching colorful plates of sushi chug around the room on a conveyor belt. Despite the hip setting, you'll find the waitstaff is very accommodating of children, especially in the early evening before the place gets really crowded. Noodle dishes, plates of tempura veggies, and panko-breaded *katsu* chicken are good choices for kids not ready for the raw stuff. Blue C even has small, interlocking chopsticks for he kids.

Cascadia, Belltown. The white tablecloths may make you nervous, but Cascadia is surprisingly kid-friendly. Chef Kerry Sear has created a three-course "tasting menu" for kids. Choices include things like chicken strips and the miniburgers that adults at the bar can't seem to get enough of. Dessert is a sundae or chocolate chip cookie and chocolate milk.

Coastal Kitchen/Five Spot/ Endolyne Joe's. These neighborhood restaurants, part of the same franchise, are very family-friendly. The Five Spot in Queen Anne is no frills and open all day, so it's good in a pinch. Coastal Kitchen in Capitol Hill is casual but more sophisticated; parents will love the inventive seafood specials, while picky eaters can get their fillets simply grilled or sautéed.

The sundaes at Endolyne Joe's in West Seattle alone are worth a trip.

Elysian Brewing Company, Capitol Hill. A reliable choice in the heart of the Hill, which has a dearth of places that seem appropriate for very young kids. Tasty pub grub including burgers, fish-and-chips, fries, and tacos.

Etta's, Belltown. Tom Douglas named this restaurant, one of three he owns, after his daughter. The jovial staff will make you feel right at home with your own daughters and sons.

Hi-Life, Ballard. Ballard families love this casual restaurant in a converted firehouse. The menu is large; basics like great burgers are well represented, but fancier fusion dishes keep parents happy, too. The waitstaff is also very friendly.

Kidd Valley. Burgers, fries, shakes, and more in an indestructible fast-food restaurant that has branches in Queen Anne (on Queen Anne Avenue), Greenlake, and the University District.

Palisade/Maggie Bluff's, Magnolia. Palisade has a big weekend brunch buffet, where kids can fill their own plates, and food for feeding the fish in the pond. Maggie Bluff's has a kid's menu and places from which to watch for sailboats.

Red Mill, Magnolia and Greenwood. Some say the burgers here are the best in town, and the Greenwood location is only blocks from the Woodland Park Zoo.

Tutta Bella, Wallingford. Though Neopolitan pizza is a bit different from the classic slice, kids don't seem to mind. You won't be the only one with kids in tow if you're here on a weekend afternoon or early evening.

SEAFOOD

$$$–$$$$ ✕**Third Floor Fish Cafe.** There are plenty of spots in Seattle proper that serve great seafood with water views, but the Third Floor is worth a trip if you want great seafood served with views of the water (Lake Washington in this case) *and* the skyline in a space that's more elegant than those you'd find in West Seattle. With the exception of the obligatory overpriced roast chicken and beef tenderloin entrées, the menu focuses completely on fresh seafood from sesame-crusted king salmon to Alaskan black cod in a shiitake vinaigrette. Diners are rarely disappointed with the daily specials. The well-thought-out seating arrangement gives almost everyone a view, but it's worth trying to request a window table. This place is pricey, but the pre-fixe menu offered on Sunday is a great deal. ⊠*205 Lake St. S, Kirkland* ☎*425/822–3553* ⊕*www.fishcafe. com* ☌*Reservations essential* ▭*AE, D, MC, V* ☙*No lunch.*

Where to Stay

WORD OF MOUTH

"The Mediterranean and Marqueen are both located in a neighborhood called Lower Queen Anne. They are about 1.5 miles from the heart of the retail core (4th and Pine). The neighborhood is near entertainment venues and, as a result, has many good reasonably priced dining options."

—happytrailstoyou

Updated
by Carissa
Bluestone

SEATTLE'S LODGING SCENE CAN OFFER endless joys or endless frustrations, depending on your budget and tastes. If you've got money to burn, you'll find plenty of ritzy, high-tech, designer hotels, all of which are clustered in the Downtown area, and some of which have amazing views of Elliott Bay, the Puget Sound, and the Olympic Mountains. Seattle is experiencing a mini–hotel boom thanks to its not-so-mini tourism boom, and the new properties that have popped up in the last few years are truly impressive—and expensive. Many older properties are rising to the call and are renovating and adding new amenities like hotel-wide Wi-Fi. On the other end of the price spectrum, Seattle has a few wonderful bed-and-breakfasts, most of which are tucked into residential areas that will give you a much different (and much better) picture of Seattle living than the Downtown core.

Another definite plus of Seattle's scene is that although the major chains like the Hilton and the Westin are well represented, many of the newest, hippest, and most interesting properties are boutique hotels or are owned by smaller, less-corporate chains. You won't find many boring rooms here—each hotel has its own style and great pains are taken to come up with unique motifs and amenities. Service is uniformly great; if you come across a snooty concierge or desk person, you should switch hotels—hostile disinterest is not the name of the game in this city's hospitality industry. So accommodating are the city's hotels that extras like pet-friendly policies and evening wine-and-cheese receptions are the norm rather than the exception.

Sounds great, right? Well, there are a few pitfalls to finding a place to stay in the city. If you want to stay anywhere else but Downtown, your options are very limited; Capitol Hill is the only residential neighborhood that has a decent selection of accommodations, and by selection we mean almost exclusively B&Bs, whose few rooms can fill up fast. Now that the Chelsea Station B&B in Fremont closed, the residential neighborhoods north of the canal have only one property of note, Greenlake Guesthouse. The city has very few interesting or cool budget spots—in high season, good luck finding a room for under $100 that has any style, especially if you haven't booked in advance. Most of the reliable, utilitarian chain motels are in awkward (and often downright ugly and unsafe) parts of town. As for the mid-range properties . . . well, what mid-range properties? In high season, the city has a noticeable dearth of hotels in the $125–$175 range. Often, shabby motels charge mid-range prices, while the hotels that offer decent mid-range accommodations charge luxury prices over $200 a night. (On the flip side, rates drop so dramatically in low season, high-end properties become reasonably affordable.)

All that said, Seattle is a small city, so there's almost no such thing as a bad location in terms of convenience (unless it's rush hour, in which there's no such thing as a good location). Some hotels in outlying areas will transport you to and from Downtown for free. Bed-and-breakfasts on Capitol Hill are a manageable walk from Downtown and are near boutiques, restaurants, bars, and movie theaters. Although the University District is inconvenient to Downtown, it's reasonably convenient to the neighborhoods above the canal, such as Fremont and Ballard, and to the northern parts of Capitol Hill. If you plan to bus it a lot, however, for your sanity's sake, don't go farther north than Queen Anne.

WHAT IT COSTS					
	¢	$	$$	$$$	$$$$
FOR 2 PEOPLE	under $100	$100–$150	$150–$200	$200–$250	over $250

Price categories are assigned based on the range between the least and most expensive standard double rooms in high season. Tax (17%) is extra.

DOWNTOWN & BELLTOWN

Downtown has the greatest concentration of hotels, many of which are new high-end high-rises, though there are also several boutique hotels and mid-range properties in historic buildings. There aren't many budget properties in the area, save for the Green Tortoise hostel and Pensione Nichols, though there are a few reliable chains in South Lake Union, which is still convenient to Downtown.

All Downtown hotels are convenient (and within walking distance) to all major sights, to Belltown to the north, and to Capitol Hill to the east (though you may opt to bus it or cab it over to this neighborhood). Although the waterfront is an integral part of Downtown, there are surprisingly few hotels directly on the water. ■ TIP➔ **Many high-rises, of course, have water views, but make sure to specify that you want a room with a view, as they're not always guaranteed, even on the higher floors.**

Belltown, slightly north and within walking distance of Downtown, has the city's trendiest hotels, including the coolest budget option in the city, the Ace Hotel, and one of the city's loveliest urban inns, the Inn at El Gaucho. Belltown's a great place to stay if you plan to hit the bars and clubs in the neighborhood; the area's weekend night activity can be good or bad depending on how you feel about navigating the congestion (made up of both traffic and drunk people) on First Avenue. Thankfully, properties like the Ändra and the Hotel Max have Belltown addresses but are far enough away from First Avenue to avoid the thick of the nightlife scene. Staying in one of these properties is good for anyone who finds Downtown a little too touristy, but still wants to stay close to the area.

DOWNTOWN

$$$$ **Alexis Hotel.** The Alexis occupies two historic buildings near the waterfront. It's a fine place to stay, with a focus on art (including a rotating collection of paintings in the corridor between wings). Subdued colors, imported Italian and French fabrics, and antiques can be found in the standard rooms and public spaces. It is, however, starting to look a little worn around the edges in some places, and it's really the specialty suites that set this property apart. The John Lennon suite is gorgeous, with framed lithographs and song lyrics, shoji screens separating the bedroom from the living room, and a wood-burning fireplace. Room 230 is also special: it's a full-blown two-bedroom

HOTEL KNOW-HOW

PRICES

Seattle's peak season is May through September, with August at the pinnacle, and prices throughout the city skyrocket then; some are nearly double what they are in low season.

The lodgings listed are the cream of the crop in each price category. Prices are based on the best high-season rates offered directly from the property; they do not take into account discounts or package deals you may find on consolidator Web sites. We always list the facilities that are available—but don't specify whether they cost extra.

Assume that hotels operate on the European Plan (EP, with no meals) unless specified that they use the All-inclusive (all meals and some drinks and activities), Continental Plan (CP, with a Continental breakfast), Modified American Plan (MAP, with breakfast and dinner), or the Full American Plan (FAP, with all meals).

BOOKING TIPS

It is imperative to book in advance for July and August, especially if you want to stay in one of the in-demand budget properties or at any bed-and-breakfast. Some B&Bs start to fill up their summer slots by March or April. The best water-view rooms in Downtown luxury hotels are often gone by mid-February. You aren't likely to have trouble booking a room the rest of the year as long as your visit doesn't coincide with major conventions, or arts or sporting events.

B&Bs fill up quickly, but it's always worth giving them a call to see what's available. Because they encourage longer stays, you may be able to get a last-minute room for a night or two to bridge the gaps that pop up as long-term guests turn over. In this case, you're doing the B&B a favor and may get a discounted rate.

All hotels listed have private bath, heat, air-conditioning, TV, and phone unless otherwise noted. In the past, air-conditioning was never a deal-breaker—mild summers and cool breezes in the evening made it unnecessary. However, Seattle's had some very hot summers recently; the heat wave in 2006 sent many an air-conditioning-hating resident running to the nearest movie theater for relief. If you're addicted to the air conditioner, make sure your room has it in summer; at the very least, make sure that windows in air conditioner–less properties open easily.

HOW TO SAVE

The best way to save? Travel off-season. Amazing deals at the hottest properties can be had in spring (and sometimes even in early June). Weather is more hit or miss this time of year than in July or August, but there are often many beautiful dry days. Rates drop dramatically again once October rolls around. Mild, picture-perfect fall days are a well-kept secret here—hiking's often good until the end of the month and the Cascades get some beautiful fall colors.

But you probably want to see the city in its late-summer glory. In that case, good luck to you. There isn't much of an upside to Seattle's high season—the best you can do is book as far in advance as possible. Midweek prices may be lower than weekend rates, but don't count on it. You'll always save more with multinight stays, particularly at B&Bs, which often have unofficial policies of giving discounts to long-term guests. The best collection of good deals is on Capitol Hill because most of its properties are B&Bs; the Queen Anne and Lake Union neighborhoods also turn up some good deals and are much closer to Downtown than the U-District, which is the other neighborhood that has a decent selection of mid-range properties.

We're extremely skeptical about special packages offered by hotels. Unless they include tangible discounts, such as reduced room rates, great deals (or credits for) spa treatments, or *dinner* credits (who needs an expensive Continental breakfast when there's a coffee shop on every corner?), they're often not worth the extra cost. We won't name names, but one hip hotel's "romance" package was nothing more than a standard room with no view, a tiny box of second-rate chocolates, and an awful bottle of Pine & Post wine that retails for under $10 in any supermarket. Ask tough questions and do the math before you get sucked into a seemingly good deal. Special amenities advertised in packages, such as late check-out times, can often be arranged without committing to a whole package.

PETS, IN. SMOKERS, OUT

Seattle is a great city for pets. A lot of people, including many B&B proprietors, have dogs, and a great many hotels accept pets; some hotels have better pet amenities than kids' programs.

Smokers, on the other hand, haven't fared so well. The city has banned smoking in most public places, including all restaurants and bars, and the new and pervasive trend is for hotels to be completely smoke-free. It's now extremely difficult to find smoking rooms; puffers may want to reconsider upgrading to that balcony room.

THE SOUND OF CHANGE

Seattle is undergoing major growth and development. It seems like every other corner in the South Lake Union and Downtown areas is the site of major construction. It's worth inquiring about such things while booking and asking how local construction projects may affect the views, noise levels, and traffic situations around your hotel.

apartment with wood floors and exposed-brick walls. Spa suites, which include in-room spa services from the Aveda spa downstairs, are a good choice if you can't splurge on a specialty suite; their bathrooms have two-person tubs and retro red-and-tan flowered wallpaper (the ones on the sixth floor also have skylights). A few rooms have restricted water views; book early to secure one of those. Downstairs, the Library bistro is one of the city's favorite lunchtime hideaways and bars. ⊠*1007 1st Ave., Downtown, 98104* ☎*206/624–4844 or 888/850–1155* ⊕*www. alexishotel.com* ⬅*73 rooms, 36 suites* ⬒*In-room: refrigerator, Wi-Fi. In-hotel: restaurant, room service, bar, gym, spa, laundry service, concierge, public Wi-Fi, parking (fee), some pets allowed, no-smoking rooms* ⊟*AE, D, DC, MC, V.*

$$$$
Fodor'sChoice
★

▨ **Fairmont Olympic Hotel.** The grande dame of Seattle hotels seems to occupy its own corner of the universe, one that feels more old New York or European than Pacific Northwest. The lobby of the elegant Renaissance Revival–style historic property has intricately carved wood paneling, graceful staircases that lead to mezzanine lounge areas, and plush couches occupied by men in suits and well-dressed older ladies— not a fleece jacket or pair of Birkenstocks in sight. Guest rooms, though lovely, are not quite as impressive as the lobby; however, major renovations, to be completed by early 2008, may change that—everything from fabrics to TVs is being replaced. The hotel assures us that repairs will not disturb guests, but if you have any concerns, ask for a floor that's far away from the one currently being renovated. Note that executive suites are kind of small for suites; deluxe rooms are nearly the same and slightly cheaper. The well-heeled traveler will find everything he or she needs here: elegant dining at The Georgian, afternoon tea in the lobby, in-room massage and spa services, and a shopping arcade that includes tux rental and couture women's wear. Though it's hard to imagine kids being truly comfortable here, the hotel does its best to accommodate families. ⊠*411 University St., Downtown, 98101* ☎*206/621–1700 or 800/441–1414* ⊕*www.fairmont.com/seattle* ⬅*232 rooms, 218 suites* ⬒*In-room: safe, refrigerator, DVD (some), ethernet. In-hotel: 3 restaurants, room service, bar, pool, gym, laundry service, concierge, public Wi-Fi, parking (fee)* ⊟*AE, D, DC, MC, V.*

$$$$

▨ **Grand Hyatt Seattle.** Adjacent to the Washington State Convention Center, this glitzy hotel appeals to business travelers. Rooms, set upward from the 10th floor, have cushy furnishings and vistas of Elliott Bay, Lake Union, and the Cascades. Three types of large suites have separate sitting rooms, and executive quarters have refrigerators and wet bars. All bathrooms have Carrara marble floors, Vesuvio granite counters, and oversize soaking tubs. The famous Ruth Chris' Steakhouse and Cheesecake Factory restaurants are downstairs. ⊠*721 Pine St., Downtown, 98101* ☎*206/774–1234* ⊕*http://grandseattle.hyatt. com* ⬅*317 rooms, 108 suites* ⬒*In-room: safe, refrigerator, ethernet, Wi-Fi. In-hotel: 2 restaurants, room service, bar, gym, laundry service, concierge, public Wi-Fi, parking (fee), no-smoking rooms* ⊟*AE, D, DC, MC, V.*

★ **$$$$**

▨ **Hotel Monaco.** The Hotel Monaco is the pet-friendliest hotel in town: not only are pets catered to with special events like canine fashion shows, but anyone who had to leave the pets at home can opt to have a goldfish (who comes with an adorable "hello my name is" introduction card) keep them company. The hotel is full of other fun touches, like bright raspberry-and-cream striped wallpaper, gold sunburst decorations, and animal prints. The bright lobby is a little less whimsical, with hand-painted nautical murals inspired by the fresco at the Palace of Knossos in Crete. There's a nightly wine reception in the lobby, which sometimes includes chair massage or fortune-telling services. Amazingly, none of this fun feels forced or contrived, and guests wishing to have a more low-key experience will be able to do so; they, however, should opt for a room with blue-and-white walls—the eclectic decor is a little easier on the eye in these than in the ones with the raspberry striped wallpaper. ⊠ *1101 4th Ave., Downtown, 98101* ☎ *206/621– 1770 or 800/945–2240* ⊕ *www.monaco-seattle.com* ⇆ *144 rooms, 45 suites* ☼ *In-room: refrigerator, DVD, ethernet, Wi-Fi. In-hotel: restaurant, room service, bar, gym, spa, laundry service, concierge, public Wi-Fi, airport shuttle, parking (fee), some pets allowed, no-smoking rooms* ☰ *AE, D, DC, MC, V.*

$$$$ **Marriott Waterfront.** Another hotel that takes advantage of Seattle's prime waterfront real estate, the Marriott has views of Elliott Bay from most rooms (half have balconies). For the best views, book the north tower. The elegant lobby has cascading Italian chandeliers, walnut detailing, glass-tile mosaic floors, and back-lighted walls of fused onyx and glass. Afternoon tea is served in the gallery, a breezeway that joins the lobby with Todd English's Fish Club Restaurant. ⊠ *2100 Alaskan Way (between Piers 62/63 and Pier 66), Belltown, 98121* ☎ *206/443– 5000 or 800/455–8254* ⊕ *www.seattlemarriottwaterfront.com* ⇆ *345 rooms, 13 suites* ☼ *In-room: Wi-Fi. In-hotel: restaurant, room service, bar, pool, gym, laundry service, concierge, executive floor, public Wi-Fi, airport shuttle, parking (fee), no-smoking rooms* ☰ *AE, D, DC, MC, V.*

★ $$$$ **W Seattle.** The W set the bar for Seattle's trendy hotels, and although its cool has been recently eclipsed by newer properties like Hotel Max and Hotel 1000, it's still an outstanding choice for hip yet reliable luxury. Candlelight and custom-designed board games encourage lingering around the lobby fireplace on deep couches strewn with throw pillows, and the hotel's bar is popular with guests and locals alike. Decorated in black, brown, and French blue, guest rooms would almost be austere if they didn't have the occasional geometric print to lighten things up a bit. The beds are exceptionally comfortable with pillow-top mattresses and 100% goose-down pillows and comforters. Floor-to-ceiling windows maximize striking views of the Puget Sound and the city. ⊠ *1112 4th Ave., Downtown, 98101* ☎ *206/264–6000 or 877/946– 8357* ⊕ *www.whotels.com* ⇆ *419 rooms, 16 suites* ☼ *In-room: safe, refrigerator, DVD, ethernet. In-hotel: restaurant, room service, bar, gym, laundry service, concierge, public Internet, public Wi-Fi , parking (fee), some pets allowed, no-smoking rooms* ☰ *AE, D, DC, MC, V.*

$$$–$$$$ **Hotel 1000.** Hotel 1000 is new to the scene, but all new luxury prop-
FodorśChoice erties will have to answer to it. The centerpiece of the small lobby is
★ a dramatically backlighted staircase (don't worry, there's an elevator)

and glass sculpture that looks like crystallized stalks of bamboo. The small sitting room off the lobby, with its elegant fire pit surrounded by mid-century modern swiveling leather stools, looks as though it's been designed for leggy Scandinavian beauties and the men in black turtlenecks who love them. The designers wanted the hotel to have a distinctly Pacific Northwest feel and they've succeeded greatly without being campy. The whole hotel is done in dark woods and deep earth tones with an occasional blue accent to represent the water. Materials like rain forest marble connect the urban space to the outdoors as much as possible. Elegant raw silk throws and fabrics in the guest rooms aren't local per se, but they could be seen as a nod to the city's sizable Thai community. Rooms are full of surprising touches, including large tubs that fill from the ceiling, and Hotel 1000 is without a doubt the most high-tech hotel in the city. Your phone will do everything from check the weather and airline schedules to give you restaurant suggestions; your TV doubles as an art gallery, displaying the greatest hits from the period of your choice; and MP3 player and iPod docking stations are standard amenities. If you ever get tired of fiddling with the gadgets in your room, there's a state-of-the-art virtual driving range programmed with some of the world's most challenging courses. ✉ *1000 1st Ave., Downtown, 98104* ☎ *206/932–3102* ⊕ *www.hotel-1000seattle.com* ⌖ *101 rooms, 19 suites* ⌂ *In-room: safe, refrigerator, DVD, Wi-Fi. In-hotel: restaurant, room service, bar, gym, spa, laundry service, concierge, public Wi-Fi, parking (fee), some pets allowed, no-smoking rooms* ▤ *AE, MC, V.*

$$$–$$$$

FodorśChoice ★

🏨 **Inn at the Market.** For its views alone, the Inn at the Market would be worthy of a Fodor's Choice. But views alone don't make a hotel great—this one has all the pieces of the puzzle from friendly service to a great location (in the north end of the market, but tucked away from the bustle of First Avenue) to simple, sophisticated guest rooms with Tempur-Pedic beds and bright, spacious bathrooms. Although the decor is nowhere as unique as at the Edgewater (the hotel's only direct competitor), if you book far enough in advance, you can get a far better deal on a water-view room here. All rooms have essentially the same decor and amenities; they're differentiated only by the types of views they offer. You certainly won't be disappointed with the Partial Water View rooms—some have small sitting areas arranged in front of the windows. The four Deluxe Water View rooms are really spectacular, though—708 and 710 are the ones to shoot for, as they share a large private sundeck. Even if you have to settle for a City Side room (a good deal even in high season), you can enjoy uninterrupted water views from the fifth-floor garden deck. The lobby is small but sweet; you won't see the water from here, but the view of a courtyard with a fountain and ivy-covered balconies is very pleasant. It's worth mentioning that room service is from Campagne, one of the city's best restaurants. The hotel has a complimentary town-car service for Downtown locations. ✉ *86 Pine St., Downtown, 98101* ☎ *206/443–3600 or 800/446–4484* ⊕ *www.innatthemarket.com* ⌖ *60 rooms, 10 suites* ⌂ *In-room: safe, refrigerator, Wi-Fi. In-hotel: 3 restaurants, room ser-*

vice, laundry service, concierge, public Wi-Fi, parking (fee), no-smoking rooms ⊟*AE, D, DC, MC, V.*

$$$–$$$$ 🏨 **Seattle Hilton.** Just west of I–5, the Seattle Hilton is a popular site for meetings and conventions. The rooms are tasteful but nondescript—you'll be paying a lot for a brand name here, reliable though it may be. Some rooms do have views over the city to Elliott Bay in the distance. Providing excellent views of the city, the Top of the Hilton bar-restaurant serves well-prepared salmon dishes and other local specialties. An underground passage connects the Hilton with the Rainier Square shopping concourse, the 5th Avenue Theatre, and the convention center. ✉*1301 6th Ave., Downtown, 98101* ☎*206/624–0500, 800/542–7700, or 800/426–0535* ⊕*www.hilton.com* 🛏*237 rooms, 3 suites* ♿*In-room: safe, refrigerator, ethernet. In-hotel: 2 restaurants, room service, bar, gym, laundry service, concierge, parking (fee), no-smoking rooms* ⊟*AE, D, DC, MC, V.*

$$$–$$$$ 🏨 **Seattle Sheraton Hotel and Towers.** Though the Sheraton will always be a powerhouse hotel, it's not one of our favorites. It may have filled a luxury hotel void at one point, but as Seattle's hotel boom brings eye-popping new places like Hotel 1000, the Sheraton seems less and less worthy of the expense. That said, you could do worse: the large, quiet accommodations are decorated in warm, honey hues, with plush carpets and bright Chihuly glass-art accents. A stay in the top five floors of either tower provides complimentary concierge service and breakfast, as well as views of Elliott Bay and Lake Union. Unfortunately, the hotel annoyingly charges for some amenities, like Wi-Fi, that should absolutely be free when you're spending so much on a room. Overall, the hotel caters primarily to business travelers and people attending events at the nearby convention center. ✉*1400 6th Ave., Downtown, 98101* ☎*206/621–9000 or 800/325–3535* ⊕*www.sheraton.com/seattle* 🛏*1,258 rooms, suites* ♿*In-room: safe, refrigerator, ethernet. In-hotel: 3 restaurants, room service, bar, pool, gym, spa, laundry service, concierge, parking (fee), no-smoking rooms* ⊟*AE, D, DC, MC, V.*

$$$ 🏨 **Hotel Vintage Park.** The fading star of the Kimpton boutique hotels (which include the Monaco and the Alexis) is again on the rise after a major 2006 renovation. The Vintage Park has always been notable for its connections to local wineries, and its devotion to the local wine scene is stronger than ever. In addition to holding weekly receptions in the lobby where winemakers are often present to discuss their products, the hotel can set up almost any wine-theme vacation you want from day tours to multiday excursions that start with you skydiving or white-water rafting to a vineyard (we're not kidding). Each guest room is named for a Washington winery, has photographs and artwork donated by the winemakers, and a color palette that includes all the hues you might encounter while walking among the vines from deep purples to pale greens and golds. The best views offered are of the Rem-Koolhaas–designed public library; ask for an "04" room. This is a smaller property with fewer facilities than some of the other nearby properties—the lobby's only interesting when the reception's in full swing. However, it's an updated place that's not another mid-century modern clone, which makes it a good choice for anyone looking for

comfort, quiet, and coziness (with just a little pizzazz) versus the latest trends and gadgets. ✉*1100 5th Ave., Downtown, 98101* ☎*206/624–8000 or 800/624–4433* ⊕*www.hotelvintagepark.com* ⇘*125 rooms, 1 suite* ♨*In-room: refrigerator, Wi-Fi. In-hotel: restaurant, room service, laundry service, concierge, parking (fee), some pets allowed, no-smoking rooms* ▭*AE, D, DC, MC, V.*

$$$ ▣ **Mayflower Park Hotel.** In a historic building, the Mayflower Park is like a smaller, less-showy version of the Fairmont Olympic. The bi-level lobby has brass fixtures and a few antiques, but it's more of a comfortable pause than a grand statement. Guest rooms are decorated in a similarly classic style, and standard rooms are on par with what you'd expect from any good mid-range chain; deluxe rooms are a little more interesting. All rooms have nice bathrooms with large mirrors and pedestal sinks. Standard rooms are on the small side, but the Mayflower Park is so sturdily constructed that it's much quieter than many modern Downtown hotels. The property is connected to the Westlake Center by a corridor, and it has its own star restaurant, Andaluca. Oliver's, a well-known martini bar, is popular with the older set for its perfectly poured drinks. ✉*405 Olive Way, Downtown, 98101* ☎*206/623–8700 or 800/426–5100* ⊕*www.mayflowerpark.com* ⇘*159 rooms, 13 suites* ♨*In-room: safe, refrigerator, Wi-Fi. In-hotel: restaurant, room service, bar, gym, laundry service, concierge, public Wi-Fi, parking (fee), no-smoking rooms* ▭*AE, D, DC, MC, V.*

$$$ ▣ **Renaissance Seattle.** Rooms at this high-rise between Downtown and I–5 are decorated in deep green, burgundy, and brown, with metal accents and dark-wood furniture. Good views of Downtown, Elliott Bay, and the Cascades can be had from rooms above the 10th floor—above the 20th, they're excellent. Rooms are attractive enough, especially for a mid-priced chain, if not terribly well laid out (standards can seem a little cramped). Guests on the club-level floors get complimentary Continental breakfast and their own concierge. The rooftop health club has a 40-foot pool. ✉*515 Madison St., Downtown, 98104* ☎*206/583–0300 or 800/546–9184* ⊕*www.marriott.com* ⇘*466 rooms, 88 suites* ♨*In-room: refrigerator, ethernet. In-hotel: 2 restaurants, room service, bar, pool, laundry service, concierge, public Internet, public Wi-Fi, parking (fee), some pets allowed* ▭*AE, D, DC, MC, V* ⓧ*CP.*

$$$ ▣ **Westin Hotel.** The flagship of the Westin chain often hosts U.S. presidents and other visiting dignitaries. Northeast of Pike Place Market, Seattle's largest hotel is easily recognizable by its twin cylindrical towers. The innovative design gives all rooms terrific views of Puget Sound, Lake Union, the Space Needle, or the city. Airy guest rooms are furnished in a simple, high-quality style. ✉*1900 5th Ave., Downtown, 98101* ☎*206/728–1000 or 800/228–3000* ⊕*www.starwoodhotels.com/westin/seattle* ⇘*822 rooms, 43 suites* ♨*In-room: safe, refrigerator, ethernet. In-hotel: 3 restaurants, room service, bars, pool, gym, laundry service, concierge, public Wi-Fi, parking (fee), some pets allowed, no-smoking rooms* ▭*AE, D, DC, MC, V.*

★ $$–$$$ ▣ **Hotel Max.** Fans of minimalism, travelers interested in cutting-edge local artists, and anyone who wants to feel like a rock star will be very happy with the Max, a superstylish hotel that swears it has created a new design esthetic, "Maximalism." The hallway of each floor is dedicated to a different local photographer and giant black-and-white photos cover each door; scenes range from Americana to live concert shots from Seattle's grunge heyday (fifth floor). A few paintings from local artists (different in each room) are all that decorate the gray walls of the guest rooms; a few carefully placed accent colors like an orange bedspread or a red cushion on a stool save the rooms from being drab. The beds are huge and heavenly—a surprising bit of substance from a hotel that prides itself on appearance. The only downside to the Max is that some of the rooms are on the small side—owing more to the constraints of being in a historic building than to tenets of minimalism—and bathrooms have very little counter space. A few rooms, however, are large enough to include black leather couches. ⊠*620 Stewart St., Downtown, 98101* ☎*206/728–6299 or 866/833–6299* ⊕*www.hotelmaxseattle.com* ⌇*163 rooms* ⌂*In-room: safe, refrigerator, Wi-Fi. In-hotel: restaurant, room service, gym, laundry service, concierge, public Wi-Fi, parking (fee), no-smoking rooms* ⊟*AE, D, DC, MC, V* ⊺⊙*CP.*

$$–$$$ ⊞**Inn at Harbor Steps.** Although it's on the lower floors of a modern high-rise residential building, this inn has a country quaint theme, with lots of florals in the guest rooms, country manor–looking plaid armchairs in the lobby, and wicker furniture in the library. Guest rooms are large, with high ceilings, gas fireplaces, and tidy kitchenettes. Bathrooms have large tubs (some of them whirlpools) and oversize glass-enclosed shower stalls. A breakfast buffet is served in the dining room. Complimentary hors d'oeuvres, wine, and tea are served each afternoon in the library. ⊠*1221 1st Ave., Downtown, 98101* ☎*206/748–0973 or 888/728–8910* ⊕*www.innatharborsteps.com* ⌇*30 rooms* ⌂*In-room: refrigerator, ethernet. In-hotel: pool, gym, laundry service, concierge, parking (fee)* ⊟*AE, MC, V* ⊺⊙*BP.*

$$–$$$ ⊞**Red Lion Hotel on 5th Avenue.** In the heart of Downtown, this former bank headquarters is a comfortable business-oriented hotel convenient to the shopping and financial districts. Service is warm and professional; the public spaces have high ceilings, tall windows, and dark-wood paneling. Lining the lobby are sitting areas with couches and overstuffed chairs upholstered in olive green and aubergine velvets and brocades. Guest rooms are midsize and are attractive enough, though decor in standard rooms is only a small step above standard chain motel; they do, however, have pillow-top mattresses, something you won't find in every chain. Rooms on the executive floors, 17–20, have exquisite views of Puget Sound or the city skyline. ⊠*1415 5th Ave., Downtown, 98101* ☎*206/971–8000 or 800/733–5466* ⊕*www.redlion.com* ⌇*287 rooms, 10 suites* ⌂*In-room: refrigerator, Wi-Fi. In-hotel: restaurant, room service, gym, laundry service, concierge, public Wi-Fi, parking (fee), some pets allowed, no-smoking rooms* ⊟*AE, D, DC, MC, V.*

$$ ⊞**Crowne Plaza.** A favorite of business travelers, the Crowne Plaza is directly off I–5, midway between First Hill and the financial district. The lobby is small and somewhat plainly appointed in teal and cream

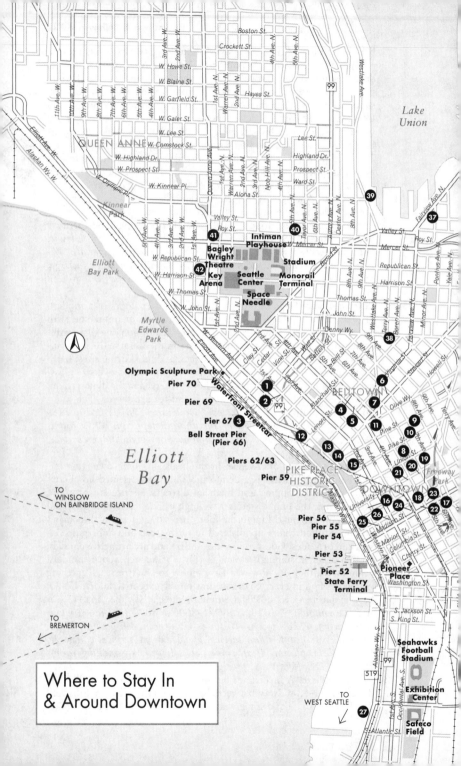

Boston St.

Crockett St.

W. Howe St.

W. Blaine St.

W. Garfield St.

Hayes St.

W. Galer St.

W. Lee St.

W. Comstock St.

QUEEN ANNE

Lee St.

W. Highland Dr.

Highland Dr.

W. Prospect St.

Prospect St.

W. Kinnear Pl.

Ward St.

Aloha St.

Kinnear Park

Valley St.

Roy St.

41

Intiman Playhouse

40

W. Republican St.

Bagley Wright Theatre

W. Harrison St.

42

Seattle Center

Stadium

Monorail Terminal

Elliott Bay Park

W. Thomas St.

Key Arena

Space Needle

W. John St.

Thomas St.

John St.

Myrtle Edwards Park

Denny Wy.

38

39

Fairview Ave. N.

37

Valley St.

Roy St.

Mercer St.

Republican St.

Harrison St.

Olympic Sculpture Park

Clay St.

Cedar

Vine St.

Pier 70

1

6

BELLTOWN

Pier 69

2

99

7

Olive Wy.

Pier 67

3

4

5

11

Pine St.

9

Bell Street Pier (Pier 66)

12

Lenora St.

10

8

Pike St.

Elliott Bay

Piers 62/63

13

14

Union St.

19

Pier 59

15

PIKE PLACE HISTORIC DISTRICT

21

20

Freeway Park

DOWNTOWN

TO WINSLOW ON BAINBRIDGE ISLAND

University

16

24

18

23

17

Pier 56

26

22

Pier 55

Madison St.

25

Pier 54

Marion St.

Columbia St.

Pier 53

Cherry St.

TO BREMERTON

Pier 52 State Ferry Terminal

Pioneer Place

Washington St.

S. Jackson St.

S. King St.

Seahawks Football Stadium

Where to Stay In & Around Downtown

Exhibition Center

TO WEST SEATTLE

27

Safeco Field

S. Atlantic St.

CLOSE UP

Bring the Kids

Most hotels in Seattle allow children under a certain age to stay in their parents' room at no extra charge, but others charge for them as extra adults; be sure to find out the cutoff age for children's discounts. Cribs are usually available upon request and hotel staff can assist you in finding a reputable babysitter.

The Fairmont Olympic Hotel has a swimming pool and offers outstanding children's amenities such as toys and games, room service menu with a Winnie-the-Pooh theme, and child-size furniture and bathrobes. Families are made welcome at the Marriott Residence Inn on Lake Union. All the guest accommodations have kitchens and bedrooms off living rooms. The large atrium-style lobby has a waterfall and several sitting areas stocked with books and games. The Silver Cloud inns are all suitable for families, especially the one on Lake Union. The Sheraton's big rooms and rooftop pool make it popular with families. In the U-District, the laid-back University Inn has an outdoor pool, free parking, and the Portage Bay Cafe—a great place to dine with kids.

with brass accents and potted plants, but at least it's modern-looking and lacking floral-print eyesores. Rooms are quiet and spacious, with lounge chairs and work areas; they're a bit more stylish than in other chains in this price category. All have views of Harbor Island to the south and Elliott Bay, Seattle Center, and the Space Needle to the north. The relaxed and friendly staff is very attentive. ✉ *1113 6th Ave., Downtown, 98101* ☎ *206/464–1980 or 800/860–7715* 🌐 *www.crowneplazaseattle.com* *415 rooms, 28 suites* *In-room: safe, refrigerator, Wi-Fi. In-hotel: restaurant, room service, bar, gym, laundry service, concierge, public Internet, public Wi-Fi, parking (fee), some pets allowed, no-smoking rooms* 💳 *AE, D, DC, MC, V.*

$–$$ **Executive Hotel Pacific.** This 1929 property maintains a low profile in a neighborhood filled with fancy hotels. Its Fourth Avenue entrance is through a coffee shop, and its Spring Street entrance is marked only by a small awning. Location (it is across the street from the public library), skilled management, and the fair price make this one of the best lodging bargains Downtown. Guest beds have tan leather headboards, sage-green spreads, and flat-screen TVs. Note that because this is an older building, rooms are small, but they all have city views. ✉ *400 Spring St., Downtown, 98104* ☎ *206/623–3900 or 888/398–3932* 🌐 *www.executivehotels.net/seattle* *159 rooms* *In-room: refrigerator, dial-up. In-hotel: restaurant, gym, concierge, public Internet, parking (fee), some pets allowed, no-smoking rooms* 💳 *AE, D, DC, MC, V* *CP.*

¢–$ **Pensione Nichols.** One of the few affordable options Downtown is also a unique and endearing place. Proprietor Lindsey Nichols attends to her guests with great enthusiasm and humor—this is a place where you can just kick back, relax, and be yourself. It's kind of like a hostel for grown-ups, or one for young people who want more privacy and style than a hostel can provide. The bed-and-breakfast is in a historic building, so the rooms are a mixed bag of sizes and layouts, but most have wrought-iron furnishings and all have new beds. Some rooms have shared bathrooms (which are clean and spacious), and most of the rooms on the third floor have skylights instead of windows (because of the building's historic status, Nichols can't renovate to add windows). Second-floor suites have their own bathrooms, as well as full kitchens and large living rooms; one suite has an enclosed balcony, the other has an accessible fire escape. Breakfast is served in the light-filled common area overlooking Elliott Bay. ✉*1923 1st Ave., Downtown, 98101* ☎*206/441–7125* ⊕*www.pensionenichols.com* ⬏*8 rooms without bath, 2 suites* ⬥*In-room: no phone, no TV, Wi-Fi. In-hotel: no elevator, public Wi-Fi, some pets allowed* ⊟*AE, D, DC, MC, V* ⦿*CP.*

★ ¢   🖪**Green Tortoise Backpacker's Hotel.** The Green Tortoise recently moved into spiffier digs and the new facilities and the impressive cleanliness of the place make this a viable option for all sorts of travelers who don't mind sacrificing a little comfort and privacy for the best deal in town. Sure, the majority of guests are in their early twenties, but the Green Tortoise does get its share of thirty- and even fortysomething travelers. Though singles and couples can rent some of the smaller dorm-style rooms as private accommodations, all rooms here share bathrooms. Bathrooms, however, are spacious, clean, and nicely tiled stand-alone units, so you don't have to worry about showering next to strangers. Each bunk bed has its own locker (bring your own lock), light, and fan. The rate includes a breakfast buffet, with waffle fixings and "unlimited eggs." Security cameras in all the halls and public spaces help to keep guests safe. ✉*105 Pike St., Downtown, 98101* ☎*206/340–1222* ⊕*www.greentortoise.net* ⬏*38 rooms without bath* ⬥*In-room: no phone, no TV, Wi-Fi. In-hotel: no elevator, laundry facilities, public Internet, public Wi-Fi* ⊟*MC, V* ⦿*CP.*

BELLTOWN

★ $$$$ 🖪**Edgewater.** Raised high on stilts above Elliott Bay—with the waves lapping right underneath it—Seattle's only hotel on the water affords spectacular west-facing views of ferries and sailboats, seals and seabirds, and the distant Olympic Mountains. The whole hotel has a rustic-chic, elegant hunting lodge look, with plaid rugs and fabrics and peeled-log furnishings. Many rooms have gas fireplaces. Note that there is a significant price jump between the waterfront rooms and the waterfront premium rooms and the upgrade is not necessarily worth it unless you want a little more space. City-view rooms are very expensive, considering, but if you prefer the hotel's unique take on lodge decor to the sleek, modern look of most Downtown hotels, the expense might be justified, especially if you really like looking at the Space Needle. Some suites have full views, overstuffed chairs, and spa tubs; or just go all-out for the enormous, party-style Beatles Suite (Room 272), where the famous Brits stayed in 1964. The elegant Six Seven restaurant, with its timber-and-river-stone setting and crystal chandeliers, has indoor-outdoor seating with a bay vista. ✉*Pier 67, 2411 Alaskan Way, Pier 67, Belltown, 98121* ☎*206/728–7000 or 800/624–0670* ⊕*www.edgewaterhotel.com* ⬏*213 rooms, 10 suites* ⬥*In-room: refrigerator, Wi-Fi. In-hotel: restaurant, room service, bar, gym, bicycles, laundry service, concierge, public Wi-Fi, parking (fee), no-smoking rooms* ⊟*AE, D, DC, MC, V.*

Sustainably Chic

It takes much more than a recycling program to make a hotel "green," and although no properties in Seattle are doing everything right, a few local luxury hotels have expanded the industry's definition of eco-friendly.

Pan Pacific: Motion detectors make sure heating and a/c units don't run when there's no one in the room. All toilets are European models that feature a half-flush option to save on the hotel's water consumption.

Fairmont Olympic: The Fairmont has a wide-reaching Green Partnership program in which all hotel employees are educated to help the hotel conserve water and energy. Initiatives range from recycling and composting programs to more inventive programs like capturing condensation from the hotel's steam heating to be used in the washing machines. Eco-conscious guests are rewarded, too—hybrid vehicles get free valet parking. **Kimpton properties:** Kimpton, whose Seattle

hotels include Hotel Monaco, Hotel Vintage Park, and the Alexis Hotel, has a far-reaching approach. Not only are recycling, towel and linen reuse, and energy conservation and water conservation schemes standard, but the company uses environmentally friendly cleaning products in all its properties and all of its printed materials are printed on recycled paper with soy-based ink.

1 Hotel & Residences: Still a mere glimmer in the city's eye, this Starwood Capital property, to be completed in late 2008, will be a fully LEED-certified green building. LEED (Leadership in Energy and Environmental Design) is a green building rating system, and certification on any of its levels is not easy to get. The hotel will combine all of the strategies mentioned above to make sure the day-to-day is as green as the building. You can track the hotel's progress at www.1residences.com.

$$$–$$$$ **Hotel Ändra.** Scandinavian sensibility and clean, modern lines define this sophisticated Belltown hotel, which is a great, less-pricey alternative to the W. The lobby is fantastic, with armchairs and couches arranged in front of a fireplace that's flanked by floor-to-ceiling bookcases. It also has a loft area, where you can retreat to if Lola, the restaurant right off the lobby, gets too boisterous. Rooms (most of which are suites) have khaki color walls and dark fabrics and woods, with a few bright accents and geometric prints here and there. Alpaca headboards and large wood-framed mirrors are interesting touches, and all the linens, towels (from Frette), and toiletries are high quality. The Ändra's clientele includes people in the creative fields and the music industry, along with Microsoft and biotech moguls in the making. ⊠ *2000 4th Ave., Belltown, 98101* ☎ *206/448–8600 or 877/448–8600* ⊕ *www. hotelandra.com* ⇆ *4 studios, 23 rooms, 92 suites* ⚷ *In-room: safe, refrigerator, ethernet, Wi-Fi. In-hotel: restaurant, room service, bar, gym, laundry service, concierge, public Wi-Fi* ⊟ *AE, D, MC, V.*

$$–$$$ **Inn at El Gaucho.** Dark, swank, and sophisticated, this luxury retro-
Fodor'sChoice   style 1950s property tops Belltown's beloved El Gaucho steak house.
★   Eighteen ultrachic suites have pale yellow walls, chocolate-color wood, workstations cleverly concealed in closets, and buttery leather furni-

ture. They're filled with such goodies as feather beds, Egyptian linens, Riedel stemware, fresh flowers from Pike Place Market, and large-screen plasma TVs. The sleek bathrooms have rain-style showers and high-end bath and body products. Rooms face either Puget Sound, the city, or the hotel's atrium; atrium rooms are quieter than those that face the street. Room 9 has the best view of the sound. Additional perks include room service from El Gaucho and in-room massages and spa services from the Hyatt's spa team. The one drawback: the flight of stairs you'll have to climb to get to the inn—there's no passenger elevator and because it's in a historic property, there won't be one anytime soon. ⊠*2505 1st Ave., Belltown, 98121* ☎*206/728–1133 or 866/354–2824* ⊕*http://inn.elgaucho.com/inn.elgaucho* ⇆*18 suites* ⌂*In-room: Wi-Fi. In-hotel: restaurant, room service, bar, no elevator, concierge, public Wi-Fi, parking (fee), no-smoking rooms* ▤*AE, MC, V* ❘○❘*BP.*

\$\$–\$\$\$ ▦**Warwick Hotel.** Service is friendly and leisurely (but not slow) at the Warwick, which is part of an international chain. The rooms are understated without being bland; most have small balconies providing Downtown views. Furnishings tend toward the traditional rather than the modern. Brasserie Margeaux, the hotel restaurant-lounge, is a welcome retreat after a day in this bustling neighborhood. The Warwick offers 24-hour courtesy transportation within Downtown. ⊠*401 Lenora St., Belltown, 98121* ☎*206/443–4300 or 800/426–9280* ⊕*www.warwickwa.com* ⇆*225 rooms, 4 suites* ⌂*In-room: refrigerator, safe, Wi-Fi. In-hotel: restaurant, room service, bar, pool, gym, concierge, public Internet, public Wi-Fi, parking (fee), no-smoking rooms* ▤*AE, D, DC, MC, V.*

★ ¢–\$\$ ▦**Ace Hotel.** The Ace is a dream come true for both penny-pinching hipsters and creative folks who appreciate the chic minimalist decor. Almost everything is white—even wood and brick elements of the original building have been painted over in some places—except for the army surplus blankets on the beds and a few pieces of art on the walls (which include murals from überhip street art luminary Shepard Fairey). The cheapest rooms share bathrooms, which are clean, stand-alone units with enormous showers. Suites are larger (some have leather couches) and have full private bathrooms hidden behind rotating walls. A small dining room hosts a Continental breakfast and has a vending machine with unusual items like Japanese snacks. The Ace has guests of all ages, but understand that this is a very specific experience and aesthetic: if you're not soothed (or stimulated) by the stripped-down, almost austere quality of the rooms or not amused by finding a copy of the *Kama Sutra* where the Bible would be, you won't enjoy this place, no matter how much money you're saving. ⊠*2423 1st Ave., Belltown, 98121* ☎*206/448–4721* ⊕*www.theacehotel.com* ⇆*28 rooms* ⌂*In-room: no a/c (some), refrigerator, Wi-Fi. In-hotel: laundry facilities, public Wi-Fi, parking (fee), some pets allowed, no-smoking rooms* ▤*AE, D, DC, MC, V.*

Lodging Alternatives

APARTMENT & HOUSE RENTALS

Renting an apartment or a house will give you access to Seattle neighborhoods that don't have a lot of traditional accommodations. A furnished rental can save you money, especially if you're traveling with a group.

Residents often list subletting opportunities on Craigslist (⊕ *http://seattle. craigslist.org*).

Sea to Sky Rentals (☎ *206/632–4210* ⊕ *www.seatoskyrentals. com*). **Vacation Rentals by Owner** (⊕ *www.vrbo.com*).

HOME EXCHANGES

You can exchange your home for someone else's by joining a home-exchange organization, which will send you its updated listings of available exchanges for a year and will include your own listing in at least one of them.

HomeLink International ☐ *Box 47747, Tampa, FL, 33647* ☎ *813/975–9825 or 800/638–3841* ⊕ *www. homelink.org* ☑ *$75 per yr.* **Intervac U.S.** ☐ *Box 590504, San Francisco, CA, 94159* ☎ *800/756–4663* ⊕ *www. intervacus.com* ☑ *$125 yearly fee.*

B&BS

Almost all of Seattle's notable B&Bs have been reviewed in this chapter, but the following services can help you find more alternatives both in the city and in outlying areas.

Bed & Breakfast Association of Seattle. ☎ *206/547–1020* ⊕ *www. seattlebandbs.com.* **Washington Bed & Breakfast Guild** (☎ *800/647–2918* ⊕ *www.wbbg.com*).

HOSTELS

There is one hostel of note in Seattle: the Green Tortoise, which is reviewed in this chapter. There was a branch of the reliable Hostelling International (HI) chain downtown, but at this writing, it was closed as the organization searches for a new location. Check the HI Web site (www.hiseattle.org) for updates.

NORTH & EAST OF DOWNTOWN

LAKE UNION

At first glance, the Lake Union area (and here we're mostly referring to the southern tip and the southwestern side of the lake) seems an awkward spot for lodgings, despite the views of the water that some of them offer. There aren't many businesses within walking distance and most of the nearby restaurants aren't worth the trip. That said, the area does have its conveniences. You're halfway between Downtown and the notable residential neighborhoods just north of the Lake Washington Ship Canal: a few minutes' drive south will put you in the middle of Downtown and a few minutes' drive north will have you crossing the Fremont Bridge.

South Lake Union is undergoing tremendous development—there are construction sites everywhere—and plans for a new streetcar service will connect the neighborhood to Downtown. The beacon of change for this area is the sparkling new, stunning Pan Pacific hotel and the enormous Whole Foods gourmet market that's part of its complex.

$$$$ ⊡**Marriott Residence Inn.** An extended-stay hotel, this Marriott is perfect for families. All accommodations are one- or two-bedroom suites, each with a living room and a fully equipped kitchen. Decorated in greens and blues, the comfortable rooms get plenty of natural light. The lobby, in a seven-story atrium with a waterfall, has many areas in which to relax, watch TV, play games, or peruse the cookbooks displayed on bookshelves. Room rates include complimentary shuttle service within a 2½-mi radius of the hotel. ⊠*800 Fairview Ave. N, Lake Union, 98109* ☎*206/624–6000 or 800/331–3131* ⊕*www.marriott. com* ⟿*234 suites* ⅏*In-room: kitchen, ethernet. In-hotel: pool, gym, laundry facilities, public Internet, parking (fee), some pets allowed, no-smoking rooms* ⊟*AE, D, DC, MC, V* ⎪⎪*CP.*

$$$$ ⊡**Pan Pacific Seattle.** This is a stunning hotel, with views that often times
Fodor's Choice eclipse the coveted Elliott Bay waterfront ones. The lobby features a
★ dramatic "floating" staircase (it leads up to meeting spaces and another small lounge), a fireplace, and plush brown suede and leather couches. The Pan Pacific went with a different color palette than most of its competitors—blond and light woods, tan marble, cinnamon accents—and the result is that every corner of the hotel feels full of light even during the gray Seattle winter. All rooms are spacious; large tubs shielded by shoji doors, Hypnos beds, and ergonomic Herman Miller chairs at the desks are standard. All corner Executive King rooms have terrific views of the Space Needle and the mountains to the west and Lake Union to the north. Of the junior suites, Rooms 10 and 11 have the best views of Lake Union—something to note if you're in town for the Fourth of July fireworks. The Pan Pacific is part of a luxury condo development that includes a large fitness center (open to hotel guests), a courtyard of high-end specialty shops, and an enormous Whole Foods, which makes up for the fact that with the exception of the excellent Marazul, the immediate area has few dining options. ⊠*2125 Terry Ave., South Lake Union, 98121* ☎*206/264-8111* ⊕*http://seattle.panpacific.com* ⟿*160 rooms, 1 suite* ⅏*In-room: safe, refrigerator, DVD (some), Wi-Fi. In-hotel: restaurant, room service, bar, gym, laundry service, concierge, public Wi-Fi, parking (fee)* ⊟*AE, DC, MC, V.*

$$–$$$$ ⊡**Marriott Courtyard.** Comfort and convenience make up for this hotel's lack of charm; however, this is yet another chain that's gotten very pricey in high season (though in this case it may have something to do with offsetting the costs of a recent renovation). The perks: Lake Union and Space Needle views, a courtesy shuttle (to and from the Space Needle, convention center, Westlake Center, Pike Place Market, and the waterfront), a cozy lobby lounge, and a pool. The property is on the southwest corner of Lake Union, directly across the street from it. Guest rooms are sunny, spacious, and done in shades of green and burgundy. ⊠*925 Westlake Ave. N (at Aloha St.), Lake Union, 98109* ☎*206/213–0100 or 800/321–2211* ⊕*www.courtyardlakeunion.com* ⟿*250 rooms, 2 suites* ⅏*In-room: refrigerator, ethernet. In-hotel: restaurant, room service, bar, pool, gym, laundry facilities, laundry service, public Internet, parking (fee), no-smoking rooms* ⊟*AE, D, DC, MC, V.*

$$–$$$ ⌧ **Silver Cloud Inn Lake Union.** Though not as attractive as its sister property on Capitol Hill, this Silver Cloud branch has something the other doesn't: views of Lake Union from many of its guest rooms as well as from a third-floor lounge. Rooms are simply and adequately furnished; some of the larger water-view rooms have nice love seats and glass doors that give them some extra light. The hotel is on the southeast corner of the lake and dining options within easy walking distance are a bit better here than on the west side. The hotel has a complimentary shuttle service to Downtown sights. Prices are reasonable considering the location, and therefore weekends in August fill up quickly. ⌧ *1150 Fairview Ave. N, Lake Union, 98109* ☎ *206/447–9500 or 800/330–5812* ⊕ *www.scinns.com* ◄ *184 rooms* ☐ *In-room: refrigerator, ethernet, Wi-Fi. In-hotel: 2 pools, gym, concierge, public Wi-Fi, parking (fee)* ☐ *AE, D, DC, MC, V* ◯*CP.*

QUEEN ANNE

Queen Anne is a large, mostly residential neighborhood. Lower Queen Anne, the part directly north of Belltown, includes the Key Arena and Seattle Center. The main drag of Queen Anne Avenue N is busier and less posh here than in its northern reaches, but the area's safe enough and actually pretty quiet at night. For now, all accommodations are in this section of the neighborhood, and although there's not much of a selection, you can find some better deals here than in Downtown and you'll still be close to everything.

$$–$$$ ⌧ **Hampton Inn and Suites.** Though it's a bit expensive in high season for a chain, it's an attractive choice if better rooms Downtown in the same range can't be found or if you plan to attend events held at the nearby Seattle Center. About half the rooms are suites, which have gas fireplaces, kitchens, and balconies. Standard rooms are furnished with desks and overstuffed chairs. Some rooms also have sofas and kitchenettes. ⌧ *700 5th Ave. N (at Roy St.), Queen Anne, 98109* ☎ *206/282–7700 or 800/426–7866* ⊕ *www.hamptoninnseattle.com* ◄ *124 rooms, 74 suites* ☐ *In-room: safe, kitchen (some), refrigerator, ethernet. In-hotel: gym, laundry facilities, public Internet, parking (no fee)* ☐ *AE, D, DC, MC, V* ◯*CP.*

$$–$$$ ⌧ **MarQueen Hotel.** At the foot of Queen Anne Hill, just blocks from the Seattle Center, the MarQueen is ideal for patrons of the opera, ballet, theater, or Key Arena sporting events. Formerly an apartment building, this 1918 brick hotel has a dark lobby with marble floors, overstuffed furniture, Asian-style lacquered screens, and a grand staircase overlooking a garden mural painted on a facing building. The spacious guest rooms, furnished with reproduction antiques, all have kitchens and sitting areas. The hotel provides complimentary van shuttle service to Downtown locations. Note that although the historic nature of the building gives the place a lot of character, it also means that it's not as sealed off from street noise (which includes several bars) as a newer hotel might be. ⌧ *600 Queen Anne Ave. N, Queen Anne, 98109* ☎ *206/282–7407 or 888/445–3076* ⊕ *www.marqueen.com* ◄ *47 rooms, 4 suites* ☐ *In-room: kitchen, refrigerator, ethernet. In-hotel: restaurant, room service, spa, no elevator, laundry service, con-*

cierge, public Wi-Fi, parking (fee), no-smoking rooms ▤*AE, D, DC, MC, V.*

$ ☷**Mediterranean Inn.** The Mediterranean Inn is a welcome addition to Queen Anne and to the Seattle lodging scene in general. It's a relatively new property, which means it's in good condition, and it's one of the best deals in town—you'll get comfortable (though not terribly spacious) studio apartments with small kitchenettes for surprisingly low prices even in high season. Sometimes, you can snag a room here for less than at the neighborhood's reigning budget spot, the Inn at Queen Anne, which isn't as new or nice as the Mediterranean. Furnishings are nothing special, though the rooms here are nicer than at some chain properties that charge more. Some rooms have views of the Space Needle and the Downtown skyline; the rooftop deck has outstanding views of both for all to enjoy. There are two supermarkets very close by to help you stock your kitchenette, and there are numerous bars and restaurants in the area. ⊠*425 Queen Anne Ave. N, Queen Anne, 98109* ☏*206/428–4700 or 866/525–4700* ⊕*www.mediterranean-inn. com* ⇋*180 studios* ⟐*In-room: no a/c (some), kitchen, ethernet. In-hotel: gym, laundry facilities, public Internet, parking (fee), some pets allowed, no-smoking rooms* ▤*AE, D, DC, MC, V.*

FIRST HILL

★ $$$$ ☷**Sorrento Hotel.** Built in 1909, the Sorrento was designed to look like an Italian villa, with a dramatic circular driveway surrounding a palm-fringed fountain. The hotel is in between Downtown and Capitol Hill and convenient to both. Though its immediate area is not terribly attractive (a lot of hospital buildings and clinics nearby), walking a few blocks north towards the excellent Frye Art Museum along tree-lined streets is a very pleasant experience. The wood-paneled lobby and adjacent Fireside Room are explosions of different fabrics: stripes, checks, chenilles, gold brocading, vividly patterned rugs, and so on. This turn-of-the-20th-century private club look certainly isn't everyone's taste, but the dark Fireside Room is undeniably cozy and tranquil. Guest rooms, on the other hand, are light, airy, and more contemporary, with only a few tasseled pillows and a few antique furnishings to tie them to the decor downstairs. The largest are the corner suites; junior suites are only marginally more expensive than the standard rooms and have a bit more space. This place is impeccable: the Italian marble bathrooms gleam, and day-of-the-week rugs in the elevators show that even those oft-neglected spaces get a daily once-over. The Hunt Club serves excellent Pacific Northwest dishes. Town-car service within the Downtown area is complimentary. ⊠*900 Madison St., First Hill, 98104* ☏*206/622–6400 or 800/426–1265* ⊕*www.hotelsorrento. com* ⇋*34 rooms, 42 suites* ⟐*In-room: safe, refrigerator, ethernet. In-hotel: restaurant, room service, bar, gym, laundry service, concierge, public Wi-Fi, parking (fee)* ▤*AE, D, DC, MC, V.*

CAPITOL HILL

Capitol Hill is a terrific neighborhood to stay in, especially if you want to get a feel for Seattle's residential life but still be close to great bars, music venues, and restaurants—and to Downtown, too. Though many of the Hill's residents are hipsters and pierced and tattooed students, almost all of the neighborhood's lodgings are demure, classically styled bed-and-breakfasts. The one hotel is the Silver Cloud Inn.

Note that many of the neighborhood's B&Bs have changed hands in the past several years, most notably the Hill House and the 11th Avenue Inn. So, familiar places may have entirely new outlooks and attitudes.

★ $$–$$$ **Silver Cloud Inn Broadway.** If you want to stay on Capitol Hill and don't like B&Bs, this is your only option—and a good one it is. Though it doesn't look like much from the outside, the Silver Cloud is full of surprises. The hotel's on a noisy intersection, but you could hear a pin drop in the spacious lobby, which is so comfortable and nicely styled in modern tans, greens, and purples that it looks like it should belong in an independent hotel, not a mid-range chain. Guest rooms are smallish and have no views to speak of due to the property's location, but they have nice furnishings like tall wooden headboards and faux granite–top desks; king rooms have plush plum-color love seats with large ottomans. King Jacuzzi rooms have large tubs and faux fireplaces (which can be set to give off just light or light and heat), but unless you really want that tub, they're not worth the extra cost as the layout is kind of odd—the tub is in what would have been a sitting area only a few feet from the bed, making the room feel cramped. Suites are well laid out and have bay windows—even though the views aren't great, the extra light is a plus. All rooms have microwaves, refrigerators, and wet bars; a shop in the lobby sells snacks and drinks. You're just steps from the Pike–Pine corridor; the hotel provides a free shuttle service to points Downtown. ⊠ *1100 Broadway, Capitol Hill, 98122* ☎ *206/325–1400 or 800/590–1801* ⊕ *www.scinns.com* ⊅ *179 rooms* ♿ *In-room: refrigerator, ethernet, Wi-Fi. In-hotel: restaurant, room service, bar, pool, gym, laundry service, concierge, public Wi-Fi, parking (fee), no-smoking rooms* ⊟ *AE, D, DC, MC, V* ⦿ *CP.*

$–$$ **Bacon Mansion.** On a tree-lined street near Volunteer Park, this 1909 Tudor is surrounded by gardens. The first-floor living room is filled with comfortable furniture and lots of natural light; it also has a grand piano. Each unique guest room is appointed with collectibles old and new. The Capitol Suite has a pine four-poster, a carved oak fireplace, and a view of the Space Needle; from the floral-theme Iris Room you can see Mt. Rainier. Several rooms have hideaway beds in addition to the queen-size beds that are the norm. The Iris Room and the Cabin Room share a nicely appointed bathroom. The restored carriage house provides larger quarters; upstairs, the former chauffeur's quarters now serve as a cozy loft. ⊠ *959 Broadway Ave. E (at E. Prospect St.), Capitol Hill, 98102* ☎ *206/329–1864 or 800/240–1864* ⊕ *www.baconmansion.com* ⊅ *11 rooms, 9 with bath; 2 suites* ♿ *In-room: no a/c, refrigerator (some), Wi-Fi. In-hotel: no elevator, public Wi-Fi, no-smoking rooms* ⊟ *AE, D, DC, MC, V* ⦿ *CP.*

★ $–$$ **11th Avenue Inn.** If your mind's-eye picture of a classic bed-and-breakfast includes antique daybeds, Oriental rugs, and a grand dining room table draped in a lace-edged tablecloth, look no further. The 11th Avenue Inn plays this role perfectly. There are Victorian touches at every turn, but there's nothing chockablock or cluttered about the place: owner David Williams has impeccable taste, and even the small den that holds two public computers and stacks of travel guides, brochures, and laminated menus from the best local restaurants is thoughtfully arranged and appointed. Modestly sized guest rooms are on two floors. The second floor has five rooms; the Citrine is our favorite for its regal antique headboard, but the Opal is a very close second because of the amount of light it gets. The Emerald and Ruby rooms share a bathroom that has a cute green claw-foot tub. The third floor has three rooms, which are closer together but bigger than those on the second floor. They have skylights, and the Garnet and Topaz rooms have window seats from which you can get glimpses of the skyline. A full breakfast is served in the elegant dining room, which is the showpiece of the house. Don't worry about using the wrong fork, though—despite its formal appearance, the inn is a warm and laid-back place, a great ambassador of Seattle hospitality. ⊠*121 11th Ave. E, Capitol Hill, 98102* ☎*206/720–7161 or 800/720–7161* ⊕*www.11thavenueinn. com* ⊨*8 rooms, 6 with bath* ⚷*In-room: Wi-Fi. In-hotel: no elevator, public Internet, public Wi-Fi, parking (no fee), no kids under 12, no-smoking rooms* ⊟*AE, D, DC, MC, V* ⦿*BP.*

\$–\$\$ 🖥**Hill House.** This small, airy B&B is barely more than a year old under its new ownership, but already proprietors Leanne and Paul Larkin have done a great job updating the place, putting fresh coats of paint everywhere (the kitchen is a spring green that's bound to put a smile on your face and the pale blue in the Narcissus Room make it the best one in the house) and adding new furnishings and pieces of art. The three rooms upstairs, named after their color palettes (the Narcissus will be renamed to match its new paint job), are all very different. The spacious Celadon has green walls, hardwood floors, and a queen bed. The Rose Room is small and cozy and best for singles. The Narcissus has its own private bath, and space enough to include a small antique writing desk. Two suites in the basement have private entrances, sitting rooms, TVs and VCRs, and they share a small patio and bamboo garden. The deck off the dining room is open to all guests. The breakfast part of the equation is taken seriously here and the owners will try to accommodate special dietary needs within reason, such as offering pastries from a vegan bakery. ⊠*1113 E. John St., Capitol Hill, 98102* ☎*206/323–4455 or 866/417–4455* ⊕*www.seattlehillhouse.com* ⊨*3 rooms, 1 with bath; 2 suites* ⚷*In-room: no phone, no TV (some), Wi-Fi. In-hotel: no elevator, public Wi-Fi, parking (no fee), no kids under 8* ⊟*AE, D, DC, MC, V* ⦿*BP.*

¢–\$\$ 🖥**Gaslight Inn.** Rooms here range from a crow's nest with peeled-log furniture and Navajo-print fabrics to suites with gas fireplaces and antique carved beds. The large common areas evoke a gentlemen's club, with oak wainscoting, high ceilings, and hunter-green carpet. One owner's past career as a professional painter is evident in the impeccable custom-mixed finishes throughout the inn. The Gaslight is more contemporary than many of its competitors and free of the cluttered feeling that most B&Bs have. That's not to say that it doesn't have any decoration—exquisite artwork on display ranges from glass art to ceramic

FodorsChoice
★

sculptures to mixed-media pieces. There's room to move around in here, including a lovely backyard, and the Gaslight has something no other B&B can claim: a heated pool. ✉ *1727 15th Ave., Capitol Hill, 98122* 📠 *206/325–3654* ⊕ *www.gaslight-inn.com* 🔄 *8 rooms* ⅄ *In-room: no a/c, no phone, refrigerator, Wi-Fi. In-hotel: pool, no elevator, laundry facilities, public Wi-Fi, no-smoking rooms* ⊟ *AE, MC, V* ⦿*CP.*

¢–$$ ⊞ **Salisbury House.** Built in 1904, this Craftsman house sits on a wide, tree-lined street. The spacious rooms contain an eclectic collection of furniture, including some antiques. The decor isn't as eye-popping as at some of its competitors, but travelers who prefer a simpler, more-contemporary look will appreciate the B&B's restraint. The basement suite has a private entrance and phone line, a fireplace, and a whirlpool bath. The Blue Room is the best of the rest: it has a private deck overlooking the garden. The Rose Room is the most traditional looking, with a canopy bed, antique armoire, and floral bed linens. One of the common areas is a sunporch with wicker furniture. The location is not as central as the other B&Bs—it's closer to Volunteer Park than to shops and restaurants—but this can be seen as a plus not a minus. After all, the farther away from the bustle of Broadway and Pike–Pine, the leafier and quieter the neighborhood. Note that the owner has two cats. ✉ *750 16th Ave. E, Capitol Hill, 98112* 📠 *206/328–8682* ⊕ *www. salisburyhouse.com* 🔄 *4 rooms, 1 suite* ⅄ *In-room: no a/c, no TV, ethernet, Wi-Fi. In-hotel: no elevator, public Wi-Fi, no kids under 12, no-smoking rooms* ⊟ *AE, DC, MC, V* ⦿*BP.*

GREEN LAKE

★ $–$$ ⊞ **Greenlake Guesthouse.** With the demise of the Chelsea Station in Fremont, the Greenlake Guesthouse is the lone representative of the residential neighborhoods north of the canal and west of the University District. Thankfully, it's outstanding in every way. The house (which actually feels like a house instead of a museum) is directly across the street from the eastern shore of beautiful Green Lake. The romantic Parkview Suite is the pièce de résistance, with a full view of the park, and pale green walls that play off the green of the leaves just outside the windows. The Cascade has a very limited view of the lake, but it has funky red walls and a gas fireplace to make up for it. All rooms have private baths with jetted tubs and heated tile floors. Owners Blayne and Julie McAfterty have put a lot of thought into everything: a public computer with Internet is available in the living room. A communal mini-bar in the hall dispenses complimentary sodas and water. Bookshelves in the upstairs hallway have an extensive DVD collection of Oscar-winning Best Pictures (along with a few guilty-pleasure action movies and some kids' favorites). To keep things interesting, the full breakfast alternates between savory (an omelet for example) and sweet (such as French toast with fresh seasonal fruit). ✉ *7630 E. Green Lake Dr. N, Green Lake, 98103* 📠 *206/729–8700 or 866/355–8700* ⊕ *www.green-lakeguesthouse.com* 🔄 *4 rooms* ⅄ *In-room: no phone, DVD, Wi-Fi. In-hotel: no elevator, public Internet, public Wi-Fi, no kids under 4, no-smoking rooms* ⊟ *DC, MC, V* ⦿*BP.*

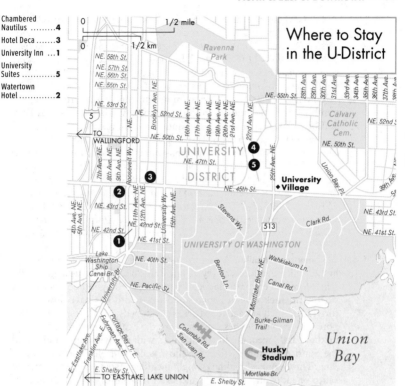

Where to Stay
in the U-District

UNIVERSITY DISTRICT

We have a love-hate relationship with the University District. On one
hand, you'll find some reasonably priced (and very nice) accommodations up here thanks to the needs of parents visiting their kids at the
University of Washington (UW). On the other hand, the area closest
to the main drag, University Avenue (The Ave) is obnoxious and may
seem a bit scuzzy if you're over the age of 21. The area on the other
side of the campus closest to megamall University Village is nicer and
more residential, but inconvenient to the rest of the city. Locationwise,
the U-District seems more cut off from Downtown than its western
neighbors of Wallingford, Fremont, and Ballard, though it's reasonably
convenient to Capitol Hill.

One plus of staying close to The Ave is the plethora of cheap ethnic
restaurants.

$$–$$$ **Hotel Deca.** Within blocks of UW, this 1931 property has been
restored to its original art deco elegance. Guest rooms are individually
decorated and have bright gem colors and bold details. Beds have floor-
to-ceiling headboards done in vibrant colors and fabrics, and some
rooms have fireplaces that look like they're encased in giant stainless-
steel picture frames. Sky Level rooms have great views of the Cascades
and the skyline to boot. The elegant District Lounge restaurant serves a

mix of tasty comfort dishes, snacks, and upscale Pacific Northwest cuisine with Mediterranean influences. ⊠*4507 Brooklyn Ave. NE, University District, 98105* ☎*206/634–2000 or 800/899–0251* ⊕*www. hoteldeca.com* ⊲*158 rooms* ⏃*In-room: Wi-Fi. In-hotel: restaurant, room service, bar, gym, laundry service, concierge, public Wi-Fi, parking (no fee), no-smoking rooms* ⊟*AE, D, DC, MC, V* ⏃⏃*CP.*

$$ ⬚**University Suites.** These cozy mini-apartments, which are perfect for families, share facilities with the adjacent Chambered Nautilus bed-and-breakfast. Each suite is unique: for example, the Ravenna has hardwood floors, an antique cast-iron bed, and herb-print kitchen tiles. The two-bedroom Cascade Suite has mountain views from its porch. All suites have DVD players and private entrances. You can wander across the lawn to the Chambered Nautilus to enjoy its breakfast room or use the business center. ⊠*5005 22nd Ave. NE, University District, 98105* ☎*206/522–2536* ⊕*www.chamberednautilus.com* ⊲*4 suites* ⏃*In-room: kitchen, refrigerator, DVD, Wi-Fi. In-hotel: no elevator, public Wi-Fi, some pets allowed, no-smoking rooms* ⊟*AE, MC, V* ⏃⏃*BP.*

$–$$ ⬚**Chambered Nautilus.** A vivid red door fronts this Georgian Revival home, which overlooks an ivy-covered hillside. In the large living room, a fireplace flickers onto classic Oriental rugs, free guest computer, and sideboard stocked with cookies and tea. Bedrooms have down comforters and such attractive extras as sleigh beds, fireplaces, and private porches. Among the best quarters are the Scallop Chamber, trimmed in khaki and green; the Rose Chamber, with its vivid floral motifs; and the Sunrise Chamber, with its yellow walls and blue-and-white bedding. Three-course breakfasts might include roasted pears with caramel sauce or individual crustless quiches in ramekins. ⊠*5005 22nd Ave. NE, University District, 98105* ☎*206/522–2536* ⊕*www.chamberednautilus.com* ⊲*6 rooms* ⏃*In-room: Wi-Fi. In-hotel: no elevator, public Internet, public Wi-Fi, no kids under 8, no-smoking rooms* ⊟*AE, MC, V* ⏃⏃*BP.*

$–$$ ⬚**Watertown Hotel.** The developer of this property is a boater and an architect, and his predilection and profession are reflected in the exposed-concrete-and-metal construction, porthole windows in bathroom doors, and the clean lines of the fountains and pools. Grasses and smooth river rocks enhance the landscaping. Public spaces are more interesting than guest rooms, though rooms do have attractive bathrooms and space-saving closets accessible from two sides and big operable windows that let in lots of light. One of the most unique features of the hotel is its "Ala Cart" menu, from which you can request a rolling cart filled with games or other goodies, depending on the theme; for example, the poker cart gives you all the accoutrements needed to start a serious game from the chips to the felt tabletop. ⊠*4242 Roosevelt Way NE, University District, 98105* ☎*206/826–4242 or 800/944–4242* ⊕*www.watertownseattle.com* ⊲*155 rooms* ⏃*In-room: safe, refrigerator, ethernet. In-hotel: restaurant, bicycles, laundry facilities, laundry service, public Internet, public Wi-Fi, parking (no fee), no-smoking rooms* ⊟*AE, D, DC, MC, V* ⏃⏃*CP.*

CLOSE UP

Seattle Spas

Although Seattle's spa scene isn't very extensive, there are several top-notch places that offer everything from haircuts and pedicures to elaborate all-day massage and body treatment packages.

Gene Juarez Salon and Spa. With both a lively hair and nail salon and a more tranquil retreat for massage and skin treatments, Gene Juarez offers one-stop shopping. The skincare menu is long and inventive; massage techniques stick to the classics like deep tissue, shiatsu, and reflexology, with some Hawaiian hot stone methods thrown in for good measure. The spa also offers a full menu of men's treatments, including hide-the-gray hair coloring and "sport" pedicures. ⊠ *607 Pine St., Downtown* ☎ *206/326–6000* ⊠ Bellevue Galleria, *550 106th Ave. NE, Bellevue* ☎ *425/455–5511* ⊕ *www.genejuarez.com.*

Habitude Salon, Day Spa & Gallery. Beamed ceilings, polished wood floors, plush furnishings, and tropical scents relax you the moment you enter. Indulge in a single treatment or in such packages as Beneath the Spring Thaw Falls (hydrating glow, massage, scalp treatment, sauna, and smoothie). Other offerings include the Hot Rocks detox sauna, Rainforest Steam Shower, delectable spa lunches, and door-to-door town car service. It's the state's only Aveda Lifestyle spa. ⊠ *2801 NW Market St., Ballard* ☎ *206/782–2898* ⊕ *www.habitude.com.*

Spa Noir. If you're not into the new age earth-tone vibe found in so many day spas, head to Spa Noir, a hip Belltown spot done in black, red, and gold. The spa specializes in facials, manicures and pedicures, and other beauty treatments, but it also offers a small menu of reasonably priced massage treatments. ⊠ *2231 2nd Ave., Belltown* ☎ *206/448–7600* ⊕ *www. spanoir.net.*

Ummelina International Day Spa. Hand-carved Javanese doors open into this tranquil, luxurious, Asian-inspired spa. Relax beneath a warm waterfall, take a steamy, scented sauna, or submit to a mud wrap or smoothing body scrub. The three-hour Equator package for couples includes all this and more. Linger over the experience with a cup of delicately flavored tea. ⊠ *1525 4th Ave., Downtown* ☎ *206/624–1370.*

3

$ 🏠 **University Inn.** This impeccably maintained inn has earned its popularity by steadfastly offering clean friendly lodging in a city where the price for a room is liable to cause sticker shock. It's mainly frequented by travelers with business at UW or the surrounding medical facilities, although leisure travelers also find themselves at home here. Traditional rooms, with small bathrooms and some balconies, were built in the 1960s; the larger deluxe and premium rooms, in a more modern wing, have pull-out sofas and kitchenettes. Guests have free use of the fitness room at the Watertown Hotel sister property, and a free shuttle runs Downtown and to the zoo. ⊠*4140 Roosevelt Way NE, University District, 98105* ☎*206/632–5055 or 800/733–3855* ⊕*www.universityinnseattle.com* ➫*102 rooms* ⚿*In-room: safe, refrigerator (some), ethernet, Wi-Fi. In-hotel: restaurant, pool, laundry facilities,* *laundry service, public Wi-Fi, parking (no fee), some pets allowed, no-smoking rooms* ☰*AE, D, DC, MC, V.*

ELSEWHERE IN SEATTLE

WEST SEATTLE

$$–$$$ ⬚**Villa Heidelberg.** Surrounded by manicured lawns and flower-filled gardens, this 1909 Craftsman has a wide porch from which you can see Puget Sound. The charms of the interior include hardwood floors, embossed wallpaper, and lace tablecloths. Rooms are appointed with comfortable Arts and Crafts furnishings and many have splendid views of the sound, garden, or mountains. Breakfast is served in the formal dining room on a table bedecked with what seem to be different sets of china, linen, and glassware each day. ✉*4845 45th Ave. SW, West Seattle, 98116* ☎*206/938–3658 or 800/671–2942* ⊕*www. villaheidelberg.com* ☞*4 rooms without bath, 2 suites* ⚴*In-room: no phone, Wi-Fi. In-hotel: no elevator, no kids under 6, no-smoking rooms* ☰*AE, MC, V* ⵔ|*BP.*

THE EASTSIDE

The Eastside suburbs have a few high-end properties of note, including Willows Lodge, which is often considered a destination in and of itself. There are also quite a few mid-priced chain hotels, but we don't list them, because unless you have business in the area or plan to spend a lot of time out here, it's really not worth staying this far from Downtown. Though the area has tons of daily commuters to Seattle, and the drive isn't always terribly annoying (especially if you hire a car and driver), rush hour traffic on the 405 and across the 520 bridge is bad. And any money you save on accommodations, you'll spend on gas, as the area is only convenient by car.

Bellevue and Kirkland have the most going on in terms of shops, eateries, and entertainment—Bellevue has its own mini-skyline—but "going on" is relative. Though the addition of a few showpiece restaurants and attractions like the Bellevue Arts Museum give the area a bit more appeal, it's got nothing on the city itself.

★ **$$$$** ⬚**Willows Lodge.** A dramatically lighted old-growth Douglas fir snag greets you at the entrance to this spa hotel. Timbers salvaged from a 19th-century warehouse lend rustic counterpoints to the lodge's sleek modern design. A stone fireplace dominates the lobby, and contemporary Native American prints and sculptures by area artists adorn the walls and gardens. Each large guest room—categorized by size and amenities as "Nice, Nicer, and Nicest"—has a gas-lighted stone fireplace, oversize soaking tub, CD and DVD players, and bathroom with freestanding stone sinks. Nicer rooms have a courtyard set over the river; the Nicest rooms add this plus a jetted tub. The famous spa provides beauty and rejuvenating treatments, and the Barking Frog restaurant is one of the Northwest's top dining venues. It's pretty far from town, but is a favorite of visitors and Seattleites alike because of its proximity to many wineries, including Chateau Ste. Michelle. Along with trying the Barking Frog, a dinner at the equally famous and nearby

CLOSE UP

Airport Hotels

There are very few reasons to stay near SEA-TAC. The airport may be close enough to the city to make getting back and forth relatively easy, but it's far enough away to make staying out here impractical for anyone who doesn't have business in the area or a particularly long layover. However, if you find yourself in need of an airport hotel, these are your best options. **Marriott Sea-Tac** (⊠ *3201 S. 176th St., Sea-Tac, 98188* ☎ *206/241–2000 or 800/643–5479* ⊕ *www.marriott. com*). The luxurious Marriott has a five-story tropical atrium complete with a waterfall, a dining area, an indoor pool, and a lounge. If you must stay in the airport environs, this is your most comfortable option.

Hilton Seattle Airport and Conference Center (⊠ *17620 Pacific Hwy. S, Sea-Tac, 98188* ☎ *206/244–4800* ⊕ *www.hilton.com*). Directly across the street from the airport, this hotel was designed with the business traveler in mind and therefore has lots of extras. Rooms are spacious and cheery.

Radisson Gateway Hotel (⊠ *18118 Pacific Hwy. S, Sea-Tac, 98188* ☎ *206/244–6666* ⊕ *www.radisson-hotels.com*). This is perhaps the best mid-range option close to the airport. Rooms have large desks and comfortable chairs, and the hotel has plenty of amenities.

Herbfarm restaurant is a must. ⊠ *14580 NE 145th St., Woodinville, 98072* ☎ *425/424–3900 or 877/424–3930* ⊕ *www.willowslodge.com* ⟿ *83 rooms, 5 suites* ⌂ *In-room: safe, refrigerator, DVD, ethernet. In-hotel: restaurant, room service, bar, gym, spa, bicycles, laundry service, concierge, public Wi-Fi, parking (fee), some pets allowed* ⊟ *AE, D, DC, MC, V* ⫪*CP*.

$$$–$$$$ ⛆**Bellevue Club Hotel.** Stunning architecture, well-trimmed grounds, and a state-of-the-art sports center create a blend of unbeatable benefits at this boutique accommodation, which is part of an exclusive club. Inside, warm earth tones and clever lighting create the illusion of sunlight even when the rainy Northwest weather arrives, and original oil paintings by local artist Mark Rediske brighten the rooms. Guest quarters have plush armchairs, cherry furnishings, and Turkish area rugs; bathrooms have limestone tiles and some have deep-soak tubs. Deluxe rooms aren't terribly exciting; upgrading is a good move here. Premium rooms have a fireplace and balcony; first-floor Club rooms have 20-foot ceilings, a CD player, and a pretty terra-cotta patio set amid landscaped gardens. The best perk, however, is access to the adjacent athletic club, with its myriad ultramodern sports facilities. Unfortunately, many guests have complained about rude and disorganized service here, so be prepared for hassles—hopefully, you'll be pleasantly surprised. ⊠ *11200 SE 6th St., Bellevue, 98004* ☎ *425/454–4424 or 800/579–1110* ⊕ *www.bellevueclub.com* ⟿ *64 rooms, 3 suites* ⌂ *In-room: safe, refrigerator, ethernet, Wi-Fi. In-hotel: 3 restaurants, room service, bar, 6 tennis courts, 2 pools, gym, spa, laundry service, concierge, public Internet, public Wi-Fi, some pets allowed, parking (fee)* ⊟ *AE, DC, MC, V*.

★ **$$$–$$$$**   🏨 **Woodmark Hotel.** The only hotel on Lake Washington's shores provides contemporary accommodations overlooking the water, a courtyard, or the street. Rooms are done in shades of café au lait, taupe, and ecru; some have balconies looking out to the water. The cheaper Marinaview rooms offer a fine middle ground, but the Creekside rooms overlook an office park. A circular staircase, descending from the lobby to the Library Bar, passes a huge bay window with a panoramic view of Lake Washington. Waters Bistro serves Pacific Rim cuisine, with dishes such as lemongrass steamed clams, and grilled halibut with roasted onion-ginger relish. ✉*1200 Carillon Pt., Kirkland, 98033* ☎*425/822–3700 or 800/822–3700* ⊕*www.thewoodmark.com* ⬦*79 rooms, 21 suites* ♿*In-room: safe, refrigerator, ethernet. In-hotel: restaurant, room service, bar, gym, spa, laundry service, concierge, parking (fee)* ▤*AE, DC, MC, V.*

$$–$$$ 🏨 **Hyatt Regency Bellevue.** Near Bellevue Square and other downtown Bellevue shopping centers, the Hyatt looks like any other sleek highrise, but its interior is adorned with huge displays of fresh flowers and such Asian touches as antique Japanese chests. Rooms are understated, with dark wood and earth tones predominating. Deluxe suites include two bedrooms, bar facilities, and meeting rooms with desks and full-length tables. You'll have access to a health club and pool that share a courtyard with the hotel. The restaurant serves excellent and reasonably priced breakfast, lunch, and dinner; an English-style pub and sports bar serves lunch and dinner. ✉*900 Bellevue Way NE, Bellevue, 98004* ☎*425/462–1234* ⊕*www.bellevue.hyatt.com* ⬦*353 rooms, 29 suites* ♿*In-room: safe, refrigerator, ethernet, Wi-Fi. In-hotel: restaurant, room service, bar, laundry service, concierge, public Internet, public Wi-Fi, parking (fee), no-smoking rooms* ▤*AE, D, DC, MC, V.*

$$–$$$ 🏨 **Westin Bellevue.** Surrounded by the boutiques and greenery of the open-air Lincoln Square shopping plaza, and a minute's drive from the city's ritzy Bellevue Mall and convention center, the shining, 42-story gold luxury tower fits in perfectly with its sophisticated surroundings. Tasteful rooms done in shades of gold are appointed with plush, all-white bedding, flat-screen TVs, and upscale baths with dual showerheads; the best have 10-foot ceilings and terraces. Suites have skyline views. The cosmopolitan Mazana Rotisserie Grill and lounge serves drinks and quick bites to elite crowds, and the opulent Cypress restaurant attracts famous names to breakfast and dinner. ✉*600 Bellevue Way NE, Bellevue, 98004* ☎*425/638–1000* ⊕*www.starwoodhotels.com* ⬦*311 rooms, 26 suites* ♿*In-room: safe, refrigerator, ethernet. In-hotel: restaurant, room service, bar, pool, gym, children's programs (ages 4–15), concierge, parking (fee), some pets allowed* ▤*AE, D, DC, MC, V.*

Nightlife
& the Arts

WORD OF MOUTH

"Check the music listings at www.thestranger.com or www.seattleweekly.com for what is going on when you are here. Your best bets for rock are the Crocodile Cafe, the Showbox, the Tractor Tavern and the Triple Door; you can check their Web sites for what's going on as well."

–christy1

Updated
by Carissa
Bluestone

SEATTLE'S MUSICAL LEGACY IS WELL known, but there's more to the arts and nightlife scenes than live music. In fact, these days, there are far more posh bars than music venues in the city. Seattle is, bluntly put, a great place to drink. You can sip overly ambitious and ridiculously named specialty cocktails in trends-of-the-moment lounges, get a lesson from an enthusiastic sommelier in a wine bar or restaurant, or swill cheap beer on the patio of a dive bar or coffeehouse. Though some places have very specific demographics, most Seattle bars are egalitarian affairs, drawing loyal regulars of all ages.

The music scene is still kicking—there's something going on every night of the week in nearly every genre of music. And today, the city's dynamic theater scene is a highly regarded proving ground for Broadway, while the Seattle International Film Festival draws the finest in world cinema here each spring. The ethereal McCaw Hall is a first-class venue for opera and ballet, and Benaroya Hall, with its outstanding acoustics, is a premier symphony hall. Families enjoy the Children's Theatre, the Northwest Puppet Center, and the many summertime folk art and music festivals.

NIGHTLIFE

Every neighborhood has a little bit of everything, save for dance clubs, which are in short supply and mostly concentrated in Pioneer Square and Belltown. The number of bars in each neighborhood increases greatly if you take into account all of the great restaurants that also have thriving bar scenes—in some cases the line between restaurant and nightspot is so blurred we had trouble determining in which chapter a property belonged.

Downtown is a great place for anyone looking to dress up a bit and hit swanky hotel bars, classy lounges, and wine bars where you don't have to be under the age of 30 to fit in. Downtown also has a smattering of pubs popular with the happy-hour crowd. Barhopping Downtown may require several taxi rides, as things can be a bit spread out, but cabs can actually be hailed on the street in this part of town.

Belltown is the trendiest part of town. It's a madhouse on weekends and most places have a distinct meat market vibe and a youngish, moneyed crowd that tends to get very, very drunk. That said, there are some lovely spaces here, a few of which stay relatively low-key even during the Saturday-night crush, as well as some quirky old neighborhood dives left over from Belltown's former life. Between them, Belltown and Downtown also have a few of the city's major music clubs.

Pioneer Square is dance club central and most places attract a very young crowd. The scene here can get pretty obnoxious, so unless you really want to dance, there are better areas in which to go barhopping.

Capitol Hill has a lot of music venues and bars and is one of the city's liveliest areas at night. The Pike–Pine corridor is base camp for hipsters drinking Pabst out of the can, though the changing face of the neighborhood has brought a few more-upscale, appearance-conscious lounges. The Hill is also the center of the city's gay and lesbian community, with the majority of gay bars and dance clubs along Pike, Pine, and Broadway. A short stretch of 15th Avenue around E. Republican Street is another mini–nightlife district, which is a bit more subdued.

Fremont has quite a few bars lining its main commercial drag of N. 36th Street, including a few spots for live music. Unfortunately, Fremont suffers from a Doctor Jekyll and Mr. Hyde syndrome. During the week, almost any of its simple bars are fine places to grab a quiet drink with a friend. Come Friday night, however, the neighborhood transforms into an extended frat party (think people throwing up in bushes and yelling "whoo hoo" as they stumble down the street) and almost no place is tolerable.

Ballard is quickly eclipsing Capitol Hill in popularity. There are at least half a dozen bars on Ballard Avenue alone. The neighborhood has quickly evolved from a few pubs full of old salts to a thriving nightlife district that has equal parts average-Joe bars, hipster haunts, music spots, wine bars, and Belltown-style lounges.

BARS & LOUNGES

In addition to its bars, Downtown and Belltown in particular have notable restaurants with separate bar areas. For example, all of Tom Douglas's restaurants have lively after-work and weekend bar scenes as do trendy hotel restaurants like BoKa in Hotel 1000. Union, a wonderful restaurant, has a nice bar, too. Most restaurants have impressive bar menus and food is often served until 11 PM, midnight, or even 1 AM in some spots.

DOWNTOWN & BELLTOWN

Alibi Room (⊠ *85 Post Alley, Downtown* ☎ *206/623–3180*), a wood-paneled bar in Pike Place Market, is where well-dressed Seattle film-industry talents sip double martinis and hash out ideas while taking in views of Elliott Bay or studying the scripts, handbills, and movie posters that line the walls. It's an ever-cool yet low-key place. Stop by for a drink or a meal, or stay to listen and dance to live music.

Black Bottle (⊠ *2600 1st Ave., Belltown* ☎ *206/441–1500* ⊕ *www.blackbottleseattle.com*) is a deliberate attempt at a gastropub and therefore it serves a carefully selected, reasonably priced, and uniformly delicious small-plates menu (as opposed to the overly heavy or overly ambitious menus found in so many upscale bars). The interior is simple—just a few black chairs and tables, and wood floors—but sleek. Because it's on the fringe of Belltown, it gets crowded on weekends, but it's less of a see-and-be-seen scene and more of a place for good friends to gather. There's a limited selection of beers on tap, but the wine list is good.

Oliver's (⊠ *405 Olive Way, Downtown* ☎ *206/382–6995*), in the Mayflower Park Hotel, is famous for its martinis. In fact, having a cocktail here is like having afternoon tea in some parts of the world. Wing chairs, low tables, and lots of natural light make it easy to relax after a hectic day.

NIGHTLIFE KNOW-HOW

THE CITY THAT GOES TO SLEEP EARLY

With very few exceptions, bars and clubs close at 2 AM. This means that last call can come as early as 1:30 AM, which depending on where you're from may be the time you're used to *starting* your evening. Seattleites don't seem to mind this too much—in a city whose residential areas are full of bungalows (often shared by multiple roommates), house parties are understandably popular—but visitors may be disappointed if they don't start their evenings early enough.

THE SMOKE WON'T GET IN YOUR EYES

An expanded smoking ban was overwhelmingly approved by Washington State voters in 2005. You cannot smoke in restaurants, bars, or clubs (the ban covers all public places and workplaces). Supposedly, you're not supposed to smoke within 25 feet of any door or window connected to a public place, but this is nearly impossible to achieve in the more-congested nightlife districts and rarely enforced.

GETTING AROUND

Program the numbers for the city's cab companies (⇨ Seattle Essentials) into your cell phone. Unless you have a designated driver or are not venturing too far from your hotel, you will need them. Expect long waits for pickups on Saturday nights. Though you'll probably be able to hail cabs on the street in the deader sections of Downtown—making a restaurant–wine bar type of trip easy enough to manage—you'll have trouble finding empty cabs in Capitol Hill, Belltown, and in the northern neighborhoods.

If you are driving around, exercise caution on the roads, especially when the bars start to let out. Unfortunately, drunk driving is kind of a fact of life, as so many people rely on their cars to get around and public transportation becomes even less frequent late at night.

Parking in Belltown is an absolute nightmare on weekend nights. The neighborhood has ample pay lots, but even those fill up, and finding a space on the street requires either a miracle or a lot of circling. Capitol Hill is almost as bad, though you should be able to find a spot in a pay lot eventually.

GOOD NEWS FOR CLUB-HOPPERS

Many Pioneer Square clubs participate in a "joint cover" pricing scheme; you pay a onetime cover charge at the first club you hit, get your hand stamped, and then are allowed into all other participating venues for free (you'll still have to pay exorbitant prices for drinks everywhere, though). If you don't know where to start, Doc Maynard's on 1st Avenue and Yesler Way usually has the info.

INFORMATION OVERLOAD

The Stranger and *Seattle Weekly* give detailed music, art, and nightlife listings, as well as hot tips and suggestions for the week's events. Friday editions of the *Seattle Times* and the *Seattle Post-Intelligencer* include weekend pullout sections detailing arts and entertainment events.

Purple Café and Wine Bar (✉ *1225 4th Ave., Downtown* ☎*206/829– 2280* ⊕*www.thepurplecafe.com*) is certainly the biggest wine bar in the city and possibly its most dramatic—despite the cavernous quality of the space and floor-to-ceiling windows, all eyes are immediately drawn to the 20-foot tower ringed by a spiral staircase that holds thousands of bottles. There are full lunch and dinner menus (American and Pacific Northwest fare), as well as tasting menus. The place does look and function more like a restaurant than a bar, but there are two actual bars to belly up to, and on busy weekend nights it's there where you'll get the better service. Though Purple is surprisingly unpretentious for a place in the financial district, it's sophisticated enough that you'll want to dress up a bit.

★ **Rendezvous** (✉*2232 2nd Ave., Belltown* ☎*206/441–5823* ⊕*www. jewelboxtheater.com*) has been around since 1924, starting out as an elite screening room for film stars and moguls. It weathered some rough times as a porn theater and a much-loved dive bar, but it's been spruced up just enough to suit the new wave of wealthy locals without alienating everyone else. An old-time feel and the great calendar of events at the bar's Jewelbox Theater (live music, film, burlesque shows) sets it apart from the neighborhood's string of cookie-cutter trendy spots.

Shorty's (✉*2222 2nd Ave., Belltown* ☎*206/441–5449*) may be one of the dingiest bars in Belltown, but it's a bright spot in a neighborhood where most bars serve $10 drinks. Along with a come-as-you-are atmosphere, you'll get pinball machines and video games, cheap beer and hot dogs, and lots of no-frills fun.

Umi Sake House (✉*2230 1st Ave., Belltown* ☎*206/374–8717* ⊕*www. umisakehouse.com*) offers a great selection of sake and sake-based cocktails in a space designed to look like someone shoehorned a real *izakaya* (a sake house that also serves substantial snacks) into a Belltown building—there's even an enclosed patio, which they refer to as the "porch," and a tatami room that can be reserved for larger parties. The sushi is good and there's a very long happy hour offered at one of the bar areas. Despite its chic interior, Umi is less of a meat market than some Belltown spots—unless you're here late on a Friday or Saturday night.

★ **Vessel** (✉*1312 5th Ave., Downtown* ☎*206/652–5222* ⊕*www. vesselseattle.com*) is the place to go if you've saved up some cash in anticipation of spending one night sampling intricate and inventive cocktails. The specialty drinks are outstanding here and you're bound to find a few concoctions that you won't find anywhere else. Service can be a bit slow on crowded weekends, but just spend the time eyeing the attractive bi-level space, which is supermodern without being a caricature of itself. The staircase leading to the mezzanine is backlighted in the type of unnatural yellow color you'd expect to find in a cocktail with 10 ingredients—it's a surprisingly nice touch. This is a sophisticated place (leave the sport sandals at home) that knows it doesn't have to trade on pretension—it's all about the drinks.

Virginia Inn (✉*1937 1st Ave., Downtown* ☎*206/728–1937*) brings Pike Place Market tourists, office workers, and Belltown residents together. It's an institution, really; the kind of place where crowds spill out onto the patio on warm summer evenings. Skip the food, which is overpriced and can be hit or miss, and cross your fingers in the hopes of getting good service—the waitstaff can sometimes demonstrate puzzling amounts of attitude.

Whisky Bar (⊠*2000 2nd Ave., Belltown* ☎*206/443–4490* ⊕*www. thewhiskybarseattle.com*) is one of Belltown's reigning dive bars. Some of its elements seem a little self-conscious—punk-rock versions of cheesecake pinup girls decorate the walls—but this place still has more edge than the hipster hellholes of Capitol Hill. There is indeed a great selection of whiskey and bourbon, as well as the obligatory terrible beers (Miller, Pabst) at supercheap prices.

W Hotel Bar (⊠*1112 4th Ave., Downtown* ☎*206/264–6000*) allows you to enjoy the hotel's signature design style even if you haven't booked a room here. You will certainly feel fabulous sipping a well-poured—if pricey—martini among the city's wealthy and beautiful. There's a bar menu that will give you a taste of the hotel's restaurant, Earth and Ocean.

★ **Zig Zag Cafe** (⊠*1501 Western Ave., Downtown* ☎*206/625–1146* ⊕*www.zigzagcafe.net*) gives Oliver's a run for its money when it comes to pouring perfect martinis and is much more eclectic and laid-back than its competitor. A mixed crowd of mostly locals hunts out this unique spot at the bottom of the Market on the Hillclimb. The Zig Zag is friendly, retro without being obnoxiously ironic, and serves up tasty, simple food and the occasional live music show to boot.

QUEEN ANNE & SEATTLE CENTER

Bricco Della Regina Anna (⊠*1525 Queen Anne Ave. N, Upper Queen Anne* ☎*206/285–4900* ⊕*www.briccoseattle.com*) is a lovely candlelit wine bar that serves a small menu of Italian snacks and entrées that change nightly. The wine list ranges all over the map, but Italian and Northwest wines are particularly well represented. Though it can get crowded on weekends, this place is unfailingly low key, despite the fact that it's popular with the moneyed Upper Queen Anne set.

The Sitting Room (⊠*108 W. Roy St., Queen Anne* ☎*206/285–2830* ⊕*www.the-sitting-room.com*) has a European-café vibe, excellent mixed drinks, and the hearts of residents of both the lower and upper parts of Queen Anne. It's quite an accomplishment to get those two very different demographics to agree on anything, but this sweet, relaxed little spot has done it with its eclectic, mismatched (but not shabby) furniture; zinc bar; sexy, dim lighting; and friendly staff.

Solo (⊠*200 Roy St, Lower Queen Anne* ☎*206/213–0080*) has a lot going on: it's part tapas bar, part art gallery, part screening room, and part music venue, where up-and-coming indie musicians perform intimate sets on a small stage. The cutting-edge artwork and music bring in a lot of Seattle's hipsters, but the bar's location near the Seattle Center and its reputation for excellent, reasonably priced tapas mean that folks without punk-rock cred often wander in, too.

The Spectator (⊠*529 Queen Anne Ave. N, Lower Queen Anne* ☎*206/599–4263* ⊕*www.thespectatorsports.com*) stands out in an area that has quite a few nondescript pubs and sports bars meant to catch pre- or postgame Sonics fans. Watch the NBA, NHL, and NFL on

15 high-definition, flat-screen TVs from comfy red leather booths. The bar also shows international broadcasts of important soccer, rugby, and cricket matches. There's a pool table and video games to keep you busy during commercials or half-times. The Spectator is about as chic and pleasant as a place with 15 TVs showing NASCAR can possibly be.

Tini Bigs (✉ *100 Denny Way, Lower Queen Anne* ☎ *206/284–0931*) attracts successful-looking couples and on-the-prowl singles, who drink martinis (there are 27 variations served here) and chat about each other through a thin, cigar-smoke haze. Black walls and shiny tables dimly lighted with pink lights ensure the stylish a proper stage.

CAPITOL HILL

★ **Capitol Club** (✉ *414 E. Pine St., Capitol Hill* ☎ *206/325–2149*) is a sumptuous Moroccan-theme escape where you can sprawl upon tasseled floor cushions and dine on Mediterranean treats. Despite this being one of the neighborhood's see-and-be-seen spots, good attitudes prevail, and the waitresses are always affable and efficient, even during busy weekend nights.

Chapel Bar (✉ *1600 Melrose Ave., Capitol Hill* ☎ *206/447–4180*) is worth a peek to see just how beautiful a former funeral parlor can be when it's resurrected as a trendy bar. This is no Goth hangout—the space is achingly hip, with white Danish modernesque chairs and banquettes offsetting dark-wood walls; a well-dressed, slightly older (late-twentysomething and thirtysomething) crowd enjoys a long list of specialty cocktails. Go during the week, if possible: the weekends get very busy and very loud and the service suffers.

Liberty (✉ *517 15th Ave. E, Capitol Hill* ☎ *206/323–9898* ⊕ *www. libertybars.com*) occupies an interesting niche—it's a neighborhood hangout that's a dark lounge rather than a comfortable pub. With good drinks made from fresh juices, good sushi, fashion and music mags scattered around, and a self-consciously laid-back vibe, it's no wonder that many Capitol Hill residents make this their "had enough of Pike–Pine" default. Thirtysomethings with media jobs and thick, black-framed glasses often reach critical mass here, but occasionally the crowd gets a little more eclectic.

★ At **Licorous** (✉ *928 12th Ave., Capitol Hill* ☎ *206/325–6947* ⊕ *www. licorous.com*) you might spend more time staring at the striking molded-tin ceiling than perusing the room for a potential date. This attractive bar has provided something that the Hill has been missing for a long time: a hip, well-designed space that attracts a true mix of the neighborhood's residents—one where everyone can feel like a grown-up and enjoy a low-key evening sipping tasty specialty cocktails. Skip the food, which is unremarkable, or just order dessert,

★ **Linda's Tavern** (✉ *707 E. Pine St., Capitol Hill* ☎ *206/325–1220*) is one of the Hill's iconic dives—and not just because it was allegedly the last place Kurt Cobain was seen alive. The interior has a vaguely Western theme, but the patrons are pure Capitol Hill indie-rockers and hipsters. The bartenders are friendly, the burgers are good (brunch is even better), and the always-packed patio is one of the liveliest places to grab a happy-hour drink.

Poco Wine Room (✉*1408 E. Pine St., Capitol Hill* ☎*206/322–9463* ⊕*www.pocowineroom.com*) deserves accolades just for taking one of the least interesting architectural spaces out there—the oddly proportioned retail space of a condo complex—and making it into a sophisticated parallel universe where a friendly crowd lounges on couches and crowds around two small bars to enjoy a competent menu of artisan Northwest wines. A selection of subtle fruit wines is a nice surprise.

FREMONT

Brouwer's (✉*400 N 35th St., Fremont* ☎*206/267–2437* ⊕*www. brouwerscafe.com*) is a Belgian-beer lovers heaven—even if it looks more like a trendy Gothic dungeon than a place with white clouds and harp-bearing angels. A converted warehouse provides an ample venue for a top selection of suds provided by the owners of Seattle's best specialty-beer shop, Bottleworks. There are plenty of German and American beers on offer, too, as well as English, Czech, and Polish selections. A menu of sandwiches, frites, and Belgian specialties help to lay a foundation before imbibing (remember that Belgian beers have a higher alcohol content). Before settling on a seat downstairs, check out the balcony and the cozy parlor room.

The George and Dragon, beloved of all Fremont residents, (✉*206 N. 36th St, Fremont* ☎*206/545–6864* ⊕*www.georgeanddragonpub. com*) is a divey English pub that sees everything from grizzled old Brits watching soccer to hipsters looking for cheap beer and whiskey to the weekend frat crowd that clogs up the front patio area. Major soccer events like the World Cup bring in huge crowds. There's a popular quiz night on Tuesday.

BALLARD

Balmar (✉*5449 Ballard Ave. NW, Ballard* ☎*206/297–0500* ⊕*www. balmar.com*) is one of Ballard's largest and most attractive bars— exposed-brick walls, hardwood floors, comfy cocoa-color couches and ottomans. The two-story space has areas to dine (serving a small-plates menu), drink, and shoot pool. It can be a bit of a fratty meat market on Saturday (it's definitely more New Ballard than Old Ballard), but other than that it's usually pretty mellow and there's room enough to accommodate all the groups of friends and coworkers who enjoy having a slightly more-upscale alternative to Ballard's neighborhood joints.

King's Hardware (✉*5225 Ballard Ave. NW, Ballard* ☎*206/782–0027*), brought to you by the owner of Linda's Tavern in Capitol Hill, has the same ironic rustic decor, the same great patio space, and the same cache with the hipster crowd. It also has good pub grub. This place gets packed to the rafters on weekends—if you want the same scene with less crowds, go two doors down to Hattie's Hat, which was the reigning hipster spot until King's showed up.

★ The **People's Pub** (✉*5429 Ballard Ave. NW, Ballard* ☎*206/783–6521*) is a Ballard institution and a great representative of what locals love about this unpretentious neighborhood. The pub (a dining room and a separate bar in the back) isn't much to look at—just a lot of wood paneling, simple wood tables and chairs, and some unfortunate floral upholstery—but it has a great selection of German beers and draws a true cross section of the neighborhood's denizens from hipsters to old-school fishermen.

Portalis (✉ *5205 Ballard Ave. NW, Ballard* ☎ *206/783–2007* ⊕ *www. portaliswines.com*) attracts serious wine drinkers who gather around communal tables and at the long bar to sample wines from around the world in this cozy, brick-lined bar. It's a full-service retail shop as well, so you can pick up a few bottles to take home. Though it's a bit stuffy for Ballard, it's a nice alternative to the frenetic scene on the upper part of Ballard Avenue.

★ If you manage to score a table at **Sambar** (✉ *425 NW Market St., Ballard* ☎ *206/781–4883*), a teeny-tiny bar attached to French restaurant Le Gourmand, you probably won't leave for hours—there's nothing else like it in Seattle. Though it claims to have French flair, the only thing that cries corner café is its small size. The interior is modern in a way that would look pretentious and stark if translated into a bigger space. Excellent cocktails are mixed with panache and made with premium liquors—just try to walk a straight line out the door when you're done. A small menu offers delicious bites from Le Gourmand, from fresh salads to guilty pleasures like the *croque monsieur* and rich desserts. The crowd is mixed and different every night; soccer moms, young professionals, and Ballard residents who are either too cool or not cool enough for the hipster joints on Ballard Avenue all show up here. A small patio adds some additional and highly coveted seating in summer.

BILLIARDS

Belltown Billiards (✉ *90 Blanchard St., Belltown* ☎ *206/448–6779*) is a spacious neighborhood restaurant with a speakeasy-like entrance, hit-or-miss southern Italian cuisine, and live music. This is not a place for people who are serious about pool—on the weekends it turns into one of the most unbearable meat markets in town. Go during the week when things are calmer or don't go at all.

★ **Garage Billiards** (✉ *1130 E. Broadway, Capitol Hill* ☎ *206/322–2296* ⊕ *www.garagebilliards.com*), built in 1928 as an auto-repair shop, is now a large, happening, chrome-and-vinyl pool hall, restaurant, and bar. The large garage doors are thrown wide open on warm evenings, making this a pleasurable alternative to other cramped places. There are 18 tournament pool tables and a small bowling alley. The place is 21 and over only.

Temple Billiards (✉ *126 S. Jackson St., Pioneer Square* ☎ *206/682–3242* ⊕ *www.templebilliards.com*) is the classic snooker joint you've seen a hundred times in the movies—you know, the one with the plaster-chipped walls and low-wattage lighting. People truly tend to focus on the action at the 11 tables. There's even a private balcony with a lone table where you can live out your Minnesota Fats fantasy. Pool fees Friday and Saturday night are $12 or $14 per hour, depending on the number of players; on Sunday and Wednesday prices drop by half and women play free.

BREWPUBS

Seattle brewpubs churn out many high-quality beers for local distribution. Most have unique house brands on tap, and those with on-site breweries also conduct tours.

Big Time Brewery (⊠ *4133 University Way NE, University District* ☎ *206/545–4509* ⊕ *www.bigtimebrewery.com*), with its neat brick walls, polished wood floors, and vintage memorabilia, is one of the best places in the U-District for a quiet beer apart from the frenetic college scene. At least 10 beers—including pale ale, amber, and porter—are always on tap; tours of the adjacent brewery tell the whole story. Skip the mediocre pub grub.

Elysian Brewing Company (⊠ *1221 E. Pike St., Capitol Hill* ☎ *206/860–1920* ⊕ *www.elysianbrewing.com*), a large, industrial-looking space with a brewery in back, lets you sample house concoctions at the copper-stamped upstairs bar or in the downstairs lounge. It's a perennial favorite of Seattleites and Capitol Hill residents and a good alternative to the hipster haunts and swanky lounges in the area. The winter and fall seasonal ales are particularly good. There's another branch in Wallingford near Green Lake on N. 55th and Meridien, but it's a bit off the beaten path unless you're staying in the area.

Hales Ales Brewery and Pub (⊠ *4301 Leary Way NW, Fremont* ☎ *206/706–1544* ⊕ *www.halesales.com*) produces unique English-style ales and the nitrogen-conditioned cream ale, special bitter, and stout. The pub's signature brews are its pale ale and amber ale; order a taster's "flight" if you want to test the rest.

McMenamins (⊠ *200 Roy St., Queen Anne* ☎ *206/285–4722*) is part of the same Portland-based brewpub chain as Six Arms, with the same brands on tap. It's a madhouse when Seattle Center events let out.

Pike Pub and Brewery (⊠ *1415 1st Ave., Downtown* ☎ *206/622–6044*) is a cavernous bar and restaurant operated by the brewers of the Pike Place Pale Ale. It also houses the Seattle Microbrewery Museum and an excellent shop with home-brewing supplies. True to its location, you might find more tourists than locals here, though it is popular with the Downtown after-work crowd.

Pyramid Alehouse (⊠ *1201 1st Ave. S, Downtown* ☎ *206/682–3377* ⊕ *www.pyramidbrew.com*), a loud festive spot south of Pioneer Square and across from Safeco Field, brews the varied Pyramid line, including a top-notch Hefeweizen and an apricot ale that tastes much better than it sounds. Madhouse doesn't even begin to describe this place during games at Safeco Field, so if you're looking for quiet and immediate seating, make sure your visit doesn't coincide with one. The brewery offers tours daily.

Six Arms (⊠ *300 E. Pike St., Capitol Hill* ☎ *206/223–1698* ⊕ *www.mcmenamins.com*), named for its six-armed Indian dancer logo, is a spacious, popular, two-story brewpub with 17 house and craft beers on tap. Two that stand out are the medium-bodied Hammerhead, and the dark Terminator Stout. As you head back to the restrooms, note the fermenting tanks painted with amusing murals.

COMEDY CLUBS

Comedy Underground (✉222 S. Main St., Pioneer Square ☎206/628–0303 ⊕www.comedyunderground.com) is literally underground, beneath Swannie's Sports Bar & Grill. Stand-up comedy, open-mike sessions, and comedy competitions are scheduled nightly at 8:30. Though it doesn't draw the big national names that Giggles does, it's a nicer venue.

Giggles (✉5220 Roosevelt Way NE, University District ☎206/526–5653) hosts local comedians and open-mike events starting at 9 PM on Thursday and Sunday (free admission before 8:30). Nationally known comedians perform on Friday and Saturday at 8 and 10. Note that national acts draw big crowds and the club gets insufferably crowded. Bring cash or an ATM card—Giggles does not accept credit cards as payment for its overpriced drinks.

Jet City Improv (✉5510 University Way, University District ☎206/781–3879 ⊕www.jetcityimprov.com), Seattle's best improv group, fuses quick wit with music and games. The audience often provides input on what the improvisational skits should be. Shows, which are all-ages, are on every Friday and Saturday at 10:30 PM; there are also 8 PM shows on most Saturdays.

Unexpected Productions (✉Market Theater, 1428 Post Alley, Downtown ☎206/781–9273 ⊕www.unexpectedproductions.org), adjacent to Pike Place Market, hosts tons of different improv events; shows may have holiday or seasonal themes or be done in the style of a certain TV or film genre like sci-fi or noir. On Friday and Saturday at 10:30 the troupe presents the long-running "TheatreSports" show, wherein skits are based entirely on audience suggestions. A family version of TheatreSports is presented on Sunday at 7.

DANCE CLUBS

The **Baltic Room** (✉1207 E. Pine St., Capitol Hill ☎206/625–4444 ⊕www.thebalticroom.net), a classy piano bar–turned–art deco cocktail lounge, is the little dance club that could—it's still popular after quite a few years on the scene and it still manages to get Seattleites of all stripes to take a few turns on the dance floor. Dress up a bit, but try to keep it comfortable. Along with top-notch DJs, skillful rock, acid jazz, and blues acts entertain dancers from a small stage. The compact dance floor gets crowded—a little too crowded—on weekends.

Century Ballroom (✉915 E. Pine St., 2nd fl., Capitol Hill ☎206/324–7263 ⊕www.centuryballroom.com) is an elegant place for dinner and dancing, with a trendy restaurant and a polished, 2,000-square-foot dance floor. Salsa and swing events often include lessons in the cover charge. Only leather-soled shoes are allowed on the floor.

Contour (✉807 1st Ave., Pioneer Square ☎206/447–7704 ⊕www.clubcontour.com) is the place to go if you're not ready to quit partying when Seattle's bars shut at 2—this small club is famous for its after-hours events that keep the doors open until 7 AM. On weekends DJs spin mostly trance and deep house, hip-hop happens on Monday and Wednesday, and Sunday's all about break beats.

The Last Supper Club (⊠*124 S. Washington St., Pioneer Square* ☎*206/748–9975*), a festive club in a hard-partying district, attracts the young and the trendy. House music and disco rock the walls, and the spacious dance floor is jammed when national and international DJs and music acts take the stage.

Pampas Room (⊠*2505 1st Ave., Belltown* ☎*206/728–1337*), hidden beneath the top-rated El Gaucho restaurant, is a first-class, 1950s-style club. The house band plays a mix of jazz, swing, and salsa into the wee hours. Weekends pack in the professional dancers; if you can't keep up, try blending into the mellower weeknight crowd. Dress way up, check your confidence, and step onto the dance floor.

Trinity (⊠*111 Yesler Way, Pioneer Square* ☎*206/447–4140* ⊕*www. trinitynightclub.com*), is a multilevel, multiroom club that offers hip-hop, reggae, disco, and Top 40. It gets packed on weekends—get there early to avoid lines or to snag a table for some late-night snacks. This is the most tasteful and interesting of the Pioneer Square megaclubs—in terms of decor, anyway.

★ **The War Room** has nothing belligerent about it (⊠*722 E. Pike St., Capitol Hill* ☎*206/328–7666* ⊕*www.thewarroomseattle.com*)—the door staff, bartenders, and patrons are all unfailingly friendly. The space is gorgeous: enormous black-and-white portraits of figures like Joseph Stalin and Richard Nixon (actually meant to be an antiwar mural) give the otherwise slick decor (deep-red walls, light-wood paneling, black leather banquettes) some character. A rooftop deck makes this *the* place to spend summer happy hours.

Washington Dance Club (⊠*1017 Stewart St., Capitol Hill* ☎*206/628–8939* ⊕*www.washingtondance.com*) invites everyone to swoosh about the refurbished 1930s Avalon Ballroom, whose 3,000-square-foot maple-wood dance floor is polished to perfection. Learn tango, swing, salsa, and ballroom moves with professional dancers, or drop in for a theme party.

GAY & LESBIAN SPOTS

Most bars are male oriented, though they welcome mixed crowds who respect the clubs and their patrons. Many establishments are on Capitol Hill.

Changes (⊠*2103 N. 45th St., Wallingford* ☎*206/545–8363*) is one of the few gay bars *not* on Capitol Hill. Locals make a night of it on karaoke Monday and Wednesday.

Cuff Complex (⊠*1533 13th Ave., Capitol Hill* ☎*206/323–1525* ⊕*www.cuffcomplex.com*) strives to be a manly leather bar but attracts all shapes, sizes, and styles. The loud, crowded dance floor is tucked away downstairs; the main-floor bar, with its patio, is the place to be on warm nights.

Girl4Girl (☎*206/709–9467 Neumo's info line* ⊕*www.girl4girlseattle. com*) organizes the largest lesbian dance parties and events in the Pacific Northwest. The party has changed venues several times over the years, but Neumo's on Capitol Hill seems to be its current haunt. Events generally take place on the third Saturday of every month. Expect a lot of dancing and drinking, and the odd burlesque performance. The crowd is often very young, but all are welcome.

Madison Pub (⊠*1315 E. Madison St., Capitol Hill* ⊕*www.madisonpub. com*) is a laid-back place to grab a drink—leave your hair gel and dancing shoes at home. Regulars shoot pool, hang out with groups of friends, and chat up the friendly bartenders. This is the antithesis of the scenester spots like Purr.

Neighbours (⊠*1509 Broadway, Capitol Hill* ☎*206/324–5358* ⊕*www. neighbours.com*) is an institution thanks in part to its drag shows, great theme DJ nights, and relaxed atmosphere (everyone, including the straightest of the straights, seems to feel welcome here). The place is packed Thursday through Saturday. The Tuesday night '80s party is popular, too.

OutDancing at Century Ballroom (⊠*915 E. Pine St., Capitol Hill* ☎*206/324–7263* ⊕*www.centuryballroom.com*) opens up Seattle's premier salsa, tango, and swing dancing venue to the city's gay and lesbian community. OutDancing events are held on the third and fourth Friday of each month and start at 8:30 with a quick dance lesson.

Purr Cocktail Lounge (⊠*1518 11th Ave., Capitol Hill* ☎*206/325–3112*) is one of the latest hot spots where beautiful men eye each other over ambitious (read: hit-or-miss) specialty cocktails. It can be kind of a meat market on weekends, but the crowd is generally good-natured and straight friends will feel comfortable here, too.

Re-Bar (⊠*1114 Howell St., Capitol Hill* ☎*206/233–9873* ⊕*www. rebarseattle.com*) is a bar, theater, dance club, and art space that is extremely friendly to all persuasions—straight, gay, lesbian, transgender, whatever. A loyal following enjoys cabaret shows, weekend stage performances, and great DJs. The place has a reputation for playing good house music, but there are many different theme nights, including a rock-and-roll karaoke. Every fourth Saturday of the month Re-Bar hosts Cherry, a popular lesbian dance party.

R Place (⊠*619 E. Pine St., Capitol Hill* ☎*206/322–8828* ⊕*www.rplaceseattle.com*) has all its bases covered—the bottom floor is a sports bar; the second floor has pool tables, pinball, and video games; and the top floor is a full-blown dance club.

The Wildrose (⊠*1021 E. Pike St., Capitol Hill* ☎*206/324–9210*) is Seattle's only dedicated lesbian bar, so expect a mob nearly every night. The crowd at weeknight karaoke is fun and good-natured, cheering for pretty much anyone. Weekends are raucous, so grab a window table early and settle in for perpetual ladies' night.

MUSIC

The Pacific Northwest's rock-and-roll heritage extends from the early '60s garage rock of The Kingsmen (who hit the big time with "Louie, Louie") to the legendary Jimi Hendrix to the grunge phenomenon of Pearl Jam and Nirvana to the present-day success of indie rock band Death Cab for Cutie. Although indie rock and alt-country rule the music scene, a thriving DJ scene and a slowly expanding jazz scene proves that Seattle is evolving.

Coffee House Culture

Some of the city's coffee shops have other lives at night, when the laptop-tapping crowds leave. The quality of the performances—from spoken word to improv jazz—vary greatly; at their worst they can be cringeworthy throwbacks to bad 1960s folk. But the experience is entirely different than that of the loud, sceney music clubs and bars, and occasionally you'll luck out and be treated to performances by the city's best budding singer-songwriters. The following spots have regular performances.

Faire (✉ *1351 E. Olive Way, Capitol Hill* ☎ *206/652–9444* ⊕ *www.faire-gallerycafe.com*). Live jazz every Sunday starting at 8 PM. Open mic night last Thursday of each month. Various other special events on other nights.

Wayward Coffee House (✉ *8570 Greenwood Ave. N, Greenwood* ☎ *206/706–3240* ⊕ *www.wayward-coffee.com*). Live music most Fridays and Saturdays starting at 8 PM. Poetry readings and open mic sessions on Sunday.

Mr. Spots Chai House (✉ *5463 Leary Ave. NW, Ballard* ☎ *206/297–2424* ⊕ *www.chaihouse.com*). Live performances almost every night of the week, ranging from funk to folk to jazz. Check their Web site for current calendar.

World Cup (✉ *5200 Roosevelt Way NE, University District* ☎ *206/729–4929* ⊕ *www.worldcupespressoand-wine.com*). Folk, blues, and acoustic pop artists most Fridays and Saturdays starting at 8 PM.

FOLK & COUNTRY

You might actually hear an Irish accent or two at **Conor Byrne Pub** (✉ *1540 Ballard Ave. NW, Ballard* ☎ *206/784–3640* ⊕ *www.conor-byrnepub.com*), along with live folk, roots, alt country, bluegrass, and traditional Irish music. There's live music almost every night of the week and great beer (including the obligatory Guinness on tap) at this laid-back pub.

The Little Red Hen (✉ *7115 Woodlawn Ave. NE, Green Lake* ☎ *206/522–1168* ⊕ *www.littleredhen.com*) is a country bar through and through. Bring your cowboy boots and hats to this divey honky-tonk, inexplicably located in one of Seattle's most gentrified and generic neighborhoods. Live country bands take the stage most nights; there are free country and line-dancing classes on Sunday and Monday nights. Don't expect anything fancy—this place has not been sanitized for tourists.

Owl n' Thistle Irish Pub (✉ *808 Post Ave., Downtown* ☎ *206/621–7777*) presents acoustic folk music on a small stage in a cavernous room. It's an affable pub near Pike Place Market, and it's often loaded with regulars who appreciate both the well-drawn pints of Guinness and the troubadours.

Tractor Tavern (✉ *5213 Ballard Ave. NW, Ballard* ☎ *206/789–3599* ⊕ *www.tractortavern.com*) is Seattle's top spot to catch local and national acts that specialize in roots music and alternative country. The large, dimly lighted hall has all the right touches—wagon-wheel fixtures, exposed-brick walls, and a cheery staff. The sound system is outstanding.

JAZZ, BLUES & R&B

For a unique experience, check out the Seattle Jazz Vespers held every first Sunday at the Seattle First Baptist Church (corner of Harvard Avenue and Seneca Street) starting at 6 PM. The event lasts about an hour and a half, with outstanding musicians playing two sets; the church's pastor give a brief sermon between sets.

Dimitriou's Jazz Alley (⌧*2033 6th Ave., Downtown* ☎*206/441–9729* ⊕*www.jazzalley.com*) is where Seattleites dress up to see nationally known jazz artists. The cabaret-style theater, where intimate tables for two surround the stage, runs shows nightly except Monday. Those with reservations for cocktails or dinner, served during the first set, receive priority seating and $2 off the combined meal-and-show ticket.

Egan's Jam House (⌧*1707 NW Market St, Ballard* ☎*206/789–1621* ⊕*www.ballardjamhouse.com*) has provided Seattle with a gift—another club devoted solely to jazz that's a neighborhood spot rather than an overpriced tourist trap. This small club and restaurant is devoted to jazz education for local high-schoolers during the day and performances from local and touring acts in the evenings.

Nectar (⌧*412 N. 36th St., Fremont* ☎*206/632–2020* ⊕*www.nectarlounge.com*) desperately wants to be a great small music venue, one that upholds Fremont's artsier ideals. During the week it's a chill place for locals to grab some happy-hour drinks and snacks or listen to live music (usually world music and funk, but the bill varies greatly). On weekends, particularly Saturday night, it gets hit with a lot of spill-over from the fratty bars down the street.

New Orleans Restaurant (⌧*114 1st Ave. S, Pioneer Square* ☎*206/622–2563*) has live music nightly, including traditional jazz, Dixieland, and zydeco. Don't let the fact that this is a restaurant turn you off—the stage dominates the room and blistering sets tend to stop conversation dead. The creole cooking isn't half bad, either.

SeaMonster Lounge (⌧*2202 N. 45th St., Wallingford* ☎*206/633–1824* ⊕*www.seamonsterlounge.com*), with its low, low lighting and wall of very secluded booths, makes the tame Wallingford neighborhood just a little bit sexier. The space is tiny—the "stage" is more like a musician holding pen sandwiched between the bar and a few tables—but that just makes it all the more intimate and friendly. The bar presents high-quality local acts, mainly of the jazz and funk variety.

ToST (⌧*513 N. 36th St., Fremont* ☎*206/547–0240* ⊕*www.tostlounge.com*), pronounced "toast," is a swank-looking but super-laid-back martini bar that just happens to have great live music many nights. This is a good place to catch a smokin' jazz, funk, or jazz-funk act, but the club also presents everything from spoken word to alt-country. Thursday nights host the popular improv soul-and-funk show Marmalade.

Tula's (⌧*2214 2nd Ave., Belltown* ☎*206/443–4221* ⊕*www.tulas.com*) is less of a production (and expense) than Dimitriou's but still manages to offer a similar lineup of more-traditional favorites as well as top-notch local and national acts. The intimate space hosts weekly Latin jazz and Big Band jazz jams and often showcases vocal artists.

ROCK

Chop Suey (✉*1325 E. Madison St., Capitol Hill* ☎*206/324–8000* ⊕*www.chopsuey.com*) tries hard to play up the kitschy Asian theme (red lanterns, laughing Buddhas, photos of Bruce Lee), but at the end of the night, all it is is a good small music club with an eclectic lineup—indie gods, hip-hop, folk rock, visiting DJs, and everything in between. Be forewarned: this place can get packed, hot, and really loud.

★ **Crocodile Café** (✉*2200 2nd Ave., Belltown* ☎*206/441–5611* ⊕*www. thecrocodile.com*) is one of Seattle's premier rock clubs, with a long, respected history. The Croc books alternative music acts nightly except Monday. The main room is usually packed; the back bar is something of a getaway. Nonconcert nights still draw throngs to munch on Mexican and American fare.

Fodor's Choice **Neumo's** (✉*925 E. Pike St., Capitol Hill* ☎*206/709–9467* ⊕*www.
★ neumos.com*) was one of the grunge era's iconic clubs (when it was Moe's), and it has managed to reclaim its status as a staple of the Seattle rock scene, despite being closed for a six-year stretch. And it is a great rock venue—sight lines and acoustics are excellent, and the roster of cutting-edge indie rock bands is the best in the city.

Showbox (✉*1426 1st Ave., Downtown* ☎*206/628–3151* ⊕*www. showboxonline.com*), near Pike Place Market, presents locally and nationally acclaimed artists. This is a great place to see some pretty big-name acts—the acoustics are decent, the venue's small enough so that you don't feel like you're miles away from the performers, and the bar areas flanking the main floor provide some relief if you don't want to join the crush in front of the stage.

Sunset Tavern (✉*5433 Ballard Ave. NW, Ballard* ☎*206/784–4880*), a Chinese restaurant–turned–bar, attracts everyone from punks to sorority chicks to postgrad nomads and neighborhood old-timers. All come for the ever-changing eclectic music acts and a karaoke night backed by a band.

The Triple Door (✉*216 Union St., Downtown* ☎*206/838–4333* ⊕*www. thetripledoor.net*) has been referred to (perhaps not kindly) as a rock club for thirty- and fortysomethings. While it's true that you'll see more world music and jazz here than alternative music, and the half-moon booths that make up the majority of the seating in the main room are more cabaret than rock, The Triple Door has an interesting lineup that often appeals to younger patrons, too.

THE ARTS

The high-tech boom provided an enthusiastic and philanthropic audience for Seattle's blossoming arts community. Benaroya Hall is now a national benchmark for acoustic design. Its main tenant is the Seattle Symphony, led by conductor Gerard Schwarz. At the Seattle Center, the ethereal Marion Oliver McCaw Hall combines Northwest hues and hanging screens in colorful light shows accompanying performances by the Seattle Opera and the Pacific Northwest Ballet.

The Seattle Repertory Theater, also at Seattle Center, hosts new and classical works, as well as preview runs of plays bound for Broadway. The celebrated Seattle Children's Theatre presents plays and musicals written for youths but polished and sophisticated enough for adults. Events for Bumbershoot, Seattle's Labor Day weekend arts festival, are held throughout the Seattle Center grounds.

Tickets for high-profile performances range from $11 to $125; fringe-theater plays and performance-art events range from $5 to $25. Many alternative theaters host "pay-what-you-can" evenings. The Seattle Symphony offers half-price tickets to seniors and students one hour before scheduled performances.

DANCE

Meany Hall for the Performing Arts (⊠ *15th Ave. NE and 41st Ave. NE, University District* ☎ *206/685–2742* ⊕ *www.meany.org*), on the UW campus, hosts important national and international companies September through May. The emphasis is on modern and jazz dance.

On the Boards (⊠ *100 W. Roy St., Queen Anne* ☎ *206/217–9888* ⊕ *www.ontheboards.org*) presents contemporary dance performances, as well as theater, music, and multimedia events. The main subscription series runs from October through May, but events are scheduled nearly every weekend year-round.

Pacific Northwest Ballet (⊠ *McCaw Hall at Seattle Center, Mercer St. at 3rd Ave., Queen Anne* ☎ *206/441–2424* ⊕ *www.pnb.org*), the resident Seattle company and school, has an elegant home at the Seattle Center. The season, which runs September through June, has traditionally included a mix of classic and international productions (think *Swan Lake* and *Carmina Burana*); however, Peter Boal, a well-known former New York City Ballet principal dancer, shook things up a bit when he took the reins as artistic director in 2006, and the lineup now includes works from celebrated contemporary choreographers like Christopher Wheeldon. Fans of *Swan Lake* and *The Nutcracker* can rest assured that those timeless productions are still part of the company's repertoire.

FILM

★ Seattle has several wonderful film festivals; the **Seattle International Film Festival** (☎ *206/324–9996* ⊕ *www.seattlefilm.com*) is the biggest one, taking place over several weeks from mid-May to mid-June. Though some highly anticipated events sell out, last-minute and day-of tickets are usually available.

★ If you're tired of 40-ounce Cokes and $10 popcorn with neon-color butter and wish that moviegoing could be a little more dignified, check out **Central Cinema** (⊠ *1411 21st Ave., Central District* ☎ *206/686–6684* ⊕ *www.central-cinema.com*). The first few rows of this charming, friendly little theater consist of diner-style booths—before the movie starts a waiter takes orders for delicious pizzas, salads, and snacks (including real popcorn with inventive toppings like curry or dill); your food is delivered unobtrusively during the first few minutes of the movie. Wash it down with a normal-size soda, a cup of coffee, or better yet a glass of wine or beer. You won't find first-run films here, but the theater shows a great mix of favorites (*Hairspray* and *E.T.*) and local indie and experimental films.

★ **Cinerama** (⊠ *2100 4th Ave., Belltown* ☎ *206/441–3080* ⊕ *www. cinerama.com*), a 1963 cinema scooped up and restored by billionaire Paul Allen, seamlessly blends the luxury of the theater with state-of-the-art technology. Behind the main, standard-size movie screen sits an enormous, 30-foot by 90-foot restored curved panel—one of only three in the world—used to screen old three-strip films like *How the West Was Won*, as well as 70-millimeter presentations of *2001: Space Odyssey*. The sight lines throughout are amazing. Rear-window captioning, assistive listening devices, audio narration, wheelchair access, and other amenities ensure that everyone has an outstanding experience.

Egyptian Theater (⊠ *805 E. Pine St., at Broadway, Capitol Hill* ☎ *206/781–5755*), an art deco movie palace that was formerly a Masonic temple, screens first-run films.

Grand Illusion Cinema (⊠ *1403 N.E. 50th St., at University Way, University District* ☎ *206/523–3935* ⊕ *www.grandillusioncinema.org*), Seattle's longest-running independent movie house, was a tiny screening room in the 1930s. It's still tiny, but it's an outstanding and unique home for independent and art films that feels as comfortable as a home theater.

Harvard Exit (⊠ *807 E. Roy St., Capitol Hill* ☎ *206/781–5755*), a first-run and art-film house, is in the former home of the Women's Century Club, hence the quaint, antiques-filled lobby.

★ The **Northwest Film Forum** (⊠ *1515 12th Ave., Capitol Hill* ☎ *206/267–5380* ⊕ *www.nwfilmforum.org*) is the cornerstone of the city's independent film scene. Its hip headquarters has two screening rooms that show everything from classics like *East of Eden* to cult hits to experimental films and documentaries.

MUSIC

Seattle Opera (⊠ *McCaw Hall at Seattle Center, Mercer St. at 3rd Ave., Queen Anne* ☎ *206/389–7676* ⊕ *www.seattleopera.org*), whose home is the beautiful Marion Oliver McCaw Hall, stages such productions as *Carmine,Ariadne auf Naxos*, and *The Girl of the Golden West* from August through May. Evening-event guests are treated to a light show from 30-foot hanging scrims above an outdoor piazza. Extra women's bathrooms and a soundproof baby "crying room" make the programs comfortable and family-friendly.

Fodor'sChoice **Seattle Symphony** (⊠ *Benaroya Hall, 1203 2nd Ave., at University St.,*
★ *Downtown* ☎ *206/215–4747* ⊕ *www.seattlesymphony.org*) performs under the direction of Gerard Schwartz from September through June in stunning, acoustically superior Benaroya Hall. This exciting symphony has been nominated for numerous Grammy Awards and is well regarded nationally and internationally.

PERFORMANCE VENUES

Benaroya Hall (✉*200 University St., Downtown* ☎*206/215–4800*) is so state of the art that the acoustics are pure in every one of the main hall's 2,500 seats. This makes seeing the Seattle Symphony, which is based here, a requisite. The four-story lobby has a curved glass facade that makes intermissions almost as impressive as performances.

Cornish College of the Arts (✉*710 E. Roy St., Capitol Hill* ☎*206/726–5066* ⊕*www.cornish.edu/events*) is the headquarters for distinguished jazz, dance, and other groups. It also hosts solid student productions.

★ **Marion Oliver McCaw Hall** (✉*Mercer St. at 3rd Ave., Queen Anne* ☎*206/389–7676 or 206/441–2424* ⊕*www.seattlecenter.org*), home of the Seattle Opera and the Pacific Northwest Ballet, is an opulent, glass-enclosed structure reflecting the skies. Inside, walls are painted in the hues of sunsets and northern lights; outside, on the piazza, occasional evening light shows are projected onto 30-foot banners dangling above a pond. (Hint: If you're not here for a performance, head atop the parking garage across the street and catch the light show for free.)

Meydenbauer Center (✉*11100 NE 6th St., Bellevue* ☎*425/637–1020* ⊕*www.meydenbauer.com*) has state-of-the-art equipment and excellent acoustics. It hosts performances by children's theater troupes, the Ballet Bellevue, the Bellevue Civic Theater, and other groups.

Moore Theater (✉*1932 2nd Ave., Downtown* ☎*206/467–5510* ⊕*www.themoore.com*), built in 1907, is Seattle's oldest theater and still hosts off-Broadway performances and music events. A quick peek at the prominent marquee clues you in to what's happening: jazz concerts, instrumental duets, hard-rock bookings, pop-music shows. The venerable hall was featured in Pearl Jam's video, *Evenflow,* and many of the big grunge music acts of Seattle's early '90s rock heyday performed here.

The **Paramount Theatre** (✉*907 Pine St., Downtown* ☎*206/682–1414* ⊕*www.theparamount.com*) opened in 1928 as a vaudeville and silent film venue. Today its 2,800 cushy seats and opulent details make it a great place to see popular music acts, top comedians, and international dance troupes. Monday night brings silent movies accompanied by the original Publix organ.

Seattle Center (✉*305 Harrison St., Queen Anne* ☎*206/684–7200* ⊕*www.seattlecenter.org*) has several halls that present theater, opera, dance, music, and performance art. Live music, theme dances, and festivals are staged monthly in the Center House. The Seattle Center is also the site of Labor Day weekend's Bumbershoot Festival, which celebrates the arts.

READINGS & LECTURES

★ **Elliot Bay Book Co.** (✉*101 S. Main St., Pioneer Square* ☎*206/624–6600* ⊕*www.elliottbaybook.com*) presents a popular series of renowned local, national, and international author readings in a cozy, basement room next to a café. Events are free, but tickets are often required.

Richard Hugo House (✉*1634 11th Ave., Capitol Hill* ☎*206/322–7030* ⊕*www.hugohouse.org*) is a haven for writers, with classes, private work areas, and readings by Northwest luminaries and authors on their way up. As it's in a Victorian building that was once a residence, it's a warm, homey place.

Christian Scientists occupied the Roman-revival-style **Town Hall** (✉ *1119 8th Ave., Downtown* ☎ *206/652–4255* ⊕ *www.townhallseattle.org*) for decades and attending lectures here does feel a bit like going to church, though the folks sharing the pews with you are liable to be among Seattle's most secular. Town Hall hosts scores of events in its spacious yet intimate Great Hall, chief among them talks and panel discussions with leading politicians, authors, scientists, and academics.

University Book Store (✉ *4326 University Way NE, University District* ☎ *206/634–3400* ⊕ *www.bookstore.washington.edu*), near the UW campus, schedules free readings by best-selling authors and academics. The second-floor space is rich with book stacks, perfect for browsing afterward. Tickets are required, and they go quickly.

THEATERS

A Contemporary Theatre *(ACT)* (✉ *700 Union St., Downtown* ☎ *206/292–7676* ⊕ *www.acttheatre.org*) launches exciting works by emerging dramatists. Four staging areas include a theater-in-the-round and an intimate downstairs space for small shows. The Apr.–Nov. season highlight is the long-running *Late Nite Catechism*.

5th Avenue Theatre (✉ *1308 5th Ave., Downtown* ☎ *206/625–1900* ⊕ *www.5thavenue.org*) opened in 1926 as a silent-movie house and vaudeville stage, complete with a giant pipe organ and ushers who dressed as cowboys and pirates. Today the chinoiserie landmark has its own theater company, which stages lavish productions Oct.–May. At other times it hosts concerts, lectures, and films. It's worth a peek—it's one of the most beautiful venues in the world.

Intiman Theatre (✉ *201 Mercer St., Queen Anne* ☎ *206/269–1900* ⊕ *www.intiman.org*), at the Seattle Center, presents important contemporary works and classics of the world stage from May through November in its 485-seat space.

Northwest Puppet Center (✉ *9123 15th Ave. NE, University District* ☎ *206/523–2579* ⊕ *www.nwpuppet.org*) encourages kids to sprawl on the floor while folktales are told by marionettes. The troupe keeps the lively stories brief (45 minutes). Puppet workshops are available.

Seattle Children's Theatre (✉ *Charlotte Martin Theatre at Seattle Center, 2nd Ave. N and Thomas St., Queen Anne* ☎ *206/441–3322* ⊕ *www. sct.org*), stages top-notch productions of new works as well as adaptations from classic children's literature. After the show, actors come out to answer questions and explain how the tricks are done.

Seattle Repertory Theater (✉ *155 Mercer St., Queen Anne* ☎ *206/443– 2222* ⊕ *www.seattlerep.org*) brings nine new and classic plays to life, split between Seattle Center's Bagley Wright and Leo K. theaters during its September-through-April season. Adoring fans flock to new takes on choice classics as well as those fresh from the New York stage. You can preorder a boxed dinner from the Café at the Rep before the show, or linger afterward over coffee and dessert.

Sports & the Outdoors

WORD OF MOUTH

"If the weather is accommodating, you might think of renting bikes and going around Alki in West Seattle or on the Burke-Gilman Trail near the UW or riding starting at Seward Park and going north along L. Washington."

—Orcas

"Hike Discovery Park's forested center down into shell- and rock-strewn beaches. Lift up rocks to watch hidden crabs scatter, and then set down the rock very carefully again. Walk back up and visit the Park's Learning Center to find out more about trees and wildlife in the Northwest."

—wabashcannonball

Updated
by Carissa
Bluestone

THE QUESTION IN SEATTLE ISN'T "Do you exercise?" Rather it's "What do you do for exercise?" Athleticism is a regular part of most people's lives here, whether it's an afternoon jog, a sunrise rowing session, a lunch-hour bike ride, or an evening game of Frisbee. The Cascade Mountains, a 60-minute drive east, have trails and peaks for alpinists of all skill levels. Snoqualmie Pass attracts downhill skiers and snowboarders. The cross-country skiing and snowshoeing are excellent at Snoqualmie Pass or across Stevens Pass. To the west of the city is the Puget Sound, where sailors, kayakers, and anglers practice their sports. Lake Union and Lake Washington also provide residents with plenty of boating, kayaking, fishing, and swimming opportunities. Farther west the Olympic Mountains beckon adventure-seeking souls to scenic wilderness.

Spectator sports are also appreciated here. To see how excited Seattle citizens can get about crew racing, stop by the Montlake Cut on the official opening day of the unofficial boating season. The University of Washington (UW) has been a rowing powerhouse since the 1930s, and tickets to Husky football games have been hot items for years. Attendance at Mariners games is at an all-time high, and the Seahawks are gaining steam as well.

Given a choice, though, most Seattleites would rather *do* than watch. More than one visitor has commented that it seems as if most Seattleites are exercising all the time. Visit Green Lake on a sunny weekend day, and you'll probably agree. Fitness is definitely a virtue in these parts, but the motivation isn't so much to look good as it is to *feel* good.

BASEBALL

The **Seattle Mariners** play in the West Division of the American League, and their home is **Safeco Field** (⊠*1st Ave. S and Atlantic St., Sodo* ☎*206/346–4000* ⊕*seattle.mariners.mlb.com*), a retractable-roof stadium where there really isn't a bad seat in the house. One local sports columnist referred to the venue—the most expensive stadium in recorded history and $100 million over budget—as "the guilty pleasure." You can purchase tickets through Ticketmaster; online or by phone from Safeco Field (to be picked up at the Will Call); in person at Safeco's box office (no surcharges), which is open daily 10–6; or from the Mariners team store at 4th Avenue and Stewart Street in Downtown. The cheap seats cost $7; the best seats cost $38–$55.

If you're in the mood for minor-league play, take I–5 roughly 30 mi either north or south of town. To the north, the **Everett Aqua Sox** play short-season Class A ball in the Northwest League. Keep an eye out for Harold the Pig, who delivers balls to the pitching mound. The Aqua Sox play at **Everett Memorial Stadium** (⊠*3900 Broadway Ave. (Exit 192 off I–5), Everett* ☎*425/258–3673* ⊕*www.aquasox.com*). Admission is $5–$12. Parking in the South Lot and on the street north of the stadium is free, but arrive about an hour early to get a space. For AAA Pacific Coast League action and a fabulous view of Mt. Rainier, head south to see the **Tacoma Rainiers.** They play at **Cheney Stadium** (⊠*2502*

CLOSE UP

How to Play

King County Parks and Recreation (☎ *206/296–4232 for information and reservations, 206/296–4171 for interpretive programs* ⊕ *www. metrokc.gov/parks*) manages many of the parks outside city limits. To find out whether an in-town park baseball diamond or tennis court is available, contact the **Seattle Parks and Recreation Department** (☎ *206/684–4075* ⊕ *www.cityofse-attle.net/parks*), which is responsible for most of the parks, piers, beaches, playgrounds, and courts within city limits. The department issues permits for events, arranges reservations for facilities, and staffs visitor centers and naturalist programs. The state manages several parks and campgrounds in greater Seattle. For more information contact **Washington State Parks** (☎ *800/233–0321 for general information, 800/452–5687 for campsite reservations* ⊕ *www.parks. wa.gov/parkpage.asp*).

5

S. Tyler, Tacoma ☎ *253/752–7700* ⊕ *www.tacomarainiers.com*). Tickets are $6–$14, but if you're totally broke, there's a grassy knoll outside left field from which you can watch the entire game. Take I–5 south to Exit 132, follow Highway 16 west for 2 mi, get off at the South 19th Street East exit; take the first right (Cheyenne Street), and follow the road to stadium parking lots. Both teams are Mariners farm clubs and offer an up-close, family-oriented baseball experience.

BASKETBALL

The men's NBA season runs from November to April. The **Seattle SuperSonics,** known simply as the Sonics, play at **Key Arena** (⊠ *Seattle Center, 1st Ave. N and Mercer St., Queen Anne* ☎ *206/283–3865, 800/462–2849 NBA* ⊕ *www.nba.com/sonics*). Tickets range from $10 to $200 for courtside seating. You can buy tickets online, at the box office, or by calling the NBA toll-free number.

The WNBA **Seattle Storm** (⊕ *www.wnba.com/storm*) has its season from mid-June to August and also plays at the Key Arena. Tickets cost $10–$47.

The **UW Huskies** represent Seattle basketball in the Pac-10 Conference. The team has had less than its share of success. The tough women's team—which enjoys a very loyal (and loud) fan base—has, however, advanced to the NCAA tournament several times in recent years. **Bank of America Arena at Hec Edmundson Pavilion** (⊠ *3870 Montlake Blvd. NE, University District* ☎ *206/543–2200* ⊕ *gohuskies.cstv.com*), known locally as "Hec Ed," is where the UW's men's and women's basketball teams play. Tickets are $6–$20.

BEACHES

With the Puget Sound to the west and 25-mi-long Lake Washington to the east, Seattle has miles and miles of waterfront, much of it speckled with beaches. In addition, smaller lakes, products of ancient glacial movements, spring forth throughout the city and the suburbs. You're never far from water. Most Lake Washington beaches in Seattle, Kirkland, and Bellevue have lifeguards on duty in summer. Free swimming lessons are given at several Seattle beaches for ages six and up. The swimming season generally runs from mid-June through Labor Day.

The general number for information on all city beaches is 206/684–4075. The City of Seattle's Web site, www.seattle.gov/parks, also has details on all parks within city limits, as well as detailed directions on how to reach them by car.

FodorsChoice
★
Alki Beach (⊠1702 *Alki Ave. SW, West Seattle*). In summer, cars inch along Alki Avenue, seeking a coveted parking space, all the passengers heading for this 2½-mi stretch of sand that has views of both the Seattle skyline and the Olympic Mountains. It's something of a California beach scene (except for the water temperature), with in-line skaters, joggers, and cyclists sharing the walkway and sun-loving singles playing volleyball and flirting. Year-round, families come to build sand castles, beachcomb, and fly kites; in winter, storm-watchers come to see the crashing waves. Facilities include drinking water, grills, picnic tables, phones, and restrooms; restaurants line the street across from the beach. To get here from Downtown, take either I–5 south or Highway 99 south to the West Seattle Bridge and exit onto Harbor Avenue Southwest, turning right at the stoplight.

Golden Gardens Park (⊠8498 *Seaview Pl. NW (near NW 85th St.), Ballard*). Puget Sound waters are bone-chilling cold, but that doesn't stop folks from jumping in to cool off. Besides brave swimmers, who congregate on the small strip of sand between the parking lot and the canteen, this park is packed with sunbathers in summer. In other seasons, beachcombers explore during low tide, and groups gather around bonfires to socialize and watch the sun go down. The park has drinking water, grills, picnic tables, phones, and restrooms. It also has two wetlands, a short loop trail, and a rugged coast with breathtaking views. From Downtown, take Elliott Avenue N., which becomes 15th Avenue W., and cross the Ballard Bridge. Turn left to head west on Market Street and follow signs to the Ballard Locks; continue about another mile to the park. Note that even though the park has two dedicated parking lots, these quickly fill up on weekends, so be prepared to circle. On weekdays the swimming beach gets packed with school and summer camp groups; go early or late in the day if you don't want to be surrounded by screaming kids.

Green Lake (⊠7201 *E. Greenlake Dr. N, Green Lake*) is best known for its ever-lively jogging path, but this beauty of a lake also has two small beach areas from which it's possible to swim. The West Beach is on the northwestern corner of the lake by N. 76th Street; the East Beach is directly across the lake on its east side around NE 72nd Street. Both beaches have diving boards, swimming rafts, and lifeguards in summer, but not much in terms of actual sand.

Houghton Beach Park (✉*5811 Lake Washington Blvd., Kirkland* ☎*425/828–1217*). On hot days, sun-worshippers and swimmers flock to this beach south of downtown Kirkland on the Lake Washington waterfront. The rest of the year, the playground attracts families, and the fishing pier stays busy with anglers. Facilities include drinking water, picnic tables, phones, and restrooms. Head to the north end of the beach if you want some distance between you and the playground. You can also rent canoes or kayaks at the docks here.

Juanita Beach Park (✉*9703 Juanita Dr. NE, Kirkland* ☎*425/828–1217*). Directly across Juanita Bay from peaceful wetlands, this beach hops: children playing in the sand, sunbathers on the dock, swimmers in the closed-in swimming area, and picnickers in the park. There are grills, picnic tables, phones, restrooms, drinking water, and a snack bar (seasonal). The beach has had problems with pollution in recent years, but a multiyear plan by the city of Kirkland is underway to revitalize the park and address the most pressing water-pollution problems.

Madison Park (✉*2300 43rd Ave. E, Madison Park*). The sandy Lake Washington beach, with easy access to the water, the sloping lawn, the playgrounds, and the tennis courts, fill quickly on warm days. There are coffee shops and other amenities nearby; the beach has drinking water, picnic tables, phones, restrooms, and showers. From Downtown, go east on Madison Street for about 3 mi, turn right on E. Howe Street and then turn left to head north on 43rd Avenue.

Madrona Park (✉*853 Lake Washington Blvd., Madrona*). Several beach parks and green spaces front the lake along Lake Washington Boulevard; Madrona Park is one of the largest. Young swimmers stay in the roped-in area while teens and adults swim out to a floating raft with a diving board. Runners and in-line skaters follow the mile-long trail along the shore. Kids clamber about the sculpted-sand garden and climb on rocks and logs. Grassy areas encourage picnicking; there are grills, picnic tables, phones, restrooms, and showers. A barbecue stand is open seasonally. From Downtown, go east on Yesler Way about 2 mi to 32nd Avenue. Turn left onto Lake Dell Avenue and then right; go to Lake Washington Boulevard and take a left.

★ **Matthews Beach Park** (✉*Sand Point Way NE and NE 93rd St., Sand Point*). On warm summer days the parking lot and nearby streets overflow with people visiting Seattle's largest freshwater swimming beach. The Burke-Gilman Trail, popular with cyclists and runners, travels through the park. Picnic areas, basketball hoops, and a big playground round out the amenities. From Downtown, take I–5 north and get off at the Lake City Way Northeast exit. Stay on Lake City Way for about 1½ mi. Turn right on to Northeast 95th Street, right onto Sand Point Way Northeast, and left onto Northeast 93rd Street.

Newcastle Beach Park (✉*4400 Lake Washington Blvd. SE, off 112th SE Exit from I–405, Bellevue* ☎*425/452–6881* ⊕*www.ci.bellevue.wa.us*). On Lake Washington in Bellevue, this large park has a big swimming beach, a fishing dock, nature trails, volleyball nets, drinking water, phones, restrooms, and a large grassy area with picnic tables.

The playground is a favorite thanks to a train that tots can sit in and older kids can climb on and hop from car to car.

Fodor'sChoice **Sand Point Magnuson Park** (⊠ *Bordered by NE 65th and 74th Sts., Sand*
★ *Point Way NE, and Lake Washington [entrances at 65th St. and 74th St.], Sand Point* ☎206/684–4946). As it was once an airport, it's not surprising that this 200-acre park northeast of the University District (U-District) is flat and open. The paved trails are wonderful for cycling, in-line skating, and pushing a stroller. Many kids have learned to ride their two-wheelers here; quite a few more have spent time on the large playground. Leashed dogs are welcome on the trails; a large off-leash area includes one of the few public beaches where pooches can swim. Farther south, on the mile-long shore, there's a swimming beach, a seasonal wading pool, and a boat launch. The park also has tennis courts, sports fields, and a terrific kite-flying hill. Be sure to look for the unique public art. *The Fin Project: From Swords to Plowshares* uses submarine fins to depict a pod of orca whales. *No Appointment Necessary* has two bright red chairs extended into the sky. *The Sound Garden* (at the neighboring National Oceanic and Atmospheric Administration campus) has steel pipes that give off sounds when the wind blows for an art display that you can hear as well as see. From Downtown, take I–5 north to the Northeast 65th Street exit, turn right and continue east to Sand Point Way Northeast.

Seward Park (⊠ *5902 Lake Washington Blvd. S, Columbia City*). Twenty minutes south of the city in the burgeoning Columbia City area, Seward Park is a relatively undiscovered gem of a park that includes trails through old-growth forest, mountain views, and a small swimming beach complete with a swimming raft. Though you feel very far away from the city here, the water is actually part of Lake Washington. There are restrooms, picnic tables, and lifeguards on duty in summer.

BICYCLING

Biking is probably Seattle's most practiced sport. Many people bike to work and seem to do their own version of the Tour de France (spandex and all) on weekends. That said, Seattle is not a particularly bike-friendly city. There are surprisingly few dedicated bike lanes, especially in the busiest parts of town. And then there are those hills—Queen Anne Hill and Phinney Ridge should only be attempted by sadists. Fortunately, all city buses have easy-to-use bike racks (on the front of the buses below the windshield) and drivers are used to waiting for cyclists to load and unload their bikes. If you're not comfortable biking in urban traffic, you can do a combination bus-and-bike tour of the city.

Seattle drivers are used to sharing the road with cyclists and with the exception of the occasional road-rage victim or clueless cell-phone talker, they usually leave a generous amount of room when passing; however, there are biking fatalities every year, so be alert and cautious, especially when approaching blind intersections, of which Seattle has many. You must wear a helmet at all times (it's the law) and be sure to lock up your bike—though there are probably more car break-ins, bikes do get stolen, even in quiet residential neighborhoods.

The Seattle Parks Department sponsors Bicycle Saturdays and Sundays on different weekends May through September. On these days, a 4-mi stretch of Lake Washington Boulevard—from Mt. Baker Beach to Seward Park—is closed to motor vehicles. Many riders continue around the 2-mi loop at Seward Park and back to Mt. Baker Beach to complete a 10-mi, car-free ride.

The trail that circles Green Lake is popular with cyclists, though runners and walkers can impede fast travel. The city-maintained Burke-Gilman Trail, a slightly less-congested path, follows an abandoned railroad line 12 mi along Seattle's waterfront from Lake Washington almost to Salmon Bay. Discovery Park is a very tranquil place to tool around in. Myrtle Edwards Park, north of Pier 70, has a two-lane path for bicycling and running. The islands of the Puget Sound are also easily explored by bike (there are rental places by the ferry terminals), though be forewarned that Bainbridge has some tough hills.

King County has more than 100 mi of paved and nearly 70 mi of unpaved routes including the Sammamish River, Interurban, Green River, Cedar River, Snoqualmie Valley, and Soos Creek trails. For more information contact the King County Parks and Recreation office.

Marymoor Velodrome (⊠*6046 W. Lake Sammamish Pkwy. NE, Redmond* ⊕*velodrom.org*). When not used for competitive racing—National Championship meets, regional Olympic trials, the Goodwill Games—the banked oval here is open to the public. Granted, it's a bit of a haul from Seattle to Redmond, but for serious speedsters, there's no substitute. Since the Burke-Gilman Trail links up in Bothell with the Sammamish River Trail (which is connected to Marymoor Park), you can ride from Seattle to Marymoor, though you may not have anything left for the track once you get here. A free junior program for ages five to eight introduces children to track cycling, with track bikes provided for free during classes and races.

The **Bicycle Alliance of Washington** (☎*206/224–9252* ⊕*www.bicycle-alliance.org*), the state's largest cycling advocacy group, is a great source for information. The **Cascade Bicycle Club** (☎*206/522–2453* ⊕*www.cascade.org*) organizes more than 1,000 rides annually for recreational and hard-core bikers. Of its major events the most famous is the Seattle-to-Portland Bicycle Classic. It offers daily rides in Seattle and the Eastside that range from "superstrenuous" to leisurely all-ages jaunts, like easy passes through the Japanese Garden at the Washington Park Arboretum. Check out the Web site for a complete list of rides and contact information. The **Seattle Bicycle Program** (☎*206/684–7583* ⊕*www.seattle.gov/transportation/bikeprogram.htm*) was responsible for the creation of the city's multiuse trails (aka bike routes) as well as pedestrian paths and roads with wide shoulders—things, in other words, that benefit bicyclists. The agency's Web site has downloadable route maps; you can also call the number above to request a printed version of the Seattle Bicycling Guide Map.

RENTALS

BikeStation (✉ *311 3rd Ave. S, Pioneer Square* ☎ *206/332–9795* ⊕ *www.bikestation.org/seattle*). This bike storage facility also offers perhaps the cheapest rentals in town. Though the selection is not as impressive as at Gregg's, you can procure a regular, mountain, or electric bike for a mere $3 per hour ($15 per day).

Gregg's Greenlake Cycle (✉ *7007 Woodlawn Ave. NE, Green Lake* ☎ *206/523–1822* ⊕ *www.greggscycles.com*). On Green Lake's northern end, this Seattle institution has been in business since 1932. It sells and rents mountain bikes, standard road touring bikes, and hybrids; helmets and locks are included with each rental. Gregg's is close to the Burke-Gilman Trail and across the street from the Green Lake Trail. Rental fees range from $20 to $50 for the day, $25 to $75 overnight, and $60 to $135 per week. Gregg's also rents in-line skates, jogging strollers, snowboarding equipment, and snowshoes.

BOATING & KAYAKING

The **Chevrolet Cup hydroplane races** (☎ *206/728–0123* ⊕ *www.seafair. com*) are a highlight of Seattle's Seafair festivities from mid-July through the first Sunday in August. Races are held on Lake Washington near Seward Park. Tickets cost $15–$25. In summer, weekly sailing regattas take place on Lakes Union and Washington. Contact the **Seattle Yacht Club** (☎ *206/325–1000* ⊕ *www.seattleyachtclub.org*) for schedules.

★ **Agua Verde Paddle Club and Cafe** (✉ *1303 NE Boat St., University District* ☎ *206/545–8570* ⊕ *www.aguaverde.com*). Start out by renting a kayak and paddling along either the Lake Union shoreline, with its hodgepodge of funky-to-fabulous houseboats and dramatic Downtown vistas, or Union Bay on Lake Washington, with its marshes and cattails. Afterward, take in the lakefront as you wash down some Tex-Mex food with a margarita. Kayaks are available March through October and are rented by the hour—$15 for singles, $18 for doubles. The third and fourth hours are free on weekdays; fourth hours are free on weekends.

★ **Center for Wooden Boats** (✉ *1010 Valley St., Lake Union* ☎ *206/382–2628* ⊕ *www.cwb.org*). Seattle's free maritime heritage museum also rents classic wooden rowboats and sailboats for short trips around Lake Union. Rowboats, pedal boats, and canoes are $15 an hour on weekdays and $25 an hour on weekends. Sloops and catboats cost $20–$45 an hour, depending on the type and size of the vessel. There's a $10 skills-check fee. Free half-hour guided sails and steamboat rides are offered on Sunday from 2 to 3 (arrive an hour early).

Green Lake Boat Rental (✉ *7351 W. Green Lake Way N, Green Lake* ☎ *206/527–0171*) is the source for canoes, paddleboats, sailboats, kayaks, sailboards, and rowboats to ply Green Lake's calm waters. On beautiful summer afternoons, however, be prepared to spend most of your time negotiating other traffic on the water as well as in the parking lot. Fees are $10 an hour for paddleboats, single kayaks, and rowboats; $12 an hour for double kayaks; and $14 an hour for sailboats and sailboards. Don't confuse this place with the Green Lake Small Craft Center, which offers sailing programs but no rentals.

Moss Bay Rowing and Kayak Center (✉ *1001 Fairview Ave. N, Lake Union* ☎ *206/682–2031* ⊕ *www.mossbay.net*). Moss Bay rents a variety of rowing craft—including Whitehall pulling boats, wherries, and sliding-seat rowboats. Single kayaks rent for $12 per hour, doubles go for $17. You can also rent kayaks to take with you on trips outside the city; daily rates are $55 for singles and $75 for doubles, weekly rates are $235 for singles and $315 for doubles. You can rent rowing shells or sailboats for $25–$35 depending on the type of craft; there is an additional $10 skills-check fee for renting these types of vessels. The center offers rowing and sailing lessons daily for $65 for a onetime private lesson; two or four lesson series cost $100 or $200 respectively. Lastly, the center also offers daily 2½-hour sailing tours of Lake Union as well as guided kayaking tours; prices start at $45 per person.

Northwest Outdoor Center (✉ *2100 Westlake Ave. N, Lake Union* ☎ *206/281–9694* ⊕ *www.nwoc.com*). This center on Lake Union's west side rents one- or two-person kayaks (it also has a few triples) by the hour or day, including equipment and basic or advanced instruction. The hourly rate is $12 for a single and $17 for a double, with daily maximums of $60 and $80, respectively. Third and fourth hours are free during the week; a fourth hour is free on weekends. If you want to find your own water, NWOC offers "to-go" kayaks; the rate for a single is $65 first day, plus $35 each additional day. Doubles cost $85 the first day and $45 for each day thereafter. In summer, reserve least three days ahead. NWOC also runs guided trips to the Nisqually Delta and Chuckanut Bay for $70 per person. Sunset tours to Golden Gardens Park ($40 per person) and moonlight tours of Portage Bay ($30 per person) are other options. Every May there are two overnight whale-watching trips to the San Juan Islands for $325 per person.

Waterfront Activities Center (✉ *3800 Montlake Blvd. NE, University District* ☎ *206/543–9433*). This center behind UW's Husky Stadium rents three-person canoes and four-person rowboats for $7.50 an hour February through October. You can tour the Lake Washington shoreline or take the Montlake Cut portion of the ship canal and explore Lake Union. You can also row to nearby Foster Island and visit the Washington Park Arboretum.

Wind Works Sailing Center (✉ *7001 Seaview Ave. NW, Ballard* ☎ *206/784–9386* ⊕ *www.windworkssailing.com*). Although members are given first picks at Wind Works, which is on Shilshole Bay, nonmembers can arrange rentals. Experienced sailors are allowed to skipper their own boats after a brief qualifying process. Sailing a 25-foot Catalina will cost you $155 on weekdays and $194 on weekends; rates for a 30-foot Hunter are $277 on weekdays and $347 on weekends.

Yarrow Bay Marina (✉ *5207 Lake Washington Blvd. NE, Kirkland* ☎ *425/822–6066* ⊕ *www.yarrowbaymarina.com/boatrental.htm*). The marina rents 19- and 22-foot runabouts for $60 an hour on weekdays and $65 an hour on weekends. There's a two-hour minimum; weekly rentals are also an option.

FISHING

Green Lake is stocked with more than 10,000 legal-size rainbow trout each year. Anglers can also vie for brown trout, largemouth bass, yellow perch, and brown bullhead catfish. The parks department maintains three fishing piers along the lake's shores: East Green Lake Drive at Latona Avenue Northeast; West Green Lake Drive North and Stone Avenue North; and West Green Lake Way North, just north of the shellhouse. You can't deny the bizarre combination of hooking one in while North Face–clad moms jog by with their toddlers in SUV-like strollers.

Lake Washington has its share of parks department piers as well. You can fish year-round for rainbow trout, cutthroat trout, and large- and smallmouth bass. Chinook, coho, and steelhead salmon are also available, but often subject to restrictions. Check regulations in the "Sport Fishing Rules" pamphlet (available at most sporting goods stores) when you buy your license. A one-day license costs about $7; the longest license you can buy is for five days and costs $17.

For saltwater fishing, Seattle has public piers along Shilshole Bay in Golden Gardens Park. Elliott Bay has public piers at Waterfront Park. Shilshole Bay charter-fishing companies offer trips to fish for salmon, rockfish, cod, flounder, and sea bass.

Adventure Charters (⊠ *7001 Seaview Ave. NW, Ballard* ☎*206/789–8245* ⊕*www.seattlesalmoncharters.com*) takes private groups out on six-person troll boats to fish for salmon, bottom fish, and crab—depending on the season. The guided trips last for six or seven hours. The price per person is $150 October–May and $160 June–September; a license, tackle, and bait are included, and your fish will be cleaned or filleted and bagged for free.

Fish Finders Private Charters (⊠*6019 Seaview Ave. NW, Ballard* ☎*206/632–2611* ⊕*www.fishingseattle.com*) takes groups of four or more out on Puget Sound for guided salmon fishing trips. The cost is $160 per person plus $7 for a fishing license. Morning trips last about six hours; afternoon trips are about five hours. All gear, bait, cleaning, and bagging are included in the fee.

FOOTBALL

The **Seattle Seahawks** play in the $430 million, state-of-the-art **Quest Field** (⊠*800 Occidental Ave., Sodo* ☎*425/827–9777* ⊕*www. seahawks.com*). Single-game tickets go on sale in July or August and all home games sell out quickly. Tickets are expensive, with the cheapest seats in the 300 section (where you actually get a really good view of the field) starting at $42. Note that traffic and parking are both nightmares on game days; try to take public transportation if possible.

Almost as popular as the Seahawks are the **UW Huskies.** The team plays at **Husky Stadium** (⊠*University of Washington, 3800 Montlake Blvd. NE, University District* ☎*206/543–2200* ⊕*gohuskies.cstv.com*), a U-shape stadium that overlooks Lake Washington, so you can arrive by boat as well as by bike, bus, or car. Tickets are $30–$65 and go on sale at the end of July.

GOLF

Gold Mountain Golf Complex (✉ 7263 *W. Belfair Valley Rd., Bremerton* ☎ 206/415-5432 ⊕ *www.goldmt. com*). Gold Mountain has two 18-hole courses, but most people make the trek to Bremerton to play the Olympic Course, a beautiful and challenging par 72 and one of Washington State's best courses. The easier Cascade Course is also popular and is lined with Douglas firs. There are four putting greens, a driving range, and a clubhouse. Prime-time green fees are $27–$35 for the Cascade and $38–$49 for the Olympic. Carts are $32. You can drive all the way to Bremerton via I–5 or you can take the car ferry to Bremerton from Pier 52. The trip will take roughly an hour and a half no matter which way you do it, but the ferry ride (60 minutes) might be a more pleasant way to spend a large part of the journey. Note, however, that the earliest departure time for the ferry is 6 AM, so this option won't work for very early tee times.

Golf Club at Newcastle (✉ 15500 Six Penny La., Newcastle ☎ 425/793-5566 ⊕ www.newcastlegolf.com). Probably the best option on the Eastside, this complex, which includes a pair of courses and an 18-hole putting green, has views, views, and more views. From the hilly greens you'll see Seattle, the Olympic Mountains, and Lake Washington. The Coal Creek course (holes; par) is the more challenging of the two, though the China Creek course has its challenges and more sections of undisturbed natural areas. This is the Seattle area's most expensive golf club—greens fees for Coal Creek range from $125 to $160 depending on the season; fees for China Creek range from $80 to $110. Newcastle is about 35 minutes from Downtown—if you don't hit traffic.

★ **Harbour Pointe Golf Club** (✉ 11817 Harbour Pointe Blvd., Mukilteo ☎ 425/355-6060 ⊕ www.harbourpointegolf.com). Harbour Pointe is about 35 minutes north of Seattle in the town of Mukilteo. Its challenging 18-hole championship layout—with 6,800 yards of hilly terrain and wonderful Puget Sound views—is one of Washington's best. Greens fees range from $20 for twilight play to $49 for prime time on weekends. Carts cost $15 per person. There's also a driving range where you can get 65 balls for $5. Reserve your tee time online, up to 21 days in advance. Inquire about early-bird, twilight, off-season, and junior discounts.

Interbay Family Golf Center (✉ 2501 15th Ave. W, Magnolia ☎ 206/285-2200 ⊕ www.seattlegolf.com). Interbay has a driving range ($7 for 68 balls, $9 for 102, $12 for 153), a 9-hole executive course ($15 on weekends, $13 on weekdays), and a miniature golf course ($7). The range

---

WORK ON YOUR SHORT GAME

If you don't want to set up a whole day of golfing, head to **Hotel 1000** (✉ 1000 1st Ave., Downtown ☎ 206/357-9485 ⊕ www.hotel1000seattle.com) to use their state-of-the-art virtual driving range. Choose from 50 of the world's best courses; private instruction is available. Rates are $30–$60 per hour per person.

HIKING 101

Considering how many people take to Washington's trails every year, there are relatively few harrowing tales or outright tragedies. That said, the state is home to some true wilderness and nearly every year you hear at least one story of a simple day hike turned struggle for survival. Below are some basic tips to help make your hiking trips safer and more comfortable.

WHAT TO BRING

The "10 Essentials." According to the Washington State Trails Association, the ten essential items all hikers should carry are: a map of the area and trail; a compass; a flashlight; at least a day's worth of food (energy bars, gorp, and hardy fruits like apples and bananas are good); warm clothing and/or rain gear (a hat and a light jacket may be needed even on hot summer days); sunglasses, especially when walking across snow patches on sunny days; a basic first-aid kit in a waterproof container or baggie; a pocket knife or multipurpose tool; waterproof matches; and a fire starter like a candle or compressed wood chips (the Pacific Northwest is a damp place and you may have trouble finding dry kindling).

Water, water, and more water. A good rule of thumb is 2 liters per person for the average day hike. Take regular water breaks—don't wait until you're very thirsty to stop.

Waterproof footwear or a change of shoes. Even if the sun is shining in Seattle, the weather may be very different at your destination. If there's even a hint of a coming rainstorm, make sure you have proper rain gear. Hiking in the rain can be exhilarating, but walking 3 or 4 mi in

sopping wet shoes is never anything but miserable.

Anything but cotton. Veteran hikers can't say enough bad things about cotton clothing. It gets soggy (and then heavy) easily and is a terrible insulator, especially when it's wet. Your cotton T will probably be fine for an easy nature walk, but if you plan to do an all-day hike, you'll fare better with wool or synthetic fabrics.

Sunblock. Even if it's cool enough to require a jacket and hat, you can still get sunburned—the sun is particularly intense above the treeline.

Toilet paper. A few squares will suffice. Though major parks usually have well-equipped public restrooms, the port-a-johns at less-traveled trailheads may not have any paper products.

Insect repellent. Rocky areas can get quite buggy with anything from gnats to horseflies. Mosquitos start biting in late afternoon. Bugs aren't always a nuisance, but carrying a small supply of repellent is advised.

Northwest Forest Pass, if necessary. Some trails require the purchase of a $5 pass (one per vehicle), which allows you to park at the trailhead. Check out www.fs.fed.us/r6/passespermits to see if your trail requires a pass; you can purchase them at any Forest Service station.

SAFETY

Don't overdo it. Injuries occur more often when you are tired and/or lack experience navigating a certain type of terrain. Know your ability and conditioning levels. The great thing about Washington is great views can be found even on relatively easy trails—not everything requires a marathon slog up a mountainside.

Don't rely on cell phones to get you out of a jam. Service is spotty at best on trails, so don't let a cell phone in your pocket give you a false sense of security.

Hike in pairs. Although you'll see plenty of solo hikers, especially on the more heavily visited trails of the major parks, it's always wise to hike in pairs or groups, especially if you're a novice.

Exercise caution on Forest Service roads. Some Forest Service roads are mere steps from major highways; others consist of miles of twisting, often-unpaved stretches. Double-check road conditions, especially in late fall or early spring or after heavy rainstorms, and make sure you have a full tank of gas before turning off main roads. If at any time you are unsure of your whereabouts, turn around and retrace your steps back to the main road.

Keep track of the time. Be sure to clock the first leg of a hike, calculate how long the return trip will take, and plan accordingly. Know what time the sun sets and remember that dense, old-growth forest trails can get dark even if the sun's still shining up top.

Share your plans with someone. Let someone know of your hiking plans, including the trail name, the approximate time you're starting the hike, and the approximate time you expect to be back.

Be bear aware. Bear sightings are rare, but black bears (and even some grizzlies) do make their homes in Washington State. Bone up on bear etiquette at www.nps.gov/noca/naturescience/bear-safety.htm.

Lock up your car. Break-ins do happen at trailhead parking areas, so always lock your car and don't leave valuables in plain view.

TRAIL ETIQUETTE

Don't litter. Even Washington's busiest trails are free of garbage. Your mantra should be: Leave no trace.

Clam up. Avoid chatter and non-emergent cell phone usage. A big part of hiking's allure is the quiet.

Stay on the trail. The delicate ecosystems of the state's busiest natural areas are under tremendous strain from all the foot traffic; wildlife habitats can also be disturbed by overzealous adventurers. Don't go off the trail, especially in spots where signs implore you to stay put.

Let horseback riders pass. Few hiking trails allow horseback riding, but if you encounter riders, step to the side and let them pass.

Let your fellow hikers pass. Step off to the side when you need a break or if you're moving slowly and sense you're causing a bottleneck on a narrow trail. In most cases, hikers going uphill have the right of way; hikers heading downhill should step aside until they pass. However, sometimes the hiker with the less-difficult or roomier path will go first to give the other hiker more time to contend with the terrain.

Smile. It's common for hikers to greet each other as they pass by. Expect to get a nod, a "hello," or all three, and return the greeting.

5

and miniature golf course are open daily 7 AM–11 PM March–October and 7 AM–9 PM November–February; the executive course is open dawn to dusk year-round.

Jefferson Park (✉ *4101 Beacon Ave. S, Beacon Hill* ☎ *206/762–4513* ⊕ *www.seattlegolf.com*). The 18-hole course has views of the city skyline *and* Mt. Rainier. The par-27, 9-hole course has a lighted driving range with heated stalls that's open from dusk until midnight. Greens fees are $33 on weekends and $28 on weekdays for the 18-hole course; you can play the 9-hole course for $8 daily. Carts are $25 and $17, and $2 buys you a bucket of 30 balls at the driving range. You can book tee times online up to 10 days in advance or by phone up to 7 days in advance.

West Seattle Golf Course (✉ *4470 35th Ave. SW, West Seattle* ☎ *206/935– 5187* ⊕ *www.seattlegolf.com*). This 18-hole course has a reputation for being tough but fair. Greens fees are $28 on weekdays, $33 on weekends. It's $25 for a cart. From the back 9 you'll get views of Elliott Bay and the skyline.

Willows Run Golf Course (✉ *10402 Willows Rd. NE, Redmond* ☎ *425/883–1200* ⊕ *www.willowsrun.com*). Willows has it all: an 18-hole, links-style course; a 9-hole, par-27 course; and a lighted, 18-hole putting course that's open until 11 PM. Thanks to an improved drainage system, Willows plays reasonably dry even in typically moist Seattle-area weather. Greens fees for 9 holes are $11 Monday through Thursday, $13 Friday through Sunday; those for 18 holes are $42 or $55. Carts cost $14 per rider. There are also two pro shops and a driving range (75 balls cost $7, 35 balls cost $4).

HIKING

Washington State has so many beautiful trails, if there was ever a state sport, hiking should be it. There are enough trails in Mt. Rainier National Park alone to keep you busy (and awestruck) for months. If hiking is a high priority for you, and if you have more than a few days in town, your best bet is to grab a hiking book or check out the site www.cooltrails.com, rent a car, and head out to the Olympics or east to the Cascades (⇨ Chapter 7 for more information on the major parks in the area). If you have to stay close to the city, don't despair, there are many beautiful walks within town and many gratifying hikes only an hour away.

Within Seattle city limits, the best trails can be found in Discovery and Seward parks and at the Washington Park Arboretum. Following the Burke-Gilman Trail from Fremont to its midway point at Matthews Beach Park (north of the U-District) would take several hours and cover more than 7 mi. You'll get a good glimpse of all sides of Seattle as the trail winds through both urban areas and leafier residential areas; the first part of the walk takes you right along the Lake Washington Ship Canal.

OUTSIDE SEATTLE

Bridle Trails State Park. Though most of the travelers on the trails in this Bellevue park are on horseback, the 28 mi of paths are popular with hikers, too. The 482-acre park consists mostly of lowland forest, with Douglas firs, bigleaf maples, mushrooms, and abundant birdlife being just a few of its features. Note that horses are given the right of way on all trails; if you encounter riders, stop and stand to the side until the horses pass. From I–90 or the 520 bridge, get on I–405 North. Take Exit 17 and turn right onto 116 Ave NE. Follow that road to the park entrance.

Cougar Mountain Regional Wildland Park. This spectacular park in the "Issaquah Alps" has more than 36 mi of hiking trails and 12 mi of bridle trails within its 3,000-plus acres. The Indian Trail, believed to date back 8,000 years, was part of a trade route that Native Americans used to reach North Bend and the Cascades. Thick pine forests rise to spectacular mountaintop views; there are waterfalls, deep caves, and the remnants of a former mining town. Look for deer, black bears, bobcats, bald eagles, and pileated woodpeckers, among many other woodland creatures. ✉ *18201 SE Cougar Mountain Dr., Issaquah* ✛ *From Downtown Seattle take I–90 east; follow signs to park beyond Issaquah.* ☉ *Daily 8 AM–dusk.*

★ **Larrabee State Park.** A favorite spot of the hippies and college students that call Bellingham home, Larrabee has two lakes, a coastline with tidal pools, and 15 mi of hiking trails. The Interurban Trail, which parallels an old railway line, is perfect for leisurely strolls or trail running. Head up Chuckanut Mountain to reach the lakes and to get great views of the San Juan Islands. ✛ *Take I–5 north to Exit 231. Turn right onto Chuckanut Dr. and follow that road to the park entrance.*

Mt. Si. A good place to cut your teeth before setting out on more-ambitious hikes or a good place to just witness the local hiking and trail-running communities in all their weird and wonderful splendor, Mt. Si offers a moderately challenging hike with views of a valley (slightly marred by the suburbs) and the Olympic Mountains in the distance. The main trail to Haystack Basin is 8 mi round-trip, but there are several obvious places to rest or turn around if you'd like to keep the hike to 3 or 4 mi. Note that serenity is in short supply here—this is an extremely popular trail thanks to its proximity to Seattle. ✛ *Take I–90 east to Exit 31 (towards North Bend). Turn onto North Bend Way and then make a left onto Mt. Si Rd. and follow that road to the trailhead parking lot.*

HORSEBACK RIDING

EZ Times Outfitters (✉ *18703 Hwy. 706, Elbe* ☎ *360/569–2449*). EZ Times has one- to three-hour guided horseback-riding trips on 20,000 acres of state forest trails near Mt. Rainier. Rates are $25 an hour. For a less strenuous outing, you can take a carriage ride, which will run you $50 an hour for two people and $10 per hour for each additional rider.

Happy Trails Horse Adventures (✉Box 32, Easton 🕾509/656–2634 ⊕www.happytrailsateastonwa.com). About and hour and a half east of Seattle, Happy Trails offers guided rides through forested hills and meadows filled with wildflowers that are part of the Cascade mountain range. Trips range from leisurely three-hour rides ($75 per person) to overnight trips ($100 per person) to two-day excursions ($165 per person; includes meals). The ranch also does pony rides year-round as well as seasonal hayrides and sleigh rides.

Tiger Mountain Outfitters (✉24508 SE 133rd St., Issaquah 🕾425/392–5090). This Eastside outfitter leads three-hour, 10-mi rides to a lookout point on Tiger Mountain. The cost is $60 per person, and rides set out at 10 AM and 3 PM in summer and 1 PM in winter.

ROCK CLIMBING

The mountains of Washington have cut the teeth (among other body parts) of many a world-class climber. So it's only natural that there are several places to get in some practice.

REI (✉222 Yale Ave. N, Downtown 🕾206/223–1944 ⊕www.rei.com). Every day around 200 people have a go at REI's Pinnacle, a 65-foot indoor climbing rock. Climbing hours are Monday 10–6, Wednesday–Saturday 10–9, and Sunday 10–5. The cost is $15 including equipment. Although reservations are a good idea, you can also schedule a climb in person. The wait can be anywhere from 30 minutes to four hours, but it's rare that you don't get to climb on the very day you sign up. Adult climbing classes ($25) are held on Tuesday nights at 6:15 PM and kids' climbing classes ($15) are held on Sunday at 5:30 PM.

★ **Schurman Rock** (✉Camp Long, 5200 35th Ave. SW, West Seattle 🕾206/684–7434 ⊕www.ci.seattle.wa.us/parks/environment/camplong. htm). The nation's first man-made climbing rock was designed in the 1930s by local climbing expert Clark Schurman. Generations of climbers have practiced here, from beginners to rescue teams to such legendary mountaineers as Jim Whittaker, the first American to conquer Mt. Everest. Don't expect something grandiose—the rock is only 25 feet high. It's open for climbs Tuesday–Saturday 10–6. Rappelling classes for kids ($150 for 15 kids for two hours) are offered year-round at Camp Long, which is also the site of Seattle's only in-city campground, whose cabins rent for $35 a night.

Stone Gardens Rock Gym (✉2839 NW Market St., Ballard 🕾206/781–9828 ⊕www.stonegardens.com). Beyond the trying-it-out phase? Head here and take a stab at the bouldering routes and top-rope faces. Although there's plenty to challenge the advanced climber, the mellow vibe is a big plus for families, part-timers, and the aspiring novice-to-intermediate crowd. The cost is $15; renting a full equipment package of shoes, harness, and chalk bag costs $9. There are "Climbing 101" classes most weekday evenings for $45.

Vertical World (✉2123 W. Elmore St., Magnolia 🕾206/283–4497 ⊕www.verticalworld.com). It opened in 1987 and claims to be nation's first indoor climbing gym. There are 14,000 square feet of climbable surface as well as a bouldering area and weight-lifting equipment. The top-rope routes max out at 32 feet, which can seem pretty darn high when you scramble up under your own power. Tuesday and Thursday nights are busiest, though rainy weekend days also breed lines. The cost is $15 a day, not including equipment rental. They often offer weekend climbing trips in Washington and Oregon and can put together custom trips, too.

RUNNING

The roughly 3-mi trail that rings picturesque Green Lake seems custom-made for running—and walking, bicycling, rollerblading, fishing, lounging on the grass, and feeding the waterfowl. Seward Park has a more-secluded, less-used 3-mi loop where the park juts out into Lake Washington in southeast Seattle. At least one pair of bald eagles is known to nest in the park, so it's not unusual for a trip around the loop to include spotting an eagle *and* Mt. Rainier.

Other good running locales are the Burke-Gilman Trail, the reservoir at Capitol Hill's Volunteer Park, and at Myrtle Edwards Park, north of Pier 70 Downtown. Discovery Park in Magnolia has a 3-mi trail that takes you "off-roading" through patches of woods and meadows, and along bluffs.

■TIP→ If you need a good pair of running shoes, check out Super Jock 'n Jill on East Greenlake Drive and 72nd Street. Staff members are extremely knowledgeable, and they'll even let you take each pair you try on out for a test run to ensure proper fit.

Club Northwest (☎*206/729–9972* ⊕*www.cnw.org*) has been around since 1972 and helped start many of the area's well-known annual races, including the Seattle Marathon, the Jingle Bell Run, the Seafair Torch Run, and others. They often host informal group runs at Magnuson park on weekend mornings. **Eastside Runners** (⊕*www.eastsiderunners. com*) has been welcoming runners of all ages and abilities in East King County since 1980. The club sponsors weekly runs and the annual Mt. Si Relay. **Seattle Frontrunners** (⊕*www.seattlefrontrunners.org*) is a gay and lesbian running and walking club that sponsors several weekly runs/walks and welcomes all participants regardless of sexual orientation or athletic ability.

SKIING & SNOWBOARDING

Snow sports may be one of the few reasons to look forward to winter in Seattle. Ski season usually lasts from November until April. A one-day adult lift ticket averages about $40, and most resorts rent equipment and have restaurants.

Cross-country trails range from undisturbed backcountry routes to groomed resort tracks. To ski on state park trails you must purchase a Sno-Park Pass, available at most sporting goods stores, ski shops, and forest service district offices. Always call ahead for road conditions, which might prevent trail access or require you to put chains on your tires.

Call for Snoqualmie Pass ski reports and news about **weather conditions** (☎ *206/634–0200 or 206/634–2754*) in the more-distant White Pass, Crystal Mountain, and Stevens Pass. You can also do online research or listen to recorded messages about **road conditions** (☎ *800/695–7623* ⊕ *wsdot.wa.gov/traffic*). For information on cross-country trails and trail conditions, contact the **State Parks Information Center** (☎ *800/233– 0321* ⊕ *www.parks.wa.gov/winter*).

Alpental at the Summit (✉ *Exit 52 off I–90, Snoqualmie Pass* ☎ *425/434– 7669* ⊕ *www.summitatsnoqualmie.com*). Alpental, part of the Summit at Snoqualmie complex, attracts advanced skiers to its many long steep runs. (Giant slalom gold medalist Debbie Armstrong trained here for the 1984 Olympics.) A one-day lift ticket will run you $39–$49; equipment is another $25–$35. The resort is 50 mi from Seattle, but it's right off the highway so you avoid icy mountain roads.

Crystal Mountain (✉ *33914 Crystal Mountain Blvd.* ☎ *360/663–3050, 800/695–7623 road conditions, 888/754–6199 snow report* ⊕ *www. crystalmt.com*). Serious skiers and boarders don't mind the 2½-hour drive here (it's about 75 mi from the city). The slopes are challenging, the snow conditions are usually good, and the views of Mt. Rainier are amazing. Lift tickets cost $48 for a half day and $53 for a full day; night skiing on Friday and Saturday costs $28. Full rental packages run $33. There are only three lodging options on or near the mountain (Crystal Mountain Hotels, Crystal Mountain Lodging Suites, and Alta Crystal Resort). They tend to fill up on busy winter weekends, so book ahead if you want to stay the night.

Hurricane Ridge (✉ *Olympic National Park, 17 mi south of Port Angeles* ☎ *360/452–0330, 360/565–3131 for road reports* ⊕ *www. hurricaneridge.net*). The cross-country trails here, in Olympic National Park, begin at the lodge and have great views of Mt. Olympus. A small downhill ski and snowboarding area is open weekends and holidays; lift tickets are $8–$20. There's also a tubing/sledding hill. The Hurricane Ridge Visitor Center has a small restaurant, an interpretive center, and restrooms. Admission to the park is $15. Call ahead for road conditions before taking the two-hour drive from Seattle.

★ The **Summit at Snoqualmie** (✉ *Exit 52 off I–90, Snoqualmie Pass* ☎ *425/434–7669, 206/236–7277 Ext. 3372 for Nordic center* ⊕ *www. summitatsnoqualmie.com*). Chances are good that a local skier took his or her first run at Snoqualmie, the resort closest to the city. With three ski areas—Summit West, Summit Central, and Summit East—gentle slopes, rope tows, moseying chairlifts, a snowboard park, and dozens of educational programs, it's the obvious choice for an introduction to the slopes. One-day lift tickets cost $39–$49; equipment packages are $25–$35 a day. The Nordic Center at Summit East is the starting point for 31 mi of cross-country trails. Guided snowshoe hikes are offered here on Friday and weekends. The $12 trail pass includes two rides on the chairlifts.

Fodor'sChoice **Whistler** (✉ *Hwy. 99, Whistler, B.C., Canada* ☎ *800/766–0449* ⊕ *www.*
★ *whistler-blackcomb.com*). Whistler, 200 mi north of Seattle, is best done as a three-day weekend trip. And you really can't call yourself a skier here and not go to Whistler at least once. (Just make sure your

car has chains or snow tires.) The massive resort is renowned for its nightlife, which is just at the foot of the slopes. You abandon your car outside the village upon arrival and negotiate the entire hotel/dining/ski area on foot. A one-day lift ticket costs about $70 (Canadian), and rental packages are about $32 (Canadian). The area includes more than 17 mi of cross-country trails, usually open November–March. For die-hard skiers and boarders who want an extended season, there's summer skiing on Blackcomb Glacier through July. Expect continued improvements to both the facilities here and to the Sea-to-Sky Highway, as Whistler ramps up for the 2010 Winter Olympics.

SOCCER

For outdoor soccer, catch the A-League Seattle Sounders at Quest Field. The season starts in early May. Tickets are $18 for reserved seating and $13 for general admission. The Seattle Sounders Select women's league team plays at the stadium, too.

SWIMMING

When flying over the suburbs of Seattle, you'll see very few backyard swimming pools. In a city where most people don't own air conditioners, swimming pools seem an unnecessary luxury. If you're in the city during a summer heat wave, however, you'll be glad to know where the nearest oasis of chlorinated aquamarine water is located. Seattle Parks and Recreation maintains eight indoor pools (Queen Anne, Ballard, Evans, Rainier Beach, Southwest, Medgar Evers, Helene Madison, and Meadowbrook) year-round and two outdoor pools (Colman and Mounger). Entrance to most is $2.75–$3.75. All have lifeguards, lockers, changing rooms, showers, and classes and special events. Because of classes and special events, schedules can change frequently; always call ahead to make sure that a pool is open to the public before heading over.

Note that all pools are heated to about 85°F, so if you want to refresh yourself in colder waters, take a dip in the Sound or in Lake Washington instead (⇨ Beaches, *above*).

Ballard Pool (✉ *1471 NW 67th St., Ballard* ☎ *206/684–4094* ⊕ *www. cityofseattle.net/parks/aquatics/ballardp.htm*). Ballard, one of Seattle's older indoor pools, has classes and public swims, including daily lap swims, adults-only swims, and water-exercise programs. Schedules change seasonally; check the Web site.

Colman Pool (✉ *8603 Fauntleroy Way SW, West Seattle* ☎ *206/684–7494* ⊕ *www.seattle.gov/parks/Aquatics/colman.htm*). Colman Pool has several unique features that make it a favorite among Seattle families: it's the area's only saltwater pool, it has a great outdoor location in Lincoln Park with the shores of the Puget Sound in view, and it has a tube slide. Public swims are held most days from around noon to 4:30, with family swims and events happening Friday–Sunday from 5 to 7 PM; however, the pool is occasional closed for private events and swim meets, so it's a good idea to call ahead and confirm its hours.

Mounger Pool (✉ *2535 32nd Ave. W, Magnolia* ☎ *206/684–4708* ⊕ *www.cityofseattle.net/parks/aquatics/mounger.htm*). Mounger is actually two pools. The "big" one is 25 yards long and has a 50-foot corkscrew slide and five lanes. The little pool is 40 feet long, warmer, and less than 4 feet deep.

Queen Anne Pool (✉ *1920 1st Ave. W, Queen Anne* ☎ *206/386–4282* ⊕ *www.cityofseattle.net/parks/aquatics/queenannepool.htm*). This 25-yard-long indoor pool is a 10-minute drive from Downtown. There are early-morning and evening lap times, adult swim sessions, family swims, and water exercise programs.

YOGA

As far as accessories go, the yoga mat is almost as ubiquitous as Gore-Tex rain gear. The city has many yoga studios that can accommodate you, whether you're a Hatha, Ashtanga, or Kundalini devotee.

8 Limbs Yoga Center (✉ *500 E. Pike St., Capitol Hill* ☎ *206/325–1511* ⊕ *www.eightlimbsyoga.com*). This center welcomes drop-ins and manages to challenge intermediate students without alienating novices. Hatha, Ashtanga, Satsang, and Viniyoga are offered. Classes cost $12 for one hour and $15 for 1½ hours.

Punk Rock Yoga (⊕ *http://punkrockyoga.com/seattle*). No, it's not yoga done to the not-so-soothing sounds of the Sex Pistols. Punk Rock Yoga is a series of classes done in several different styles from basic Hatha yoga to hybrid styles that incorporate Thai massage techniques or belly dancing. Classes are held in several different venues around town, usually in either Capitol Hill or Fremont. Purists and overachievers need not apply: as founder Kimberlee Jensen Stedl told *Seattle Weekly,* she aims to "scrub the elitism and rigidity out of modern yoga." All ages and fitness levels are welcome. Live music often accompanies classes thanks to a rotating cast of local musicians. Check the Web site for current schedules and locations.

Samadhi Yoga (✉ *1205 E. Pike St., Capitol Hill* ☎ *206/329–4070* ⊕ *www.samadhi-yoga.com*). Samadhi combines yoga with an aerobic workout surrounded by statues of Hindu deities. Classes have an Ashtanga focus. Classes are $10–$15, less if you buy a multiclass card.

Yoga Life Studio (✉ *7200 Woodlawn Ave. NE, Green Lake* ☎ *206/529–0581* ✉ *8 Boston St., Queen Anne* ☎ *206/283–9642* ⊕ *www.yogalife.com*). This relaxing studio offers various types of yoga classes throughout the day and welcomes both beginners and experienced practitioners. Prenatal yoga, Reiki, and a monthly "TranceDance" combining yoga and music are also on the schedule, and massage and yoga therapy is available. As a drop-in you pay $14 a class; multiclass cards are available.

Shopping

WORD OF MOUTH

". . . In the middle of Pioneer Square, stop in at Elliott Bay Books or any of the galleries on 1st or Occidental . . . make your way up Fifth and Sixth to the Nordstrom HQ and the Pacific Place shopping center for any retail therapy needs. "

–Gardyloo

Updated
by Carissa
Bluestone

YES, A GOOD NUMBER OF its citizens still wear polar fleece and sport sandals, but Seattle is finally starting to come into its own as a shopping destination. As appropriate for a city that can at times feel like a small town, most of Seattle's best stores are cute neighborhood boutiques; however, the city also has quite a few malls and we defy you to name a major national store that isn't represented in the 5th Avenue shopping district.

Shopping in Seattle is something best done gradually. Don't expect to find it all in one or two days worth of blitz shopping tours. Downtown is the only area that allows for easy daylong shopping excursions. Within a few blocks along 5th Avenue, you'll find the standard chains (The Gap, Urban Outfitters, Nordstrom, Anthropologie, Old Navy), along with Nike's flagship store, and a few more-glamorous high-end stores, some featuring well-known designers like Betsey Johnson. Belltown is also an easy area to patrol—most stores of note are within a few blocks along 1st and 2nd avenues. But to find the stores that are truly special to Seattle—boutiques featuring local designers, independent record stores, cozy used-book shops with the requisite resident cat sleeping in the corner—you'll have to branch out and hit Capitol Hill and the northern neighborhoods. Every neighborhood has at least one or two must-stop shops.

DOWNTOWN

Seattle's retail core might feel business-crisp by day, but it's casual and arts-centered by night, and the shopping scene reflects both these moods. You'll find department store flagships, high-gloss vertical malls, and dozens of upper-echelon boutiques. Fifth Avenue is the heart of Downtown's shopping district and there are so many retail outfits around Pike and Pine streets, the whole area looks like it could be one big mall. Label hounds will be happy, as will shoppers coming from smaller towns that don't have their own Nordstrom or Old Navy. Anyone looking for something they can't get in any midsize city in the country will want to head over to Belltown or Capitol Hill first.

There are tons of shops around Pike Place Market, too, though many of them sell cheap trinkets and souvenirs; we've listed the shops that are worth a special visit.

Best shopping: 4th, 5th, and 6th avenues between Pine and Spring streets, and 1st Avenue between Virginia and Madison streets.

ANTIQUES & COLLECTIBLES

Antiques at Pike Place. Well stocked with vintage objects of all styles from dozens of vendors, this is the kind of antiques shop that's fun for everyone to browse in—there are plenty of small, affordable treasures to take home, from jewelry to vases to clocks to ceramic pieces. ⊠ *92 Stewart St., Downtown* ☎ *206/441–9643* ⊕ *www.antiquesatpikeplace.com.*
Big People Toys. The Madison Street store offers 18th- and 19th-century Asian antiques focusing on furniture from China. You'll find the stan-

CLOSE UP

The Most Bang for Your Buck

Shopping becomes decidedly less fun when it involves driving around and circling block after block for parking. You're better off limiting your all-day shopping tours to one of several key areas than planning to do a citywide search for a particular item. The following areas have the greatest concentration of shops and the greatest variety—you can park once and have plenty to keep you busy for the day.

Fifth Avenue & Pacific Place. Depending on where you're staying, you probably won't need to drive to this area, but if you do, the parking garage at Pacific Place always seems to have a space somewhere (it also has valet parking). Tackling either the Pacific Place mall or the four blocks of 5th Avenue between Olive Way and University Street could keep you very busy for a day; put them both together, and well, good luck to you.

First Avenue, Belltown. From Bell Street to Stewart Street (four blocks), you'll find a bunch of clothing boutiques, shoe stores, and some sleek home and architectural design stores. If you exhaust these possibilities, two more blocks down 1st Avenue brings you to the Pike Place Market. There are numerous pay lots on both 1st and 2nd avenues.

Fremont & Ballard. Start in Fremont's small retail center, which is mostly along 36th Street. You may be able to snag street parking; if not, you can park in PCC Natural Market's garage (the first 90 minutes is free). If you don't find what you're looking for in Fremont's clothing boutiques, gift shops, and music and book stores, it's an easy drive over to Ballard. Ballard Avenue is chockablock with great shops, and has a lot of home-furnishings stores, along with clothing and shoe stores. Finding parking in Ballard can be tricky on weekends (there aren't many lots to fall back on), but it's still easier than in Capitol Hill.

Pike–Pine corridor, Capitol Hill. Forget tacky Broadway, the best shopping in the Hill is on Pike and Pine streets between Melrose Avenue and 10th Avenue E. Most of the stores are on Pike Street; Pine's best offerings are clustered on the western end of the avenue between Melrose and Summit. There are pay lots on Pike (by Broadway) and one on Summit by E. Olive Way (next to the Starbucks).

6

---

dard lacquered trunks and small boxes and carved wooden pieces, but what will really get your attention is the stunning collection of insects under glass. ⊠*90 Madison St., Downtown* ☎*206/749–9016* ⊕*www. bigpeopletoys.com.*

Carolyn Staley Fine Japanese Prints. This simple, elegant space showcases rare antique *ukiyo-e* (17th- to 19th-century paintings and prints depicting scenes from everyday life) and modern Japanese woodblock prints. ⊠*2001 Western Ave., Suite 320, Downtown* ☎*206/621–1888* ⊕*www.carolynstaleyprints.com.*

★ **Honeychurch Antiques.** Known for its high standards of quality and service, this striking gallery has several rooms of Asian art, artifacts, and furniture ranging from museum-grade antiques to early-20th-century decorative pieces. The owners also oversee Glenn Richards, which has a similar focus and equally impressive collection of Asian antiques.

It's three blocks south of Honeychurch, around the corner on Denny Avenue. ⊠*411 Westlake Ave. N, Downtown* ☎*206/622–1204* ⊕*www.honeychurch.com.*

Walker-Poinsett Antiques. High-quality 17th- to 19th-century furniture, 16th-century brass candlesticks, and early-19th-century Sheffield plate adorn this Downtown gallery. ⊠*1405 5th Ave., Downtown* ☎*206/624–4973* ⊕*www.walkerpoinsett.com.*

BOOKS & PRINTED MATERIAL

Arundel Books. An attentive staff of dedicated bibliophiles are happy to guide you through this well-balanced mix of new, used, and rare titles. ⊠*1001 1st Ave., Downtown* ☎*206/624–4442* ⊕*www.arundelbooks.com.*

Left Bank Books. The bookstore for activists, Left Bank has progressive (often antiestablishment) political and social books covering everything from environmental issues to race relations to gay and lesbian rights. It's a not-for-profit shop, owned and operated by its staff. ⊠*92 Pike St., Downtown* ☎*206/622–0195.*

Metsker Maps. A massive selection of books, globes, charts, and atlases range from antique maps to prints of satellite images. Don't let the store's location in the middle of the Pike Place Market melee fool you: this is a Seattle institution, not a tourist trap. ⊠*1511 1st Ave., Downtown* ☎*206/623–8747* ⊕*www.metskers.com.*

★ **Peter Miller Architectural & Design Books and Supplies.** A floor-to-ceiling stock of architecture, art, and graphic design books in this urbane store attracts a stylish clientele. Sleek notebooks, bags and portfolios, drawing tools, and gifts are on hand for the discerning designer or businessperson, including Le Corbusier stencils. ⊠*1930 1st Ave. , Downtown* ☎*206/441–4114* ⊕*www.petermiller.com.*

CLOTHING

Alhambra. The interior at this pricey boutique may be Moorish-inspired, but the clothes are strictly now (and slightly European). If you need a party dress, you should definitely take a look here, though you'll also find sophisticated separates casual enough for the office or for brunch. The clothing here appeals to a wide age range—the connective thread is the emphasis on fine fabrics and detailing. ⊠*101 Pine St. , Downtown* ☎*206/621–9571* ⊕*www.alhambranet.com.*

Baby and Co. Taking style inspiration directly from the major fashion houses of Europe and Japan, this longtime Seattle favorite dresses women in esoteric fashions by Girbaud, Ishiko, and Lilith. You'll pay a lot for the privilege of being ahead of the trends. ✉ *1936 1st Ave. , Downtown* 📞*206/448–4077.*

Butch Blum. The attentive staff at this decidedly upscale retailer for men and women gives expert guidance on cultured creations by Giorgio Armani, Ermenegildo Zegna, Yohji Yamamoto, and Jil Sander—just to drop a few names. ✉ *1408 5th Ave., Downtown* 📞*206/622–5760* 🌐*www.butchblum.com.*

You're probably not going to browse for couches and coffee tables while on vacation, but if you're in the market for such things, Western Avenue between Union and Seneca streets has several high-end home-furnishings showrooms, which make up an informal "Furniture Row."

Flora and Henri. For parents who can't bear to outfit their kids in the Gap, Flora and Henri offers pricey vintage-inspired children's garments made from high-quality fabrics. Though the clothes are decidedly more sophisticated than most playground duds, they're still playful and age appropriate. Details mean hand stitching mean they're also sturdy enough to survive long enough to make gorgeous hand-me-downs. There is another branch in Capitol Hill. ✉ *717 Pine St., Downtown* 📞*206/749–9698* 🌐*www.florahenri.com.*

Ian. Selling hot brands for young men and women—Juicy Couture, Miss Sixty, Nice Collective, and G-Star among them—Ian offers urban streetwear that's a little tamer and more put together than the disheveled hipster look, but can easily be dressed up for the clubs. There is another, smaller branch in Fremont on 36th Street. ✉ *1919 2nd Ave., Downtown* 📞*206/441–4055.*

Isadora's Antique Clothing. It may look like every other vintage store, but Isadora's has built up quite a reputation for its excellent-quality vintage apparel (much of it from big-name designers like Dior and Halston), outrageous party dresses, and vintage and estate jewelry. ✉ *1915 1st St., Downtown* 📞*206/441–7711* 🌐*www.isadoras.com.*

★ **Mario's of Seattle.** Known for fabulous service and designer labels, this high-end boutique treats every client like a superstar. Men shop the ground floor for Armani, Zegna, and Dolce & Gabbana; women ascend the ornate staircase for Prada, Vera Wang, and Marc Jacobs. A freestanding Hugo Boss boutique sells the sharpest tuxedos in town. ✉ *1513 6th Ave., Downtown* 📞*206/223–1461* 🌐*www.marios.com.*

Nancy Meyer Fine Lingerie. Elegant European lingerie designs by La Perla, Fernando Sanchez, and others fill every nook and cranny of this tiny shop. The prices are sky high, but the goods are exquisite. ✉ *1318 5th Ave., Downtown* 📞*206/625–9200* 🌐*www.nancymeyer.com.*

Sway and Cake. The clothes come in two styles—tight and tighter—at this boutique for young, body-conscious fashionistas. Though the store claims it pulls from both coasts, styles often seem more Los Angeles than New York. Prices are high, but not outrageous. ✉ *1631 6th Ave., Downtown* 📞*206/624–2699* 🌐*www.swayandcake.com.*

★ **Tulip.** This sweet boutique is all about flirtatious clothing that has a much longer shelf life (and more dignity) than the trends-of-the-moment goods populating most of the Downtown stores. Even if you don't find anything, you'll be glad you stepped off busy 1st Avenue to browse in this lovely space—with soothing earth tones, a few pieces of Indonesian furniture, and a supremely laid-back vibe, Tulip feels more like a spa than a store. ✉*1201 1st Ave., Downtown* ☎*206/223–1790* ⊕*www.tulip-seattle.com.*

DEPARTMENT STORES

Macy's. The last of the true Downtown department stores, this retail anchor is a reliable source for clothing, housewares, cosmetics, and furniture. ✉*3rd Ave. and Pine St., Downtown* ☎*206/506–6000.*

★ **Nordstrom.** Seattle's own local retail giant sells good-quality clothing, accessories, cosmetics, jewelry, and lots of shoes—in keeping with its roots in footwear—including many hard-to-find sizes. Deservedly renowned for its customer service, the busy Downtown flagship has a concierge desk and valet parking. ■TIP➔ **The Nordstrom Rack store at 1st Avenue and Spring Street by Pike Place Market has great deals on marked-down items; new merchandise arrives every Tuesday.** ✉*500 Pine St., Downtown* ☎*206/628–2111.*

FOOTWEAR

A Mano. Ped, a superpopular shoe store closed and morphed into . . . another shoe store. Like its predecessor, A Mano sells high-quality shoes from all over the world, many of them handmade, along with some jewelry from local designers and other accessories. The space is still lovely: colorful handbags hang on exposed-brick walls and patrons can sit on comfy emerald-green couches while trying things on. ✉*1115 1st Ave., Downtown* ☎*206/292–1767* ⊕*www.shopamano.com.*

John Fluevog. You'll find the store's own brand of fun, funky boots, chunky leather shoes, and urbanized wooden sandals here in men's and women's styles. ✉*205 Pine St., Downtown* ☎*206/441–1065* ⊕*www.fluevog.com.*

Maggie's Shoes. The shop itself isn't very inspiring, but the owner (Maggie) makes special trips to Italy to ensure she's stocking the best and most fashionable men's and women's shoes in fine Italian leather. You'll also find a few select pieces of women's Italian sportswear and purses. ✉*1927 1st Ave., Downtown* ☎*206/728–5837* ⊕*www.maggiesshoes.com.*

GIFTS & HOME DECOR

★ **Great Jones Home.** Though refurbished vintage furniture is one of the store's specialties, most shoppers come to Great Jones Home to browse through the stylish housewares (French candles, dishes, bath products) in this spacious, skylighted store. One whitewashed wall is devoted to imported fabrics. ✉*1921 2nd Ave., Downtown* ☎*206/448–9405* ⊕*www.greatjoneshome.com.*

★ **Peter Miller Details.** Streamlined Alessi housewares and brightly printed Marimekko bags are part of the well-edited stock of indispensable *objets* for home and office in this lifestyle gallery. ✉*1924 1st Ave., Downtown* ☎*206/441–4114* ⊕*www.petermiller.com.*

☾ **Schmancy.** At first glance, the toys here seem a little too hip for kids under the age of 20. After all, not many kids would want to foster stuffed animals that come with not only their own names but their own psychiatric disorders: Kroko the crocodile clutches his pillow as he fights off paranoid hallucinations. But not all the figurines and toys in this tiny, adorable store are so troubled—the plush cupcakes and donuts seem very content. ⊠ *1932 2nd Ave., Downtown* ☎*206/728–8008* ⊕*www.schmancytoys.com.*

Sur La Table. Culinary artists have flocked to this popular Pike Place Market destination since 1972. It's packed to the rafters with some 12,500 kitchen items, including an exclusive line of copper cookware, endless shelves of baking equipment, tabletop accessories, cookbooks, and a formidable display of knives. ⊠ *84 Pine St., Downtown* ☎*206/448–2244* ⊕*www.surlatable.com.*

Urchin. Good industrial design inspires this eclectic shop, which sells everything from spun-aluminum lamps and vases to messenger-style diaper bags. Look for stylish business-card holders and mobiles so pretty you could hang them in the living room after they're no longer needed over the crib. ⊠ *1922 1st Ave., Downtown* ☎*206/448–5800* ⊕*www.urchinseattle.com.*

Watson Kennedy Fine Living. This jewel box of a store in the courtyard of the Inn at the Market stocks luxurious bath products and aromatic gifts. The sister store on 1st Avenue and Madison Street has vintage furniture, tableware, gourmet olive oil, and its own line of beeswax candles. ⊠ *86 Pine St., Downtown* ☎*206/443–6281* ⊕*www.watsonkennedy.com.*

JEWELRY

Turgeon Raine sells gems and jewelry in a spacious contemporary gallery. It's Washington's exclusive representative for Patek Philip watches. ⊠ *1407 5th Ave., Downtown* ☎*206/447–9488* ⊕*www.turgeonraine.com.*

MALLS

★ **Pacific Place.** Shopping, dining, and an excellent movie multiplex are wrapped around a four-story, light-filled atrium, making this a cheerful destination even on a stormy day. The mostly high-end shops include Cartier, Tiffany & Co., MaxMara, Coach, and Brookstone, though you'll find some standards here like Victoria's Secret and Eddie Bauer. A third-floor sky bridge provides a rainproof route to Nordstrom. One of the best things about the mall is its parking garage, which is surprisingly affordable given its location and has valet parking for just a few bucks more. ⊠ *600 Pine St., Downtown* ☎*206/405–2655* ⊕*www.pacificplaceseattle.com.*

Westlake Center. Westlake is like the ugly stepsister to Pacific Place's glitzy Cinderella. More than 60 stores and food vendors are open for business in a four-story glass pavilion that's also the Downtown link for the monorail to Seattle Center, but most of them are the standard mall fare like Nine West and Talbots. Best bets: fill a gift basket with Northwest specialty foods and crafts at Made in Washington, take a spin around Japanese department store Daiso for low-cost imports, and find quirky gifts and locally made jewelry at Fireworks. ⊠ *1601 5th Ave., Downtown* ☎*206/467–1600* ⊕*www.westlakecenter.com.*

OUTDOOR CLOTHING & EQUIPMENT

North Face. You can't swing a salmon in this town without hitting a North Face jacket. North Face must be doing something right, because they seem to provide the garments of choice for residents who don't believe in umbrellas. Besides the ubiquitous slickers, you'll find plenty of outdoor equipment. ✉ *1023 1st Ave., Downtown* ☎ *206/622–4111* ⊕ *www.thenorthface.com.*

Fodor'sChoice **REI.** REI (for the record, Recreational Equipment, Inc., but nobody
★ calls it that) is Seattle's sports-equipment mecca. The enormous flagship store has an incredible selection of outdoor gear and its own 65-foot climbing wall. The staff is extremely knowledgeable and there always seems to be enough help on hand even when the store is busy. You can try things out on the mountain-bike test trail or in the simulated rain booth. ■TIP➔ **REI also rents gear such as tents, sleeping bags, and backpacks in case you don't want to lug all your camping stuff across the country.** ✉ *222 Yale Ave. N, Downtown* ☎ *206/223–1944* ⊕ *www.rei.com.*

WINE & SPECIALTY FOODS

Delaurenti Specialty Food Markets. If you're planning any picnics, you might want to swing by here first. Imported meats and cheeses crowd the deli cases, and packaged delicacies pack the aisles. Hard-to-find items like truffle-infused olive oil will be great additions to your kitchen at home. The wineshop upstairs has excellent Italian vintages. ✉ *1435 1st Ave., Downtown* ☎ *206/622–0141.*

★ **Pike & Western Wine Shop.** Pike & Western is one of the two best wine-shops in the city (the other is McCarthy & Schiering in Queen Anne). It has a comprehensive stock of wines from the Pacific Northwest, California, Italy, and France—and expert advice from friendly salespeople to guide your choice. ✉ *1934 Pike Pl., Downtown* ☎ *206/441–1307* ⊕ *www.pikeandwestern.com.*

Rose's Chocolate Treasures. This cute shop on a quiet stretch of Post Alley is a nice break from the busier end of the market. Although some of the truffles are overly sweet for a gourmet shop, some of the more-savory flavors like wasabi or basil and blueberry are quite good, as are seasonal fruits dipped in chocolate. ✉ *1906 Post Alley, Downtown* ☎ *866/315–7673.*

The Tasting Room. A handful of Washington State boutique wineries are represented at this tasting room and wineshop. Most of the wines featured are handcrafted and/or reserve vintages. At the northern end of Post Alley, this quiet, tucked-away shop is a great place to sequester yourself from the mania of the market and try a few bottles you probably won't find in any other wineshop. ✉ *1924 Post Alley, Downtown* ☎ *206/770–9463* ⊕ *www.winesofwashington.com.*

BELLTOWN

Belltown has quite the growing collection of hip boutiques, most of them conveniently located on 1st Avenue. Thanks to the area's growing population of scenesters with money to burn, you'll find plenty of pricey women's wear and home accessories in the mix. However, true

CLOSE UP

Seattle Souvenirs

FOOD & DRINK

McCarthy & Schiering is the place to go for Pacific Northwest wines. Pick up delectable organic chocolates from **Theo** (✉ *400 Phinney Ave. N, Fremont* ☎ *206/632–5100*), Fremont's own little chocolate factory.

Seafood isn't the easiest thing to bring home, but if you go to **Pike Place Fish Market** the friendly, fish-flinging experts here will not only wrap up your purchase but will also ship it across the country for you.

Look for "Rub with Love" spice rubs from Seattle's favorite celebrity chef, Tom Douglas. They're sold at many souvenir shops, gourmet stores, and high-end supermarkets.

To bring home some beans, pop into a coffee shop—most offer ground coffee by the bag. Caffe Vita, Victrola, Lighthouse Roasters, and Caffe Fiore all roast their own brands (⇨ Coffeehouses *in* Dining).

MUSIC & LITERATURE

Staff recommendations at **Sonic Boom Records** will help you discover the Northwest's up-and-coming musicians. **Elliott Bay Book Company** has a good, well-organized selection of local literature and history books, with handwritten staff recommendations to help you pick out the real gems.

NOVELTIES & FUN STUFF

The **SpaceBase Gift Shop** (✉ *400 Broad St., Queen Anne* ☎ *800/809–0902*) has the city's ultimate icon, the Space Needle, rendered in endless ways. Among the officially licensed goods are bags of Space Needle Noodles, towering wooden pepper grinders, and artsy black T-shirts.

SPORTS STUFF

At the **Seattle Team Shop** (✉ *1029 Occidental Ave. S, Sodo* ☎ *206/621–1880*) you can kill three teams with one stone: the Sonics, the Seahawks, and the Mariners. The **Dawg Den** (✉ *4509 University Way NE, University District* ☎ *206/547–6005*) has University of Washington Huskies jerseys, as well as general "U-Dub" merchandise.

T-SHIRTS

Before you buy a teenage relative—or anyone else for that matter—an oversize T-shirt that says "Seattle!" head up to Fremont to **Desteenation** (✉ *3412 Evanston Ave. N, Fremont* ☎ *206/324–9403*). The store sells T-shirts with the names of independent, local businesses. Each shirt has a tag attached with information about and pictures of the business it's advertising. Note that not all of the shirts are for Seattle shops, so read the tag carefully or ask if you need help selecting a gift.

to the neighborhood's more-humble origins, many of the shops here are a little artier, and a little more Seattle than their Downtown counterparts. Many local, independent designers are represented here, too, though the clothing tends to be more upmarket than the crafty, DIY goods offered in say, Capitol Hill or Ballard.

Best shopping: Along 1st Avenue between Virginia and Bell streets

CLOTHING

Endless Knot. If your wardrobe consists entirely of blacks and grays, get thee to the Endless Knot. The store is a color explosion; even if you can't handle a batik dress, you're sure to find a scarf or handbag to brighten up your look. ⊠*2300 1st Ave., Belltown* ☎*206/448–0355.*

Gian DeCaro Sartoria. Gian DeCaro has a reputation for single-handedly saving many of Seattle's techies from the "casual Friday" downward spiral. Custom-tailored suits, his specialty, may come at prices only Bill Gates can handle, but his shop is also full of elegant ties, cuff links, and other accessories, as well as ready-to-wear clothing in luxurious fabrics. ⊠*2025 1st Ave., Belltown* ☎*206/448–2812.*

Karan Dannenberg Clothier. Though the clothes here aren't cheap, this is one of the most egalitarian boutiques in Seattle. Dannenberg stocks sophisticated, modern clothing, but doesn't bow to useless trends, meaning that items will last more than one season. She also stocks a lot of plus sizes, something you don't see in many boutiques. Belltown party girls can find the perfect pair of jeans and executives can find classy work-appropriate clothes. The store also stocks glamorous formal wear. ⊠*2232 1st Ave., Belltown* ☎*206/441–3442.*

Kuhlman. This tiny store on the same ultrahip block as the Ace Hotel has a careful selection of urban street wear that includes hard-to-find designers—it's sophisticated while still maintaining an edge. If you've got some time, Kuhlman is best known for creating unique custom jeans, pants, and jackets, often from superb European and Japanese fabrics. ⊠*2419 1st Ave., Belltown* ☎*206/441–1999* ⊕*www.kuhlmancompany.com.*

Margaret O'Leary. Gorgeous hand-loomed cashmere knits here appeal to women of all ages, and fine cotton and linen apparel rounds out the collection. Be prepared for sticker shock. ⊠*2025 1st Ave., Suite B, Belltown* ☎*206/441–6691* ⊕*www.margaretoleary.com.*

Monica Gutweis. Gutweis herself makes each one-of-a-kind garment in this tiny gallery; her fabrics and detailing have earned her a cult following. If you want to let your inner rock star out without letting go of your dignity, come to this store. Gutweis is a little bit Goth, a little bit punk, and not one bit pretentious; therefore, her pieces are dramatic, but never impractical. She also stocks jewelry and accessories from other local designers. ⊠*2405 1st Ave., Belltown* ☎*206/956–4620.*

Patagonia. If the person next to you on the bus isn't wearing North Face, he or she is probably clad in Patagonia. This popular and durable brand excels at functional outdoor wear—made with earth-friendly materials such as hemp and organic cotton—as well as technical clothing everyday and sporty enough for those who don't actually do sports. The line of whimsically patterned fleecewear for children is particularly charming. ⊠*2100 1st Ave., Belltown* ☎*206/622–9700* ⊕*www.patagonia.com.*

FOOTWEAR

★ **J. Gilbert Footwear.** Wrap your feet in comfort and European styling by designers Thierry Rabotin, Anyi Lu, and Taryn Rose. Along with limited-edition deluxe cowboy boots, you'll find glove-soft leather jackets and chic, casual clothing. ✉*2025 1st Ave., Belltown* ☎*206/441–1182* ⊕*www.jgilbertfootwear.com.*

GIFTS & HOME DECOR

Chartreuse International. Savvy collectors shop here for authentic mid-century modern furniture and accessories by Harry Bertoia, Arne Jacobsen, Isamu Noguchi, and other design luminaries. ✉*2609 1st Ave., Belltown* ☎*206/328–4844* ⊕*www.modchartreuse.com.*

Egbert's. The smooth lines of Italian and Scandinavian furniture are enlivened by African tribal art and textiles in this elegant gallery. Essential housewares include sinuous vases by Alvar Aalto and colorful Murano glass. ✉*2231 1st Ave., Belltown* ☎*206/728–5682.*

Velocity Art & Design. Velocity's showroom has a little bit of everything: furniture, bedding, lighting, accessories, and artwork from local artists. It all follows a mid-century esthetic, whether a piece is an overt homage to an icon of the area or just coyly retro new creation from one of today's hippest designers. Prices are high, but so is the quality of the selection. ✉*2118 2nd Ave., Belltown* ☎*206/781–9494* ⊕*www. velocityartanddesign.com.*

MUSIC

Singles Going Steady. If punk rock is more to you than a catchall adjective for odd hairstyles, you must stop at Singles Going Steady. Punk and its myriad subgenres on CD and vinyl are specialties, though they also stock rockabilly, indie rock, and hip-hop. It's a nice foil to the city's indie-rock-dominated record shops and a good reminder that Belltown is still more eclectic than its rising rents may indicate. ✉*2219 2nd Ave., Belltown* ☎*206/441–7396* ⊕*www.singlesgoingsteady.com.*

PAPER GOODS

Blu Canary Stationery. If you'd rather commit a social faux pas than send a schmaltzy supermarket greeting card, head to this cheerful little shop and stock up on cards that actually approximate real human emotions. The store, of course, stocks beautiful papers and journals, as well as many fun gift items. ✉*2331 2nd Ave., Belltown* ☎*206/443–3328.*

Paperhaus. Paperhaus is so put together you expect the stacks of three-ring binders to yell at you for slouching. Form and function reign here: you won't find any unicorns or sparkly stars on these notebooks. Unless you're redoing your home office from afar, you probably won't find too much of interest here, but they do carry some sleek writing instruments, photo albums, and laptop and messenger bags that are worth a peek. ✉*2008 1st Ave., Belltown* ☎*206/374–8566* ⊕*www.paperhaus.com.*

PIONEER SQUARE

Although this neighborhood has more than a few tourist traps hiding in its attractive brick buildings, it also has a few of the city's most beloved stores (Elliott Bay Book Company and Bud's Jazz Records chief among them), as well as many galleries and galleryesque shops selling high-end furniture and collectibles. Serious art collectors should see the Exploring chapter for a full list of galleries; here we've listed only the shops selling antiques and collectibles, not high-priced artwork.

Many pay lots in the neighborhood participate in the "Parking Around the Square" program, which works with local businesses to offer shoppers validated parking; the Web site www.pioneersquare.org lists the lots and stores that offer it.

Best shopping: 1st Avenue S between Yesler Way and S. Jackson Street, and Occidental Avenue S between S. Main and Jackson streets.

ANTIQUES & COLLECTIBLES

Chidori Asian Antiques. So packed full of stuff it looks more like a curio shop than a high-end antique seller, Chidori offers high-quality Asian antiques, pre-Columbian and primitive art, and antiquities from all over the world. ⊠*108 S. Jackson St., Pioneer Square* ☎*206/343–7736.*

Flury & Company. View one of the largest collections of vintage photographs by Edward Curtis, along with Native American antiques, traditional carvings, baskets, jewelry, and tools in a historic space that's as interesting as the store's wares. ⊠*322 1st Ave., Pioneer Square* ☎*206/587–0260* ⊕*www.fluryco.com.*

Jean Williams Antiques. Eighteenth- and 19th-century English and French furniture is arranged formally in an elegant space. This is the polar opposite of exploring cluttered Asian antiques stores—less an adventure and more a serious appointment with your checkbook. ⊠*115 S. Jackson St., Pioneer Square* ☎*206/622–1110* ⊕*www.jeanwilliamsantiques.com.*

★ **Kagedo Japanese Art and Antiques.** The finest quality Japanese antiques and works by modern masters are on display in this influential gallery. Among the treasures are intricately carved *okimono* (miniature figures rendered in wood, ivory, or bronze), stone garden ornaments, studio basketry, and textiles. The gallery itself is worth a look—it's beautifully laid out, and includes a small rock garden and rice-paper screens that cover the storefront's picture windows. ⊠*520 1st Ave. S, Pioneer Square* ☎*206/467–9077* ⊕*www.kagedo.com.*

Kibo Galerie. African art from tribal masks to statuary to textiles fill this bi-level space. ⊠*323 Occidental Ave. S, Pioneer Square* ☎*206/442–2100* ⊕*www.kibogalerie.com.*

Laguna. Watch your step as you navigate through this colorful, crowded shop; it's wall-to-wall collectible 20th-century American dinnerware, art pottery, vintage linens, tiles, and garden pieces. ⊠*116 S. Washington St., Pioneer Square* ☎*206/682–6162* ⊕*www.lagunapottery.com.*

BOOKS & MUSIC

★ **Bud's Jazz Records.** Bud's is a Seattle institution (it's over 20 years old), and the store almost makes up for the fact that the city doesn't have a great jazz scene. A narrow set of stairs leads to a tightly packed underground store that sells just jazz (equal parts vinyl and CDs) and lots of it, including hard-to-find recordings. And there's always something good playing on the sound system, making this a great place for a leisurely browse. ⊠*102 S. Jackson St., Pioneer Square* ☎*206/628–0045.*

Fodor'sChoice ★ **Elliott Bay Book Company.** Many Seattleites consider this enormous independent bookstore the literary heart of the city. More than 150,000 titles are arranged on rustic wooden shelves in a labyrinth of brick-lined rooms. A side room contains used books—about 22,000 of them—on all subjects; some are signed first editions. The store is well known for its popular lectures and readings by local and international authors. As you enter, check out the great selection of Pacific Northwest history books and fiction titles by local authors, complete with handwritten recommendation cards from staff members. ■TIP➜ **The café in the basement is one of neighborhood's best options for lunch or a quick bite.** ✉101 S. Main St., Pioneer Square ☎206/624–6600 ⊕www.elliottbaybook.com.

Wessel & Lieberman. This handsomely fitted shop in a historic building specializes in first editions, Pacific Northwest history and literature, Western Americana, book arts, and fine letterpress. This is also a good alternative if you can't handle the masses at Elliott Bay. ✉208 1st Ave. S, Pioneer Square ☎206/682–3545 ⊕www.wlbooks.com.

CLOTHING

Betty Blue. Big-ticket designer labels at deep discount prices are snapped up quickly at this boutique. You'll find last season's runway creations by Prada, Stella McCartney, Jil Sander, Michael Kors, Balenciaga, and many others. The store carries men's clothing, too. ✉608 2nd Ave., Pioneer Square ☎206/442–6888 ⊕www.shopbettyblue.com.

Ebbets Field Flannels. Wear your bit of baseball history: here you'll find faithful reproduction team jackets, jerseys, and caps from the 1920s to '60s, with an emphasis on the Negro Leagues, minor leagues, and the Pacific Coast League. ✉404 Occidental Ave. S, Pioneer Square ☎206/262–0260.

Ragazzi's Flying Shuttle. For women who want to add some whimsy and color to their wardrobe without veering into crazy cat-lady territory, Ragazzi's offers locally crafted, handwoven clothing in bold colors, as well as chunky, get-noticed jewelry. ✉607 1st Ave., Pioneer Square ☎206/343–9762.

Synapse 206. A near-seizure-inducing jumble of every imaginable fabric and color, Synapse 206 throws arty, innovative, and often audacious designs from local and international designers under one roof. Prices are actually reasonable, and whether or not you walk out with something, you'll have fun poking around in here. ✉206 1st Ave. S, Pioneer Square ☎206/447–7731 ⊕www.synapse206.com.

Violette. The owner of this lovely little boutique has a penchant for vintage and accordingly, many of pieces sold here are made with vintage fabrics or affect a vintage style. Clothes are fresh, functional, and girlie in a good way—just like the best fashions from the '40s and '50s. The store also carries handbags and some home-decor items. ✉602 2nd Ave., Pioneer Square ☎206/652–8991 ⊕www.violetteboutique. blogspot.com.

FOOTWEAR

Clog Factory. For better or for worse, earth mothers, soccer moms, men in ponytails, gardeners, fans of back support, and hipster girls who can make anything "hot" clomp down to this store, where clogs of all sizes, shapes, and colors are lined up on high, exposed-brick walls. There's not much more to say: it's a store filled with clogs—it's fun, and though the fashion mags may not thank you, your feet probably will. ✉*217 1st Ave. S, Pioneer Square* ☎*206/682–2564.*

Glass House Studio. Seattle's oldest glassblowing studio and gallery lets you watch fearless artisans at work in the "hot shop." Studio pieces and other works on display are for sale. ✉*311 Occidental Ave. S, Pioneer Square* ☎*206/682–9939* ⊕*www.glasshouse-studio.com.*

Northwest Fine Woodworking. More than 20 fine Northwest craftspeople are represented in this large, handsome showroom. Even if you're not in the market for new furniture, stop in for a reminder of how much personality wood pieces can have when they're not mass-produced. The store also carries gifts like chess sets and ornate hand-crafted kaleidoscopes and more-practical household items like wooden bowls and utensils. ✉*101 S. Jackson St., Pioneer Square* ☎*206/625–0542* ⊕*www.nwfinewoodworking.com.*

Grand Central Arcade. This former gold rush–era hotel has a vaulted, exposed-brick interior courtyard and one or two interesting shops. The Grand Central Bakery is the main attraction here; you'll see its breads and pastries featured in stores, coffee shops, and restaurants throughout the city. On the ground floor, A. J. Smith & Co. is a fun place to sift through vintage prints and collectibles. Go downstairs to see the wares (and the artists at work) at the Pottery School, sigh over the Japanese paper art at Tai Designs, or just take a load off on one of the benches. ✉*214 1st Ave. S , Pioneer Square* ☎*206/623–7417.*

INTERNATIONAL DISTRICT

The megamarket Uwajimaya (reviewed in the Exploring chapter) is the major shopping attraction of the International District. The rest of the neighborhood warrants browsing, too. Here you can pick up Chinese pastries, jade and gold jewelry, Asian produce, and Eastern herbs and tinctures. Little souvenir shops, dusty and deep, sell Japanese kites, Vietnamese bowls, Chinese slippers, Korean art, and tea or dish sets.

Best shopping: S. King Street between 5th and 8th avenues South

Eileen of China. The labyrinth of rosewood furniture and lacquered cabinets in this enormous warehouse of Asian art and antiques is peppered with porcelain vases, wood and jade carvings, snuff bottles, and small gift items. ✉*519 6th Ave. S, International District* ☎*206/624–0816.*

★ **Kobo at Higo.** Housed in what used to be a 75-year-old five-and-dime store, this distinctive gallery has fine ceramics, textiles, and exquisite crafts by Japanese and Northwest artists; you can also see artifacts from the old store. Items range from something as simple as incense from Kyoto to an enormous antique chest. ✉*602 S. Jackson St., International District* ☎*206/381–3000* ⊕*www.koboseattle.com.*

QUEEN ANNE

There are actually two shopping areas in this hillside neighborhood—around the Seattle Center at the bottom of the slopes and along Queen Anne Avenue N at the top. East from the Seattle Center along Queen Anne and Mercer avenues are tiny cafés, bookstores, antiques and consignment shops, and bike stores. The cluster of businesses at the top of the hill includes crafts shops and home-decor shops.

Best shopping: Along Queen Anne Avenue N between W. Harrison and Roy streets, and between W. Galer and McGraw streets.

ANTIQUES & COLLECTIBLES

Crane Gallery. This well-respected gallery at the base of Queen Anne Hill houses top-notch Japanese, Chinese, Korean, Tibetan, and Southeast Asian antiques and art objects, including bronzes, porcelain, and textiles. ✉*104 W. Roy St., Queen Anne* ☎*206/298–9425* ⊕*www.cranegallery.com.*

BOOKS & MUSIC

Easy Street Records. Hip and huge, this lively independent music store at the base of Queen Anne Hill has a well-earned reputation for its inventory of new releases, imports, and rare finds. ✉*20 Mercer St., Queen Anne* ☎*206/691–3279* ⊕*www.buymusichere.net.*

⟳ **Queen Anne Books.** The friendly staff at this general-interest neighborhood bookstore is full of suggestions for good reads. Reflective of the number of families in Queen Anne, the store has a good children's section, and there are storytelling sessions on the third Sunday of every month. It holds the added bonus of being adjacent to El Diablo coffee shop. ✉*1811 Queen Anne Ave. N, Queen Anne* ☎*206/283–5624* ⊕*www.queenannebooks.com.*

CLOTHING

Adelita. With the closing of beloved La Femme, Adelita is now the best boutique in the neighborhood. This is as edgy as Upper Queen Anne gets: strong yet accessible designs by Petro Zillia, Lulu Guinness, and Tarina Tarantino, among others. You'll also find children's clothing, spa products, and a single pale pink barber's chair for on-the-spot haircuts and makeup applications. ✉*1527 Queen Anne Ave. N, Queen Anne* ☎*206/285–0707* ⊕*www.adelitastyle.com.*

GIFTS & HOME DECOR

Four Winds. Stores selling Tibetan and Indonesian crafts under pseudo-spiritual names usually make us groan, but Four Winds has a terrific and thoughtful selection of fine jewelry, textiles, furniture, and gifts—probably because the owner selects most items personally during frequent travels. There are, of course, more than 50 varieties of incense. ✉*1517 Queen Anne Ave. N, Queen Anne* ☎*206/282–0472.*

Stuhlbergs Fine Home Accessories. Fine Italian pewter, Salviati crystal, brightly colored European pull toys, fancy votive candles, and Petit Bateau baby clothes all coexist peacefully in this charming Craftsman-style cottage. ✉*1801 Queen Anne Ave. N, Queen Anne* ☎*206/352–2351* ⊕*www.stuhlbergs.com.*

WINES & SPECIALTY FOODS

★ **McCarthy & Schiering Wine Merchants.** This is the best wineshop in the city. The selection of Northwest wines is large and carefully selected and the knowledgeable staff is attitude-free. ✉ *2401 Queen Anne Ave. N, Queen Anne* ☎ *206/282–8500* ⊕ *www.mccarthyandschiering.com.*

Teacup. In a city full of coffee drinkers, Teacup boldly salutes the overlooked leaf. More than 100 varieties of tea are sold loose by the pound and the excellent selection includes special blends formulated to boost energy levels without causing jangled nerves. The place has a few tables if you want to sample some teas in-house. ✉ *2207 Queen Anne Ave. N, Queen Anne* ☎ *206/283–5931* ⊕ *www.seattleteacup.com.*

CAPITOL HILL

Capitol Hill is one-stop shopping for hipster accoutrements, whether you're looking for retro kicks, ironic-slogan T-shirts, hard-to-find CDs and vinyl, or sleek, slightly mod home furnishings. Broadway is popular among college students because of its cheap clothing stores, including standbys Urban Outfitters and American Apparel. The Pike–Pine corridor holds the majority of the neighborhood's interesting and superhip shops.

Best shopping: E. Pike and E. Pine streets between Boren Avenue and Broadway Avenue E, E. Olive Way between Bellevue and Broadway avenues East, and Broadway Avenue E between E. Olive Way and E. Roy Street

ANTIQUES

★ **David Weatherford Antiques and Interiors.** Shop for fine French, English, and Asian antiques in this gracious 1894 Queen Anne–style mansion. ✉ *133 14th Ave. E, Capitol Hill* ☎ *206/329–6533* ⊕ *www.davidweatherford.com.*

BOOKS & MUSIC

Bailey/Coy Books. Handwritten recommendations guide you through a thoughtful selection of diverse topics; there's a substantial section of gay and lesbian literature. ✉ *414 Broadway Ave. E, Capitol Hill* ☎ *206/323–8842.*

Horizon Books. Book lovers and claustrophobes will start to palpitate upon entering this tiny cottage. A kind of order rules the chaos of the tall stacks, but it may not be apparent to the casual observer. Thankfully, the owners know where every book is, so just ask if you can't find what you're looking for. ✉ *425 15th Ave. E, Capitol Hill* ☎ *206/329–3586.*

Twice Sold Tales. This excellent used-book store has more shelf space than most and the best sleeping-cat-to-customer ratio in the city. As only a Capitol Hill business could afford to do, the shop stays open until 2 AM on Friday, with 20% discounts offered between 11 PM and closing. ✉ *905 E. John St., Capitol Hill* ☎ *206/324–2421.*

Wall of Sound. World-music enthusiasts who can't bear to listen to another Putumayo release will love this small, neatly organized boutique. From Japanese avant-rock to the latest club hits of Ghana to local artists warping folk music into something palatable, if it's obscure, experimental, and good, you'll find it here. ✉ *315 E. Pine St., Capitol Hill* ☎ *206/441–9880* ⊕ *www.wosound.com.*

CLOTHING

Atlas Clothing. Atlas is loaded with previously appreciated shirts, jackets, and tees; stacks of new and vintage denim; must-have sneakers from the '70s and '80s; and tons of accessories. This is not over-the-top costume vintage; visit Red Light for that. ✉ *1515 Broadway, Capitol Hill* ☎ *206/329–4460.*

♻ **Bootyland.** There's nothing "whatever fits" about children's clothes at this store that caters to Capitol Hill residents as they transition from communal housing to mortgage payments. Although not all the T-shirts are screen-printed with punk-rock themes, the collection overall is as close to hip as something that will inevitably be covered in food stains can be. But even if you think the duds are a bit over-the-top, it's worth taking a look at the toys, which are made of all-natural materials (no off-gassing plastics) and adorned with nontoxic paint. And the onesies and simple vintage-looking tees made from organic hemp are adorable and not terribly overpriced. ✉ *1317 E. Pine St., Capitol Hill* ☎ *206/328–0636* ⊕ *www.bootylandkids.com.*

Juniper. Slightly off the beaten path in the eastern neighborhood of Madrona—you'll have to drive here from Capitol Hill—this sleek boutique offers high-priced "haute green" clothing and accessories from designers as diverse as American Apparel and Anna Cohen, a Portland-based designer and current darling of green fashion. Sustainable materials are turned into sophisticated fashions—if you can't believe that bamboo can be made into a dress, head here. ✉ *3314 E. Spring St., Madrona* ☎ *206/838–7496* ⊕ *www.juniperinmadrona.com.*

★ **Le Frock.** It may look like just another overcrowded consignment shop, but Le Frock is Seattle's favorite vintage store. Among the racks, you'll find plenty of labels, and the store has a good shoe selection as well. Prices are reasonable and there are frequent sales. ✉ *317 E. Pine St., Capitol Hill* ☎ *206/623–5339* ⊕ *www.lefrockonline.com.*

Pretty Parlor. You'd better like pink if you're going to step into this boutique. Being a fan of tutus and lace doesn't hurt either, though the parlor's mix of vintage, used, and new clothes isn't nearly as precious as its interior. The creative, one-off pieces from local designers are usually the best things in stock, though the used and vintage sections often have outrageous party dresses that are fun to try on even if you have nowhere to wear them. Jewelry, handbags, shoes, and hats round out the store and there's even a competent selection of men's clothes. ✉ *119 Summit Ave. E, Capitol Hill* ☎ *206/405–2883* ⊕ *www. prettyparlor.com.*

★ **Red Light Clothing Exchange.** Nostalgia rules in this cavernous space filled with well-organized, good-quality vintage clothing. Fantasy outfits from decades past are arranged by era or by genre. There's plenty of denim, leather, and disco threads alongside cowboy boots and evening wear. There's a smaller branch in the University District. ✉ *312 Broadway E, Capitol Hill* ☎ *206/329–2200* ⊕ *www.redlightvintage.com.*

FOOTWEAR

Capitol 1524. Savvy "sneakerheads" come here to buy limited-edition Nikes, Pumas, Adidas, and New Balance kicks and reissued styles from the 1980s. Vintage shoes are also on sale at premium prices. This is one of the few stores in the neighborhood where you'll hear hip-hop playing instead of indie rock. ✉ *1524 E. Olive Way, Capitol Hill* ☎ *206/322–2307* ⊕ *www.capitol1524.com.*

Edie's Shoes. Plop down on the big purple couch and try on trendy but sensible footwear by Camper, Puma, J. Shoes, and more in this basic but well-organized shop. You won't find any outrageous designs or one-of-a-kind items here, but it does have a good selection of favored brands in perhaps a few more styles than you'd find at Nordstrom. ✉ *319 E. Pine St., Capitol Hill* ☎ *206/839–1111* ⊕ *www.ediesshoes.com.*

GIFTS & HOME DECOR

Area 51. Anything might materialize in this 6,000-square-foot industrial space, from Eames replicas to kitschy coffee mugs, but it will all look like it's straight out of a hipster's handbook to the design trends of the 1960s and '70s. ✉ *401 E. Pine St., Capitol Hill* ☎ *206/568–4782.*

Galactic. Like the retail equivalent of cotton candy, Galactic offers sweet, frivolous home accessories and clothing, displayed on white racks and pale pink and blue walls. T-shirts have graphic prints or sassy slogans—or both. Gift items might include night lights in the shape of Chinese lanterns or flowerpots painted with fat Dr. Seuss stripes. Items are simple, fun, and, unlike in many other gift shops, affordable. ✉ *1213 Pine St., Capitol Hill* ☎ *206/749–9167* ⊕ *www.galacticboutique.com.*

Kobo. On the most dignified offshoot of the Broadway shopping district is this lovely store, selling artisan crafts from studios in Japan and in the Northwest. You'll find a similar stock here as in the International District branch: tasteful home wares, cute but functional gifts, and the odd piece of furniture. After a long day of looking at retro and ironic items, this place will cleanse your palate. ✉ *814 E. Roy St., Capitol Hill* ☎ *206/726–0704* ⊕ *www.koboseattle.com.*

Square Room. The Square Room sells furniture, objets d'art, jewelry, and home accessories that are hip but never gimmicky. The art here often imitates nature and many of the store's wares are made from either eco-friendly or recycled materials. The two owners often contribute their own artwork to the mix. ✉ *910 E. Pike St., Capitol Hill* ☎ *206/267–1214* ⊕ *www.squareroom.us.*

Standard Home. Investment-quality mid-century modern furniture and housewares by such luminaries as George Nelson, Charles and Ray Eames, Russel Wright, and Hans Wegner crowd this informative gallery. ✉ *1108 Pike St., near Boren Ave., Capitol Hill* ☎ *206/464–0850.*

FREMONT

Just across the Fremont Bridge, you'll find a great cluster of shops as you enter the neighborhood's main commercial area. Though pricey clothing boutiques are reaching critical mass, the neighborhood's still got a good mix, including independent music and book shops, vintage stores, and gift shops where you can buy a trinket for $5 or a substantial piece of art for $500. The weekly summer Sunday market along the waterfront (with free parking nearby) is hit or miss, but worth a look if you're in the area.

Best shopping: Blocks bound by Fremont Place N and Evanston Avenue N to N. 34th Street and Aurora Avenue N

ANTIQUES & COLLECTIBLES

Deluxe Junk. Looking like an old Hollywood movie prop shop, this labyrinth of vintage furniture, retro bric-a-brac, and racks of costume-ready clothing requires lots of time for worthwhile browsing. This is sometimes a great place to find kitschy Seattle souvenirs. ⊠*3518 Fremont Pl. N, Fremont* ☎*206/634–2733.*

Fremont Antique Mall. Decades of popular American culture are stuffed into every conceivable corner of this bi-level space. The clothing selection might not look that impressive, but it sometimes yields incredible finds. The dishes, furniture, toys, and other cool stuff are fun to look through whether you're a serious collector or just an innocent bystander. It's easy to walk right past this place—look carefully for the door and then proceed down the flight of stairs. ⊠*3419 Fremont Pl. N, Fremont* ☎*206/548–9140.*

BOOKS & MUSIC

★ **Ophelia's Books.** Ophelia's may have the lowest-profile of Seattle's many excellent used-book stores, but it's our favorite. The tight quarters are cozy without being oppressive, the tiny spiral staircase leading to the basement space is a very sweet detail, and the resident cat is always asleep on a stack somewhere. But what sets Ophelia's apart is its excellent (and manageable) selection of major titles from best-selling and well-known authors. Other shops may have many more shelves—and more rare or obscure works—but lack a good selection of the types of books that send most of us to bookstores in the first place. Also, it has a poetry section that's more than five books big. ⊠*3504 Fremont Ave. N, Fremont* ☎*206/632–3759.*

★ **Sonic Boom Records** Though now something of a mini-chain (there are branches in Ballard and Capitol Hill), Sonic Boom is an independent shop through and through. It carries a little bit of everything, but the emphasis is definitely on indie rock. Handwritten recommendation cards from the staff help you find local artists and the best new releases from independent Northwest labels. The store has listening stations as well. Sonic Boom recently expanded: the vaunted "vinyl annex" was brought street level into an adjacent space, which also includes books, gifts, and other indie paraphernalia. ⊠*3414 Fremont Ave. N, Fremont* ☎*206/547–2666* ⊕*www.sonicboomrecords.com.*

CLOTHING

Flit. In spite its name, this tiny new boutique seems to have a solid head on its shoulders. The selection, which includes denim, some outerwear, and gorgeous casual dresses, is cohesive and modern but still practical—clothing for women who want to stand out, but not too far out. Some of the brands you'll regularly find here are Odyn, Voom, and the classiest pieces from the Triple Five Soul line. Prices can be high, but they can also sometimes be surprisingly reasonable. ✉3526 Fremont Pl. N, Fremont ☎206/547-2177 ⊕http://flitboutique.blogspot.com.

Fritzi Ritz Vintage Clothing. If you manage to catch Fritzi Ritz on a day when it's actually open, you'll be pleasantly surprised to find well-organized racks of vintage goodies. Hipsters can pick up bowling shirts and Converse; dramatic dressers can pick up all manner of poofy skirts and suede, fringed apparel. ✉750 N. 34th St., Fremont ☎206/633-0929.

Horseshoe. The Western theme is mostly just a nod to the owner's ties to the Midwest, but Horseshoe does feel like that down-to-earth cousin who saunters through life in cowboy boots reminding us that clothes should be comfortable and jeans should come in sizes larger than 4. Though you'll pay a pretty penny for all the premium denim on offer here, casual tops, T-shirts, and wrap dresses are much more affordable. The owner also sells her own line of jewelry. ✉720 N. 35th St., Fremont ☎206/547-9639.

Impulse. At first it looks like this stark basement space doesn't have much of a selection, but as you make your way around the racks, you notice how each piece flows effortlessly into the next, and how each selection is impeccable. You'll find some denim and footwear here, but you'll find better elsewhere; Impulse excels at sophisticated slacks, skirts, dresses, and outerwear that often seem subdued or basic until you notice an interesting seam line here or a hand-stitched detail there. You'll find some big names here, too, like Alice Roi and Vivienne Westwood. ✉621 N. 36th St., Fremont ☎206/545-4854 ⊕www.impulseseattle.com.

★ **Les Amis.** The best-looking boutique in Fremont, Les Amis is like a pop-up from a little girl's storybook set in a French country cottage. The over-35 set will breathe a sigh of relief when they see that the racks are not just filled with low-rise jeans but with sophisticated dresses, gorgeous handknits, and the makings of great work outfits. Younger fashionistas come here, too, to snap up unique summer skirts and ultrasoft T-shirts. Everyone seems to love the lingerie collection. Les Amis carries some top designers such as Lulu Guinness and Nanette Lepore; accordingly, this is the most expensive store in Fremont. You know prices are high when even the bargain bin discounts don't seem like a good deal. ✉3420 Evanston Ave. N, Fremont ☎206/632-2877 ⊕www.lesamis-inc.com.

FOOTWEAR

Gift shop Burnt Sugar also has a small but good selection of shoes.

Lola Pop. Shoes that make the grade at this chic little shop must be exceedingly stylish *and* comfortable; that's a lot to ask of sexy, strappy heels, but they and their lower-heeled shop mates meet the strict standards set by their French-born proprietress, who picks up all her wares on annual buying trips to France and Italy. ✉*711 N. 35th St., Fremont* ☎*206/547–2071.*

GIFTS & HOME DECOR

Bitters Co. Textiles, linens, tableware, and jewelry—whose organic forms speak of the human touch—fill this unique general store. There are handcrafted goods from Guatemala, Indonesia, and the Philippines, and an in-house line of tables made from reclaimed Douglas fir. ✉*513 N. 36th St., Fremont* ☎*206/632–0886* ⊕*www.bittersco.com.*

Burnt Sugar. Look for the store on the corner with the rocket on the roof: that's where you'll find a funky mélange of handbags, greeting cards, soaps, candles, jewelry, toys, and other eclectic baubles you never knew you needed. There's a makeup counter, and half the store is devoted to a small but cool selection of men's and women's shoes. ✉*601 N. 35th St., Fremont* ☎*206/545–0699.*

Essenza. A gurgling stone fountain stands in the center of this light-filled boutique, whose airy displays showcase delicately scented European bath products by Santa Maria Novella, Tocca, and Père et Fils. You'll find the complete line of Fresh cosmetics, handmade bed linens, women's silk and cashmere loungewear, delicate jewelry, and exquisitely detailed children's clothing. ✉*615 N. 35th St., Fremont* ☎*206/547–4895.*

Frank & Dunya. Named after the owners' dogs, this cheerful shop sells colorful, locally crafted art. Gift items range from hand-painted switch-plate covers and elaborate night lights to pillowcases and coffee mugs. Although there's a lot of kitsch here, the paintings, prints, and mixed-media pieces displayed on the far wall are less whimsical and often very good. ✉*3418 Fremont Ave. N, Fremont* ☎*206/547–6760.*

BALLARD

Ballard is quickly eclipsing its neighbor Fremont as the best shopping destination north of the canal. For every pricey women's clothing boutique in Fremont, there's a pricey furniture or home-accessories store in Ballard. In between furniture shops you'll find men's and women's boutiques, a branch of Sonic Boom Records, a wineshop, a great tea store, and more. If you want a taste of the old neighborhood, NW Market Street still has a few shops selling Scandinavian goods and souvenirs.

If you really fall in love with the neighborhood, Ballard Mail & Dispatch (✉*1752 NW Market St., Ballard* ☎*206/789–4488*), also known as the Sip & Ship, has T-shirts, hoodies, coffee mugs, and other hip accessories emblazoned with the neighborhood's name.

Best shopping: Ballard Avenue between 22nd Avenue NW and 20th Avenue NW; Northwest Market Street between 20th and 24th avenues.

CLOTHING & ACCESSORIES

↻ **Clover.** This precious store has unusual and high-quality toys, games, and children's clothes that you won't find at Toys "R" Us and The Gap. However, unlike Toys "R" Us, the space isn't exactly conducive to playing in the aisles, so you might want to make sure the kids have burned off some energy before taking them here. ✉ *5335 Ballard Ave. NW, Ballard* ☎*206/782–0715* ⊕*www.clovertoys.com.*

Merge. "Fashions that last" should be Merge's tagline. Like Impulse in Fremont, Merge offers women's clothes that are thoroughly modern, keeping Seattleites up with what's going on in New York and San Francisco, but simple and sophisticated enough to hang in the closet for years to come. Designers include Chaiken, Harkham, Nicholas K, among many others, and a few local brands. ✉ *5000 20th Ave. NW, Ballard* ☎*206/782–5335.*

Olivine. Olivine is like a mini–department store: you'll find everything from evening wear to footwear to lingerie to bath products and makeup in one airy space. The clientele is mostly young, but some of the items are sophisticated enough for women who don't want to dress like college students. The prices are somewhat high, though competitive for the brands on offer. Service, unfortunately, is bad—not unfriendly, just completely disinterested. ✉ *5344 Ballard Ave. NW, Ballard* ☎*206/706–4188* ⊕*www.olivine.net.*

★ **Velouria.** The owner of Velouria, Tess de Luna, is a designer herself. She adds the best of her line to the racks, along with unique creations from independent West Coast designers. Overall, the clothes have a crafty, DIY feel—lots of appliqués and deliberately off-kilter hems and seams—but some of the separates would work well in any wardrobe. Even if you can't rock the hipster look, pop in to this friendly little store to check out the handbags, wallets, and jewelry. ✉ *2205 NW Market St., Ballard* ☎*206/788–0330* ⊕*http://shopvelouria. tripod.com.*

FOOTWEAR

re-souL. Stocking cool but comfortable shoes from Paul Smith, Palladium, and Roberto de Carlo, as well as its own line, this hip space offers a small selection of boots, sneaks, and high heels for real humans at reasonable (or at least competitive) prices. In keeping with the "little bit of everything" trend so popular with Seattle boutiques, re-souL also sells great jewelry pieces, as well as a few CDs and the odd piece of furniture. They carry both men's and women's shoes and accessories. ✉ *5319 Ballard Ave., Ballard* ☎*206/789–7312* ⊕*www.resoul.com.*

GIFTS & HOME ACCESSORIES

★ **Archie McPhee.** Leave it to Seattle to have a novelty store that sells gag gifts that are subversive and often wickedly funny. Barista action figures, demon rubber duckies, and homicidal unicorns share the shelves with more-sedate items like rubber bouncing balls in all sizes and colors, bandages adorned with T-bone steaks or ninjas, and tiki-theme glasses and coasters. ✉ *2428 NW Market St., Ballard* ☎*206/297–0240* ⊕*www.mcphee.com.*

Camelion Design. The most affordable (and "affordable" is relative) modern home-accessories store in Ballard is crammed showroom style with furniture, accessories, and gift items. It's a good place to get living-room envy or just pick up an area rug, vase, or picture frame. Another sufferer of Seattle boutique schizophrenia, Camelion also sells jewelry, bath products, and stationery. ✉ *5330 Ballard Ave. NW, Ballard* ☎ *206/783–7125.*

Dandelion Botanical Company. Apothecary isn't a term you hear often these days, but that's what Dandelion calls itself, and rightfully so—the store sells Chinese and ayurvedic herbs and essential oils, along with its own line of bath salts and aromatherapy products. Most of the items they sell are made of all natural materials (for example, nontoxic candles) and many ingredients and herbs are certified organic. If you're picturing a claustrophobic Chinatown shop or dingy co-op, don't worry—the space is that of a high-end if down-to-earth boutique. ✉ *5424 Ballard Ave., Ballard* ☎ *206/545–8892* ⊕ *www. dandelionbotanical.com.*

Romanza. The eccentric aunt of the Ballard gift shops, Romanza is the polar opposite of the neighborhood's sleek, mid-century modern-influenced home stores. Jam-packed with pricey accessories that are either of the frilly, glittery, over-the-top, or faux-European varieties, this is a terrific place to indulge those "I'm on vacation" impulse purchases. ✉ *2206 NW Market St., Ballard* ☎ *206/706–1764* ⊕ *www.romanza-gifts.com.*

Venue. Venue is the chic version of the Made In Washington stores: it only stocks goods made by designers from within the city's borders (some of whom have their studios in the sleek bi-level space), but you won't find anything resembling a tacky souvenir here. Artisan chocolates, custom handbags, hand-painted silk pillows, and prints and photographs are just a few examples of the gift items being produced right under our noses. ✉ *5408 22nd Ave., Ballard* ☎ *206/789–3335* ⊕ *www.venueballard.com.*

WINE

Portalis. This sophisticated little wine bar is also a full shop that sells nearly 400 wines, with origins that span the globe, including a few choice Pacific Northwest bottles. They offer tastings every Sunday from noon to 3 PM. ✉ *5205 Ballard Ave. NW, Ballard* ☎ *206/783–2007* ⊕ *www.portaliswines.com.*

PHINNEY RIDGE & GREENWOOD

These adjacent neighborhoods, north of Fremont and east of Ballard, aren't shopping destinations per se. Most of the stores in this area are spread out along the long stretch of Greenwood Avenue, between 75th Street and 85th Street—too spread out to form a compact shopping district. However, a few clothing boutiques are giving it a go, and the shops up here are generally more affordable than the specialty shops of Fremont and Ballard.

CLOTHING

Frock Shop. The Frock Shop offers vintage shopping for people who hate musty consignment shops, and carries elegant fashions for people who hate spending $200 on a tank top. The attractive space looks like a particularly well-organized walk-in closet, where everything has its place: vintage finds on that rack, new clothes on this one, hats lined up above, jewelry in the armoire, and cards and stationery on the writing desk. ✉ *6500 Phinney Ave. N, Phinney Ridge* ☎ *206/297–1638.*

Lemon Meringue. This boutique aims to outfit Seattle women in all stages of their lives: there are young, hip fashions for the going-out days, maternity wear and baby clothes for the mom stage, and clothes to bridge the gap between the two phases. The connective thread in the narrative is high-quality, hip, and comfortable fashions, many from European designers. Clothes come in a range of prices, too—a nod to the fluctuating salaries of the average woman. The store, owned by two friends, is homey and inviting, and has a small play area for kids. ✉ *7720 Greenwood Ave. N, Greenwood* ☎ *206/297–6071* ⊕ *www. lemonmeringue.us.*

★ **Tweed.** The duds at Tweed deftly toe the line between very different looks: depending on the style of the woman wearing them, they can either be hipster chic or office chic. Sportier looks from Penguin hang next to sophisticated, boldly patterned silk blouses and dresses. There's a table piled with jeans, a small shoe selection, and a cabinet full of lovely jewelry from local designers. Service is unfailingly friendly and helpful. The shop offers tailoring with a quick turnaround time. ✉ *8350 Greenwood Ave. N, Greenwood* ☎ *206/784–4444* ⊕ *www. tweedboutique.com.*

NOVELTIES & GIFTS

☾ **Greenwood Space Travel & Supply Co.** The name of this shop baffled Greenwood residents for months until it was revealed as part of 826 Seattle, a branch of novelist Dave Eggers' national creative-writing program for kids. The small store has kooky items purported to be space-travel essentials (freeze-dried meals), many of which are obvious nods to kitschy science fiction movies (check out the ray guns). It also carries 826 T-shirts, and all of the proceeds go to the writing center. ■TIP→ **While you're here, check the bulletin board for notices about upcoming events and single-session workshops.** Note that this is not a full-blown toy store: go in with a sense of humor and an imagination because much of the cleverness is literary—standard toys and items given ridiculous new names to sound like important instruments of space travel. Everyone will enjoy filling out the hilarious space-traveler screening questionnaires and spaceship accident reports. ✉ *8414 Greenwood Ave. N, Greenwood* ☎ *206/725–2625* ⊕ *www.826seattle.org.*

UNIVERSITY DISTRICT

The U-District's parallel shopping corridors are along Roosevelt Way NE and University Way NE. Each has a line of worn-looking but well-stocked book, clothing, and accessories stores. University Way NE has more shops and small, inexpensive ethnic restaurants, as well as the venerable main branch of the University Bookstore. Though the heart of the U-District isn't a terribly exciting shopping area, it does offer some bargains, as well as a few college-age standbys like American Apparel.

The main shopping attraction in the neighborhood is actually the enormous University Village mall, east of the main campus area. It's something of an eyesore, but it does have quite a selection.

> A POEM EMPORIUM
>
> Wallingford's commercial district along NE 45th Street has yet to make any serious waves in the Seattle shopping scene, but **Open Books** (✉ *2414 N. 45th St., Wallingford* ☎ *206/633–0811* ⊕ *www.openpoetrybooks.com*) deserves mention: It's one of only two poetry-only bookstores in the country. The serene space is conducive to hours of browsing; when you're ready to interact the owners are always happy to answer your questions, make suggestions, or chat about the titles you've selected. There's also a good selection of magazines as well as chapbooks from local writers.

Best shopping: University Way NE between NE 42nd and 47th streets, and University Village at 25th Avenue NE and NE 45th Street

BOOKS & MUSIC

Cellophane Square. Buy, sell, or trade your used CDs and vinyl in this bastion of indie rock, punk, and garage-band releases. Great finds in the used bins are what have made this formerly independent shop a worthy stop, but it also sells new releases. ✉ *4538 University Way NE, University District* ☎ *206/634–2280.*

Cinema Books. Catering to film fans and TV junkies, this esoteric shop is filled with new, rare, and collectible books relating to movies and the people who make them. ✉ *4753 Roosevelt Way NE, University District* ☎ *206/547–7667.*

Half Price Books. This national chain lives up its name by offering new and used titles on all subjects at half the current list price. Two floors of closely packed shelves make up this indispensable source of discounted reading material. ✉ *4709 Roosevelt Way NE, University District* ☎ *206/547–7859* ⊕ *www.halfpricebooks.com.*

★ **University Book Store.** Campus bookstores are usually rip-offs to be endured only by students clutching syllabi, but the University of Washington's store is a big exception to that rule. This enormous resource has a well-stocked general book department in addition to the requisite textbooks. Author events are scheduled all year long. Check out the bargain-book tables and the basement crammed with every art supply imaginable. ✉ *4326 University Way NE, University District* ☎ *206/634–3400* ⊕ *www.bookstore.washington.edu.*

CLOTHING

American Apparel. This big, two-story branch of the hip national chain that offers clothing with a conscience (i.e., sweatshop-free) is some of the best shopping in a neighborhood that has few good clothing stores. Outfit the whole family in good-quality, classic T-shirts, cotton skirts, fleece pants, and hoodies. Their "Sustainable Edition" label uses organic cotton. ⊠*4345 University Way NE, University District* ☎*206/547–0399.*

★ **Buffalo Exchange.** This big, bright shop of new and recycled fashions is always crowded—and it takes time to browse the stuffed racks—but the trendy rewards are great: embellished jeans, leather jackets, and vintage-style dresses. As with all thrift stores, the selection can be hit or miss, but trust-fund kids from UW often unload last season's labels here, so you can find some pretty great deals on high-quality clothing. ⊠*4530 University Way NE, University District* ☎*206/545–0175* ⊕*www.buffaloexchange.com.*

Moksha. Culling mostly from local designers, Moksha sells hip little skirts and dresses fashioned out of old Indian saris and embellished with gossamer overlays and intricate beading. Or maybe you'd prefer cute T-shirts and trendy denim. It's all unique and affordable. ⊠*4542 University Way NE, University District* ☎*206/632–1190.*

Pitaya. Catering to trendy young women, this polished boutique has an in-house brand of jeans, tops, dresses, skirts, and accessories—all priced just right for students. ⊠*4520 University Way NE, University District* ☎*206/548–1001.*

Red Light Clothing Exchange. Nostalgia rules in this cavernous space filled with well-organized, good-quality (if sometimes pricey) vintage clothing. Fantasy outfits from decades past—complete with accessories—adorn the dressing rooms, though you won't find the full-on costumes that the Capitol Hill branch has. ⊠*4560 University Way NE, University District* ☎*206/545–4044* ⊕*www.redlightvintage.com.*

FOOTWEAR

5 Doors Up is a destination for fashion-forward sports-shoe fans of both sexes. Look for limited editions of Puma's Mihara line, Fly London for men, and ultra-high-top Converse sneakers usually available only in Japan. ⊠*4309 University Way NE, University District* ☎*206/547–3192.*

M.J. Feet. If you're shocked to hear that Birkenstocks come in more styles than the standard tan hippie sandal, you'll be floored by M.J. Feet, which carries the comfortable brand in dozens of different styles and colors. You'll also find pricey but coveted sandals and shoes by Masai Barefoot Technology. ⊠*4334 University Way NE, University District* ☎*206/623–5353.*

GIFTS & HOME DECOR

Burke Museum of Natural History and Culture. Traditional and contemporary Northwest Coast Native American works and exhibits related to the cultural heritage of the Pacific Northwest are displayed at this important historical resource, located on the northwest corner of UW.

Visit the museum store for books and extraordinary mementos. ✉*17th Ave. NE and NE 45th St., University District* ☎*206/543–5590.*

Snow Goose Associates. Alaskan Eskimo, Canadian Inuit, and Northwest Coast Native American artists are represented through carvings, jewelry, baskets, masks, boxes, and prints. ✉*8806 Roosevelt Way NE, University District* ☎*206/523–6223.*

SHOPPING CENTER

University Village. Trees, fountains, and whimsical animal sculptures are scattered among the more than 80 upscale shops and restaurants in an attempt to make this outdoor mall look more like a shopping "village." The result is as artificial as the polite smiles people plaster on their faces as they drive around and around looking for parking. ■TIP→ **Go immediately to the free parking garage even if it means you have to walk farther.** U-Village (as it's known to locals) does, however, have branches of all the major national chains: Barnes & Noble Booksellers, Pottery Barn, Williams-Sonoma, Banana Republic, Crate & Barrel, Sephora, Aveda, Restoration Hardware, and the list goes on. Smaller operations like Anthropologie and Kiehl's are also represented, as are upscale staples like Coach. Lastly, until Apple gets its act together and opens a Downtown store, the mall has the only Apple Store in town. If you like driving out of your way to deal with crowds, awful parking situations, slamming on your brakes every five minutes to allow pedestrians to cross the "village," and generally viewing the folly of suburban sprawl planning, you won't be disappointed. If you're looking for anything special, unique, or "Seattle," don't waste the gas on the trip. ✉*NE 45th St. and 25th Ave. NE, University District* ☎*206/523–0622* ⊕*www.uvillage.com.*

BELLEVUE

The core of Bellevue's growing shopping district is Bellevue Square Mall and the cluster of upscale shops and restaurants on the mall's southwest corner. Bellevue Galleria and Bellevue Place are two smaller malls that also have some upscale shops, along with restaurants, movies, and parking. The community's retail strip stretches from Bellevue Square between NE 4th and 8th streets to the enormous, department store–anchored Crossroads Shopping Center several miles to the east.

As the presence of so many malls may suggest, Bellevue offers much of what you can find in any major city in the country—and in many of the shops in Seattle proper. Label hounds, however, will appreciate the high-end stores represented in the malls and the new boutiques that are popping up to compete with them.

Best shopping: Bellevue Square—it really does seem to have it all.

Bellevue Galleria. Although small as malls go, it's a convenient satellite to the bigger Bellevue Square Mall. Stores include Habits for the Home, Men's Warehouse, Sahara Fine Arts, and Tower Records, but it's best to come for a day of spa pampering at Gene Juarez rather than for a whole day of shopping. There's plenty of evening entertainment, too, with four restaurants and the Regal Cinemas. ✉*550 106th Ave. NE, Bellevue* ☎*425/452–1934.*

Bellevue Square. More than 200 stores fill Seattle's favorite outskirts mall. Notables include Nordstrom, Macy's, Pottery Barn, Crate & Barrel, Aveda, Banana Republic, Coach, Esprit, and Swatch. The wide walkways and benches, the many children's clothing stores, the first-floor play area, and the third-floor children's museum make this a great place for kids, too. You can park for free in the attached garage. ✉*Bellevue Way, Bellevue* ☎*425/454–8096* ⊕*www.bellevuesquare.com.*

Crossroads Shopping Center. Sixty shops—including Bed Bath & Beyond, Gottschalks, and Old Navy—surround the open Public Market Stage where there's free live music 7:30–10 PM on Saturday, and an open mike on Friday 6:30–10 PM. A giant chessboard and playground are nearby, and the Crossroads Cinema anchors the southeast corner. If you're hungry, there are more than 20 restaurants. ✉*15600 NE 8th St., Bellevue* ☎*425/644–1111* ⊕*www.crossroadsbellevue.com.*

Side Trips
from Seattle

WORD OF MOUTH

"I'm not an expert on places to stay on the San Juans, as we normally stay in our boat, but I will say that it might be nice to stay on two islands, Orcas and San Juan Island. Those are really the two main islands. Lopez Island would be fun to visit (Best to see by bike, which can be rented), but with limited time, you might want to stay on the other two."

—Orcas

Updated
by Carissa
Bluestone

THE BEAUTY OF THE CITY is enough to wow most visitors, but it's nothing compared to the beauty of the state that surrounds it. You simply must put aside a day or two to venture out to one of the islands of the Puget Sound or to do a hike or scenic drive in one of the spectacular mountain ranges a few hours outside the city.

If you head west to Olympic National Park, north to North Cascades National Park, or east to the Cascade Range, you can hike, bike, or ski. Two-and-a-half hours southeast of Seattle is majestic Mt. Rainier, the fifth-highest mountain in the contiguous United States. Two hours beyond Rainier, close to the Oregon border, is the Mt. St. Helens National Volcanic Monument. The state-of-the-art visitor centers here show breathtaking views of the crater and lava dome and the spectacular recovery of the areas surrounding the 1980 blast.

You can get a taste of island life on Bainbridge, Whidbey, or Vashon—all easily accessible for day trips—or settle in for a few days on one of the San Juan Islands, where you hike, kayak, or spot migrating whales and resident sea lions and otters.

THE ISLANDS OF THE PUGET SOUND

The islands of the Puget Sound—particularly Bainbridge, Vashon, and Whidbey—are the most obvious and popular day trips for Seattle visitors. They're easy to get to, easy to get around, and all three offer spectacular scenery (starting with the ferry ride over from Seattle) and a way of life that is even more laid-back than in the city itself. Though each island has a smattering of inns and campsites, very few people stay the night—it's just too easy to get back to Seattle in time for dinner. Of the three, Whidbey requires the biggest time commitment to get to (it's 30 mi northwest of Seattle), but it has the most spectacular natural attractions. Bainbridge is the most developed island—it's something of a moneyed bedroom community—with a few decent restaurants and even a small winery rounding out its natural attractions. Vashon is the slowest and most pastoral of the islands—if you don't like leisurely strolls and bike rides, you might get bored there quickly.

Bainbridge and Whidbey get tons of visitors in summer. Though you'll usually be able to snag a walk-on spot on the ferry, spaces for cars can fill up, so arrive early. You'll want a car on Whidbey (you can actually drive there, too) and on Bainbridge if you want to tour the entire island. You can also tour Bainbridge on bicycle (just beware the hills), while Vashon is best enjoyed on bicycle.

BAINBRIDGE ISLAND

❶ *35 mins northwest of Seattle by ferry.*

Bainbridge Island is developed enough to have rush-hour traffic problems, but in many parts it manages to retain a small-town vibe. Longtime residents work hard to keep parks and protected areas out of the hands of condominium builders, and despite the increasing number of stressed-out Seattle commuters, the island still has resident artists, craftspeople, and old-timers who can't be bothered to venture into the big city. Though not as dramatic as Whidbey or as idyllic as Vashon, Bainbridge always makes for a pleasant day trip.

The ferry drops you off in Winslow. Along its compact main street, Winslow Way, it's easy to wander away an afternoon among the antiques shops, art galleries, bookstores, and cafés. There are several bike rental shops by the ferry terminal, too, if you plan on touring the island on two wheels. Getting out of the busy terminal area can be a bit nerve-wracking, but you'll soon be on quieter country roads. Be sure to ask for maps at the rental shop, and if you want to avoid the worst of the island's hills, ask the staff to go over your options with you before you set out.

The Chamber of Commerce operates a visitor's kiosk close to the ferry terminal.

Bainbridge Island Vineyard and Winery (⊠ *8989 Day Rd. E* ☎ *206/842– 9463* ⊕ *www.bainbridgevineyards.com*) has 8 acres of grapes that produce small batches of pinot noir, pinot gris, and siegerrebe; fruit wines are made from the seasonal offerings of neighboring farms. It's open for tastings Friday–Sunday 11–5. Tours are offered on Sunday at 2. If you first grab lunch provisions, you can picnic on the pretty grounds.

★ The 150-acre **Bloedel Reserve** has fine Japanese gardens, a bird refuge, a moss garden, and other gardens planted with island flora. A French Renaissance–style mansion, the estate's showpiece, is surrounded by 2 mi of trails and ponds dotted with trumpeter swans. Dazzling rhododendrons and azaleas bloom in spring, and Japanese maples colorfully signal autumn's arrival. Reservations are essential, and picnicking is not permitted. ⊠ *7571 NE Dolphin Dr., 6 mi west of Winslow, via Hwy. 305* ☎ *206/842-7631* ⊕ *www.bloedelreserve.org* ⊠ *$10* ☉ *Wed.–Sun. 10–4 (last reservation at 2).*

On the southwest side of the island is the 137-acre **Fort Ward State Park.** There are 2 mi of hiking trails through forest, a long stretch of beach, and even a spot for scuba diving. Along with views of the water and the Olympic Mountains, you might be lucky and get a crack view of Mt. Rainier. A loop trail through the park is suitable for all ability levels and will take you past vestiges of the park's previous life as a military installation. There are picnic tables in the park, but no other services are available. ⊹ *Take Hwy. 305 out of Winslow. Turn west on High School Rd. and follow signs to park* ☎ *206/842-3931* ⊕ *www.parks. wa.gov* ☉ *Daily 8* AM*–dusk.*

Twice a year, the island's artists and craftspeople are in the spotlight with the **Bainbridge Island Studio Tour** (☎ *206/780-3528* ⊕ *www.bistudiotour.com*). Participants put their best pieces on display for these three-day events and you can buy everything from watercolors to furniture directly from the artists. Even if you can't make the official studio tours—held in mid-August and again in late November—check out the Web site, which has maps and information on studios and shops throughout the island, as well as links to artists' Web sites. Many of the shops have regular hours and you can easily put together your own tour.

WHERE TO EAT

Most of the island's most reliable options are in Winslow—or close to it. You'll also find a major supermarket on the main stretch if you want to pick up some provisions for a picnic, though you can also easily do that in Seattle before you get on the ferry.

$–$$$ ✕ **Café Nola.** Café Nola is the best option for something a little fancier than pub grub or picnic fare. The bistro setting is pleasant—pale yellow walls, white tablecloths, jazz playing softly in the background—and there's a small patio area for outdoor dining. The food is basically American and European comfort cooking with a few modern twists. At lunch you can get sandwiches—duck with Brie and cranberry jam; grilled cheese made with fontina, Brie, and mozzarella—or something hearty like barbecue pork or beef Stroganoff. At dinner seafood dishes like guava-glazed ahi and pan-seared scallops in a roasted pepper sauce are recommended. The restaurant is within walking distance of the main ferry terminal. ⊠ *101 Winslow Way E, Winslow* ☎ *206/842–3822* ⊕ *www.cafenola.com* ☲ *AE, MC, V.*

$ ✕ **Harbor Public House.** An 1881 estate home overlooking Eagle Harbor was renovated to create this casual restaurant at Winslow's public marina. Seafood tacos, pub burgers, and grilled flatiron steak sandwiches are typical fare, as are key lime pie and root beer floats. This is where the pleasure-boating and kayaking crowds come to dine in a relaxed, waterfront setting. Things get raucous during Tuesday-night open-mike sessions. ⊠ *231 Parfitt Way, Winslow* ☎ *206/842–0969* ⊕ *www.harbourpub.com* ☲ *AE, DC, MC, V.*

¢–$ ✕ **Blackbird Bakery.** A great place to grab a cup of coffee and a snack before exploring the island, Blackbird serves up rich pastries and cakes along with a few light lunch items and a good selection of teas and espresso drinks. Though there is some nice window seating that allows you to watch the human parade on Winslow Way, the place gets very crowded, especially when the ferries come in, so you might want to take your order to go. ⊠ *210 Winslow Way E, Winslow* ☎ *206/780–1322* ☲ *MC, V* ☉ *No dinner.*

VASHON ISLAND

❷ *20–35 mins by ferry from West Seattle.*

Vashon is the most peaceful and rural of the islands easily reached from the city, home to fruit growers, rat-race dropouts, and a few Seattle commuters.

Biking, strolling, picnicking, and kayaking are the main activities here. A tour of the 13-mi-long island will take you down country lanes and past orchards and lavender farms. There are several artists' studios and galleries on the island, as well as a small commercial district in the center of the island, where a farmers' market is a highlight every Satur-

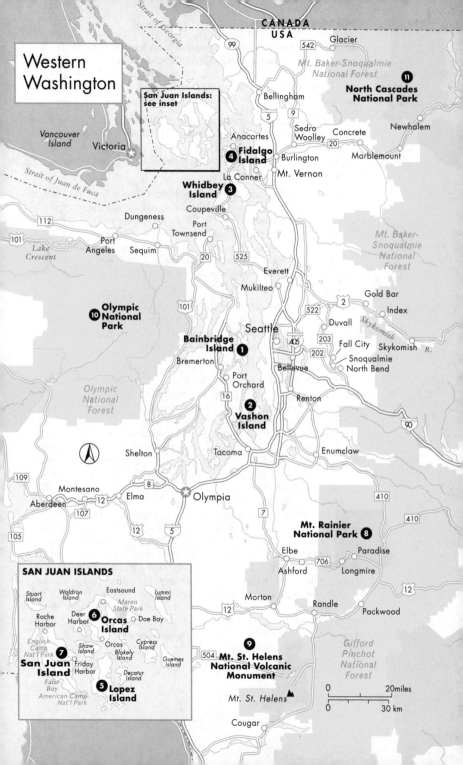

Western Washington

San Juan Islands:
see inset

Strait of Georgia

CANADA
USA

542

Glacier

Mt. Baker-Snoqualmie National Forest

⓫ North Cascades National Park

99

Vancouver Island

Victoria

Bellingham

5

9

Sedro Woolley

Concrete

20

Newhalem

Strait of Juan de Fuca

Anacortes

⓸ Fidalgo Island

La Conner

Burlington

Mt. Vernon

Marblemount

112

Dungeness

⓷ Whidbey Island

Coupeville

101

Lake Crescent

Port Angeles

Sequim

Port Townsend

20

525

Mt. Baker-Snoqualmie National Forest

Everett

Mukilteo

2

Gold Bar

Index

⓾ Olympic National Park

101

522

Duvall

Skykomish R.

Seattle

405

203

Fall City

Skykomish

⓵ Bainbridge Island

Bremerton

Port Orchard

202

Snoqualmie

North Bend

Bellevue

90

16

Renton

⓶ Vashon Island

Olympic National Forest

Shelton

Tacoma

Enumclaw

109

Montesano

8

Elma

Olympia

Aberdeen

12

410

107

105

7

12

410

⓼ Mt. Rainier National Park

Elbe

706

Paradise

Ashford

Longmire

12

SAN JUAN ISLANDS

Stuart Island

Waldron Island

Eastsound

Lummi Island

Maren State Park

Morton

Randle

Packwood

Roche Harbor

Deer Harbor

⓺ Orcas Island

Doe Bay

12

504

English Camp Nat'l Park

Shaw Island

Orcas

Cypress Island

⓽ Mt. St. Helens National Volcanic Monument

⓻

Blakely Island

Guemes Island

Gifford Pinchot National Forest

San Juan Island

Friday Harbor

Decatur Island

False Bay

American Camp Nat'l Park

⓹ Lopez Island

Mt. St. Helens

0   20 miles

0   30 km

Cougar

day from May to October. The popular Strawberry Festival takes place every July. The **Vashon-Maury Island Chamber of Commerce** (⊠ *19021 Vashon Hwy. SW* ☎ *206/463–6217* ⊕ *www.vashonchamber.com*) is open Tuesday, Wednesday, and Thursday from 9 to 3. The site www.vashonmap.com is also a good source of information.

The car ferry leaves from Fauntleroy in West Seattle for the 20-minute ride. A passenger-only ferry from Pier 50 in Downtown Seattle takes 35 minutes. Note that passenger-only ferries are infrequent, so be sure to plan ahead and double-check the return schedule. Both ferries dock at the northern tip of the island.

Vashon has many parks and protected areas. **Jensen Point** has trails, a swimming beach, and boat and kayak rentals. From the ferry terminal, take Vashon Highway SW to SW Burton Drive and turn left. Turn left on 97 Avenue SW and follow it around as it becomes SW Harbor Drive. You can stroll along the beach at **Point Robinson Park**, which is very picturesque thanks to **Point Robinson Lighthouse** (☎ *206/463–0920*). Free tours of the lighthouse are given from 12:30 to 4 on Sunday; call to arrange private tours at other times.

Blue Heron Art Center (⊠ *19704 Vashon Hwy.* ☎ *206/463–5131* ⊙ *Tues.–Fri. 11–5, Sat. noon–5*) is the best representative of the island's diverse arts community, presenting monthly exhibits that span all mediums. The gift shop sells smaller items like jewelry.

WHERE TO EAT

$–$$ ✕ **Hardware Store.** The restaurant's unusual name comes from its former incarnation as a mom-and-pop hardware shop—it occupies the oldest commercial building on Vashon and certainly looks like a relic from the outside. Inside you'll find a charming restaurant that's a cross between a bistro and an upscale diner. On the lunch menu you'll find simple sandwiches, salads, and burgers; dinner includes hearty old-standbys like buttermilk fried chicken, pasta, meat loaf, and grilled salmon. A decent wine list focuses on Northwest and Californian wines. Breakfast is served on Sunday. ⊠ *17601 Vashon Hwy. SW* ☎ *206/463–1800* ⊕ *www.thsrestaurant.com* ▭ *MC, V* ⊙ *Closed Tues.*

$–$$ ✕ **Sound Food Café.** Both a bakery and a restaurant, Sound Food offers made-from-scratch pastries and coffee for breakfast; sophisticated salads and sandwiches (prosciutto, artichoke, and Havarti or grilled chicken with curried apples and tarragon aioli) for lunch; and fresh fish and seafood, pan-roasted pork, chicken, and duck dishes for dinner. Tuesday night brings an all-Italian menu and Thursday is all Thai. Ingredients are fresh, local, and often organic. Despite the dark red paint on some walls, the dining room is cheerful and homey; a beautiful garden out back provides some outdoor seating. ⊠ *20312 Vashon Hwy.* ☎ *206/463–0888* ⊕ *www.soundfoodcafe.com* ▭ *AE, DC, MC, V* ⊙ *Closed Sun. and Mon.*

WHIDBEY ISLAND

❸ *20 mins by ferry from Mukilteo (5 mi south of Everett) across Posses-sion Sound to Clinton.*

Whidbey is a blend of low pastoral hills, evergreen and oak forests, meadows of wildflower (including some endemic species), sandy beaches, dramatic bluffs, and a few pockets of unfortunate suburban sprawl. It's a great place for taking slow drives, for viewing sunsets over the water, for taking ridge hikes that give you uninterrupted views of the Strait of Juan de Fuca, and for boating or kayaking along the protected shorelines of Saratoga Passage, Holmes Harbor, Penn Cove, and Skagit Bay.

The best beaches are on the west side, where wooded and wildflower-bedecked bluffs drop steeply to sand or surf—which can cover the beaches at high tide and can be unexpectedly rough on this exposed shore. Both beaches and bluffs have great views of the shipping lanes and the Olympic Mountains. Maxwelton Beach, with its sand, drift-wood, and great views across Admiralty Inlet to the Olympic Moun-tains, is popular with the locals. Possession Point includes a park, a beach, and a boat launch. West of Coupeville, Ft. Ebey State Park has a sandy spread; West Beach is a stormy patch north of the fort with mounds of driftwood.

You can reach Whidbey Island by heading north from Seattle on I–5, west on Route 20 onto Fidalgo Island, and south across Deception Pass Bridge. The Deception Pass Bridge links Whidbey to Fidalgo Island. From the bridge it's just a short drive to Anacortes, Fidalgo's main town and the terminus for ferries to the San Juan Islands. On a nice day, a pleasant excursion is a ferry trip across Possession Sound, 30 mi north-west of Seattle. It's a great way to watch gulls, terns, sailboats, and the occasional orca or bald eagle—not to mention the surrounding scenery, which takes in Camano Island and the North Cascades.

LANGLEY
7 mi north of Clinton.

The village of Langley is above a 50-foot-high bluff overlooking Sara-toga Passage, which separates Whidbey from Camano Island. A grassy terrace just above the beach is a great place for viewing birds that are on the water or in the air. On a clear day, you can see Mt. Baker in the distance. Upscale boutiques selling art, glass, jewelry, and clothing line First and Second streets in the heart of town.

WHERE TO
STAY & EAT
$–$$

✕ **Café Langley.** Terra-cotta tile floors, antique oak tables, and the aroma of garlic, basil, and oregano set the mood at this Mediterranean res-taurant with Northwest touches. The tables are small but not too close together. Exotic dishes include rich hummus and baba ghanoush, egg-plant moussaka, stuffed grape leaves, Mediterranean seafood stew, and lamb or chicken shish kabob. For Northwest fare, try the Dungeness crab cakes, Penn Cove mussels, or a seafood salad. Green or Greek salads accompany all entrées. The staff is friendly, professional, and helpful. ✉113 1st St. ☎360/221–3090 ▭AE, MC, V.

$$$-$$$$ ✕▥ **Inn at Langley.** Langley's most elegant inn, the concrete-and-wood
Fodor'sChoice Frank Lloyd Wright–inspired structure perches on a bluff above the
★ beach. Asian-style guest rooms, all with fireplaces and balconies, have
dramatic marine and mountain views. Stark yet comfortable rooms
contrast beautifully with the lush landscape. The Chef's Kitchen res-
taurant ($$$$; reservations essential), with its double-sided river-rock
fireplace and full-view kitchen, is set above a pretty herb garden. In
summer it serves sumptuous six-course dinners on Friday and Satur-
day at 7 and on Sunday at 6. ⊠*400 1st St., 98260* ☎*360/221–3033*
⊕*www.innatlangley.com* ⤺*26 rooms* ⚲*In-hotel: restaurant, spa, no
elevator* ▭*MC, V* ⦿*CP.*

$-$$ ▥ **Saratoga Inn.** At the edge of Langley, this cedar-shake, Nantucket-style
accommodation is a short walk from the town's shops and restaurants.
Wood-shingle siding, gabled roofs, and wraparound porches lend the
inn a neatly blended Euro–Northwest ambience. This theme extends to
the interior, with wood floors and fireplaces. The carriage house, which
has a deck as well as a bedroom with a king-size bed, a bathroom
with a claw-foot tub, and a sitting area with a sleep sofa, offers more
privacy. Included in the price is breakfast and a daily wine reception
with hors d'oeuvres. ⊠*201 Cascade Ave., 98260* ☎*360/221–5801 or
800/698–2910* ⊕*www.saratogainnwhidbeyisland.com* ⤺*15 rooms,
1 carriage house* ⚲*In-room: no a/c. In-hotel: no-smoking rooms, no
elevator* ▭*AE, D, MC, V* ⦿*BP.*

SHOPPING At **Blackfish Gallerio** (⊠*111 Anthes Ave.* ☎*360/221–1274*) you can
see pieces by Kathleen Miller, who produces enamel jewelry and hand-
painted clothing and accessories; and Donald Miller, whose photographs depict the land and people of the Northwest; as well as works
by other regional artists. The **Cottage** (⊠*210 1st St.* ☎*360/221–4747*)
stocks vintage and imported men's and women's clothing.

Meet glass and jewelry artist Gwenn Knight at her gallery, the **Glass
Knight** (⊠*214 1st St.* ☎*360/221–6283*), which also exhibits work
by other Northwest artists. **Karlson/Gray Gallery** (⊠*302 1st St.*
☎*360/221–2978* ⊕*www.karlsongraygallery.com*) exhibits and sells
paintings, jewelry, pottery, and sculpture by established and emerging
artists in a variety of media. Exhibits change on the first Saturday of
the month. The **Museo** (⊠*215 1st St.* ☎*360/221–7737* ⊕*www.museo.
cc*), a gallery and gift shop, carries contemporary art by recognized
and emerging artists, including glass artists, of which there are many
on Whidbey.

GREENBANK
14 mi northwest of Langely.

About halfway up Whidbey Island is the hamlet of Greenbank, home
★ to the 125-acre **Greenbank Farm,** a loganberry farm encircled by views
of the Olympic and Cascade ranges. You can't miss the huge, chest-
nut-color, two-story bar with the wine vat out front, the centerpiece to
this picturesque property. Volunteers harvest the loganberries—which
are a cross between blackberries and raspberries—and turn them into
rich jams and loganberry wine–filled chocolates. Greenbank's dessert

wines can be sampled daily in the tasting room. The adjacent Whidbey Pies Café creates gourmet confections, which disappear quickly as visitors head for the scattered picnic tables, twisted mountain trails, and shimmering pond. Besides wildlife, be on the lookout for the herd of fluffy alpacas raised on-site by the Whidbey Island Alpacas company. The 1904 barn, which once housed a winery, is now a community center for farmers' markets, concerts, flea markets, and other events, including the famous Loganberry Festival each July. ✉*657 Wonn Rd.* ☎*360/678–7700* ⊕*www.greenbankfarm.com* ⌨*Free* ☉*Daily 10–5.*

The 53-acre **Meerkerk Rhododendron Gardens** contain 1,500 native and hybrid species of rhododendrons and more than 100,000 spring bulbs on 10 acres of display gardens with numerous walking trails and ponds. The flowers are in full bloom in April and May. Summer flowers and fall color provide interest later in the year. The 43 remaining acres are kept wild as a nature preserve. ✉*Hwy. 525 and Resort Rd.* ☎*360/678–1912* ⊕*www.meerkerkgardens.org* ⌨*$5* ☉*Daily 9–4.*

WHERE TO
STAY
★ $$–$$$$

🏠 **Guest House Cottages.** Surrounded by 25 acres, each of these six private log cabins, resembling cedar-sided barns with towering stone chimneys, come with a feather bed, a hot tub, country antiques, a kitchen, and a fireplace. The Cabin and the Tennessee and Kentucky cottages are built like classic log cabins; the Carriage House has stained-glass windows and a private deck; and the Farm Guest House is done in a blend of country and colonial styles. The log cabin–style Lodge has comfortable Northwest-style furnishings set around a river-rock fireplace. Rates include a country-style breakfast on the first two days of your stay, and winter brings three-nights-for-the-price-of-two specials. ✉*835 E. Christianson Rd., 98253* ☎*360/678–3115* ⊕*www. guesthouselogcottages.com* ⌨*6 cabins* ⌂*In-room: no phone, kitchen, DVD. In-hotel: pool, gym, no kids* ▭*No credit cards.*

COUPEVILLE

On the south shore of Penn Cove, 15 mi north of Greenbank.

Restored Victorian houses grace many of the streets in quiet Coupeville, Washington's second-oldest city. It also has one of the largest national historic districts in the state, and has been used for filming movies depicting 19th-century New England villages. Stores above the waterfront have maintained their old-fashioned character. Captain Thomas Coupe founded the town in 1852. His house was built the following year, and other houses and commercial buildings were built in the late 1800s. Even though Coupeville is the Island County seat, the town has a laid-back, almost 19th-century air.

☼ The **Island County Historical Museum** has exhibits on Whidbey's fishing, timber, and agricultural industries, and conducts tours and walks. The square-timber **Alexander Blockhouse** outside dates from the Puget Sound Indian War of 1855. Note the squared logs and dovetail joints of the corners—no overlapping log ends. This construction technique was favored by many western Washington pioneers. Several old-time canoes are exhibited in an open, roofed shelter. ✉*908 NW Alexan-*

der St. ☎*360/678–3310* 🎟*$3* ⏱*May–Oct., Wed.–Mon. 10–5; Nov.–Apr., Fri.–Mon. 1–4.*

☾ **Ebey's Landing National Historic Reserve** encompasses a sand-and-cobble beach, bluffs with dramatic views down the Strait of Juan de Fuca, two state parks, and several (privately held) pioneer farms homesteaded in the early 1850s. The reserve, the first and largest of its kind, holds nearly 100 nationally registered historic structures, most of them from the 19th century. Miles of trails lead along the beach and through the woods. Cedar Gulch, south of the main entrance to Ft. Ebey, has a lovely picnic area in a wooded ravine above the beach.

Ft. Casey State Park, on a bluff overlooking the Strait of Juan de Fuca and the Port Townsend ferry landing, was one of three forts built after 1890 to protect the entrance to Admiralty Inlet. Look for the concrete gun emplacement and a couple of 8-inch "disappearing" guns. The Admiralty Head Lighthouse Interpretive Center is north of the gunnery emplacements. There are also grassy picnic sites, rocky fishing spots, and a boat launch. ✉*2 mi west of Rte. 20* ☎*360/678–4519* ⊕*www.parks.wa.gov* 🎟*Free, parking $5* ⏱*Daily sunrise–sunset.* In late May **Ft. Ebey State Park** blazes with native rhododendrons. West of Coupeville on Point Partridge, it has 22 acres of beach, campsites in the woods, trails to the headlands, World War II gun emplacements, wildflower meadows, spectacular views down the Strait of Juan de Fuca, and a boggy pond. ✉*3 mi west of Rte. 20* ☎*360/678–4636 or 800/233–0321* ⊕*www.parks.wa.gov* 🎟*Free, parking $5* ⏱*Daily sunrise–sunset.*

WHERE TO
STAY & EAT
$$–$$$ ✕**The Oystercatcher.** The town's top seafood spot turns out sophisticated dinners from a modest little storefront shop along the main street. Once you dine here you're hooked—and you'll never tire of coming back to see what's on the menu, as the menu changes twice monthly. Although the emphasis is on seafood, dishes start from basic fish, fowl, meat, and vegetarian themes, then blossom into artfully arranged fare. ✉*901 Grace St. NW* ☎*360/678–0683* ▭*AE, MC, V* ⏱*Closed Mon. and Tues. No lunch.*

$–$$ ✕**Christopher's.** A warm and casual place, Christopher's is in a house one block from the waterfront. The new location is more modern than the eclectic former space—walls are painted soft browns and deep reds, white tablecloths have been discarded in favor of sleeker bare-wood tabletops—but the menu is largely the same, featuring local oysters and mussels, and such flavorful fare as raspberry barbecued salmon, bacon-wrapped pork tenderloin with mushrooms, lamb stew, and grilled ahi tuna. The wine list is extensive. ✉*105 NW Coveland* ☎*360/678–5480* ▭*AE, MC, V* ⏱*Closed Sun.*

¢–$$$ 🛏**Captain Whidbey Inn.** Almost a century old, this venerable madrone lodge on a wooded promontory offers a special kind of hospitality and charm now rarely found. Gleaming fir-paneled rooms and suites, which have pedestal sinks but share bathrooms, are furnished with antiques and modern amenities; quarters on the north side have views of Penn Cove. More-luxurious Lagoon Rooms, in a separate cedar motel, overlook a quiet, marshy expanse. A cluster of small, one-bedroom cabins have stone fireplaces, private baths, and share a hot tub, while the two-bedroom cottages each have a fireplace, hot tub, and kitchen. ⊠*2073 Captain Whidbey Inn Rd., off Madrona Way, 98239* ☎*360/678–4097 or 800/366–4097* ⊕*www.captainwhidbey.com* ⌨*23 rooms, 2 suites, 4 cabins, 3 cottages* ⌂*In-room: no a/c (some), no phone (some), no TV (some). In-hotel: restaurant, bar* ⊟*AE, MC, V.*

$ 🏨**Compass Rose Bed and Breakfast.** Inside this 1890 Queen Anne Victorian, a veritable museum of art, artifacts, and antiques awaits you. The proprietor's naval career carried him and his wife to all corners of the globe, from which they have collected the inn's unique adornments. The innkeepers' friendliness will make your stay all the more enjoyable and interesting. ⊠*508 S. Main St., 98239* ☎☎*360/678–5318* ☎*800/237–3881* ⊕*www.compassrosebandb.com* ⌨*2 rooms* ⌂*In-room: no a/c, no phone, no TV. In-hotel: no-smoking rooms, no elevator* ⊟*No credit cards* ⏐❍⏐*BP.*

OAK HARBOR
10 mi north of Coupeville.

Oak Harbor itself is the least attractive and least interesting part of Whidbey—it mainly exists to serve the Whidbey Island Naval Air Station and therefore has none of the historic or pastoral charm of the rest of the island. It is, however, the largest town on the island and the one closest to Deception Pass State Park. In town, the marina, at the east side of the bay, has a picnic area with views of Saratoga Passage and the entrance of Penn Cove.

★ ☺ **Deception Pass State Park** has 19 mi of rocky shore and beaches, three freshwater lakes, and more than 38 mi of forest and meadow trails. The park occupies the northernmost point of Whidbey Island and the southernmost tip of Fidalgo Island, on both sides of the Deception Pass Bridge. Park on Canoe Island and walk across the bridge for views of two dramatic saltwater gorges, whose tidal whirlpools have been known to swallow large logs. ⊠*Rte. 20, 7 mi north of Oak Harbor* ☎*360/675–2417* ⊕*www.parks.wa.gov* ✉*Park free, campsite fees vary* ☉*Apr.–Sept., daily 6:30* AM*–dusk; Oct.–Mar., daily 8* AM*–dusk.*

WHERE TO EAT ✕**Island Grill.** This friendly roadside café in the woods south of Decep-
$–$$ tion Pass serves fresh and flavorful American fare such as salads, burgers, and fish-and-chips. You can enjoy your meal in the comfortable dining room, or pick up food from the take-out window for a picnic on the waterfront at adjacent Deception Pass State Park. ⊠*41020 Rte. 20* ☎*360/679–3194* ⊟*MC, V.*

FIDALGO ISLAND

❹ *15 mi north of Oak Harbor.*

The Deception Pass Bridge links Whidbey to Fidalgo. Anacortes, Fidalgo's main town, has some well-preserved brick buildings along the waterfront, several well-maintained old commercial edifices downtown, and many beautiful older homes off the main drag.

The frequently changing exhibits at the **Anacortes History Museum** focus on the cultural heritage of Fidalgo and nearby Guemes Island. ✉ *1305 8th St., Anacortes* ☎ *360/293–1915* ⊕ *www.museum.cityofanacortes. org* ✇ *Free* ☉ *Thurs.–Mon. 1–5.*

West of Anacortes, near the ferry landing, **Washington Park** has dense forests, sunny meadows, trails, and a boat launch. A narrow loop road winds through woods to overlooks with views of islands and saltwater. You can picnic or camp under tall trees near the shore. ✉ *12th St. and Oakes Ave.* ☎ *360/293–1927* ✇ *Free, camping $12–$15* ☉ *Daily sunrise–sunset.*

WHERE TO EAT

$–$$$ ✕ **Randy's Pier 61.** The dining room's nautical theme is in keeping with the waterfront setting. From here you can see across the channel to Guemes Island and the San Juans; don't be surprised if a sea lion looks up from the tide rips or if a bald eagle cruises by. Specialties include seafood gumbo, crab cakes, salmon Wellington, crab-stuffed prawns, and a beautifully flavored (and expertly cooked) apples-and-almond salmon. The staff is professional and friendly. ✉ *209 T Ave., Anacortes* ☎ *360/293–5108* ▭ *AE, D, MC, V.*

SHOPPING

Compass Wines (✉ *1405 Commercial Ave., Anacortes* ☎ *360/293–6500* ⊕ *www.compasswines.com*) is one of the state's premier wine shops, with lots of hard-to-find vintages from small wineries whose annual releases sell out quickly. Besides wines, Compass purveys artisan cheeses, provisions yachts and charter boats, and assembles delectable lunch baskets.

THE SAN JUAN ISLANDS

There are 176 named islands in the San Juan archipelago, although these and large rocks around them amount to 743 at low tide and 428 at high tide. Sixty are populated (though most have only a house or two) and 10 are state marine parks, some of which are accessible only to kayakers navigating the Cascadia Marine Trail. The three largest islands, Lopez, Orcas, and San Juan, are served regularly by ferries and seaplanes and get packed with visitors in summer. These islands support a little fishing and farming, but tourism generates by far the largest revenues.

Serene, well-appointed inns cater to visitors, and creative chefs operate small restaurants, serving food as contemporary as anything in Seattle. Each of the San Juans maintains a distinct character, though all share in the archipelago's blessings of serene farmlands, unspoiled coves, blue-green or gray tidal waters, and radiant light. Because of the travel time from Seattle and the variety of activities available on the San Juans, almost everyone spends a few days here.

Since the 1990s, gray whales have begun to summer here, instead of going north to their arctic breeding grounds; an occasional minke or humpback whale can also be seen frolicking in the kelp.

Ferries stop at the four largest islands: Lopez, Shaw, Orcas, and San Juan. Others, many privately owned, can be reached be commuter ferries from Bellingham and Port Townsend. Seaplanes owned by local airlines regularly splash down near the public waterfronts and resort bays around San Juan, Orcas, and Lopez, while charters touch down in private waters away from the crowds.

■ TIP→ Orcas and San Juan islands are extremely popular in high season; making hotel and ferry reservations in advance is essential.

LOPEZ ISLAND

5 *45 mins by ferry from Anacortes.*

Known affectionately as "Slow-pez," the island closest to the mainland is a broad, bay-encircled bit of terrain amid sparkling blue seas, a place where cabinlike homes are tucked into the woods, and boats are moored in lonely coves. Of the three San Juan islands with facilities to accommodate overnight visitors, Lopez has the smallest population (approximately 2,200), and with its old orchards, weathered barns, and rolling green pastures, it's the most rustic and least crowded during high season. Gently sloping roads cut wide curves through golden farmlands and trace the edges of pebbly beaches, while peaceful trails wind through thick patches of forest. Sweeping country views make Lopez a favorite year-round biking locale, and except for the long hill up from the ferry docks, most roads and designated bike paths are easy enough for novices to negotiate.

The only settlement is Lopez Village, really just a cluster of cafés and boutique shops, as well as a summer market and outdoor theater, visitor information center, and grocery store. Other attractions—such as seasonal berry-picking farms, small wineries, kitschy galleries, intimate restaurants, and isolated bed-and-breakfasts—are scattered around the island.

The **Lopez Island Historical Museum** has relics from the region's Native American tribes and early settlers, including some impressive ship and small-boat models and maps of local landmarks. ⊠ *28 Washburn Pl., Lopez Village* ☎ *360/468–2049* ⊕ *www.rockisland.com/~lopezmuseum* 🖾 *Donations accepted* ☉ *May–Sept., Wed.–Sun. noon–4.*

Spencer Spit State Park is on former Native American clamming, crabbing, and fishing grounds. The spit is a stop along the Cascadia Marine Trail for kayakers, and it's a good place for summer camping. It's also one of the few Washington beaches where cars are permitted. ✛ *2 mi northeast of Lopez Village via Port Stanley Rd.* ☎ *360/468–2251* 🖾 *Free* ☉ *Mar.–Oct., daily 8–dusk.*

★ A quiet forest trail along beautiful **Shark Reef** leads to an isolated headland jutting out above the bay. The sounds of raucous barks and squeals mean you're nearly there, and eventually you may see throngs of seals and seagulls on the rocky islets across from the point. Bring binoculars to spot bald eagles in the trees as you walk, and to view sea otters frolicking in the waves near the shore. The trail starts at the Shark Reef Road parking lot south of Lopez Village, and it's a 15-minute walk to the headland. ⊹ *Off Shark Reef Rd., 2 mi south of Lopez Island Airport* ☎*360/856–3500 or 800/527–3305* ⊠*Free* ☉*Daily dawn–dusk.*

Lopez Island Vineyard is spread over 6 acres about 1 mi north of Lopez Village. The winery produces chardonnay, merlot, and cabernet sauvignon–merlot blends, as well as sweeter wines, such as those made from raspberries, blackberries, and other local fruits. ⊠*Fisherman Bay Rd. north of Cross Rd.* ☎*360/468–3644* ⊕*www.lopezislandvineyards. com* ⊠*Free* ☉*July and Aug., Wed.–Sat. noon–5; May, June, and Sept., Fri. and Sat. noon–5; Apr. and Oct.–Dec., Sat. noon–5.*

WHERE TO STAY & EAT

$$–$$$ ✕**Bay Café.** Boats dock right outside this pretty waterside mansion at the entrance to Fisherman Bay. In winter, sunlight streams into the window-framed dining room; in summer you can relax on the wraparound porch before a gorgeous sunset panorama. Seafood tapas, such as basil-and- goat-cheese-stuffed prawns with saffron rice, or sea scallops with sun-dried tomatoes, delightfully tickle the palate. Homemade sorbet and a fine crème caramel are among the desserts. Weekend breakfasts draw huge crowds. ⊠*9 Old Post Rd., Lopez Village* ☎*360/468–3700* ⊕*www.bay-cafe.com* ⊟*AE, DC, MC, V* ☉*Closed Mon. and Tues. Oct.–May. No lunch.*

★ **¢–$** ✕**Holly B's Bakery.** Tucked into a small, cabinlike strip of businesses set back from the water, this cozy, wood-paneled dining room is the highlight of daytime dining in the village. Fresh-cooked pastries and big homemade breakfasts are the draws. Sunny summer mornings bring diners out onto the patio, where kids play and parents relax. ⊠*Lopez Plaza* ☎*360/468–2133* ⊕*www.hollybsbakery.com* ⊟*No credit cards* ☉*Closed Dec.–Mar. No dinner.*

$$ ▦**Edenwild.** This large Victorian-style farmhouse, surrounded by gardens and framed by Fisherman's Bay, looks as if it's at least a century old, but it actually dates from 1988. Large rooms, each painted or papered in different pastel shades, are furnished with simple antiques; some have claw-foot tubs and brick fireplaces. The sunny dining room is a cheery breakfast spot. In summer you can sip tea on the wraparound ground-floor veranda or relax with a book on the garden patio. ⊠*132 Lopez Village Rd., Lopez Village, 98261* ☎*360/468–3238 or 800/606–0662* ⊕*www.edenwildinn.com* ⇆*6 rooms, 2 suites* ⬧*In-hotel: no kids under 12, no elevator* ⊟*AE, D, MC, V* ��❘*BP.*

$$ ▦**Mackaye Harbor Inn.** This former sea captain's house, built in 1904, rises two stories above the beach at the southern end of the island. Rooms have golden-oak and brass details and wicker furniture; three have views of Mackaye Harbor. Breakfast includes Scandinavian specialties like Finnish pancakes; tea, coffee, and chocolates are served in the evening. Rooms are simple, with colorful coverlets. The Harbor

Suite has a private bath, deck, and fireplace. Kayaks are available for rent, and mountain bikes are complimentary. ✉*949 MacKaye Harbor Rd., Lopez Village, 98261* ☎*360/468–2253 or 888/314–6140* ⊕*www.mackayeharborinn.com* ⇆*4 rooms, 2 with bath; 1 suite* ♿*In-room: no phone, no TV. In-hotel: beach, bicycles* ▭*MC, V* ☉*Closed Oct.–Apr.* ⚞*BP.*

SPORTS & THE OUTDOORS

BICYCLING Mountain bike rental rates start at around $5 an hour and $25 a day; tandem, recumbent, and electric bikes are $13–$20 an hour or $42–$65 per day. Reservations are recommended, particularly in summer.

The **Bike Shop on Lopez** (✉*Lopez Village* ☎*360/468–3497*) makes free deliveries to the ferry docks or to your hotel. **Cycle San Juans** (✉*Hwy. 1* ☎*360/468–3251*) offers rentals and tours. **Lopez Bicycle Works** (✉*2847 Fisherman Bay Rd.* ☎*360/468–2847* ⊕*www.lopezbicycleworks.com*), at the marina, can bring bicycles to your door or the ferry.

SEA KAYAKING **Elakah! Expeditions** (☎*360/734–7270 or 800/434–7270* ⊕*www.elakah. com*), a family-run sea-kayaking company, leads kayaking clinics on Lopez and two- to five-day trips ($225 to $495) around the San Juans. Specialty trips, such as those for women only, are also organized. **Lopez Kayaks** (☎*360/468–2847* ⊕*www.lopezkayaks.com*), open May to October at Fisherman Bay, offers a four-hour tour of the southern end of Lopez for $75 and a two-hour sunset tour for $35. Kayak rentals start at $15 an hour or $40 per day, and the company can deliver kayaks to any point on the island for an additional $10 fee.

SHOPPING

The **Chimera Gallery** (✉*Village Rd.* ☎*360/468–3265*), a local artists' cooperative, exhibits and sells crafts, jewelry, and fine art. **Fish Bay Mercantile** (✉*Lopez Rd.* ☎*360/468–2126*) is a fun, quirky gallery full of hand-carved wooden masks and furnishings, handwoven shawls and blankets, handmade jewelry, and scenic paintings by island artists—plus quirky international stuff like the Hindu lunchbox collection. **Grayling Gallery** (✉*3630 Hummel Lake Rd.* ☎*360/468–2779*) displays the paintings, prints, sculptures, and pottery works of nearly a dozen Lopez Island artists. **Islehaven Books** (✉*Village Rd.* ☎*360/468–2132*), which is supervised in part by the owner's pack of five Russian wolfhounds, is stocked with publications on San Juan Islands history and activities, as well as books about the Pacific Northwest. There's also a good selection of mysteries, literary novels, children's books, and craft kits, plus greeting cards, art prints, and maps. Many of the items sold here are the works of local writers, artists, and photographers.

ORCAS ISLAND

❻ *75 mins by ferry from Anacortes.*

Roads on flower-blossom–shape Orcas Island, the largest of the San Juans, sweep through wide valleys and rise to gorgeous hilltop views. Spanish explorers set foot here in 1791, and the island is named for their ship—not for the black-and-white whales that frolic in the surrounding waters. The island was also the home of Native American tribes, whose history is reflected in such places as Pole Pass, where the Lummi people used kelp and cedar-bark nets to catch ducks, and Massacre Bay, where in 1858 a tribe from southeast Alaska attacked a Lummi fishing village.

Today, farmers, fishermen, artists, retirees, and summer-home owners make up the population of about 4,500. Houses are spaced far apart, and towns typically have just one major road running through them. Resorts dotting the island's edges are evidence of the thriving local tourism industry. Orcas is a favorite place for weekend getaways from the Seattle area any time of the year, as well as one of the state's top settings for summer weddings.

Eastsound, the main town, lies at the head of the East Sound channel, which nearly divides the island in two. Small shops here sell jewelry, pottery, and crafts by local artisans. Along Prune Alley are a handful of stores and restaurants.

The **Funhouse** is a huge, nonprofit activity center and museum for families. Interactive exhibits on age, hearing, kinetics, and video production, among other subjects, are all educational. Kids can explore an arts-and-crafts yurt, a climbing wall, a library, Internet stations, and a big metal "Jupiter" tree fort. Sports activities include indoor pitching cages and games, as well as an outdoor playground. Kids and adults can also take classes on music, theater, digital film, and poetry. There are free programs for preteens and teenagers on Friday and Saturday nights (hint to mom and dad, who might want to enjoy dinner alone on this romantic island). ⊠ *30 Pea Patch La., Eastsound* ☎ *360/376–7177* ⊕ *www.thefunhouse.org* ⊠ *$5* ☉ *Sept.–June, weekdays 3–5:30, Sat. 11–3; July and Aug., Mon.–Sat. 11–5.*

★ **Moran State Park** comprises 5,000 acres of hilly, old-growth forests dotted with sparkling lakes, in the middle of which rises 2,400-foot-high Mt. Constitution, the tallest peak in the San Juans. A drive to the summit affords exhilarating views of the islands, the Cascades, the Olympics, and Vancouver Island. You can explore the terrain along 14 hiking trails and choose from among 151 campsites if you'd like to stay longer. ⊹ *Star Rte. 22; Head northeast from Eastsound on Horseshoe Hwy. and follow signs* ⊕ *Box 22, Eastsound, 98245* ☎ *360/376–2326, 800/452–5678 for reservations* ⊠ *Camping $17 plus $2 per night* ☉ *Daily dawn–dusk.*

WHERE TO STAY & EAT

$$$–$$$$ ✕ **Christina's.** Copper-top tables and paintings by island artists enhance this cozy bayside spot. The seasonal menu focuses on local seafood, prepared with fresh herbs and served with vegetables. Look for delicacies like spring greens with fennel and Samish Bay cheese; roast chicken with mushroom bread pudding; and curry coconut fish stew. Fine views of the East Sound make for a romantic dinner on the rooftop terrace or the enclosed porch. An excellent wine list and a bevy of rich desserts complement every meal. ⊠ *310 N. Beach Rd., Eastsound*

☎360/376–4904 ⊕*www.christinas.net* ▤*AE, DC, MC, V* ⊗*Closed Tues. Oct.–mid-June. No lunch.*

¢–$ ✕**Bilbo's Festivo.** Stucco walls, colorful tiles, and wood benches reflect this restaurant's Tex-Mex inclinations. And believe it or not, the food here is healthful. The fresh, delectable burritos, enchiladas, and cha- lupas are lard-free. There's also fabulous homemade guacamole and locally grown organic salad greens. Margaritas are served in the court- yard in summer, and you can warm your hands around the patio fire pit on cool autumn evenings. Kids dash immediately to the outdoor play area. ⊠*N. Beach Rd. and A St., Eastsound* ☎360/376–4728 ⌂*Reservations not accepted* ▤*AE, MC, V* ⊗*No lunch Oct.–May.*

★ $$$–$$$$ ⌂**Spring Bay Inn.** Two former park rangers run this woodland B&B at the edge of private Spring Bay. All rooms have water views, wood- burning fireplaces, feather beds, and sitting areas; the Ranger Suite has an outdoor hot tub. A hearty breakfast in the morning will fortify you for the free, two-hour kayaking trips around the island's craggy edges, or for hiking the trails that meander through the property. Afterward, there's an enormous complimentary brunch. Advance reservations are a must; summer slots start to fill up by May. ⊠*Obstruction Pass Trail- head Rd. off Obstruction Pass Rd., Olga, 98279* ☎360/376–5531 ⊕*www.springbayinn.com* ⇆*5 rooms* ⌂*In-room: no phone, no TV. In-hotel: beachfront, public Wi-Fi* ▤*D, MC, V* ⦿*BP.*

$–$$$$ ⌂**Deer Harbor Inn.** This lodge has eight wood-paneled rooms, each with a balcony and peeled-log furniture. Four cottages—including one with three bedrooms—and the Harborview Suite have whirlpool tubs and propane fireplaces; two houses have kitchens and laundry facilities. The century-old apple orchard is lovely, making it a favorite spot for weddings. ⊕*5½ mi southwest of West Sound via Deer Harbor Rd.* ☎360/376–4110 or 877/377–4110 ⊕*www.deerharborinn.com* ⇆*8 rooms, 1 suite, 4 cottages, 2 houses* ⌂*In-room: no phone, kitchen (some), no TV (some), Wi-Fi. In-hotel: restaurant, laundry facilities, public Wi-Fi* ▤*AE, MC, V* ⦿*CP.*

$$$ ⌂**Rosario Spa & Resort.** Shipbuilding magnate Robert Moran built this Mediterranean-style mansion on Cascade Bay in 1906. It's now on the National Register of Historic Places and worth a visit even if you're not staying here. The house has retained its original Mission-style furniture and numerous antiques; its centerpiece, an aeolian organ with 1,972 pipes, is used for summer concerts in the ballroom. Some of the rooms are compact and basic; others are luxurious suites with outdoor decks, Jacuzzis, gas fireplaces, and kitchens. You can hike, kayak, and scuba dive nearby or stay in for a day of pampering in the downstairs Avanyu Spa. From your room you can watch seaplanes splash down in the bay and fishing and sailboat charters come into the marina. With prior notice, a Rosario shuttle will meet you at the ferry dock and take you to the hotel. ⊠*1 Rosario Way, Eastsound, 98245* ☎360/376–2222 or 800/562–8820 ⊕*www.rosarioresort.com* ⇆*111 rooms, 4 suites* ⌂*In-room: kitchen (some), Wi-Fi (some). In-hotel: 2 restaurants, bar, 2 tennis courts, 3 pools, gym, spa, concierge, children's programs (ages 5–13), public Internet* ▤*AE, DC, MC, V.*

$–$$ 🖼 **Turtleback Farm Inn.** Eighty acres of meadow, forest, and farmland in the shadow of Turtleback Mountain surround this forest-green inn. Rooms are divided between the carefully restored late-19th-century green-clapboard farmhouse and the newer cedar Orchard House. All are well lighted, and have hardwood floors, wood trim, and colorful curtains and quilts, some of which are made from the fleece of resident sheep. The inn is a favorite place for local weddings. Breakfast is in the dining room or on the deck overlooking the valley. ⊠*1981 Crow Valley Rd., Eastsound, 98245* 📞*360/376–3914 or 800/376–4914* ⊕*www.turtlebackinn.com* ↪*11 rooms* ⚐*In-room: no phone, no TV. In-hotel: bar, no elevator* ☰*MC, V* ⊚|*BP.*

SPORTS & THE OUTDOORS

BICYCLES & MOPEDS   Mountain bikes rent for about $30 per day or $100 per week. Tandem, recumbent, and electric bikes rent for a bout $50 per day. Mopeds rent for $20 to $30 per hour or $60 to $70 per day.

The Boardwalk (⊠*Orcas Village* 📞*360/376–2791* ⊕*www.orcasisland-boardwalk.com*), at the ferry landing, rents road and mountain bikes. **Dolphin Bay Bicycles** (⊠*Orcas Village* 📞*360/376–4157 or 360/376–6734* ⊕*www.rockisland.com/~dolphin*), at the ferry landing, rents road, mountain, and BMX bikes for children and adults. **Orcas Moped Rentals** (⊠*Orcas Village* 📞*360/376–5266*), at the ferry landing, rents mopeds and bicycles. **Wildlife Cycles** (⊠*Eastsound* 📞*360/376–4708* ⊕*www.wildlifecycles.com*) rents bikes and can recommend routes all over the island.

BOATING & SAILING   **Amante Sail Tours** (⊠*Deer Harbor* 📞*360/376–4231*) offers half-day sailing trips for up to six people for $35 per person. **Deer Harbor Charters** (⊠*Deer Harbor* 📞*360/376–5989* ⊕*www.deerharborcharters.com*), an eco-conscious outfitter (they're the only one in the San Juans to use biodiesel), has several small sailboats making half-day cruises around the San Juans for marine wildlife viewing. Rates are $45 to $75 per person. Outboards and skiffs are also available, as is fishing gear. **Orcas Boat Rentals** (⊠*Deer Harbor* 📞*360/376–7616* ⊕*www.orcasboats.com*) has sailboats, outboards, and skiffs for full and half-day trips. They also rent paddleboats for $25 for the first hour and $15 each additional hour. **West Beach Resort** (✛*3 mi west of Eastsound* 📞*360/376–2240 or 800/937–8224* ⊕*www.westbeachresort.com*) rents motorized boats, kayaks and canoes, and fishing gear.

SCUBA DIVING   **Island Dive & Water Sports** (⊠*Rosario Resort, Eastsound* 📞*360/378–2772 or 800/303–8686* ⊕*www.divesanjuan.com*) has a dive shop with rentals and offers a complete program of services, including instruction, air fills, and charter trips. Two custom dive boats make two-tank dives for $79 with gear; resort packages are available. **West Beach Resort** (⊠*West Beach* 📞*360/376–2240 or 877/937–8224*) is a popular dive spot where you can fill your own tanks.

SEA KAYAKING   All equipment is usually included in a rental package or tour. One-hour trips cost around $25; three-hour tours, about $45; day tours, $95–$120; and multiday tours, about $100 per day.

Crescent Beach Kayaks (⊠*Eastsound* ☎*360/376–2464* ⊕*http://crescent-beachkayaks.com*) caters to families with free instruction and kayak rentals. **Orcas Outdoors Sea Kayak Tours** (⊠*Orcas Village* ☎*360/376–2222* ⊕*www.orcasoutdoors.com*) has one- and three-hour journeys, as well as day trips and rentals; a second branch is based at the Outlook Inn in Eastsound. **Osprey Tours** (⊠*Eastsound* ☎*360/376–3677* ⊕*www.ospreytours.com*) uses handcrafted wooden Aleutian-style kayaks for half-day, full-day, and overnight tours of the islands. **Shearwater Adventures** (⊠*Eastsound* ☎*360/376–4699* ⊕*www.shearwaterkayaks.com*) holds kayaking classes and runs three-hour, day, and overnight tours from Rosario, Deer Harbor, and Doe Bay resorts.

WHALE-
WATCHING
Cruises, which run about four hours, are scheduled daily in summer and once or twice weekly at other times. The cost is around $50 per person and boats hold 20 to 40 people. Wear warm clothing and bring a snack.

Deer Harbor Charters (☎*360/376–5989 or 800/544–5758* ⊕*www.deer-harborcharters.com*) has whale-watching cruises around the island straits. **Eclipse Charters** (☎*360/376–6566* ⊕*www.orcasislandwhales.com*) searches around Orcas Island for whale pods and other wildlife. **Whale Spirit Adventures** (⊠*West Sound Marina* ☎*360/376–5052 or 800/376–8018*) offers whale-sighting tours to the accompaniment of new-age chanting or flutes.

SHOPPING

Crow Valley Pottery (⊠*2274 Orcas Rd., Eastsound* ☎*360/376–2351 or 800/684–4297* ⊕*www.crowvalley.com*) carries ceramics, metalworks, blown glass, and sculptures. **Darvill's Rare Print Shop** (⊠*Eastsound* ☎*360/376–2351*) specializes in maps and unique bird and floral prints. **Orcas Island Artworks** (⊠*Main St., Olga* ☎*360/376–4408* ⊕*www.orcasisland.com/artworks*) displays pottery, sculpture, jewelry, art glass, paintings, and quilts by resident artists.

SAN JUAN ISLAND

❼ *45 mins by ferry from Orcas Island, 75 mins by ferry from Anacortes.*

Lummi Indians were the first settlers on San Juan, with encampments along the north end of the island. North-end beaches were especially busy during the annual salmon migration, when hundreds of tribal members would gather along the shoreline to fish, cook, and exchange news. Many of the Lummi tribe were killed by smallpox and other imported diseases in the 18th and 19th centuries. Smallpox Bay was where tribal members plunged into the icy water to cool the fevers that came with the disease.

The 18th century brought explorers from England and Spain, but the island remained sparsely populated until the mid-1800s. From the 1880s Friday Harbor and its newspaper were controlled by lime-company owner and Republican bigwig John S. McMillin, who virtually ran San Juan Island as a personal fiefdom from 1886 until his death in

1936. The town's main street, rising from the harbor and ferry land-ing up the slopes of a modest hill, hasn't changed much in the past few decades, though the cafés and shops are snazzier now than they were in the 1960s and '70s. San Juan is the most convenient Pacific Northwest island to visit, since you can take the ferry here and explore the entire island by public transportation or bicycle.

⟳ A stairwell painted with a life-size underwater mural leads you to the **Whale Museum.** Models of whales and whale skeletons, recordings of whale sounds, and videos of whales are the attractions. Head around to the back of the first-floor shop to view maps of the latest orca pod trackings in the area. ✉ *62 1st St. N, Friday Harbor* ☎ *360/378–4710* ⊕ *www.whale-museum.org* 🖃 *$6* ☉ *June–Sept., daily 9–6; Oct.–May, daily 10–5.*

The **San Juan Historical Museum,** in an old farmhouse, presents island life at the turn of the 20th century through historic photography, documents, and buildings. ✉ *405 Price St.* ☎ *360/378–3949* ⊕ *www. sjmuseum.org* 🖃 *$3* ☉ *Oct.–Apr., Tues. and Thurs. 10–2; May–Sept., Thurs.–Sat. 1–4.*

To watch whales cavorting in Haro Strait, head to **Lime Kiln Point State Park,** on San Juan's western side just 6 mi from Friday Harbor. A rocky coastal trail leads to lookout points and a little white 1914 lighthouse. The best period for sighting whales is from the end of April through August, but a resident pod of orcas regularly cruises past the point. ✉ *6158 Lighthouse Rd.* ☎ *360/378–2044* 🖃 *Free* ☉ *Daily 8* AM– *10* PM; *lighthouse tours May–Sept. at 3 and 5.*

★ ⟳ **San Juan Island National Historic Park** commemorates the Pig War, in which the United States and Great Britain nearly went to war over their respective claims on the San Juan Islands. The dispute began in 1859 when an American settler killed a British soldier's pig, and escalated until roughly 500 American soldiers and 2,200 British soldiers with five warships were poised for battle. Fortunately, no blood was spilled and the disagreement was finally settled in 1872 in the Americans' favor, with Emperor William I of Germany as arbitrator.

The park comprises two separate areas on opposite sides of the island. English Camp, in a sheltered cove of Garrison Bay on the northern end, includes a blockhouse, a commissary, and barracks. A popular (though steep) hike is to the top of Young Hill from which you can get a great view of northwest side of the island. American Camp, on the southern end, has a visitor center and the remains of fortifications; it stretches along driftwood-strewn beaches. Many of the American Camp's walk-ing trails are through prairie; in the evening, dozens of rabbits emerge from their warrens to nibble in the fields. Great views greet you from the top of the Mt. Finlayson Trail—if you're lucky, you might be able to see Mt. Baker and Mt. Rainier along with the Olympics. From June to August you can take guided hikes and see reenactments of 1860s-era military life. ✉ *American Camp: 6 mi southeast of Friday Harbor; English Camp: 9 mi northwest of Friday Harbor. Park Headquarters: 125 Spring St., Friday Harbor* ☎ *360/378–2902* ⊕ *www.nps.gov/sajh*

🕮*Free* ◷*American Camp visitor center: June–Sept., daily 8:30–5; Oct.–May, Wed.–Sun. 8:30–4:30. English Camp visitor center: June–Sept., daily 9–5.*

★ ⊙ The **Westcott Bay Institute for Art & Nature** is essentially a 19-acre open-air art gallery within the spectacular Westcott Bay Reserve. You can stroll along winding trails to view more than 80 sculptures spread amid freshwater and saltwater wetlands, open woods, blossoming fields, and rugged terrain. The park is also a haven for birds; more than 120 species nest and breed here. Art workshops and events are scheduled throughout the year in the tented area. ✉*Westcott Dr. off Roche Harbor Rd.* ☎*360/370–5050* ⊕*www.wbay.org* 🕮*Free* ◷*Daily dawn–dusk.*

It's hard to believe that fashionable **Roche Harbor** at the northern end of San Juan Island was once the most important producer of builder's lime on the West Coast. In 1882 John S. McMillin gained control of the lime company and expanded production. But even in its heyday as a limestone quarrying village, Roche Harbor was known for abundant flowers and welcoming accommodations. McMillin transformed a bunkhouse into private lodgings for his invited guests, who included such notables as Teddy Roosevelt. The guesthouse is now the Hotel de Haro, which displays period photographs and artifacts in its lobby. The staff has maps of the old quarry, kilns, and the Mausoleum, an eerie Greek-inspired memorial to McMillin.

McMillin's heirs operated the quarries and plant until 1956, when they sold the company to the Tarte family. Although the old lime kilns still stand below the bluff, the company town has become a resort. Locals say it took two years for the limestone dust to wash off the trees around the harbor. McMillin's former home is now a restaurant, and workers' cottages have been transformed into comfortable visitors' lodgings. With its rose gardens, cobblestone waterfront, and well-manicured lawns, Roche Harbor retains the flavor of its days as a hangout for McMillin's powerful friends—especially since the sheltered harbor is very popular with well-to-do pleasure boaters.

⊙ On **Krystal Acres Alpaca Farm,** an enormous swathe of farmland on the west side of the island, keep an eye out for the dozens of alpacas from South America. In the big barn, the shop displays beautiful, high-quality clothing and crafts, all handmade from alpaca hair. ✉*152 Blazing Tree Rd., Friday Harbor* ☎*360/378–6125* ⊕*www.krystalacres.com* 🕮*Free* ◷*Apr.–Dec., daily 10–5; Jan.–Mar., Fri.–Mon. 11–5.*

At **Pelindaba Lavender Farm,** a spectacular 20-acre valley is smothered with endless rows of fragrant purple-and-gold lavender blossoms. The oils are distilled for use in therapeutic, botanical, and household products, all created on-site. If you can't make it to the farm, stop at the outlet in the Friday Harbor Center on First Street, where you can buy their products and sample delicious lavender-infused baked goods and beverages. ✉*33 Hawthorn La., Friday Harbor* ☎*360/378–4248* ⊕*www. pelindaba.com* 🕮*Free* ◷*May–Sept., daily 10–5; Oct., Fri.–Sun. 10–5; Nov.–Dec., Wed–Sun. 10–5.*

WHERE TO STAY & EAT

$$$–$$$$
Fodor'sChoice
★

✕**Duck Soup Inn.** Blossoming vines thread over the cedar-shingled walls of this restaurant. Inside, island-inspired paintings and a flagstone fireplace are the background for creative meals served at comfortable booths. Everything is made from scratch daily, including sourdough bruschetta and ice cream. You might start with Thai-style prawn roll-ups, made with peanuts, scallions, coconut, hot chilies, lime, and fresh mint; or perhaps apple-wood-smoked Westcott Bay oysters. For a second course, you might have grilled quail or chiles rellenos. Vegetarian options and child portions are available. Northwest, California, and European wines are also on hand. ⊠ *50 Duck Soup La.* ☎ *360/378–4878* ⊕ *www.ducksoupinn.com* ▭ *MC, V* ⊗ *Closed Nov.–Mar; Mon.–Thurs. Oct., Apr., and May; Mon. and Tues. in June; Mon. July–Sept. No lunch.*

¢–$

✕**Blue Dolphin Café.** The best-known breakfast spot in town might be tiny, but the portions that emerge from the kitchen would satisfy the hungriest sailor. Stacks of pancakes, big egg scrambles, crisp bacon, and tender sausages are turned out with astonishing speed, often in carry-out boxes for travelers rushing to make the next ferry. Side dishes and sandwiches turn up at lunchtime, but the whole operation shuts down mid-afternoon. ⊠ *185 1st St., Friday Harbor* ☎ *360/378–6116* ▭ *No credit cards* ⊗ *No dinner.*

¢–$

✕**Front Street Ale House.** This dark, woodsy English-style alehouse serves traditional pub fare: bangers and mash (sausages and mashed potatoes), bubble and squeak (grilled cabbage and mashed potatoes), and a terrific shepherd's pie. A draft from the adjacent San Juan Brewing Company is the perfect accompaniment—try the Pig War Stout or Royal Marine Pale Ale. If you can't decide what to drink, choose the beer sampler, which comes with five types of drafts served in shot glasses. The second-floor Top Side area has a dance floor and great harbor views. ⊠ *1 Front St., Friday Harbor* ☎ *360/378–2337* ⊕ *www.sanjuanbrewing.com* ⌂ *Reservations not accepted* ▭ *AE, MC, V.*

$$$–$$$$

▦**Friday Harbor House.** This contemporary hotel takes advantage of its bluff-top location with floor-to-ceiling windows that overlook the marina, ferry landing, and San Juan Channel below. Sleek, modern, wood furnishings and fabrics in beige hues fill the rooms, all of which have fireplaces, deep jetted tubs, and at least partial views of the water. The elegant restaurant serves seasonal meals and special wine-tasting dinners, often to a backdrop of glowing sunsets in summer. ⊠ *130 West St., Friday Harbor, 98250* ☎ *360/378–8455* ⊕ *www.fridayharborhouse.com* ➲ *23 rooms* ⌂ *In-room: refrigerator, Ethernet. In-hotel: restaurant, no-smoking rooms* ▭ *MC, V* ⊙*CP.*

★ **$$–$$$**

▦**Kirk House Bed and Breakfast.** Steel magnate Peter Kirk had this Craftsman bungalow built as a summer home in 1907. Rooms are all differently decorated: the Garden Room has a botanical motif, the sunny Trellis Room is done in soft shades of yellow and green, and the Arbor Room has French doors leading out to the garden. You may take breakfast in the parlor—or have it in bed, served on antique Limoges china. Bountiful wicker-basket picnics, with all the trimmings, can be prepared for a day's excursion. There is a two-night minimum stay in high season. ⊠*595 Park St., Friday Harbor, 98250* ☎*360/378–3757 or 800/639–2762* ⊕*www.kirkhouse.net* ⤸*4 rooms* ◊*In-room: no a/c, no phone, DVD, Wi-Fi. In-hotel: no kids under 10, no-smoking rooms* ⊟*MC, V* ⑩*BP.*

$–$$$ ⊞**Roche Harbor Resort.** First a log trading post built in 1845, and later an 1880s lime-industry complex, including hotel, homes, and offices, this sprawling resort is still centered around the lime deposits that made John S. McMillin his fortune in the late 19th century. Rooms are filled with notable antiques, like the claw-foot tub where actor John Wayne used to soak. Luxury suites in the separate McMillan House have fireplaces, heated bathroom floors, and panoramic water views from a private veranda. The beachside Company Town Cottages, once the homes of lime company employees, have rustic exteriors but modern interiors. Elsewhere are contemporary condos with fireplaces; some have lofts and water views. Walking trails thread through the resplendent gardens and the old lime quarries. ⊠*4950 Reuben Memorial Dr., 10 mi northwest of Friday Harbor off Roche Harbor Rd., Roche Harbor, 98250* ☎*360/378–2155 or 800/451–8910* ⊕*www.rocheharbor.com* ⤸*16 rooms without bath, 14 suites, 9 cottages, 20 condos* ◊*In-room: kitchen (some), refrigerator (some), DVD (some), no TV (some). In-hotel: 3 restaurants, tennis court, pool, spa* ⊟*AE, MC, V.*

SPORTS & THE OUTDOORS

BEACHES   **American Camp** (⊕*6 mi southeast of Friday Harbor* ☎*360468–3663)*, part of San Juan Island National Historical Park, has 6 mi of public beach on the southern end of the island. **San Juan County Park** (⊠*380 Westside Rd., Friday Harbor* ☎*360/378–2992)* has a wide gravel beachfront where orcas often frolic in summer, plus grassy lawns with picnic tables and a small campground.

BICYCLES &   You can rent standard, mountain, and BMX bikes for $30 per day or
MOPEDS $100 per week. Tandem, recumbent, and electric bikes rent for about $50 per day. You can rent mopeds for $20 to $30 per hour or $60 to $70 per day. Make sure to reserve bikes and mopeds a few days ahead in summer.

Island Bicycles (⊠*380 Argyle St., Friday Harbor* ☎*360/378–4941* ⊕*www.islandbicycles.com)* is a full-service shop that rents bikes. **Island Scooter & Bike Rental** (⊠*Friday Harbor* ☎*360/378–8811)* has bikes and scooters for rent. **Susie's Mopeds** (⊠*125 Nichols, Friday Harbor* ☎*360/376–5244 or 800/532–0087)* rents mopeds and bicycles. There is another location in Roche Harbor near the airport.

BOATING &   Fees for moorage at private docks are $8 per night for boats under 26
SAILING   feet long and $11 per night for larger vessels. Moorage buoys are $5 a night. Fees are paid in cash on-site, while annual permits ($50–$80) are available from shops in Friday Harbor. At public docks, high-season moorage rates are 70¢–$1.35 per foot (of vessel) per night.

Port of Friday Harbor (☎*360/378–2688* ⊕*www.portfridayharbor. org)* provides marina services including guest moorage, vessel assistance and repair, bareboat and skippered charters, overnight accommodations, and wildlife and whale-watching cruises. **Roche Harbor**

7

Marina (☎360/378–2155 ⊕*www.rocheharbor.com*) has a fuel dock, pool, grocery, and other guest services. **Snug Harbor Resort Marina** (☎360/378–4762) provides marina services and van service to and from Friday Harbor, including ferry and airport shuttle service, and rents small powerboats.

CHARTERS   Charter sailboat cruises start at about $225 per day and run up to $400 per day for deluxe vessels. Charter powerboat trips start at about $150 per day. Extra costs for overnight cruises may include skipper fees ($150–$175), meals ($10–$15 per person daily), preboarding fees ($50–$100), and so on.

Amante Sail Tours (☎360/376–4321) leads morning and afternoon sails for two to six guests. **Cap' n Howard's Sailing Charters** (☎360/378–3958 or 877/346–7245) hires out full-size vessels for sailing excursions around the islands. **Charters Northwest** (☎360/378–7196 ⊕*www. chartersnw.com*) offers three-day and weeklong full-service sailboat and powerboat charters. **Harmony Charters** (☎360/468–3310 ⊕*www. interisland.com/countess*) conducts daylong and multiday sailboat charters throughout the San Juan Islands and the Pacific Northwest. **Kismet Sailing Charters** (☎360/468–2435 ⊕*www.rockisland.com/~sailkismet*) leads overnight excursions through the San Juans and southwest Canada on a 36-foot-long customized yacht.

SCUBA DIVING   **Island Dive & Water Sports** (✉*Friday Harbor* ☎360/378–2772 ⊕*www. divesanjuan.com*), at the waterfront, is a full-service dive shop with classes, equipment, air fills, and charters. Two-tank dives cost $79, with gear included. Overnight adventure packages with two days of diving start at $200.

SEA KAYAKING   Many kayakers bring their own vessels to the San Juans. If you're a beginner or didn't bring your own kayak, you'll find rentals in Friday Harbor, as well as outfitters providing classes and tours. Be sure to make reservations in summer. One-hour trips start at $25, three-hour tours run about $45, day tours cost $90–$125, and overnight tours cost $80–$100 per day with meals. Equipment is always included in the cost.

A Leisure Kayak Rentals (☎360/378–5992 or 800/836–8224) will shuttle you from the ferry to the start of your kayaking class; hourly, daily, and overnight tours are also scheduled. **Crystal Seas Kayaking** (☎360/378–4223 or 877/732–7877/625–7245 ⊕*www.crystalseas.com*) has many trip options including sunset tours and multisport tours that might include biking and camping. **Discovery Sea Kayaks** (☎360/378–2559 or 866/461–2559 ⊕*www.discoveryseakayak.com*) offers both sea-kayaking adventures, including sunset trips and multiday excursions, and whale-watching tours. **San Juan Kayak Expeditions** (☎360/378–4436 ⊕*www.sanjuankayak.com*) runs kayaking and camping tours in two-person kayaks. **Sea Quest** (☎360/378–5767 or 888/589–4253 ⊕*www. sea-quest-kayak.com*) conducts kayak ecotours with guides who are trained naturalists, biologists, and environmental scientists.

WHALE-
WATCHING

Whale-watching expeditions run three to four hours and around $50 per person. ■**TIP➜ For the best experience, look for tour companies with small boats that accommodate no more than 20 or 30 people**; if booking on a larger vessel, inquire as to whether or not they always fill the boat to capacity or leave a little breathing room. Bring warm clothing even if it's a warm day.

Salish Sea Charters (☎*360/378–8555 or 877/560–5711 ⊕www.salish-sea.com*) has three tours per day from April through September that get you right up next to the orcas. **San Juan Excursions** (☎*360/378–6636 or 800/809–4253 ⊕www.watchwhales.com*) offers daily whale-watching cruises. **Western Prince Cruises** (☎*360/378–5315 or 800/757–6722 ⊕www.orcawhalewatch.com*) operates a four-hour narrated whale-watching tour.

SHOPPING

Friday Harbor is the main shopping area, with dozens of shops selling a variety of art, crafts, and clothing created by residents, as well as a bounty of island-grown produce. From May to September, the **San Juan Island Farmers' Market** (✉*2nd St., Friday Harbor* ☎*360/378–5240 ⊕www.sanjuanisland.org*) fills a parking lot two blocks northwest of town on Saturday from 10 to 5.

Rainshadow Arts (✉*144 Panorama Pl., Friday Harbor* ☎*360/378–1813 ⊕www.rainshadow-arts.com*) displays Pacific Northwest arts and crafts: baskets, pottery, watercolors, sculpture, photographs, and clocks. **Waterworks Gallery** (✉*315 Spring St., Friday Harbor* ☎*360/378–3060 ⊕www.waterworksgallery.com*) represents eclectic, contemporary artists.

Near Friday Harbor, the **San Juan Vineyards** (✉*3136 Roche Harbor Rd.* ☎*360/378–9463 ⊕www.sanjuanvineyards.com*), 3 mi north of Friday Harbor, has a winery, tasting room, and gift shop, and organizes such special events as May barrel tastings, "Bottling Day" in July, volunteer grape-harvesting in October, and winter wine classes and tastings. Visit **Westcott Bay Sea Farms** (✉*904 Westcott Dr., off Roche Harbor Rd.* ☎*360/378–2489 ⊕www.westcottbay.com*), a rustic oyster farm tucked into a small bay 2 mi south of Roche Harbor, for some of the tasty oysters, especially from November through April.

7

SAN JUAN ISLANDS ESSENTIALS

To research prices, get advice from other travelers, and book travel arrangements, visit www.fodors.com.

BY AIR

Port of Friday Harbor is the main San Juan Islands airport, although there are also small airports on Lopez, Shaw, and Orcas islands. Seaplanes land on the waterfront at Friday Harbor and Roche Harbor on San Juan Island, Rosario Resort and West Sound on Orcas Island, and Fisherman Bay on Lopez Island. San Juan Islands flights are linked with mainland airports at Anacortes, Bellingham, Port Angeles, and Seattle-Tacoma International Airport.

The small propeller jets and seaplanes of Island Air and San Juan Airlines hop among the San Juans. Kenmore Air has seaplane flights from Seattle to all the main islands. Northwest Seaplanes has service from Renton, south of Seattle, to San Juan, Orcas, and Lopez. Sound Flight also connects the islands with Renton. All airlines have charter and sightseeing flights.

Island Air (☎ 360/378–2376 ⊕ www.sanjuan-islandair.com). **Kenmore Air** (☎ 425/486–1257 or 866/435–9524 ⊕ www.kenmoreair.com). **Northwest Seaplanes** (☎ 425/277–1590 ⊕ www.nwseaplanes.com). **San Juan Airlines** (☎ 800/690–0086 ⊕ www.sanjuanairlines.com). **Sound Flight** (☎ 425/254–8063 or 866/921–3474 ⊕ www.soundflight.net).

BY BOAT & FERRY

Washington State ferries depart from Anacortes, about 76 mi north of Seattle, to the San Juan Islands. The drive to Anacortes takes about 1½ hours. Sunny weekends and summer months mean long lines of cars at ferry terminals all around the San Juan Islands. No reservations are accepted (except for the Sidney–Anacortes run from mid-May through September). Passengers and bicycles load first, and loading stops two minutes before sailing time. For walk-on passengers, it's $13.15 from Anacortes to any point in the San Juan Islands. From Anacortes, vehicle and driver fares to the San Juans are $32–$36 to Lopez Island, $38–$43 to Orcas and Shaw islands, $46–$51 to Friday Harbor.

Clipper Navigation operates the passenger-only *Victoria Clipper* jet catamaran service between Pier 69 in Seattle and Friday Harbor. Boats leave daily in season at 7:45 AM; reservations are strongly recommended. The journey costs $42–$47 one way. The *San Juan Island Commuter* has daily scheduled service in season to Orcas Island and Friday Harbor, as well as Lopez Island and a few other smaller islands. Ferries depart at 9:30 AM from the Bellingham Cruise Terminal (about 1½ hours by car from Seattle). One-way fares start at $49.50. The ferry also carries kayaks, bicycles, and camping equipment.

Boat & Ferry Information **Clipper Navigation** (☎ 250/382–8100 in Victoria, 206/448–5000 in Seattle, 800/888–2535 in the U.S. ⊕ www.victoriaclipper.com). **San Juan Island Commuter** (✉ Bellingham Cruise Terminal, 355 Harris Ave., No. 104, Bellingham ☎ 360/738–8099 or 888/443–4552 ⊕ www.whales.com). **Washington State Ferries** (☎ 206/464–6400, 888/808–7977, 800/843–3779 automated line in WA and BC ⊕ www.wsdot.wa.gov/ferries).

BY BUS

On San Juan Island, San Juan Transit & Tours operates shuttle buses from mid-May to mid-September. Hop on at Friday Harbor, the main town, to get to all the island's significant points and parks, including the San Juan Vineyards, Pelindaba Lavender Farm, Lime Kiln Point State Park, and Snug and Roche harbor resorts. Tickets are $5 one-way, $8 round-trip, or $15 for a day pass.

Info **San Juan Transit & Tours** (☎ 360/378–8887 ⊕ http://sanjuantransit.com).

BY CAR

To reach the San Juan Islands from Seattle, drive north on I–5 to Exit 230. From here, head west on Route 20 and follow signs to the ferry terminal in Anacortes. You may have to wait in long lines to take your car on the ferry. You can avoid the lines by leaving your car on the mainland and arranging for pickup service at the island ferry terminal. Most B&B owners provide this service with prior arrangement.

Island roads have one or two lanes, and all carry two-way traffic. Slow down and hug the shoulder when passing another car on a one-lane road. Expect rough patches, potholes, fallen branches, wildlife, and other hazards—plus the distractions of sweeping water views. Be on the lookout for deer and rabbits. Carry food and water, since you may want to stop frequently to explore.

There are few car rental agencies on the islands. Angie's is the only office on Lopez. M&W is the only agency on Orcas, and they also have an office on San Juan. Susie's Mopeds rents cars and mopeds on San Juan. Summer rates for rentals run $50–$70 per day.

Info **Angie's Cab Courier** (☎ *360/468–2227*). **M&W Rental Cars** (☎ *360/376–5266 Orcas, 360/378–2886 San Juan* ⊕ *www.sanjuanauto.com*). **Susie's Mopeds** (☎ *360/376–5244 or 800/532–0087* ⊕ *www.susiesmopeds.com*).

VISITOR INFORMATION

Tourist Information **Lopez Island Chamber of Commerce** (☎ *360/468–4664* ⊕ *www.lopezisland.com*). **Orcas Island Chamber of Commerce** (☎ *360/376–2273* ⊕ *www.orcasislandchamber.com*). **San Juan Islands Visitors Bureau** (✉ *Box 98, Friday Harbor 98250* ☎ *360/468–3701 or 888/468–3701* ⊕ *www.guidetosanjuans.com*).

THE PARKS

Washington State's vast wilderness leaves the day-tripper with far too many choices. The major parks—Mt. Rainier National Park, Mt. St. Helens National Volcanic Monument, Olympic National Park, and North Cascades National Park—are all spectacular, and very different from each other.

Mt. Rainier is perhaps the most popular destination: it's close enough to Seattle to be an easy day trip; it has plenty of facilities for armchair or novice naturalists, as well as extremely challenging hikes and climbs; and the park is so beautiful that even the drive up to the visitors' center is often reward enough for the effort.

Mt. St. Helens, close to Mt. Rainier and once just as popular, is slowly regaining attention as more of its climbing routes and hiking trails reopen. Although viewing the devastation of the 1980 eruption is still a major attraction, witnessing the rebirth underway in many areas of the park is also a major reason to go. If you've seen Mt. Rainier and want something a little different, Mt. St. Helens is a feasible day trip with plenty to offer.

Mt. Rainier, however, is really only rivaled in popularity by the Olympic Peninsula. Wilderness covers much of the rugged peninsula, which is the westernmost corner of the continental United States. Its heart of craggy mountains and a 60-mi stretch of its ocean shore are

HIKING SAFETY

For tips on how to make your hiking trips safer and more comfortable, see the "Hiking 101" feature in Chapter 5.

safeguarded in Olympic National Park. Here, you'll find mythic coastline and dense rain forest, two things not immediately associated with the Seattle area. Many people plan their vacations around camping and hiking in the Olympics, partly because the area is much farther from Seattle than say, Mt. Rainier, and many of its attractions could not be seen during a day trip—unless your "day" started at dawn.

With all the fuss made about the Olympic Peninsula, the North Cascades National Park may not make it onto the radar of many visitors, which is unfortunate since the region is considered by some the most spectacular mountain scenery in the lower 48 states. The park is by no means a *hidden* gem—plenty of people visit each year—but it feels in many parts less-discovered than Mt. Rainier or the coast. If you're willing to commit to a long (though beautiful) drive, you'll hit some amazing trails about 3 hours outside of Seattle. Its hard to beat the experience of hiking in this region.

MT. RAINIER NATIONAL PARK

8

Fodor's Choice
★

Approximately 95 mi southeast of Seattle (about 2½ hours)

Rainier is so massive that its summit is often obscured by its own shoulders. When the summit *is* visible—from up-close vantage points—the views are breathtaking. The impressive volcanic peak stands at an elevation of 14,411 feet, making it the fifth highest in the lower 48 states. More than 2 million visitors a year return home with a lifelong memory of its image. Douglas fir, western hemlock, and western red cedar—some more than 1,000 years old—stand in cathedral-like groves. Dozens of thundering waterfalls are accessible from the road or by a short hike.

Rainier is an episodically active volcano, showing off every thousand years or so, and steam vents are still active at its summit. With more than two dozen major glaciers, the mountain holds the largest glacial system in the continental United States. The winter tempests that bring the snow so much resemble those of the Himalayas that Everest expeditions train here. But that's on the mountain's face above 10,000 feet; most visitors see a much-more-benign place with an unmatched spirit. Wildflower season in the meadows at and above the timberline is mid-July through August, depending on the exposure (southern earlier, northern later) and the preceding winter's snowfall. Most of the park's higher-elevation trails aren't snow-free until late June.

The major roads to Mt. Rainier National Park—Routes 410, 706 and 123—are paved and well-maintained state highways. They eventually, however, become mountain roads and wind up and down many steep slopes. Drive with caution. Vehicles hauling large loads should gear down, especially on downhill sections. Even drivers of passenger cars should take care not to overheat brakes by constant use. That said, be courteous of other drivers by trying to keep up with speed limits; nothing is more irksome to a hardcore Rainier hiker than being stuck for miles behind a swerving sedan full of tourists doing 15 mi under the speed limit. If you want to drive really slow and sightsee, pull over in turnout areas to give the cars behind you a chance to pass. Storms can cause delays at any time of year, and you can expect to encounter road-work several times if you are circumnavigating the mountain in summer. ⚠ **Major flooding in the winter of 2006 washed out many roads and trails. Though many repairs had been completed at this writing, some roads were still closed, so double check all routes.**

> ### GROVE OF THE PATRIARCHS
>
> On an island in the Ohanapecosh River, is one of Mt. Rainiers's most popular attractions, the Grove of the Patriarchs. Protected from the fires that periodically sweep the area, this small grove contains many 1,000-year-old trees. A 1½-mi loop trail heads over a small bridge through old-growth Douglas fir, cedar, and hemlock. The grove is just north of the Stevens Canyon entrance, 13 mi north of Packwood, via Route 123 and U.S. 12.

Crowds are heaviest in July, August, and September, when the parking lots often fill before noon. Weekends during this time are particularly bad—try to plan your hike for midweek if possible. The Sunrise entrance to the park is generally slightly less crowded than Paradise or Longmire, but you can expect crowds there, too. Fortunately, crowds start to thin midway through most of the more-challenging hikes and some of the valley loops can be completely deserted even if there are hundreds of people on the higher elevation hikes. During high season, campsites are reserved several months in advance, and other lodgings are reserved as much as a year ahead. Washington's rare periods of clear winter weather bring lots of residents up for cross-country skiing.

Mt. Rainier is open 24 hours a day but with limited access in winter. Gates at Nisqually (Longmire) are staffed in daylight hours year-round. Facilities at Paradise and Ohanapecosh are open daily from late May to mid-October, and Sunrise is open July to early October. Access to the park in winter is limited to the Nisqually entrance. The Jackson Memorial Visitor Center at Paradise is open on weekends and holidays in winter.

During off-hours you can buy passes at the gates from machines that accept credit and debit cards. The entrance fee is $15 per vehicle, which covers everyone in the vehicle for seven days. Motorcyclists and bicyclists pay $5 per person. Annual passes are available for $30. Climbing permits are $30 per person per climb or glacier trek. Wilderness

Lay of the Land

Mt. Rainier National Park has several different entrances, and several parking areas with visitors centers (the main ones being Longmire, Paradise, and Sunrise). Most visitors arrive at the Nisqually entrance on the southwest corner of the park—it's the closest entrance to I-5 (via Route 706) and the one that provides the most direct access to Longmire and Paradise.

You can also enter the park from the east, via Route 410. An eastern route is best to reach the Sunrise visitor

center, going through the White River entrance. Highway 123 enters the park from the southeast, and goes through the Stevens Canyon entrance and past the Ohanapecosh Visitor Center. All but Carbon River Road and Route 706 to Paradise are closed by snow in winter. Most roads open by late April or May, but exactly when is entirely dependent on the weather.

It's a long drive between visitor centers, so be certain of which one is closest to your trail before you commit to a route.

camping permits, which must be obtained for all backcountry trips, are free, but advance reservations are highly recommended and cost $20 per party.

There are public phones and restrooms at all park visitor centers (Sunrise, Ohanapecosh, and the Jackson Memorial Visitor Center at Paradise) as well as at the National Park Inn in Longmire and the Paradise Inn at Paradise. The only fully accessible trail in the park is Kautz Creek Trail, a ½-mi boardwalk that leads to a splendid view of the mountain.

VISITOR INFORMATION

Fantastic mountain views, alpine meadows crisscrossed by nature trails, a welcoming lodge and restaurant, and an excellent visitor center combine to make Paradise the first stop for most visitors to Mt. Rainier National Park. There are visitor services, a ranger station, and lodging at 5,400 feet. The **Jackson Memorial Visitor Center at Paradise** has 360-degree views of the park, information, displays, and seasonal programs. The Stevens Canyon Road from Paradise east to Ohanapecosh is truly spectacular, with close-up views of the mountain, wildflowers, and the red and yellow fall foliage of huckleberry, mountain ash, and alpine dwarf willow. ⊠ *Rte. 706, 9 mi east of Longmire* ☎ *360/569–6036* ⊕ *www.nps.gov/mora* ✉ *Free* ☉ *May–Sept., daily 7–6.*

At the **Ohanapecosh Visitors Center,** in the southeastern part of the park and south of the Grove of the Patriarchs, you can learn about the region's dense old-growth forests through interpretive displays and videos. ⊠ *Rte. 123, 11 mi north of Packwood, 1½ mi south of Stevens Canyon entrance* ☎ *360/569–6046* ☉ *Late May–Oct., daily 9–5.*

The town of Longmire, east of the Nisqually entrance, is the main southern gateway to Mt. Rainier National Park. Glass cases in the **Longmire Museum** contain plants and animals from the park, including a large, friendly looking stuffed cougar. Photographs and geographical displays provide an overview of the park's history. The visitor center, next to the museum, has some perfunctory exhibits on the surrounding forest and its inhabitants, as well as information about park activities. ⊠ *Rte. 706, 17 mi east of Ashford and 6 mi east of Nisqually entrance* ☎ *360/569–2211 Ext. 3314* 💰 *Free with park admission* ☉ *July–Labor Day, daily 9–5; Labor Day–June, daily 9–4:15.*

As you head north from the Grove of the Patriarchs you'll reach the White River and the park entrance that's named after it. At the **Sunrise Visitor Center,** to the east, you can watch the alpenglow fade from Rainier's domed summit. You can also view exhibits on this region's alpine and subalpine ecology. Nearby loop trails lead you through alpine meadows and forest to overlooks that afford broad views of the Cascades and Rainier. ⊠ *Sunrise Rd., 15 mi east of White River park entrance* ☎ *360/663–2425* ☉ *July 4–Oct. 1, daily 9–6.*

WHERE TO STAY & EAT

Many people do Mt. Rainier as a day trip from Seattle. Thanks to long hours of daylight in summer, if you get a reasonably early start (on the road by 8 or 9 AM), you'll have plenty of time to complete one of the park's longer hikes and be back in Seattle at a reasonable time. The food offered at the park's visitor centers is mediocre and overpriced—the best plan of action is to pack enough food to get you through your hike and back on the road to Seattle, where you'll find simple roadside restaurants and cheaper fast-food options.

The two national park lodges are attractive and well maintained, but unless you've made summer reservations nearly a year in advance, getting a room in peak season is a challenge. There are dozens of motels and cabin complexes near the park entrances, but most are plain, overpriced, or downright dilapidated. If you want to spend a few days in Rainier, and can't get a reservation at one of the properties listed below, camping may be your best bet.

★ $–$$ ✕🏨 **Alexander's Country Inn.** Serving guests since 1912, Alexander's offers comfortable lodging just a mile from Mt. Rainier. Antiques and fine linens lend the main building romance. Two adjacent guesthouses are also for rent. Rates include a hearty breakfast and evening wine. The cozy restaurant ($–$$; closed weekdays in winter), the best place in town for lunch or dinner, serves fresh fish and pasta dishes; the bread and the desserts are baked on the premises. Box lunches are available for picnics. ⊠ *37515 Rte. 706 E, 4 mi east of Ashford, Ashford, 98304* ☎ *360/569–2300 or 800/654–7615* ⊕ *www.alexanderscountryinn.com*

⇗12 *rooms, 2 3-bedroom houses* ⌂*In-hotel: restaurant, spa* ▭*MC, V* ⚊*BP.*

$–$$ ✕⊞ **National Park Inn.** A large stone fireplace takes pride of place in the common room of this otherwise generic country inn, the only one of the park's two lodgings that's open year-round. Such rustic details as wrought-iron lamps and antique bentwood headboards adorn the rooms. The fare in the restaurant ($–$$) here is simple American. For breakfast, don't miss the home-baked cinnamon rolls. For lunch there are hamburgers, soups, and sandwiches. Dinner entrées include maple hazelnut chicken and grilled red snapper with black bean sauce and corn relish. The inn is operated as a B&B from October through April. ✉*Longmire Visitor Complex, Rte. 706, 10 mi east of Nisqually entrance, Longmire, 98304* ☎*360/569–2275* ⊕*www.guestservices. com/rainier* ⇗*25 rooms, 18 with bath* ⌂*In-room: no a/c, no phone. In-hotel: restaurant* ▭*MC, V.*

¢–$ ✕⊞ **Paradise Inn.** With its hand-carved Alaskan cedar logs, burnished parquet floors, stone fireplaces, Indian rugs, and glorious mountain views, this 1917 inn is a sterling example of national park lodge architecture. German architect Hans Fraehnke designed the decorative woodwork. In addition to the full-service dining room, there's a small snack bar and a snug lounge. Lunches are simple and healthful: grilled salmon, salads, and the like. For dinner, you might find the signature bourbon buffalo meat loaf, Mediterranean chicken, and poached salmon with blackberry sauce. Summer sees leisurely Sunday brunches. The inn sustained heavy damage from winter storms in 2006; it is undergoing renovations and will reopen in May 2008. ✉*Rte. 706, Paradise* ⌖*c/o Mount Rainier Guest Services, Box 108, Star Rte., Ashford98304* ☎*360/569–2275* ⊕*www.guestservices.com/rainier* ⇗*127 rooms, 96 with bath* ⌂*In-room: no phone, no TV. In-hotel: restaurant, bar* ▭*MC, V* ☉*Closed Nov.–mid-May.*

¢–$ ⊞ **Inn of Packwood.** Mt. Rainier and the Cascade Mountains tower above this inn surrounded by lawns at the center of Packwood. Pine paneling and furniture lend the rooms rustic charm. You can swim in an indoor heated pool beneath skylights or picnic beneath a weeping willow. ✉*13032 Hwy. 12, Packwood, 98361* ☎*360/494–5500* ⊕*www.innofpackwood.com* ⇗*34 rooms* ⌂*In-room: kitchen (some), refrigerator (some). In-hotel: pool, spa* ▭*MC, V* ⚊*CP.*

★ ¢–$ ⊞ **Wellspring.** The accommodations here include tastefully designed log cabins, a tree house, and a room in a greenhouse. All guest quarters are individually decorated. There's a queen-size feather bed suspended by ropes beneath a skylight in the Nest Room; the Tatoosh Room has a huge stone fireplace and can house up to 10 people. Also available are a variety of spa facilities, as befits a property created by a massage therapist. ✉*54922 Kernehan Rd., Ashford, 98304* ☎*360/569–2514* ⇗*9 units* ⌂*In-room: no phone, kitchen (some), refrigerator (some), no TV. In-hotel: spa, no-smoking rooms, no elevator* ▭*MC, V.*

¢–$ ⊞ **Whittaker's Bunkhouse.** This 1912 motel once housed loggers and mill workers. In those days it was referred to as "the place to stop on the way to the top." In the early 1990s famed climber Lou Whittaker bought and renovated the facility. Today it's a comfortable hostelry, with inexpensive single bunks with shared baths as well as larger private rooms with private baths. ⊠*30205 Rte. 706 E, Ashford, 98304* ☎*360/569–2439* ⊕*www.whittakersbunkhouse.com* 🛏*20 rooms* ⚷*In-room: no phone, no TV. In-hotel: restaurant, public Wi-Fi* ⊟*AE, MC, V.*

¢ 🛏**Cowlitz River Lodge.** You can't be beat the location of this comfortable two-story family motel: it's just off the highway in Packwood, the gateway to Mt. Rainier National Park *and* the Mt. St. Helens National Volcanic Monument. A lodgelike construction and a large stone fireplace in the great room add some character—a good thing as guest rooms have standard motel furniture and bedding. ⊠*13069 U.S. 12, Packwood, 98361* ☎*360/494–4444 or 888/305–2185* ⊕*www.escapetothemountains.com* 🛏*32 rooms* ⚷*In-hotel: laundry facilities* ⊟*AE, DC, MC, V* ⫶⊙⫶*CP.*

¢ 🛏**Nisqually Lodge.** Fires in the grand stone fireplace of this lodge hotel a few miles west of Mt. Rainier National Park lend the great room warmth and cheer. Guest rooms are comfortable and have standard motel decor. ⊠*31609 State Rd., Ashford, 98304* ☎*360/569–8804* ⊕*www.escapetothemountains.com* 🛏*24 rooms* ⚷*In-hotel: laundry facilities, no-smoking rooms* ⊟*AE, MC, V* ⫶⊙⫶*CP.*

CAMPING FACILITIES

There are five drive-in campgrounds in the park—Cougar Rock, Ipsut Creek, Ohanapecosh, Sunshine Point, and White River—with almost 700 sites for tents and RVs. None of the park campgrounds has hot water or RV hookups; showers are available at Jackson Memorial Visitor Center.

For backcountry camping you must obtain a free wilderness permit at one of the visitor centers. Primitive sites are spaced at 7- or 8-mi intervals along the Wonderland Trail. A copy of *Wilderness Trip Planner: A Hiker's Guide to the Wilderness of Mount Rainier National Park*, available from any of the park's visitor centers or through the superintendent's office, is an invaluable guide if you're planning backcountry stays. Reservations are available for specific wilderness campsites, from May 1 to September 30, for $20. For more details, call the Wilderness Information Center at 360/569–4453.

The park experienced severe storms and flooding in the winter of 2006. Many backcountry sites and trails and even some of the more-accessible campgrounds were damaged. Be sure to double-check your options with park officials. As of this writing, Sunshine Point was closed indefinitely and Ipsut Creek was walk-in only because of road closures.

⚠**Cougar Rock Campground.** This secluded, heavily wooded campground with an amphitheater is one of the first to fill up. Reservations are accepted for summer only. ⊠*2½ mi north of Longmire* ☎*800/365–2267 or 301/722–1257* ⊕*reservations.nps.gov* 🛏*173 sites* ⚷*Flush toilets, dump station, drinking water, fire grates, ranger station* ⊙*Closed mid-Oct.–late May.*

⚠**Ipsut Creek Campground.** The quietest park campground is also the most difficult to reach. It's in the park's northwest corner, amid a wet, green, and rugged wilderness; many self-guided trails are nearby. The campground is theoretically open year-round, though the gravel Carbon River Road that leads to it is subject to flooding and potential closure at any time. Reservations aren't accepted here. ⊠ *Carbon River Rd., 4 mi east of Carbon River entrance* ☎ *360/569–2211* ⤴ *31 sites* ⚲ *Pit toilets, running water (non-potable), fire grates.*

⚲ **La Wis Wis Campground.** Alongside a small creek in Gifford Pinchot National Forest, this forest service campground is a few miles from the Ohanapecosh gateway to Rainier. ⊠ *Off Rte. 12, 7 mi northeast of Packwood then ½ mi west on Forest Service Rd. 1272* ☎ *360/494–5515* ⤴ *100 sites* ⚲ *Drinking water, picnic tables* ▤ *No credit cards* ☾ *Closed Oct.–Apr.*

⚲ **Mowich Lake Campground.** This is Rainier's only lakeside campground. It's at 4,959 feet and is, by national park standards, peaceful and secluded. It's accessible only by 5 mi of convoluted gravel roads, which are subject to weather damage and potential closure at any time. Reservations not accepted. ⊠ *Mowich Lake Rd., 6 mi east of park boundary* ☎ *360/568–2211* ⤴ *30 sites* ⚲ *Pit toilets, running water (non-potable), fire grates, picnic tables, ranger station* ☾ *Closed Nov.–mid July.*

⚲ **Ohanapecosh Campground.** In the park's southeast corner, this lush, green campground has a visitor center, amphitheater, and self-guided trail. It's one of the first campgrounds to open. Reservations are accepted for summer only. Several sites were washed out by flooding in winter 2006, but the campground is open. ⊠ *Ohanapecosh Visitor Center, Rte. 123, 1½ mi north of park boundary* ☎ *800/365–2267 or 301/722–1257* ⊕ *reservations.nps.gov* ⤴ *189 sites* ⚲ *Flush toilets, dump station, drinking water, fire grates, ranger station* ☾ *Closed late Oct.–May.*

⚲ **White River Campground.** At an elevation of 4,400 feet, White River is one of the park's highest and least wooded campgrounds. Here you can enjoy campfire programs, self-guided trails, and partial views of Mt. Rainier's summit. Reservations not accepted. ⊠ *5 mi past White River entrance* ☎ *360/569–2211* ⤴ *112 sites* ⚲ *Flush toilets, drinking water, fire grates, ranger station* ☾ *Closed mid-Sept.–late June.*

SPORTS & THE OUTDOORS

HIKING It's almost impossible to experience the blissful beauty of the alpine environment or the hushed serenity of the old-growth forest without getting out of your car and walking. The numerous trails in and around Mt. Rainier range from low-key one-hour nature strolls to the legendary Wonderland Trail, which circles the mountain and takes two weeks to complete. Although the mountain seems benign on calm summer days, each year dozens of hikers and trekkers lose their way and must be rescued. Weather that approaches cyclonic levels can appear quite suddenly, any month of the year. With the possible exception of the short loop hikes listed below, you should carry day packs with warm clothing, plenty of water, food, and other emergency supplies on all treks.

Nisqually Vista Trail. This gradually sloping, 1¼-mi round-trip trail is popular with hikers in summer and cross-country skiers in winter. It heads out through subalpine meadows to point overlooking Nisqually Glacier. In summer, listen for the shrill alarm calls of the area's marmots. ⊠*Jackson Memorial Visitor Center, Rte. 123, 1 mi north of Ohanapecosh, at the high point of Rte. 706.*

Skyline Trail. This 5-mi loop, one of the park's highest, beckons daytrippers with a cinemagraphic vista of alpine ridges and, in summer, meadows filled with brilliant flowers and birds. At 6,800 feet, Panorama Point, the spine of the Cascade Range, spreads away to the east, and Nisqually Glacier grumbles its way downslope. ⊠*Jackson Memorial Visitor Center, Rte. 123, 1 mi north of Ohanapecosh at the high point of Rte. 706.*

Sourdough Ridge Self-Guiding Trail. The mile-long loop of this easy trail takes you through the delicate subalpine meadows. A gradual climb to the ridgetop yields magnificent views of Mt. Rainier and the more-distant volcanic cones of Mounts Baker, Adams, Glacier, and Hood. ⊠*Sunrise Visitor Center, Sunrise Rd., 15 mi from White River park entrance.*

Trail of the Shadows. This ½-mi trek is notable for its glimpses of meadowland ecology, its colorful soda springs (don't drink the water), James Longmire's old homestead cabin, and the foundation of the old Longmire Springs Hotel, which was destroyed around 1900. ⊠*Rte. 706, 10 mi east of Nisqually entrance.*

Van Trump Park Trail. You gain an exhilarating 2,200 feet while hiking through a vast expanse of meadow with views of southern Puget Sound. The 5-mi trail provides good footing, and the average hiker can make it up in three to four hours. ⊠*Rte. 706 at Christine Falls, 4.4 mi east of Longmire.*

★ **Wonderland Trail.** All other Mt. Rainier hikes pale in comparison to this stunning 93-mi hike, which completely encircles the mountain. The trail passes through everything from the old-growth forests of the lowlands to the wildflower-studded alpine meadows of the highlands. Be sure to pick up a mountain goat sighting card from a ranger station or information center to help in the park's ongoing effort to learn more about the park's goat population. Wonderland is a rugged trail; elevation gains and losses totaling 3,500 feet are common in a day's hike, which averages 8 mi. Most hikers start out from either Longmire or Sunrise and take 10–14 days to cover the 93-mi route. Wilderness permits are required and reservations are strongly recommended. ⊠*Longmire Wilderness Information Center, Rte. 706, 17 mi from Ashford; Sunrise Visitor Center, Sunrise Rd., 15 mi from White River park entrance.*

MOUNTAIN CLIMBING   Climbing Mt. Rainier is not for amateurs. Near-catastrophic weather can occur quite suddenly at any time of the year. That said, if you're experienced in technical, high-elevation snow, rock, and ice-field adventuring, climbing Mt. Rainier can be memorable. Experienced climbers can fill out a self-registration climbing card at the Longmire, Paradise, White River, or Carbon River ranger stations and lead their own groups of two or more. In winter, the Paradise Climbing Ranger Station has self-registration available 24 hours a day, seven days a week. You must register with a ranger before leaving and check out upon return.

There's a $30 annual climbing fee no matter how many climbs are made per year. This applies to anyone venturing above 10,000 feet or onto one of Rainier's glaciers.

Rainier Mountaineering Inc., a highly regarded concessionaire, cofounded by Himalayan adventurer Lou Whittaker, makes climbing the Queen of the Cascades an adventure open to anyone in good health and physical condition. The company teaches the fundamentals of mountaineering at one-day classes held during climbing season, from late May through early September. Participants are evaluated on their fitness for the climb; they must be able to withstand a 16-mi round-trip with a 9,000-foot gain in elevation. Winter ski programs are also offered. Costs run $100–$200 for the guide's Glacier Hike, one-day climbing school, and crevasse rescue school. The three-day summit climb package is $805, including classes. ⊠*Jackson Memorial Visitor Center, Rte. 123, 1 mi north of Ohanapecosh, at the high point of Rte. 706* ☎*360/569–2227 or 888/892–5462* ⊕*www.rmiguides.com.*

SKIING **Crystal Mountain Ski Area.** The state's biggest and best known area is
★ ♿ open in summer for chairlift rides ($15) that afford sensational views of Rainier and the Cascades. In winter, daily lift rates are $53. Crystal Mountain has 1,300 acres of serviced lift area and 1,000 acres of backcountry. ⊠*Crystal Mountain Blvd. off Rte. 410, Crystal Mountain* ☎*360/663–2265* ⊕*www.crystalmt.com* ♥*June–Sept. (summer chairlift), daily 10–4; mid-Nov.–Apr., weekdays 9–4, weekends 8:30–4.*

Longmire Ski Touring Center. Longmire, which is adjacent to the National Park Inn, rents cross-country ski equipment and provides lessons from mid-December through Easter, depending on snow conditions. A set of skis, poles, and boots is $15 per day. Snowshoe rental is $12 per day. Lessons range from $16 for a two-hour group lesson to $20 for a four-hour guided tour. ⊠*Rte. 706, 10 mi east of Nisqually entrance, Longmire* ☎*360/569–2411, 360–569–2271 midweek* ♥*Thanksgiving–Easter, daily 9–5.*

♿ **Paradise Ski Area.** Here you can cross-country ski or, in the Snowplay Area north of the upper parking lot at Paradise, sled using inner tubes and soft platters from December to April. Check with rangers for any restrictions that may apply. Ranger-led snowshoe walks are held from here and several cross-country ski trails, from novice to advanced, lead from Paradise. ⊠*Accessible from Nisqually entrance at park's southwest corner and from Stevens Canyon entrance at park's southeast corner (summer only)* ☎*360/569–2211* ⊕*www.nps.gov/mora* ♥*May–mid-Oct., daily sunrise–sunset; mid-Oct.–Apr., weekend sunrise–sunset.*

♿ **White Pass Village.** This ski area has 54 privately owned condominiums and is about 10 mi east of the Stevens Canyon entrance. White Pass summit is about 6,000 feet. There are 18 trails, including a Nordic network. A beginner lift allows novice skiers to stand for the 70-foot ride up the hill. An all-day lift ticket is $43. ⊠*On U.S. 12* ☎*509/672–3101* ⊕*www.skiwhitepass.com* ♥*Nov.–Apr., daily 8:45 AM–4 PM; night skiing Jan. and Feb., weekends 4 PM–10 PM.*

CLOSE UP

Two Scenic Drives

Most people travel to Mt. St. Helens via the Spirit Lake Memorial Highway (Route 504), whose predecessor was destroyed in a matter of minutes in 1980. This highway has unparalleled views of the mountain and the Toutle River valley. However, from the town of Randle (midway between Mt. Rainier and Mt. St. Helens), forest service roads run through national forest land to the east side of Mt. St. Helens and the Windy Ridge Viewpoint, the best place from which to observe the destruction wrought by the eruption and the dramatic renewal of the natural landscape. To reach Randle from Seattle, take I–5 to Highway 12; at Randle head south on Forest Service road 25. Turn onto Forest Service road 99 and follow it until you reach the Windy Ridge parking area. Note that heading to Windy Ridge will add at least a half hour on to your driving time from Seattle.

MT. ST. HELENS

❾ *Approximately 155 mi southeast of Seattle (about 3 hours)*

It was once a premier camping destination, with a Mt. Fuji–like cone and pristine forest. But the May 18, 1980, eruption blew off its top and stripped its slopes of forest. The 8,365-foot-high mountain, formerly 9,665 feet high, is one of a string of volcanic Cascade Range peaks that runs from British Columbia's Mt. Garibaldi south to California's Mt. Lassen.

The mountain has recently been reopened to climbers after activity, including a 36,000-foot plume of steam and ash, closed it to climbs in early 2005. Most people come to the park to explore the numerous hiking trails that offer views of the mountain, and scenes of devastation and renewal.

The U.S. Forest Service operates the Mt. St. Helens National Volcanic Monument. The user fee is $3 per day per visitor center within the monument or $6 per day for a multicenter pass. Monument passes are available at visitor centers, Ape's Headquarters, and Cascade Peaks Restaurant and Gift Shop on Forest Road 99. You'll also need a Northwest Forest Pass to park at trailheads, visitor centers, and other forest facilities. The pass costs $5 per vehicle per day.

Route 504 is the main road through the Mt. St. Helens National Volcanic Monument. The Castle Rock Exit (No. 49) of I–5 is just outside the monument's western entrance. Follow 504 into the park. You can access the park from the north by taking Forest Service Road 25 south from U.S. 12 at the town of Randle. Forest Service Road 25 connects with Forest Service Road 90, which heads north from the town of Cougar. The two forest service roads are closed by snow in winter.

VISITOR INFORMATION

For information on park attractions and road and trail conditions, check out the U.S. Forest Service's Mt. St. Helens Web site www.fs.fed.us/gpnf/mshnvm.

On the east side of the mountain are two bare-bones visitor centers, Windy Ridge and Ape Cave. On the south side of the mountain there's a center at Lava Canyon. The three centers along Route 504 on the forest's west side—Mt. St. Helens Visitor Center (at Silver Lake), Coldwater Ridge Visitor Center Complex, and Johnston Ridge Observatory—are open daily in summer. Johnston Ridge closes from October until May; the other centers remain open daily. Silver Lake has hours from 9 to 6, and Coldwater and Johnson Ridge operate from 10 to 6; hours may be slightly different in winter.

Castle Rock's location on I–5 at the Spirit Lake Highway makes it a major point of entry for the Mt. St. Helens National Monument. The site takes its name from a tree-covered knob that once stood on the banks of the Cowlitz River and served as a navigational landmark for Hudson's Bay Company trappers and traders. The landscape changed dramatically when the 1980 eruption filled the Toutle and Cowlitz rivers with hot volcanic mush. A local **visitor center** (⊠ *Hwy. 504, Castle Rock* ☎ *360/274–2100*) has an exhibit hall portraying the history of Castle Rock and Mt. St. Helens. *The Eruption of Mount St. Helens*, a 30-minute giant-screen film, plays every 45 minutes from 9 AM to 6 PM at the **Cinedome Theater** (⊠ *Exit 49 off I–5, Castle Rock* ☎ *360/274– 9844*). Admission is $6.

The **Mt. St. Helens Visitors Center** (⊠ *Rte. 504, 5 mi east of I–5, Silver Lake* ☎ *360/274–2100*) doesn't have great views of the mountain, but it has exhibits documenting the eruption and a walk-through volcano.

★ ☺ **Weyerhauser/Hoffstadt Bluff Visitors Center** (⊠ *Rte. 504, 27 mi east of I–5* ☎ *360/274–7750*) has picnic areas; a helicopter-tour operator; hiking trails; and the Memorial Grove, which honors the 57 people who lost their lives during the 1980 eruption. Admission is free. ■TIP➔ **Weyerhauser also has the only full-service restaurant along Route 504.**

Exhibits at the **Coldwater Ridge Visitors Center** (⊠ *Rte. 504, 43 mi east of I–5* ☎ *360/274–2131*) document the great blast and its effects on the surrounding 150,000 acres—which were devastated but are going through a remarkable recovery. The center has a small concession area, and a ¼-mi trail that leads to Coldwater Lake.

★ ☺ The **Johnston Ridge Observatory** (⊠ *Rte. 504, 53 mi east of I–5* ☎ *360/274–2140*) in the heart of the blast zone has spectacular views of the crater and lava dome. Exhibits here interpret the geology of Mt. St. Helens and explain how scientists monitor an active volcano.

SPORTS & THE OUTDOORS

CLIMBING   Climbing is limited to the south side of the mountain. The most popular route delivers you to the crater's rim. Though this climb is not as technical as Mt. Rainier, making it more accessible to a wider range of visitors, climbers should be in good shape and be comfortable with traversing rugged terrain and rock scrambles. A round-trip climb takes a minimum of seven hours.

Permits (good for one day only) are required year-round. From November to March permits are free and can be obtained at any time at the

Climber's Register (✉ *Outside Jack's Restaurant, 13411 Lewis River Rd., Ariel* ☎ *360/231–4276*). Permits for high season, from April to October must be purchased in advance and cost $22 per person. Permits are only sold online through the **Mt. St. Helens Institute** (⊕ www.mshinstitute.org). The Web site also has a good FAQ about climbing the mountain.

HIKING

Mt. St. Helens also has plenty of beautiful trails—more than 200 miles worth—that require less of a commitment than climbing the crater. Below are a few of the most popular trails; for a full list of options, check out the Mount St. Helens National Volcano Monument Trail guide, which can be downloaded from the park's Web site or purchased from the park's visitor centers and at other select Forest Service offices.

⚠ **At this writing some roads and trails were closed for maintenance; double-check all routes before setting out.**

★ **Ape Cave.** Ape Cave is the longest continuous lava tube in the continental United States, and one of the park's outstanding attractions. Two routes traverse the tube: the lower route is an easy hour-long hike, while the upper route is challenging (expect uneven ground and some scrambles) and takes about three hours. Be sure to bring your own light source and warm clothing—temperatures in the cave don't rise above the mid-40s. In high-season ranger-led walks are sometimes available; inquire at the headquarters. There are several above-ground trails in the area, including the Trail of Two Forests, which includes easy walks to see the remains of a lava-ravaged ancient forest and an optional 45-foot "crawl" through a tree mold. ✛ *Headquarters: From I–5 head east on Hwy. 503 and Forest Service road 90. Turn left on Forest Service road 83, then left again onto Forest Service road 8303 and follow that road to the parking lot.*

Lava Canyon. During the 1980 eruption Lava Canyon was engulfed in a tremendous mudflow. Today evidence of the destruction is overshadowed by new growth and the many waterfalls of the Muddy River, which is no longer that muddy. The level of difficulty varies: the upper part of the trail is an easy ½-mile walk that includes a boardwalk; the middle and lower sections of the trail can be slippery and include crossing a suspension bridge and climbing a ladder. ✛ *Trailhead: From I–5 head east on Hwy. 503 and Forest Service road 90. Turn left on Forest Service road 83 and go 12 mi (trailhead is 1 mi beyond Lahar Viewpoint).*

Truman Trail 207. This moderately challenging 5.7-mile trail gives you a good view of the devastation caused by the 1980 eruption, along with views of Spirit Lake, Mt. Margaret, and, of course, the crater. New growth can be seen as well, and in summer you'll spy wildflower patches. Note that Truman ends at the junction with Boundary Trail 1, another very popular (though more difficult) trail, so if you can continue on if you haven't had your fill. The Truman Trail takes about four hours round-trip. ✛ *Trailhead: Access from the Windy Ridge Viewpoint. From I–5 take Hwy. 12 east to Forest Service road 99 and follow it to the parking area.*

OLYMPIC NATIONAL PARK

10 *Port Angeles: 84 mi (2½ hours) northwest of Seattle. Forks: 141 mi (4 hours) northwest of Seattle. Lake Quinault: 156 mi (3½ hours) southwest of Seattle.*

One of the largest, most remote, and least developed protected areas in the United States, Olympic National Park preserves 922,651 acres of the peninsula's magnificent mountainous interior and wave-stung shoreline. In the center rises a crown of glacier-topped peaks, almost as difficult to traverse now as it was a century ago.

Olympic's most popular panoramas, such as the view from atop Hurricane Ridge north to Vancouver Island, or the seascape at Ruby Beach, are best viewed during the clear-sky, sunny months of July, August, and September. Misty, rain-splashed days, however, add indelible atmosphere to the rain-forest valleys and the Pacific coastline, and they are truer representations of the area's character, even if they obscure distant views. Rain is possible any time of year, but it's most common from November through April.

U.S. 101 encircles most of the park's interior, although many of the best trails are accessed via winding Forest Service roads that branch inward toward the mountains and outward toward the beaches.

The park's six entrances are open 24 hours year-round, and most gate stations are staffed daily from 9 to 4. The vehicle admission fee is $15, which gives you a pass good for seven days at any park entrance. Parking at Ozette, the trailhead for one of the park's most popular hikes, is $1 per day. June through September are peak months, when the park receives 75% of its annual visitors. Its most popular sites, such as Hurricane Ridge, can approach capacity by 10 AM. But don't let that scare you away—there are so many remote trails that with the help of a good hiking book, you can still find uncrowded routes and plenty of serenity. May and October are much less crowded and have generally favorable weather, though you'll need warm clothing, including a hat and gloves, to hike during those months. Winter brings persistent cloudiness, frequent rain, and chilly temperatures; crowds are almost nonexistent from Thanksgiving to Easter. When it snows, the slopes draw skiers and snowshoers, although Hurricane Ridge Road is closed from Monday to Thursday, November through March.

WHAT TO SEE

Lake Crescent. Almost everyone who visits the park sees Lake Crescent, as U.S. 101 winds along its southern shore, giving way to gorgeous views of azure waters rippling in a basin formed by Tuscan-like hills. In the evening, low bands of clouds caught between the surrounding mountains often linger over its reflective surface. Along the lake's 12-mi perimeter are campgrounds, resorts, trails, and places to canoe and fish. ⌧*U.S. 101, 16 mi west of Port Angeles and 28 mi east of Forks* ☎*360/928–3380.*

The Sol Duc Valley is one of those magical, serene places where all the Northwest's virtues seem at hand—lush lowland forest, a sparkling river, salmon runs, and quiet hiking trails. Native Americans dipped into the soothing waters of **Sol Duc Hot Springs** for generations. Today, visitors come from all areas to soak in the three hot mineral pools, ranging in temperature from 98°F to 104°F, which are part of Sol Duc Hot Springs Resort. The resort, built in 1910, has simple cabins for overnight visitors, plus a restaurant and hamburger stand. You need not patronize the resort to use the hot springs. The most popular hike is the Sol Duc Trail, which goes up to the Sol Duc Falls; the main trailhead is at the end of Sol Duc River Road. ⊠*Soleduck Rd. on Lake Crescent, 12 mi south of Fairholm* ☎*360/327–3583 or 888/476–5382* ⊕*www.visitsolduc. com* ⚟*$10 for springs* ☉*Apr.– mid-May and Oct., daily 9–5; mid-May–Sept., daily 9–9.*

> ### OVERNIGHTING IN THE OLYMPICS
>
> The Olympics and camping were made for each other, but if you'd rather not rough it under the stars, head north to Port Angeles, the Olympic Peninsula's largest town, which has sophisticaled restaurants and hotels; however, visiting the coast and the interior of the park will still require quite a bit of driving. Another option is Lake Quinault on the southern tip of the park. It has only a few lodgings and feels remote, but it's more convenient to the coastline than Port Angeles. In between the two are a smattering of lodges and motels.

Lake Ozette, the third-largest glacial impoundment in Washington, anchors the coastal strip of Olympic National Park at its north end. The small town of Ozette, home of a coastal tribe, is the trailhead for two of the park's better one-day hikes. Three-mile trails lead over boardwalks through swampy wetland and coastal old-growth forest to the ocean shore and uncrowded beach. The northernmost trail reaches shore at Cape Alava, westernmost point in the continental United States. Wet weather makes the boardwalks slippery, so watch your step. ⊠*At end of Hoko-Ozette Rd., 26 mi southwest of Rte. 112 near Sekiu* ☎*360/963–2725.*

★ An 18-mi spur road winds from U.S. 101 to the **Hoh River Rain Forest,** where spruce and hemlock trees soar to heights of more than 200 feet. Alders and big-leaf maples are so densely covered with mosses they look more like shaggy prehistoric animals than trees. Look for elk browsing in shaded glens. And be prepared for rain: the region receives 140 inches or more a year (that's 12 feet and up). The Hoh Visitor Center, near the campground and the trailheads, has maps and information. The 18-mi Hoh River Trail, one of the most popular in the park, follows the Hoh River to the base of Mt. Olympus, which rises 7,965 feet above the forest floor. Two other much shorter trails lead through the forestland around the visitor center. Naturalist-led campfire programs and walks are conducted almost daily in July and August. ⊠*From U.S. 101 (about 20 mi north of Kalaloch) take Upper Hoh Rd. 18 mi east to Hoh Rain Forest Visitor Center* ☎*360/374–6925.*

Lake Quinault, 4½ mi long and 300 feet deep, is partly in Olympic National Park, partly in Olympic National Forest, and partly on the

7

Quinault reservation. The glimmering lake is the first landmark you reach when driving the west-side loop of U.S. 101. The rain forest is at its densest and wettest here, with moss-draped maples and alders, and towering spruces, firs, and hemlocks. Enchanted Valley, high up near the Quinault River's source, is a deeply glaciated valley that's closer to the Hood Canal than to the Pacific Ocean. A scenic loop drive circles the lake and travels around a section of the Quinault River. There are several short hikes in the surrounding woods and the lake is a terrific place to kayak—the water is clear and usually calm and you get a view of a few craggy peaks of the Olympics. Quinault Lodge is on the southeast side of the lake, while several public and private campgrounds border the northwest side. ⊠ *U.S. 101, 38 mi north of Hoquiam* ☎ *360/288–2444* ☯ *Ranger station May–Sept., daily 8–5.*

VISITOR INFORMATION

At the **Olympic National Park Visitor Center**, park rangers provide advice on where to go and how to maximize your time, as well as information on campgrounds, wildlife movement in the park, programs, weather forecasts, and almost anything else you might want to know. You can pick up free road and trail maps, information pamphlets, and the park's newspaper, the *Bugler*, as well as buy books, postcards, and souvenirs. Ranger talks, guest programs, children's events, and other activities are scheduled throughout the year. ⊠ *600 E. Park Ave., Port Angeles, 98362* ☎ *360/565–3130, 360/565–3131 24-hour road and weather information* ⊕ *www.nps.gov/olym* ☯ *May–Sept. daily 9–5; Oct.–Apr., Thurs.–Mon. 10–4.*

The park's premier scenic drive is from the Port Angeles visitor center to **Hurricane Ridge**. The road climbs steeply to 5,242 feet, from the thick fir forest in the foothills to alpine meadow at the top of the ridge. As you drive upward, you may notice marmots and goats ambling along the roadsides. Meanwhile, ever-larger panoramas reveal spectacular views on all sides. From the Hurricane Ridge visitor center at the top, you can see the heart of the mountains to the south and Canada to the north, across the Strait of Juan de Fuca. Trails on Hurricane Ridge take you through alpine meadows covered with wildflowers in spring and summer. In winter, the area has miles of cross-country ski and snowshoeing routes, and even a modest downhill-ski operation. ⊠ *Hurricane Ridge Rd., 17 mi south of Port Angeles* ☎ *360/565–3130, 360/452–0329 for snow conditions* ☯ *Visitor center daily 9–4.*

WHERE TO STAY & EAT

Port Angeles has some lovely cafés and restaurants. Elsewhere near the park, you'll have to settle for simpler fare and fast food, though you'll be able to find grocery stores in which to pick up picnic supplies. Note that there are some long stretches of Highway 101 where you'll find no facilities, so remember to keep some snacks in the car.

Both Port Angeles and Forks have a range of chain hotels and budget motels.

★ $$–$$$ ✕ **C'est Si Bon.** Far more formal and more French than is typical on the Olympic Peninsula, this first-rate restaurant stands out for its setting.

Tables cloaked in white linen are set above views of a rose garden, and ornate chandeliers illuminate European oil paintings on bold red walls. The menu—think onion soup, Cornish hen, filet mignon, and lobster tail—is written by the French expatriate owners. The wine list is superb, with French, Australian, and American choices, including Washington wines. ⊠*2300 U.S. 101 E, 4 mi east of Port Angeles* ☎*360/452–8888* ⊕*www.cestsibon-frenchcuisine.com* ⌕*Reservations essential* ⊟*AE, DC, MC, V* ⊘*Closed Mon. No lunch.*

$$–$$$ ✕**Toga's International.** The European-inspired cuisine at this classy restaurant, in a former home, melds world flavors and cooking styles with the best local ingredients. Mountain views from the dining room and patio harken images of the chef-owner's former home in Germany's Black Forest. For an unusual treat, have your meal cooked on a *Jagerstein* (hunting stone) right at your table. This is one of the few places west of Seattle where you can order cheese, meat, or seafood fondue (with a day's notice). ⊠*122 W. Lauridsen Blvd., Port Angeles* ☎*360/452–1952* ⌕*Reservations essential* ⊟*MC, V* ⊘*Closed Sun. and Mon. and Sept. and Jan.*

★ $–$$ ✕**Dupuis Restaurant.** Flower-filled gardens surround this old-time seafood spot on U.S. 101 between Port Angeles and Sequim. One of the dining rooms was a tavern in the 1920s. Close-set tables in the elegant main dining room are lighted by small chandeliers overhead. Windows frame views of the well-tended gardens. Grilled local fish, steamed crabs and oysters, seafood sautés, and a selection of Continental choices, like cheese-topped French onion soup, round out the menu. ⊠*256861 U.S. 101, Port Angeles* ☎*360/457–8033* ⊕*www. dupuisrestaurant.com* ⊟*AE, MC, V* ⊘*No lunch.*

$ ✕**Forks Coffee Shop.** This modest restaurant on the highway in downtown Forks serves terrific, home-style, classic American fare. From 5 AM onward you can dig into giant pancakes and Sol Duc scrambles (eggs, sausage, hash browns, and veggies all scrambled together). At lunch, there's a choice of soups, salads, and hot and cold sandwiches. Dinner specials come with free trips to the salad bar and may include entrées like baked ham, baby-back ribs, grilled Hood Canal oysters, and spaghetti. ⊠*U.S. 101, Forks* ☎*360/374–6769* ⊟*MC, V.*

$$–$$$ ✕▨**Kalaloch Lodge.** A two-story cedar lodge overlooking the Pacific, Kalaloch has 20 cabins and five lodge rooms with sea views. Log cabins have either fireplaces or woodstoves, knotty pine furnishings, earthtone fabrics, and kitchenettes; the ones on the waterfront also have deep couches looking seaward out of a picture window. To suit the rustic ambience, no phones or TVs are in the rooms, but there's a common area where guests gather for entertainment. The restaurant's menu ($–$$) changes seasonally, but usually includes local oysters, crab, and salmon. Dinner is served in the main dining room and in the upstairs cocktail lounge—which, like the restaurant, has unobstructed ocean views. ⊠*157151 U.S. 101* ✎*HC 80, Box 1100, Forks, 98331* ☎*360/962–2271 or 866/525–2562* ⊕*www.visitkalaloch.com* ⇦*10 rooms, 44 cabins* ⌕*In-room: no phone, kitchen, no TV. In-hotel: restaurant, bar, some pets allowed, no elevator* ⊟*AE, MC, V.*

$–$$$ ✕🏠**Lake Quinault Lodge.** On a lovely glacial lake in Olympic National Forest, this beautiful early-20th-century lodge complex is within walking distance of the lakeshore and hiking trails in the spectacular old-growth forest. A towering brick fireplace is the centerpiece of the great room, where antique wicker furnishings sit beneath ceiling beams painted with Native American designs. In the rooms, modern gadgets are traded in for old-fashioned comforts, such as claw-foot tubs and fireplaces. The lively bar is a good place to unwind after a day spent outdoors. The restaurant ($–$$) serves upscale seafood entrées like baked salmon with capers and onions. ⊠*S. Shore Rd.* ⌂*Box 7, Lake Quinault, 98575* ☎*360/288–2900 or 800/562–6672* ⊕*www. visitlakequinault.com* ⇄*92 rooms* ♿*In-room: no phone, VCR (some), no TV (some). In-hotel: restaurant, bar, pool, some pets allowed, no-smoking rooms* ☐*MC, V.*

¢–$$ ✕🏠**Lake Crescent Lodge.** Deep in the forest at the foot of Mt. Storm King, this comfortable farmhouse-style lodge, built in 1916, has a wraparound veranda and picture windows framing the lake's sapphire waters. Rooms in the rustic Roosevelt Cottage have polished wood floors, stone fireplaces, and lake views, while Tavern Cottage quarters resemble modern motel rooms. Second-floor rooms in the historic lodge, a former pub, have shared baths. The lodge's fir-paneled dining room ($–$$$) overlooks the lake, and the adjacent lounge is often crowded with campers. Seafood dishes like grilled salmon or steamed Quilcene oysters, as well as classic American fare, highlight the restaurant menu. ⊠*416 Lake Crescent Rd., Port Angeles, 98363* ☎*360/928–3211* ⊕*www.lakecrescentlodge.com* ⇄*30 motel rooms, 17 cabins, 5 lodge rooms without bath* ♿*In-room: no phone, no TV. In-hotel: restaurant, bar* ☐*AE, DC, MC, V* ⊗*Closed Nov.–Apr.*

★ $$–$$$$ 🏠**Colette's Bed & Breakfast.** A contemporary mansion curving around 10 acres of gorgeous waterfront property, this B&B offers space, service, and luxury equaled by no other property in the area. Leather sofas and chairs and a river-rock fireplace make the great front room a lovely spot to watch the water through expansive 20-foot windows. The suites—with names like Iris, Azalea, and Cedar—also overlook the water and have fireplaces, balconies, CD and DVD players, and two-person Jacuzzis. A specially made outdoor fireplace means you can enjoy the deck even in winter. Multicourse breakfasts include espresso-based drinks and fresh fruit. ⊠*339 Finn Hall Rd., 10 mi east of Port Angeles, 98362* ☎*360/457–9197 or 888/457–9777* ⊕*www.colettes. com* ⇄*5 suites* ♿*In-room: refrigerator, DVD, Wi-Fi. In-hotel: no kids under 18, no-smoking rooms, no elevator* ☐*MC, V* ⦿*BP.*

★ $–$$$ 🏠**BJ's Garden Gate.** A gingerbread-style porch fronts this waterfront Victorian home on 3 acres of landscaped grounds. Exquisitely appointed guest rooms include Victoria's Repose, which has a finely carved half-tester English oak bed and a balcony with a private two-person hot tub. All rooms have fireplaces, Jacuzzis, CD players and VCRs, plus panoramic water views. Antiques are artfully arranged throughout the living and dining rooms, which have expansive views of the strait. Gorgeous flower gardens, which have been featured in national commercials, help make this an ideal romantic getaway. ⊠*397 Monterra*

Dr., Port Angeles, 98362 ☎*360/452–2322 or 800/880–1332* ⊕*www. bjgarden.com* ↩*5 rooms* ⚒*In-room: VCR, dial-up. In-hotel: no kids, no-smoking rooms, no elevator* ▤*AE, MC, V* ⍾❙*BP.*

$–$$ 🏛**Miller Tree Inn Bed and Breakfast.** Built as a farmhouse in 1916, this pale yellow B&B is still bordered on two sides by pastures. Numerous windows make the rooms bright, cheerful places to relax amid antiques, knickknacks, and quilts. Premier rooms have king-size beds, gas fireplaces, hot tubs for two, and VCRs. A separate apartment has a private entrance and kitchenette. One parlor has a library and piano, the other has games. In summer, lemonade and cookies are served on the lawn or the wide front porch. From October through April, nearby rivers offer prime salmon and steelhead fishing. ✉*654 E. Division St., Forks, 98331* ☎*360/374–6806 or 800/943–6563* 🖷*360/374–6807* ⊕*www.millertreeinn.com* ↩*6 rooms, 1 apartment* ⚒*In-room: no a/c, no phone, kitchen, VCR (some), no TV (some). In-hotel: some pets allowed, no kids under 7, no-smoking rooms, no elevator* ▤*MC, V* ⍾❙*BP.*

$ 🏛**Tudor Inn.** This 1910 Tudor-style B&B stands behind a white picket fence in a residential neighborhood. Several gathering spots throughout the house—a piano parlor, an antiques-filled sitting room, a front porch, and a back deck—encourage mingling. Guest rooms, all with views of the water or Hurricane Ridge, have themes like Country, Wedgewood, and Oriental. Yours might have a fireplace, balcony, or claw-foot bathtub. Candlelight breakfast and afternoon tea are included. ✉*1108 S. Oak St., Port Angeles, 98362* ☎*360/452–3138 or 866/286–2224* ⊕*www.tudorinn.com* ↩*5 rooms* ⚒*In-hotel: no kids under 12, no-smoking rooms, no elevator* ▤*MC, V* ⍾❙*BP.*

¢–$ 🏛**Forks Motel.** The town's largest motel has been around since 1955, offering friendly service and pleasant, simple accommodations, from small rooms with showers to two-bedroom suites with kitchens and Jacuzzis. The well-kept pool is open from May through September. ✉*351 S. Forks Ave., Forks, 98331* ☎*360/374–6243 or 800/544–3416* 🖷*360/374–6760* ⊕*www.forksmotel.com* ↩*61 rooms, 12 suites* ⚒*In-room: no a/c (some), kitchen (some), Wi-Fi. In-hotel: pool, laundry facilities, some pets allowed, no-smoking rooms, no elevator* ▤*AE, D, DC, MC, V.*

CAMPING   Campgrounds in Olympic National Park range from primitive back-
FACILITIES   country sites to paved trailer parks with nightly naturalist programs. Each designated site usually has a picnic table and grill or fire pit, and most campgrounds have water, toilets, and garbage containers. Park campgrounds have no hookups, showers, or laundry facilities. Firewood is available from camp concessions, but if there's no store you can collect dead wood within 1 mi of your campsite. Dogs are allowed in campgrounds but not on trails or in the backcountry. Trailers should be 21 feet long or less. There's a camping limit of two weeks.

Intrepid hikers can camp virtually anywhere along the park's shoreline or in its forested areas. The required overnight wilderness-use permit costs $5, plus $2 per person per night. Passes are available at visitor centers and ranger stations. Note that when you camp in the backcountry, you must choose a site at least ½ mi inside the park boundary.

With the exception of the Kalaloch Campground, all campsites are first-come, first-served. Reservations for Kalaloch can be made online through the National Park Service's Web site, www.nps.gov.

🏕 **Altaire Campground.** This small campground sits amid an old-growth forest by the river in the narrow Elwha River valley. A popular trail leads downstream from the campground. ⊠*Elwha River Rd., 8 mi south of U.S. 101, Olympic National Park* 🕾*No phone* 🛏*30 sites* ♿*Flush toilets, drinking water, fire grates* ▤*No credit cards* ⊘*Closed Nov.–Mar..*

🏕 **Dosewallips Campground.** Popular with hikers, and hunters in fall, this small, remote campground lies beneath Mt. Constance, one of the most conspicuous peaks in the park. The campground is in old-growth forest along the river. Note that this is a hike-to site only (3½ mi) ever since Dosewallips Road washed out. ⊠*Dosewallips River Rd., 15 mi west of Brinnon, Olympic National Park* 🕾*No phone* 🛏*30 sites* ♿*Pit toilets, fire grates* ▤*MC, V* ⊘*Closed Nov.–Apr..*

🏕 **Elwha Campground.** The larger of the Elwha Valley's two campgrounds, this is one of Olympic's year-round facilities, with two campsite loops in an old-growth forest. ⊠*Elwha River Rd., 7 mi south of U.S. 101, Olympic National Park* 🕾*No phone* 🛏*41 sites* ♿*Flush toilets, drinking water, fire grates, public telephone, ranger station* ▤*MC, V.*

🏕 **Hoh Campground.** Crowds flock to this rain-forest campground under a canopy of moss-draped maples, towering spruce trees, and morning mist. ⊠*Hoh River Rd., 17 mi east of U.S. 101, Olympic National Park* 🕾*No phone* 🛏*89 sites* ♿*Flush toilets, dump station, drinking water, fire grates, public telephone, ranger station* ▤*MC, V.*

🏕 **Hoh River Resort Campground.** Spruce trees shade this all-around sportsman's hangout along the Hoh River. Fishing and hiking are nearby. ⊠*175443 U.S. 101, 20 mi south of Forks* 🕾*360/374–5566* 🛏*13 sites with hookups, 7 tent sites* ♿*Flush toilets, full hookups, drinking water, showers, picnic tables, electricity, public telephone, general store* ▤*MC, V.*

🏕 **Kalaloch Campground.** Kalaloch is the biggest and most popular Olympic campground. Its vantage of the Pacific is duplicated nowhere on the park's coastal stretch, although the campsites themselves are set back in the spruce fringe. ⊠*U.S. 101, ½ mi north of the Kalaloch Information Station, Olympic National Park* 🕾*No phone* 🛏*177 sites* ♿*Flush toilets, dump station, drinking water, fire grates, public telephone, ranger station* ▤*MC, V.*

🏕 **Lake Quinault Rain Forest Resort Village Campground.** Sprawled on the south shore of Lake Quinault, this campground has ample recreation facilities, including beaches, canoes, ball fields, and horseshoes. ⊠*S. Shore Rd., 3½ mi east of U.S. 101, Lake Quinault* 🕾*360/288–2535* 🛏*30 RV sites* ♿*Flush toilets, full hookups, drinking water, showers, picnic tables, electricity, public telephone, general store* ▤*MC, V* ⊘*Closed Nov.–Mar..*

⚿**Ozette Campground.** Hikers heading to Cape Alava, a scenic promontory that's the westernmost point in the lower 48 states, use this lakeshore campground as a jumping-off point. There's a boat launch and a small beach. ✉*Hoko-Ozette Rd., 26 mi south of Rte. 112, Olympic National Park* ☎*No phone* ⛺*15 sites* ♿*Pit toilets, fire grates, ranger station* ▭*MC, V.*

⚿ **Sol Duc Campground.** Sol Duc resembles virtually all Olympic campgrounds except for one distinguishing feature—the famed hot springs are a short walk away. The nearby Sol Duc River has several spots where visitors can watch spawning salmon work their way upstream. ✉*Sol Duc Rd., 11 mi south of U.S. 101, Olympic National Park* ☎*No phone* ⛺*80 sites* ♿*Flush toilets, dump station, drinking water, fire grates, public telephone, ranger station, swimming (hot springs)* ▭*No credit cards* ⊗*Closed Nov.–Mar..*

⚿ **South Beach Campground.** The first campground travelers reach as they enter the park's coastal stretch from the south, this is basically an overflow campground for the more-popular and better-equipped Kalaloch a few miles north. Campsites are set in the spruce fringe, just back from the beach. There is no water. ✉*2 mi south of Kalaloch information station at southern boundary of park, U.S. 101* ☎*No phone* ⛺*50 sites* ♿*Pit toilets, fire grates* ▭*No credit cards* ⊗*Closed Oct.–Apr..*

SPORTS & THE OUTDOORS

Serene **Lake Crescent,** surrounded by the Olympic mountain forests, is one of the park's most popular places to boat. Besides canoeing and kayaking, you can drive motorboats and water-ski here. Speedboats are not permitted around the designated swimming area at the west end of the lake.

Fairholm General Store (✉*U.S. 101, Fairholm* ☎*360/928–3020*) rents rowboats and canoes for $10 to $45 on Lake Crescent. The store is at the west end of the lake, 27 mi west of Port Angeles. It's open May through September, daily 9 to 6. **Lake Crescent Lodge** (✉*416 Lake Crescent Rd.* ☎*360/928–3211*) rents rowboats for $8.50 per hour and $35 per day.

Lake Quinault has boating access from a gravel ramp on the north shore. From U.S. 101, take a right on North Shore Road, another right on Hemlock Way, and a left on Lakeview Drive. There are also plank ramps at Falls Creek and Willoughby campgrounds on South Shore Drive, near the Quinault Ranger Station. Since there's only one access road to Lake Ozette, it's a good place for overnight trips. Only experienced canoe and kayak handlers should travel far from the put-in, since fierce storms occasionally strike, even in summer.

FISHING Rainbow and cutthroat trout are found in the park's streams and lakes, and salmon ply the rivers and shores. You don't need a state fishing license to fish in the park; however, anglers must acquire a salmon-steelhead punch card when fishing for those species. The Bogachiel, Hoh, Quinault, Skokomish, and Dosewallips rivers are world-famous steelhead streams. Ocean fishing and shellfish and seaweed harvesting require licenses, which are available at sporting goods and outdoor-supply stores. Fishing regulations vary throughout the park and some areas are regulated by Native American tribes; check regulations for each location.

Jim Leons Outdoor Adventures (✉*382 Elk Valley Rd., Forks* ☎*360/374–3157* ⊕*www.jimleons.com*) conducts fishing and hunting trips around the Olympic Peninsula. **Mike Schmitz Olympic Peninsula Fishing Guides** (✉*Box 2688, Forks 98331* ☎*360/364–2602 or 888/577–4656* ⊕*www.mikeschmitz.com*) runs fishing trips on the Hoh, Sol Duc, and other rivers. The **Quillayute River Guide Service** (✉*Box 71, La Push 98350* ☎*360/374–2660* ⊕*www.forks-web.com/jim*) focuses on steelhead fishing on the Quillayute and Hoh rivers.

HIKING Wilderness beaches provide the park's most unusual hiking experience: an opportunity to explore an essentially unaltered Pacific coastline. Major entry points are at La Push, Rialto Beach, and Cape Alava. Be sure to read the tide tables before starting out on beach trails. Plan your route carefully or you risk being trapped by the ocean. Park rangers and volunteers at the visitor centers can show you how to read the tide tables and warn you of any dangerous areas.

In the interior, trails embedded in forested river valleys provide perfect warm-ups for the intense climbs into alpine country. The Elwha, Dosewallips, Skokomish, Quinault, Hoh, and Sol Duc valleys all have developed trails that wend upstream, finally climbing into high passes and a glacier-rimmed alpine basin where they link up with each other.

Boulder Creek Trail. The 5-mi round-trip walk up Boulder Creek leads to the Olympic hot springs, a half dozen pools of varying temperatures; some are clothing-optional. ✉*End of Elwha River Rd., 4 mi south of Altaire Campground.*

Cape Alva Trail. Beginning at Ozette, this 3-mi trail leads from forest to wave-tossed headlands. Be careful on the often-slippery boardwalks. ✉*End of Hoko–Ozette Rd., 26 mi south of Rte. 112, west of Sekiu.*

Fodor'sChoice **Hoh Valley Trail.** Leaving from the Hoh Visitor Center, this rain forest jaunt takes you into the Hoh Valley, wending its way alongside the river, through moss-draped maple and alder trees, and past open meadows where elk roam in winter. ✉*Hoh Visitor Center, 18 mi east of U.S. 101.*

Hurricane Ridge Trail. A ¼-mi alpine loop, most of it wheelchair accessible, leads through wildflower meadows overlooking numerous vistas of the interior Olympic peaks to the south and the Strait of Juan de Fuca panorama to the north. ✉*Hurricane Ridge visitor center, Hurricane Ridge Rd., 17 mi south of Port Angeles.*

★ **Sol Duc Trail.** This easy, 1½-mi gravel path off Sol Duc Road winds through thick Douglas fir forests toward the thundering, three-chute Sol Duc Falls. Just 1/10 mi from the road, below a wooden platform over the Sol Duc River, you come across the 70-foot Salmon Cascades. In late summer and autumn, thousands of salmon negotiate 50 mi or more of treacherous waters to reach the cascades and the tamer pools near Sol Duc Hot Springs. The popular 6-mi **Lovers Lane Loop Trail** links the Sol Duc falls with the hot springs. You can continue up from the falls 5 mi to the **Appleton Pass Trail**, at 3,100 feet. From there you can hike on to the 8½-mi mark, where views at the High Divide are from 5,050 feet. ⊠*Sol Duc Rd., 11 mi south of U.S. 101.*

KAYAKING & **Olympic Raft and Kayak** (☎*360/452–1443 or 888/452–1443 ⊕www.*
RAFTING *raftandkayak.com*), based in Port Angeles, is the only rafting outfit allowed to venture into Olympic National Park. The company makes seasonal white-water rafting excursions along the Elwha River, and twice-daily trips on the Hoh River from July to September. They also organize guided kayak, canoe, and camping trips to Lake Ozette, and to Lake Aldwell and Freshwater Bay along the north coast of the Olympic Peninsula. **Rainforest Paddlers** (☎*360/374–5254 ⊕www.rainforestpaddlers.com*), in Forks, takes kayakers down the Lizard Rock and Oxbow sections of the Hoh River from May through September. **Adventures Through Kayaking** (☎*360/417–3015 ⊕www.atkayaking.com*), also in Port Angeles, runs kayaking lessons, and runs white-water river trips and lake-kayaking excursions around the island and coastal waters of the region.

Snow is most likely to fall from mid-December through late March on the Olympic Peninsula. For recorded road and weather information from November through April, call 360/565–3131. **Hurricane Ridge** is the area to head to for downhill and cross-country skiing. The most popular route for day mushers is the 1½-mi Hurricane Hill Road, west of the visitor center parking area. A marked snow-play area with trails and gentle hills has been set aside near the visitor center for cross-country skiers, snowshoers, and inner tubers. There's a weekend and holiday ski lift that runs from 10 to 4, plus two rope tows and a ski school. Cross-country trails start next to the downhill area and Hurricane Ridge Lodge. Free guided snowshoe walks take place Friday through Sunday at 2, with sign-ups at the lodge an hour beforehand. There's also a supervised tubing area, open Friday through Sunday, ¼ mi before the parking area on the right side of the road, as well as a children's tubing area across from the lodge. Ski and snowshoe rentals cost $12 to $35 at the Hurricane Ridge visitor center.

NORTH CASCADES NATIONAL PARK

⑪ *North Cascades Visitor Center in Newhalem, approximately 117 mi (2½ hrs) northwest of Seattle*

Countless snow-clad mountain spires dwarf glacial valleys and lowland, old-growth forests in North Cascades National Park. the untrammeled expanse covers 505,000 acres of rugged mountain land. Only Route 20 (North Cascades Highway) traverses the park, and it's closed by snow at Diablo Lake half the year. Furthermore, it's within the Ross Lake National Recreation Area and Okanogan National Forest and never touches the park itself, which is almost entirely roadless.

Area towns include La Connor (68 mi north of Seattle), where Morris Graves, Kenneth Callahan, and other painters set up shop in the 1940s;

Wildlife on the Trails

The best times to view wildlife are at dawn and dusk, when animals can often be spotted at forest's edge. Keep in mind that all wild animals are just that—wild—and both people and animals benefit by keeping their distance.

MT. RAINIER

You're not as likely to see Rainier's wildlife—deer, elk, black bears, coyotes, and other creatures—as often as you might at other parks. The only critters to routinely show their faces are marmots, and seeing these cute, pudgy rodents waddle along trails and sun themselves on rocks just adds to the charm of the mountain's lower trails. Squirrels are also common: Douglas' squirrels have dark reddish brown fur and appear in forested areas; golden-mantled ground squirrels look like overgrown chipmunks and are often spotted on trails. Red foxes have been spotted in the Paradise and Longmire areas.

Mountain goats can occasionally be spotted on the quiet and misty upper reaches. Columbian black-tailed deer are regular residents of the park; fawns are born in May. The bugling of bull elk on the high ridges can be heard in late September and October, especially on the park's eastern side.

More than 200 species of birds, particularly Stellar's jays and common ravens, make their home in the park. The lower reaches of the park (below 3500 feet) are home to northern spotted owls and marbled murrelets.

MT. ST. HELENS

The animal populations of Mt. St. Helens were devastated—if not completely wiped out—by the 1980 eruption. Today life has returned in the form of Roosevelt elk, black-tailed deer, and a few small mammals, such as the northern pocket gopher, the Pacific jumping mouse, and golden-mantled ground squirrels. Several bird species live here, including the common raven, mountain bluebird, white-crowned sparrow, the American robin, hairy woodpecker, and the red-breasted nuthatch.

OLYMPIC NATIONAL PARK

South and east of U.S. 101, the interior's thick forests of spruce, fir, and cedar spread out, supporting a thriving population of black bears, cougars, deer, elk, and numerous small animals. West of U.S. 101 the park claims 65 mi of wild coastline, where bald eagles, osprey, blue herons, and hawks soar the skies, and migrating whales, sea lions, sea otters, and seals swim off-shore. Even though few roads penetrate very far into the park, you can still see many of Olympic's larger wild animals by roadsides and at meadow edges at dawn and dusk. Bears are most commonly seen in May and June, and in fall when they prowl berry patches. Elk spend the summer in the high country and return to lowland valleys in autumn.

NORTH CASCADES

Grizzly bears and wolves are believed to inhabit the North Cascades, along with other endemic wildlife. Bald eagles are present year-round along the Skagit River and the various lakes. In December, they flock by the hundreds to the Skagit to feed on a rare winter salmon run, remaining through January. Black bears are often seen in spring and early summer along the road in the high country, feeding on new green growth. Deer and elk are often seen in early morning and late evening.

Mount Vernon, an attractive riverfront community 11 mi northwest of La Connor; and Sedro-Woolley, a former mill and logging town that's 9 mi northeast of Mount Vernon and is a gateway to park. ■ TIP→ **Note that you're better off making Mount Vernon or even La Connor a hub for park exploration: Sedro-Woolley's hotels and restaurants reflect the fact that the town is in something of a slump.** The park never closes, though access is limited by winter snows. Summer is peak season—and up here, summer begins in July and ends around Labor Day—especially along the alpine stretches of the North Cascades Highway. Wildflowers paint the mountain meadows, hummingbirds and songbirds pepper the forest air, and even the high ridges are pleasantly warm. Although the views are best this time of year—when the usual spate of Pacific storms moderates—valleys can still start the day shrouded in fog.

Autumn brings crisp nights and many cool, sunny days. The North Cascades Highway is a popular drive in September and October, when the changing leaves—on larch, the only conifer that sheds its leaves, as well as aspen, vine maple, huckleberry, and cottonwood—make a colorful show. Snow closes the North Cascades Highway by November, and the road doesn't fully reopen until late April.

Visitor centers—with pay phones, bathrooms, park information, nature walks, lectures, and children's programs—are found along the North Cascades Highway in Sedro-Woolley, in Marblemount, Newhalem, and Winthrop, and in Stehekin (accessible only by boat, plane, or on foot) at the head of Lake Chelan. Several trails are also accessible along this route, including Sterling Munro, River Loop, and Rock Shelter, three short trails into lowland old-growth forest, all at Mile 120 near Newhalem; and the Happy Creek Forest Trail at Mile 134. Campgrounds aside, there are no lodging facilities in the park; for a hotel or restaurant you'll have to head to a nearby town.

A free wilderness permit is required for overnight backcountry activities; you can acquire one—in person only—at the Wilderness Information Center in Marblemount or at park ranger stations.

From Sedro-Woolley, **North Cascades Highway** (Route 20) winds through the green pastures and woods of the slowly narrowing upper Skagit Valley. As the mountains close in on the river and the highway, the road climbs only imperceptibly. Skagit Valley, like other valleys of the North Cascades, was cut below sea level by the glaciers of the last ice age, some 15,000 years ago. Close to sea level, the largely flat valley floor was created when the gash was filled in with alluvial deposit carried down from the mountains by the rivers. Beyond Concrete, a former cement-manufacturing town, the road begins to climb into the mountains, to Ross and Diablo dams.

East of Ross Lake, several turnouts offer great views of the lake and the snowcapped peaks surrounding it. The whitish rocks in the road cuts are limestone and marble. Meadows along this stretch of the highway are covered with wildflowers from June to September; nearby slopes are golden and red with fall foliage from late September through October. The pinnacle point of this stretch is 5,477-foot-high Washington Pass, east of which the road drops down along Early Winters Creek to the Methow Valley in a series of dramatic switchbacks (with vista turnouts).

From the Methow Valley, Route 153 takes the scenic route down the Methow River, with its apple, nectarine, and peach orchards, to Pateros on the Columbia River. From here, you can continue east to Grand Coulee or south to Lake Chelan.

VISITOR INFORMATION

North Cascades National Park Headquarters, the major administrative center, is a good place to pick up passes and permits, as well as to obtain information about current conditions. ⊠ *810 Rte. 20, Sedro-Woolley* ☎ *360/854–5200* ⊕ *www.nps.gov/noca* ⊘ *Mid-Oct.–mid-May, weekdays 8–4:30; late May–mid-Oct., daily 8–4:30.*

The **North Cascades Institute** (NCI) offers classes, field trips, and wilderness adventures such as backpack trips to hot springs within the Cascades. Contact them for information about these events or for a comprehensive catalog of books, guides, maps, and other materials. Especially popular are hiking guides such as *Best Easy Day Hikes in the North Cascades* and *100 Hikes in the North Cascades.* ⊠ *810 Rte. 20, Sedro-Woolley* ☎ *360/856–5700 Ext. 209* ⊕ *www.ncascades.org.*

The **North Cascades Visitor Center** has an extensive series of displays on the natural features of the surrounding landscape. You can learn about the history and value of old-growth trees, the many creatures that depend on the temperate rain-forest ecology, and the effects of human activity. Park rangers frequently conduct programs; check bulletin boards for schedules. ⊠ *Rte. 20, Newhalem* ☎ *206/386–4495 Ext. 11* ⊘ *Memorial Day–Labor Day, daily 9–4:30; Labor Day–Memorial Day, weekends 9–4:30.*

WHERE TO STAY & EAT

Mount Vernon has several Best Western properties along with many other reliable chain motels.

$$–$$$ ✕ **Kerstin's.** The intimate dining room overlooks the channel. The menu, which changes seasonally, includes portobello mushrooms roasted with pesto, pan-braised fresh king salmon, pork tenderloin, rib-eye steak with Indonesian spices, halibut, and lamb shank with port wine sauce. The oysters baked in garlic-cilantro butter and finished with Parmesan are particularly popular. ⊠ *505 S. 1st St., La Conner* ☎ *360/466–9111* ⊟ *AE, DC, MC, V* ⊘ *Closed Tues.*

$ ✕ **Skagit River Brewing Company.** A former produce warehouse now houses one of western Washington's best microbreweries, along with a pub serving better-than-average food. Highlights include wood-fired pizzas, a half-pound pub burger, and a big bean burrito. Hewn-wood tables and comfortable couches make lounging inviting. There's a barbecue grill right outside, where the chef will prepare your ribs or chicken wings. ⊠ *404 S. 3rd St., Mount Vernon* ☎ *360/336–2884* ⊕ *www.skagitbrew.com* ⊟ *AE, MC, V.*

★ ¢–$ ✕**Calico Cupboard.** This storefront bakery-café turns out some of the best pastries in Skagit County. It's very popular for breakfast and lunch and can become uncomfortably crowded on summer weekends (in which case you can buy the goodies at the take-out counter for a picnic in the park). There's another branch in Mount Vernon on Freeway Drive. ⊠*720 S. 1st St., La Conner* ☎*360/466–4451* ⊕*www. calicocupboardcafe.com* ▤*MC, V* ⊘*No dinner.*

$$–$$$ ⌂**La Conner Channel Lodge.** La Conner's only waterfront hotel is an understated modern facility overlooking the narrow Swinomish Channel. Each room has a private balcony and a gas fireplace and is decorated in subdued gray tones with wooden trim; 12 rooms have whirlpool baths. ⊠*205 N. 1st St., La Conner, 98257* ☎*360/466–1500* ⊕*www.laconnerlodging.com* ⇦*29 rooms, 12 suites* ▤*AE, D, DC, MC, V* ⦿*CP.*

$–$$ ⌂**Wild Iris.** Right next to the slightly less-expensive Heron, this B&B is a large, sprawling, modern (1992) Victorian-style inn. Most of the rooms are suites, and these have CD players, robes, fireplaces, whirlpool spa tubs, and private decks or balconies. Breakfast is served in the large restaurant-style dining room. ⊠*121 Maple Ave., La Conner, 98257* ☎*360/466–1400* ⊕*www.wildiris.com* ⇦*4 rooms, 12 suites* ⌃*In-room: no a/c, DVD, dial-up. In-hotel: restaurant, public Wi-Fi, no elevator* ▤*AE, MC, V* ⦿*BP.*

¢–$$ ⌂**Heron.** This B&B, in a replica Victorian house, has a stone fireplace in the parlor. The rooms are spacious, and the homemade breads and muffins served with breakfast in the formal dining room are scrumptious. The on-site Watergrass Day Spa offers organic skin-care treatments and massage services are available there or in your room. ⊠*117 Maple Ave., La Conner, 98257* ☎*360/466–4626* ⊕*www.theheron. com* ⇦*9 rooms, 3 suites* ⌃*In-room: no a/c. In-hotel: spa, some pets allowed, no elevator* ▤*MC, V* ⦿*BP.*

CAMPING
FACILITIES

⛺**Newhalem Creek Campground.** With three loops, a small amphitheater, a playground, and a regular slate of ranger programs in summer, Newhalem Creek is the main North Cascades campground. Above the Skagit River in old-growth forest, it is adjacent to the visitor center, and close to several trails that access the river and the surrounding second-growth forest. ⌃*Flush toilets, dump station, drinking water, fire grates, picnic tables, public telephone, ranger station* ⇦*116 RV/ tent sites* ⊠*Rte. 20 along access road to park's main visitor center* ☎*360/854–7200* ⊕*www.nps.gov/noca* ▤*No credit cards* ⊘*Closed Mid-Oct.–mid-Apr.*

SPORTS & THE OUTDOORS

Cascade Pass. Perhaps the most popular park hike, this much-traveled, moderate, switchbacked, 3 2/3-mi trail leads to a divide from which dozens of peaks can be seen. The meadows here are covered with alpine wildflowers in July and early August. A Northwest Forest Pass is needed. On sunny summer weekends and holidays, the trailhead parking lot can fill up; it's best to arrive before noon. The trip up and back will take the average hiker less than four hours, but allow plenty of extra time at the summit for admiring the wildflowers and gawking at the surrounding peaks. ✛*End of Cascade River Rd., 14 mi from Marblemount.*

Rainy Pass. An easy and accessible 1-mi paved trail leads to Rainy Lake, a waterfall, and a glacier-view platform. ✛*Rte. 20, 38 mi east of visitor center at Newhalem.*

Skagit River Loop. One of the most notable hikes in the park, this 1⅘-mi handicapped-accessible trail loops through stands of huge, old-growth firs and cedars, dipping down to the Skagit River and out onto a riverside gravel bar. ✛*Near North Cascades visitor center.*

Thornton Lakes Trail. A 5-mi climb into an alpine basin with two pretty lakes, this steep and strenuous hike takes about five to six hours round-trip. Northwest Forest Pass needed. ✛*Rte. 20, 3 mi west of Newhalem.*

★ **Trail of the Cedars.** Only ½ mi long, this trail winds its way through one of the finest surviving stands of old-growth Western red cedar in Washington. Some of the trees on the path are more than 1,000 years old. ✛*Near North Cascades visitor center.*

Seattle Essentials

PLANNING TOOLS, EXPERT INSIGHT, GREAT CONTACTS

There are planners and there are those who, excuse the pun, fly by the seat of their pants. We happily place ourselves among the planners. Our writers and editors try to anticipate all the issues you may face before and during any journey, and then they do their research. This section is the product of their efforts. Use it to get excited about your trip to Seattle, to inform your travel planning, or to guide you on the road should the seat of your pants start to feel threadbare.

GETTING STARTED

We're really proud of our Web site: Fodors.com is a great place to begin any journey. Scan Travel Wire for suggested itineraries, travel deals, restaurant and hotel openings, and other up-to-the-minute info. Check out Booking to research prices and book plane tickets, hotel rooms, rental cars, and vacation packages. Head to Talk for on-the-ground pointers from travelers who frequent our message boards. You can also link to loads of other travel-related resources.

▌ RESOURCES

ONLINE TRAVEL TOOLS
The tourist boards sites will no doubt be your first stops. The home page for the Seattle Convention and Visitor's Bureau is ⊕*www.visitseattle.org*. For insight on the entire state, head to Washington State Tourism's ⊕*www.experiencewashington.com*. Information straight from the city's leaders is at ⊕*www.cityofseattle.net/html/visitor*. Forget driving. Take public transportation—including the bus, streetcar, and water taxi. This site tells you how: ⊕*transit.metrokc.gov*. OK. So you have to drive. The site ⊕*www.wsdot.wa.gov/traveler.html* will help you deal with Seattle's horrific traffic problems.

Almost every neighborhood in Seattle has its own Web site, but some are more useful than others. The Downtown Seattle Association offers the very professional-looking ⊕*www.downtownseattle.com*, with a great calendar page and a helpful "Getting Around" page with good maps. You can view Pioneer Square through rose-colored glasses at ⊕*www.pioneersquare.org*. Ignore the hard sell from the Pioneer Square Community Association—though the portrait of the neighborhood isn't entirely accurate, the site has excellent maps of the area along with detailed info on parking and on the popular monthly art walks. Ballard's surprisingly sleek ⊕*www.*

inballard.com has up-to-date listings and reviews of the neighborhood's major businesses and sights, complete with pictures of each. Navigating ⊕*www.fremont.com* requires some patience, but the calendar and listings are usually kept up to date and the "Urban Myths" section gives you the backstories on the neighborhood's iconic public art. Find out what's going on around the University of Washington by logging on to ⊕*www.udistrictchamber.org*. The site isn't terribly exciting, but it has a good collection of links and a list of merchants that validate parking. Since Capitol Hill's apparently too cool to have its own site, instead check out ⊕*www.georgetownneighborhood.com*. Georgetown will be too far off the beaten path for most folks, but any site that uses the tagline "Seattle's Fiesty, Intensely Creative Neighborhood" is worth a look. To learn more about Bellevue, a rapidly growing mini-city in the Eastside suburbs, look to ⊕*www.bellevuechamber.org*.

NWSource (www.nwsource.com), which is affiliated with the *Seattle Times,* is an easy-to-search database with information on all neighborhoods (and their businesses) in Seattle and the Eastside. It's like a local version of Citysearch—packed with information, at least half of which is up to date. To delve a little too deeply into the daily minutiae of Seattle residents, check out ⊕*www.seattlest.com*. Among the snark and obsessive commentary on local sports teams, you'll find decent restaurant reviews and the weekly "Get Out" posts, listing the best events in the city from readings at the Elliott Bay Book Company to concerts at Neumo's.

The *Seattle Post-Intelligencer* Web site (⊕ *www.seattlepi.com*) is full of breaking local and national news. The *Seattle Times* daily newspaper is one of the country's largest independently owned. Its Web site (⊕ *www.seattletimes.com*) has frequently updated local news and entertainment information. The site run by the irreverent free weekly newspaper *The Stranger* (⊕ *www.thestranger.com*) is a good place to find fun things to do—especially at night. The *Seattle Weekly* (⊕ *www.seattleweekly.com*) focuses on local political coverage and entertainment.

ALL ABOUT SEATTLE

Safety Transportation Security Administration (*TSA*; ⊕ *www.tsa.gov*).

Weather Accuweather.com (⊕ *www.accuweather.com*) is an independent weather-forecasting service with good coverage of hurricanes. **Weather.com** (⊕ *www.weather.com*) is the Web site for the Weather Channel.

VISITOR INFORMATION

The Seattle Convention and Visitor's Bureau is really pulling out all the stops these days. Not only have they coined a new cringe-worthy yet oddly appropriate tagline for Seattle—"Metronatural"—but they have rebranded their visitor center as the "Citywide Concierge Center." The service, which has an office in the Washington State Trade and Convention Center on Pike Street (between 7th and 8th avenues) can help you plan all aspects of your trip from securing events tickets to making accommodations and restaurant reservations to arranging ground transportation and other services. They're set up to accept drop-ins (open weekdays 9–1 and 2–5) and you can also contact them before your trip with questions and requests.

If you're having trouble planning a side trip out of the city, call Washington State Tourism; you can request brochures or speak with a travel planner weekdays from 8 to 5 PST.

Contacts Seattle Convention and Visitor's Bureau (☎ *206/461–5840 or 206/461–5888* ⊕ *www.visitseattle.org*). **Washington State Tourism** (☎ *800/544–1800* ⊕ *www.experiencewashington.com*).

■ THINGS TO CONSIDER

GEAR

Summer days in Seattle are often sunny and warm (and sometimes very hot), however, to be ever prepared for the cool, overcast day or odd rain shower, Seattleites have become masters of the art of layering. So, bring the shorts and T-shirts but also bring a light jacket and sweater or fleece, and long pants. If you're visiting in fall or winter, you'll need rain gear, too, and a real winter coat. Seattle is known for its mild if drizzly winters, but the city does experience cold snaps in December and January. Comfortable walking shoes are a must in any season.

Dining out is usually an informal affair, and even fancier restaurants rarely require a jacket and tie. That doesn't mean you won't feel more comfortable getting a little dressed up to dine in Seattle's finest eateries, but unless you're going on a cruise, you can leave the tux at home.

If you plan on hiking or camping during the summer, insect repellent is a must, as are *sensible* clothing and shoes. We can't tell you how many times we've seen tourists trudging up rocky trails in Mt. Rainier National Park in beachwear and flip-flops or worse—looking like they should be sipping cocktails at a yacht club. The locals may look like idiot savants in all their color-coordinated, waterproof gear, but they know their state and its trails well, and most of the time they have very good reasons for their fashion choices. Sturdy sneakers or hiking shoes are a must and hats are a good idea, too, not only to block out the strong sun, but to keep your head warm at chillier elevations. If you're camping, you'll definitely need more than a windbreaker to keep you warm at night. Packing these items will save you money, but there are also plenty of places to pick up supplies once you hit the city. Note that REI is just one of the sporting-goods stores that rents equipment like tents and sleeping bags to visitors so you don't have to schlep them on the plane or explain your ice ax to a TSA officer.

You'll have no problem finding your favorite sundries and toiletries—and organic, all-natural versions of them, too. Sunblock is a must in summer; the lovely breezes coming off the water will fool you into thinking you're not getting burned to a crisp.

TRIP INSURANCE

What kind of coverage do you honestly need? Do you even need trip insurance at all? Take a deep breath and read on.

We believe that comprehensive trip insurance is especially valuable if you're booking a very expensive or complicated trip (particularly to an isolated region) or if you're booking far in advance. Who knows what could happen six months down the road? But whether or not you get insurance has more to do with how comfortable you are assuming all that risk yourself.

Comprehensive travel policies typically cover trip-cancellation and interruption, letting you cancel or cut your trip short because of a personal emergency, illness, or, in some cases, acts of terrorism in your destination. Such policies also cover evacuation and medical care. Some also cover you for trip delays because of bad weather or mechanical problems as well as for lost or delayed baggage. Another type of coverage to look for is financial default—that is, when your trip is disrupted because a tour operator, airline, or cruise line goes out of business. Generally you must buy this when you book your trip or shortly thereafter, and it's only available to you if your operator isn't on a list of excluded companies.

Expect comprehensive travel insurance policies to cost about 4% to 7% of the total price of your trip (it's more like 12% if you're over age 70). A medical-only policy may or may not be cheaper than a comprehensive policy. Always read the fine print of your policy to make sure that you are covered for the risks that are of most concern to you. Compare several policies to make sure you're getting the best price and range of coverage available.

PACKING 101

Why do some people travel with a convoy of huge suitcases yet never have a thing to wear? How do others pack a duffle with a week's worth of outfits *and* supplies for every contingency? We realize that packing is a matter of style, but there's a lot to be said for traveling light. These tips help fight the battle of the bulging bag.

Make a list. In a recent Fodor's survey, 29% of respondents said they make lists (and often pack) a week before a trip. You can use your list to pack and to repack at the end of your trip. It can also serve as record of the contents of your suitcase—in case it disappears in transit.

Think it through. What's the weather like? Is this a business trip? A cruise? Going abroad? In some places dress may be more or less conservative than you're used to. As you create your itinerary, note outfits next to each activity (don't forget accessories).

Edit your wardrobe. Plan to wear everything twice (better yet, thrice) and to do laundry along the way. Stick to one basic look—urban chic, sporty casual, etc. Build around one or two neutrals and an accent (e.g., black, white, and olive green). Women can freshen looks by changing scarves or jewelry. For a week's trip, you can look smashing with three bottoms, four or five tops, a sweater, and a jacket.

Be practical. Put comfortable shoes atop your list. (Did we need to say this?) Pack lightweight, wrinkle-resistent, compact, washable items. (Or this?) Stack and roll clothes, so they'll wrinkle less. Unless you're on a guided tour or a cruise, select luggage you can readily carry. Porters, like good butlers, are hard to find these days.

Check weight and size limitations. In the United States you may be charged extra for checked bags weighing more than 50 pounds. Abroad some airlines don't allow you to check bags over 60 to 70 pounds, or they charge outrageous fees for every excess pound—or bag. Carry-on size limitations can be stringent, too.

Check carry-on restrictions. Research restrictions with the TSA. Rules vary abroad, so check them with your airline if you're traveling overseas on a foreign carrier. Consider packing all but essentials (travel documents, prescription meds, wallet) in checked luggage. This leads to a "pack only what you can afford to lose" approach that might help you streamline.

Rethink valuables. On U.S. flights, airlines are liable for only about $2,800 per person for bags. On international flights, the liability limit is around $635 per bag. But items like computers, cameras, and jewelry aren't covered, and as gadgetry can go on and off the list of carry-on no-no's, you can't count on keeping things safe by keeping them close. Although comprehensive travel policies may cover luggage, the liability limit is often a pittance. Your home-owner's policy may cover you sufficiently when you travel— or not.

Lock it up. If you must pack valuables, use TSA-approved locks (about $10) that can be unlocked by all U.S. security personnel.

Tag it. Always tag your luggage; use your business address if you don't want people to know your home address. Put the same information (and a copy of your itinerary) inside your luggage, too.

Report problems immediately. If your bags—or things in them—are damaged or go astray, file a written claim with your airline *before leaving the airport*. If the airline is at fault, it may give you money for essentials until your luggage arrives. Most lost bags are found within 48 hours, so alert the airline to your whereabouts for two or three days. If your bag was opened for security reasons in the States and something is missing, file a claim with the TSA.

Trip Insurance Resources

INSURANCE COMPARISON SITES		
Insure My Trip.com	800/487–4722	www.insuremytrip.com
Square Mouth.com	800/240–0369	www.quotetravelinsurance.com
COMPREHENSIVE TRAVEL INSURERS		
Access America	866/807–3982	www.accessamerica.com
CSA Travel Protection	800/873–9855	www.csatravelprotection.com
HTH Worldwide	610/254–8700 or 888/243–2358	www.hthworldwide.com
Travelex Insurance	888/457–4602	www.travelex-insurance.com
Travel Guard International	715/345–0505 or 800/826–4919	www.travelguard.com
Travel Insured International	800/243–3174	www.travelinsured.com
MEDICAL-ONLY INSURERS		
International Medical Group	800/628–4664	www.imglobal.com
International SOS	215/942–8000 or 713/521–7611	www.internationalsos.com
Wallach & Company	800/237–6615 or 504/687–3166	www.wallach.com

BOOKING YOUR TRIP

Unless your cousin is a travel agent, you're probably among the millions of people who make most of their travel arrangements online.

But have you ever wondered just what the differences are between an online travel agent (a Web site through which you make reservations instead of going directly to the airline, hotel, or car-rental company), a discounter (a firm that does a high volume of business with a hotel chain or airline and accordingly gets good prices), a wholesaler (one that makes cheap reservations in bulk and then resells them to people like you), and an aggregator (one that compares all the offerings so you don't have to)?

Is it truly better to book directly on an airline or hotel Web site? And when does a real live travel agent come in handy?

▌ ONLINE

You really have to shop around. A travel wholesaler such as Hotels.com or Hotel-Club.net can be a source of good rates, as can discounters such as Hotwire or Priceline, particularly if you can bid for your hotel room or airfare. Indeed, such sites sometimes have deals that are unavailable elsewhere. They do, however, tend to work only with hotel chains (which makes them just plain useless for getting hotel reservations outside major cities) or big airlines (so that often leaves out upstarts like jetBlue and some foreign carriers like Air India).

Also, with discounters and wholesalers you must generally prepay, and everything is nonrefundable. And before you fork over the dough, be sure to check the terms and conditions so you know what a given company will do for you if there's a problem and what you'll have to deal with on your own.

▌TIP➔ To be absolutely sure everything was processed correctly, confirm reservations made through online travel agents, discounters, and wholesalers directly with your hotel before leaving home.

Booking engines like Expedia, Travelocity, and Orbitz are actually travel agents, albeit high-volume, online ones. And airline travel packagers like American Airlines Vacations and Virgin Vacations—well, they're travel agents, too. But they may still not work with all the world's hotels.

An aggregator site will search many sites and pull the best prices for airfares, hotels, and rental cars from them. Most aggregators compare the major travel-booking sites such as Expedia, Travelocity, and Orbitz; some also look at airline Web sites, though rarely the sites of smaller budget airlines. Some aggregators also compare other travel products, including complex packages—a good thing, as you can sometimes get the best overall deal by booking an air-and-hotel package.

▌ WITH A TRAVEL AGENT

If you use an agent—brick-and-mortar or virtual—you'll pay a fee for the service. And know that the service you get from some online agents isn't comprehensive. For example Expedia and Travelocity don't search for prices on budget airlines like jetBlue, Southwest, or small foreign carriers. That said, some agents (online or not) *do* have access to fares that are difficult to find otherwise, and the savings can more than make up for any surcharge.

A knowledgeable brick-and-mortar travel agent can be a godsend if you're booking a cruise, a package trip that's not available to you directly, an air pass, or a complicated itinerary including several overseas flights. What's more, travel agents that specialize in a destination may have exclusive access to certain deals and insider information on things such as charter flights. Agents who specialize in types of travelers (senior citizens, gays and lesbians, naturists) or types of trips (cruises, luxury travel, safaris) can also be invaluable.

■TIP→ Remember that Expedia, Travelocity, and Orbitz are travel agents, not just booking engines. To resolve any problems with a reservation made through these companies, contact them first.

Unless Seattle is just one stop in a complicated Northwest itinerary, you probably won't need a travel agent to plan your trip here. The lowest fares for domestic flights to Seattle are usually found online, and usually by booking directly from an airline's Web site. Many airlines and consolidator sites have deals with car-rental agencies that can help you save a few bucks on that expense. Accommodations may be hard to come by if you don't book in advance for high season, but it's a common practice for Seattle concierges to help you find a property of equal price and excellence if they are booked up when you call. Furthermore, the restaurants and events really worth visiting are rarely the ones included in package deals. The beauty of Seattle is that it takes very little planning to create a great city itinerary, and no itinerary in this laid-back city should be too rigid.

All that said, you might want to give your agent a call if you plan to stay on Orcas or San Juan islands in peak season to see if they have any good deals that might include discounts on ferry rides and resort stays.

Agent Resources **American Society of Travel Agents** (☎ *703/739–2782* ⊕ *www. travelsense.org*).

■ ACCOMMODATIONS

These days luxurious, eye-popping designer hotels seem to outnumber any other type of accommodation in the city. Seattle's hotel industry is booming, and if you've got money to burn, you'll be thrilled with all of your choices. Seattle also has a number of bed-and-breakfasts, though rooms at them tend to go quickly since they represent the best deals in the city during high season. Almost all B&Bs are in Capitol Hill, whereas almost all hotels are Downtown. Though the city does have its share of standard budget chain hotels and motels, most of them are terribly overpriced in high season and in awkward spots in the city. The best rule of thumb to get the room that you want is to book as far in advance as possible.

For more information about lodging options and for prices, ⇨Chapter 3, Where to Stay.

Most hotels and other lodgings require you to give your credit-card details before they will confirm your reservation. If you don't feel comfortable e-mailing this information, ask if you can fax it (some places even prefer faxes). However you book, get confirmation in writing and have a copy of it handy when you check in.

Be sure you understand the hotel's cancellation policy. Some places allow you to cancel without any kind of penalty—even if you prepaid to secure a discounted rate—if you cancel at least 24 hours in advance. Others require you to cancel a week in advance or penalize you the cost of one night. Small inns and B&Bs are most likely to require you to cancel far in advance. Most hotels allow children under a certain age to stay in their parents' room at no extra charge, but others charge for them as extra adults; find out the cutoff age for discounts.

■TIP→ Assume that hotels operate on the European Plan (EP, no meals) unless we specify that they use the Breakfast Plan (BP,

Online Booking Resources

AGGREGATORS

Kayak	www.kayak.com	also looks at cruises and vacation packages.
Mobissimo	www.mobissimo.com	
Qixo	www.qixo.com	also compares cruises, vacation packages, and even travel insurance.
Sidestep	www.sidestep.com	also compares vacation packages and lists travel deals.
Travelgrove	www.travelgrove.com	also compares cruises and packages.

BOOKING ENGINES

Cheap Tickets	www.cheaptickets.com	a discounter.
Expedia	www.expedia.com	a large online agency that charges a booking fee for airline tickets.
Hotwire	www.hotwire.com	a discounter.
lastminute.com	www.lastminute.com	specializes in last-minute travel; the main site is for the U.K., but it has a link to a U.S. site.
Luxury Link	www.luxurylink.com	has auctions (surprisingly good deals) as well as offers on the high-end side of travel.
Onetravel.com	www.onetravel.com	a discounter for hotels, car rentals, airfares, and packages.
Orbitz	www.orbitz.com	charges a booking fee for airline tickets, but gives a clear breakdown of fees and taxes before you book.
Priceline.com	www.priceline.com	a discounter that also allows bidding.
Travel.com	www.travel.com	allows you to compare its rates with those of other booking engines.
Travelocity	www.travelocity.com	charges a booking fee for airline tickets, but promises good problem resolution.

ONLINE ACCOMMODATIONS

Hotelbook.com	www.hotelbook.com	focuses on independent hotels worldwide.
Hotel Club	www.hotelclub.net	good for major cities worldwide.
Hotels.com	www.hotels.com	a big Expedia-owned wholesaler that offers rooms in hotels all over the world.
Quikbook	www.quikbook.com	offers "pay when you stay" reservations that let you settle your bill at check out, not when you book.

OTHER RESOURCES

Bidding For Travel	www.biddingfortravel.com	a good place to figure out what you can get and for how much before you start bidding on, say, Priceline.

10 WAYS TO SAVE

1. Join "frequent guest" programs. You may get preferential treatment in room choice and/or upgrades in your favorite chains.

2. Call direct. You can sometimes get a better price if you call a hotel's local toll-free number (if available) rather than a central reservations number.

3. Check online. Check hotel Web sites, as not all travel sites list chains.

4. Look for specials. Always inquire about packages and corporate rates.

5. Look for price guarantees. For overseas trips, look for guaranteed rates. With your rate locked in you won't pay more, even if the price goes up in the local currency.

6. Look for weekend deals at business hotels. High-end chains catering to business travelers are often busy only on weekdays; they often drop rates on weekends.

7. Ask about taxes. Verify whether local hotel taxes are included in quoted rates. In some places taxes can add 20% or more to your bill.

8. Read the fine print. Watch for add-ons, including resort fees, energy surcharges, and "convenience" fees for such things as unlimited local phone service you won't use or a free newspaper in a language you can't read.

9. Know when to go. If your destination's high season is December through April and you're trying to book, say, in late April, you might save money by shifting your dates a bit. Ask when rates go down, though: if your dates straddle peak and nonpeak seasons, a property may still charge peak-season rates for the entire stay.

10. Weigh your options. Weigh transportation times and costs against the savings of staying in a cheaper but more far-flung hotel.

with full breakfast), Continental Plan (**CP,** Continental breakfast), Full American Plan (**FAP,** all meals), Modified American Plan (**MAP,** breakfast and dinner) or are all-inclusive (**AI,** all meals and most activities).

▍ AIRLINE TICKETS

Most domestic airline tickets are electronic; international tickets may be either electronic or paper. With an e-ticket the only thing you receive is an e-mailed receipt citing your itinerary and reservation and ticket numbers.

The greatest advantage of an e-ticket is that if you lose your receipt, you can simply print out another copy or ask the airline to do it for you at check-in. You usually pay a surcharge (up to $50) to get a paper ticket, if you can get one at all.

The sole advantage of a paper ticket is that it may be easier to endorse over to another airline if your flight is canceled and the airline with which you booked can't accommodate you on another flight.

▍ RENTAL CARS

For a city that prides itself on being forward-thinking, Seattle has some major catching up to do when it comes to its public transportation options. The bus and monorail are fine for getting around Downtown, and each neighborhood in itself is very walkable, but the sad truth is that if you want the freedom to fully explore the neighborhoods north of the Lake Washington Ship Canal, off-the-beaten-path destinations, or the Eastside, you'll want to rent a car. If you plan to go to any town outside the city or do day trips to places like Mt. Rainier, a rental car becomes mandatory.

Rates in Seattle begin at $21 a day and $110 a week for an economy car with air-conditioning, automatic transmission, and unlimited mileage. This does not include the car-rental tax of 18.5%.

Try to avoid renting a car from a major agency at the airport, where rental fees are higher and an additional airport tax is charged. Most major rental agencies have offices Downtown or along the waterfront, within easy reach of the main hotel area. Of the major agencies at the airport, Thrifty often has the lowest rates because it does not have a counter in the airport (it's a short shuttle bus ride away).

Booking in advance is always a good idea—and a must on holiday weekends when Seattleites flee the city—but if you're not sure you'll need a car, don't feel compelled to rent one until you're here and you know what your needs are. Last-minute reservations may not yield the best rates, but renting a car only to pay for it to sit in your hotel's parking garage (almost no hotels offer free parking) isn't the greatest of deals either.

Almost no popular hiking trips require special vehicles—the road to Mt. Rainier, for example, is paved the whole way—but if driving 20 mi down a bumpy Forest Service dirt road to reach a remote trailhead sounds like something you want to try, you might want to make sure the vehicle you rent can handle it.

Unless you're hauling around kayaks, rent the smallest car possible, especially if you plan to do a lot of city driving. Downtown has plenty of parking garages, but they're expensive, pay lots are scarcer in other neighborhoods and often have very tight spots that require a lot of maneuvering to get into, and street parking is a headache in all but the quietest residential areas. The smaller the car, the easier it'll be to find a space.

In Washington State you must be 21 and hold a major credit card (many agencies accept debit cards with the MasterCard or Visa logo) to rent a car. Rates may be higher if you're under 25. You'll pay about $3 per day per child seat for children under age four or 40 pounds, or per booster seat for children ages four to six

10 WAYS TO SAVE

1. Nonrefundable is best. If saving money is more important than flexibility, then nonrefundable tickets work. Just remember that you'll pay dearly (as much as $100) if you change your plans.

2. Comparison shop. Web sites and travel agents can have different arrangements with the airlines and offer different prices for exactly the same flights.

3. Beware those prices. Many airline Web sites—and most ads—show prices *without* taxes and surcharges. Don't buy until you know the full price.

4. Stay loyal. Stick with one or two frequent-flier programs. You'll rack up free trips faster and you'll accumulate more quickly the perks that make trips easier. On some airlines these include a special reservations number, early boarding, access to upgrades, and more roomy economy-class seating.

5. Watch those ticketing fees. Surcharges are usually added when you buy your ticket anywhere but on an airline Web site. (That includes by phone—even if you call the airline directly—and paper tickets regardless of how you book.)

6. Check early and often. Start looking for cheap fares up to a year in advance. Keep looking till you find a price you like.

7. Don't work alone. Some Web sites have tracking features that will e-mail you immediately when good deals are posted.

8. Jump on the good deals. Waiting even a few minutes might mean paying more.

9. Be flexible. Look for departures on Tuesday, Wednesday, and Thursday, typically the cheapest days to travel. And check on prices for departures at different times and to and from alternative airports.

10. Weigh your options. What you get can be as important as what you save. A cheaper flight might have a long layover, or it might land at a secondary airport, where your ground transportation costs might be higher.

Car Rental Resources

AUTOMOBILE ASSOCIATIONS		
American Automobile Association	315/797–5000	www.aaa.com; most contact with the organization is through state and regional members
National Automobile Club	650/294–7000	www.thenac.com; membership open to CA residents only
LOCAL AGENCIES		
Ace ExtraCar	800/227–5397 or 206/246–7844	www.bnm.com
Advantage	800/777–5500	www.arac.com
Best Rent-a-Car	206/784–2378	bestrent-a-car.com
Express Rent-A-Car	866/443–6825	www.expressrentacar.com
MAJOR AGENCIES		
Alamo	800/462–5266	www.alamo.com
Avis	800/331–1084	www.avis.com
Budget	800/472–3325	www.budget.com
Hertz	800/654–3131	www.hertz.com
National Car Rental	800/227–7368	www.nationalcar.com
Thrifty	877/283–0898 Sea-Tac, 206/878–1234 Downtown	www.thrifty.com

or under 60 pounds, both of which are compulsory in Washington state.

When you reserve a car, ask about cancellation penalties, taxes, drop-off charges (if you're planning to pick up the car in one city and leave it in another), and surcharges (for being under or over a certain age, for additional drivers, or for driving across state or country borders or beyond a specific distance from your point of rental). All these things can add substantially to your costs. Request car seats and extras such as GPS when you book.

■ TIP→ **Make sure that a confirmed reservation guarantees you a car. Agencies sometimes overbook, particularly for busy weekends and holiday periods.**

CAR-RENTAL INSURANCE

Everyone who rents a car wonders whether the insurance that the rental companies offer is worth the expense. No one—including us—has a simple answer. It all depends on how much regular insurance you have, how comfortable you are with risk, and whether or not money is an issue.

If you own a car and carry comprehensive car insurance for both collision and liability, your personal auto insurance will probably cover a rental, but read your policy's fine print to be sure. If you don't have auto insurance, then you should probably buy the collision- or loss-damage waiver (CDW or LDW) from the rental company. This eliminates your liability for damage to the car.

Some credit cards offer CDW coverage, but it's usually supplemental to your own insurance and rarely covers SUVs, minivans, luxury models, and the like. If your coverage is secondary, you may still be liable for loss-of-use costs from the car-rental company (again, read the fine print). But no credit-card insurance is valid unless you use that card for *all* transactions, from reserving to paying the final bill.

■TIP→ **Diners Club offers primary CDW coverage on all rentals reserved and paid for with the card. This means that Diners Club's company—not your own car insurance—pays in case of an accident. It** *doesn't* **mean that your car-insurance company won't raise your rates once it discovers you had an accident.**

You may also be offered supplemental liability coverage; the car-rental company is required to carry a minimal level of liability coverage insuring all renters, but it's rarely enough to cover claims in a really serious accident if you're at fault. Your own auto-insurance policy will protect you if you own a car; if you don't, you have to decide whether you are willing to take the risk.

U.S. rental companies sell CDWs and LDWs for about $15 to $25 a day; supplemental liability is usually more than $10 a day. The car-rental company may offer you all sorts of other policies, but they're rarely worth the cost. Personal accident insurance, which is basic hospitalization coverage, is an especially egregious rip-off if you already have health insurance.

■TIP→ **You can decline the insurance from the rental company and purchase it through a third-party provider such as Travel Guard (www.travelguard.com)—$9 per day for $35,000 of coverage. That's sometimes just under half the price of the CDW offered by some car-rental companies.**

∎ VACATION PACKAGES

Packages *are not* guided excursions. Packages combine airfare, accommodations, and perhaps a rental car or other extras (theater tickets, guided excursions, boat trips, reserved entry to popular museums,

10 WAYS TO SAVE

1. Beware of cheap rates. Those great rates aren't so great when you add in taxes, surcharges, and insurance. Such extras can double or triple the initial quote.

2. Rent weekly. Weekly rates are usually better than daily ones. Even if you only want to rent for five or six days, ask for the weekly rate; it may very well be cheaper than the daily rate for that period of time.

3. Don't forget the locals. Price local companies as well as the majors.

4. Airport rentals can cost more. Airports often add surcharges, which you can sometimes avoid by renting from an agency whose office is just off airport property.

5. Wholesalers can help. Investigate wholesalers, which don't own fleets but rent in bulk from firms that do, and which frequently offer better rates (note that you must usually pay for such rentals before leaving home).

6. Look for rate guarantees. With your rate locked in, you won't pay more, even if the price goes up in the local currency.

7. Fill up farther away. Avoid hefty refueling fees by filling the tank at a station well away from where you plan to turn in the car.

8. Pump it yourself. Don't buy the tank of gas that's in the car when you rent it unless you plan to do a lot of driving.

9. Get all your discounts. Find out whether a credit card you carry or organization or frequent-renter program to which you belong has a discount program. And confirm that such discounts really are a deal. You can often do better with special weekend or weekly rates offered by a rental agency.

10. Check out packages. Adding a car rental onto your air/hotel vacation package may be cheaper than renting a car separately.

transit passes), but they let you do your own thing. During busy periods packages may be your only option, as flights and rooms may be sold out otherwise.

Packages will definitely save you time. They can also save you money, particularly in peak seasons, but—and this is a really big "but"—you should price each part of the package separately to be sure. And be aware that prices advertised on Web sites and in newspapers rarely include service charges or taxes, which can up your costs by hundreds of dollars.

■TIP→ Some packages and cruises are sold only through travel agents. Don't always assume that you can get the best deal by booking everything yourself.

Each year consumers are stranded or lose their money when packagers—even large ones with excellent reputations—go out of business. How can you protect yourself?

First, always pay with a credit card; if you have a problem, your credit-card company may help you resolve it. Second, buy trip insurance that covers default. Third, choose a company that belongs to the United States Tour Operators Association, whose members must set aside funds to cover defaults. Finally, choose a company that also participates in the Tour Operator Program of the American Society of Travel Agents (ASTA), which will act as mediator in any disputes.

You can also check on the tour operator's reputation among travelers by posting an inquiry on one of the Fodors.com forums.

Organizations **American Society of Travel Agents** (*ASTA* ☎ 800/965–2782 or 703/739–2782 ⊕ www.astanet.com). **United States Tour Operators Association** (*USTOA* ☎ 212/599–6599 ⊕ www.ustoa.com).
■TIP→ Local tourism boards can provide information about lesser-known and small-niche operators that sell packages to only a few destinations.

▌CRUISES

Seattle's expanding cruise industry now welcomes some of the world's largest ships to docks on Elliott Bay. The city's strategic location along the West Coast means that it's just a day's journey by water to Canada or California, and you can reach Alaska or Mexico in less than a week. In addition to the major cruise lines, you can also sail around Elliott Bay, Lake Union, Lake Washington, or along a combination of local waterways.

Of the large ships, Norwegian Cruise Line offers seven-day summer cruises from Seattle to Alaska, as well as five-day cruises from Los Angeles to Vancouver, B.C. that stop in Seattle. The ships dock at Pier 66, the Bell Street Pier Cruise Terminal. Holland America Line, which has seven-day cruises to Alaska on the *MS Amsterdam,* and Princess Cruises, which offers seven-day Alaska cruises on the *Star Princess,* both dock at the Terminal 30 Cruise Facility south of Downtown.

Cruise Lines **Carnival Cruise Line** (☎ 800/227–6482 or 305/599–2600 ⊕ www.carnival.com). **Holland America Line** (☎ 877/932–4259 or 206/281–3535 ⊕ www.hollandamerica.com). **Norwegian Cruise Line** (☎ 800/327–7030 or 305/436–4000 ⊕ www.ncl.com). **Princess Cruises** (☎ 800/774–6237 or 661/753–0000 ⊕ www.princess.com).

TRANSPORTATION

Seattle can be a bit baffling at first, especially if you delve into its residential neighborhoods—and you should. Use the transportation advice in this section to help you plan your wanderings around the city's sometimes illogical layout.

I NAVIGATING SEATTLE

Rule #1: Downtown is the easiest neighborhood to explore and is therefore the one part of the city where you're least likely to need—or want—a car. Also bear the following tips in mind as you navigate the city.

—Water makes the best landmark. Both Elliott Bay and Lake Union are pretty hard to miss. When trying to get your bearings Downtown, Elliott Bay is a much more reliable landmark than the Space Needle.

—Upper Queen Anne and the northern and eastern areas of Capitol Hill are the most confusing spots to drive around in as the streets lose their grid pattern and start to go off in all different directions. You'll need a map for these areas—Seattleites often do.

—Remember that I–5 literally bisects the city and there are limited places at which to cross it (this tip goes for pedestrians, too). From Downtown to Capitol Hill, cross using Pike, Pine, Madison, James, or Yesler; from Lake Union or Seattle Center to Capitol Hill, use Denny; above the canal, 45th, 50th, and 80th are the major streets running all the way east–west.

—The major north–south routes connecting the northern part of the city to the southern part are I–5, Aurora Avenue/99, 15th Avenue NW (Ballard Bridge), and Westlake (Fremont Bridge) and Eastlake avenues. With the exception of some difficult on-ramps, I–5 is easy to navigate. Note that Aurora has a limited number of signed exits north of the canal (mostly

you just turn directly onto side streets) and a limited number of exits in general Downtown (after the Denny exit if you're heading north to south). Some of the Downtown exits are on the left-hand side, making this road a bit more confusing if you don't know where you're going.

—Public buses provide a sufficient if frustrating system that's best used to move between Downtown and Capitol Hill or Queen Anne. To get from Downtown to Seattle Center, use the monorail. To get from Downtown to Pioneer Square use the bus or trolley. Walking is often the fastest solution around Downtown and Belltown. Using the bus system to get from Downtown to the neighborhoods above the canal can sometimes be a slow process.

Streets in the Seattle area generally travel east to west, whereas avenues travel north to south. Downtown roads are straightforward: avenues are numbered west to east (starting with 1st Avenue by Elliott Bay and ending with 39th Avenue by Lake Washington), streets are named, and a rough grid pattern can be discerned. Above the Lake Washington Ship Canal, east to west streets are mostly numbered, starting with N. 34th Street in Fremont and going up into the 100s as you head into the northern suburbs. Here, the system for avenues makes much less sense; they're mostly named, but a few are numbered. West of I–5, 1st Avenue NW starts in Fremont and numbers increase as you go west toward Shilshole Bay, ending with 36th Avenue NW. East of I–5, 1st Avenue NE starts in Wallingford and the numbers increase as you go toward Lake Washington, ending at 50th Avenue NE.

Directionals are often attached to street names. N (north), as in N. 34th Street, is for Queen Anne, around the Seattle Center, and Fremont, Wallingford, and Green Lake. NE (northeast) is for the University

District, and NW (northwest) designates Ballard. S. (south) marks Downtown streets around Pioneer Square and the International District, as well as neighborhoods south of the city—although SW (southwest) means West Seattle. E. (east) designates Capitol Hill; W. (west) means Queen Anne and Magnolia.

Directionals are noted as prefixes to streets and suffixes to avenues; thus, if someone says "NW 67th," it is safe to assume they are referring to NW 67th *Street,* not avenue. Conversely, if someone says a destination is on "33rd E," they are referring to 33rd *Avenue* East.

▌BY AIR

Nonstop flying time from New York to Seattle is approximately 5 hours; flights from Chicago are about 4–4½ hours; flights between Los Angeles and Seattle take 2½ hours; flights between London and Seattle are about 9½ hours.

Seattle is a hub for regional air service, air service to Alaska, Hawaii, and Canada, as well as for some carriers to Asia. It's also a convenient North American gateway for flights originating in Australia, New Zealand, and the South Pacific. But it's a long westbound flight to Seattle from Europe. Such flights usually stop in New York; Washington, D.C.; Boston; or Chicago after crossing the Atlantic.

▌TIP→ **If you travel frequently, look into the TSA's Registered Traveler program. The program, which is still being tested in several U.S. airports, is designed to cut down on gridlock at security checkpoints by allowing prescreened travelers to pass quickly through kiosks that scan an iris and/or a fingerprint. How sci-fi is that?**

Airlines & Airports **Airline and Airport Links.com** (⊕ *www.airlineandairportlinks.com*) has links to many of the world's airlines and airports.

Airline Security Issues **Transportation Security Administration** (⊕ *www.tsa.gov*) has

answers for almost every question that might come up.

AIRPORTS
The major gateway is Seattle–Tacoma International Airport (SEA), known locally as Sea-Tac. The airport is south of the city and reasonably close to it—non-rush-hours trips to Downtown sometimes take less than a half hour. Sea-Tac is a midsize, modern airport that is usually very pleasant to navigate through. Our only complaint: inexplicably long waits at the baggage claim, especially at night when they seem to send all flights to one or two carousels.

Sea-Tac has a few restaurants, but no fancy facilities, so don't arrive hours before your flight and expect to be entertained.

Charter flights and small carriers like Kenmore Air that operate shuttle flights between the cities of the Pacific Northwest land at Boeing Field, which is between Sea-Tac and Seattle.

Airport Information **Boeing Field** (☎ *206/296–7380* ⊕ *www.metrokc.gov/airport*). **Seattle–Tacoma International Airport** (☎ *206/433–5388* ⊕ *www.portseattle. org/seatac*).

Sea-Tac is about 15 mi south of Downtown on I–5 (from the airport, follow the signs to I–5 North, and take the Seneca Street Exit for Downtown). Although it can take as little as 30 minutes to ride between Downtown and the airport, if you're traveling during either rush hour, it's best to allow at least an hour for the trip in case of traffic snarls.

Metered cabs cost around $30 (not including tip) between the airport and Downtown, though some taxi companies offer a flat rate to Sea-Tac from select Downtown hotels. Expect to pay $35–$40 to Capitol Hill, Queen Anne or the neighborhoods directly north of the canal. Seattle has a small cab fleet, so expect long waits if a lot of flights arrive at the same time, especially late at night.

FLYING 101

Flying may not be as carefree as it once was, but there are some things you can do to make your trip smoother.

Minimize the time spent standing in line. Buy an e-ticket, check in at an electronic kiosk, or—even better—check in on your airline's Web site before leaving home. Pack light and limit carry-on items to only the essentials.

Arrive when you need to. Research your airline's policy. It's usually at least an hour before domestic flights and two to three hours before international flights. But airlines at some busy airports have more stringent requirements. Check the TSA Web site for estimated security waiting times at major airports.

Get to the gate. If you aren't at the gate at least 10 minutes before your flight is scheduled to take off (sometimes earlier), you won't be allowed to board.

Double-check your flight times. Do this especially if you reserved far in advance. Schedules change, and alerts may not reach you.

Don't go hungry. Ask whether your airline offers anything to eat; even when it does, be prepared to pay.

Get the seat you want. Often, you can pick a seat when you buy your ticket on an airline Web site. But it's not guaranteed; the airline could change the plane after you book, so double-check. You can also select a seat if you check in electronically. Avoid seats on the aisle directly across from the lavatories. Frequent fliers say those are even worse than back-row seats that don't recline.

Got kids? Get info. Ask the airline about its children's menus, activities, and fares. Sometimes infants and toddlers fly free if they sit on a parent's lap, and older children fly for half price in their own seats. Also inquire about policies involving car seats; having one may limit seating options. Also ask about seat-belt extenders for car seats. And note that you can't count on a flight attendant to produce an extender; you may have to ask for one when you board.

Check your scheduling. Don't buy a ticket if there's less than an hour between connecting flights. Although schedules are padded, if anything goes wrong you might miss your connection. If you're traveling to an important function, depart a day early.

Bring paper. Even when using an e-ticket, always carry a hard copy of your receipt; you may need it to get your boarding pass, which most airports require to get past security.

Complain at the airport. If your baggage goes astray or your flight goes awry, complain before leaving the airport. Most carriers require this.

Beware of overbooked flights. If a flight is oversold, the gate agent will usually ask for volunteers and offer some sort of compensation for taking a different flight. If you're bumped from a flight *involuntarily*, the airline must give you some kind of compensation if an alternate flight can't be found within one hour.

Know your rights. If your flight is delayed because of something within the airline's control (bad weather doesn't count), the airline must get you to your destination on the same day, even if they have to book you on another airline and in an upgraded class. Read the Contract of Carriage, which is usually buried on the airline's Web site.

Be prepared. The Boy Scout motto is especially important if you're traveling during a stormy season. To quickly adjust your plans, program a few numbers into your cell: your airline, an airport hotel or two, your destination hotel, your car service, and/or your travel agent.

Shuttle Express has the only 24-hour door-to-door shared van service. Rates vary depending on destination, number of people in your party, and how many bags you have, but a one-way trip to the Downtown hotel area for one adult with two bags is around $27. You can make arrangements at the Shuttle Express counter upon arrival or make advance reservations online or by phone. For trips to the airport, make reservations at least 24 hours in advance. Gray Line Downtown Airporter offers shuttle service to select Downtown hotels for $10.25 one way or $17 round-trip. The last shuttle leaves Sea-Tac at 11 PM. Express Car and Atlas Towncar have limo service to and from the airport. The fare is $45 to Downtown and can be shared by up to four passengers.

Your least-expensive transportation option ($1.50–$2; cash only, exact change in bills or coins) is a Metro Transit city bus. If you don't have a lot of luggage, this is a fantastic option for reaching Downtown cheaply. You can catch a bus outside the baggage claim areas for the 30- to 45-minute ride into town. Take Express Tunnel Bus 194 or regular Bus 174. Metro Transit's Web site has a great trip planner that provides door-to-door itineraries, explaining any connections you may have to make if you're not staying Downtown; representatives can also help you plan your trip over the phone.

Various other shuttle services exist to take passengers directly to surrounding towns and even out to places like the islands or Mt. Rainier. Check out Sea-Tac's Web site for a list of special shuttles and buses.

Contacts Atlas Towncar (☎ 888/646–0606 or 206/860–7777 ⊕ www.atlastowncar.com). **Gray Line Airport Express** (☎ 800/426–7532 recorded schedule info, 206/626–6088 ⊕ www.graylineseattle.com). **Metro Transit** (☎ 206/553–3000 ⊕ http://transit. metrokc.gov). **Shuttle Express/Express Car** (☎ 425/981–7000 ⊕ www.shuttleexpress.com).

FLIGHTS

American, Continental, Delta, Northwest, and United are among the many major domestic airlines that fly to Seattle from multiple locations. Alaska Airlines and its affiliate Horizon Air provide service from many states including Alaska and often have the best fares.

USAirways has flights from Philadelphia, Charlotte, Las Vegas, and Phoenix. Frontier Airlines has flights from Denver to Seattle. JetBlue has nonstop service to Seattle from New York and Boston. Hawaiian Airlines flies daily from points in Hawaii. Southwest Airlines has flights from many East Coast and Midwestern cities.

Air Canada flies between Seattle and Vancouver, British Columbia. Kenmore Air has scheduled floatplane flights from Seattle's Lake Union to the San Juan Islands, Victoria, and the Gulf Islands of British Columbia.

Airline Contacts Air Canada (☎ 888/247–2262 ⊕ www.aircanada.ca). **Alaska Airlines** (☎ 800/252–7522 or 206/433–3100 ⊕ www.alaskaair.com). **American Airlines** (☎ 800/433–7300 ⊕ www.aa.com). **Continental Airlines** (☎ 800/523–3273 for U.S. and Mexico reservations, 800/231–0856 for international reservations ⊕ www.continental. com). **Delta Airlines** (☎ 800/221–1212 for U.S. reservations, 800/241–4141 for international reservations ⊕ www.delta. com). **Frontier** (☎ 800/432–1359 ⊕ www. frontierairlines.com). **Hawaiian Airlines** (☎ 800/367–5320 ⊕ www.hawaiianair. com). **jetBlue** (☎ 800/538–2583 ⊕ www. jetblue.com). **Kenmore Air** (☎ 800/543–9595 ⊕ www.kenmoreair.com). **Northwest Airlines** (☎ 800/225–2525 ⊕ www.nwa.com). **Southwest Airlines** (☎ 800/435–9792 ⊕ www. southwest.com). **United Airlines** (☎ 800/864–8331 for U.S. reservations, 800/538–2929 for international reservations ⊕ www.united.com). **USAirways** (☎ 800/428–4322 for U.S. and Canada reservations, 800/622–1015 for international reservations ⊕ www.usairways.com).

▌ BY FERRY

Ferries are a major part of Seattle's transportation network, and they're the only way to reach such points as Vashon Island and the San Juans. Ferries also transport thousands of commuters a day from Bainbridge Island, Bremerton, and other outer towns to their jobs in the city. For visitors, ferries are one of the best ways to get a feel for the region and its ties to the sea. You'll also get outstanding views of the skyline and the elusive Mt. Rainier from the ferry to Bainbridge.

Passenger-only speedboats depart from Seattle's Pier 50 weekdays on runs to Vashon Island. It's $8.50 from Seattle; the return trip is free. From May 1 through September 30, the Elliott Bay Water Taxi makes a quick, 12-minute journey from Pier 54 to Seacrest Park in West Seattle for $3 each way. Clipper Navigation operates the passenger-only *Victoria Clipper* jet catamaran service between Seattle, the San Juan Islands, and Victoria. These longer journeys are fairly expense: $76–$89 one way to Victoria, $42–$47 one way to the San Juans. Note that *Victoria Clipper* fares are slightly cheaper if you book at least one day in advance.

The Washington State Ferry system serves the Puget Sound and San Juan Islands area. Peak-season fares are charged the first Sunday in May through the second Saturday in October. However, ferry schedules change quarterly, with the summer schedule running mid-June through mid-September. Ferries around Seattle are especially crowded during the city's weekday rush hours and holiday events, while San Juan Islands ferries can be jammed on weekends, holidays, and all of mid-June through September. Be at the ferry, or have your car in line, at least 20 minutes before departure—and prepare to wait several hours during heavily traveled times. Walk-on space is always available; if possible, leave your car behind.

You can pick up sailing schedules and tickets on board the ferries or at the terminals, and schedules are usually posted in local businesses around the docks. The Washington State Ferry (WSF) automated hotline also provides travel details, including weekly departure and arrival times, wait times, cancellations, and seasonal fare changes. To ask questions or make international reservations for journeys to Sidney, British Columbia, call the regular WSF hotline. Note that schedules often differ from weekdays to weekends and holidays, and departure times may be altered due to ferry or dock maintenance, severe weather or tides, and high traffic volume.

Peak-season walk-on fares from Seattle are $6.70 to Bainbridge and Bremerton, and from Edmonds to Kingston; $4.30 from Fauntleroy in West Seattle to Southworth or Vashon Island; $3.95 from Mukilteo to Clinton, on Whidbey Island; and $2.60 each way between Port Townsend and Keystone. It's $13.15 from Anacortes to any point in the San Juan Islands, or $16 to Sidney, British Columbia; tolls are collected on westbound routes only. Seniors (age 65 and over) and those with disabilities pay half fare; children 5–18 get a 30% discount, and those under age 5 ride free.

Peak-season vehicle fares (including one adult driver) are $14.45 from Seattle to Bainbridge and Bremerton, and from Edmonds to Kingston; $18.50 from Fauntleroy to Vashon Southworth, and Point Defiance in Tacoma to Vashon; $11.15 from Port Townsend to Keystone, and from Fauntleroy to Southworth; and $8.60 from Mukilteo to Clinton. From Anacortes, vehicle and driver fares through the San Juans are $32–$36 to Lopez Island, $38–$43 to Orcas and Shaw islands, $46–$51 to Friday Harbor, and $53.70 to Sidney, British Columbia.

For all fares, you can pay with cash, major credit cards, debit cards with MasterCard or Visa logos, and traveler's checks.

Information **Clipper Navigation**
(☎ 800/888–2535 in the U.S., 250/382–8100 in Victoria, 206/448–5000 in Seattle ⊕ www. victoriaclipper.com). **Elliott Bay Water Taxi** (☎ 800/542–7876 in WA, 206/553–3000 ⊕ http://transit.metrokc.gov/tops/oto/ water_taxi.html). **Washington State Ferries** (☎ 800/843–3779 automated line in WA and BC, 888/808–7977, 206/464–6400 ⊕ www. wsdot.wa.gov/ferries).

▌ BY BUS

ARRIVING & DEPARTING
Greyhound Lines and Northwest Trailways have regular service to points throughout the Pacific Northwest, the United States, and Canada. The regional Greyhound/Trailways bus terminal at 9th Avenue and Stewart Street is convenient to all Downtown destinations.

Greyhound buses travel several times daily to major towns along I–5 and I–90. Main routes head south from Seattle through Tacoma (45 minutes, $7 one way), Olympia (1 hour and 45 minutes, $11.50 one way), and Portland (3½–4½ hours, $25 one way). Buses going north from Seattle pass through Mount Vernon (1½ hours, $10.50 one way), Everett (40 minutes, $8 one way), and Bellingham (2 hours, $17 one way), close to the Canadian border. Eastern routes head to Yakima (3 hours, $27.50 one way), Spokane (6–8 hours, $32 one way), and many points in between and beyond. Fares are slightly less on weekdays and for round-trip tickets. Ask about companion rates, advance purchase savings, and seasonal discounts.

Northwest Trailways also has daily buses within Washington, including from Seattle south through Tacoma ($6), north through Everett ($6), and east through Spokane ($29), as well as long-haul service from points in Idaho.

Long-haul Bus Info **Greyhound Lines** (☎ 800/231–2222 or 206/628–5526 ⊕ www. greyhound.com). **Northwest Trailways** (✉ 811

Stewart St., Downtown ☎ 800/366–3830 ⊕ www.trailways.com).

GETTING AROUND SEATTLE
The Metropolitan Transit's transportation network is inexpensive and fairly comprehensive. So why do so many Seattleites own cars? Well, buses still take twice as long to make any trip, especially if transfers are involved or traffic is particularly bad; there are long gaps in off-peak schedules; and although the commercial centers of every neighborhood are well connected, there are too few stops within residential areas. So, when you factor in wait time, transit time, and the time it takes to hoof it from your house to the bus stop, a trip that takes 10 minutes by car can take 40 by bus. That said, if you're only using the buses to travel around Downtown and over to Capitol Hill, then you'll probably find navigating the system easy and fairly quick. Traveling to the commercial centers of Fremont and Ballard by bus from Downtown is also relatively easy; from Pike Place Market it takes at least 20 minutes to get to Fremont center and 25–35 minutes to get to NW Market Street and Ballard Avenue in Ballard. It takes at least 30 minutes to get from Pike Place Market to the University District.

Most buses, which are wheelchair accessible, run until around midnight or 1 AM; some run all night, though in many cases taking a cab late at night is a much better solution than dealing with sporadic bus service. The visitor center at the Washington State Convention and Trade Center has maps and schedules or you can call Metro Transit directly. Better yet, if you have Internet access, you can make use of Metro Transit's excellent trip planner feature. You simply type in your starting and ending addresses and the approximate time you want to start your trip or arrive at your destination and you'll get three or four options and detailed information on bus stop locations.

Most bus stops have simple schedules posted telling you when buses arrive; bus stops Downtown often have route maps and more information. Drivers are supposed to announce all major intersections, and you won't have to worry about signaling for a stop at hubs or during peak hours (someone else will probably do it or there will be people waiting at each stop, so the bus will have to pull over). At less-traveled stops in residential neighborhoods and during off-peak hours, you may have to signal for the driver to pull into your stop, so don't fall asleep.

Between 6 AM and 7 PM, city buses are free within the Metro Bus Ride Free Area, bounded by Battery Street to the north, 6th Avenue to the east (and over to 9th Avenue near the convention center), S. Jackson Street to the south, and the waterfront to the west; you'll pay as you disembark if you ride out of this area. Throughout King County, both one-zone fares and two-zone fares at off-peak times are $1.25; during peak hours (6 AM–9 AM and 3 PM–6 PM), one-zone fares are $1.50 and two-zone fares $2. Unless you travel outside the city limits, you'll pay one-zone fares. Onboard fare collection boxes have prices posted on them. The $5 King County Visitor Pass is a bargain if you're doing a lot of touring. Valid for one day, it includes rides on King, Pierce, and Snohomish county buses, the waterfront trolley, and the Elliott Bay Water Taxi. You can purchase online or at Metro offices. Transfers between most lines are free; if you think you'll need one, make sure you ask the driver for a transfer slip when you get on the bus.

Fares for city buses are collected in cash or by prepaid tickets and passes *as you board* the bus heading into Downtown, and *as you exit the bus* on the way out of Downtown. There's usually a sign posted on the fare collection box that tells you when you pay. Fare boxes accept both coins and bills, but drivers won't make change, so don't board the bus with a $5 bill and a hapless grin. If your bus pass has a magnetic strip, just run it through the reader on the fare box; if not, hand it to the driver. You can only buy bus passes at Metro offices or online, not on the vehicle; cash, debit cards, MasterCard, and Visa are accepted at all offices.

One thing you should prepare yourself for when taking the bus is the overwhelming possibility that there will be at least one crazy or drunk person loudly disturbing the peace. Though Seattleites have countless stories about eventful bus rides, very few of those stories involve actual threats or crimes, so you don't have to worry too much about safety. Just know that commuters rarely want to chat with strangers, so if you respond to that person who's trying a little too hard to get your attention, you're probably in for a 20-minute screed about the government or a way-too-detailed description of a health problem.

Other than that, riding the buses is only unpleasant during the rush hours when they're packed with annoyed residents and helmed by frazzled drivers trying to stay on schedule despite the traffic.

City Bus Information **Metropolitan Transit** (☎800/542-7876, 206/553-3000, 206/287-8463 for automated schedule line ⊕transit.metrokc.gov).

BY CAR

If you aren't staying in a central location, you may find Seattle's transit system frustrating. Access to a car is *almost* a necessity if you want to explore the residential neighborhoods. If you want to do side trips to the Eastside, Mt. Rainier, or pretty much any sight or city outside the Seattle limits (with the exception of Portland, Oregon, which is easily reached by train), you will definitely need a car. Before you book a car for city-only driving, ask your hotel if they offer car service. Many high-end hotels offer complimentary town-car service around Downtown and the immediate areas.

The best advice about driving in Seattle is to avoid driving during rush hour whenever possible. The worst tangles are on I–5 and I–90, and any street Downtown that has a major on or off ramp to I–5. The Fremont Bridge and the 15th Avenue Bridge also get tied up. Aurora Avenue/99 gets very busy but often moves quickly enough. Other than that, you should find driving around Seattle a lot less anxiety-inducing than driving around other major cities. Though you'll come across the occasional road rager or oblivious driver who assumes driving an SUV makes one invincible, drivers in Seattle are generally courteous and safety-conscious—though you'll want to pay extra attention in the student-heavy areas of Capitol Hill and the U-District. The biggest hazard is the lack of strict cell phone laws—every other driver has one glued to his or her ear, and it's amazing there aren't more accidents because of this.

If the phrases "traffic calming devices" and "always stop for pedestrians" are new to you, be sure to read Road Conditions and Rules of the Road, *below.*

GASOLINE

Gas stations are conveniently located throughout Seattle. If you are looking for gas Downtown, you'll find stations around Safeco stadium, on Dearborn in the International District, on Denny in north Belltown, and on Broadway in Capitol Hill. Above the ship canal, there are several stations on 45th Street: two on the corner of Fremont Avenue and several more as 45th heads into Wallingford toward I–5. There's a Shell station on Leary Way between Fremont and Ballard. Fill up before getting on I–5, particularly if you're heading south—service stations don't readily appear until you're well south of the city and there's always the possibility that you'll waste a lot of gas in stop-and-go traffic. Almost all stations are self-serve, and major credit and

debit cards are widely accepted. Prices get slightly cheaper as you head south toward Tacoma, but don't count on it—as gas prices continue to soar, the difference between pumps in the city and in the suburbs is negligible. Gas is much more expensive on the islands and the closer you get to Canada.

Seattle, like many major West Coast cities, also has several biodiesel stations. Biodiesel, an environmentally conscious fuel made with renewable resources (most often vegetable oil) instead of petroleum, can be used in most diesel cars without making engine modifications (some pre-1990 models require minor modifications). Around Seattle, you'll see plenty of Volkswagens of all stripes and ages and older BMWs with bumper stickers proudly stating that they run on biodiesel. Biodiesel users can find station locations at www.laurelhurstoil.com.

PARKING

Parking is a headache and a half in Seattle. Street parking is only guaranteed in the quietest residential areas—even leafy parts of Capitol Hill are crammed full of cars all hours of the day. The city has a good share of pay lots and garages in the central core of the city, but even the pay lots can fill up on weekend nights, particularly in Belltown and Capitol Hill. Metered street parking exists in Downtown Seattle and the commercial stretches of Capitol Hill, but consider yourself lucky if you manage to snag a spot. Meters are $1.50 per hour and although there are a few old-style coin-only meters left here and there, most pay stations are electronic and take either coins or debit and credit cards. You get a printed sticker noting the time your parking is up, which you affix to the curbside passenger window. Pay stations are clearly marked by signs with big white Ps in blue circles; there is usually one machine per block of parking spaces. Parking is free Sunday, holidays, and after 6 PM weekdays and Saturday. The maximum meter time is two hours, so if you plan to be Downtown longer and won't be nearby to refill the meter, find a parking lot or garage.

Pay lots are the next price tier up, though Downtown they are often just as expensive as garages. Rates vary greatly, but expect to pay at least $5 or $6 for a few hours in Capitol Hill and $8 or $9 for the same amount of time in Downtown or Belltown. Some pay lots have electronic pay stations similar to metered parking—use bills or a debit or credit card to pay at the station and place the printed ticket on the driver's side dashboard—but some lots still use old-fashioned pay boxes where you shove folded-up bills into a tiny slot with the same number as the space you parked in. So make sure you have some cash on you if you're trolling for pay-lot parking. Very few pay lots have attendants; the ones that do have dedicated pay booths and uniformed employees.

Most Downtown malls and high-rises have garages. Lot and garage rates begin at $3 an hour and cap off between $15 and $25 for the day. Park before 9 AM to take advantage of early-bird specials, which typically run $12 to $15. One of the best garages to park in is the Pacific Place mall lot: rates are reasonable, spaces are plentiful, and there's even a valet parking service for a few dollars more. Many merchants in the mall, as well as other local businesses, offer parking validation. Most garages take credit and debit cards.

Evening and weekend parking rates are usually cheaper than those on weekdays, around $5 for parking between 6 and midnight and $5–$12 for parking all day on weekends. After 5 PM, it's just $3 to park at Pacific Place for up to four hours. The Public Market Parking Garage at Pike Place offers free parking after 5 PM for anyone patronizing many of the area's restaurants, including the Alibi Room, Le Pichet, the Pink Door, and Campagne.

About two dozen major Downtown stores participate in the CityPark program, in which shoppers who spend at least $20 at their location get a $1 discount token for use at participating CityPark garages and lots. Tokens may also be used on King County Metro, Community Transit, and Sound Transit buses. A CityPark logo designates shops that are part of the program; garages and lots include those in the Ampco, CPS, Diamond, Imperial, Key Park, Republic, Standard, and U-Park systems. In the International District, look for the dragon parking sign in shop windows; these stores also provide discount parking tokens that can be used in specific neighborhood lots.

Important: No matter where you park, always lock your car and never leave valuables in your vehicle. The city has plenty of problems with break-ins. Don't be fooled by the laid-back suburban feel of some of the residential areas—they all experience waves of car theft and vandalism.

Lastly, you may be tempted to park in large private lots like those belonging to supermarkets. You're really rolling the dice: you may get away with it at small businesses and banks during non-business hours when no one's around to enforce the rules, but large businesses like grocery stores tend to have someone patrolling the lot. If you end up getting a ticket, you'll pay $35, far more money than you'll pay at a garage or pay lot.

ROAD CONDITIONS

Seattle's roads are generally pretty good, though amusingly enough they can get very flooded during heavy rainstorms (you'd think someone would have figured that one out by now). Note that many side streets in residential areas are extremely narrow due to people parking on both sides of the street—what should technically be a one-way street is actually a two-way. The basic rule of thumb when you're faced with oncoming traffic on a very narrow stretch is that whoever has space on their side pulls over to let the other driver pass.

Drive slowly around the Pike Place Market area—there are stretches of slippery cobblestones, as well as unmarked dips in the road as you crest the hills from west to east that can really bottom out a car.

Residential areas have many blind intersections, some without any stop signs or traffic circles. Sometimes cars are parked so close to the intersection that you have to pull way out into it in order to see what's coming—just another reason to rent a compact car with a short front end.

There are a lot of construction and road projects going on in the city right now, but detours are usually well signed and reasonably logical.

Note that some Forest Service roads are paved but many are dirt or gravel and can become treacherous during or after extreme weather conditions—severe rainstorms in the winter of 2006 even washed out a major road into Mt. Rainier National Park. Before heading out to a remote trailhead, always check road conditions. The same goes for any trip heading east over the mountain passes.

Winter snowfalls in the city are not common (generally only once or twice a year), but when snow does fall, traffic grinds to a halt, schools and businesses close, and the roadways become treacherous (mostly because many Seattleites don't know how to drive on snow and ice) and stay that way until the snow melts.

Tire chains, studs, or snow tires are essential equipment for winter travel in mountain areas such as Mt. Rainier. If you're planning to drive to high elevations, be sure to check the weather forecast beforehand. Even the main highway mountain passes can be forced to close because of snow conditions. In winter months, state and provincial highway departments operate snow-advisory telephone lines that give pass conditions.

Road-Condition Reports Washington State Road Condition Reports (☎ *888/766–4636* ⊕ *traffic.wsdot.wa.gov*).

ROADSIDE EMERGENCIES

Seattle AAA is a full-service travel agency that offers maps and roadside service for an enrollment fee.

Emergency Services Auto Impound Hotline (☎ *206/684–5444*). **Emergency Resource Center** (☎ *206/684–3355*). **Emergency Roadside Assistance** (☎ *800/AAA–HELP national number*). **Seattle AAA** (☎ *206/448–5353*).

RULES OF THE ROAD

Speed limits within Seattle vary between 25 and 45 mph. Right turns are allowed on most red lights after you've come to a full stop, and left turns on red are allowed on adjoining one-way streets. Note that the speed limit on much of I-5 within Washington State is 65–70 mph and fellow drivers expect you to keep up. To avoid a harrowing trip, stay in the right lane if you want to drive 55. Freeway on-ramps in the city are regulated by stoplights during morning and evening rush hours.

Seattle has many one-way streets—sometimes it seems like you can't make a left turn anywhere—but they are usually clearly marked. Be on the lookout for signs that prohibit left turns during certain hours of the day (usually 4–6 PM).

All residential neighborhoods have traffic calming devices at most intersections, usually in the form of traffic circles. A few rules apply: if you approach the circle at the same time as another driver, you yield to the driver on your right. If a driver is entering the circle as you approach it, they have the right of way. Technically, you're supposed to travel around the circle to complete a left turn, though most residents cut the turn if it's clear that there's no oncoming traffic. Be sure to use your blinker, as it'll make the whole process less confusing and less dangerous for everyone.

Pedestrians always have the right of way, even if they are not at a crosswalk. At some of the busier streets in the commercial districts of residential neighborhoods, crosswalks are clearly marked with illuminated signs; in less-traveled areas, crosswalks can be very hard to see, especially at night. Pay attention when approaching any crosswalk: pedestrians in this city are used to having cars stop on a dime to let them cross and tend to rely on drivers for their safety more than they should. What's more, on a two-way street, the Seattleite driving the oncoming car will most likely slam on his or her brakes to let the pedestrian pass, so if you blow through a crosswalk when the other lane of traffic has stopped, not only do you risk injuring a pedestrian, but you'll just look like a jerk.

▌ BY MONORAIL

Built for the 1962 World's Fair, the Seattle monorail is a quick, convenient link for tourists that travels an extremely short route between the Seattle Center and Downtown's Westlake Mall, located at 4th Avenue and Pike Street. Making the 1-mi journey in just 2 minutes, the monorail departs both points every 10 minutes from 11 AM to 9 PM daily. The round-trip fare is $4; children age four and under ride free. During weekends, Seattle Sonics basketball games, and the Folklife, Bite of Seattle, and Bumbershoot festivals—which all take place at the Seattle Center—you can park in the Macy's garage at 3rd Avenue and Stewart Street, take the monorail, and present your monorail ticket stub when you return for discounted parking rates of $5 on Friday and Saturday and $4 on Sunday and Monday.

Information **Seattle Center Monorail** (☎ *206/905–2620* ⊕ *www.seattlemonorail. com*).

▌ BY STREETCAR

The Waterfront Streetcar line of vintage 1920s-era trolleys from Melbourne, Australia, runs 1.6 mi south along Alaska Way from Pier 70, past the Washington State Ferries terminal at Piers 50 and 52, turning inland on Main Street, and passing through Pioneer Square before ending on South Jackson Street in the International District. It runs at about 20-minute intervals daily from 7 AM to 9 or 10 PM (less often and for fewer hours in winter). The fare is $1.25 from 9 to 3 and after 6, $1.50 during peak commuting hours. The stations and streetcars are wheelchair accessible. At this writing, construction on a new station has slightly disrupted streetcar service—the service still exists, but the trolleys have been replaced by green-and-beige buses clearly marked WATERFRONT STREETCAR LINE. The route is slightly different, so consult Metro Transit for updated schedule information.

As of this writing, a new streetcar system was under construction. The first section, which will travel from South Lake Union down Westlake Avenue to the Westlake Center, was slated for completion by late 2007. Basically another version of the monorail a few paces east, this will hardly solve any of Seattle's traffic problems (unless, of course, rumors that they're going to extend the project into the neighborhoods above the ship canal pan out). It will, however, make all of those luxury condos and hotels and office buildings sprouting in the South Lake Union area more accessible to the Downtown retail core.

Information **Metropolitan Transit** (☎ *206/553–3000, 206/287–8463 for automated schedule line* ⊕ *transit.metrokc.gov*).

▌ BY TAXI

Seattle has a pretty small taxi fleet; taking a cab is not a major form of transportation in the city. Most people only take cabs to and from the airport and when they go out partying on weekends. You'll often be able to hail cabs on the street in Downtown, but anywhere else, you'll have to call. Expect long waits on Friday and Saturday nights.

Rides generally run about $2 per mile, and unless you're going a very short distance, the average cost of a cab ride in the city is $10–$12. The meter drop alone is $2.50 and you'll pay 50¢ per minute stuck in traffic. Soaring gas prices may add a surcharge of $1 to the total. The nice thing about Seattle metered cabs is that they almost always accept credit cards and an automated system calls you on your cell phone to let you know that your cab has arrived. All cab companies listed below charge the same rates.

Metered cabs are not the best way to visit the Eastside or any destination far outside the city—if you get stuck in traffic, you'll pay dearly for it. Ask your hotel for car service quotes concerning short side trips outside city limits.

Taxi Companies **Orange Cab** (☎ *206/522-8800*). **Red Top Cab** (☎ *206/789-4949*). **Yellow Cab** (☎ *206/622-6500*).

▐ BY TRAIN

Amtrak, the U.S. passenger rail system, has daily service to Seattle from the Midwest and California. The *Empire Builder* takes a northern route from Chicago to Seattle. The *Coast Starlight* begins in Southern California, makes stops throughout western Oregon and Washington, including Portland, and terminates its route in Seattle. The *Cascades* travels from Eugene, Oregon up to Vancouver, British Columbia, with several stops in between. If you want to spend a day or two in Portland, taking the train down instead of driving is great way to do so. It's fast and comfortable and the Amtrak station in Portland is centrally located. Sit on the left side of the train on the way down for stunning views of Mt. Rainier. All Amtrak trains to and from

Seattle pull into King Street Station off of S. Jackson Street in the International District.

Trains to and from Seattle have regular and business-class compartments. Cars with private bedrooms are available for multiday trips (such as to Chicago), while "Custom Class" cars provide more legroom and complimentary refreshments on shorter routes (to Portland, for example). Reservations are necessary, and major credit cards are accepted.

Sounder Trains (commuter rails), run by Sound Transit, are still a new phenomenon in Seattle—and as such, you can only travel during peak hours on weekdays, into the city in the mornings and out of the city in the evenings. Trains leave Tacoma at 5:45 AM, 6:20 AM, 6:48 AM, and 7:10 AM, with stops in Puyallup, Sumner, Auburn, Kent, and Tukwila prior to Seattle. Southbound trains leave Seattle at 4:20, 4:45, 5:10, and 5:40 PM. Sounder Trains from Everett leave at 6:10 and 6:40 AM, stopping in Edmonds, and make the return trip from Seattle at 4:33 and 5:13 PM. (Note that there is daily Amtrak service from most of these cities, offering more departure times.)

It's $2 for one zone, $3 for two zones, and $4 from endpoint to endpoint; kids under six ride free. Tickets can be purchased at machines inside the stations or by mail. Transfers from Sounder Trains are accepted on buses throughout the region.

Information **Amtrak** (☎ *800/872-7245 or 206/382-4125* ⊕ *www.amtrak.com*). **Sound Transit** (☎ *800/201-4900 or 206/398-5000* ⊕ *www.soundtransit.org*).

ON THE GROUND

▮ COMMUNICATIONS

INTERNET

Seattle is a very wired city. Almost every hotel has some form of Internet access, be it building-wide Wi-Fi, Ethernet in rooms, or a business center with computer stations and laptop hookups. Even many B&Bs have at least one computer station—if they don't have Wi-Fi. What's more, many hotels offer free Wi-Fi or Ethernet to their clients, a practice that should be standard worldwide, especially if you're paying $300 a night for a room. Some large corporate chains like the Hilton do charge extra for Internet, so be sure to inquire when you book. Paying for hotel Internet is only for the business traveler—so many coffeehouses (and a few bars and restaurants) in Seattle offer unlimited free Wi-Fi, there's no reason to shell out $10 a day for it at your hotel if you just want to check your e-mail a few times. Some coffeehouses charge for Wi-Fi or only give you an hour of usage per purchase. For a detailed list of our favorite coffeehouses, *see* Chapter 2, Where to Eat. For a broader list of coffeehouses with Wi-Fi and/or computer stations, check out ⊕*www.seattle.wifimug.org.*

For a list of free Wi-Fi hot spots offered by the City of Seattle, check out ⊕*www. seattle.gov/html/citizen/wifi.htm.* Wi-Fi is available on Washington State Ferries and at Sea-Tac, but both entities charge high rates for usage.

▮ DAY TOURS & GUIDES

BICYCLING

Terrene Tours organizes private day trips for groups of up to five for $580, which includes bike rental, guide, support van, lunch, and drinks. They can also set up overnight tours of the surrounding countryside and islands.

BOAT

Argosy Cruises sails around Elliott Bay (1 hour, from Pier 55, $15–$19), the Ballard Locks (2½ hours, from Pier 56, $28–$36), and offers a cruise between Lake Union and Lake Washington (2 hours, from AGC Marina in South Lake Union, $22–$28). Let's Go Sailing permits passengers to take the helm, trim the sails, or simply enjoy the ride aboard the *Obsession* or the SC70 *Neptune's Car,* both 70-foot ocean racers. Three 1½-hour excursions ($25) depart daily from Pier 54. A 2½-hour sunset cruise ($40) is also available. Passengers can bring their own food on board.

BUS TOURS

Gray Line of Seattle operates bus and boat tours, including a six-hour Grand City Tour ($39) that includes many sights, lunch in Pike Place Market, and admission to the Space Needle observation deck. The hop-on, hop-off double-decker buses ($19) that do one-hour-long loops of the city core from the Seattle Center to Pioneer Square are the best bet for travelers who want to experience the city from outside of a bus, too. They also do day trips to Mt. Rainier and Mount St. Helens, though note that these tours only stop at scenic lookouts and visitor centers—you won't actually have the chance to do any hiking or exploring in either park.

CARRIAGE

Sealth Horse Carriages narrated tours ($50 per half hour, $100 per hour) trot away from the waterfront and Westlake Center.

ORIENTATION

For $39, Show Me Seattle takes up to 14 people in vans on three-hour day tours of the major sights. Though they bill the tour as Seattle "as the natives see it," this is an extremely touristy program that makes stops at places like the flagship

Eddie Bauer store and the first Starbucks, and the *Sleepless in Seattle* floating home (what year is it, again?). The tour is comprehensive—it takes in the views at Kerry Park in Queen Anne and heads above the canal to see Fremont, Ballard, and Green Lake—but don't expect this tour to be any more authentic than the others. For $42, Seattle Tours also has similar day tours of the city in vans, with stops for picture taking. The Seattle Skyscrapers Tour visits all the major buildings of Downtown in about two hours for $12.

PLANE

Seattle Seaplanes' 20-minute scenic flight for $67.50 per person takes in views of Woodland Park Zoo, Downtown Seattle, and Lake Washington. The company also schedules flying lessons, charter trips, and dinner flights to the San Juans and area islands. Take a 20-minute air tour with Seattle Flight has several different tours of the area ranging from 20 minutes to an hour; prices range from $27–$65 per person (no more than three passengers). Kenmore Air makes scenic flights over the city, as well as to the San Juan Islands and Victoria, British Columbia.

SELF-GUIDED

One way to tour Seattle at your own pace is with the Go Seattle Card, which provides admission to more than 30 of the city's top attractions. The credit-card-style ticket comes with a map and guidebook, and then you're off to explore the Space Needle, Museum of Flight, and other famous sights. Slightly discounted cards are available for children, students, and seniors, and if you're not up for a one-day whirlwind sweep through the city, they also come in two-, three-, five-, and seven-day increments. But before you buy one, think seriously about how many admissions costs you'll encounter each day—the cards start at $49 for one day of sightseeing and jump to $79 for two days and $109 for three days. Unless you're doing a lot of hopping around between museums and major sights like the Space Needle, it may not be that great a deal.

WALKING

Chinatown Discovery Tours offers 1½-hour walking tours of the neighborhood that may include a presentation at the affiliated Wing Luke Asian Museum; tickets are $16.95. Seattle Walking Tours creates customized, 2½-hour itineraries that cover specific areas of the city. These cost $15 per person for a minimum of three guests.

Tour Companies **Argosy Cruises** (☎800/642–7816 or 206/623–1445 ⊕www. argosycruises.com). **Chinatown Discovery Tours** (☎206/623–5124). **Go Seattle Card** (⊕www.goseattlecard.com) **Gray Line of Seattle** (☎800/426–7532 or 206/624–5077 ⊕graylineseattle.com). **Kenmore Air** (☎866/435–9524 or 425/486–1257 ⊕www.kenmoreair.com). **Let's Go Sailing** (☎800/831–3274 or 206/624–3931 ⊕www. sailingseattle.com). **Sealth Horse Carriages** (☎425/277–8282). **Seattle Flight** (☎206/767–5234 ⊕www.seattleflight.com). **Seattle Seaplanes** (☎800/637–5553 or 206/329–9638 ⊕www.seattleseaplanes.com). **Seattle Skyscrapers Tour** (☎206/667–9184). **Seattle Tours** (☎206/768–1234 ⊕www. seattlecitytours.com). **Seattle Walking Tours** (☎425/885–3173 ⊕www.seattlewalking-tours.com/walk_tour.htm). **Show Me Seattle** (☎206/633–2489 ⊕www.showmeseattle. com). **Terrene Tours** (☎206/325–5569).

▌HOURS OF OPERATION

Normal banking and office hours are weekdays from 9 to 6; some bank branches are also open on Saturday morning.

The majority of gas stations in Seattle and immediately off I–5 in suburban areas are open 24 hours.

Museums are generally open from 10 to 5 Tuesday through Saturday, with longer hours on first Thursdays and shorter hours on Sunday. Most major sites are open daily from 9 to 5 or later except on Christmas, New Year's Day, and Easter Sunday. Woodland Park Zoo and the Seattle Aquarium are open every day of the year.

There are a handful of 24-hour pharmacies in the Seattle area; others generally operate from 9 AM to 9 PM.

Most department stores and shops in malls are open 10 to 9 weekdays and Saturday, 11 to 6 on Sunday.

The hours of boutiques and small business can be erratic, a testament to the laid-back nature of the city. Never assume a store is open on Sunday; many smaller shops have truncated Saturday hours as well. To make matters more confusing, most smaller stores close one day during the week (usually Monday or Tuesday, but it varies), and some stores don't open until 11 AM, noon, or even 1 PM. Thankfully, coffeehouses tend to keep regular and long hours, so you'll have no problem finding one to kill time in if you have to wait for a store to open.

▌ MONEY

Almost all businesses and attractions accept debit and credit cards, though small surcharges may apply for charges under $5. The only exceptions are some smaller restaurants and bakeries.

Many metered cabs also accept credit cards or debit cards with the MasterCard or Visa logo.

Prices throughout this guide are given for adults. Substantially reduced fees are almost always available for children, students, and senior citizens.

Throughout this guide, the following abbreviations are used: **AE**, American Express; **D**, Discover; **DC**, Diners Club; **MC**, MasterCard; and **V**, Visa.

▌ SAFETY

Seattle is generally safe. The airport, ground transit links, ferries, and popular sights are well monitored by guards and cameras, and the city's knowledgeable travel personnel are on hand to help set visitors in the right direction. Tight rules apply as to what you can bring into stadiums, arenas, and performance venues; expect bag searches, X-ray machines, and/or metal detectors.

Use common sense and you'll avoid trouble. Always lock your car (there are plenty of break-ins, especially in residential areas), and park in lighted areas after dark; be careful when walking alone Downtown during late hours; don't flash cash or valuables in heavily touristed areas where petty theft might occur. Keep your laptop in the hotel safe when it's not in use.

Panhandlers tend to frequent Pioneer Square, Belltown, the U-District, and some area parks. Even visitors and transplants who come from other major cities with large homeless populations are surprised by how aggressive (and at times, verbally abusive) Seattle's panhandlers can be. You may pass your entire vacation without incident, but don't be surprised if someone curses you out after you refuse to give them money.

▌ TAXES

There is a 15.6% hotel tax in Seattle for hotels with more than 20 rooms, 8.6% for properties with fewer than 20 rooms. Hotel tax is approximately 7.9% in areas outside the city limits. There is an added 11% tax for renting cars at the airport.

The sales tax in Washington is 8.8% and is applied to all purchases except groceries and prescription drugs. At restaurants you'll pay a 9.2% meal tax.

FOR INTERNATIONAL TRAVELERS

CURRENCY

The dollar is the basic unit of U.S. currency. It has 100 cents. Coins are the penny (1¢); the nickel (5¢), dime (10¢), quarter (25¢), half-dollar (50¢), and the very rare golden $1 coin and even rarer silver $1. Bills are denominated $1, $5, $10, $20, $50, and $100, all mostly green and identical in size; designs and background tints vary. You may come across a $2 bill, but the chances are slim.

CUSTOMS

Information **U.S. Customs and Border Protection** (⊕www.cbp.gov).

In Seattle **Sea-Tac U.S. Customs and Immigration office** (☎206/553–7960 customs, 206/553–0467 immigration).

DRIVING

Gas prices at this writing are about $2.69–$3.10 per gallon. Stations are plentiful, and stay open 24 hours along the highways.

All but the most rural or wooded roads are paved. Multilane, interstate highways I–5 (north–south) and I–90 (east–west) are the fastest routes to and from Seattle. Highways with three-digit numbers (like the 405 and 520 routes through Bellevue) encircle urban areas, which may have other limited-access expressways, freeways, and parkways.

Driving in the United States is on the right. Speed limits are posted in miles per hour (usually between 55 mph and 70 mph). Watch for lower limits in small towns and on back roads (usually 30 mph to 40 mph). Most states require front-seat passengers to wear seat belts; many states require children to sit in the backseat and to wear seat belts. In major cities rush hour is between 7 and 10 AM; afternoon rush hour is between 4 and 7 PM. To encourage carpooling, some freeways have special lanes, ordinarily marked with a diamond, for high-occupancy vehicles (HOV)—cars carrying two people or more.

ELECTRICITY

The U.S. standard is AC, 110 volts/60 cycles. Plugs have two flat pins set parallel to each other.

EMERGENCIES

For police, fire, or ambulance, dial 911 (0 in rural areas).

EMBASSIES

Contacts **Australia** (☎202/797–3000 ⊕www.austemb.org). **Canada** (☎202/682–1740 ⊕www.canadianembassy.org). **United Kingdom** (☎202/588–7800 ⊕www.brit-ainusa.com).

Canada **Canadian Consulate** (✉1501 4th Ave., Suite 600, Downtown ☎206/443–1777 ⊕http://geo.international.gc.ca/can-am/seattle).

New Zealand **New Zealand Consulate** (✉10649 N. Beach Rd., Bow, WA ☎360/766–8002 ⊕www.nzembassy.com).

HOLIDAYS

New Year's Day (January 1); Martin Luther King Day (third Monday in January); Presidents' Day (third Monday in February); Memorial Day (last Monday in May); Independence Day (July 4); Labor Day (first Monday in September); Columbus Day (second Monday in October); Thanksgiving Day (fourth Thursday in November); Christmas Eve and Christmas Day (December 24 and 25); and New Year's Eve (December 31).

MAIL

You can buy stamps and aerograms and send letters and parcels in post offices. Stamp-dispensing machines can occasionally be found in airports, bus and train stations, office buildings, drugstores, and convenience stores. U.S. mailboxes are stout, dark-blue steel bins; pickup schedules are posted inside the bin (pull down the handle to see them). Parcels weighing more than a pound must be mailed at a post office or at a private mailing center.

Within the United States a first-class letter weighing 1 ounce or less costs 41¢; each additional ounce costs 17¢. Postcards cost 26¢. Postcards or 1-ounce airmail letters to most countries cost 90¢; postcards or 1-ounce letters to Canada or Mexico cost 69¢.

To receive mail on the road, have it sent c/o General Delivery at your destination's main post office (use the correct five-digit ZIP code). You must pick up mail in person within 30 days, with a driver's license or passport for identification.

There are post offices throughout Downtown Seattle and in surrounding neighborhoods. They're generally well staffed, and the lines move quickly. You can also post letters and packages from any UPS, FedEx, or Mail Boxes, Etc. store.

Contacts **DHL** (☎800/225–5345 ⊕www. dhl.com). **Federal Express** (☎800/463–3339 ⊕www.fedex.com). **Mail Boxes, Etc./The UPS Store** (☎800/789–4623 ⊕www.mbe.com). **United Parcel Service** (☎800/742–5877 ⊕www.ups.com). **United States Postal Service** (⊕www.usps.com).

PASSPORTS & VISAS

Visitor visas aren't necessary for citizens of Australia, Canada, the United Kingdom, or most citizens of European Union countries coming for tourism and staying for fewer than 90 days. If you require a visa, the cost is $100, and waiting time can be substantial, depending on where you live. Apply for a visa at the U.S. Consulate in your place of residence; check the U.S. State Department's special Visa Web site for further information.

Visa Information **Destination USA** (⊕www.unitedstatesvisas.gov).

PHONES

Numbers consist of a 3-digit area code and a 7-digit local number. Within many local calling areas you dial only the 7 digits; in others you dial "1" first and all 10 digits—just as you would for calls between area-code

regions. The same is true for calls to numbers prefixed by "800," "888," "866," and "877"—all toll free. For calls to numbers prefixed by "900" you must pay—usually dearly.

For international calls, dial "011" followed by the country code and the local number. For help, dial "0" and ask for an overseas operator. Most phone books list country codes and U.S. area codes. The country code for Australia is 61, for New Zealand 64, for the United Kingdom 44. Calling Canada is the same as calling within the United States, whose country code, by the way, is 1.

For operator assistance, dial "0." For directory assistance, call 555–1212 or occasionally 411 (free at many public phones). You can reverse long-distance charges by calling "collect"; dial "0" instead of "1" before the 10-digit number.

Instructions are generally posted on pay phones. Usually you insert coins in a slot (usually 25¢–50¢ for local calls) and wait for a steady tone before dialing. On long-distance calls the operator tells you how much to insert; prepaid phone cards, widely available in various denominations, can be used from any phone. Follow the directions to activate the card, then dial your number.

CELL PHONES

The United States has several GSM (Global System for Mobile Communications) networks, so multiband mobiles from most countries (except for Japan) work here. Unfortunately, it's almost impossible to buy a pay-as-you-go mobile SIM card in the United States—which allows you to avoid roaming charges—without also buying a phone. That said, cell phones with pay-as-you-go plans are available for well under $100.

Contacts **Cingular** (☎888/333–6651 ⊕www.cingular.com). **Virgin Mobile** (☎No phone ⊕www.virginmobileusa.com).

CON OR CONCIERGE?

Good hotel concierges are invaluable—for arranging transportation, getting reservations at the hottest restaurant, and scoring tickets for a sold-out show or entrée to an exclusive nightclub. They're in the know and well connected. That said, sometimes you have to take their advice with a grain of salt.

It's not uncommon for restaurants to ply concierges with free food and drink in exchange for steering diners their way. Indeed, European concierges often receive referral *fees*. Hotel chains usually have guidelines about what their concierges can accept. The best concierges, however, are above reproach. This is particularly true of those who belong to the prestigious international society of Les Clefs d'Or.

What can you expect of a concierge? At a typical tourist-class hotel you can expect him or her to give you the basics: to show you something on a map, make a standard restaurant reservation (particularly if you don't speak the language), or help you book a tour or airport transportation.

Savvy concierges at the finest hotels and resorts can arrange for just about any goods or services imaginable—and do so quickly. You should compensate them appropriately. A $10 tip is enough to show appreciation for a table at a hot restaurant. But the reward should really be much greater for tickets to that U2 concert that's been sold out for months or for those last-minute sixth-row-center seats for *The Lion King*.

▍TIME

Washington State is in the Pacific Standard Time zone, which is 2 hours later than Chicago, 3 hours later than New York, 8 hours later than London, and 18 hours later than Sydney.

▍TIPPING

Tips and service charges are usually not automatically added to a bill in the United States. If service is satisfactory, customers generally give waiters, waitresses, taxi drivers, barbers, hairdressers, and so forth, a tip of from 10% to 20% of the total bill. Bellhops, doormen, and porters at airports and railway stations are generally tipped $1 for each item of luggage. In Seattle there is no recognized system for tipping concierges. A gratuity of $2–$5 is suggested if you have the concierge arrange for a service such as restaurant reservations, theater tickets, or a town car, and $10–$20 if the service is more extensive or unusual, such as having a large bouquet of roses delivered on a Sunday.

EFFECTIVE COMPLAINING

Things don't always go right when you're traveling, and when you encounter a problem or service that isn't up to snuff, you should complain. But there are good and bad ways to do so.

Take a deep breath. This is always a good strategy, especially when you are aggravated about something. Just inhale, and exhale, and remember that you're on vacation. We know it's hard for Type A people to leave it all behind, but for your own peace of mind, it's worth a try.

Complain in person when it's serious. In a hotel, serious problems are usually better dealt with in person, at the front desk; if it's something quick, you can phone.

Complain early rather than late. Whenever you don't get what you paid for (the type of hotel room you booked or the airline seat you pre-reserved) or when it's something timely (the people next door are making too much noise), try to resolve the problem sooner rather than later. It's always going to be harder to deal with a problem or get something taken off your bill after the fact.

Be willing to escalate, but don't be hasty. Try to deal with the person at the front desk of your hotel or with your waiter in a restaurant before asking to speak to a supervisor or manager. Not only is this polite, but when the person directly serving you can fix the problem, you're more likely get what you want quicker.

Say what you want, and be reasonable. When things fall apart, be clear about what kind of compensation you expect. Don't leave it to the hotel or restaurant or airline to suggest what they're willing to do for you. That said, the compensation you request must be in line with the problem. You're unlikely to get a free meal because your steak was undercooked or a free hotel stay if your bathroom was dirty.

Choose your battles. You're more likely to get what you want if you limit your complaints to one or two specific things that really matter rather than a litany of wrongs.

Don't be obnoxious. There's nothing that will stop your progress dead in its tracks as readily as an insistent "Don't you know who I am?" or "So what are you going to do about it?" Raising your voice will rarely get a better result.

Nice counts. This doesn't mean you shouldn't be clear that you are displeased. Passive isn't good, either. When it comes right down to it, though, you'll attract more flies with sugar than with vinegar.

Do it in writing. If you discover a billing error or some other problem after the fact, write a concise letter to the appropriate customer-service representative. Keep it to one page, and as with any complaint, state clearly and reasonably what you want them to do about the problem. Don't give a detailed trip report or list a litany of problems.

INDEX